D0119854

Ruth Rendell

THE KEYS TO THE STREET

ROAD RAGE

THE KEYS TO THE
STREET

For Don

Chapter One

Iron spikes surmount each of the gates into the Park, twenty-seven of them on some, eighteen or eleven on others. For the most part the Park itself is surrounded by thorn hedges but thousands of feet of spiked railings still remain. Some of these spikes are blunted, as on those enclosing the gardens of Gloucester Gate, some are ornamented and some take a bend in the middle. On the tall railings outside one of the villas the spikes have claw-like protuberances, six on each, curved and sharp as talons. A certain terrace has spikes on pillars, splaying out and blossoming like thorn trees. If you started counting spikes in the region of the Park and its surroundings you could reach millions. They go well with the Georgian architecture.

By night the Park is closed to people. Of the living creatures which remain within its confines most are zoo animals and waterfowl. The spiked gates open every morning of the year at six and close every evening at dusk, which is at four-thirty in winter but not until nine-thirty in May. Its 464 acres of land fill a circle. Inside the ring of streets which surrounds it lies another ring and within this, widely separated, the equilateral triangle of the London Zoo, the lake with its three arms and four islands, and around the ornamental gardens a road which on the map looks like a wheel with two projecting spokes.

The Park is deserted by night. That is, the intention

is that it should be deserted. The Park Police patrol between dusk and dawn, paying special attention to the restaurant areas that make likely shelters and to the Park residences, the villas, the expensive properties and Winfield House where the American Ambassador lives. No vagrant could sleep undisturbed under the lee of the pavilions or the bandstand but the police cannot search everywhere every night. The canal bank remains as a place of concealment and the wide green spaces and, in summer, the long grass under the trees.

To the north of the Park, beyond the zoo and Albert Road lie Primrose Hill and St John's Wood; here are St John's Wood Church, Lord's Cricket Ground and, turning southeastwards, the London Mosque. Park Road runs down towards Baker Street and Sherlock Holmes by way of the London Business School and St Cyprian's Church – Anglo-Catholic, white and gold inside and scented with incense. The Marylebone Road, the Planetarium, Madame Tussaud's waxworks – most popular of all London's tourist attractions, more visited than the Tower and Buckingham Palace – the Royal Academy of Music, Park Crescent and Park Square with their secret gardens and the tunnel passing under the road that links them. And so the Park is encircled, here by Albany Street, running from Great Portland Street Station due north, as straight as a Roman road, to meet Albert Road and Gloucester Avenue. The streets of Primrose Hill form a shape like a tennis racquet and Gloucester Avenue is its handle. There are railings everywhere, their spikes straight and pointed, twisted at a right angle or ornate and blunted.

Albany Street is not leafy and sequestered like almost every other street in the vicinity of the Park, but wide, grey, without trees. Barracks fill much of one side but beyond the other side of it lie the grandest and most lavish of the terraces – Cambridge, Chester and Cumberland, with their colonnades, their pediments, their statuary and their wealthy occupants. Beyond the barracks on the other side the area quickly becomes less respectable, though it has a long way to go before sinking to the level of Somers Town between Euston and St Pancras Stations. From one of these streets, near St James's Gardens, a young man was walking across Munster Square, heading for Albany Street.

The name everyone called him by was Hob, the three letters of which were the initials of his two given names and his surname. Apart from this, the feature that distinguished him from his contemporaries was the size of his head. His body was solid and thickset but his head still looked too big for it. When he reached fifty, if he ever did, his jowls would be down on his shoulders. His fair hair was cut an inch long all over his big head and gleamed in the yellowish chemical light. It was an unusual combination, that of fair hair and brown eyes. His eyes were a curious textured brown, like chocolate mousse, and the pupils were sometimes as big as a cat's and sometimes the size of a full stop on a keyboard.

Hob had a job to do, for which he had just been paid half his fee of fifty pounds. That is, he had been paid twenty-five pounds. This he intended to put with everything else he had, to buy what he needed before he could do anything at all. Often he wished he were a woman, because for women making money was quick and, as far as he could see, easy. One of the first things he remembered hearing from a grown-up – it was an uncle, his mother's boyfriend – was that every woman is sitting on a fortune.

He was in a state. That was how he put it to

himself, the phrase he always used for his present condition. One of his stepsisters had described her panic attacks to him and in her description he recognised his own state. But his was longer-lasting and somehow *bigger*. It took in the whole world. It made him afraid of everything he could see and hear and just as frightened of what he couldn't see and of silence. As the state intensified a huge bubble of fear like a glass ball enclosed him so that he wanted to beat and thrash at its curved walls. Sometimes he did, even out in the street like this, and people crossed the road to avoid this madman who punched at the empty air.

He did not yet have pain or nausea. But beyond walking to his destination, up this long, wide, grey street where at present there were no people to avoid him or to stare, he could have done nothing; certainly not the job for which he had received half the fee. Walking became mechanical. Even in a state he sometimes thought he could have walked for ever, on and on, over the dark lawns, the green peak, the hills of north London, to the fields and woods far beyond.

But walking miles would be unnecessary. Gupta or Carl or Lew would be on the other side of the Cumberland Gate where the Chinese trees were. He walked through the wells and alleys and up the slope at Cumberland Terrace. His shadow was a lumbering black cut-out on wrinkled cobbles. Lights shone up on walls and behind cascades of leaves.

The Outer Circle, so busy by day, was deserted at night and no single car was parked on its gleaming surface. The great terraces, palaces in woodland, slept heavily behind dark foliage, and though many of their eyes were shuttered, some were alive with orange light. Lamps were lit along the pavements as far as he could see in each direction. The spaces between them were filled with shiny darkness. He crossed the road. The Cumberland Gate was locked and had been for nearly three hours.

The railing of which the gate was made was topped with iron spikes, eighteen on each gate. When he was well – the term he used for his condition when not in a state – he would have thought nothing of climbing the gate. Now he scrambled over it like an old man with an old man's caution and fear of puncturing flesh and breaking bones. On the other side an expanse of half-dark lay – grey lawn, pale paths, black trees, spindly black Chinese trees that made him think of scorpions.

The police patrolled in cars, on foot, on bicycles, sometimes with dogs. It was a principle of his, and of Carl's, that they cannot ever be everywhere. Mostly they were not where he was or Carl was. He walked into the trees. He meant not to make a sound but when a young scorpion leapt off its parent's back and grew wings and turned into a pterodactyl – it was a pigeon flying from a treetop – he let out a cry of fear.

A hand came from behind and went over his mouth. He wasn't afraid, he knew who it was. Gupta said:

'Are you crazy?'

'I'm not well.'

Even in the dark he could see Gupta's bloody teeth when he spoke. They looked as if he'd been chomping on raw steak but in fact it was betel he chewed. All the money Hob had was exchanged for what Gupta produced, a zip-lock bag holding a small block of something like a white pebble but rough and irregular, not smoothed by the sea. Automatically, he thought of his strength and Gupta's frailty and of the other white stones in the yogurt carton, enough to keep him well for a long time. But it was no use.

Retribution would be swift. He'd carried out some of it for them so he knew. They'd start by breaking his legs. He doubted if he would even get beyond the first thump of his fist into Gupta's skinny belly.

It was strange, but he had stopped trying to understand it. The state was so awful, so why did he want to prolong it? He always did. That uncle – or one of them – would have said it was like banging your head against a wall: it was so good when you stopped. But that wasn't quite how he felt; rather it was as if the pain and the state, the panic and the total meaninglessness of everything, became pleasure when he knew he had the means of ending them. The state became almost enjoyable and he walked inside his glass bubble, rolling his head and mouthing something like a smile.

If he headed for Chester Road and the Inner Circle he would be bound to encounter the police, so he turned back. But instead of climbing the Cumberland Gate once more, he kept close along the dark grass under the hedge, aware now that he was cold. The night was cold as nights in April are. The sweat which kept on breaking out on his face and chest dried cold and salty. He could taste the salt when he licked his dry upper lip.

Soon, if the state were too long prolonged, trembling would start, and the sick feeling, and the great weakness as if he was ageing years in as many minutes. It was a matter of striking the happy medium. Again he climbed a spiked railing – this time at the Gloucester Gate – and this time it was harder; he was an even older man with worse arthritis and more frightened bones.

He got over the gate and waited at the lights at the top of Albany Street. Some seconds, a whole minute probably, passed before he understood that the lights had changed from red to green and back to red

6

again. A solitary car stopped and waited. He went across, holding on to the wall of the bridge now, just another drunk to passers-by, turning clumsily into Park Village East and pushing open the gate into the ruined garden.

They were doing up the house that loomed above him in darkness. Its windows were gone, leaving black pits. The builders' materials lay in heaps – timber, bricks, a ladder. He nearly blundered into a concrete mixer, a thing like a great pale zoo animal with heavy backside and tiny stupid head. Down the slope, black but with the gleam of water in its depths, lay the Grotto. He scrambled down, scratching his hands on brambles, trying to avoid the coils of barbed wire. There, at the bottom, his seat on the coping lit by a thin shaft from a lamp on the bridge, he shivered and hunched his body before feeling in the pocket of his jacket for his materials.

They were kept in a red velvet drawstring bag, the kind of thing a box containing a ring or necklace is put into in a jeweller's shop. He had found it in a waste bin in York Terrace where the rubbish is of high quality. From the bag he took first another find, the metal rose from a galvanised iron watering can, then a tin lid that by chance (he had searched for quite a long time) exactly fitted over the rim of the rose. Then came the screwtop from a vodka bottle with *Purveyors to the Imperial Russian Court* and the dates 1887–1917 printed on it in red, then a drinking straw still in its plastic wrapping (he had helped himself to this from the counter at the refreshment place near the Broad Walk), and finally a cigarette lighter.

First he took the white crystalline substance he had bought from Gupta between finger and thumb. His hand was shaking but that didn't matter as all he had to do was crumble the substance up. He dropped it through the neck of the rose on which he had bored two holes about a centimetre apart. He removed the drinking straw from its wrapping, cut it in half with nail scissors and inserted the two halves to a length of about three centimetres into the holes in the neck. It was just light enough to see to do this, but he could have done it in pitch darkness.

Having checked by feel that the straw halves were inserted to the correct length – very important this – he struck the cigarette lighter and set the flame to the perforations on which the rock rested. The second it caught he closed the lid over the base of the rose, took the straws into his mouth and drew in a deep inhalation. At this, the first draw, he always made a noise. It was a sound of joy, of orgasmic happiness, but to others it would have seemed like a groan of despair.

No one heard him. There was no one to hear. When educating him to work for them, Lew had told him jumbo took just ten seconds to reach the brain. He told him it would change him from one kind of person into another kind and he had been right. Hob grunted his satisfaction. A car passed along the bridge and the trees shook a little. The state began to recede like something evil in a dream being sucked away out of a door. It struggled as it went but the door closed and clouds of warmth filled its space, and sweet singing and hope. He closed his eyes. Once, when he first used the watering can rose, he had simply turned it upside down and inhaled through the perforations, but he found you wasted a lot that way. Waste was a crime.

After a while he removed the vodka cap from the neck of the rose, shook out the rose and the lid, put them back into the jewel bag and threw the straws away into the bushes. He had begun to feel strong and immensely happy. That was just the start.

8

Traffic was at its lightest – no heavy lorries or containers, only private cars. There are always some private cars. There are always people in Camden High Street, no matter what the hour. After midnight, for a while, London throbs softly but it still throbs. Chemical lamps colour the darkness greenish-white and dull orange, and the traffic lights change from green to amber to red to amber again and to green silently and often to an empty street. At such a place, where the lights changed to no purpose, to a deserted roadway, he crossed to Albert Road, to Parkway. When he was well he was a different person and he walked springily.

The different person, the person who was not in a state, was a joker, facetious, a user of peculiar slang. Everything made him laugh. He was strong; he could do anything. He could certainly do the job for which he had received half-payment. The watch he had often been tempted to sell told him it was twelve minutes past one.

The mark was due to arrive in London on the nine-twenty-five train from Shrewsbury which comes into Euston Station at one-fourteen. Euston was less than a mile away, the nearest of all the London termini. If the train was on time and a taxi was waiting, he had just enough time to make it to St Mark's Crescent – nice time, in fact. A mark living in St Mark's Crescent was something else to make him laugh, and he did so, but quietly, to himself.

He walked up Gloucester Avenue, took the fork into Regent's Park Road and up the fork to the right. The Park was invisible, though lying only a few yards behind the tree-shaded walls. Dark shadows and leaves that scarcely rustled. Dustbins awaiting emptying. A cat that padded as silently as the place was silent, listened, froze, smelt or intuited him, and streaked, quick as a weasel, over the wall.

9

Lights were on in the houses, but not many. There were no lights on any floor of the house that was his destination. It had a dingy front garden, thick with weed bushes. He knew some of these were brambles because they caught on his clothes as he dropped down among them. A briar tugged at the back of his hand, scratching and puckering, making a zip fastener of blood on the skin.

It was so quiet that he heard the taxi when it was still in Regent's Park Road. He felt very calm and happy, wishing only that he had someone to talk to and clown with, maybe put on his hit-man act, talking like a TV actor. The taxi turned the corner and pulled up outside the garden where he was hiding. Its light shone right on him, into his eyes. He kept as low down as he could get. He heard the exchange.

'Take three.'

'Thanks very much, guv.'

The gate opened. The taxi started, moved, began to turn. If the driver had waited till the front door came open he didn't know what he'd have done. A suitcase was pushed in on to the path, and the gate closed behind it and its owner with a soft click. The lights of the taxi dwindled, disappeared and the throb of its engine faded.

He stood up and used his bare hands, first his hands, then his feet. One hand over the mouth from behind, a stranglehold armlock to bring him down, and when he was on the ground, the kicking. Not enough to kill or permanently disable but enough to injure, break a couple of the mark's ribs, maybe not improve the future prospects of his spleen. Some dental work would probably also be needed.

He enjoyed it. He admired himself for doing it so well, particularly his skill in doing it in silence. Long practice and the use of his hands had ensured not a sound escaped from that mouth out of which blood now trickled in a thin stream. He knelt down. There was nothing in his brief about robbing the man but when you came to think of it the fee was laughable. He was entitled. He put his hand inside the jacket, felt in the pocket and found a wallet. Credit cards were no use to him. There was only one thing he wanted to buy and neither Carl nor Gupta would take Visa. Ten pounds, twenty and another twenty ... Joy began to fill the spaces of his body with warmth. Eighty pounds. He stuffed it into his pocket alongside the red velvet bag.

Then, because he liked a joke and was feeling cheerful, he opened the suitcase and took a look inside. Not surprisingly, it was full of clothes. The surprise was that they were women's, mostly women's underwear. It now came back to him that he had heard there was something funny about the mark, though he'd half-forgotten what.

He set about hanging the stuff on the bushes – red silk bikini pants, French knickers, a black bra, a black lace nightie. It looked as if a couple of girls were camping there and had done their washing before they kipped down for the night. Whatever the name of the black see-through thing was – a sort of all-in-one with a fastening in the crotch – he didn't know but he draped it over the gate and dropped a couple of suspender belts on the mark's recumbent body.

The faint groaning coming from that half-open mouth meant it was dangerous to remain any longer. He left the garden, licking the blood off the scratch on the back of his hand, walking fast, going in the opposite direction this time, towards Primrose Hill. His spirits had begun to sink. Lew had told him about the ten-second effect but said nothing about depression coming back half an hour later. It was too late now. Gupta would no longer be among the

Chinese trees but Carl or Lew might be on the Hill or the Macclesfield Bridge. He headed that way, his gains in his pocket.

'Jumbo, jumbo,' muttered Hob, and then he sang it to keep his spirits up. 'Jumbo, jumbo . . .'

Chapter Two

The letter came the day she left. There was a postcard from her grandmother, a bill for water and this letter in a brown envelope with the Harvest Trust logo that looked like a scarlet mushroom, but was not of course that, was something quite other than that. She postponed opening it. Her grandmother's postcard was from a place called Jokkmokk in the north of Sweden. It said: *Dear Mary, I shall be back in London next Thursday, by which time you will be settled in Park Village. Will phone. Surprising heat here and midnight sun, Much love . . .*

'I'll want a cheque for your half of the water,' Alistair said, very sour and cross, truculent with resentment.

Mary said nothing about having paid all the electricity bill herself. He had got hold of the other envelope and was looking at the red logo.

'May I have my letter, please?'

He handed it to her reluctantly. 'They want more, I suppose.'

'Very unlikely.' She was trying to keep everything she said to him brief, civil, equable. The rows were in the past. 'It will just be the update. They keep in touch.'

'I hope it's to say he's dead,' said Alistair viciously.

It was hard to stay calm in the face of this. 'Please don't say that.'

'It would be the best and ultimate way to show

13

you how you've wasted your time and rubbished your body.'

'I'm going to finish packing,' she said.

He followed her into the bedroom. There were two open suitcases on the bed, one half-filled with her clothes. She put the letter and the postcard on top of a blue T-shirt and laid her trouser suit, folded with tissue, on top of that. A week had gone by since she had slept in that bed with him. During that week, he had slept in the bed and she had had the sofa-bed in the living room. It was easier that way, if her aim was a quiet life – for what was left of it for the two of them together, anyway. She found her cheque book in a drawer and wrote him a cheque for half the water rate.

A nod, no smile, no thanks, and he had put it in his pocket. 'If you hadn't this plushy place to go to you wouldn't be going, would you? If it was a furnished room, for instance? Or back to Grandma?'

'We've been through all that, Alistair.'

'And when they come back from this protracted holiday – what then? When they kick you out of glitzville? You'll come back here and say you've made a mistake and can you have your old bed back.'

'Perhaps, though I don't think so. This is supposed to be a separation.'

'A *trial* separation.'

'If you like.' Why did she always weaken, compromise? 'We may both feel differently after four months.'

'You'll allow for that, will you? That *I* may feel differently. That I may no longer want to marry you? That's going now, you know, that's been on the wane ever since you deceived me over that Harvest thing I'm not supposed to mention. Since you deliberately made yourself ill for nothing, for no more than to get

14

on a feel-good high, to be a martyr, to have "done some good in this world" – wasn't that the phrase?'

'Not used by me,' she said, and she felt her temper going, slipping away, a ball dropped on a slope, running downhill. She made a grab at it, hung on. 'I never said any of those things, never.' Thank God, I never married you, she thought. Things could be worse, I could have married you.

She closed the lid of one suitcase, started filling the other. He watched her, his upper lip slightly curled back, an animal's expression she had never seen when first they knew each other. 'If my grandmother phones, will you give her this number? I'm sure she has it but just in case.'

She had written it down along with the address: Charlotte Cottage, Park Village West, Regent's Park, London NW1.

'Cottage!' he said.

'The house was thought small when it was first built.'

'Pretentious,' he said. 'A sort of Petit Trianon.'

'It's near my work,' she said. 'I can walk to work from there.' As if that was why she was doing it, as if proximity to the museum was her reason.

He had an uncanny way of intuiting these things, of picking up on a weakening. His face changed and he wheedled. He had never wheedled when first they met. 'You'll ask me over, won't you? Come to that, there's no reason why I shouldn't move in there too.'

'There is a reason,' she said quietly. Her temper was back with her. It had never had much independence, was almost incapable of getting lost; a timid thing like its owner, not much good at standing up for itself. She fastened the second suitcase, picked up her bag, put it down again to get into her jacket.

15

'There are quite a few reasons, Alistair, but there isn't any point in talking about it.'

'You don't seriously believe I'd ever –' he hesitated, looking for a word, a silly word perhaps, a baby word, something that reduced violence to play '– smack,' he said, 'smack you again, do you?'

Yes, she did. Not that there had been much of that but there had been enough. Enough to change her from the woman, typical, normal, who says, *He wouldn't hit me twice*, who says of abused women, *Why do they stay*? to the half-accepting kind, the it-was-only-once kind, even the kind who says, *He was provoked beyond bearing*. Except that she wasn't staying or accepting or bearing but getting out.

He stood in the doorway, between her and the hall, and she had to pass him. What was I thinking of, she asked herself then and there, what was I thinking of, staying for even five minutes with a man who frightens me? An unreasonable man who thinks he owns me, body and soul?

She took a suitcase in each hand and walked by him, every muscle tense, her breath held. Instead of stepping back, he stood his ground and she had to push past him. He didn't touch her with his hands. Once, she remembered, he had stuck out a foot and tripped her up. That had been in the early Harvest days, when he first found out. He had extended a foot and sent her sprawling and said when she picked herself up, 'That wasn't me, that was your bones; you've weakened your bones, you've made yourself into an old woman.'

But he didn't touch her. 'Alistair, goodbye,' she said, a safe distance from him.

He put out a hand, then both hands, his head a little on one side. 'Kiss?'

And if he seized hold of her, struck her face with one hand, then the other, shook her, threw her to the

16

floor, used his fists . . . ? He had never done anything like that, nothing on that scale, but she found herself shaking her head. She opened the front door. Outside by the lift someone was waiting. Thank God . . . Alistair said, in his old warm voice, 'Goodbye, darling. Keep in touch,' but whether it was for her benefit or the listener at the lift she couldn't tell.

She had forgotten to call for a cab to take her to the tube. She lugged the suitcases round the corner, to a point invisible from any window in the flat, and sat on the low wall in front of the estate agent's, waiting for a taxi to come.

Devonshire Street was the farthest south any of Bean's dogs lived. This was Ruby the beagle. The next one was Boris the borzoi in Park Crescent, rich dogs both of them, well-fed, with top-grade veterinary insurance, sleek and proud and indulged. But all Bean's dogs were like that or they wouldn't have been his dogs. It would have been unthinkable for him to walk a cross-breed or a mongrel.

With Boris and Ruby on the double leash, he made his way down the slope that leads to the Nursemaids' Tunnel. This passage connects Park Crescent Gardens on the southern side with Park Square to the north. It passes above the Jubilee Line of the Underground and under the Marylebone Road. By day and night the traffic here is heavy, thundering westwards to the Westway, the M40, and eastwards to Euston and King's Cross. It never really ceases, not even at three and four in the morning, but in the early mornings and the late afternoons, the times when Bean took his dogs out, it was heaviest. Boom-boom-boom it went above the tunnel roof, shaking this subterranean lane whose brownish walls and damp stone floor were lit by natural light from the open entrances at each end.

17

Crossing the road by the other possible means was difficult at any time. The green prancing man was lit up for almost too short a time to get to the island and thence to the other side when you had two dogs with you, both inclined to stop for a sniff without warning. As a resident of the Crown Estates, Bean had his own key to the gardens and hence the tunnel. It was once used by nannies and their young charges and as a place of assignation for lovers. Bean doubted if anybody much used it now but him.

His route was carefully organised so that the most athletic dogs had the longest run and the small short-legged ones the shortest. He started with the beagle at three-forty-five, the borzoi five minutes later and proceeded to pick up Charlie the golden retriever in St Andrew's Place and Marietta the chocolate poodle in Cumberland Terrace, marching them through the terrace passages and out into Albany Street.

It was a sunny afternoon in late April, not warm but with a chilly wind blowing clouds across the blue face of the sky. The trees were in tender spring leaf and flowers were coming out in window boxes. Bean, at seventy, was a strong, spry though small man who looked fifty-five from a little way away. Applying, back in 1986, for the last employment he was ever to have, he had given his age as forty-nine and been believed. By design he dressed young, but not absurdly so. Though possessing several of the late Maurice Clitheroe's suits – all altered to fit him – well-pressed blue jeans, a roll-necked jumper and a blue padded jacket were his winter attire. Ne'er cast a clout till May be out, they said, and April wasn't out yet. His hair he had always kept militarily short but these days he shaved his head to achieve a dense whitish stubble.

Bean stipulated that he wouldn't take old dogs or fat dogs or dogs with health problems. Six was his maximum number, never to include dogs the law required to be muzzled. Making a pretty good living at what he did – much more than a supplement to the retirement pension – he had quite a lot of rules. He had to be strict, as he explained to a Mrs Goldsworthy in Albany Street, whose scottie he was taking out for the first time.

'Seven days' notice of the dog going away on its holidays, madam,' he said to her, 'and a month for termination of contract. Except in a case of illness, naturally. And if anyone else or your good self takes the animal walkies that's as well as not instead of, if you take my meaning.'

'Oh, yes, of course.'

'So this is McBride, is it? Game little dogs, scotties, but a bit short in the leg so he'll come in for the medium scale run along with Lady Blackburn-Norris's Shih Tzu.' Bean dropped names unashamedly. It was good for business. 'We'll see you in three-quarters of an hour then.'

Bean (in his own words) was as fit as a fiddle from all that walking, the old ticker as good as one thirty years younger, and he strode up the long straight street at four miles an hour. He was a vegetarian and it was only on Friday nights that he drank a drop of anything stronger than Coke. Health-conscious and regarding the streets merely as exercise equipment for himself and 'his' dogs, he was unaware of the history of the place and its architecture, or of the Park itself. He noticed little of that distinguished building of the Sixties, Lasdun's Royal College of Physicians, and never noticed that the point at which he crossed the road was outside the Danish Church of St Katharine's, a not entirely successful copy of King's College chapel in Cambridge.

The crescent called Park Village West, and also called, especially by those who live there, the most

19

beautiful street in London, debouches from Albany Street at the Camden Town end. Albany Street is a much frequented thoroughfare, free of heavy traffic only by night and on Sunday mornings, but Park Village West is a little haven of peace and rustic charm. It is something like a cross between a country lane and a cathedral close and in the springtime it smells of flowering trees and narcissi and wallflowers.

Bean and his dogs turned in there under the overhanging trees. 'Disarming villas', these 1840-ish houses have been called, 'masterpieces of the Nash school'. Each one stands alone in its embowering garden and each one is different with its own style of classical ornament, blank windows, storied urns, imperatorial busts, Della Robbia medallions, gazebos, weather vanes and garages disguised as temples to Olympian gods.

The house where his next call was to be made was separated from the pavement first by a spacious front garden, then by a low wall, freshly painted and with Charlotte Cottage incised in its stucco. Bean secured the handle of his leash to a gatepost, and bidding his charges sit quietly, went into the garden and up the path. Last petals were falling from red tulips, baring their sooty calixes. Pansies and auriculas were out and the laburnum soon would be. A clematis with flat blooms like dull blue satin spread its tendrils across the creamy, faintly glossy, façade of the house. Fluted columns stood on either side of the blue front door, supporting a pediment with Nash's gods and goddesses disporting themselves in creamy relief on a blue ground. A downstairs window was open and a woman of about Bean's age or older put her head out.

'Is that the time?' she said. 'I wouldn't have put it at a minute after three.'

'It's four-sixteen, Lady Blackburn-Norris,' said Bean in his invariably polite way, for good manners cost you nothing.

She retreated and after a few seconds opened the front door, carrying the Shih Tzu, the chrysanthemum dog. Gushi's coat of golden fronds, petallike and flopping into his eyes, resembled his owner's strawberry blonde hair, her fringe restrained by a pair of blue-framed mirror sunglasses. 'Whatever is that beagle doing to the borzoi?'

'Best ignore it, madam,' said Bean. If she didn't know by this time he wasn't in the business of telling her. He took the Shih Tzu from her and as he was attaching a free branch of the leash to its collar, fending off Ruby's overtures, a taxi came round the corner and drew up outside Charlotte Cottage.

The young woman who got out of it, and lugged out two suitcases from the seat next to the driver, must be the Blackburn-Norrises' house-sitter. She looked very young to Bean, though he admitted that the greater part of the population looked young to him, and he could no longer tell whether someone was eighteen or thirty. This woman – girl, he thought – had an appearance of fragility, as if the wind could blow her away. She was slim and for some reason made him think of a lily, long-necked, white-skinned and very fair. Not the sort to take Gushi out for long walks herself by the looks of her, and that was all to the good.

He nodded and said good afternoon. He could see that many would have called her attractive, even beautiful, but she held no attraction for him. What he had known of sex, particularly in later years, had seemed to him at best grotesque and at worst frightening. When Maurice Clitheroe died he put all thoughts of it away for ever with a sigh of something stronger than relief. It crossed his mind to help the young lady up the path with her cases – crossed it

21

and fled. His hands were full with the dogs. Besides, she shouldn't bring heavy suitcases with her if she couldn't handle them herself, and if she tipped him it would be the average woman's ludicrous offering, twenty pee or at most fifty.

By this time the dogs were straining and pulling, impatient to be off, anxious for the real outing to begin. He crossed the street and the Outer Circle, taking them into the Park by the Gloucester Gate, and on the broad expanse of green south of the zoo he unfastened the leashes and let them run free.

In the distance the woman who exercised a dozen dogs, but behaved more like a nanny with her charges, was playing ball with three labradors and a boxer. Bean gave her one of his looks but she was much too far away to see.

'We are starting out in Brazil,' said Lady Blackburn-Norris, 'then on to Mexico and Costa Rica. California after that, Utah for the great national parks or whatever they call them, and New England for the autumn colours. We shall be back by early September, shan't we, darling?' Her husband had a face and figure very much like the borzoi Mary had seen at the gate, even to the spindly legs, bent shoulders and anteater's proboscis of a nose.

'If it hasn't killed us,' he said. 'I expect we seem far too ancient to you, Miss Jago, to be doing this at all. And you would be right. I am eighty-two and the madam is seventy-nine.'

'My grandmother is older and she still travels a lot,' Mary said.

'Oh, dear Frederica! If only she was coming with us! But she's still in Sweden and apparently she has a long-standing engagement to go with the Trattons to Crete next month. I can't tell you how grateful we are to her, Miss Jago, for bringing us you. Without

22

someone really reliable in the house we couldn't be going away at all, could we, darling?'

Sir Stewart Blackburn-Norris said in his dry restrained way that indeed they could not. Frequently, in the past weeks, he had entertained murderous thoughts towards his wife's best friend Frederica Jago for making this protracted trip of theirs possible. Notifying the police was all very well and they had a dog – if Gushi could be called a dog – but nothing equalled *someone in the house*. Without *someone in the house* even his wife would have thought twice about going. Of course he didn't want to go. With his intimates he made no secret of it. He wanted to stay here, to stroll down to his club in Brook Street every morning and lunch there; every afternoon to take a cab back to Park Square for a chat with his friend, the director of the Crown Estates, in his sanctum, a temple-like building next to the Nursemaids' Tunnel entrance; to go on eating his dinner at Odette's three times a week, at Odin's three times a week and at the Mumtaz on Sundays.

'It was not to be,' he said aloud but didn't explain when Frederica's granddaughter looked enquiringly at him.

He showed her how to work the heating and his wife showed her how to work the video recorder. They gave her the list of useful phone numbers and indispensable services. She was instructed on no account to take Gushi out between eight and nine in the morning or four-fifteen and five-fifteen in the afternoon, Bean would do that, but she could take him out at other times if she – and he – felt like it and had the strength.

'I doubt if I will,' said Mary. 'I'll be at work during the day.'

'Oh, yes, you work, don't you?' said Sir Stewart as if he had just about heard of women pursuing this

23

freakish course, as if maybe one in a thousand did so due to esoteric pressures or rare idiosyncracy. 'At that Sherlock Holmes place in Baker Street, wasn't it?'

Mary laughed. 'No, no. Not Sherlock Holmes. Irene Adler. I work at the Irene Adler Museum in Charles Lane.' She thought the name might mean something to them but it evidently didn't. 'That's St John's Wood. I can walk to work from here.'

Sir Stewart insisted on looking it up in his Geographer's London Atlas. He was calculating the distance, deciding perhaps whether it might be too far for her to walk, too far for *anyone* to walk, let alone someone as fragile-looking as she, when Bean came back with the dog. Introductions were made and Bean said:

'I'll see you at eight-fifteen am then, miss.'

No one had ever called her 'miss' before. It made her feel like the daughter of the house in a Victorian novel. Fondled and spoken to nicely, Gushi launched himself at her, licking and snuggling, settling into her arms like a bunch of chrysanthemums.

'Get down, bloody dog,' said Sir Stewart.

Mary said, 'Why Gushi? I mean, where does the name come from.'

'Gushi Khan ruled Tibet in the seventeenth century, didn't he, darling?'

'God only knows,' said Sir Stewart. 'His first owner named him. I'd have called him Sam.'

Mary wandered through the rooms while the Blackburn-Norrises put the final touches to their packing. It was a pretty house, comfortable and elegant, furnished charmingly yet indistinguishably from the interiors of a thousand houses and flats that bordered on the Park. Chintz, velvet, Wilton, Chinese porcelain, Georgian silver, poppy heads and peacock feathers, button-back chairs, chaise longues, rent tables, Hope chairs and one that might have been a Duncan Phyfe. She knew about these things, sometimes hoped wistfully for something different, to come upon an interior that might surprise or delight. One day, no doubt, she would have a house of her own to furnish.

There were shutters at the windows and these would help with security. No lace curtains hid the lattices or obscured the view. She stood looking out on the garden with its pergolas, and its ornamental pond, and beyond it to the green space that divides the two segments of the village.

At this time of the year trees and shrubs were luxuriant, flowering creepers sprawling across every wall and height, brickwork hidden under a complicated leafy tapestry, so that nothing could be seen that might not have been in the depths of countryside. If skyscraping towers were somewhere out there, the trees clothed in fresh green and jade and golden-green hid them. Aircraft trails that scored broken white lines across the blue sky might have been streaks of cirrus.

In the garden a white lilac thrust its spires of blossom between those of a late forsythia and the snowy net of a spiraea. For some reason, the beauty of it added to her sudden, unexpected loneliness. It was a long time since she had lived alone and in half an hour she would be quite solitary. Except, of course, for Gushi, but Mary was not one of those who find the companionship of an animal equal to that of human beings. She stroked the dog's head, for the thought seemed a shade treacherous.

The taxi came early. Mary opened the door to the driver. The Blackburn-Norrises were still upstairs. Sir Stewart, as soon as he heard voices, began shouting for the driver to come up and lend a hand with the cases. Five minutes of chaos ensued, the driver arguing and grumbling about his back, Lady

25

Blackburn-Norris fluttering in circles and suddenly, surprisingly, kissing Mary goodbye, Sir Stewart inexplicably choosing this final moment to tell her how the window locks worked.

They went. The dog had gone to sleep. Mary continued to look out of the window until long after the taxi had disappeared. It was very quiet, silent as the country, and though she strained to listen she could hear nothing of the throb and hum of London. Alistair came into her mind and she thought of what it meant to be afraid of someone you had once loved and admired. He would very likely phone this evening. She wondered what would happen if she failed to answer it, if she let it ring, and the caller was a friend of the Blackburn-Norrises.

The idea of speaking to Alistair was suddenly very terrible. Perhaps she could go out for a walk or go to the cinema. There was a cinema by Baker Street Station and two in Camden Town. Wouldn't it be irresponsible to leave the house and the dog immediately she had got here? She went upstairs and began to unpack.

Her bedroom looked out over the garden and the gardens of Park Village East and across the railway line to Mornington Crescent. A gas balloon, segmented red and yellow, floated up in the sky over Euston Station. She emptied the first case and hung things up in a mahogany wardrobe with claw feet. The clothes on the top of the second case went into drawers. She lifted out the trouser suit. Underneath were the postcard from Jokkmokk and the letter from the Harvest Trust.

Mary sat on the bed and looked at the envelope in her hands for a few moments before opening it. This was normal for her with letters from the Trust. She wanted to know and she dreaded to know, so she always hesitated like this, bracing herself, being

26

prepared. Could you prepare? Wouldn't the worst thing, the thing she dreaded, be a shock, however much she anticipated it?

Alistair had said he hoped the man she knew only as 'Oliver' was dead. No doubt he had not absolutely meant that – he was illogical, unreasonable, about everything to do with the donation – but 'Oliver' might be dead. This letter might be telling her so.

When had she last heard? She thought back. Before Christmas, October or November, more than six months. But that, of course, was normal, the way things should be. She had asked the Trust to supply information after three months, after six, nine, twelve and eighteen months. It must now be more than eighteen months, nearer twenty, since the harvest was taken.

He might be dead. The success rate was only twenty to fifty per cent. In fact, he was rather more likely to be dead than alive. Prepared, or as near prepared as she was likely to be, she opened the envelope quickly, tearing at the flap with her thumbnail.

The letter was from the Harvest Trust's donor welfare officer. It reminded her that she had 'requested anonymity be relaxed after one year and a half if all continued to go well'. Therefore, subject to her consent, her name and address would be supplied to 'Oliver' and his, with his consent, to her. Or, having obtained 'Oliver's' address, she might go ahead and make contact with him herself. It was advisable for the parties to correspond with each other before arranging a meeting. The donor welfare officer would be happy to assist in every possible way. She hoped 'Helen' would consult her if she had any problems, and she signed herself, Deborah Cox.

Mary read it again. She had been given something to occupy her first evening.

Chapter Three

Irene Adler, adventuress, beauty, one-time mistress of the King of Bohemia, resided, according to Conan Doyle, at Briony Lodge, Serpentine Avenue, St John's Wood. But this is fiction and the only street in London designated Serpentine is in West Two not North-West Eight, so the founders of the museum that bears her name had to be content with a house in a turning off St John's Wood High Street.

It holds no memorabilia of her. How could it? The only woman that Sherlock Holmes ever loved – or at least, admired – appears in one single story. No sooner had he set eyes on her than she had married Mr Norton, leaving nothing behind but a photograph of herself for Holmes to treasure. But the objects in the museum are the kind of things she might have possessed: a collection of late nineteenth- and early twentieth-century dresses, Pre-Raphaelite paintings, numberless exercises in the Art Nouveau, furniture of the kind with which the Blackburn-Norrises furnished their house, jewellery in silver and jet, pinchbeck, cairngorms and moonstones, a few treasured copies of the *Yellow Book*, Swinburne, Watts-Dunton, a great many Beardsley drawings and a first edition of *Zuleika Dobson*.

Mary Jago's introduction to it was soon after she left art school and set up on her own, restoring costumes. It had not been a lucrative business but it brought her into contact with Dorothea Borwick who ran the Irene Adler and who later offered her a partnership. For the museum, largely ignored by Londoners, was a success with tourists, particularly Americans. Sometimes Mary and Dorothea even had to restrict admittance, roping off the entrance for half an hour, their hearts gladdened by the sight of a queue forming and extending round the corner into St John's Wood Terrace.

Dorothea never came in on Mondays just as Mary never did on Saturdays, and when she got there it was still only twenty-past nine and Stacey who sat at the ticket office and served in the shop, had not yet arrived. Mary had left Charlotte Cottage as soon as the dog-walker had brought Gushi back. She was uncertain as to the whereabouts of a pillar box in which to post her letter to the Harvest Trust, but she had found one at once, at the point where Park Village West debouched from Albany Street.

A good deal of thought and careful deliberation had preceded the writing of that letter. It had taken up most of the evening, causing her to give up ideas about a visit to the cinema. Did she, for instance, want the Harvest Trust to have her new address? Was there any point when it was only temporary? The Blackburn-Norrises would be back by early September and then, unless she felt very differently, unless she was utterly changed and had decided to go back to Alistair, she must find a place of her own.

But the reply to this letter would be very important, the revealing at last of 'Oliver's' identity. She almost decided to phone instead, but would they tell her on the phone? Of course not – she might be anyone, an investigative journalist, a spy. No one at the Trust would recognise her voice. Back to the letter then, the blank sheet of paper on which she had not yet even written an address. If she put Chatsworth Road, Willesden, now she no longer lived there, would Alistair send the Trust's reply on to her? Or would he take pleasure in destroying it?

The simplest plan would be to head the paper with her grandmother's address. She had a key to the house and, besides, Frederica would be home in a day or two. After this letter from the Trust, there would very likely be no more, for information about his condition would come to her straight from 'Oliver'. She wrote c/o Mrs F.M. Jago in the top right-hand corner, Lamballe House, Belsize Park Gardens, London NW3. The substance of the letter was to ask for 'Oliver's' real name and his home address.

This way it would be out of Alistair's reach. In the past year and a half he had become angrier and more resentful of what she had done, not less so. In some curious way he had seemed to want revenge on this man he had never seen and she had never seen, whose only offence had been to suffer from Acute Myeloid Leukaemia. As she walked across the Park, crossing the Broad Walk, and took the path that runs along the southern boundary of the zoo, she thought once more of Alistair's inexplicable behaviour. She thought of how her action had seemed to change him and turn him into an unreasonable and at times cruel man.

The Harvest Trust had recommended a discussion with one's family before the decision to be a donor was finally taken. Alistair and her grandmother were her family – she had no other – but while her grandmother had been supportive once she'd conquered her initial anxiety, from Alistair she had had nothing but anger, incredulity, rejection.

The Trust's very name had provoked shudders. He seemed to have a gift for picking out from its literature every point that might be construed as ominous.

30

'A harvest, they call it a harvest what they do. Doesn't that tell you something? They're harvesting the marrow out of your bones.'

And then, 'They insure you for a quarter of a million pounds. Look, it says so here. Do you think they'd do that if it wasn't dangerous?'

'I'm young and healthy,' she had said. 'They wouldn't take me if I wasn't suitable. I just look fragile but I'm not.'

And that was before she had been asked to give the donation, when she had only put her name on the register. To give in to him, to what was after all a quite unreasonable demand, she had felt would be weak and positively wrong. She knew that she belonged in the victim category, the quiet gentle type, usually female, who yields for the sake of peace, who placates and smiles and who, of course, brings out the worst in the bully. It was a casting, a role, she had lately been setting out to resist. But when the Trust came back to her with a potential recipient and asked her to attend the centre for a medical examination, she had not been able to stand up for herself.

She said nothing to Alistair. She went for the medical in her lunch hour. Of course, she still intended to tell him. Ironically, if things had been going badly for them she might have told him. She might have been made stronger by adversity, but their relationship was in a successful and happy period – why spoil it? Just the same, she meant to tell him well in advance of the harvest date. She would have to tell him, she knew that.

The bank sent him to Hong Kong. He was to be away a week and it was during that week that the donation was to be made. Donors should be met, it was advised, on leaving the hospital and accompanied home. She would have to do without that, or

31

she would have to do without Alistair. Dorothea would meet her, Dorothea was discreet and would say nothing. Perhaps Alistair need never know. Whatever advances she had made, she had by then reverted to type, and telling herself she was a coward and a fool made no difference.

Mary relived all this as she walked through the Park to the Monkey Gate, over the canal bridge and into Charlbert Street. It had been a day like this, sunny and breezy, but autumn not spring, when she went to the hospital for the harvest collection. The only risk, contrary to what Alistair suggested, was that associated with general anaesthetic, the same as if undergoing any operation. She was 'out' for about two hours, during which time they took a litre of marrow and blood, or five per cent of the total in her body.

Coming round, she had felt at first excitement. It was done, she had done it. She had been able to do it, use her own good health to repair someone else's ill-health, to mend nature's mistake. If she had done nothing much up till now, no good deeds, if she did none in the years to come, she had performed this one act to justify her existence. To no one on earth would she actually have said those words; to Dorothea when she came in to visit she made light of it, saying it was nothing, a breeze. But in her heart she experienced a deep satisfaction. Even if it failed, if the transplant was useless, she would have tried. She would have done what all philosophies and all religions told us we were here to do: love our neighbour and with positive intent.

This emotional high was not long enduring. The words she had used, though silent and unspoken, now embarrassed her. She came back swiftly to practical things. Dorothea accompanied her home in a taxi, made a meal and shared it with her, telling her to take it easy, not to come back to the museum till the following week. Mary had been tired and a little stiff but otherwise well. She ate three meals a day, went for gentle walks, took the iron pills prescribed for her and waited for Alistair to come home.

It was something she had never been able to account for, to explain to herself, why she had not once looked at the place on her body from which the harvest had been taken. She knew precisely where it was: the cavity of the hip, the iliac crest. It would have been normal surely, natural, to have studied these punctures on the smooth pale skin, even though she had been assured they would not leave a scar. Some revulsion, if not regret – never that – must have kept her eyes from the spot while she undressed, while she took a shower. Some unwillingness to see what altruism had done to a body that was perfect, without a blemish?

Alistair saw the marks. He saw them when they made love and the bedroom was flooded with autumn sunshine, soft golden light falling on her nakedness, her whiteness and its single flaw ...

The first-comers made straight for the shop where Stacey sold them calendars and postcards of Lillie Langtry and Eleanora Duse, leather-bound reissues of the novels of Ada Leverson, painted fans, beaded bags, batik, appliqué work and very expensive mock-Fortuny Knossos scarves. Mary set to work in the hat room, mending a silk brim, reattaching black ostrich feathers. 'A crab shelled in whalebone' was Aldous Huxley's description of the Edwardian lady and he called her plumed hat 'a French funeral of the first class'. There were more than twenty such hats in this room, all huge gateau-like confections, pearly-white, rose-pink, blue, yellow, black, festooned with roses, ribbons, feathers. On one wall was a *Vogue* cartoon from 1909 of a tiny woman wearing a hat as big as an umbrella on whose brim sat a rabbit gobbling up a cabbage.

When she was in here or in the corset room, Mary often thought Irene Adler's incursions into male attire – as when she whispers 'good evening' to Holmes in Baker Street – entirely understandable. The crab in whalebone could have known comfort only in bed at night, never by day in the S-shaped whalebone stays, the buckled and webbed bodices, the crustaceous layers, and those furbelowed cartwheel hats. Other pictures on the walls showed Edwardian women attempting to mount stairs, board trams and manage their hats on windy days.

The first visitors began wandering through and Mary put her work aside. The Americans asked the most questions and there was a preponderance of Americans. She had expected a quiet, slack day, as Monday usually was, failing to take into account that the tourist season was approaching its height.

'How did they handle those trailing skirts in the rain?' someone asked. It was a stock question and one she could scarcely answer.

'What about ordinary women?' was another. It was asked more and more often. 'What did the poor do? The ones who couldn't afford maids to dress them and cabs to ride in? How did they manage?'

And always, 'Who was Irene Adler?'

They sold more copies of the Sherlock Holmes story *A Scandal in Bohemia* (Irene as crab on the front cover and in jacket and breeches on the back) than all the catalogues and brochures put together. A favourite place was the facsimile of Irene's drawing room, as it must have been at Briony Lodge with the secret panel by the fireplace where the compromising photograph was kept hidden, open for all to see the secret spring. Gustav Klimt had not painted her, for he was real and she was fiction, but the mock-Klimt portrait of Irene in sequins and pearls posed against a gold-leaf screen, framed in narrow gilded wood, went back to hang on the walls of many a Midwest condo.

Business was too brisk at lunchtime for Mary to leave the museum. It even looked at one point during the afternoon as if admission would have to be restricted for half an hour. But the crowd dwindled as five approached, by which time the shop had run out of calendars and Knossos scarves and Stacey was on the phone to the sales rep. Mary worried a little about Charlotte Cottage. Would Bean have let himself in satisfactorily at four-fifteen, found Gushi and by now have brought him back? Would he have secured the front door behind him?

She considered taking a taxi back, for she had had one good walk that day. But the sun was still shining and the wind had dropped, and once she had entered the Park she forgot about a reluctance to walk, she forgot about Charlotte Cottage and Gushi and turned southwards across the broad open space. Strange, how seldom she had come in here while she lived in Willesden, and, though working at the museum, had scarcely ever crossed the canal or even set foot south of Prince Albert Road.

Taking the path that leads down to the boating lake, she noticed for the first time how open the Park was, how relatively treeless in its centre, a great plain of green fringed with the towers and landmarks of London: the gold dome of the Mosque, the slender column of the minaret beside it, the Art-Deco edifice of the Abbey National in Baker Street, the Post Office Tower, and behind her, the Mappin Terraces of the zoo. There were trees on the north bank of the lake and at its shallow rim a cluster of waterfowl, pochards, mandarins and a black swan, squabbling over the spilled slices from a cut loaf.

She crossed the Long Bridge and paused for a while to look at the heron perched on one of the island trees. It should have been possible to turn left and head for the Cumberland Gate but there was no way through.

She was learning that this was characteristic of the Park, perhaps inevitable in a design based on two circles, one within the other, that were not concentric. Paths seldom led where you thought they would, and it was very easy, especially in this vicinity, to take what you thought were all the right directions yet find yourself heading back for the zoo and St John's Wood. *Through the Looking Glass* was what it was like, the bit where Alice notices that the path which seems to lead straight to the garden does not and is afraid of going back through the glass into the old room. I, at any rate, shall not go back to the old room, the old life, Mary thought, and with that she came out into the Inner Circle by the Open Air Theatre.

It was a short distance from there, through the golden gates and along Chester Road, to the Broad Walk. The new fountains were playing. Flowers spilled over the rims of the lion tazze and the Roman vases. The flowerbeds, formal rectangles that flanked the wide path, were filled with polyanthus in bloom, with pansies and yellow jonquils. All the way along, from Park Square to Chester Road, and up beyond where there were no flowers but only trees and a certain wildness, seats faced each other, most of them occupied by two or three people. But on the seat nearest to the point where the road crossed the Broad Walk a man was sitting alone.

People of his sort always did sit alone, unless another of their kind joined them. No one would choose to sit on the same seat as he. Mary, approaching along the path from the west, sought about in her mind as she had often done before, for the right word for him. Dosser? Street person? Street sleeper? Not beggar, he wasn't begging. Not tramp, that was from her grandmother's time. Perhaps there was no word and perhaps there should be none.

He was reading. That made him different, set him apart. He seemed oblivious to everything and everyone, concentrating on his book. The barrow that contained his possessions rested against the metal arm of the seat. From the rag tied round his neck to the boots on his feet, his clothes were well-worn denim, rumpled wool and threadbare polyester. He wore a dark-coloured quilted jerkin. His hair was dark, the thick bushy beard that covered the greater part of his face iron-grey. She thought she had seen him somewhere before without being able to remember where. It was his hands which recalled this previous sighting or meeting. They were long, narrow, beautiful hands, sun-browned but smooth, and on the left one was a gold wedding ring.

He looked up as she passed and for a moment, infinitesimal, fleeting, their eyes met. His were blue, a strong sea-blue. He lowered his eyes almost immediately to his book and turned the page in a precise controlled movement. Trying to remember where she had seen him that first time – in Baker Street? Outside Madame Tussaud's? But she hardly ever went that way – Mary walked along the path where the gingko trees grow, the Chinese Maidenhair trees, towards the Cumberland Gate. Had he asked her for money? Had he perhaps been selling the *Big Issue*?

At the sound of her key in the lock, Gushi made three sharp barks. She called his name and he came running. If he was tired from his walk he gave no sign of it. She squatted down and he jumped into her arms, nestling there and burying his chrysanthemum face in her neck and shoulder.

If Mary Jago failed to remember where she had previously seen Roman Ashton, he had no trouble in placing her. She was the young woman who, arriving two hours earlier than usual at the museum in Charles Lane, had come upon him waking up on the doorstep. Irene Adler, the place was called. It had a glass-covered porch outside its front door that extended to the pavement across a small forecourt. For several nights he had slept there, dry and secluded, but he never went back after she had discovered him.

'I'm so sorry,' she had said, not wanting to step over him, also perhaps afraid. A great many people were afraid of them, himself and his kind. 'I woke you up. I didn't know anyone was sleeping here.'

It was a principle of his not to speak to the 'public', to speak only to his fellows, though that had its own problems, its own guilt. There was no reason for him to speak to people. He had no need to beg and never did, so if they addressed him he merely nodded or shrugged or gave no sign of having heard them. This delicate-looking slender girl, fair and somewhat fey-like, merited more than that. She had spoken to him as politely as if he had been a respectable house-holder. So he nodded, got to his feet and rolled up his bedding in a quick deft movement, stepping aside to let her pass.

'Sorry about that,' he said. 'I'm going.'

She must have heard it as a mutter, a low growl. She was not to know those were the first words he had uttered to anyone apart from the street sleepers for a year. The first sentence to escape him since he had closed up his house and taken to the outdoors.

And now he had seen her again. For a moment he thought she was going to speak to him and he wondered what reply to make, if any; whether to be as he once had been – a pleasant, courteous, easy-going sort of man – or as he now was, forbidding, grave, dour. But she had not spoken; she had not recognised him. It was just as well. Conversation with ordinary people was not for him; they spoke different languages.

For a little while he continued to read *Dead Souls*, or tried to read it, but the doings of Chichikov no longer held his attention. He had been distracted, not so much by the sight of the pale fair-haired girl with the swinging stride as by the emotion and the reflections thinking back to that earlier time had evoked.

He put the book into his buggy, a wooden barrow with four wheels and a handle like the shaft of a spade, and, pushing it ahead of him, began ambling along one of the paths in a westerly direction. He had no clear idea where he was going, a common state for him to be in, for one of the benefits of his condition was perfect freedom.

It was a warm still afternoon and this he enjoyed after the winds of the past weeks, the cold spring, the long damp winter. If happiness was denied him for ever, was something exclusively for others, he could feel pleasure and that sometimes more intensely and sensuously than those who lived under roofs and slept in beds. His appreciation of the sun on his face and the soft balmy air was luxurious and profound. It almost made him smile.

Another of his principles was never to make plans during the afternoon or evening as to where he would sleep that night, for to do so was to abrogate that freedom, and freedom was all he had. Every-thing else had been taken away or he had taken it away himself. He would give some thought to his night's 'lodging' when it was dark and the streets were empty, the cars had gone, the pubs had closed and those like himself came into their own.

He crossed over York Bridge and entered the sequestered part of the Park on the southern shore of the lake. On the seats along here his fellows were often to be found – Effie with her bundles wrapped in green plastic; Dill who would be accompanied by his dog but encumbered by so little, a nylon backpack, a couple of coats tied round his middle by their sleeves – but there was no one today. He knew Dill could live that way because he mostly had a bed in the Marylebone Road shelter or the one in the Edgware Road, something Roman's guilt and sense of being always a phony and a fake would never allow him to have. After all, how many of those others had possessed a house of their own; possessed it, sold it and banked the money?

For much of each day Roman lived in the past. And this was deliberate, a purposeful exploration of the time of his happiness, a reliving. Sometimes this dreaming occupied him for several hours on end as he walked across the Park and along the streets which made a network like the weaving of a nest around its centre. He would select a particular happening from that past and enter it again. It might be the birth of one of his children and the things he said to Sally and she to him, or even earlier, his first meeting with Sally at university.

Once he had been quite unable to do this, had been afraid to do it, more than afraid, terrified. The sight of that delicate fair girl reminded him that when they first encountered each other had been the time of his beginning this process of recall. Walking away from her, his bedding in the buggy, he had thought that speaking to an ordinary person, a dweller in the

40

world he had left, should serve as a sign for him and there and then he decided to put an end to the time of denial. Total change, absolute alteration of circumstances, utter abandonment of the past – all these had served their purpose. Now it was time to move on and take the plunge into pain. He would rip the scar tissue off the wound and lay a cold probe against the rawness. He had nothing to lose. It had to be done and now was the time to begin.

He had started by a kind of meditation, his eyes on his wedding ring, the symbol of what had been and what was lost. Since then, in this world he had chosen for himself, both unreal and more real than any reality he had ever known, he had re-experienced every day his lovely history, a chapter of it or part of a chapter, and it did not heal the pain or come near healing it. But something else was happening. He was more aware than he had ever been of what it was to be a human being and it was as if, in all his joyous and contented days, he had never really known this before. And self-pity, so rebellious and consuming, was utterly gone. He had become unaccommodated man, perhaps even what those existentialists said man should be – free, suffering, alone, and in control of his own destiny.

Now he chose for his excursion into the past a holiday he and Sally and Elizabeth had had in Crete. It was ten years before, almost exactly ten years. Elizabeth had been four or five. They had chosen May for the wild flowers that cover the island with blossom at that time and because the sun was warm but not yet hot. He chiefly remembered from that holiday the colour of the sea, the blue of Elizabeth's eyes, the languor and the sweet idleness and his and Sally's lovemaking, the best since their honeymoon. They had been the young ardent lovers of seven years before and in those two weeks Daniel had been conceived. With a pain that made him gasp Roman remembered their bed and waking in the morning naked, uncovered by bedclothes, and Sally naked beside him. Like gods they were, discovered by the morning light.

As he left the Park by the Clarence Gate, he found himself able to summon up from that past time the things they had said to each other and even the expression in Sally's eyes, the tranquillity and sometimes the passion. He remembered walking on the beach with his daughter and carrying her because the sand was too hot on the soles of her small tender feet. 'Daddy, Daddy,' she had said, lifting up one foot, 'my soul is burning!' Or that was what it sounded like and they laughed, he and Sally, for what did he know then of burning souls and hellish torment?

Across Gloucester Place he walked and into the hinterland of Marylebone Station where the shabby streets make so extreme a contrast with Nash's palatial terraces. He took the steps down into Boston Place and through Blandford Square into Harewood Avenue. The sight of a corner shop reminded him that he must buy food for his supper. Sometime or other it must be done, but shops were always open till all hours in these streets. He came into Lisson Grove and turned south, conjuring Elizabeth's face in his mind, its innocence and its rapture, and as sometimes happened, the tears came into his eyes and fell down his cheeks.

Other people took no notice. They expected him to be different from them, demented, drug-crazy, drunk, ungoverned, mad. It was because of these things that he was where he was and they were where they were. Only Pharaoh, leaning against the door of a shop closed for the night, eyed him with some feeling of kinship and holding out the bottle

42

from which he had been drinking, said, 'Here, mate, want a sup?'

Roman had long ago ceased to worry about catching things from drinking out of other people's bottles and though he didn't want it – God knows what it was – he accepted and took a swig. Rioja and meths, he thought. Wiping his mouth on his sleeve, the way he had learnt from Dill and Effie, he sat down on the stone step and looked up at Pharaoh. He never stopped hoping to see some change in the man's face, some improvement. By that he meant that madness would be less evident there, that the slipping away of sanity would have halted so that something human still remained, some kindly light in the feral bloodshot eyes, some relaxing of the mouth so that the lips were neither curled back nor sucked together in a whitened rigidity.

But there was no change and the sign of humanity Pharaoh had given in offering a drink to a man in tears, was a rare happening. Soon even that would cease. He squatted down and thrust his haunted face into Roman's, his black beard that he streaked with dark blue dye into Roman's beard.

'Have you got a key for me?' he said.

Roman shook his head. Anyone who looked more closely at Pharaoh – no one ever looked closely – would have seen the hundreds of keys which hung round him, strung there on the rope which served him as a belt, pinned to his clothes with safety pins: brass and steel and chrome, Yale keys and Banhams, front-door keys and back-door keys, keys for opening suitcases and keys for locking padlocks. From the irregular bulges in his clothes Roman suspected his pockets too were filled with keys. He clinked and rattled when he walked, shuffling in and out of doorways, going where his voices sent him in search of the ultimate key.

43

Where did they come from? Whose had they been? Pharaoh never said and Roman never asked.

'The keys of the kingdom,' Pharaoh said.

His black eyes rolled. When he looked about him he made jerky startled movements. One of his voices told him that when Christ said, 'I will give unto thee the keys of the kingdom of heaven,' it was an actual bunch of keys that He handed to Peter. These were lost, had been lost for two thousand years, but it was Pharaoh's mission to find them. He speculated constantly as to their nature and appearance.

'They'll be made of gold, won't they? Purest gold? Only gold'd unlock the gates of heaven.'

Pharaoh should not be here at all, an outsider, on the street, but in the kind of place that had no existence these days, a place that was comfortable and clean and civilised, where he could have some dignity, where caring people looked after him and doctors well-versed in the tragedy of his existence put him on a regimen of drugs. Roman had no idea whether he was autistic or schizophrenic or mentally handicapped. He preferred the word 'mad' to all these because he knew that he too was mad and that being mad was a prerequisite of what he had done in becoming an outsider.

Patting Pharaoh on the shoulder – from which the man with the blue-streaked beard started back, recoiling and snarling like a wildcat poked with a stick – Roman got up and continued on his course towards the Marylebone Road and across it back into Gloucester Place. It amused him to reflect that being addressed by Pharaoh would once have alarmed him very much. He would have been frightened, though not admitted it, would have pretended not to hear. And to have entered into a conversation with such a creature would have been unthinkable. He was such a creature himself now, or not far off.

Turning into Crawford Street, he waited before crossing the road for the red and white food delivery van to pass. What would Express Tikka and Pizza say if he phoned from a call box and asked for a delivery of Chicken Masala to the third seat on the left going up the Broad Walk from Chester Road? A verbal equivalent, he supposed, of the look he got in the sandwich bar where he asked for cheese and pickle.

They looked askance but they served him. It was his accent, Roman knew; it made them think that maybe they were wrong, that this was no dosser but an eccentric, an absent-minded professor who forgot to have baths. He would have lost his accent if he could but his attempts to do so sounded like grotesque parodies. Tomorrow, he was reminded, he had better have an all-over wash, in a public convenience somewhere. Keeping clean, or avoiding utter filthiness, was one of the grimmer problems the outsider faced and one which no insider ever took into account.

Turning into Old Quebec Street, wondering where to settle down and eat his supper, he came under the windows of Talisman, the environmentalist publishers. He wore no watch but told the time by the state of the light and traffic and the movement of people and he guessed it was seven. The staff, such as it was, would have gone home an hour ago. To the front door Talisman's logo of a lyre-tree leaf was attached with its name and that of its editor-in-chief, Tom Outram. Once his name had been there too, but that, like so much in his old life, was water under the bridge, flowing into the sea of his memories.

Chapter Four

No one but Alistair would phone so early. Urgency was always implicit in phone calls made before nine in the morning.

Bean had called and collected Gushi. It was half-past eight. Mary thought she knew who her caller must be and she hesitated before picking up the receiver. But there was always her grandmother to think of. Her grandmother was strong and healthy but very old.

'How are you settling in?'

He had never spoken to her like that before. It was the phrase of an elderly parent delivered in a tone that was solicitous but querulous too and aggrieved. She tried to sound brisk and cheerful.

'Fine,' she said. 'I'm all right. It's nice here. I've been walking a lot.'

As soon as she had said it she knew it was an unwise thing to say, for he immediately countered by telling her not to overdo things. She was not strong, she was a fragile creature. He managed, without putting this into words, to imply that by her irresponsible and thoughtless conduct she had put her health in jeopardy.

'When am I to be allowed to come and see you?'

'Alistair,' she said, 'we're having a separation, remember?'

'A *trial* separation.'

She tried again. 'I have left you. We're apart.

We've discussed it, we decided. My coming here was to mark the beginning of our separation.'

'Oh, come on,' he said, 'that's just a figure of speech. The mistake was mine in giving any of that stuff credence. Absence makes the heart grow fonder, that's the real reason, isn't it?'

Hers or his? There was no need to ask. He implied that being parted from him would increase her affection for him. Affection – that lukewarm word. Even of that she felt very little. If you were like her, receptive, anxious to please – euphemisms, she told herself, for passive and ingratiating – you found it hard to understand how anyone thought love could be won by bullying. He set about bullying her now.

'You can't escape me so easily, you know, Mary. I'm not the kind of man to wreck two people's lives for a woman's whim. Haven't I proved in the past that I know what's best for us?'

She should have refuted that but she feared the storm that would ensue. She had left him, hadn't she? That great step had been taken; she need not learn to fight him. She told him she was in a hurry and must go.

'All right. I know that tone of voice. There's no getting a word out of you when you've decided to sulk. You'll soon get over that. I'll be over very soon.'

As if she had invited him . . .

'No,' she managed to say. 'Please no.' The effort of refusing always made her tired as if she really was the delicate creature she looked.

'I'll drop in one evening,' he said as if she hadn't spoken. 'I'll take you out somewhere.'

Mary went back into the kitchen and poured herself a second cup of coffee. It was going to be harder getting away from him than she had thought. The strength of will she hoped she was learning would be needed, but what of the strength that

47

women can never acquire? She would never come near to matching him physically. Like stigmata appearing at certain triggers, her face suddenly stung from the blow on the cheek he had given her when he saw those puncture marks. She looked in the mirror and saw the flush that bloomed there, brighter on the right side than the left. Alistair was left-handed.

They had been making love. He drew away from her and, extending his right hand, touched those marks with the tips of his fingers.

'What's that?' he said. The tone told her he knew. 'Scorpion bit you? Poison Ivy? Barbed wire?'

There is something terrible about the mood of lovemaking – so tender, languorous, exciting in that uniquely warm and breathless way – being broken by a harsh voice, sarcasm, barely suppressed rage. Nothing comes so quickly as sexual desire and nothing ebbs so fast as sexual willingness. It was like feeling cold water poured over her body.

She turned her face away. 'The bone marrow harvest,' she said. 'I told you I meant to do it.'

'You deceived me,' he said and, taking hold of her face in an iron grip with fingers that dug, struck her cheek with the flat of his hand, the hardest blow she had ever received. Until then, the *only* blow.

It was not quite a beating up he gave her. You could hardly call a slap on the face, a shaking, another slap, a pulling upright and a throwing to the ground, beating someone up. She had crawled away and shut herself in the bathroom. Her cheek was bruised next day and she had bruised her leg when she fell.

He apologised to her; he crawled. He didn't know what had come over him, only that it never would again. Predictably, he showed the other aspect of the bully's character. It was this wretched temperament of his, he excused himself, his love of physical perfection, his worship of the ideal.

'You're so perfect, I can't bear to think of your body assailed, plundered.' He was almost crying. 'I can't bear to think of all that beauty endangered.'

Except by him, she thought later, except by him. He had touched her bruised cheek with tears in his eyes . . .

Still, that would never happen again. None of it would happen; it was all over. She had left and, under another roof, could withstand any onslaught. Upstairs she dabbed at her cheek with pale powder, as if it was still red and marked by Alistair's hand. Her eyes had that panicky look he had lately induced in them but as she made herself breathe deeply, her face smoothed and grew calmer, her shoulders relaxed.

Gushi was brought back just as she was leaving. She showed him his freshly filled water bowl, gave him a quick caress, and running now, caught up with Bean and his troop on the corner of Albany Street: Boris the borzoi, Charlie the golden retriever, Marietta the chocolate poodle, McBride the scottie. Only Ruby the beagle was absent.

'Gone on her holidays to Ilfracombe,' said Bean. He had a camera on a strap round his neck, like a tourist. 'She'll be missing the Park. Them hounds need a lot of exercise.'

'Won't she be able to run on the beach?'

He never answered questions. She wondered why she bothered to ask. Bean countered questions with a statement or a question of his own as competently as any politician trained to do this on television. Sometimes his statements were relevant, sometimes not.

'A hound can run twenty miles and think nothing of it,' he said.

49

She felt like saying: But can hounds think? Instead, she remarked on Bean's expertise in the handling of so many dogs. He nodded, accepting the praise as his due, and said in the tone that sounded disparaging, though probably was not:

'I'll say goodbye then, miss. We mustn't detain you.'

'Goodbye.'

'Mind how you cross the road. The traffic's very treacherous in these parts.'

Had he once been a butler? Perhaps. His manner was that of a superior upper servant – well, a superior upper servant in a film of the Fifties. Her experience of the real thing was non-existent. The grandparents who had brought her up, though comfortably off, had lived modestly, with a cleaner coming in twice a week. She took the lower path, the one that runs close up against the fence of the Abika Paul Memorial Gardens, the better to see the cattle and deer. Her grandmother had sometimes brought her in here as a child, had once taken her to the zoo with a friend who lived in Primrose Hill. A sheltered childhood and youth it had been, she supposed. Her grandparents had been discreetly wealthy, what they called 'comfortably off'. Such strange expressions, 'comfortably off', 'well off' – off what? Off the poverty line, the breadline?

Their income had never been mentioned, money never talked about. Even now she had no idea how much Frederica had, even if she was rich or genteely poor. Alistair had shown an interest but her grandmother had never been forthcoming to Alistair, had never liked him. If she had agreed with Alistair in anything it had been over the bone marrow donation and her opposition had been mild compared to his, had been no more than a fear of 'unnecessary' anaesthesia and a conviction – despite all evidence to the contrary – that Mary must be as vulnerable as she looked.

People were a mixture of subtle contrasts. Malleable, weak, diffident she might be, but she had gone ahead with her resolution. She had persisted. It's a man, the Trust had told her, twenty-two years old, suffering from Acute Myeloid Leukaemia. The donation would take place in this country, they said, but they had not told her whether the recipient was British or of some other nationality.

After the transplant they gave him the card she had written to him and they gave her the letter he had written to her. Both were unsealed; both had been scrutinised to make sure identification of either donor or recipient was impossible. His name was Oliver, but they smiled when they said it, making clear this was a pseudonym. Her name, that she was told to put on the card, was Helen, and they had told him she was twenty-eight and in perfect health. She had chosen 'Helen' because it was her dead mother's name and she wondered why he had picked 'Oliver' or if it had been chosen for him.

She had not known what to write on the card, so had done no more than call him 'Dear Oliver', wish him a speedy recovery, and sign herself, 'Yours sincerely, Helen'. It was rather ridiculous. What could it mean to him? His letter to her was typed, not very expertly. It was formal, lifeless. 'Dear Helen, I want to thank you for what you have done for me,' but ended as if emotion had broken through, 'In undying thankfulness, Oliver', and she wondered that they hadn't demurred at that, that most unfortunate word, for he very likely would die, in spite of the donation.

Then came the updates from 'Oliver's' transplant centre. He was well at three months and at six. There was a delay – she heard nothing for six months and

51

was sure he was ill again, was dying – then the nine-month report and the twelve-month came simultaneously: 'Oliver' continued well. She kept the updates away from Alistair but inadvertently let out that 'Oliver' was thriving.

Alistair claimed to have seen a decline in her own health since the donation and a fading of her looks. She told him she was perfectly well, she looked just the same. Her grandmother, in spite of earlier opposition, had remarked favourably on her appearance. Perhaps it was bringing Frederica into it that had set him off. He took hold of her by the shoulders.

'You need some sense shaking into you,' he had said, and had proceeded to shake her, gently at first, then with a kind of frenzy.

She fell against a table, dislodging a glass vase which broke and cut her leg. He had to take her to hospital, to Casualty, and when her leg was stitched and strapped up, wept all over her, bemoaning the loss of her beauty, the draining away of her 'life-blood'.

'Why did you make that stupid sacrifice? Why did you destroy your health and your looks? Now you can see what it's led to.'

It was the beginning of the end. Some of the worst of it for Mary was the realisation of her own poor judgement. How could she have loved him or even have thought she loved him? Why hadn't she detected this behaviour in him before? And then there came back to her the slight unease she had always felt when he seemed to judge people by their physical appearance. She met his mother and found this ageing woman doing the same thing. Like Sir Walter Elliot in *Persuasion*, Marina Winter remarked constantly on the propensity of those around her 'to lose something of their personableness when they cease to be quite young', and made irrelevant comments on 'freckles, and a projecting tooth, and a clumsy wrist'.

Discovering where this trait in Alistair had come from went some way to excusing it in Mary's eyes, but later on she came to wonder how it would be if they stayed together and she too aged and began to lose her looks. Would he call her a dog as she had once or twice been shocked to hear him describe an older woman? Would everything else she was – her closeness to him, the sexual life they enjoyed, the gentle tranquillity she knew was hers, her skills as a craftswoman – would all this go for nothing when lines came on her face and gravity pulled her earthwards?

She had found out sooner than she expected. He punished physical diminution, not with words but with blows. Remembering, she felt the blood mount into the cheek where he had struck her. She felt it settle there and burn the skin.

Chapter Five

With Gushi in her lap, Frederica Jago said, 'Where will you go then when the Blackburn-Norrises come back?' And without waiting for an answer, 'Come back and live with me.'

Mary laughed. 'That's a rash invitation. I might take you up on it.'

'It's your home, my dear. Where else would it be natural for you to go?'

'To a place of my own.'

'Of course my house is much bigger but it's not in the same league as this one. But what is, when you come to think of it? Still, you would have the run of it and you'd often have it to yourself. You know I'm always away.'

It was true. While Mrs Jago's husband was alive they had never set foot west of Cornwall or east of Suffolk, for Lucian Jago had a fear of flying and a tendency to seasickness. Since his death and Mary's departure, if she had not wandered the earth, she had taken every available package tour – to India, to Tashkent and Samarkand, the rose-red city of Petra, up the Yangtse and down the Nile, California, New England. Lately, as she passed eighty, she had restricted her travelling to Europe, forsaking the travel agent's recommendations and visiting out-of-the-way places.

She was a small, thin, pretty woman, bird-faced with a crest of white wavy hair, her granddaughter's green eyes, and indeed very much as Mary would one day be, her bones more apparent than her flesh, the shape of her body still uncannily like a young girl's.

Having arrived at Charlotte Cottage in a taxi with a gift for Mary from Lapland and a bottle of champagne, she renewed her friendship with Gushi. She had brought him a dog-chewing bar, that she assured him was made from reindeer skin, and feeling for it in her bag, brought it out first and then an envelope.

'I nearly forgot. This came for you.'

Mary took it. 'I was going to ask but I thought it would be too soon.'

'Too soon for what?' Frederica gave Gushi the chewing bar and he rolled on his back on the carpet, grasping it in his paws and growling. 'What is it? More about your bone marrow man?'

'I hope it's his name and address.' She hesitated, as she had done with the Trust's last communication, turning the envelope in her hands, looking at the logo, the stamp, the postmark. 'I shall know at last. It's rather daunting.'

'Don't be daunted. Would you like me to open it?'

'No. No, I don't think so.'

'My darling Mary, you don't have to open it in my presence. I shan't be offended. Keep it till I've gone.'

Mary shook her head. 'I'm going to open it now.'

It would, after all, only be a name. An ordinary sort of name, probably, and a number and a street anywhere in the country, in a city or a town or a village. She had been told it was in the British Isles, that he was British; that was all.

There was no need, this time, for preparation, for bracing herself. Timidity was ridiculous when the contents of this envelope could not possibly contain any threat. Frederica handed her a paper knife from

55

the desk, ivory handled, with a long thin blade. She had probably seen the Blackburn-Norrises use it. Mary slit along the top of the flap and took out the enclosure.

The letter was short. It said:

Dear Ms Jago,

We note that you have not asked us to pass your own name and address on to 'Oliver' and therefore assume you will do this yourself. He is now willing to be identified. His name is Leo Nash and his address Flat 24, Redferry House, Plangent Road, London NW1. I should like to take this opportunity of wishing you a pleasant and rewarding meeting with Mr Nash.

Yours sincerely,
Deborah Cox

Mary read it aloud. She said: 'How very strange. Plangent Road can't be far from here. It's North-West One like this is.'

'Maybe, but it's not much like this,' Frederica said drily. 'It's Somers Town. And you know nothing else about him? Nothing except that he's twenty-three and male?'

'Twenty-four by now,' said Mary. 'Do you know, all these months I've longed to meet him, and now I can I don't know whether I want to or not. It's a mistake to meet people in these circumstances, isn't it? One's always disappointed.'

'These circumstances aren't within my experience, Mary. I don't know. It's old-fashioned to say this but I am old-fashioned. It would be unnatural if I wasn't.'

'Say what?'

'I was going to say, I *am* saying, that it's best to meet people through being introduced by your friends or family. Or at work perhaps, only I've never been to work, so I can't say. This young man owes you a lot, he is under a great obligation to you, and that isn't the best basis for a friendship.'

'A friendship!' said Mary. 'He may not even answer my letter. If he feels he's under an obligation he probably won't want to meet me.'

'Is it true that we dislike those who have done us a service?' Frederica asked. 'If so, the greater the service perhaps the greater the dislike. And it's hard to imagine a greater service than saving someone's life. He may feel he owes you more than he could ever repay. And then if he sees – how shall I put this? Mary, you're very pretty and – well, graceful and sweet; you're obviously educated and gifted and living in a lovely place. Won't that be a burden for him too? A poor, sick, deprived young man from what sounds like a council estate behind Euston Station?'

Mary looked at her. She felt stricken by a small panic. 'I wish you hadn't been away,' she said. 'I wish we could have had this conversation before I asked for his address.'

'And if I'd advised you, would you have taken my advice? Of course you wouldn't.'

'It isn't too late,' Mary said slowly. 'I haven't been in touch with him. I just know his name and where he lives. What would your advice be?'

Frederica laughed. 'Are you passing the buck? Laying the responsibility on me?'

'I don't know. Perhaps. I'm in the habit of doing that. Or I used to be. Advise me.'

'Tear the letter up, give me the pieces and on my way home I'll drop them in a litter bin.'

'So that I couldn't get them out and piece them together again? It wouldn't be any use, I'm afraid. I know his name now. I have the address by heart.

Wouldn't I always regret it if I didn't write to him? But perhaps he won't answer.'

Frederica laughed. 'He'll answer.'

On the front doorstep in Albany Street Edwina Goldsworthy gave Bean formal notice that she would be going away on holiday in ten days' time and McBride be taking up residence in kennels. Bean disapproved of kennels and his manner became chilly. But he had to go inside for the necessary paperwork, having first tied his dogs up to a lamppost, and this delayed him.

'Don't be surprised if he loses weight in there, madam,' he said, and he cast a critical eye over Mrs Goldsworthy's bulky form before adding, 'Pining does more than diets, as I always say.'

She was dependent on him; she couldn't say much. None of them could. They were in his power. Without him they would have to leave their beds an hour earlier, sacrifice their cocktail hour, get up off their arses and muddy their shoes. Bean smiled to himself. Power was not something he had personally experienced in his years as the late Anthony Maddox's and then the late Maurice Clitheroe's servant, but now he was making up for lost time. Absolute reliability, 'sirs' and 'madams' sprinkled among his remarks, a genuine love of dogs, punctilious punctuality – all this made him indispensable. He disliked being even five minutes late, for this detracted from his power, and he quickened his pace as he and the dogs made for Cumberland Terrace, home of Marietta, the chocolate poodle.

The actress Lisl Pring hadn't noticed the time. She kissed Marietta and had her make-up licked off. Bean had never seen anyone as thin as this woman, except in famine photos. They said telly made a person look fatter, which was no doubt the reason.

He wondered how she did it. Lived on salad, no doubt, or maybe she was like that model he'd read about who had nothing in her fridge but a lemon.

He reminded her of his seven-days-notice-of-holidays rule and she shrieked something about never having a moment to go anywhere, darling. If it wasn't shooting it was rehearsals from five am till midnight, believe it or not. Bean nodded. He didn't really believe it. She must be rich. Up here in the hinterland of the terrace was like being in some Georgian spa, Leamington or Cheltenham, all mellow stone and ivy, blossom coming out and ferns uncurling, a smell like the country, green and sharp. Bean thought he wouldn't half mind living here himself, only he'd never afford it the way things were. He must put his power to wider use.

The bag lady with the green plastic bundles was meandering slowly up the Outer Circle as he came out of Cumberland Terrace. Her name, he knew, was Effie but in his mind Bean called her a horrible cow. Boris and Charlie and the rest of them always wanted to sniff her. This propensity of theirs, sometimes seeming to prefer people who smelt nasty to people who smelt nice, was his only objection to dogs. He tugged the leashes away with an artificial shudder. The bag lady told him to fuck off and gave him instructions about the kind of sexual activity he and his dogs might mutually engage in. Bean thought it a pity that the cleaning-up of London, begun some three years before, had not included purging the streets of dossers, beggars and foul-mouthed slags.

Before returning him to Mr and Mrs Barker-Pryce in St Andrew's Place, Bean took a photograph of Charlie the golden retriever. He was a handsome dog and made quite a picture standing there, head raised, tail up, in the sunshine. Charlie's owner answered the door himself, cigar in hand. Mr Barker-Pryce was a Member of Parliament for some London constituency and it was a wonder how he managed in the House of Commons chamber, having to go without his cigars for maybe a whole two hours. Bean and the borzoi proceeded on alone to Park Square. Here Bean used his key to let himself into the gardens in the centre of the square.

These gardens, nothing to look at from the street – a wire fence, a scrubby (but impenetrable) hedge, the tops of trees – are a park themselves when you get inside. They might be the grounds of some great country house with their green lawns, curved flower-beds, tall trees and flowering shrubs, lovely in their peace and tranquillity. Bean never noticed the beauty but he liked the exclusivity. He liked anything that put him among an elite, permitted privileges and pleasures few might enjoy. Here was an opportunity for another shot, a red blaze of flowering shrub that might serve for someone's Christmas card.

The path to the Nursemaids' Tunnel descends in a shallow sloping curve between brick walls to the portico which is the tunnel entrance. It gave Bean a bit of a shock to find himself not alone in the tunnel. There was someone in there, far up ahead. He would have thought nothing of this if the figure had been on the move, striding towards him or away from him, but whoever it was was leaning against the wall on the left-hand side at the Park Crescent end, holding a bottle to his lips. A street sleeper. Another of Effie's ilk. Like most people, Bean was afraid of the street people, and particularly afraid when with one in a confined space. He was a small man, far from young, and borzois, though large dogs, bred to hunt the wolf, are fine-boned and seldom aggressive.

Bean could have turned back. He could have gone back and crossed the Marylebone Road at the lights by Regent's Park tube station. But he didn't want the man with the bottle to see this happen, to see him turn tail and of course understand perfectly why he had retreated. For he, Bean, was a man of power and if he turned he would have yielded power into the hands of this dirty reject, this piece of flotsam fit for nothing but a city's sewers. He imagined broken drunken laughter echoing down the passage, reverberating off the damp walls.

He hadn't much money on him but he didn't want to lose his camera. It was a Pentax and, like so much in Bean's possession, had once belonged to Maurice Clitheroe. If he'd only thought of it five minutes before he could have slipped the camera inside his jacket.

How had the man got in here? They were careful with their keys, the Crown Estates. In order to obtain one you had to be a resident of the Square or the Crescent, or the adjacent terraces and mews. He touched the camera like someone fingering an amulet, and quickly drew his hand away. He walked on, somewhat more slowly than he would have done if the man with the bottle hadn't been there, but not so slowly as to show his fear. The borzoi took its normal delicate steps, loping on tiptoe, but very steady in its progress.

The light at the end showed Bean a gaunt thin figure with long black hair and a beard stained blue. A momentary flashback took him sixty years into the past and a village school in Hampshire, the teacher telling them how in the distant past the inhabitants of these islands had painted their bodies with woad. Maybe the blue stuff on this roughneck's beard was woad. Bean determined not to look as he passed him, to walk past at a steady pace as if the man wasn't there or as if for some reason he hadn't *noticed* that he was there. He pulled the leash tight so that Boris was close up to him on his right side. This was the kind of thug that wouldn't think twice about kicking a dog.

The man turned his head to stare when Bean was about two yards from him. And Bean had to look; he had to return that stare for a single second before jerking his eyes away. In that second he received an impression of metal, of glitter, as of the man being covered in slivers of metal. It reminded him, unpleasantly but irresistibly, of Maurice Clitheroe's indulgence in S-M – Bean had no idea what those initials stood for but he knew what it was all right – and of some of those who came to the flat in Mr Clitheroe's time. Leather, zip fasteners, body piercing – there had been a lot of that – and a great deal of metal in many shapes and forms, most of it sharp.

Thinking of all this got Bean past the man, and the dog past the man, up the steps and out into the light. His mind had been distracted at exactly the right time. Safe, unmolested, his camera safe, he indulged himself in a spot of what the late Anthony Maddox called *l'esprit de l'escalier* and thought what he might, ought to, have said. Like, 'What authority do you have to use this tunnel?' or 'By whose permission are you in this private foot passage?'

James Barker-Pryce CMG, MP would have done that. So would Bertram Cornell. They had the right accent; they had been to the kind of school where they taught you to think of yourself as a king of the earth. Money did that for you too. As Bean walked out of the gardens and crossed the road to the Park Crescent pavement, he realised what those metal things were. They were keys. The man had keys hanging off him everywhere and no doubt one of them was the key to this garden. Something would have to be done.

Boris's home was not the house where the blue

plaque testified to Marie Tempest's having once lived there, but a few doors along. The Cornells' housekeeper did what she always did and opened the basement door in the area. What was wrong with the front door? If she didn't know it, his days of being treated like a servant were over. Her attitude meant he had to go round the corner into Portland Place and all the way down the iron staircase.

The borzoi trotted in, ignoring the housekeeper, leaving Bean without the least sign of affection, without a backward glance. It pushed a door open with its long nose and disappeared into the room beyond, a cold dog with no feelings.

'It's Russian, you see,' said the housekeeper as if that explained everything.

Bean nodded. 'Mr and Mrs Cornell away, Valerie?'

The housekeeper said her employers were in France, coming back tomorrow. Even they called her Miss Conway. Apart from her friends, only Bean took upon himself the right to call her by her given name. She was getting up her nerve to tell him not to, but she hadn't got it up yet. Her revenge was to make him walk down those steps and necessarily, of course, up them again. She told him there had been another burglary in the Crescent, two in fact, one of them only next door.

'That must make you nervous being here on your own,' said Bean.

It did. But she disliked being reminded of it. 'I've got the dog.'

Bean laughed lightly, shaking his head. 'More of a pussy cat, that one,' he said. 'There are some rough characters about. I just saw something barely human in the tunnel, more like an alien. You don't want to open your front door to no one.'

'Thanks a bunch,' said Valerie.

She slammed the door. Bean winced a little to

63

show his sensitivity for the benefit of any passers-by who might be watching. He favoured the statue with a passing glance, Queen Victoria's father, Prince Edward, Duke of Kent, standing on a plinth at the end of the gardens and looking down Portland Place. Someone had once told Bean he was the spitting image of the Duke and after that he had never passed the bronze figure without giving it a look.

He lived a little way away in York Terrace East. Normally, he would have gone back by way of the tunnel but he didn't want to encounter the key man again. Better brave the Marylebone Road, wait a good two minutes for those lights to change, then belt across before they changed back again. It was easier without dogs pulling him like in some chariot race.

He let himself into his flat. Neat as a pin, spotlessly clean, it was furnished exactly as it had been in the days of Maurice Clitheroe, its former owner, with heavy, highly polished late-nineteenth-century pieces, red and blue Turkey rugs, and in the living room a newish three-piece suite covered in tan-coloured hide. This and the huge television and video reflected Bean's own taste. His kitchen was carefully geared for the freezer-microwave culture. There was no oven and there were no pans. The lot had gone on the day of Mr Clitheroe's memorial service, along with the piano, the whip and gun collection and the pictures of two saints undergoing particularly revolting forms of martyrdom.

Maurice Clitheroe had left Bean his duplex in recognition of services rendered. These had some-times been onerous, particularly in the area of punishment, though here he had always been the executant, never the recipient. He had known where to draw the line, as for example in refusing to gratify Mr Clitheroe's demand that both of them should wear spiked dog collars while at home alone. And in spite of this setting of limits, the flat had still been left to him according to a promise frequently made but never entirely taken seriously.

In relation to the flat he loved – he called it a maisonette – and in which he now settled down contentedly to microwave a Linda McCartney vegetarian platter, Bean had only one regret. He had no opportunity to impress his clients with his address, no chance of presenting them with invoices on paper headed York Terrace, NW1. For since the owners of dogs were unable to claim income tax relief on what they paid him, every penny he received was black money, money in the back pocket, handed over in cash. His earnings from Mr Clitheroe had never reached the tax floor, for all was found for him – his board, his lodging, even his clothes. The Inland Revenue probably thought he was dead or, more likely, had never been born.

He had a look at the camera and checked that there were three frames left on the film.

In her third week at Charlotte Cottage Mary was twice invited out to dinner. Her grandmother gave rather a grand dinner party for her. The nine guests and Frederica Jago sat down to deep-fried *Crottin de Chavignol* with cranberry sauce, roast guinea fowl and French apple tart with clotted cream. A heavy meal suitable for old-fashioned old people. Everyone but Mary and one of the men she sat next to was very old, so it was plain that the young or youngish man had been invited for her sake.

Much the same thing happened at the other dinner party. This was given by Dorothea in Charles Lane where she lived with her husband Gordon in the house next door to the Irene Adler Museum. Everyone among the eight guests was young, so they ate

65

roquette and corn salad in an orange and walnut dressing, red mullet with couscous and deep-fried sage leaves, followed by cherimoya sorbet with a sharon fruit coulis. Couples were either married or living together in long-term relationships, so it was apparent to Mary that the single (divorced) man she sat next to had been invited for her sake.

Of these two men, Frederica's protégé and Gordon's friend, the former rang Mary up next day and asked if she would go to the cinema with him to see *The Madness of King George*. She said no. It was not only that she had seen the film, but that of all activities likely to improve two people's knowledge of each other, cinema-going must be the least effective. You met in the foyer; you sat side by side in the dark in silence; you had a drink afterwards and said goodnight. Not that she wanted to improve her knowledge of him, nor apparently did he of her, for he suggested no alternative outing. The other man, Dorothea's, didn't get in touch at all.

'It's humiliating,' Mary said to Dorothea next day in the Irene Adler drawing room. 'I wish you hadn't done it. I wish my grandmother hadn't done it.'

'Oh, come on. I didn't do anything. The poor man's just getting over the trauma of his wife's running off with the VAT inspector. Gordon and I try to include him in as much as we can.'

'And you thought this poor girl was just getting over the trauma of her boyfriend knocking her about, is that it? They'd be just right for each other? Well, he didn't think so. I haven't heard a word from him. And that is humiliating, Dorrie.'

Nearly as humiliating as writing to Leo Nash and getting no reply. She had been so sure of a prompt answer to her letter. What a fool, to imagine the man longing to hear from her, desperate for a word, only waiting with bated breath for the chance to get in touch!

'You're overreacting,' said Dorothea, and she stood back, trying to decide if the framed photograph of Irene Adler looked best displayed on the mantelpiece or semi-concealed behind the half-open secret panel. It was a question which had exercised her ever since the drawing room had been created in its present mode. 'He's probably just too unhappy to even think of anyone else at the moment.'

'Yes, I daresay. But to me it seems he must have gone home saying to himself, they needn't think they can catch me so easily. I know a trick worth two of that. And then he forgot me.'

As Leo Nash must have looked at the Charlotte Cottage address and the writing paper and wondered what form her patronage of him would take?

'Look, if you fancy him we can maybe manage . . .'

'I don't fancy him in the least. I'll just go on going to the cinema by myself.'

She said nothing to Dorothea about being lonely. Dorothea would have asked her round to Charles Lane every evening, given a dinner party for her every week. School friends, college friends would have rallied round if she had got in touch. Her cousin in Surrey had invited her for the weekend but she had said no because of Gushi. Being alone and minding it wasn't the best training for someone who was trying to be strong and independent.

The weekends were the worst. There had only been three of them but they were very bad. She got up late, she read, she walked Gushi until he was exhausted and had to be carried, she walked about the West End, went to the Wallace Collection and the Planetarium. In the evenings she worked on the new catalogue and brochure she was compiling for the museum.

It was better on weekday evenings. She and Gushi watched television or played the Blackburn-Norrises' CDs. At bedtime she had stopped shutting Gushi up in the kitchen where his basket was but took him upstairs with her and let him sleep on her bed. During the night he edged closer and closer up towards the bedhead and now when she woke in the mornings it was to find his frondy face on the pillow beside her and as often as not her arms embracing him.

For the first week, in the mornings, she had awaited the post, but nothing came except junk mail, hire car and taxi cards, fliers from a food delivery service. Her phone number was on the writing paper and when the phone rang she half-expected a diffident, anxious male voice. But the only voice, and it wasn't diffident, was Alistair's.

After the early morning call, he phoned three times. The first was to say he was coming to see her: he would be over the following evening to take her out to dinner. Her protests, her reminder that they were separated, had no effect. If not tomorrow, then the next day, he said. In the end she agreed to the second suggestion and went through agonies all next day and the next, wondering how to deal with him if he came back with her and wanted to stay the night.

Seven came and seven-thirty and at seven-thirty-five he phoned to say he couldn't make it. She was relieved and at the same time angry. Angry with herself as much as with him for the two miserable days she had spent. That afternoon she had been so distracted that she had told an American tourist Irene Adler had lived in St John's Wood Terrace and her royal lover had been the King of Serbia.

Alistair phoned for the third time to say he was worried about her health. He had made an appointment for their GP to see her.

'It's at eight-thirty on Thursday morning.'

'Alistair, as you know, I haven't got a car. Do you really think I'm coming to Willesden at that hour?'

'Of course you'd stay the night here.'

'I'm perfectly well. I don't need a doctor.' She tried to speak pleasantly to him, to be polite but firm, but when she said goodbye his furious shouting down the receiver made her tremble.

All of it made her ask herself if she had been right to take on this dog-sitting and house-minding at Charlotte Cottage. Of course she could not have stayed with Alistair, that was plain, but should she perhaps have gone first to her grandmother, and then found herself a place in a shared flat? To be with other people . . .

It was too late now. Outside it was sunny again, a warm still evening. Two people walked by, on their way out into Albany Street, their arms round each other. Loneliness was worse on fine evenings when the red sun went down over the horizon of a great city and the night sky grew purple, though with no chance of seeing the stars. She took Gushi on her lap and watched television.

The little dog was out with Bean and the others when the post came in the morning. A flier from a company selling exercise trampolines, another from Express Tikka and Pizza, and an envelope post-marked NW1. Her habitual hesitation at opening letters she told herself to abandon now; stop it once and for all. It was all part of the fearful temperament she had to learn to overcome. In a cool controlled way she went into the living room, picked up the paper knife and slit open the envelope.

She looked at the photograph first. A passport size photograph taken in one of those station or super-market kiosks of a man's pale thin face in front of a pleated curtain. To herself she was calling it anaemic before she realised what she was saying. Of course he was anaemic. Anaemia had nearly killed him ... The eyes were light and clear, the hair so fair as to be almost white, the features regular, classical: thin lips, straight nose, very high smooth forehead.

A handwritten letter from the Plangent Road address.

Dear Mary Jago, she read, *I am the man whose life you saved with your more than generous donation. You not only saved it, you made it good again, worth living. I want you to know that I am well now, thanks to you.*

Since you have given me your name and address, I think you must want us to get in touch. I hope I am not being presumptuous in saying that you may want us to meet as much as I want it.

I will not put you to the trouble of phoning me or writing back. In fact, I should make a confession and tell you I have no phone. Today, as I write, is Monday and you will get this letter by Wednesday at the latest. If I do not hear from you to tell me you would rather not meet me, I will be at an outside table at the Rose Garden restaurant in Regent's Park, the one north of the lake, from 5.30 till 6.00 on Friday.

I won't say, do come. But I hope you will come.
Yours sincerely,
Leo Nash

Chapter Six

Most of the street sleepers, the dossers, the dropouts, the jacks men, were on the street because they had nowhere else to be. They were without roofs of their own, or roofs rented, to put over their heads. This was not true of Roman, who had had a roof, who had had his own home, but who was on the street because he had no more choice than those others, because the outside was the only option if he was to continue to live.

If he was to live. An alternative there had been, the alternative open to all. 'Skipping out' on the canal bank, he had thought many times of sliding into the cold water one night, having first ripped his brain and his senses apart with the meths and water mixture, cloudy white fluid the jacks men called milk. The faith he no longer had stopped him. His Polish mother had brought him up a Catholic and if all of it was gone now, all dispelled by reason and science, vestigial fear remained, some absurd awe of the sin against the Holy Ghost.

So the street it had to be. Because home was unlivable in, a hollow place that howled at him, empty, empty, never to be filled again. A place so haunted that he had to hide his face from the staring walls and stuff bedding into his mouth to keep himself from crying out. And not just that house of his, but any house, flat, hotel, shelter, he might move to.

71

It was as if claustrophobia of a kind never before experienced had come to him with loss. Just as an inability to work had come, to go about among ordinary people. He was obliged to avoid every aspect of life as he had known it, if he was to survive and not curl up somewhere into a foetus that screwed up its eyes and hid its face in its frog's paws. Only the outside was feasible to him, where those he encountered took it for granted that he was set apart, that he was to some degree mad. This was the point, that he should be the Wandering Jew, or Oedipus. And if he had not put out his own eyes, nor had he his daughter with him as companion.

It was possible to have been too happy. He knew that now and because, at first, after it first happened, he lamented that he had been as happy as that, wished his had been a bad or broken marriage, his children ugly and stupid – because of these indefensible thoughts he had cut himself off from everything, expelled his family from his mind, and then expelled everything else from his life. The idea was to have nothing to remind him, to make everything different; no roof over his head, no job, no friends, no social life, no familiar things around him. If he was going to run away, and he was, it had to be a proper running away, complete, absolute, the old life shed in every aspect.

Until the fair girl spoke to him and he spoke to her.

He had been up to Primrose Hill where nuns give out tea and bread and butter to the homeless at five in the afternoon. It was in some novel of Graham Greene's that he had come upon that phrase 'a phony and a fake', and he applied it often to himself. For he had a home he had put into the hands of agents and sold. The money derived from that sale stopped him using the hostels and the day centres, to which others had a better right than he; it stopped him taking money passers-by offered him; but he drew the line at the nuns' tea. He drank the tea and ate the bread and butter and left a pound coin on the table.

A lot of Irishmen were up there from the gloomy Victorian hostel in Camden Town. Their life expectancy, he had read somewhere in Talisman Press days, was forty-seven. The meths would do for them – that and the cold and the poor diet. What you learn when you drop out of life! Roman wandered down Regent's Park Road and took the St Mark's Bridge over the canal. He counted seven houseboats moored alongside each other in Cumberland Basin and one in front of the Chinese teahouse. On its flat roof a woman lay sunbathing in a green bikini.

The finger of the minaret pointed into a pale blue sky on which the tiny clouds made a net. He thought of Omar Khayyam and the Sultan's turret caught in a noose of light. The sun made the Mosque's golden roof too bright to look at. He crossed the Outer Circle and came into the Broad Walk. It was wild and thickly treed up here, no flowerbeds, the neat lawns distant.

Roman sat down for a while on one of the seats by Sir Cowasjee Jehangir's drinking fountain. An engraved legend told him it had been put there from gratitude for a benevolent Raj's mercy to Parsees. A man's face in stone looked out from the column above the inscription. Since its foundation, how many thousands had drunk its water, how many horses once refreshed themselves at its troughs? The Parsees placed their dead on towers of silence for the vultures to take, to eat and pick their bones. He had been so placed, awaiting his fate.

From the zoo behind him came an animal sound, a loud grunt or trumpeting. He and Sally had never brought their children to the zoo but had taken them only to parkland where the big cats run free, to Woburn and Longleat. Slipping into his meditative mood, his remembering time, he recalled the Longleat day: the glorious weather, Elizabeth drawing pictures of a lioness and cubs on her sketch pad, the whole of it rather marred for him by his ridiculous anxiety.

The car's windows opened automatically at the press of a switch; they weren't the wind-down kind. He had heard of those windows going wrong, of sticking either in the open or the shut position. What if something should go wrong, one of the children open a window and the window refuse to close again? If lions surrounded the car, if the car broke down ... Later, when they were home again, he discovered that Sally had been thinking in just the same way, with exactly the same fears. But it was often so. They had shared thoughts, fears, happiness, read each other's minds.

Strange then that he had never prevised what had actually happened to his children, to his wife. His fears had been no more than fantasies or sops to a providence in whom he had no belief. They were never actual anticipations of real disaster with the corollary of: what will I do if they are all taken from me? How will I feel? How will I survive? And when it happened he had been without fear for some time, had rid himself of all but normal anxiety now Elizabeth was nearly fifteen and Daniel eight.

Roman did not usually think of that day. He did not relive the moments in which the news had been brought to him. For one thing, he could hardly remember what his feelings had been. An amnesia had descended and left him with a memory of beforehand and – horribly, agonisingly – twelve hours afterwards. The lost hours between he no longer tried to recapture.

But he did think sometimes – and he thought now, as he got up again and walked away from the stone column, the tower of silence – of that later aftermath, of the awful recurring disbelief, of sleep which came so readily and so easily, sleep in which everything could be buried, but which had to be resisted, for when he woke the truth returned as fresh and new as when it was first told him. Sleep, which is supposed to be a blessing, the 'balm of hurt minds', could be a curse too. Who would want a pain-killing drug that when its effects wore off, brought worse suffering?

It was different now. Denial was past and forgetfulness never came. He lay down to sleep on some doorstep in the full acceptance of what had happened and his waking was to the naked knowledge of their doom and his fate. There was no longer room for illusion. But in those early days, before he took to the street, he would wake in the morning, turn to the pillow beside his and wonder where Sally was, up so early. Then, like some slow rumbling explosion, growing in magnitude before the final roar, it had all returned to him and he groaned aloud his irrepressible pain. He whimpered and groaned and relived his homecoming that evening – the arrival of the police on his doorstep, their kindness and their total inability to soften what they called 'the blow'. That was when he had taken his decision to deny, expel, bury, pretend.

Now he had reached a point in the progression of his survival when he could control his memories. He was no longer at the mercy of these things bursting and breaking into the fabric of his general sadness. They were there, always there, the trigger of his madness, but he need not relive them nor see what in reality he had never seen: the crash explode, metallic

75

and black and red, on his inner eye. He could expel them and think instead of another happy time – of Daniel's last birthday, dinner at McDonald's for fifteen little kids and *Beauty and the Beast* at the cinema afterwards. Elizabeth had come, a great concession, a considerable kindness, from a teenager to a small boy . . .

Roman turned into Chester Road and entered the Inner Circle by the golden gates. Sally had always liked the Rose Garden, but later than this, a month later, when the roses were in bud and their scent was still a delicate breath on the air. The precision of the garden had pleased her, its order, the considerable taste that had gone into its arrangement. He left the gardens by the gate at the Open Air Theatre and walked on. As he crossed the Long Bridge over the northern arm of the lake he heard footsteps behind him and looked back. It was the fair girl. She was late, she was running, and he wondered if she was meeting someone.

It surprised him very much that she spoke to him. This was their third encounter and in any other circumstances that would have been enough to merit a greeting. But Roman had learned that street people merit nothing and those who see them every day still ignore them with averted eyes. Thousands never see them at all, any more than they notice the litter that lies everywhere. So when she smiled and said, 'Hallo,' he was too astonished to reply. He could only stare at her.

'It's a lovely day,' she said.

He found his lost voice. 'Yes,' he said. 'Yes, it is. Lovely.'

Instead of continuing to walk, he paused and leant against the parapet of the bridge. He didn't want her to think he was following her and perhaps be frightened. For a moment she had made him feel like a man again, an insider, and he was not at all sure that he wanted that.

The Rose Garden restaurant had a romantic sound. It turned out to be a building like a cluster of mushrooms, little domed roofs bunched together, and on a terrace little hexagonal tables. Mary took care to approach from the direction he wouldn't expect her to come from. She wanted to see him before he saw her. Not that there was any idea in her mind of turning tail if it should be someone who appeared uncongenial sitting there, but rather to prepare herself.

Preparations were a commonplace in her life. She prepared herself before opening envelopes for what might be inside them, before answering the phone, before meeting someone new. She must make sure. She must compose her face, her smile. There might be several lone men sitting at tables, waiting for women. All she knew of him was from that photograph and that he was six years younger than herself.

He would expect her to come from the Inner Circle or perhaps up the path and past the kiosk on Holme Green. Instead, she came out of the gardens. Most of the tables outside the restaurant were occupied, couples, foursomes, two men together, three women together, one man alone, but he was forty at least. She was standing still now, her eyes travelling from table to table. Then she saw him. It was a boy she expected but this was a man, yet unmistakably the original of the photograph. Unexpected heat came up into her face and she felt it colour her cheeks. As she had thought, he was watching for her to come from past the lake and across the road, but he turned his head as if that flush had communicated itself to him. She moved then and made her way to his table.

He stood up and held out both his hands, a tall very thin man.

'Mary Jago,' she said.

'Leo Nash,' he said, 'or Oliver.'

He had dropped his left arm as if he thought the act of taking both her hands, which he had evidently planned to do, was too forward. She put her hand into his and found it cold. He looked older than his age, a little worn, which was natural after so much illness and stress and surely fear. His features would have been handsome but for his pallor. Light grey eyes met her green eyes and she thought, with a little shock, that he and she were alike to look at; they might have been brother and sister.

'Now I'm here and you're here,' he said, 'I don't know what to say. And that's ridiculous because I've rehearsed things to say so many times. I've made speeches to myself, trying to express my gratitude, but I'm dumbstruck in your presence.'

'Not quite.' She tried a laugh but she was breathless. 'I'd call you highly articulate.'

'Only in a nothing-to-say kind of way. At least I can ask you if you'd like some tea. Would you? Or a drink? Or tea and cakes? What would you like?'

He hadn't a phone which meant he was seriously poor. His clothes were just the young man's uniform, jeans, a T-shirt, a sweatshirt draped over his shoulders, giving nothing away.

'Tea would be fine,' she said.

While he gave the order to a waitress, she sat looking at him in silence. Whatever she had expected it was not this. His appearance, yes, but not her feelings. The knowledge that this fragile, thin, pale man's body contained the marrow from her own bones, a healing elixir which had restored his health, affected her so profoundly that she felt almost faint.

She hung forward in her chair and closed her eyes.

78

It was as if she had slept with him the night before for the first time – no, it was more than that, almost as if she were in love with him . . .

He spoke gently: 'Are you all right?'

Her hands were over her eyes. She took them away and looked at him. His face was concerned, a little taken aback. 'I'm sorry,' she said. 'You must think me an awful fool.'

He shook his head. 'You expected someone different?'

'Oddly enough, no. I can't say I expected you but you're not a surprise. I had your photograph.' She made a great effort. 'I mean, I'd prepared myself to see you and I had a good idea what you'd be like, but really seeing you, really sitting here with you – well, it's a strange sensation.'

'Strange, but good. For me, at any rate.'

'Would you – would you tell me how it's been for you. I mean, your recovery. Or is that an intrusion on your – well, your privacy?'

He laughed, but gently. She was finding it hard not to look directly into those clear grey eyes. The spell of them was broken by the arrival of tea. Cakes came for him, fruit tarts, a cream horn.

'I am supposed to eat a lot,' he said. 'Eat well, they're always saying to me. I expect they mean fruit and vegetables, not cream cakes.'

This time she could smile. 'Would you tell me about it?'

'The transplant, do you mean?'

'Yes, I think so. The whole thing. Your illness, the transplant, all of it. I want to hear. From you.'

'Wouldn't that be very self-indulgent on my part?'

Her self-confidence was growing. 'Think of it as indulging me.'

'All right. That certainly makes it easier.'

He hesitated. He was eating a cream slice with a

79

child's enjoyment. It amused her to see him lick the cream from his fingers, look up and give her a wide frank smile.

'I'd just finished university,' he said. 'I was looking for work. I was getting anxious I'd never find anything, and at first I thought the pain was – well, nerves. That's how it started, with this awful pain.' He wrinkled up his eyes, remembering. 'A sharp pain in my side. I thought it was nerves and then I thought it was appendicitis. I went to my GP and he said it was gastro-enteritis. But I'd never had anything like it before; I couldn't believe what he said. Then the pain got intense, acute. Do you really want to hear this?'

'Of course I do.'

'I've got an older brother. He's important to me – he's like a best friend. I told him and he rushed me to Casualty. The hospital found my spleen was three times its normal size. It had a lot to cope with. It had taken over the function of my white blood cells. They told my brother and then they told me.'

'It must have been a great shock.'

'Like being stunned by a totally unexpected blow. One minute I was a normal healthy man, or so I thought, a man with a pain in his stomach, and then – this. They operated and took out my spleen. They told me I had AML – Acute Myeloid Leukaemia. I thought it was a death sentence.'

'But you went to the Harvest Trust?'

'Not at first. I'd been told I should have a bone marrow transplant. With siblings the chance of matching tissue is one in four so I was hoping against hope my brother would match. He was willing.' She saw him clench his hands. He spoke with intensity. 'He was more than willing. He was longing for the chance to help me. We're very close.'

'But his tissue didn't match?'

'As I said, I'd felt under sentence of death. When they told me about this one in four chance all that changed. I was so sure it would be all right. You know, if you were told you had to have surgery and there was a one in four chance of not coming out of the anaesthetic you'd be sure you'd die, wouldn't you? I would. I was sure one in four meant my brother's tissue would match. I was so confident I didn't even think much about it. He was my brother; we had the same genes, the same colouring, the same sort of looks. I knew it would be all right.

'They tested him and he wasn't compatible. I couldn't believe it at first. I thought they must have made a mistake. But they hadn't.' He sighed, then brightened. 'Still, if my brother had been able to make the donation I wouldn't have met you.'

'I doubt if that would have bothered you much,' Mary said. 'You wouldn't have known I existed.'

He put his head a little on one side, as if considering what she had said.

'My brother tried to find a donor. He had leaflets printed and put them through a thousand doors. Can you imagine? Most people just ignored them but a lot came forward for tests. One of them was compatible, but he turned out not to be suitable. I knew I'd die unless a donor was found. That's a very unpleasant feeling. It throws you into a panic, knowing you've got something that can be cured, or at any rate arrested, and the drug, serum, whatever, is everywhere, maybe even quite common, but you can't find it. It's hidden away; it may be inside lots of people you see in the street but you can't get at it. Then the hospital told us about the Trust.'

'Go on.'

He recalled the day the Harvest Trust told him there was someone prepared to make the donation and his happiness at this good news, his excitement, later on his realisation of reprieve.

'I'd lived with the dread that I'd never see twenty-two. That was going to be my next birthday. Now here was a bunch of people telling me the chances were I would. I'd tried to get used to despair, to my fate, and now I had to get used to hope.'

There was a setback when they were afraid his condition had deteriorated too far for him to be eligible for the transplant. But he seemed stable and they had gone ahead. While this was going on, he said, he thought of her all the time.

'I thought of "Helen". Maybe I'm a bit of a hero-worshipper. I worshipped my brother, still do, and now here was this woman for me to worship, this unknown woman. You were a saviour to me, a sort of saint.'

She disliked the ease with which she blushed. Never in her life before had she had such cause for blushing. Her face flooded with colour.

'But it was *nothing*,' she said, surprising herself by her own vehemence. 'It was *nothing*.'

'I'm not at all sure *I* would have done it,' he said. 'Getting over the transplant, I had a lot of leisure to think. I thought about that a lot – what would I have done if I could have made a donation, and I decided I wouldn't have. I'd have been afraid.'

His eyes seemed filled with adoration. Embarrassed, awkward, but unable to stop looking at him, she tried to leave the subject, to deflect things.

'What about work? You couldn't have worked while all this was going on. How have you lived?' Again she had perhaps gone too far. 'I'm sorry, I shouldn't ask . . .'

'You can ask me anything.'

The words fell calmly. His total openness was almost frightening. The sense of intimacy made her

82

shiver a little, for although they had been there less than half an hour it was as if she had known him for a long long time.

'No, I'm sorry,' she said again, weak now with attempting she hardly knew what. 'I have no right to pry like this.'

'*You* can ask me anything. After all, I'm yours, aren't I?'

'What do you mean?' she said.

'Nothing to make you look so – so fearful. Don't you know that when you save a man's life he belongs to you? Like a servant. In the true sense of that word, I mean. Someone who will devotedly serve you.'

Her hands were on the table surface and he put his over them. The hands he had reached out to take hers and had withdrawn from shyness or some sense of decorum, he now placed over her hands and let them rest there with increasing pressure. The touch was extraordinarily comforting.

'My brother kept me,' he said. 'I have a job now. It's only part-time and it's not much. I work for him, my brother. It's not the kind of thing I had in mind. I'd been to a great university, I had high hopes of my future, but still, it's work. I was glad of anything once I knew I was going to live.'

She waited for him to say what he did, what the work was, but he didn't say. The bill came. As he was taking it from the waitress's hand, Mary said:

'No, let me.'

This time he laughed. The girl was standing there listening, but he didn't seem to mind. 'You're remembering I said I hadn't a phone. I only meant I hadn't a phone of my own. I've been sharing a flat with my brother since I got ill. I had to, I couldn't manage on my own.'

Her hands felt cold now he had taken his away.

She was aware that with the coming of evening it was no longer warm. She stood up.

'I'll walk you to Park Village, shall I? Oh, don't look like that. I'm quite well. You've made me well, remember? I can walk long distances, Mary.'

It was the first time he had used her name and she was unprepared for the rush of pleasure it brought her. They passed into the Broad Walk and made their way northwards. The bearded man she had encountered earlier was once more on one of the seats, once more reading. She prepared to smile at him and say hallo, but he kept his eyes on the page. Leo began to talk of the curious coincidence of their living so near to each other. He called her Mary again and managed to give the name a prettier sound than anyone else had.

She looked back once but the man on the seat had gone.

Chapter Seven

There had not even been a period of wondering where they all were, of apprehensiveness, doubt, the tickle of speculation, fear growing from unexplained absence and the silent phone. He knew, or thought he knew. They were in Woodbridge, at his mother-in-law's. It was school holidays, the October half-term, and Sally had driven herself, Elizabeth and Daniel, up into Suffolk to see her mother who had been ill. They were to stay overnight.

Afterwards, in a kind of mad obsession with figures, dates, sums, he had tried to calculate how often she had made that journey in the previous fifteen years; how often she and he and all of them had made it. Two hundred times? More? Looking back over the years, consulting his diary, he eventually came to the precise figure of two hundred and twenty-three times. Anything to distract his mind, keep it, if only for minutes, in the emotionless drought of measurements and number.

That number of times she had driven it without incident, without event almost, with nothing approaching a narrow escape. He hadn't been anxious. Of course he hadn't. Not once had he been tempted to pick up the phone and check. They were there with Sally's mother. Perhaps they would phone him and then again perhaps they wouldn't. When he had eaten he might phone Sally's mother and ask how she was.

But he doubted later if he had thought those things at the time. He hadn't been thinking of them at all. His mind had been elsewhere, concerned with a manuscript purporting to be the diary of a runaway slave who had married a Havasupai woman that Talisman might buy if it could be authenticated and the price wasn't too high. He had brought a copy of it home with him. It lay on the kitchen table, open at page four. Strange that now he couldn't even remember whether or not Tom Outram had bought that book.

He was pottering about, getting himself a meal. Not defrosted pizza but baked beans, because he preferred tins to the microwave. He read another paragraph while he was opening the tin. There was a bottle of Meursault in the fridge, half-full (or half-empty if you were a pessimist, though he never had been), its neck corked with one of those wine-saver stoppers. He had poured himself a glass of wine while he was heating up the beans. The slave's diary probably wasn't genuine, was fiction, but might be all the more publishable for that . . .

The doorbell rang at one minute to seven. He thought it was someone collecting for a charity. He went to the door feeling for his wallet in his pocket.

The police officers gave him no details then. That came later. He learned all about it later. Then, at one minute to seven, his glass of wine half-drunk, his baked beans burning on the stove till the police-woman turned off the plate, they asked him to sit down; they told him of an accident, then of serious consequences, then of fatality. He had stared at them. He remembered asking them to repeat what they had said, he was so certain his hearing was playing tricks. He *couldn't* have heard that, this *couldn't* be happening to him.

For a long time he associated the smell of burnt

tomato sauce with the collapse of his life, the loss of all that made his happiness. Once he had smelt it in a workmen's café in Camden Town and felt as sick as if he had swallowed poison.

The day after the police came he learned that Sally had been driving carefully, prudently, obeying all the rules, within the speed limit. Elizabeth was beside her in the passenger seat, Daniel in the back. The car had come to a stop at a level crossing over the Eastern Region railway line somewhere near Ipswich. It was at the foot of a hill. The lorry behind her, a twenty-ton container from the docks at Felixstowe with defective brakes, came down the hill too fast and slid into the back of the car, precipitating it through the closed crossing gates into the path of the oncoming train.

The three of them were killed instantly. The driver of the train was injured but all the passengers were unhurt. As for the lorry driver, he had a bang on the head and badly bruised knuckles. Two hundred and twenty-three times it had been all right and all those times that two hundred and twenty-fourth time had been waiting to happen, coming nearer every time, with the force of destiny. If you believed that sort of thing. Roman didn't.

He didn't go to the inquest but he went to the funeral. He *was* the funeral. Sally's dying mother was there and Sally's sister but he hadn't wanted anyone else and had told people not to come. He slept heavily that night and woke in the belief that Sally had got up early, would appear in a minute with tea for him. The knowledge and the pain pouring back tore from him cries of violent protest.

Two weeks afterwards, having resigned from the Talisman Press, he put his house on the market and took to the outdoors.

The funeral, that surreal occasion, was the event he

thought had tipped him over the edge into insanity. Or whatever the condition was he had developed and had lived with. The three coffins, carried up the aisle of that stark crematorium by men in black coats, made a picture Ernst might have painted, or perhaps Magritte. He saw the scene over and over as such a picture, stuck somewhere on the other side of reality in that world where bad dreams live and drug-induced hallucinations.

Curiously, since he had admitted the past, it was liable to come back at all sorts of odd times and print itself in front of his eyes. Now was one of those times as he walked across Prince Albert Road, making for St John's Wood churchyard, called 'Church Gardens'. Cars had stopped for him at the pedestrian crossing but he hardly saw them. One of them hooted to hurry him along. Before his eyes the three coffins passed, carried by strong young men, the kind of young men only seen dressed like that at funerals, their fresh faces lugubrious, their eyes downcast.

There had been no flowers. Of course not. How could anyone suggest anything so ludicrous? Well, no one had suggested it. His whole life, his past, his present and his future, lay in three wooden boxes. He sat, unresponsive, in a pew, looking at the boxes, while a very young man with an Adam's apple like a swallowed toffee going up and down in his throat, talked in a Potteries accent about the resurrection and the life.

The picture dimmed as he reached the opposite pavement. By now the light was fading as the cruel vision had faded. The churchyard would soon be closed. Police patrolled the Park to clear it of vagrants before and after closing time but Roman had found he could sometimes elude them in this shady place outside its gates and make himself a bed among the old tombs.

He blinked his eyes and saw only the green turf, the flowerbeds, and the trunks of plane trees, their bark like grey skin peeling here and there to show the lemon colour beneath. The leaves of planes, the beeches and the whitebeams, looked very pale and tender in the fading light. All white things shone with a curious radiance.

Having walked many miles this fine day, Roman walked further. He did as he always did in the church gardens and looked at the grave of John Sell Cotman, the watercolourist who had died a hundred and fifty years ago, and at Joanna Southcott's, the religious visionary, she of 'the Box', dead before the Battle of Waterloo. On most of the grey gravestones the lettering was no longer decipherable but eroded by time and weather. The bluebells were nearly over but the borage aped their colour and the cow parsley shimmered as in a country lane.

He sat down on one of the seats, leant back his head and closed his eyes. Once he had been a man very conscious of comfort, one who chose a mattress with care, sparing no expense. Armchairs had to be soft and have footrests. But in his wanderings he had lost all interest in comfort and scarcely noticed whether he lay down to sleep on paving stones or on the comparative luxury of a lawn.

After a while he was aware of the presence of someone else in the gardens. Not the police, that was not their tread. It was Effie's footsteps that he heard. He opened his eyes. She came up to the seat and sat down on the other end of it, giving him a shy sideways glance, looking away, saying nothing. Only another dosser sits on the seat where a dosser already is.

She was quite a young woman, younger than he, though at first he had taken her for old. Her stoop made him think so – that and her wizened hands and

89

thick bandaged legs. But when she took off the old cap she wore and unwound the woollen scarf from her head, it was a round unlined face he saw with a full vulnerable mouth and the ox eyes the Greeks said Hera had.

It was in his own first winter that he first encountered her, for she had been on the street a shorter time than he. A mild March had still been March, damp and by night very cold. In this same churchyard, though not on this same bench, she had sat beside him and as darkness came – it seemed like night but it was only six – laid her hand first on his knee, then shifted it to close the fingers between his legs. Once he would have been shocked. He would have recoiled from her and left in haste. But a mild interest was all he felt, that and curiosity and a wonder that after long celibacy, after five months of banishing sexual thoughts, his flesh responded to this tramp woman's touch and it was a full erection she held in her warm, surprisingly feminine hand.

Even then he had not shaken off his old, ingrained sense of superiority, of belonging to an elite, and as he moved with her on to her blanket spread on the grass, into the well of darkness between tombstones, it was a favour he felt he was doing her. He was being kind. He was enduring the earthy smell of her, the fishy smell, the burrowing of her hands, out of generosity. The unknown, dark and glutinous place into which he slid was honoured by him; God knew what he risked, by this grace of his.

But when it was over and for the first time since he had known her he saw her smile, felt the arms that had gone round him squeeze in a hug, he understood in a blinding revelation that she believed *she* had been generous to *him*. Hers was a proud smile and the arms that held him almost maternal. Out of pity perhaps or empathy, she had given him the only thing she had to give. It was a lesson to him. He was ashamed. Only later, when she had left the church-yard, dragging her bundles, he recalled with a shiver of relief at whatever had reprieved him, how near he had been to paying her, to handing over a ten-pound note with a word of thanks.

Now, with Effie seated beside him again, he felt nothing of what he had once felt before he was married and encountered by chance and alone a woman with whom he had had a one-night stand: embarrassment, awkwardness, a threatening pres-ence. The streets and the street people had changed him. Social graces and social inhibition had departed and with them the fear of what others might say or think. He would have no more sex with Effie but it would cost him no embarrassment to tell her so or show her so. Turning his head, he smiled at her, and reaching into the bag in his barrow, said:

'Do you want a drink? I've only got Coke.'

She shook her head. She was one of those who had bad days and, less often, good days, and he could tell from the way she contemplated her hands, turning them palms uppermost, then on to the palms and back again, muttering softly, that this day was bad. What it was she saw on her hands – blood perhaps, or a rash, stigmata or ineradicable dirt – he could not tell. The hands looked like any woman's to him, but rough and prematurely aged. She turned them over and back, over and back, examining them more and more closely.

'I'm going to bed now,' he said. 'I'm going to sleep.'

She turned her hands, looked at the dirty nails with the concentration of a woman who has just painted hers and admires them.

'Goodnight, Effie.'

He would have been surprised if she had answered.

She put her hands on her knees, then sat on them. She aimed a kick at one of her bundles as if it disgusted her, its weight, the need always to carry it, the ugly mud-green colour of the plastic. The bundle rolled a few feet away along the path. Roman sometimes felt the streets were one vast sprawling psychiatric ward and he just as much an inmate as any of them.

He got up, walked for a little and found himself a place to sleep between two flat granite slabs, from which the lettering had disappeared. The turf in there was composed of short grass and moss in equal proportions. Beyond the railings, lit now by the wash from yellow lamps, loomed the fronts of a huge block of flats, Byzantine, white and terracotta.

The traffic climbing up to Hampstead on the Lord's side sounded like the sea, the tide coming in over a shingle beach. But in here now it might have been a country churchyard, Stoke Poges perhaps, quiet, serene, with that indefinable air of resignation and rest and deep peace that prevails in all places where graves are. Roman spread his groundsheet, for he had experienced the results of doing without one, and over it his sleeping bag. Into this he climbed and lay relaxed, looking out at the red brickwork and the white stucco between the long slender stems of churchyard weeds. He had long forgone the use of a pillow. Because it was appropriate he recited what he could remember of Gray's *Elegy*.

'Perhaps in this neglected spot is laid
Some heart once pregnant with celestial fire;
Hands, that the rod of empire might have sway'd,
Or waked to ecstasy the living lyre.'

Halfway through the next verse he fell asleep.

Darkness is not long enduring in the middle of May and dawn comes at five. It was growing light but not yet sunrise when Effie woke him, shaking his shoulders, her face close up to his face. At first he thought this was another overture she was making to him, though even by the standards of her world and his, it would have been a rough method.

'No, Effie,' he said. 'No.' And because any excuse he might make or reason he might give would be false and a prevarication, he said, 'That was just for once. No more of that.'

For answer, she grasped a handful of the pullover and T-shirt covering his right shoulder, and with her other hand flung out, pointed northwards towards Wellington Place. It was a gesture melodramatic, almost Gothic, in intensity. Her face worked. She always found speech difficult, from some natural impediment or later trauma, and now she managed only:

'On the rails! See the rails!'

He made an immediate association with trains. She must mean the Jubilee Line that passed underneath them on its way to St John's Wood Station. He got to his feet, stretched his stiff legs and flexed his arms. Sleeping outdoors sometimes felt good but it left a dull numbness in the bones. One had a clear head but aching limbs and back. He rubbed his eyes. He followed Effie along the path where she preceded him with steps that flagged more and more until they stopped altogether.

'Where is it, Effie?'

She was shaking her head, not to deter him but as if the only hope for her was to deny what she had seen, what she wanted to show him.

'Where do you want me to go?'

She pointed. Her plump vulnerable face, turned to him with pleading in every feature, was full of grief. The finger she extended trembled. On an impulse he seized her hand and held it tightly in his own.

93

The sky was lightening but here among the trees, in the dense boskiness, it was still dark, the shadows blacker than they ever are by day. She seemed to be leading him to the churchyard's northern boundary. There was no sound of traffic, no wind blowing, only a heavy silence. He seldom saw the early morning, for he slept most deeply in those hours just before and just after dawn. The sky astonished him. It was a clear jewel-like unclouded blue.

Effie clutched his sleeve. She pulled him up the path towards the main gate in Wellington Place that faces Cochrane Street. There, on the railings to the left of the gates, he saw it. The rails, she had said, the rails. Now he saw what she meant.

The man's body seemed to be impaled on the spikes of the railing. The upper part of it hung head downwards into Wellington Place and a single hand showed, half-clenched, claw-like. The lower part of the body was on this side, in the churchyard. Booted feet drooped and thin bony ankles showed below the ragged hems of dark dirty jeans. Effie began to make gibbering sounds, throwing her hands about. He hesitated, his heart beating fast. Then he went up to the railing, reached between the bars and touched the dead man's cold hand. That was how he knew he was dead, because the hand was so cold.

He fancied he recognised the face but he couldn't be sure. The clothes that were nearer to rags showed him to be one of the street people. There was never any mistaking that.

When he saw the place where the spike had entered the body and the blood, now dry and black, encrusting spike, rags and wound, he turned away from that tower of silence and looked instead up at the clear, blue, remorseless sky.

94

Chapter Eight

Most callers at the Irene Adler that day and the next and the next came to ask directions to the site of the murder. They bought entrance tickets but few of them lingered. It was the murder scene they wanted, and to waste no time getting there.

'Turn left into St John's Wood Terrace, left again into the High Street and take the first turning on your right. You'll know it by the scene-of-crime tapes.'

Mary and Dorothea could have recited that formula in their sleep, though neither of them had been to look at the site. If for nothing else, it was good for business. Apart from the direction seekers, there was a troop of tourists who had come on from Wellington Place, anxious to sample what else was on offer in the neighbourhood: first the boutiques of St John's Wood High Street, the cafés for a drink; then the Irene Adler; finally the murder site to round off a day's entertainment.

'I shall throw up,' said Dorothea, 'if anyone else tells me that poor devil died of knife wounds and the spike was just incidental decoration.'

Mary was squeamish and disliked hearing about it, even in reported speech, but it had not occurred to her to feel nervous about walking through the churchyard or the Park. The visitors did their best to make her afraid.

'I wouldn't set foot in the Park now,' said a

95

woman in the Hat Room. 'Alone or accompanied. Not even with my Great Dane. You're asking for trouble if you take a short cut that way.'

'But it didn't happen in the Park,' said Mary.

'Not that one, no. But how do you know the next one won't?' The woman began closely examining a rose-coloured hat, swathed in pink ostrich feathers. 'Women were safer in those days, weren't they? Not allowed out much, protected, respected by men, always in a carriage.'

Mary wanted to say, not if you were working class and how about Jack the Ripper, but she didn't. It seemed unlikely that anyone who chose to kill one of the meths drinkers from the canal bank would single her out as his next victim. When she had first heard of the murder she had thought at once of the man she had met in the Park and then she remembered the morning she had found him waking up on the Irene Adler doorstep. It was absurd the way she found herself hoping quite desperately that the corpse on the railings was not he. A photograph in the evening paper was no help. One dark-haired bearded man looks very like another, and this blurred print gave no more clues to identity than his name: John Dominic Cahill.

'Irish,' said the woman, now studying a black hat with a white egret apparently flying from its crown. 'I suppose one mustn't be prejudiced.'

Mary wondered if it were she or some other visitor to the Irene Adler who had left behind, by accident or perhaps sinister design, a sheet of paper listing crimes reported in the Park during the previous year and the year before that. Stacey found it on the counter, lying beside the guides.

'One grievous bodily harm, three actual bodily harms,' read Dorothea aloud. 'Two assaults on the

police, two indecent assaults, four indecent expo-
sures – why tell *us* – nine cases of criminal damage,
seven cases of misuse of drugs, sixteen burglaries.
But last year there weren't any bodily harms or
assaults on the police, and only five criminal damages, but *thirteen* misuses of drugs.'

'It doesn't seem very much, any of it,' Mary said.
'Not in a year.'

She walked home by her accustomed route. As on
this evening and the one before that, she was hoping
to see the man that in her own mind she called
Nikolai. She had read in the paper, among the many
stories about vagrants and beggars that had
appeared, that the street people all had nicknames.
Whether this was true she didn't know but she
named the bearded man Nikolai from that moment
because that was Gogol's name and he had been
reading *Dead Souls*.

His voice interested her. Perhaps she was a snob,
but she had not expected a man such as he to have a
voice and an accent like his. Nor to have been
reading what he was reading, come to that. She
looked for him on her way home, hoping he was not
John Dominic Cahill, whose nickname, the paper
said, was Decker. She hoped very much that Decker
and Nikolai were not one and the same.

But he was nowhere to be seen. She even took the
long route, crossing the Long Bridge and entering the
Inner Circle. It was dull and rather windy, therefore
unlikely that he would be on one of the seats in the
Broad Walk. She made a detour through the shady
shrubberies in the southeast corner but he was not
there either. A waste of time, she told herself, and
then that it would have been rather awkward if he
had been there and they had suddenly come face to
face along one of the dark paths.

Leo Nash was taking her out to dinner. He had

phoned and asked her two evenings before. Mary was gratified because she had thought her behaviour to him, her reticence, her caution, might have discouraged him. And now she hardly knew where that coolness had come from or what purpose it had served.

He had walked back to Park Village West with her, leaving the Park by the Gloucester Gate. It all seemed familiar to him and when she asked he told her he had always lived near the Park and always, since a small boy, loved the terraces, the villas, the lake, the glimpses of wild animals behind the zoo fencing.

'And you're called Nash!' she had said.

He looked at her, uncomprehending. 'That's right.'

'Nash,' she said, 'John Nash. He was the architect of the Park.'

'Ah. I've never thought of that before. I never made the connection.'

'Perhaps he was an ancestor.'

He laughed but she thought he looked disconcerted. 'There are an awful lot of us in the phone book.'

They passed the Grotto and took the turn into the crescent of Park Village that was the longer way round. The lilac was past and it was too early for the roses. Crimson and gold wallflowers and the orange Siberian kind scented the air. Someone was cutting a lawn, the buzzing of the motor a country or suburban sound. It smelt like a florist's shop, he said, as if he had never been in a garden before and had only known cut flowers, forced flowers in pots and boxes. Mary stopped outside the gate of Charlotte Cottage. The rock garden was a mass of white and yellow and blue alpines and the first geraniums were coming out in the tubs.

'What a lovely garden,' he said.

'The house is pretty nice too.'

She fancied the look he gave her was a strange one, puzzled, as if he were suddenly adrift. She had been on the point of asking him in. For a drink, a cup of coffee. We have to have these excuses, she thought, or women do. But something stopped her, some sudden feeling of distance between them. The rapport she had felt up till then was gone, reminding her that he was a stranger. After all, she didn't know him. They had only just met. What did they have in common but shared marrow in their bones?

'It has been very good to meet you at last,' she said, as if such warm words would soften her rejection of him. At once, in her own ears, they sounded like cold words. They sounded rigidly formal. She held out her hand, making things worse. 'I hope we'll see each other again.'

She could see she had hurt him. He pursed his lips the way a man may do when he feels he has committed some solecism, when he has put a foot wrong but does not know where or how.

'I hope that too. May I phone you?'

'Of course.'

'Then I will. Soon.'

'Thank you for walking me home,' she said, and she had gone quickly to let herself into the house, picking up Gushi and hugging him the moment she was inside.

After that it was a relief when he phoned. She could repair the damage, make all things well between them. She had waited for him to phone but wouldn't have been surprised if he hadn't, and then she would have had to think how to get in touch with him. But he had phoned, and surely at the earliest opportunity that he could have done so without seeming too eager. His voice had been warm and friendly and had evoked from her just such a warm response.

99

The call seemed to have released her to talk about him. When her cousin Judith phoned she spoke to her of the new friend she had made, the man who was the recipient of her transplant. She told Dorothea, who wanted to know if he was 'personable', if he was 'fanciable' – when was she seeing him again?

'That would be one in the eye for old Alistair.'

'I've only met him once, Dorrie.'

She told her grandmother. Frederica Jago was going to Crete on the following day with some people called Tratton, old friends who had a house there.

'I know one shouldn't ever say I told you so but I did tell you he'd reply, he just took a long time about it. And he's nice?'

'I think so. I think he's very nice.'

'Not a – what do they call them? – not a yob? My darling Mary, you needn't look like that. We do judge people by the neighbourhoods they come from.'

'He's a clever, well-educated, quiet and, I think, rather sensitive man.'

'And you found that out in how long? An hour?'

Mary laughed. 'A bit less. Perhaps you can meet him when you get back from Crete. I must go. I've been here much longer than I meant to.'

Frederica insisted on calling a taxi for her. She was not to wait out in the street. The murder had been too near for comfort.

'And take her right to the door, please,' she said to the driver. 'Into the crescent and right to the door, not just to the Albany Street corner.'

Mary kissed her. Her grandmother smelt delicately of vanilla. She had looked back at the house and waved as the cab pulled away, at the great late Victorian pile, stucco, red shingles, red tiles, all gleaming in yellow lamplight, and Frederica's neat tiny figure on the steps under the big bulbous portico.

Leo was a little early. He had a taxi waiting, and though he came in, it was only to the hall while she shut Gushi into the drawing room. He wore a suit and this reminded her of Alistair, who dressed formally most of the time. She came back to find him studying a framed print of Christ Church in a series of Oxford college etchings on the hall wall.

'I was at the House,' he said. 'It looks just the same.'

Did people still call Christ Church that? 'Yes, you said you were taken ill just after you'd got your degree.'

He smiled at her. The smile pulled his young face into a network of radiating lines. She thought he looked ill, suddenly aged, pale as a sick old man.

'Are you all right?'

'Yes. Why? I'm naturally a bit wan. It's the curse of the very fair-skinned.'

He took her to an Italian restaurant in Paddington Street, off Marylebone High Street. It was a place recommended by a friend of his brother's. The distance could easily have been walked. But was he fit to walk half a mile? She very much wanted to ask him how he was now. Would he stay well? Was he, in fact, *cured*? She doubted if such a thing was possible.

As soon as they entered the simple little restaurant Mary sensed that the food would be good, the service efficient and discreet. It was a pretty place, with wooden tables and comfortable seats instead of the rickety glass and wrought-iron kind, mirrors and paintings on the walls, flowers on every table and candles lit.

While they ate he talked of the first donor who had

101

come along. Their tissue was compatible. In fact, it was a perfect match, as close as a brother or sister. But the man was generally in poor health and he was found medically unfit to donate marrow.

'It was the most appalling disappointment. I was sure I was going to die. I tried to teach myself to be resigned to it. I even wrote out instructions for the kind of funeral I wanted to have.'

'Your mother wasn't compatible?'

His face was impassive. He no longer met her eyes. 'My mother wasn't tested. She – well, she was afraid of the anaesthetic, of going under. She's never had anaesthesia. I can understand.'

This had been *her* grandmother's fear. Perhaps it was common, this dread of loss of consciousness, loss of control, a brief experience of death. 'There were no other relatives, then?'

'Cousins. Two were tested but it was no use. Then you came along.' He smiled. 'In the nick of time.'

'I'm sure there would have been others.'

'No, I think not. You were the only one in the world.'

There was an intensity in the way he said it and the look he gave her that made her glance away. He seemed to sense her embarrassment and began to talk of indifferent things – his brother's business, a vague merchandising that meant nothing to her; the place they lived in that he would like to leave when he could, but which had come to them when their mother moved out. A roof over one's head was not something to be lightly abandoned.

The bill came and she offered to go halves. His expression became stern, a little impatient. 'No. Don't suggest it again, please.'

She recoiled. His severity was unexpected and, gentle herself, she reacted painfully to brusqueness in others. It was almost like being struck and she put up her hand to her cheek, remembering Alistair, fearing verbal attack almost as much as physical. Leo's smile, warm and somehow conspiratorial, a small, sharing, intimate smile, restored them to where they had been before.

'The only one in the world,' he said again. 'You may not care for the idea but I can't help feeling that makes for a special relationship.'

She hesitated, then said quietly as they came out into the street, 'Oh, no, I feel that too. I don't see how anyone in our situation could escape feeling that.'

'Shall we walk back?'

It was not for her, she felt, to suggest he might be incapable of walking. But now the half-mile she had first thought of as the distance between here and Park Village, in a more realistic estimate became at least a mile.

'If you like.'

She tried to say it grudgingly. Her unwilling tone was assumed to give him the impression walking found no favour with her. If it did he chose to ignore it and they walked side by side up towards the Marylebone Road and the York Gate.

To her relief he had said nothing about the murder. He was the only person she had spoken to in the past three days who had not talked of the murder. Even her grandmother had touched on it with her injunction to the taxi driver. She asked Leo about his parents and he told her his father was dead and his mother lived in Scotland, had married again after his father's death. His brother Carl was ten years older than he, a clever gifted man, he said, and he added with a smile that he was nearly as much a life-saver as she. Though Leo didn't say so, Mary had the impression Carl was gay. Leo only said that he was rather solitary, mysterious about his private life.

At the utterance of this last word, the word 'life',

Leo put out one hand to support himself against a shop front. In the artificial light it was hard to see but Mary thought his pallor had intensified. He stood there, breathing carefully, then lowered himself to sit on a wall that reached to waist height.

'You shouldn't be walking,' she said. 'It's too far. It's too much for you.'

He nodded. 'I'm afraid it is. I'll be all right in a moment.' The smile he managed reassured her. 'This still happens. They warned me it would go on happening.' He seemed to be considering whether what he wanted to say would be wise. The words came out in a rush. 'I'm on low-dose chemotherapy. It's –' he sought for a word '– a bore.'

'We'll get a taxi.'

Quite a long time passed before one came. It was nearly eleven and Mary, who had been determined this time to ask Leo in, make coffee for him, explain to him how she came to be there and show him over the house, now saw that all this must be postponed. He opened the taxi door for her and she heard him tell the driver to take them first to Park Village West and then take him on alone to Plangent Road.

'May I see you again tomorrow?' he said. 'To make up for making a fool of myself tonight? In a subtle sort of way you warned me not to try walking, didn't you?'

'I wanted to make you believe *I* was reluctant. I couldn't do more.'

He turned away and said in a muffled voice, 'You do everything quite perfectly.'

She blushed in the dark. Her cheeks burned. She wanted to tell him how glad she was he hadn't mentioned the murder, but to say anything about it would defeat the purpose of the remark. As the taxi turned into Park Village West he took both her hands

104

in his. His hands felt warmer tonight. They exerted a strong pressure on her, not the grip of a sick man.

'Tomorrow then.'

'Tomorrow's Saturday,' she said.

'All the better. May I come in the morning? May I come at ten?'

'Of course.' Things seemed to be progressing very fast, but why not? What harm could it do? What had she to lose? 'Look after yourself,' she said. 'Rest. Have a good night's sleep.'

She was aware of the chill of the night as she stood there for a moment. All the flowers were out, gleaming monotone in the pale cold light from street lamps. From a house nearby music was coming softly but she heard a window close and then all was silent.

The inside of Charlotte Cottage felt warm and Gushi like a soft comforting muff. She buried her hands in his golden fur. The weekend ahead would be the first one she had spent there that would not be lonely and herself forlorn. She took Gushi up to bed with her and dreamed of Leo Nash, a dream in which she came upon him sitting in the Park in front of an easel. He was making an architect's drawing of Sussex Place with its ten oriental domes and array of Corinthian columns. As she approached he tore the sheet off a drawing block and handed it to her, saying:

'You may like to see a compatible tissue-type.'

The thin paper was icy in her hands and before she could look at the drawing it had melted like snow and dripped from her fingers.

A clock somewhere that she hadn't yet located was striking the last note of ten when he arrived. He put out his hand as if for a formal hand-shaking but when he placed hers in it, covered it with the other in a warm intimate gesture. The little dog came running out and without hesitation he picked it up and held it in his arms.

'He is just the sort of dog I'd expect you to have.'

'Why?'

'Small but strong, gentle and appealing, loving, childlike. Not *like* you but the sort of things you like. Am I right?'

'About the things I like or his being my dog?'

They had come into the living room and sat down. He had glanced at the work Mary had been doing on the Irene Adler brochure and she expected him to ask her about it but instead he said, looking a little disconcerted:

'Isn't he yours?'

Raised eyebrows, a half-smile, his hands deep in the dog's fur. She had never seen such clear eyes, like glass, water in a smoked glass. He was in jeans this morning, a check shirt, a denim jacket. These boy's clothes restored his youth.

'I am beginning to wish he was,' she said. 'I've got very fond of him.'

'You're looking after him for someone?'

'The owners of this house. Did you think this house was mine, Leo?'

He looked about the room, his eyes resting on a vase, a cabinet, then meeting hers again. 'I suppose so. Isn't it yours?'

'I'm looking after it for an old couple who are friends of my grandmother.'

He smiled. 'The assumptions one makes!'

'They've gone on holiday to Central America. They've no children and no one to look after the house and the dog. My grandmother's away too, but only for a couple of weeks. She lives in Hampstead and she's not up to coming in here every day. She's over eighty.'

106

'I'm glad you don't own this house.'

'Why?'

He was serious now. A pair of frown lines appeared between his eyebrows.

'You haven't seen where I live. I thought you might be rich. I'll tell you something. When I saw your address on the letter I almost didn't reply.'

'Is that why it took you so long?'

It was a question, she now understood, that had bothered her for weeks. Why he had waited; why he had condemned her to waiting for the post, to rushing to the phone when it rang. She just stopped herself saying, 'So that's why!'

'I wanted to reply, I wanted desperately to meet you. You still don't fully realise the depths of my gratitude. But when I saw that address I was – well, deeply disappointed. Taken aback, that may be a better way to put it. I came down here, you know. I came one evening and sneaked a look at the house.'

'How devious,' she said lightly.

'I concluded you were rich and privileged. It was a natural assumption to make. You were rich and therefore not for me, never for me.'

'For *you*?' she said, the colour flooding into her face.

'A figure of speech,' he said. 'I'm sorry. Already I – I think of us as close. I can't help it. You know what the Victorians used to say, flesh of my flesh and bone of my bone.'

'That was husbands and wives. That was the one flesh of the old marriage service.'

'They didn't have transplants then.' His sidelong glance and half-smile took away her discomfort. 'It's a lovely day. Where shall we have lunch?'

'You must let me give you lunch.'

'Why not? I will now I know you're not rich.'

107

Chapter Nine

Roman's children had been fond of the British Museum. Elizabeth seemed to have passed her affection for it on to Daniel and several times they had accompanied him, both particularly attracted by Egyptian antiquities. It was the Museum then that drew him when he felt the need to absent himself for a few days from his usual haunts, and he set up the nearest thing to a home he had on a doorstep in Great Russell Street.

The temperature had dropped and it was cold, but not cold like winter. He passed a lot of his time in Coram Fields, reading Bunin's stories which he bought in a second-hand shop in Theobald's Road. One day, after a visit to the baths and an attempt at smartening up, he went into the Museum and on another, unprecedentedly, to the cinema. His flight from Regent's Park had been brought about by the discovery of Decker's body, though he had not known it was Decker then.

For a few minutes he and Effie had stood there, not looking at it, but aware more than they were aware of anything, that it was there. In spite of himself and in spite of what he thought of as his new toughness, the result of true street wisdom, Roman had felt his throat rise and the awful black weakness that precedes vomiting take hold of him. But he had turned his eyes from that hand with the clawed fingers, from those booted feet and the blackened blood on the railing, and looked up at the cold purity of the morning sky. And slowly, while he held on to Effie and she clutched him, the nausea had passed. Whatever Effie felt, trembling and pale, looking up at him for help, also passed. He heard her sigh throatily.

The street was still deserted, the place still silent. Only now was the traffic beginning to swell in Wellington Road and its muted thunder to reach them. A van passed, its driver staring straight ahead.

'You go, Effie,' he said. 'Go into the Park. Go back through the churchyard into the Park. And say nothing. You haven't seen this. You haven't been here. Say nothing.'

There was little fear of that. No doubt she could speak but she seldom did more than mutter or curse passers-by who cringed from her. He looked into her face. It was blank, snub-nosed, the eyes round and protuberant, the pink-brown skin smooth like a child's. The woollen scarf that wrapped her head smelt of old damp sheep.

So ingrained was his middle-classness, his education, his *gentility*, that it was impossible for him ever to feel the same towards a woman as he had before he made love to her. Strange term for what had passed between him and Effie, but what other to use that would not also revolt his middle-classness? He and Effie, though in grotesque circumstances, had performed that act that must make him for ever feel some tenderness for her. He could never be otherwise than aware of a bond between them, though she hadn't spoken his name, was probably unaware of what it was.

He put his arms round her, hugged her tightly and sent her off with a gentle push along the path. Then he too left the churchyard, uncertain what to do, uncertain whether to do anything. What he and Effie

109

had seen on the railings back there he was very nearly sure no one else had seen before them. Except whoever had done this deed, always excepting him.

He tramped up St John's Wood High Street – the meaning of the word 'tramp' had been made manifest to him this past year and a half – until he came to a phone box. There he calculated his chances. All calls could be quickly traced, he was sure of that, but he had his voice to rely on. An anonymous call made in the accent of Westminster School and Cambridge would hardly lead police to the vagrant with his barrow.

He made his call. He reported a dead body impaled on the railings in Wellington Place. The second time they asked his name, he put the receiver back. Once, in the past, he had spent several nights asleep on the doorstep, under the Corinthian portico of the Connaught Chapel, once a church, now film studios – O times! O customs! – but it was too obvious, too open. Instead, in Ordnance Hill, in the garden of an empty house with uncurtained windows and a 'sold' sign outside, he made his bed on concrete steps and rolled himself into his sleeping bag. Chilled and suddenly hungry, he was unable to sleep, and after a few minutes, perhaps ten, he heard the wail of sirens on police cars.

Later in the day, he crossed into the Park by the Macclesfield Bridge. The canal walkways here were narrow lanes, for the embankments were so thickly overgrown as to be like woodland descending to the water. Planes and limes and hornbeams grew there, their trunks buried among the greenery and white fronds of cow parsley. Something less than two years ago he had brought the children here and told them how an earlier bridge had been destroyed when a gunpowder boat blew up underneath it in 1874. Now he stood on the centre of the three segmental arches, looking down on to the narrow paving below him where police were questioning the jacks men. They were not in uniform but he could tell they were police. Their denim jeans were pressed and their leather jackets glossy; they were well-fed and they would not die at forty-seven.

Roman thought it foolish to mock or vilify the police but he didn't love them either. His taking to the streets had removed him from that law-abiding company whose side they are on to another society that lies beyond the pale and where the police are enemies. He watched one of the jacks men, a thin grey-faced Ulsterman he had once or twice talked to, go sluggishly off with the two policemen to the car parked up in Albert Road. To help in their enquiries, no doubt, to be questioned until his meths-addled brain reached a point of incorrigible confusion.

The moment they spoke to him, Roman, they would know he was different. A crank, a dropout, therefore suspicious. His voice would alert them to his eccentricity while his clothes and barrow proclaimed his vagrant status. He walked on, going southwards, through the Park, out the other side into the Marylebone Road, across it and through what Dickens, he remembered, had called 'the awful perspectives of Wimpole Street, Harley Street, and similar frowning districts'. Four or five days should do and then he would go back. The sky was grey and the ramparts of these tall Georgian houses grey too, not a tree in sight, the traffic a river of shiny metal running down to Cavendish Square.

When Saturday came he returned. In the sunshine of early June he came back into the Park by the York Gate, turning immediately to the left, to the water's edge and bobbing ducks, the tree-shaded lawns and the seats where Effie sometimes sat. But she was not there this morning. There was no one but the dog

111

man with a borzoi, a beagle and a golden retriever tugging on his leash.

They had gone out and had their lunch. He had let her pay for it, repeating his remark about its being all right because she wasn't rich. Afterwards they walked down to Covent Garden in the sunshine and listened to a students' orchestra playing Mozart. The Flute and Harp Concerto, Leo said, the only one for these instruments Mozart wrote, composed for a rich patron and his daughter to play together. When the music stopped and the players began packing up their instruments, he had taken her hand. Not in a handshake but gently lifted as if he meant to bring it to his lips.

She looked at him, into his eyes, wondering with a small flutter of excitement, what next? What will he say next? What shall we do now?

He squeezed the hand he was holding, let it fall. 'I'm going to leave you here.'

She almost thought she had misheard.

'I must go,' he said. 'I have to meet my brother.'

Did he mean her to come too? 'We can get the tube if you like.'

She fancied a note of impatience. 'No, I thought I said. I have to meet my brother. Alone.' Then, belatedly, 'Will you be all right?'

'Of course.'

Disappointment came later. At first she was only astonished at this sudden departure. A kiss on the cheek was to be expected but he didn't kiss her. She watched him go off in the direction of Floral Street and the tube, that casual loose-limbed walk of his, his thinness so that his bones showed through whatever he wore, his bright fair hair. He didn't turn back to wave.

She was left to go home on her own at that worst

time of the week to be alone, five on a Saturday afternoon. Walking back, at last getting into the tube herself, she reflected that he had said nothing about seeing her again, seeing her soon, phoning her. In an age when the merest business acquaintances kissed at a second meeting, he hadn't kissed her.

She tried to think what she had said, done, implied, how she might have offended. Nothing came to mind.

I didn't know it till now, she thought, but I want to see him again. I want to see him very much.

Chapter Ten

No man had ever brought her flowers before. She had believed it an outdated custom. Why did Alistair have to be the first? The flowers were carnations and that white stuff with myriad tiny blossoms whose name she could never remember.

Alistair had turned up without warning. There had been no more phone calls. She had even allowed herself to think there would be no more. He had given up, she had thought. Perhaps he had met someone else.

'How absolutely over a man, sick and tired and done with him you must be,' Dorothea said, 'when you find yourself hoping he's met someone else.'

'It would be simple relief. I don't think I'd have a moment's regret.'

A fantasy she had while walking across the Park involved a nice strong-minded woman for Alistair, handsome in a no-nonsense kind of way, someone who would laugh at him and stand up to him. The difficulty lay in imagining Alistair's response. Was the sad fact that he was a bully who needed not a worthy adversary but a victim?

She was thinking about him as she approached the house so that seeing him on the doorstep, peering through the letter box as if he thought she was hiding from him, was like a thought miraculously and unpleasantly made real. Holding up the bunch of flowers and looking constricted in his dark suit, with his black hair slick and short, he seemed like an illustration to P.G. Wodehouse. And in a Wooster-ish way he said:

'Aren't you going to let us in?'

'Oh, Alistair . . .'

She was distracted; she hardly knew what to say.

It was Leo she had hoped would come this evening. She might have been thinking about Alistair but it was Leo she wanted to see, Leo who had made no sign since the previous Saturday of wanting to see her. But in spite of his absolute silence, she half-expected him and still half-expected him. It was impossible that a man should have said the things he had said, looked as he had looked, and then quitted her life with a quick touch of the hand.

There was no question, though, but to let Alistair in. That fantasy woman might have shut the door in his face but she was different. She took the flowers from him, standing aside to let him come in.

'I wished you'd phoned,' she managed to say.

'Do people in our situation really need to phone and make appointments?'

She wanted to say, what situation? We are in no situation. We are separated, this is a separation that we are in, and that word 'trial' was just a sop to both of us. But she said nothing. He was looking round him at the hall, up the stairs, into the living room, his eyebrows rising.

'Go in,' she said. 'I'll put the flowers in water.'

Which vases were for use and which for decoration only? The Chinese ones looked valuable and frail. She opened cupboards, found a pottery jar and a glass vase and tried to arrange the flowers. Irene Adler could probably have done it but now it was a lost art. She carried vase and jar into the living room.

Alistair was sitting on the sofa in the act of repelling Gushi's advances with the toe of his shoe. It

115

was such a classic tableau, the former lover now cast as villain proving his worthlessness by kicking the dog, that she found it impossible not to laugh. Gushi had scarcely made contact with Alistair's shoe. She knew very well that he disliked dogs. But she laughed, thinking of Leo who was already Gushi's best friend, and the scene briefly endeared Alistair to her.

'What's funny?' he said.

'Nothing. Poor Gushi. Shall I put him outside?'

He shrugged. 'This is quite a place you've secured for yourself.'

'Hardly for myself, Alistair. The owners will be back in September.'

'Didn't you say they'd no children? No family at all?'

'So far as I know.' The flicker of tenderness she had felt for him was dwindling. 'Would you like a drink?'

'I thought I could take you out to dinner,' he said rather peevishly.

She was in a dilemma. Having dinner with Alistair was not the way she would have chosen to spend the evening. On the other hand, she didn't much want Leo to phone while Alistair was in the house. If he phoned he might suggest coming over. It was not so much a matter of the men as rivals – Leo was a friend only, through the whole weekend they had barely touched hands – as the awkwardness of introducing him to Alistair as 'Oliver', the recipient of the transplant. What would Alistair do? Insult Leo? Abuse him? *Hit* him?

'I'll phone a restaurant and book a table,' Alistair said. 'Have you any ideas? You live here.'

A quick decision must be made. She must not involve herself in prevarication, plotting, strategy, but tell herself the truth, that she had nothing to

116

hide. Wouldn't it be wonderful if Leo came, whoever else might be here, whatever the consequences? And it was nonsense to think of Alistair hitting anyone. She had magnified a mild belligerence into a full-blown tendency to unprovoked violence.

'We'll stay here,' she said. 'I'll cook something.'

He put the phone receiver down. 'I hoped you'd say that. I mean that we could stay in. I don't care about food. Bread and cheese will do for me and we can have a bottle of wine. You do have wine?'

She nodded. Suddenly she had no idea what to say to him. No topic of conversation presented itself. The idea of spending a whole evening with him was dismaying, as if they were strangers, as if they hadn't lived together for nearly three years. What had they talked about? How had they passed a thousand evenings? She found herself looking at him in despair, a misery not apparent, it seemed, from her expression for he said in a jovial way:

'You don't know how I've missed you.' He looked at her sideways. 'That flat in Willesden,' he said as if it were a place he had remotely heard of, not somewhere he and she had lived in for so long, 'it's grim. It's a dump. I can't tell you how depressing I find it. And of course it's much worse now you're not there.'

'If you dislike it so much you'll have to move.' She heard her grandmother's briskness in her own tone and was glad of it.

'Yes,' he said. 'Yes, you're right. The fact is, darling, I want to do what I should have insisted on doing in the first place . . .'

'I'll get that wine,' she said. 'I've got a salad made and there's some salmon. Will wine do or do you want gin or something?'

'I should have insisted,' he said as if she hadn't spoken, 'on moving in here with you.'

117

The confrontation she had hoped to avoid was approaching, was almost there. 'I'd rather not talk about that. I'll get the wine.'

She opened the bottle in the kitchen, so that he couldn't wrest it from her and demonstrate male skills. Leo came into her mind, Leo opening just such a bottle of wine for them to share before lunch that Saturday. He had raised his glass and said, 'To you!' She tried to understand how so much warmth had changed abruptly to indifference, to an apparent need to get away quickly from her presence. How much of that was her imagination and how much real? Every time the phone rang she thought it must be he but it rang seldom and once or twice she had found herself willing it to ring into the oppressive silence.

She put the bottle and glasses on a tray, took the food out of the fridge, refilled Gushi's water bowl, washed her hands. Alistair was exploring the room, examining the Blackburn-Norrises' porcelain.

'What on earth have you been doing?' he said. 'Been down the cellar, selecting a choice vintage?'

'I buy my own wine. I don't drink theirs.'

He made her churlish. He brought out the worst in her. She handed him a glass with a forced smile. He raised it and said:

'To us!'

There is no 'us', she thought, but she said nothing, drinking in silence. Leo had said, 'To you!' but, like Alistair's toast, it had meant nothing . . .

'For one thing,' he said, 'I don't like you being alone here, not with people getting murdered in the vicinity.'

'One person. A man. Some poor down-and-out. And St John's Wood is hardly "the vicinity".' She must stop being tactful, discreet, cowardly. It was hard but a beginning must be made somewhere.

'Alistair, that's just an excuse. Why don't you say what you mean? You want to live with me again. Well, I'm afraid I don't want to live with you.'

He was looking disbelieving. Not hurt or angry but simply incredulous. 'Then why did you?'

'That was three years ago,' she said. 'People change. I've changed. I don't know if you have. I think you have but it may be that I never really knew you. And you may never have known me.'

His answer was cut off by the phone ringing.

Mary jumped, as she had known she would if the phone rang, but she was powerless to prevent the reaction. Her heart began to pound. It must be Leo. Leo, who had made no contact with her since Saturday, was phoning to ask her out or even to tell her he was on his way to Park Village. Alistair, on his feet again, put his hand out to lift the phone.

'No!'

She had never, in all their time together, spoken to him with such force. She had hardly ever spoken to anyone so peremptorily. Astonishment stopped him in his tracks and he turned on her a shocked look.

She picked up the receiver, said a quiet 'Hallo' and gave the number.

The voice was not Leo's but a woman's, elderly, educated, gentle. Mary was aware at first only of a huge disappointment, a let-down that made her want to cry out in frustration. She had no idea who this was. The name Celia Tratton meant nothing.

'We have met, once, a few years ago. At Frederica's. At your grandmother's.'

'Yes, of course.' Enlightenment came quickly. 'I do remember. I'm so sorry. My grandmother's staying with you, isn't she?'

'Mary, I have very bad news. I'm sorry.'

'Bad news? She's ill?'

'Well, yes, she was ill. I suppose she was.'

119

Mary said flatly, 'She's dead.'

'Yes. This afternoon. She can have known nothing about it. We were sitting out on the terrace, in the shade. One moment she was talking to us and the next she was dead. A stroke. It was so absolutely sudden, a terrible shock . . .'

She had been as near as a mother. Mary spoke the necessary formal mechanical words. She replaced the receiver with slow deliberation, then shifted it, making sure it was correctly in its rest. Her mind had emptied and she felt cold. She was aware of Alistair's arm sliding round her shoulders and Alistair's hot cheek pressed against hers. Gushi came over and sat close up against her leg. Alistair tried to toe him away.

'Oh, stop doing that!' Mary cried. 'Leave him alone. Why do you have to act so in character?' She began laughing and crying at the same time. She expected him to smack her face but he didn't.

'I'm sorry,' he said. 'I didn't want him bothering you.'

'My grandmother died. Did you realise that?'

'Of course.'

She moved her face from his, took his arm away.

'Darling,' he said, 'she was old. She'd had her life. She was bound to die soon anyway.'

Mary thought, I would like to get up and point to the door and tell him to go, to get out; I would like to have the power and the clout to do that. Instead, she leant back, closing her eyes, and saw her grandmother quite vividly, her bright lined face, the sharp green eyes that were full of youth, and thought, she can't be dead. It can't be true; there must be a mistake.

'She must have been all of eighty-five,' said Alistair, pursuing his technique of comforting. 'She

120

felt no pain. She was just snuffed out like a candle. We should all be so lucky when our time comes.'

'Yes, all right.'

'Imagine how it would have been if she'd lingered for months. Think what you'd have been through, seeing to all that, nursing her – you'd have had to, you were all she'd got.'

'Yes, all right, Alistair. I know.'

'She'd had a good life and a lot of people would say she'd made a fortunate end.'

I am a poor meek thing, Mary thought, and I like quiet, meek, gentle people like myself. I liked, I *loved*, my grandmother who treated men's and women's feelings as if they were made of brittle glass and who handled them with fine dextrous fingers. I like people who go slowly and feel their way and are discreet and careful of their words, people who move delicately and tread on no one's dreams. 'Civilised' is my favourite word. That being so, how could I have lived for years with this man? And why can't I tell him to go away?

Alistair brought her some wine and she sipped it. He told her she really should eat something and when she said she couldn't said that *he* would.

'I'm hungry and I don't mind admitting it. Life has to go on.'

He brought himself a plate of salmon and salad with a hunk of granary bread. While he ate he talked about his day at work to 'distract' her. Not listening to what he said, she put Leo in his place, wondering what Leo would be saying if he were here now, imagining sensitivity but not the form it would take.

After a while she excused herself and went upstairs. The door had a lock and a key, so she locked it in case Alistair came up. Then she unlocked it because locking it was absurd. She lay on the bed and thought, I would like Dorothea here, or Judith. I

121

would like someone just to be with me. I would like Leo. I hardly know him, I've only spent a few hours with him but I would like him here now. Anyone but Alistair. Why does it have to be Alistair?

She can't be dead. But of course she can be. She was old, very old.

The age of the person who has died doesn't make any difference to those left behind. It's just as bad for them to lose someone of 85 as someone of 45 or 25. Leo would understand. He knew about death and she needed someone who knew about it. When she went downstairs again Alistair was watching television. He turned his head.

'Feeling a bit better?'

She nodded, though the nod meant nothing.

'There's nothing for you to do. I washed up my own plate and our glasses.'

It was an effort to stop herself thanking him but she made the effort and succeeded.

'I'm going to stay the night here with you, Mary. You shouldn't be alone.'

'Really, that's not necessary, Alistair.'

'I'm going to stay the night. I should never forgive myself if I abandoned you.' In the tone of someone who expects to be told no spare room would be needed, he could sleep with her, he said archly, 'Isn't there a spare bedroom going begging?'

She suddenly remembered telling her grandmother that she and Leo must meet when her holiday was over. Tears came into her eyes. She said goodnight, picked up Gushi and took him upstairs to bed with her. She locked the door and this time it stayed locked. After a while she heard Alistair padding about, searching for an airing cupboard, then fumbling in it for bedlinen.

The night was long but she slept at last.

122

Chapter Eleven

In the days when he lived in Bryanston Square as manservant to the late Anthony Maddox, Bean had come to hate his employer. Anthony Maddox had a dog, a spaniel, whom he never treated with much kindness, though it was an affectionate creature, and when one day during a bout of teasing it bit him, Maddox made Bean take it to the vet to be destroyed.

It was not in Bean's nature to feel self-disgust, but he many times reproached himself for obeying Maddox's order in this matter. He should have said no. He should have given in his notice rather than have Philidor put down. Meekly, though with sorrow in his heart, he had taken the spaniel to the veterinary surgery and asked for the deed to be done. But after that he took a slow, if largely concealed and invisible, revenge. In ways of which Maddox knew nothing until the day before his death, Bean made his life a misery.

He never guessed that into every bowl of soup Bean brought him, his manservant had first spat. Nor that a spoonful of Bean's urine went into cups of tea and coffee. The caterpillars which Bean harvested from plants in the Park (and in relation to which Maddox had a phobia) he did see, only to be told by Bean that increasing short-sightedness made cleansing lettuce of these creatures impossible. Maddox was very fond of salad but he stopped eating it. He was three times summoned for non-payment of rates because, unbeknownst to him, Bean had appropriated the local authority's demands before they reached him.

He parked his car on the Residents' Parking to which he had a right in the City of Westminster but many times, during the night, Bean moved it on to a double yellow line. Valuable books he borrowed from the London Library unaccountably disappeared. His electric blanket caught fire. Bean contaminated his goose liver pâté with a culture he had made out of a ham and cheese waffle removed from a Park dustbin and gave him gastro-enteritis. At first the doctor thought it was salmonella and this pulled Bean up short. He didn't want to kill the man and be done for murder.

Anthony Maddox had a stroke on his sixty-sixth birthday. It seriously affected his speech. Bean cared for him devotedly but on the day before Maddox was due to be transferred permanently to a nursing home, he unburdened himself totally to his employer.

Maddox was having his lunch. That is, it was lunchtime and Bean was feeding him, or about to feed him, soup followed by peach yogurt. The soup was a delicate pale green, prepared by Bean from fresh Aldeburgh asparagus, chicken stock and cream. He was quite aware of the incongruity of these three ingredients with the fourth. It was from such anomalies that he derived his entertainment. He would have called it his sense of humour.

A damask napkin, washed, starched and ironed by Bean, was spread across Anthony Maddox's shrivelled throat, concave chest and protuberant belly. The old man's mouth was drawn down to one side and his eyes bulged. They seemed, but probably were not, fixed upon the glorious prospect visible through the long Georgian window, of Sir Robert

124

Smirke's church, St Mary's, Wyndham Place, its pediment, its columns and its Tower-of-the-winds capitals. The sun shone upon its cupola, turning the brownish stone to a rich coppery gold.

Lifting the spoon to his employer's parted lips – they were always parted these days – Bean said:

'I spat in this soup while I was heating it up, sir. It's been a habit of mine to do that these fifteen years.'

Maddox's eyes bulged further and he recoiled from the spoon. His mouth worked.

'Some mornings I've brought up a lot of phlegm, sir, and that's gone into your soup too.' Bean spoke in his customary deferential tone. 'Smarmy' was the word applied to it by one of Maddox's friends. 'I've pissed in your tea and coffee. Not every cup, probably every third cup. You drink rather a lot of those beverages, sir, and I couldn't keep pace.'

Maddox vomited the soup he had already taken. His face was paper-white. Bean was very tender with him, giving him a blanket bath, making him comfortable, but Maddox had a heart attack and died in the night.

Few people kept a manservant in the Eighties. Single men living on their own got in a team of cleaners once a fortnight, ate takeaway or TV dinners from the microwave, had their washing done and delivered by the mobile laundry and never needed to make their beds because they used duvets. Bean had his name on the agency's book for months. He was living on his savings in a rented room over a newsagent's in Lisson Grove. Anthony Maddox had left him nothing in his will, which made Bean even more pleased with himself for confessing about the spit and urine.

One day he got a job offer. The man who interviewed him was, in Bean's own words, 'weird'.

He was plump and bald with a fringe of thin reddish hair growing round the naked pate and although it was ten in the morning, wore a black silk suit over a shirt with a frilly jabot. The apartment – you couldn't call something on two floors a flat – had weapons hanging round the walls, mostly whips, but guns too with ornamental stocks. There was a picture of a nearly naked young man with a halo round his head and his body stuck full of arrows and an even larger one of another haloed man being grilled like a piece of steak. Not that Bean ever ate steak but he sometimes cooked it – and sometimes spat on it – for Anthony Maddox.

His interviewer was called Maurice Clitheroe, a stockbroker, though he told Bean nothing of this at their first meeting. His voice was high and fluting and his way of speaking rather puzzled Bean because it seemed that everything was 'painful' to him and he 'suffered' a lot.

'I am *painfully* aware of the need of someone to *look after* me,' he said. 'Of course I realise that you would *contribute* to my *sufferings* but that I could *endure* if not with equanimity, with *resignation*. I am afraid you may find me rather a *sore subject*.'

Bean had no idea what all this meant but he took the job. Beggars can't be choosers and, living in Lisson Grove, he saw quite a lot of beggars. On bad days he imagined joining them, sitting in a porch, cap on the pavement, a dog maybe to keep him company and supply pathos. It was at first a matter of regret that Maurice Clitheroe had no dog but later, when he understood about the whips, the visitors to the apartment and the meaning of Clitheroe's funny talk, he was glad. God knows what might have become of a dog in all the excitement that was so often the order of the day in York Terrace.

The boys who came had been in the straightforward beating business and some of them hardly knew their own strength. Several times Bean had to put Clitheroe to bed with arnica on his bruises and cortisone cream on his weals. The young ladies were more refined, put saddle, bridle and bit on Clitheroe and rode him up the stairs and through the bedrooms. Once or twice since his employer's timely death and his coming into his inheritance, Bean had happened to see one of those visitors in the street. He was out and about so much, it was inevitable.

She was soliciting in Baker Street and wearing very poor quality thigh boots and a mini-skirt with a broken zip. Bean was in his new bomber jacket and baseball cap. Taking him for an American, she asked him in a mid-Atlantic accent if he would like to buy her a cocktail. For answer, he gave her one of his looks, a stare and then a sudden swift baring of the teeth. She recoiled before telling him to sod off. That look of his always made people wince and few recovered as fast as this girl.

He went into Europa Foods, which stays open late, and bought himself some pot noodles, a jar of minced sun-dried tomatoes, button mushrooms in brine, a blueberry and almond practically fat-free yogurt and a can of Sprite. The only other person of his acquaintance he met on the way home was the Cornells' housekeeper out with a man friend. They looked as if they were on their way to the Screen on Baker Street for the eight-fifteen showing. Remembering how she had sent him up and down those area stairs some four hours earlier and again some three hours earlier, Bean said loudly:

'Good evening, Valerie. Lovely evening.'

From the pavement newsstand in the Marylebone Road opposite the station he bought an *Evening Standard*. He wasn't a newspaper reader, or indeed much of a reader at all, but stuff whizzed past so quickly on the telly that sometimes you couldn't take in the details. The story about the impalement on the churchyard railings had by now been relegated to an inside page. An inquest had found that John Dominic Cahill, known as Decker, had died of stab wounds, principally of a stab wound that pierced the left ventricle of the heart. The body's being stuck on the railing spikes was merely an artistic touch, what the coroner described as evidence of the perpetrator's 'evil and degraded sense of humour'.

Bean read all about it while the microwave was heating up his pot noodle, dried tomatoes and button mushroom mixture. The verdict was of murder. No nonsense, Bean observed, about 'unlawful killing' or manslaughter. He was a hundred per cent in favour of the death penalty himself. If he had his way executions would be in public, not to mention putting lesser offenders in the stocks.

Drinking his Sprite, which had had five minutes in the freezer for a quick chill, he read an interview with Cahill's sister, a Bernadette Casey from County Offaly, who though admitting she hadn't set eyes on her brother or spoken to him for twenty-eight years, described him as a 'lovely person' whose death had devastated her and all his other eight brothers and sisters. It was incredible to her that Johnny should have been living rough on the streets of London and she still hoped and prayed there was some mistake.

The police hadn't got very far with finding who had done it. You could read that between the lines. Of course, it was probable that, like him and any other law-abiding citizen, they didn't *care* who had done it. Wasn't this just another bit of human detritus swept up off the streets and thrown away like litter?

Bean switched on the television. It was news time

but the murder no longer merited space on the national news. He leaned back in his chair and gave himself up to dreams: the dog of his own he wanted and would one day have when he had decided on the breed and could afford a pedigree animal, sired by a Crufts champion; ways of augmenting his income; could he manage a third daily round of dog-walking?

At this point Bean's thoughts turned to his clientele, to the Barker-Pryces, the Blackburn-Norrises, Mrs Goldsworthy, Lisl Pring and the rest of them. He had hoped to discover, when he first began walking these people's dogs, secrets of their pasts, incidents they would not want known and might pay to keep secret. But they barely admitted him to their houses; they never confided in him; they presented to him only blank and blameless façades. He sometimes thought that living for eight years with Maurice Clitheroe had given him an exaggerated idea of what the average West End dweller's homelife was like. Perhaps they really were all innocent, happily married (or happily celibate), chaste, incorruptible, exemplary citizens.

As to the secrets he did know, if they were secrets, there was no use threatening with exposure the girl who had approached him in Baker Street, for she would very likely regard this as welcome publicity and in any case she had no money. He cheered up a bit when the notion came to him that Lisl Pring might well be bulimic. Now she was starring in a successful sitcom, she might not be thrilled to see the *Sun* running a story about how she binged and then stuffed her fingers down her throat.

Bean went out to the kitchen to fetch his yogurt. Next time he went to fetch Marietta he'd give the place a good sniff, checking for vomit.

*

The hamburger stall outside Madame Tussaud's smelt the same as human sweat. Very strong human sweat. Bean knew all about it. He had smelt plenty of it in Maurice Clitheroe days, especially when one of the young men came round. The hamburger stall was doubly offensive to him, for that reason, and because it emanated from meat. He wondered what had possessed him to come this way round instead of taking York Gate or Park Square, and as he passed the stall, pushing his way through the milling throng of adolescents from all over Europe, he held a tissue ostentatiously over his nose or mouth. Nobody noticed, or if they did they thought he was protecting himself from traffic emissions in the Marylebone Road.

Waxworks. Bean couldn't see the point. He had been in there once, into the Chamber of Horrors – where else? – with Maurice Clitheroe to look at someone hanging up on a hook and that French chap stabbed to death in his bath. Maurice Clitheroe liked that sort of thing and frequented Tussaud's. Bean fancied it had been less busy seven or eight years ago. These days it was almost impossible to make one's way along the pavement, but he refused to be driven into the road and used his elbows. A young woman with three rings in her left ear and two in her right tried to sell him a copy of the *Big Issue* but drew back at the glare she got and the bared teeth.

The beggar with the dog – that was how Bean thought of him – was sitting in his usual place, halfway between Tussaud's and York Gate. A plastic box that had once held a video cassette lay open on the pavement for the receipt of alms and the dog sat on the man's knees, sleeping, snuggled up with its nose in a jacket pocket. The dog Bean's expert eye identified as a beagle, lemon and white, a pedigree without a doubt.

He bared his teeth at this man too. It was a grimace that was always effective, due perhaps to its shock value. People always recoiled. Armed as usual with his camera, he stepped back to the pavement edge and took a photograph. The beggar put his arms up over his face but by that time it was too late.

Boris the borzoi was the first dog he picked up. As usual Valerie Conway made him walk all the way down the area steps. She had a message for him, she said, from Mr and Mrs Cornell, to keep his wits about him because there had been an epidemic of dog-stealing.

'Those dossers pinch dogs, you know,' said Valerie. 'They want them to keep them warm at night and then there's the pathos factor.'

'The what?' said Bean.

'I mean, the British feel more sorry for a dog than a human, don't they?'

Bean stored up everything he learned on the chance it might come in useful and when he came to the flat in Portland Place to collect Ruby the beagle, he passed on this new information to Erna Morosini.

'Beagles are particularly in demand,' he said. 'For example, that down-and-out sits outside Tussaud's, he's got a beagle. You can see it's registered at the Kennel Club.' His powers of invention came into play. 'They drug them to keep them quiet all day. Valium's the favourite but Largactil runs it a close second.'

'I wish you hadn't told me,' said Mrs Morosini.

'We all have to face facts, don't we, madam? I'll be taking some photos of Ruby in the coming week. If you're interested they'll be very reasonably priced.'

The eyes of the Duke of Kent met his as he came back into Park Crescent and Bean composed his features into a similar stern and haughty expression. He let himself into the gardens and he and the two dogs made their way down the sloping path to the Nursemaids' Tunnel. On this mild afternoon of hazy sunshine it was deserted as usual and there was no sign of the key man. The gardens of Park Square were equally empty but for pigeons and sparrows on the sunlit grass and a squirrel which ran down the trunk of one tall green tree and up the trunk of another. It being Saturday, the Park itself would be crowded.

Bean told Mr Barker-Pryce about the street people stealing dogs, in his version substituting golden retrievers for beagles. Barker-Pryce said nastily that since Charlie only went out twice a day and always with Bean it was up to him to see that no such theft took place.

Bean said, 'You're right, sir,' but with rage in his heart. He didn't mention photographing Charlie and obviously the time wasn't right to say anything to Lisl Pring about pictures of Marietta. He'd told her poodles were currently the beggars' favourite prey and she'd reacted unexpectedly.

'They can have her. She's just shat all over my kilim.'

'You don't mean that, Miss Pring.'

Bean was shocked, by the sentiment and the language.

Waiting in the hall while she went to fetch Marietta, sniffing like a hound, he opened a door that looked as if a cloakroom would be on the other side, but it was only a cupboard. A long embroidered dress on a dummy and a suit of armour, standing up as if it had a man inside it, startled him and he closed the door quickly. Remembering what Lisl Pring had said, he was deterred from saying anything to Mrs Goldsworthy about scotties as dogs coveted for their pathos factor or bed-warming value.

The tall dosser with the beard and the Oxbridge

132

accent passed him as he walked up Albany Street. This, at least, was one that didn't smell. Caught short one morning, Bean had tied his dogs up to the railings and popped into the public convenience just off the Broad Walk. The tall one had been in there, strip-washing himself and drying his hair under one of the hand dryers. Bean hadn't spoken to him and he didn't now. He looked the other way. These people were a health hazard. Who knew *why* he'd been washing?

The young lady that was house-sitting Charlotte Cottage looked a bit peaky this afternoon. She was wearing black, which meant little on its own, but she had someone in there Bean recognised as one of the undertakers from a firm in the Marylebone Road. His curiosity, always active, quickened.

As he took Gushi from her, he said in his most respectful tone, 'No bad news of Sir Stewart and Lady Blackburn-Norris, I hope, miss?'

She wasn't the sort to pin your ears back and he despised her for her gentleness.

'Oh, no, no,' she said in a sad abstracted way. 'I'm sure they're fine. I had a card from Costa Rica.'

Bean decided not to pursue it. He wasn't interested in her personal tragedies. He hustled the dogs up to the Gloucester Gate and let them off on the broad expanses beyond the Parsee's fountain. The Park was as crowded as he had expected, young people lying about on the grass in various stages of undress, though the weather was far from hot and the sun kept going in. Charlie was the most friendly and uninhibited of the dogs and it brought Bean a good deal of amusement to see him go up to some of those cuddling couples and poke his nose into their crotches and bottoms. They shrieked and cursed him. Gushi and Marietta found a picnic party and Marietta ran off into the bushes with half a Swiss roll.

133

Usually, Bean preferred the Park to be deserted but this was the next best thing – a real crowd, most of whom seemed irritated and incommoded by the activities of dogs.

Even the sight of the woman walker with her orderly troop strolling the long path that bisects the Park couldn't entirely dispel his mood of cheerfulness. It was payday. He would collect from everyone on the way back, as he always did on Saturdays.

The undertaker had left by the time he took Gushi back. The young lady's eyes were red. Either she'd been crying or it was conjunctivitis. He reminded her he needed paying, and she actually apologised to him when she handed over the notes. With one hand Mrs Goldsworthy pulled McBride into the house and with the other thrust his money at him. It sounded as if she had a drinks party on the go which Bean thought decadent at five-fifteen on a summer afternoon. He'd have bared his teeth at Lisl Pring if he hadn't relied on her custom, her goodwill and the money she owed him. She came to the door in shorts and a halter top, skinny midriff bare as the day she was born, and a fellow behind her also in shorts with his arms round her waist.

Mr Barker-Pryce stank of cigars so badly that even the dog flinched. He counted out Bean's money very slowly and then, like a bank cashier, did it all over again. Bean had to tug at the notes to extract them from the nicotine-stained fingers.

He said, 'Thank you very much, sir,' and the door was shut smartly in his face.

Digging out the key from under the new wads of money, he let himself into the gardens of Park Square. A squirrel ran across the path no more than three feet from him and Ruby the beagle gave a great tug on the leash in pursuit of it. She nearly pulled Bean over. The borzoi growled at her and curled back his lips in much the same way as Bean did when displeased by the sight of someone or something.

In spite of the number of keys to the gardens which must be in circulation, the lawns and walks were deserted and the seats were empty. The wind had dropped, or had dropped in here in the sunlit space between tall trees. Flowers, unidentifiable by Bean, scented the air and almost masked the stench of fumes from the Marylebone Road. A blackbird sang.

The grass was not worn away by many feet and there was no litter to disfigure the walks or overflow from bins. A pity dogs were not allowed to run free in here. If they were he'd never go into the Park again. He made his way down the steep walled path to the tunnel, Boris and Ruby padding side by side ahead of him.

He never came down this path without a frisson of tension. His muscles always flexed and he had to keep his hands from tightening into clenched fists. But there was no sign of the key man. The tunnel was empty as it almost always was. And it was never dark at this hour, even in the middle, but invariably quite adequately lit with natural light from both ends. A momentary nasty idea came then, that the key man might be waiting at the other end, outside, just round the corner, and would step out, glittering and clinking, to fill the tunnel mouth as he reached it.

But he gave no thought to what might be behind him and was almost at the other end, having heard no footfalls, no indrawn breath, when something struck him on the crown of his head. It was like hitting his head on the beams of a low ceiling or the lintel of a door. But rather worse, for he staggered and fell over, first to his knees, then sprawled on his back. There was a moment of darkness with dazzle-ment, a seeing of stars, tailed comets and satellites whizzing across a black sky, and in it he must have relinquished his hold on the leash.

Bean thought he felt a hand fumbling in the pocket of his bomber jacket. He groaned and made feeble movements. Then he did hear footsteps, running away, back into Park Square. He sat up. His baseball cap had fallen off but it had been on his head when he was struck and Bean had no doubt it had saved him from worse damage. Gingerly, he felt his scalp and looked at his fingers. There was no blood. He hated the idea of falling and wondered if he could have broken something. Osteoporosis was not con-fined to elderly ladies, he had read in a health magazine.

His camera! It was gone. For a moment he thought that perhaps for once he had left it at home, but he knew its strap had been round his neck when he took the money from Barker-Pryce. As for his keys ... They had been in his jeans pocket: the key to York Terrace, the keys to Charlotte Cottage and Lisl Pring's and the one to these gardens. He ran his hand down the side of his leg, feeling for the ridges of metal, then thrust his hand inside. The keys were all there, but the pocket of his bomber jacket was empty. The wad of notes from four of his clients was gone and with it the best part of two weeks' retirement pension. Bean's stomach turned over. It was just as if his stomach had dropped on to the floor and done a somersault, turned itself over its heels.

At any rate he could get up. His legs were all in one piece. And he could see. The blow hadn't detached his retinas, which was another thing his extensive medical reading had told him could hap-pen. The two dogs were gone. Bean told himself they couldn't get out of the gardens and dismissed wild imaginings of the two of them under the wheels of container lorries in the Marylebone Road. In vain he called them, his voice weak and reedy.

Of course he had to go looking for them himself. Boris he found rolling on the rotting corpse of a pigeon and Ruby, still attached to him by the leash, running round in angry circles. Wearily he picked up the leash, his head throbbing.

One thing was for sure, he refused to go down the steps. When the Cornells' housekeeper appeared in the area he shouted at her that if she didn't open the front door he would leave Boris tied to the railings.

'What's got into you?' she said.

'I've been mugged, that's what's got into me. Open the front door, Valerie. I'm not feeling at all well. I've probably got concussion.'

After rather a long while the front door was opened. Bean saw white carpet, gilded furniture and red lilies in a Venetian glass bowl. He unclipped the leash and Boris entered the house, as if he always went that way, padding silently, to push a door open with his long nose.

'I don't have to remind you my remuneration is due, do I, Valerie?'

It was appalling to think of the sum that had been taken from him. He would have to plunder his savings. And the camera. Why had he never thought to insure the camera? He put up one hand to massage the lump that was swelling up on his scalp. The housekeeper came back with his money in an envelope. She seemed to be keying herself up to say something unpleasant.

'I'll see you tomorrow morning,' said Bean.

'And when you do, I'll thank you to call me Miss Conway!'

She had gone red in the face with the effort of it. Bean shrugged, pocketed the envelope and walked

137

home to York Terrace. If you lost consciousness, however briefly, it was concussion and you were supposed to go to the doctor. But had he lost consciousness? On the whole he thought not. As soon as he was inside he phoned the police and told them he had been assaulted and all his money stolen.

An officer would call, they said. Meanwhile he should see a doctor.

'I know who my assailant is,' said Bean.

'You saw him?'

'I didn't exactly see him but I know him. He's a vagrant, a down-and-out, goes about all covered with keys.'

'Your own keys are missing?'

Bean admitted they were not but he was tired of this officer sounding so bored and indifferent, and said he would come down to the police station himself.

Chapter Twelve

Mary had thought people would take the loss of a grandmother less seriously than, say, the death of a parent, but it had not turned out like that. Dorothea's husband had a week's holiday due to him and he took over her job. The Trattons in Crete saw to the arrangements for returning Frederica Jago's body. The undertakers were helpful if grimly lugubrious. Alistair arrived and shepherded her to the registering of the death, the ordering of flowers, the passing on of the news to solicitors.

'It's just the same as if you'd lost your mother,' he said, his attitude quite changed from what it had been that evening the news came. 'It's the same kind of grief. We do wrong when we judge the bereaved person's feelings by some level of kinship.'

This man was the same one that only a week before had told her she should be thankful not to have had to nurse her grandmother through a lingering end. Alistair had not mentioned money or the disposal of the house in Belsize Park. He had not mentioned sex either or staying overnight. And nothing had been said about the transplant or the Harvest Trust.

There had been nothing from Leo. She had met him only three times but she missed him. 'Desperately' was the word that came to mind. She told herself not to be so extreme, hysterical almost. How could she feel an intense longing for the company of someone she hardly knew? She had begun to dream about him, once in an erotic and romantic scenario that shocked her awake.

Flesh of my flesh, she remembered, bone of my bone. Those words of his had been the high point of an emotional moment when she had felt briefly that years of intimacy lay behind them. Was it unnatural or presumptuous to have believed then that years of closeness lay ahead of them?

He had disappeared into nothingness. The day after the dream in which he held her, kissed and caressed her, she had the strange feeling that if she never saw him again, if he had gone from her life as swiftly as he had entered it, those few hours they had spent together would remain with her always.

Sorrow at her grandmother's death competed with the emotions Leo had aroused, but it failed to drive him from her mind. If he had come to her she could have talked to him about Frederica Jago. He would have listened, would have wanted to hear. Alistair cut short her reminiscences. Memories and recollections weren't to his taste.

'I did know your grandmother, darling. I knew her a lot better than I know my own relations.'

And Dorothea said dwelling on the past was upsetting. Once the funeral was over she should put all that behind her.

'I don't agree with all this talking things through. It just makes it worse. Look at all those people who talked things through and discovered they'd been abused as kids. Wouldn't they have been better off not knowing?'

'It isn't that kind of talking I mean. I don't want a therapist.'

'You want to live in the present,' said Dorothea.

Leo, Mary somehow guessed, would have listened and asked all the right questions, would have been patient with her, spent hours if necessary hearing about the grandmother who had been a mother and friend and a great consolation for the trials of life and whom no one could replace. But she was half-afraid now that she would never see Leo again.

She went back to work before the funeral. It was better to be at the Irene Adler than in Charlotte Cottage alone. An evening talking to Celia Tratton – who had come back from Crete the day before – made her feel calmer, more able to accept. The number of tourists visiting the museum had fallen off since the murder had ceased to be a talking point and no longer had its place in newspapers, and Mary used a half-hour when no one came to try to phone Leo.

It had taken a good deal of self-persuasion to get her to this point. She had reminded herself of all the things he had said to her, the kind and flattering things, how almost everything he had said at that first meeting and on the Friday, had indicated that he wanted them to be friends. His last words, tinged with impatience, she tried to put from her mind. She did her best to banish the picture she had of his abrupt departure. Something had happened to prevent his getting in touch, perhaps something to do with his brother. Or it might be that he had tried to phone her but had given up because the line had been so frequently engaged since her grandmother's death. Reminding herself of that, she had on the previous evening attempted to phone him at his brother's number, three times, but there had been no reply.

Had she ever told him precisely where she worked? He had told her only that he was employed by his brother and had a part-time job. Whether that was at home or in some office he hadn't said. There was no mystery about it, of that she was sure; there simply had been no occasion to go into details about the job.

By now she was beginning to ask herself what she would say if he did answer. Why haven't I heard from you? Can we meet? I would like to see you again? All were impossible for someone like her. She wanted an explanation but knew she was incapable of asking a man she had only met three times why he had dropped her. He could hardly be put into the category of an inconstant lover. Perhaps she could just ask him how he was, make some bland empty enquiry. She dialled the number and again there was no reply.

It rained on the day of the funeral. Alistair took time off work and was there to hold an umbrella over her. The man she had met at Frederica's dinner and who had asked her to the cinema with him came to the church with a woman who was clearly a girlfriend. The elderly friends were there, all but the Blackburn-Norrises. Mary made a mental note to phone their hotel in Acapulco and break the news gently to them. Frederica's solicitor, who had also been at that dinner with his wife, sat in a front pew, and when it was all over, and the dismal gathering afterwards in Belsize Park was all over, he stayed behind.

Mary wondered why, vaguely thinking that perhaps she had done something wrong in inviting mourners to a place which was not hers, or not yet legally hers. But she had supposed it would be even more heinous to hold any sort of party in Charlotte Cottage. However, Mr Edwards had remained behind for a very different reason and one which Alistair, refilling his sherry glass, seemed to know all about. Suddenly a staginess took over from the funereal atmosphere. Mr Edwards whispered something to Alistair and Alistair said:

142

'I am sure my fiancée is quite up to hearing it now.'

The two of them retired with measured tread to Frederica's dining room. Mary was so indignant at being called Alistair's fiancée that she hardly noticed the door had closed and they were in there together. It opened after a few seconds; Alistair put his head out and he asked Mary in a low, very serious voice if she would come in and join them.

Mr Edwards had seated himself at the head of the table. Alistair sat at the foot. But when Mary came in he got up, held a chair out for her and stood behind it. He went on standing behind it after she had sat down, like a husband in a Victorian wedding photograph, she thought.

'Mr Edwards is going to tell you the contents of your grandmother's will, my dear.'

'My dear' was another departure. The two of them were taking her over in a patronising paternalistic sort of way and the idea came to her that if only Leo were there he would stop this happening. But she restrained herself, nodded to Mr Edwards and told him please to go ahead.

With a small deprecatory cough, he told her what she knew already, that this house was now hers, and told her too what she had never dreamed of, that her grandmother had left her everything she possessed: just under two million pounds.

If Mary had for a moment thought that somehow – she couldn't begin to guess how – Alistair had *known*, that he and the solicitor had been in cahoots, one look over her shoulder at his face dispelled that. It was like someone else's face, someone she had never known, for it had crumpled and grown soft, his eyes very wide open, his mouth slack. He pulled out the chair next to hers and sat down on it. She half-expected him to throw his arms across the table and lay his head on them, but he remained quite still, staring at a picture on the opposite wall.

Mr Edwards was talking about small bequests, little sums to little charities. She scarcely heard him. She was asking herself why it was she had never guessed her grandmother had had so much. He stopped talking quite suddenly and turned on her a bright, almost gleeful smile, as if he had not, some two hours before, attended the funeral of an old and valued friend and client.

'Thank you,' Mary said.

Alistair took hold of her hand and held it hard. She saw Mr Edwards looking at them benevolently, as at a young couple on the threshold of their married life, made happy by a windfall of gargantuan proportions. They could hardly realise it yet, he must be thinking, the joyful shock had half-stunned them, but in a few moments . . .

Even the tone of his voice had changed as he began talking about probate, the law's delays. Mary nodded. Alistair found the tongue that she thought must have been cleaving to his palate and said:

'Yes, absolutely. My fiancée is in no immediate need. And afterwards – well, I am in banking as no doubt you know, and I can take care of all that.'

The rain had begun again by the time Mr Edwards left. He put up his umbrella and made his way at a half-run towards the street and a taxi. Alistair had phoned for one for them. They travelled back to Charlotte Cottage in silence. Having closed the front door, he turned to her and tried to take her in his arms. Worms turn, she thought, and I have not even been quite a worm, more of a trapped insect that can still sting. She held his hands, took them down from her shoulders and stepped back.

'It's a strange thing,' she said, 'that while I was

living with you I was your girlfriend and now I've left you I'm your fiancée. How do you account for that?'

'You're going to say it's the money, aren't you?'

'No, I'm not going to say that, Alistair. You've said it. You've said what I couldn't bring myself to say.'

'Perhaps it's slipped your mind that I've been here seeing to things practically every day since your grandmother died. I didn't know what kind of money she'd left.'

'You made an intelligent guess. You're a banker, as you told Mr Edwards; you know about these things.'

'Darling,' he said, 'darling, I want to marry you. All right, I didn't know that until you'd left me. Is that so bad? I didn't value you as you should be valued while you were with me, but when you'd gone I missed you so desperately.'

'"Darling" and "my fiancée" – I think of them as expressions people use when they don't want to say someone's name.'

He said angrily, 'What's that got to do with it? I said I wanted to marry you. I told you why. You've no right to hold the past against me. Those things will never happen again, I've promised you that.' He clenched his hands. 'You haven't even noticed, have you?'

'Noticed what?'

'That I haven't once mentioned the transplant, that harvest thing, whatever you call it. I've put that behind me. I made myself a promise never to say any more about it and I've kept to that. What more do you want?'

It grew easier with every sentence. Her strength increased at an almost alarming rate. 'I don't want anything, Alistair.'

'What does that mean?'

'From you. I don't want anything. I thought I'd explained that.'

'No, you've got everything, haven't you? What you've been waiting for. Independence. You don't *need* me is what you mean.'

He made a kind of running jump at her, taking her by surprise. He seized her by the shoulders and began to shake her. His face had changed back to what it used to be, flushed dark red, the eyes very black.

'You're mine; you can't get away from me like that. Just because you're rich now, you think you don't need me, after everything I've done for you, after what we've been . . .'

The doorbell rang. His hands tightened, then faltered and she twisted away from him. Her teeth were chattering. She put up her hand to cover her mouth as if its pressure would stop the shaking. The bell rang again and she went to answer it, speechless, trembling, unable to speak to Bean who stood on the doorstep, wearing his polite obsequious smile.

'Good afternoon, miss. Little fellow ready for his walkies, is he?'

The borzoi, the beagle, the golden retriever, the chocolate poodle and the scottie were tied to the gatepost. A large sticking plaster covered most of the bald part of Bean's head. Mary looked at it in a dazed sort of way before fetching Gushi. Alistair followed her to the door, said a hearty 'Good afternoon' to Bean and that it was far from ideal weather for dog-walking.

'Needs must, sir, when the devil drives,' said Bean ambiguously.

Mary shut the door. Alistair was leaning against the wall.

'Look, I'm sorry about that. But you can be so

146

exasperating I get carried away. I suppose I just have this feeling I can shake some sense into you.'

'You ought to know by now that you can't.'

She opened the door again. She was struggling hard not to cry and succeeded better with the door open, with Bean and the dogs still visible, with the man in the house opposite braving a shower to deadhead his roses.

'I'd like you to go. Please just go.'

There was a moment, no more than a few seconds, in which it seemed he might wrench the door from her, slam it shut and lean against it, confronting her. He must have thought of it, then maybe postponed such action until a later date. Something had struck him as dumb as she had been with Bean, perhaps a too-late realisation of what he had done, how he had reverted to the behaviour he said he had put behind him. He took his raincoat from the hallstand and went out into the rain, walking very fast.

Alone, she could cry now but she found she no longer wanted to. She went into the living room, sat at Lady Blackburn-Norris's desk and began writing a letter to Leo.

The nuns on Primrose Hill had dispensed tea to Pharaoh the key man at five on Saturday afternoon along with Racker and Dill and some of the jacks men and himself. Roman told the police all this and that he had spoken to Pharaoh, insofar as it was possible to have a conversation with anyone so distracted and strange and out of touch with reality as the key man was. He understood that he had supplied Pharaoh with an alibi for something that had occurred at five, though no one told him what.

When he asked what had happened, in his middle-class way, the way that expects explanation from authority, they said they were unable to tell him that.

147

For a moment he thought the officer was going to call him 'sir'. Bewildered by his accent and perhaps by a very different manner from that of the jacks men, the young policeman was indeed on the verge of calling him 'sir', until he reminded himself this was a vagrant he was talking to.

Roman might have told the police something of Pharaoh's life but they hadn't asked him and he had learned, while on the street, not to offer gratuitous information. There was no reason for them to suspect him of being the repository of Pharaoh's secrets, if indeed he was; if the story told him one night on the canal bank was even true. Roman believed it was. Francie Quin who had recounted it was no more drunk on 'milk' than he normally was and he offered the story without bursting into the jacks men's mad laughter or their occasional growling belligerence.

Everyone knew Pharaoh's real name was Jimmy Clancy but only Quin had discovered where his sobriquet came from. Back in the Seventies, when very young, when still in his teens, he had been attached to a religious cult that roamed the country in battered vans and trucks, and like strolling players of old, performed on the roadside or in a field its own version of miracle and mystery plays. In one such play, a dramatised 'Moses in the Bulrushes', Clancy had played the King of Egypt whose daughter finds Moses and brings him up. The title had stuck and he was Pharaoh thereafter.

It was in those days too that he had first, as was fashionable, put the blue tint on his hair. Or rather, his sister, a hairdresser, had done it for him. Quin fancied he had been schizophrenic since his teens, since before the time he joined the cult. Most of the members heard God talking to them, so there was nothing strange to be noted in Pharaoh's behaviour.

'Though it was more Satan than God, if you ask

148

me,' said Quin. 'An imp of Satan tormenting him. He was supposed to find the Keys of the Kingdom, whatever they might be.'

'The Keys of the Kingdom of Heaven. Christ is said to have given them to Peter,' said Roman, and because he didn't want to seem a fount of knowledge, 'or that's what I've heard. Something like that. The Pope would have them now.'

'They real then, are they? I mean, like what they lock up the Park with?'

Roman said he didn't think so, more a symbol, or a way of speaking, but Quin seemed to know what he meant. In the dark canal a full moon was reflected, like a round white light under the water. Trees trailed thin branches across its surface as if to catch the moon in their net. It could have been some broad sluggish river they sat beside, with dense vegetation growing down to its banks, a mass of complex leafiness that might have stretched, for all that could be seen, back across the city for miles, covering buildings in a dark wilderness. Perhaps the Nile had been like that, where Moses floated in his rushy cradle.

A reddish London sky was all scudded over with wisps of black cloud. Distantly the tall Edwardian blocks, palely lit with sodium and neon, gleamed like palaces, the castles in the sleeping wood. The sounds of the city, as light as they ever became, thinned and rarefied, throbbed softly through the earth.

The rest of the jacks men had gone home to their hostel in Camden, a place Quin avoided if he could elude the police and sleep in the Park. He had collected his DSS money that day, so had brown ale instead of meths and water and he passed the bottle. Roman took a swig so as not to be stand-offish.

'When he got bad they sectioned him and he was in this bin for most of the Eighties. He come out four

149

or five years back to what they call care in the community.' Quin gave a soft derisive laugh. 'His mum gave him a bed for two nights. After that her and his stepfather changed the locks and he couldn't get back in. He didn't know and he came back and tried his keys in the locks. Them was the keys he started with, the ones that wouldn't open her door.'

'Where does he get them from? The rest of the keys, I mean?'

'Nicks them, God knows. He don't never *use* them. They're not the right ones, they don't open the doors he wants open.'

'Lift up your heads, O ye gates,' Roman muttered, wishing immediately afterwards that he hadn't.

But Quin seemed gratified. 'That's right. Say some more.'

So Roman said, 'Lift up your heads, O ye gates, and be ye lift up, ye everlasting doors, and the King of Glory shall come in . . .'

'You want to say that to Pharaoh,' said Quin. 'He'd like that, would Pharaoh.'

But remembering the religious cult, Roman said, 'I've no doubt he knows it already.'

Whether the police had actually spoken to Pharaoh he couldn't tell. He looked at newsboards, half-expecting to read of another murder, but there was nothing. Of Effie there had been no sign since the day they found John Dominic Cahill's body and he had told her to leave the gardens. But he sensed among the men and the occasional woman who slept rough on the borders of the Park, a new tension, an awareness of danger and threat, as if nemesis had come to disturb their precarious peace.

The weather was mild, though still cold at night. He took his clothes and one of his blankets to the launderette in Baker Street. His old winter-worn trainers he threw away and bought a new pair. The best time of year was coming for the street sleepers. It was not until you slept on doorsteps that you realised real summer only comes to England after midsummer is past, and in those short months perhaps a mere four or five nights will be warm.

On one of those, in the first week of June, he slept in the open on Primrose Hill, hoping to see the stars. But even up there the sky was overcast by some unnatural vapour and suffused from below by a reddish artificial light. He lay awake for a long time, remembering Elizabeth's interest in astronomy and how he had read it up to keep pace with her, just as he had bought himself a book on pondlife so that he might know what Daniel was talking about. But very little life of any kind remained in English ponds – fertilisers and insecticides had seen to that – and the stars were no longer visible from a West Hampstead garden.

He could conjure up their three faces as they had been when last he saw them, but now as he did so he thought how he had frozen them in the ice of his present. Had they lived they would no longer look like that. Sally might but Elizabeth would be nearly seventeen now, a young woman, and as for Daniel – at perhaps no time once babyhood is past does the face change so much as it does between eight and ten and Daniel would be ten now. So he, their father, was looking at a mirage, at outdated photographs, at lost lives gone beyond any real recall.

For the first time since he had taken to the street he thought of the future. Up until this moment there had only been the past and the present, for he had supposed, though he had never put this into uttered or silent words, that he would not long survive, that life could not support so much pain. Men have died from time to time, he quoted to himself, and worms have eaten them, but not for love. Not of grief either,

151

it seemed. The future stretched before him, the door to it had opened at last, and on the other side he saw, white and rolling uphill, an infinite street on which the homeless slept and he among them.

If Carl had said it once he had said it a hundred times, that he didn't want Hob coming upstairs. Well, he could come up for a social call if he wanted, but Hob never made social calls. He only wanted one thing and Carl was ready enough to supply it, but not at home, not in front of Leo.

Hob knew all that but he was desperate. He wasn't just in a state; this was the mother of all states. It was the worst he'd ever known since that time he'd spent all one night in a cell and they wouldn't give him anything, not even one of those new type antihistamines. They'd had a good laugh at his expense. It had been the funniest thing they'd seen in months.

He knew he was getting bad when he could hear the mice. According to Carl there was a mouse for every person in the British Isles, which made about fifty-eight million, and most of them lived in the walls of Redferry House. Or that was Hob's opinion. Another thing he'd heard was that no matter where you were, city or countryside, you were never more than six feet from a rat. His sister had told him you could be sitting somewhere really up-market, like the bar of a classy hotel, and there'd be a rat lurking inside the wall behind you or outside the window with the velvet curtains. But it was mice he heard, running around and scratching behind the skirting board. Or, rather, he heard them when he was in a state. The rest of the time he didn't hear them or else he didn't care. He'd start feeling shaky, weak and old, and his muscles would jump and then he'd hear the scratching.

It was hard to say what came first, the panic attack

152

when everything frightened him – the air itself, the light, just having his eyes open, any sort of movement – or the mice scratching. There was very little furniture in his first-floor flat, only a brown vinyl couch with Mickey Mouse scatter cushions and the mattress he slept on and of course the TV, and there was never much food. He usually kept in a packet of Weetabix and one of cream crackers, for his health's sake. But the night before he'd drunk a lot of vodka in lieu of anything better, eaten a Weetabix to get something on his stomach and fallen asleep in the middle of it.

When he woke up at dawn or something like that, light anyway, there'd been droves of mice round his feet eating crumbs. He'd yelled out and they'd fled but he felt so bad that afterwards he'd wondered if they were real mice or not. And if they were real, could he have seen fifty of them, which was what he thought?

So what with the mice and nothing in the flat but the last of the vodka and six morphine tabs prescribed for his stepfather's ex-wife's cancer, he had to go upstairs and see Carl. The way he saw it he didn't have a choice. For once, the lift was working. If it hadn't been he reckoned he'd have lain down on the floor and died. His mother's nan, who was ninety-five, sang a song that went:

> I have no pain, dear Mother, now,
> But oh, I am so dry,
> Attach me to a brewery,
> And leave me there to die.

It wasn't a brewery he wanted, more like a chemistry lab, but the song writer had the right idea. He growled the tune, going up in the lift, but had to stop because he was shrieking. Carl and Leo lived on the seventh floor. Carl had painted the front door quite a nice shade of yellow but someone had tried to break in and though they hadn't succeeded, they'd gouged a great slash out of the woodwork from the keyhole to the letter box.

A long time passed before the door was answered. Carl came at last. He looked Hob up and down.

'I thought I told you not to come here.'

'I'm in a state,' Hob said.

'My home base is out of bounds, Hob,' Carl said. 'You know that.'

'I'm in a state. I just want one rock to see me through the weekend.' He pushed past Carl into the flat. 'I got to have it, you know me.'

'One rock wouldn't see you through a revolving door,' said Carl sadly. 'Say hallo to Leo. He's not feeling too good.'

'Him and me both. Hi. I got to have it, Carl, don't fuck me over.'

Leo was lying on the sofa. He didn't look any worse than usual, or not in Hob's opinion. When Hob was in a state he hadn't much time for other people's ailments. Leo was reading a letter. He looked terrible when he laughed, his face more like a skull than usual.

'Now you're here you'd better sit down. Turn your visit into a social call, right? How about a cup of tea?'

Hob shook his head feebly. Sitting down in the brothers' flat he could sometimes convince himself he was in a kindly rehab centre. There was carpet on the floor, and armchairs, and if the rest of the furniture was of a slightly lower standard than the kind you see exposed for sale on the pavements of Kilburn High Road, it was furniture and it gave some semblance of home to the place. Carl kept it warm too, for Leo's sake. Last year, just before Leo came home from hospital, Carl had made an attempt to paint this room but had abandoned the task halfway through, so that two of the walls were green, one white and one half green and half white.

Hob's mum, who'd known Leo all his life, said Carl was more like a father to him than a brother, thought the world of him, worshipped the ground he walked on – which wasn't much like Hob's experience of the paternal role. And Carl didn't have a very tender heart where others were concerned. Now he had Hob seated in a chair with a mug of tea in front of him, he was back conversing with Leo as if there wasn't anyone else there.

Hob didn't know who this woman was they were talking about and cared less. The tea tasted like mice piss, anyway. The woman had written to Leo, it sounded like; she was halfway to being his girlfriend, which was crazy on account of everyone knew Leo was on his way out. Carl wasn't going to talk about it in front of him anyway – Hob might be in a state but he didn't miss that tiny shake of the head Carl gave Leo. Maybe he'd mouthed something about walls having ears, only Hob couldn't see. His voice came out in a whine.

'I got to have something, Carl.'

'The fountain then, the old drinking fountain. Ten. When it's dark. If it's not me it'll be Gupta.'

'You not got nothing now? No shit?'

Carl said remotely, 'Absolutely no shit, Hob, in all senses of the word.'

'A couple of Es? Some cycles?'

'You're the expert, Hob. I don't even know what cycles are but I bet they're on the controlled list.'

'Some jellies?' Hob said hopefully.

'You're too scared of the needle, you know that,' said Carl. 'It's time I took payment in kind again, I think.' He took the letter from Leo. 'Nice handwriting she's got.'

'She's got nice things to say.'

Carl laughed. He put the letter in his pocket. 'I've never done a violent act,' he said conversationally. 'Never drawn a drop of blood or caused a moment's pain in anger. The pain I caused gave infinite pleasure. How does it feel, Hob, doing what you do?'

'I don't know,' said Hob. 'I'm in a state. I'm fucked.'

'I'll have a job for you one of these days. How would you like that, Hob? A job that was big enough to keep you in rocks or that elephant dope for the rest of your life?'

Hob said with as much eagerness as he could muster, 'Have you got a job for me, Carl? I don't mind work, I'll work all the hours God gave.'

Carl started laughing. 'I bet you will. You're a scream, did you know that? You know that old dog man, the one in the baseball cap that walks the dogs?'

'I don't know him. Why would I?'

'I can't tell you why you would, Hob. Can't you stop that shaking? You're rocking the room and Leo's not a well man. The old dog man may have something for you if you're in the Park around half-four in the afternoon. Mind you, I'm only guessing but I reckon he'll have something. It's what I've heard. You'd better go now. I'll see you later or Gupta will.'

Leo was looking at him with those great glassy eyes in his skull face. Hob was beginning to feel very sick. He knew he wouldn't be sick because he hadn't eaten anything to bring up, but he needed to be out in the air. Carl kept the flat very warm for Leo's sake.

'Say goodbye nicely to Leo,' said Carl. 'He's not feeling very bright.'

Downstairs again, Hob forgot about the fresh air. He'd had an idea. There was just a chance, not much

156

of one but a faint chance, that he'd left a tab or even some blow – who was he kidding? – in the pockets of his clothes.

Everything he possessed lay in heaps on the bedroom floor, some of it piled on the blankets on the end of his mattress to help keep him warm on cold nights. The best he had came from charity shops; the worst, which was his daily wear, out of litter bins or off skips. He started fumbling through the smelly welter of garments – the pockets of an old red cardigan, stiff with dirt and food stains; jeans with missing knees and ragged hems; a scuffed leather jacket that had been his grandfather's decades ago. The pockets yielded nothing but dead matches and old scratch cards.

His searching became manic and, frustrated, he flung stuff across the room: aged T-shirts that were greyish or blackish, sagging vests, a pair of striped pyjama pants. The movement must have disturbed the mice, for the scraping noises began again, and a scurrying and a faint high-pitched squeaking.

Hob lay down on the mattress as the panic attack started and buried his face in the old clothes, uncertain now whether the sounds he heard were made by the mice or by himself. A huge empty loneliness isolated him and he whimpered. He pounded his fists on the floorboards and all the mice fled like an army in the full tilt of retreat.

Chapter Thirteen

Boris and Ruby lugged Bean across the Marylebone Road at the lights between Park Square and Park Crescent. They were never red for long enough to satisfy him and he bared his teeth and shook his fist at impatient drivers. But he wasn't going back through that tunnel while the key man was still at large.

He had given the police a precise description, from the long black hair and beard dyed a fierce cobalt blue to the feet in split and filthy leather boots. The keys, he believed, were fastened to his clothes with safety pins, and he described them as like an armour plating, a kind of chain mail worn for protection. Several times, because no arrest was made and nothing seemed to be done, Bean went back to the police and harried them. He wanted an identity parade so that he could pick the key man out. They told him they were working on his case and if anything developed they would get back to him. Bean had no faith in them.

Though he knew a large number of people, he had few friends, and those he had were acquaintances he met in the Globe on a Friday night, the only evening out he had. There was Freddie Lawson, who worked as odd-job man for the Crown Estates, and Peter Carrow, a Park attendant, whose life had changed very much for the better when he was issued with a vacuum cleaner for sucking up the litter in the Broad

158

Walk and round the pavilions. Lawson, a widower, and Carrow, whose wife had left him long ago, both drank far more than Bean did, drank away their wages in the Globe or the Allsop Arms every night, but it was on Friday that they met him in the Globe and it was there that Bean recounted to them his experiences with the key man. Carrow, who knew most of the dossers by sight at least, immediately recognised Bean's description and was even able to tell him the key man's name.

By now Bean had convinced himself he had seen Clancy when he was mugged. He believed it. The two encounters had become blurred in his mind and he told Lawson and Carrow that it was just after he passed Clancy in the tunnel that the key man had stepped away from the wall and struck him on the back of the head. A number of other people, including the inevitable tourists, heard him say this.

'And the Bill won't do nothing for you?' said Lawson.

Lawson always called the police the Bill. Carrow called them the Filth.

'They're protecting him,' said Bean, 'for reasons of their own.'

He tried to enlist the help of Valerie Conway. Since their confrontation over the matter of her given name, Bean had called her nothing. All kinds of styles and titles were in his repertoire – Miss, Miz, Madam, Ma'am, as well as surnames preceded by Miss or Miz – but he called her nothing now and she perceived that he had won that round. Therefore she was on her guard when he asked her if it wasn't a fact that he had described to her his encounter with Clancy, calling him an 'alien'.

'That wasn't the same time as when you were mugged,' said Valerie.

'Oh, please,' said Bean. 'Don't give me that. I came

159

here with the dog and for once you opened the front door to me on account of me being in such a state. I was on my knees, I couldn't hardly see straight.'

'Maybe, but you never said who'd done it to you. If you want my opinion, you're confused. You can't expect me to make a fool of myself going to the police with a story that's a figment of your imagination.'

'Perhaps you'll fetch the dog,' said Bean.

Victory to Valerie, she thought, shutting the area door behind them. Bean crossed the road and went to pick up Charlie the golden retriever in St Andrew's Place. James Barker-Pryce, a wet dead cigar plugged into the left corner of his mouth, brought the dog to the door. Bean advised him to be careful if he was thinking of going out. There was a dangerous vagrant at large, identifiable by his blue-dyed hair and the keys pinned all over him. Barker-Pryce said he hoped Bean hadn't been drinking. He never gave credence to anything told him by a member of the working class, never had and never would; they had always been mentally subnormal and were now even more reduced by television and drugs.

Bean told his tale to Mrs Goldsworthy and then to Lisl Pring.

'I wouldn't like anything to happen to Marietta,' was all she said.

Incensed, Bean forgot his usual deference. 'Thanks very much,' he said. 'Never mind me.' He added, ridiculously, a belated, 'Miss.'

Lisl Pring started laughing. When she laughed she sucked in her diaphragm and you could count her ribs. She wouldn't have cared what Bean said to her so long as the poodle got its walks.

'I shall be going on my holidays to my sister in Brighton the first week of August,' he said and watched her face fall. 'I'm telling you well in advance so as you can make other arrangements.'

Up in Park Village Miss Jago showed more sympathy. She asked him if he was fully recovered, if the police had found whoever was responsible. Bean wondered what she was after. He had no belief in altruism. Maybe she was running short of cash in the absence of Sir Stewart and Lady Blackburn-Norris and thought soft soap might secure her a discount.

'There's no doubt who was responsible, miss,' he said darkly, shaking his head in the way people do when they wish to convey exasperation and disillusionment. 'The kind of alien a lady like yourself would no more notice than you would a bit of muck on the pavement. I wouldn't even ask you if you'd come in contact with him.'

She came back with the dog in her arms, cuddling him like a baby.

'Every penny I'd got on me he took. And my camera. Luckily, I used up the film with the shots on it of these lovely dogs. Would you be interested in acquiring a portrait of the little Shih Tzu?'

She said it wasn't her dog. That was a matter for Sir Stewart and Lady Blackburn-Norris. He had guessed she'd say that and didn't much care. Mrs Goldsworthy had said she'd love a portrait of McBride or even an album of pictures.

It was common knowledge he was to be found in the Park every day around eight-thirty in the morning and four-thirty in the afternoon, say a quarter of an hour on either side of those times. Bean thought afterwards that this must account for it. But before the man came up to him he had set the dogs free and was walking the long exposed path towards the bridge and the new pond by the Hanover Gate. It was warm enough to do without his bomber jacket and he tied it round his middle by its sleeves the way

161

the youth did. For the baseball cap, smart protection from the sun's heat on his poor head, he was starting to feel a greater affection than he had for any human being. It had probably saved his life when Clancy attacked him.

By the railings that enclosed the grounds of The Holme, the big house that overlooked the lake, the woman was walking her dozen dogs. Not one of them was on the lead and all walked sedately, the little ones at her heels, the bigger ones in as orderly a fashion as if they had all been to training classes. Perhaps they had. The woman wore jodhpurs and a check shirt and her long dark hair flowed down her back. She must have one of those whistles inaudible to the human ear, for when a labrador lagged behind Bean saw her put something to her lips and the labrador come running obediently.

Three of his dogs were close at his heels and the other three at the lake's edge – Marietta barking at a red-headed duck, the Shih Tzu and the scottie drinking from the scummy brown water – as Bean stepped on to the bridge that here crosses a loop of the lake enclosing an island. It was shady and dim, a dusty place, overshadowed by tall trees. Birds thronged the nearly stagnant water, pochards, mandarins, swans, mallards, pintails, coots and divers. Even in the winter a sour smell rose from the water and now, in the mild humidity of June, there was a powerful stench of decaying vegetable matter. He was halfway across when a man approaching from the other end stopped in front of him and asked for a light.

Bean might have said, 'Sorry' or 'I'm afraid I don't carry one,' but in fact he said, 'I don't smoke,' in such a way as to put smoking on a par with snorting cocaine.

Instead of passing on, the man looked him in the

162

eye. He was young, skinny but with a jowly face, a round head and a crew cut, too young and strong for Bean to push past him. He had the sort of eyes Bean had heard addicts had, dull and with pinhead pupils. A flicker of fear plucked at his chest. But he was not alone. He could see Sunday crowds on the sunlit grass by the Hanover pond; footsteps were approaching behind him and two girls with linked arms had come on to the bridge ahead.

'My mate heard you shooting the shit,' the man said. 'Or it come over the grapevine.'

'I done *what*?'

The man took no notice. 'I'm not talking about wasting. If you want him attended to it'll cost you a Hawaii.'

Bean managed a mental translation but the last bit escaped him.

'Fifty smackers.'

'Chance'd be a fine thing,' said Bean. 'I haven't got it. It was three times that he took off of me. And my camera. Bastard with blue hair and all over keys.' He tried to collect his thoughts. 'Fifty – that's a lot of money.'

'Suit yourself. If you change your mind I'll be here next Sunday. Same time, same place.'

It wasn't true he hadn't got it, but he couldn't easily afford to part with it. Once again Bean thought how imperative it was to find ways of augmenting his income. He watched the round-headed man return the way he had come and head towards the Hanover Gate.

The idea that someone young and strong might 'attend to', which presumably meant 'beat up', the key man was very inviting. With recollections of certain episodes in the domestic life of Maurice Clitheroe – once he had spent three days in bed as the result of an encounter with a young giant from

163

Salisbury Street – Bean thought longingly of Clancy in a similar state. And in Clitheroe's case it had been *play*. It was only the cost that stopped him running after the round-headed man. Of course it was cheap at the price, but only if parting with the price didn't hurt.

The golden dome of the Mosque, heaving into view, was somehow reassuring. The man would be there again next Sunday.

It was a week since she had written to him but he hadn't even phoned. What had happened that first time she had written to him, disclosing her identity, giving her address, was happening again. Dorothea, in whom up to a point she confided, said that perhaps he was one of those men who only want women who are hard to get. Women who were forthcoming and made overtures frightened them away. That wasn't much comfort to Mary, who was remembering with some degree of shame the warm phrases in her own letter and how she had reminded him of the special friendship they had. It had been to some extent an appeal, her own loneliness cited and her bereavement.

When Saturday came she had given up. He had dropped her. She had said or done something to upset him or he had changed his mind about her. Alistair had phoned and asked her to have dinner with him and though she had refused, putting the phone down after a quick goodbye, she had wondered if next time she would yield, if Alistair with his small violent acts, his petty aggression and his overbearing ways wasn't better than no one at all. When she thought of those small violences the blood came up and heated the cheek he had slapped.

She was looking at herself in the mirror, at that phenomenon of the reddening cheek, watching the

164

colour die away, when the doorbell rang. For once she didn't speculate as to who it might be. She heard a taxi move off as she was opening the door.

Leo stood on the doorstep, paler than she had ever seen him, even his lips drained of colour.

'I've been in hospital,' he said. 'I didn't want you to know.'

The explanation she should have thought of but hadn't. 'But why not, Leo?'

He hesitated. 'May I come in?'

'Of course. Of *course*.' She remembered what Dorothea had said but she couldn't help herself. 'I'm so glad to see you.'

He came in diffidently. She closed the door. Already she was wondering how she could have listened to Dorothea's reasoning, could have doubted her own judgement.

'I felt I'd failed you,' he said. 'I'd let you down. You've done so much for me and I'd reneged on you. I'd been overdoing things, apparently. I know I had, I'm well aware of it. But you must be able to guess why I had.'

She shook her head.

'How shall I put it? I don't want to upset you, Mary.' He paused and seemed to be thinking what to say that would not be hurtful. 'I've been overexerting myself because I'd met you,' he said. 'There. I've said what I've been afraid to say. I so wanted to be a – a normal man for you.'

'Leo . . .' She took both his hands in hers.

He let them lie passively. His eyes were bright, too bright, as with fever. 'I was going to – well, to let things slide between us. Slip away out of your life, if you understand me. It means so much to me that you should never see me as ungrateful or indifferent but at the same time, I'd rather you felt that than that – you – you saw your donation had been in vain.'

'But you've said you're all right. You've said – I think you've said – the leukaemia hasn't come back.'

'I didn't know that when they took me in.' He turned his face away. 'I was so afraid, Mary.'

She tightened her grip on his limp hands. This time he made her a small return of pressure. 'Then your letter came. You'd said very little but I think I knew what your grandmother meant to you. I couldn't stay away any longer.'

Their faces were very close. He reached a little forward and kissed her on the lips. It was just such a kiss as she might have given him in the unimaginable situation of her making the first advance, light, gentle, dry but lingering. He put his arms round her and held her close to him in a brotherly hug. She felt his bones through the meagre flesh, birdlike, fragile. A pulse in his neck was beating fast. Still holding her shoulders, but feather-lightly, in a ghost's clasp, he looked into her face.

'I am afraid to say too much, Mary. When you've been ill, like I have, when you've been so near death and thought you were near death again, your emotions get very – very febrile, very wild and hot, you think and fancy all sorts of things. But you mustn't – I mustn't – express them too soon. I have to keep telling myself, there *is* time, I *have* got years ahead.'

Leo went into the living room, sat on the sofa, perfectly still, as if in a trance. Unusually for him, he put out no hand to fondle the little dog as it pressed itself against his legs. He said in a curiously intense tone:

'Tell me about your grandmother. Tell me all about her and your childhood and everything.'

It was what she had wanted. She began talking to him of things never previously aired. The idea of telling Alistair of the day when, newly orphaned but

166

not yet knowing it, she had been brought to her grandparents, how she had felt, was unthinkable. But she could tell Leo, who sat listening intently, his eyes sometimes meeting hers, his lips sometimes parting in a smile. She spoke of those early days. Frederica had seemed old but when you are eight all grown-ups seem old. Children are quickly won over and a devotion in them easily awakened. The oddest thing was that from the first Frederica was nicer than her own mother had been.

'It seems disloyal. It's something people don't say, that their adoptive parents were better than their natural parents. But mine were. My parents were very young; my mother was only twenty-one when I was born. They only married because I was going to be born. And afterwards they wanted to go on living the same sort of life they always had. I think my mother must have resented me. I remember her as indifferent and rather rejecting. Why am I telling you all this?'

'Because I asked you.'

'And that's enough? Maybe it is. My parents died when someone's private plane they were flying in from an airfield in Essex to France came down in the Channel. I was unhappy at first, of course I was. I think my grandparents were very unhappy, they'd lost their only child, but they never showed it to me. She was called Helen, my mother. That's why I took the name when I had to write that note for you. Guilt, I expect it was, though, not love.

'I loved my grandparents. I adored my grand-mother. And, you know, the air crash which was so terrible for them and supposed to be for me – I once overheard a woman say to my grandmother that it was the great tragedy that had blighted my child-hood – it was romantic. It was something to have and almost to boast about; it set me apart in a rather dashing way from the other girls at school. If some power, some genie, had asked me if I would like my parents back, I'd have said no. But I'd never have told anyone, I'd have been ashamed.'

'But you're not ashamed to tell me?'

'No. Strange, isn't it?'

He said: 'I want you to think you can tell me anything. I want to be the person you can talk to.' He stood up, a little unsteadily, she thought, and for a moment he put his hand on his forehead. 'I must go now. May I come back tomorrow?'

'I've tired you,' she said.

'No. You're the last person to tire me. You refresh me.' He spoke like a child, a very young boy. 'Can I have a proper kiss?'

She nodded. He put his arms round her and kissed her, but very softly, very gently. His mouth tasted of some scented spice, cinnamon perhaps or cardamom. Afterwards she thought it had been like no other kiss she had ever known and if she had had to explain what she meant she would have said it was non-physical, like a kiss in the mind, or like kissing someone not of this world, a wraith, a spirit, a ghostly visitant.

'You will come back?' she said eagerly.

'I promise.'

He looked less ill next day, though his thinness was extreme. She had the illusion that she could see through him as he passed through the hall and came into the living room, could see the shapes of furniture and the colours of cloth through his transparent form. They drank wine and she made lunch for them. He told her about his feelings for his brother.

'I love him and he loves me,' he said. 'Does that sound terrible to you, coming from a man?'

'Of course it doesn't.'

168

'He's done everything for me. Given up everything too. He was at drama school, he's a wonderful actor, but he gave that up to be with me every day when I was so ill, so that I'd never be alone. He's been more than a father to me.'

'I'd like to meet him.'

He didn't answer that but said rather abruptly, 'I'm moving out, I'm getting a place of my own.'

'But why, if you get on so well?'

'Because it's not fair on him, Mary. I drag him down. I spoil his privacy. Besides, it's his place but he gives up the bedroom to me and sleeps on the sofa.'

He had found a flat in Primrose Hill, in Edis Street, no more than a room with kitchen area and shower really, but it would do. She searched her mind for ways of putting it, finally came out with:

'Leo, I haven't told you but I'm going to be quite rich. My grandmother left me a lot of money. If there is anything I could . . .'

He cut her short. It was like that time in the Italian restaurant when he had reacted so peremptorily to her offer of paying her share of the bill. 'Absolutely not. Please don't even think of it.'

They had left the table and were once more side by side on the sofa, Gushi at their feet.

'I very much dislike the idea of your being rich,' Leo said. There was an unprecedented distaste in his voice, though rather than rising in volume it had sunk almost to a whisper. 'You may say that it's none of my business but – but I want things about you to be my business, Mary.'

He looked deep into her eyes. She felt her face flood with colour. Seeing the flush, he put up one finger to touch her cheek. The other hand followed. He took her face in his hands and kissed her with the gentleness of a woman kissing a child. Then, when

169

she was unresistant, began a soft delicate kissing, his lips on hers, then brushing her cheek, the tip of her nose, her mouth once more. The gentleness of it, the slowness, aroused her. She expected every moment a crushing embrace, hard lips, a tongue that prised her mouth open and reached chokingly, like some surgical probe, for the back of her throat. Leo kissed her lips and stroked her cheek. Her body, that she now felt to have been stiff and tense for weeks, the muscles held rigidly, began to slacken and melt.

'There is something I would very much like to do,' he whispered. 'May I ask you? If you say no, we'll just go on sitting here, but if you say yes . . .'

'What is it, Leo?'

'I would like to lie down and hold you. That's all, just hold you.'

She nodded.

'I mean just hold you,' he said. 'Not anything more.' He gave a dry unhappy laugh. 'That has to be all, I think.'

They went upstairs. He seemed quite unselfconscious when he took off his outer clothes. She looked at a skeletal but still beautiful body, straight, smooth, as white as her own. It would have seemed ridiculous, in anticipation or retrospect, to go to bed with a man in her underclothes, he in underpants, she in bra and tights, but in the present, as a happening, it was natural. She wondered where he had received the transplant but could see no mark on him.

In bed he held her in his arms. She had always found this position a difficult one with Alistair, for if maintained for more than a few minutes, the arm under his body would 'go to sleep', as would his under her, while the other possibility, that of embracing him with one arm and folding the other behind her, brought an intolerable ache to her shoulder. But Leo held her without demanding that she hold him.

170

She laid one arm across his chest, the other on her own breasts. He held her firmly but not tightly and if the arm under her body grew numb he gave no sign of it. He did not speak. She had to remind herself that he was six years younger than she, for he held her as an innocent father might hold his child.

Not since she was a child herself, not since those days when she was laid down for a rest in the afternoon – by that mother who was only too glad, if the truth were known, for an hour of peace – had Mary slept in the daytime. But she slept now and Leo slept. His, she thought, waking after the unbelievable period of two whole hours, was the heavy slumber of a man who has missed out on sleep for too long and has a hundred hours to make up. She raised herself on one elbow and looked at his face, the narrow lips relaxed in sleep, the pale skin in places prematurely lined, the veined lids over his closed eyes, membranes like purplish leaves. When he was a child his hair must have been white, for even now it was only faintly coloured, the shade of sun-bleached straw.

Something told him she had moved away, for blindly in sleep he reached for her. But not in the way other men had done, not as Alistair had done, seizing her roughly and pulling her down into a hard embrace and bruising kisses that made her lips sore and her gums bleed. Without opening his eyes, Leo felt for her hand and taking it in his, brought it to his mouth. He kissed her hand gently, the wrist, the back of it, the knuckles. She thought, what is happening to me? Am I falling in love with him? Is it the strangeness of him that fascinates me, or is it that I feel an ever and ever stronger need to look after him?

I do need that. I need to bring him here and care for him. It is as if I have begun the process of healing him and I must carry it through. Soon I must let him go, I must let him go home, but I am afraid that

171

when he goes, when he is out of my sight and my care he will fail and fall and become ill again. Oh, if only I could keep him here I know I could restore him and then, one day . . .

Bean was back. The bell rang once, then again insistently. She put on a dressing gown, picked Gushi up into her arms and went down to answer the door. Bean smiled his obsequious smile, his eyes cold and empty. He thrust a package into her hand.

'Photos of the little chap, miss,' he said. 'Just to take a look. No obligation to purchase.'

Chapter Fourteen

While in Maurice Clitheroe's employ Bean had drunk heavily. Sometimes he had drunk to excess. There was always a lot of liquor in the house and he had helped himself. If Clitheroe knew, and he must have known, he never said anything. Perhaps he understood that Bean couldn't do the job he did without a stimulant and a sedative. It was no joke, as Bean often said to himself, being the companion, servant, pimp and nurse of a serious masochist.

Most of the young people who came to the house in York Terrace were in it only for the money. They took no more pleasure in beating a fat old man than Bean did in doing his shopping and cooking his *tournedos*. But one or two were different. Bean, admitting them to the house, could see it in their faces and in the fixed stare of their half-mesmerised eyes. They were sadists and when the whip or the cane was in their hands there was no stopping their frenzy.

It was then, hearing Clitheroe's screams and unable to sort pain from pleasure – or were they the same? – that Bean took the brown ale chasers with glass after glass of cheap Spanish brandy. Sometimes he was almost too far gone to see the visitor off the premises, but he had to persevere. He had to keep as steady as he could, for it was afterwards that Clitheroe needed his ministrations.

Once he found him unconscious. On another

occasion he wanted to take his employer to Casualty, but Clitheroe, gasping on the floor, open weals on his naked back that bled into the Turkey carpet, fortunately predominantly crimson already, forbade his phoning for an ambulance on pain of dismissal. Bean passed out himself later, on brandy and brown ale.

There was one young man, nameless but called by him The Beater, that he particularly remembered. If the eyes were the windows of the soul, as Anthony Maddox said they were, he had no soul, for looking into his eyes was like looking into empty holes. There was nothing beyond. The tip of his nose and his upper lip were pinkish as if he had rubbed them with sandpaper. He walked gracefully, his body straight and relaxed, his shoulders permanently lifted and his knees ever so slightly bent. After his visits Maurice Clitheroe was in a worse state than after any other beatings or being ridden up the stairs or having sharp objects threaded into soft parts of his body.

He was sixty-seven, Bean's own age. His body was covered with scars, as a constantly abused slave's must be. Bean had never seen anything like it. He advised Clitheroe not to let The Beater come again but his employer took no notice. Bean was not fanciful – he admitted with some satisfaction that he had no imagination – yet he thought to himself that, peculiar though it was, Clitheroe was *in love* with The Beater. He was obsessed by him. He desperately needed him. And The Beater killed him.

Or that was Bean's view of it. The beating Clitheroe got that evening was the worst Bean had ever known. Of course he was not a witness to it – he never was – and when the screams began, he swigged brandy directly out of the bottle and hid himself in his bed with the quilt stuffed into his ears.

The Beater let himself out and Bean never saw him again. Clitheroe had a haemorrhagic stroke.

His doctor, from Harley Street, just across the road, knew all about Clitheroe's proclivities. He didn't look at the old man's body below the neck. By the time Clitheroe died ten days later the worst of the evidence had faded, though Bean had sometimes wondered what the undertakers thought.

So long as no one blames *me*, was his philosophy, and no one did. He gradually stopped drinking once the funeral was over. He was interested in getting fit before it was too late, and now it had come down to one whisky and two bottles of brown ale in the Globe on a Friday night. Freddie Lawson called the Globe 'a real pub, all spit and sawdust and sausage sandwiches', and Bean's dinner on a Friday was not exactly a sausage but a veggie-burger sandwich with Branston pickle and sometimes a plate of chips.

He wanted to find out the identity of the round-headed man who had asked for a light on the bridge last Sunday. Freddie knew nothing about it and Peter Carrow refused to say anything until Bean told him why he needed to know. The air in the Globe was blue with smoke. It made Bean hoarse and he had to raise his voice. Several people stared at him.

'Who d'you think you're looking at?' Bean said belligerently.

An American tourist turned his face away. Bean glared at those who kept on staring. One of them was maybe the mate of the round-headed man.

'You been drinking before you come in here?' said Carrow.

'I'm not pissed, so don't make insinuations.' Bean dipped a chip in Branston pickle and popped it into his mouth. 'There's a feller I'm on the lookout for. Got a pal with a head like Mussolini.'

'Who?' said Carrow, who was a mere forty-five,

and without waiting to hear, 'What d'you want him for?'

Bean told him, not lowering his voice much. 'It must be him overheard me talking in here.'

Freddie Lawson started laughing.

'A Hawaii! Where did he get that from? A Hawaii!'

'I can't afford it,' said Bean. 'Shame, because I reckon Mussolini'd do a good job.'

'It's a terrible thing,' said Carrow, 'when a working man has to do the filth's dirty work for them.'

The American tourist, on his way out, whispered to Bean, 'Hawaii Five-O, right?'

'And you can keep your nose out of my business,' said Bean.

The round-headed man's friend failed to declare himself and Bean had to go home unsatisfied. While he was out at the shops next morning he considered walking over to the cash dispenser outside Barclays in Baker Street. Perhaps Mussolini wouldn't want it all at once but would accept twenty-five before the assault on Clancy and twenty-five after the deed was done. He started to cross the Marylebone Road before the lights changed but he was too late and retreated angrily when a van nearly mowed him down. The driver stuck up two fingers in response to Bean's raised fist.

A few years back, someone *had* been hit by a van just about here. Well, in Luxborough Street, same difference. A laundry and dry-cleaner's van it was. The one who was in the way had only been one of those beggars, so it didn't matter much. After that the van had skidded and hit a wall and the driver, who wasn't wearing a seat belt, had been thrown out and found by the ambulance men draped over the spiked railings of the mansion flats. Bean remembered the case well and Mr Clitheroe reading it out

176

of the paper to him as he often did; he liked reading aloud.

The beggar had been killed instantly – hadn't felt a thing, no doubt – but the driver, for all he'd three broken ribs, had been found guilty of manslaughter, not just careless driving, and he'd gone to prison. Not for all that long, though going to prison at all Bean thought a monstrous injustice. But it went to show how dangerous the streets were round here.

With Clancy incapacitated he would be able to use the tunnel again.

Mr Cornell came to the door. In the time it had taken Bean to exercise Boris, Valerie Conway had gone away on her summer holidays. Cornell, at any rate, was a gentleman, coming to the front door, not expecting Bean to go down into the area. Bean told him about the photos he'd taken of Boris and Mr Cornell seemed interested, said that if Bean would drop a selection in sometime he'd like to have a look.

With no Valerie to needle or be needled by and no stairs to climb, he got to Devonshire Street five minutes early and saw through a downstairs window Erna Morosini kissing a man. They were both in dressing gowns. The man wasn't her husband, Bean was sure of that, and maybe he could make something of it; maybe it would lead to an augmentation of his funds. The trouble was that Mrs Morosini looked not at all disconcerted when she answered his ring, but was all smiles, happier than he'd ever seen her.

'I'd love to see photos of Ruby. Will you drop them in. Not naughty ones, mind!'

That made up his mind for him. He could afford it. He was going to increase his income, would buy a new camera and draw out fifty pounds for Mussolini. The beggar with the beagle was sitting outside the Screen on Baker Street when he got over there and talking to him, or standing beside him and wearing a typically evil expression, was Clancy, the key man. His hair had the blue sheen of a peacock's feather and the sun shining on his keys made a breastplate of them and made Clancy look, in Bean's eyes, like some demon god in a Hammer film. Bean went into one of the Sherlock Holmes souvenir shops and bought the red baseball cap with a picture of Holmes in a white circle he'd seen in the window. It was summer weight, with a perforated crown.

On Sunday he felt quite excited. It started to rain as soon as he got into the Park. He was wearing his heavier weight cap and over his jacket a raincoat of clear plastic, so he was all right. Just the same, he would have preferred to keep under the trees but that would mean staying in those parts of the Park where dogs were not permitted to run loose, Queen Mary's Rose Garden or the surroundings of the lake. But once their pads touched grass Charlie and the borzoi pulled so hard that Bean could scarcely keep his feet. He had to set them free and the others with them.

A veil of rain, low hanging clouds of it, half-obscured the Mappin Terraces of the zoo, brown man-made mountains, and the ranged blocks of flats of St John's Wood, red and white and Sixties grey rough-cast. The few high-rise buildings loomed out of the mist and to the south the spaceship head on the stalk of the Post Office Tower stood out distinct, but greyer and uglier than on a sunny day. Bean stuffed his hands in his pockets, feeling the roll of notes. Water began to drip off the peak of his cap, so he turned it backwards, the way he'd seen kids do in American TV programmes.

He took pride in doing his job well but there were limits. The rain had come on more heavily and now the Mappin Terraces and all the trees to the north had disappeared behind a grey-out. None of the dogs seemed to notice except for Gushi, who stood close to Bean's feet, shaking himself and whimpering. Bean began calling them. As was always the case with dogs – except the woman walker's – some were obedient and some were not. Experience told him Charlie wouldn't come. He whistled shrilly while clipping Gushi, Marietta and McBride on to the leash. Ruby bounded up, throwing herself on top of the scottie in a simulated act of sexual intercourse, gender not much affecting role in dogs.

Bean shouted at her and resumed his whistling. All the dogs shook themselves, their loose skin rattling. Bean wished he had invested in waterproof trousers when he bought the plastic raincoat. There wasn't a sign of Charlie, though Boris suddenly appeared out of the gloom, like the Hound of the Baskervilles Bean had seen in a Sherlock Holmes film. He padded up with lowered head and dripping ears, growling unpleasantly when Bean grabbed his collar.

He thought he had allowed plenty of time but he looked at his watch and saw that it was nearly twenty to five. With five dogs on the leash, he stood not knowing which direction to go in. Where would Charlie go? One of the refreshment places maybe, to root about in a bin or beg for food. Not that anyone would be eating out-of-doors in this weather.

Neither was in the direction Bean wanted to go. Right up till this moment, he had been in two minds about Mussolini, hoping to meet him and give him the go-ahead and fearing to meet him. But now doubt had fled and he desperately wanted to see the man again, to reach the bridge, carry out his negotiations and set the process in motion. As he plodded along the path, tugged by his troop of dogs, he saw the key man once more in his mind's eye, the blue hair and beard, the cruel eyes, the clanking chain mail. He mustn't miss his chance of teaching the key man a lesson . . .

Charlie was nowhere around the restaurant. Did that mean he had to traipse all the way back to the Broad Walk? Ahead of him the path led down to the Long Bridge, crossing a different arm of the lake from the one where Mussolini would soon arrive, where he might already be . . . Bean had never lost a dog, never had a dog go missing for more than a minute or two. But Charlie had disappeared, had been absent now for a quarter of an hour. It was five to five.

To the north of the lake, where ducks disported on the sodden grass or bounced on the little waves, Bean stood and cursed. The dogs, taking advantage of a pause, shook themselves vigorously. Bean began whistling again. Whatever happened, whatever he must forgo, he couldn't go back to Mr Barker-Pryce and his bristling eyes and cigar without Charlie.

There was a sound of scuffle and splashing, a quacking and honking, as three pink-footed geese and a white duck rose in a flurry of panic-stricken feathers from the water's edge. Charlie was behind them, joyously leaping, his paws muddied to the hocks, his appearance so changed by total immersion that he looked as thin as the borzoi and as dark as the poodle. Bean made a grab for him and the retriever, understanding that the game and the glories of liberty were over, drew his whole body together and relaxed it in a massive series of shakes. Bean and the other dogs were soaked in water and flying mud. Even Bean's face was spattered with mud, his hands red and wet, his feet squelching in inundated shoes.

But he ran. With all six dogs galloping ahead of him like a husky team – if only he had a sledge! – he made for the bridge over the loop of the lake. The sky was lightening and the rain easing up. Under the trees that led to the bridge it was almost dry. Bean took a deep breath and clenched the fist that held the leash. But of course Mussolini wasn't there; even if he had been there he wouldn't be any longer, not at five past five, not half an hour after the appointed time.

He ran across the rest of the span. The rain had almost stopped and the sun was coming out through the drizzle. Bean took the path towards the Mosque, whose golden dome the sun had set glittering like an old coin, like a coin when they still made them of precious metals. He fancied this was the way Mussolini had gone last time. But there was no sign of him. There was scarcely a soul about but for the man tying up the paddle boats to the island in the Hanover pond.

He was never late but he was going to be late getting his dogs back. Their owners would worry. They wouldn't listen to excuses about Charlie's truancy. Bean hurried to the path that runs parallel to the Outer Circle towards the Clarence Gate, and lifting his eyes to scan the green prospect and the lake edge, searching still for the round-headed man, saw a rainbow form itself in a brilliant arc, one end in Madame Tussaud's and the other far away in Camden Town.

Chapter Fifteen

In a cold winter, on a Saturday, when Daniel was five and Elizabeth twelve, he had taken them to the Planetarium, for which his son was a little too young, but his daughter had enjoyed it. Afterwards, after lunch at a place in Baker Street, the sun had come out and they had walked to St John's Wood tube station through the Park. Frost still lingered on the grass and there were patches of snow in shady places.

The lake was frozen over. Elizabeth, who was a skater and had received a new pair of skates for Christmas, wanted to know why no one was on the ice and Roman had told them, not going into too many details because Daniel was so young, of the disaster on the ice of February 1867, since which time no one had been allowed to skate there. Several hundred people had been on the ice when it began to break, for they had persisted in spite of warnings from the man from the Humane Society who cried to them, 'For God's sake get off, or there will be a great calamity!'

'Were they drowned?' Daniel asked.

'Some were.' Roman didn't say how many; he didn't say forty. He didn't say that a hundred and fifty people went into the water and forty died. 'The lake was deeper then. It was twelve feet deep between the islands, and the ice was never thick enough. The Tyburn river flowed through it and a fast current stops thick ice forming.'

The children had looked across the lake to the great house called The Holme and at the islands lying below it. Swans and geese and ducks congregated on their banks. Elizabeth wanted to know how the people were got out of the water.

'They sent down divers. Afterwards the lake was drained and remade and now it's no more than four feet deep anywhere.'

'Are there ghosts?' said Daniel. 'In the night do the ghosts of drowned people come out of the water?'

'Ghosts don't exist, Daniel,' said Roman.

But now he wondered, for in his winter dreams he had sometimes seen the people from the ice disaster rising from the black water and the ice floes, as in that Pre-Raphaelite painting of the sea giving up its dead, and once among the faces had been his children's, wan in death, and his wife's.

Often, while the children were still alive, he had regretted even the expurgated version of events he had given Daniel, for the boy would revert to it in cold weather and Roman thought he too had dreamed about it. The bombing of the bandstand, another horror, had taken place within Elizabeth's lifetime, though she had been only about three and had known nothing of the IRA bomb that killed and injured so many bandsmen. At least, he had never told them that. They had never in their Park walks passed the spot where the bandstand stood on the northern bank of the lake, flanked now by memorial willows.

Was this, what was happening now, another Park tragedy? Yet he had noticed, and wondered if others had, that the two murders, very obviously linked, had both taken place outside the Park, if on its perimeter.

It was on a newsboard opposite Baker Street Station and outside the Globe that he first read of the second one. Typically, the news on it was couched in ambiguous terms. You had to buy the paper to know the true facts. 'Second Homeless Man Horror', said the newsboard. 'Horror' could mean many things. The ice disaster and the bandstand bombing were both horrors.

Roman should have bought the paper but he didn't, not then. He was on his way to the launderette in Paddington Street to wash his clothes, after which he would return to the men's toilets just off the Broad Walk, wash himself all over and put on clean T-shirt, denims and sweater. Forty minutes in front of the rotating machines, another ten in the second-hand bookshop swapping *Dead Souls* for *Kim*, and he was resolved on buying the *Standard* on his way back.

It was on sale outside the station. Roman bought a copy and sat down on the low wall to read it. The dead man had not yet been named. His body, like John Dominic Cahill's, was found impaled on railings near Regent's Park, but as in Decker's case, death was not thought to be due to impalement. He had been stabbed first by a knife with a six-inch long blade. He was found in the early hours of the morning by a man returning to his home in Primrose Hill from an eighteenth birthday party. This man wasn't named either.

Roman hoped the body wasn't Dill's. He folded up the paper, put it in his pocket, and walked up past Madame Tussaud's under the scaffolding. They had been refurbishing, decorating, renovating the building for months. He found he had been holding his breath and now he expelled it thankfully.

Dill was sitting on the pavement with his beagle beside him and a paper bag of dog biscuits that the animal was busily eating. Roman sat beside him and showed him the *Standard*. Dill said he'd seen it on the telly. They had an old black and white television set in the shelter where he sometimes slept.

'They never said railings,' Dill said. 'They said broken glass on top of a wall.'

'Where was it?'

'Primrose Hill somewhere. They never said. It scared me.'

Dill had a thin pale face and eyes whose swollen lids seemed pulled down by the epicanthic fold, but he was too white and his sparse hair too fair to be oriental. Roman had never known him to drink. He often seemed afraid and now his fear had intensified to the point of straining and shrivelling the skin of his face. His age, Roman thought, was probably no more than twenty-five.

'I don't like the sound of that glass,' he said. 'Glass going into you, lace-, lacer-, lacernating you. That's what they said.'

A woman dropped a fifty pee coin into the hat on the pavement. 'Thank you very much,' Dill said. The dog sniffed the coin and wagged his tail. 'It's us he's after,' said Dill. 'Our sort.'

He offered no definition, used none of the many descriptive words, but Roman understood. The newspaper had said much the same and as cagily. The two men, murdered within a month of each other, had both been homeless . . .

'You go to St Anthony's, don't you?' St Anthony's was the shelter in Lisson Grove. 'Better stay there every night. You'll be safe then. Till he's been caught.'

Roman could see in Dill's wistful look that in the summer he preferred the open air. If it wasn't wet or too cold he would rather sleep under the stars, or what passed for them, the reddish milky way of reflected light. But he nodded, somewhat comforted, and he put out his arms to pull the dog on to his lap.

Making his way into the Park by the York Gate, Roman turned to follow the southern shore of the lake. An old woman in a tracksuit was feeding a black swan and her cygnets with broken biscuits. A heron took flight from a tree on the island and flew westwards, its wings wide, its neck in an S-bend. The sun had brought the people out. They strolled desultorily along the lake shore or sat on the seats. No fear showed in their faces. There was nothing to indicate the violent death that had taken place half a mile from here the night before.

It was warmer, hotter even, than it had been all year. Real summer had come, you would say if you were a visitor or a tourist and unaware that real summer may never come, nor real winter for that matter, and that the weather is fickle, arbitrary – hot today and cold tomorrow, dry now and wet later. The Park was a pattern of green light and shade, not much other colour. Men and women wear bright colours in hot climates, but blue and grey here, brown and black and gravel beige. The water of the lake was a gleaming grey, glassy and calm.

Roman asked himself if he shared Dill's fear. As vulnerable as Dill (or Pharaoh or Effie or the jacks men), was he afraid to die, stabbed through the heart and the lungs and the great vessels round the heart, then impaled on a fence? He found himself unable to answer. Once he could have answered, once he would have welcomed death meted out by someone else. Was he afraid to die? It frightened him that he had changed, that he could no longer give an unqualified no, that he must give half a yes.

Because surely the opposite of saying no was, 'I want to live . . .'

In the men's toilets he washed himself all over. He waited until the sun was setting and most of the visitors had gone and then he washed himself at a

186

basin, the top half first, then, discreetly, the lower half, with his towel clean from the launderette wrapped round his waist. Two men came in but he knew from experience they would ignore him. They would fear him. He was a dosser who might beg from them, gibber and wave his arms or shout imprecations. When they had gone he washed his hair and part-dried it under the hand dryer.

Being clean brought an unprecedented sense of well-being. He emerged, dirty clothes rolled up in his barrow, and sat on a seat at the top of the Broad Walk by the Parsee's fountain, looking at the weathered carvings of birds and animals and at the worn pink marble pillars. He drank the pint of milk he had bought, wished it were wine, and read *Kim*.

The police came round and shooed him out at nine-thirty, by which time it was too dark to read. He had no idea where to sleep the night, thought of but rejected the Irene Adler's porch as being too near the site of the first murder, and Regent's Park Road as being too near (presumably) the second. Leaving the Park by the Gloucester Gate and the deserted children's playground, he paused as he always did on this spot to look at Joseph Durham's figure in bronze of a pretty young girl, winsome, sweet-faced, standing on an artistic arrangement of rocks. Shading her eyes with one hand, she seemed to be gazing at Gloucester Terrace. Hers was precisely the face of a girlfriend he had once had, long before he met Sally. To look at this girl, set upon her rocky perch a hundred and twenty years ago, was to see his girlfriend again, to remember and feel a trace of nostalgia. Once or twice, while looking, he had wondered what his reaction would have been if that were Sally's face or Elizabeth's. Would he linger in front of the statue or shun it, dreading to look it full in the eye?

187

He crossed the road and peered down into the leafy dale, once perhaps an ornamental garden, known as the Grotto. The low wall of the bridge over a defunct arm of the canal bore a bronze bas-relief commemorating the martyrdom of St Pancras, the saint with uplifted radiant face attacked by a lioness that looked mild and friendly and who jumped up at him like a dog.

There were rocks down there and a stone-coped pool, figure eight-shaped, its water brown and coated with a network of scum. Among the laurels and rhododendrons litter lay or was caught on branches – shreds of plastic, newspaper soaked and dried and soaked again, beer bottles, torn dark rags. Tangles of barbed wire and chain-link fencing muddled together seemed to serve no purpose.

Roman looked about for a way in. He walked along past the bas-relief and turned a little way into Park Village East, where a big Victorian villa was in the process of renovation. Builders' skips, ladders, concrete mixer and timber stood about. He pushed open a gate in the wall and made his way into the derelict garden which overlooked the Grotto.

From this direction it was possible to avoid most of the wire entanglements. He had long since discovered that barbed wire does a poor job of keeping out intruders if the intruders don't mind getting their clothes torn. It was a neglected, decaying, private place that he found himself in. He plucked a couple of drinking straws, or a drinking straw unaccountably cut in half, from between the leaves of a bush. His groundsheet spread out on leaf mould, he prepared his bed, sheltered from the bridge by rhododendrons, from the night sky by the branches of a taller tree. In the damp leafy shade it was cold and he pulled on a sweater before he climbed into his sleeping bag.

At this time of the year the dawn came before four-thirty. He saw the brilliance of a sunrise between leaves, a white dazzlement behind a tracery of black, but the first thing he thought of was the death of one of 'our sort', and it surprised him that he had been able to sleep so peacefully. It was as if he had only just lain down, had this minute closed his eyes, and the whole night had passed in seconds.

Often he had no morning meal but today he went into one of the early-opening cafés in Camden Town and, like the condemned man he was, ate a hearty breakfast, eggs and bacon, sausages and fried bread. A glass of something bitter and thin he had learned to call orange juice came with it and strong henna-coloured tea. He would have felt self-conscious in there once, but no longer. Most of the customers looked like him. At least he had had a wash and changed his clothes the afternoon before.

At the Talisman Press they had published a book about the old farmlands of North London. He remembered it now as he walked along Albert Road, recalling the engravings of Chalk Farm and Primrose Hill. The only thing that looked remotely the same was the hill itself, rising out of the level ground more like a man-made tumulus than a natural formation. Once he had looked up there and seen a figure standing on the summit, his hands upraised to the sky. Suddenly the figure flung itself down, waving its arms and kicking its legs, before rising again and once more seeming to implore help from heaven. Roman had guessed it was Pharaoh, but he was too far away to see the blue on his hair or the glint of his keys.

The old farmland trees must have gone sometime in the nineteenth century. It was all planes now and a few hornbeams, ornamental trees that looked incongruous to him with lush tall grass growing close to their trunks. He took the paths along the eastern side, recalling the account of a murder from that same book. Sir Edmund Godfrey's body had been found in a ditch on the south side of Primrose Hill one day at the end of the seventeenth century. Though his sword was thrust through his body, strangulation had caused his death. Nothing had been taken from him, his money was in his pocket, but he was all over bruises and his neck was broken. Medals were struck to commemorate his death, on one of which he was shown as walking with a broken neck and a sword running him through.

Roman thought he remembered reading of several people being executed for the murder and reading too of duels fought on the hill. He told himself he had come in there to find somewhere pleasant and peaceful to sit and read his Kipling but he knew he had another reason. That accounted for his dwelling on the violent deaths of the past.

There was no one on the summit today. It was windy, the planes' thready branches blowing and the hornbeams ruffled. He walked along the northern perimeter and saw the blue and white crime tape on the railings far ahead of him. Long before reaching the place he went out into Primrose Hill Road. A row of cars were parked, obvious police cars and probable police cars. On the opposite side of the road a small crowd stood, waiting, watching, though there was nothing to watch.

The tape cordoned off several yards of pavement but the railing itself was swathed in sheeting. A bunch of flowers, wrapped in clear film, lay on the pavement outside the cordon. Someone, then, had cared for this derelict and Roman wondered who. He looked about him and saw railing everywhere. There must be miles of it in the Park's vicinity, the spiked kind like this and the kind with blunted spikes. Here railings separated gardens from pavements and gardens from other gardens, skirted churches, made confining barriers along paths. Where in other places fences might be or hedges or walls, here were iron railings, straight, plain, usually painted black, crossed with two horizontal bars at foot and top, crowned with spikes.

This murderer could have no difficulty in finding a site for a crime. Sites proliferated. If all he needed was a homeless man and a stretch of railings, his activities could be infinite. Roman stood with the crowd, watching faces, but these gave nothing away. They were blank, apathetic, patient. A policeman who had been doing something to the tape, adjusting it or shortening it or pulling it in some different direction, got into his car and drove away. The red and white van of Express Tikka and Pizza slowed a little as the driver passed the spot but quickly moved on. A woman in the crowd lit a cigarette.

Roman turned back on to the hill and sat on a seat that was sunny and sheltered from the wind. He tried to read but his concentration was poor and his thoughts wandered back to Sir Edmund Godfrey, whose murder seemed as pointless as these, whose apparent killers had protested their innocence to the last and whose ghost was believed to haunt the Hill. That reminded him of his son, brought Daniel before him, Daniel who half-believed in the ghosts of the drowned rising through the broken ice.

After a while he was on the move again, in quest as he had been on the previous day of a newspaper. It was not much after ten but the *Standard* was already on the streets. He bought a copy and, leaning against a long sweep of railings, read that the second victim of the man they were calling the Impaler had been identified.

He was James Victor Clancy, aged thirty-six, of no fixed address, known to some as the key man and to others as Pharaoh.

Chapter Sixteen

The American tourist asked for a list of items to be shipped to Cincinnati for himself and his wife: Irene Adler's best tea service, the framed picture that looked like a Klimt, the photograph she had given to Holmes, two lace tablecloths and a heap of wax fruit under a glass dome. Mary was making sure he understood they were all replicas, not antiques, all the *kind* of thing a woman such as Irene might have possessed in 1885, when Stacey came in to tell her a man had called for her.

'To take you home,' Stacey said. 'Well, it's gone five.'

'What's his name? Didn't he give his name?'

'I never asked.'

It must be Leo. He was taking two days off to settle into his new flat and on a fine afternoon, might walk from Edis Street to Charles Lane without too much exertion. The colour came up into her face and from the way the American smiled she thought he had noticed and drawn his own conclusions.

'I'll come as soon as I've finished here.'

She wrote the things down in the order book. The man from Cincinnati gave her his card. Just as he was leaving – he had taken a few steps towards the shop door – he asked her where she thought the next murder would be located. Someone on their tour favoured the zoo and they were laying bets.

'I say in back of the theatre and my wife she's all for those big kinda gates by the rose garden.'

Mary didn't know what to say so she only smiled, or tried to. Dorothea had already gone. Mary turned the notice on the shop door to 'closed' and hoped Stacey had done the same for the museum. She and Leo might go out to eat this evening and perhaps he would stay overnight with her. He had never yet done this, he had never made love to her, but it would come soon. This slow approach tantalised her, yet in some ways she wanted to prolong it, for the enhancement of a mounting sexual excitement. Three times now they had lain side by side in her bed at Charlotte Cottage and at last he had begun to caress her very softly and gently, with an interest that seemed more like pleasure than patience. She had whispered to him not to stop, that all would be well, he had nothing to fear.

'Next time,' he had said.

Next time was this time. She was a little aware of her seniority and more than a little of the gratitude he owed her, but she managed at least for the time to dismiss all that. She had looked in one of Irene Adler's mirrors, gilt-framed with cherubs and curlicues, and thought that she looked better, younger, prettier, than at any time since she heard of her grandmother's death. The sun had turned her hair from straw to gold. She came out into the hall to greet Leo with a smile and her hands outstretched.

The man waiting was Alistair.

The smile that was not for him encouraged him to throw his arms round her. He would have kissed her mouth if she hadn't turned it quickly away and presented her cheek. Stacey watched avidly.

'Surprise?' he said.

'I didn't expect you, Alistair.'

'Until they catch this man I don't want you walking to and fro on your own.'

She shrugged, could think of nothing to say that hadn't already been said.

'I'm thinking of you. Of your safety. While you're still coming here, if I can't be here you get a taxi, is that understood?'

Some women, presumably, were flattered by this sort of hectoring manner, by being told what to do and then asked if a simple command wasn't beyond their comprehension. No one, not her grandfather, nor from what she could remember, her father, had ever talked to her like this. Impossible to imagine Leo capable of the words or the tone without breaking down into helpless laughter.

'Oddly enough, Alistair,' she said, trying to keep her voice light, 'I can look after myself.'

'I wonder how many foolhardy women have said that before coming to grief? Now why wouldn't you dine with me last week, Mary? I think I deserve an explanation.'

'I'm sorry,' she said. 'I haven't got one. I haven't got an explanation.'

She walked ahead of him out of the museum, thinking fast, making up her mind how to handle his presence and the plans he had no doubt made for the evening to come. Go out with him to eat somewhere she would not, nor take him back with her to Charlotte Cottage. Somehow she must shake him off.

He was hastening to the corner of St John's Wood Terrace, his right arm already upraised for a taxi.

He said over his shoulder, 'We have to talk about this, but of course you'll give up the –' He was seeking a polite word, '– the shop, museum, whatever you call it. You won't *need* to work.'

'Alistair,' she said.

There must have been something in her tone he

195

had never heard before. She was aiming at that and it looked as if she had succeeded. He said, 'Yes, what?'

'I'm not going in a taxi with you. I'm not going back to Park Village. I'm on my way to see a friend.'

'What friend?' He spoke abstractedly, watching the departing taxi with disappointment.

She took a deep breath. 'The man who had my transplant.' She tried again, not looking at him. 'The man who received my bone marrow donation.'

'You are not serious.' His voice was cold and smooth as water. It was a strange voice to emerge from those thick lips, that flushed hot face.

He can't shake me out here, she thought. He can't hit me in the street. 'I am perfectly serious. I have met him and I – I like him and we are –' How to say it? What words to choose? '– seeing each other.'

He came close up to her. She saw his hands move to take hold of her and fall again as his sense of the conventions inhibited him. He trembled with impotence.

'You're not fit to be left alone if that's what happens when you're alone.'

'And you're not my judge, Alistair.' She spoke bravely but her voice was small. 'I don't want you to – to pronounce on what I do, who I see.'

He was shrill with indignation. 'Someone must. You're not fit to do it yourself.'

She shook her head, trying to be dismissive. 'I don't want to see you again, Alistair.'

'I am not hearing this,' he said.

'We said our goodbyes before I left. We went through everything. We decided – we *both decided* – it was best. It was all over. Don't you remember? You were happy to see me go, you said. And then you came back. It wasn't my wish and it isn't now. I hope we can be friends one day but it can't be yet. I don't want to see you – can't you understand that?'

'I think it's generally true of you, Mary, that you don't know what you want.'

'We shouldn't be having this – this discussion out here, in public.'

'Then why are we? You began it.'

She hesitated. 'I would be afraid to have it indoors, that's why. Do you understand? I'd be afraid of you.'

He made an impatient gesture. 'Where does he live?'

Again she shook her head.

'You said you were going to him, so I ask you, where does he live?'

Had his manner always been so hectoring? Not when he got his own way. Of course not then. And he had nearly always, then always, got his way when they were together. If he had never raised his hand to her she would be meekly married to him by now.

She felt a dread of being captured by him, forced into a cab, taken home, browbeaten there, perhaps struck. Turning away, she began to walk, rather aimlessly, down Charlbert Street towards the Park. Alistair came after her, taking bold purposeful strides. He grabbed hold of her arm with a hard hand and started to march her along. It was the way she had sometimes seen, and deeply disliked seeing, a parent manhandle a child of perhaps eight years old that was misbehaving in a shopping centre. Like that parent, Alistair jerked her arm while keeping it pressed by his own hand close against her side. His voice had become abrupt, clipped.

'Tell me where he lives, this con man of yours.'

'Why do you call him that?'

'Please. Be your age. How long have you been here? How long is it since you told that Harvest Trust place this Oliver could be told who you were? Six weeks? Seven? And in that time he hasn't just made himself known to you, he's got to the point of –

what's your phrase – "seeing you". Does that mean sleeping with? I sincerely hope not, Mary, I sincerely do, for your sake and his. In that time your grandmother died and made you a rich woman. Doesn't that tell you what he's after?'

'It tells me what you are, Alistair,' she said quietly. 'Perhaps what you've always been after. Oliver – I don't want to tell you his name – would prefer me poor, only I'm not and he has to put up with me as I am. Now will you please let go of my arm?'

For a moment she stood frozen, then pulled herself away from him and began to run. The gesture was so sudden that he was startled and briefly incapable of movement, stunned by her unaccustomed decisiveness and rejection of him. She ran across the road and he was unable to follow her for the traffic from the Park end, three cars coming along almost nose to tail. One of them started to double-park, holding the rest up.

Mary ran without aim westwards along Allitsen Road. When she had told Alistair she was going to Leo, this had been no more than an escape ploy and as she now saw, an unwise one. There had been no real intention of visiting Leo's new flat and there was none now. She wanted only to elude Alistair and somehow hide herself from him until he grew tired and went home. But as she ran across Avenue Road – he was pursuing her but once again had been held up and frustrated by traffic, this time a stream of rush hour cars pouring towards the Park and the Macclesfield Bridge – she asked herself why not go to Leo, why not shake off Alistair and go to Leo?

It was a long time since she and her grandmother had been to call for that friend in Primrose Hill and she had no clear idea how to find her way to Edis Street, only a notion that it might be a turning off Gloucester Avenue. Since the second murder the

198

thought of the open greens of Primrose Hill frightened her, but it was light, the broadest daylight, and bright and sunny too. If she had ever been in there before, perhaps twenty years ago, she had forgotten the place.

The man with the beard that she had come upon reading *Dead Souls* was crossing the green towards the Ormonde Terrace Gate. He smiled at her. She said a breathless, 'Hallo', wanted to tell him, if he saw Alistair, to send him off in the opposite direction. But of course she couldn't do that. There was no time to pause and read the map at the gate. She looked back once, then rushed into Primrose Hill and hid herself behind the plane trees in the long grass.

It was quite unlike Regent's Park, wilder, nearer to Hampstead Heath. The hill rose up, a pronounced green peak, out of green slopes and plains, and all around its borders were tall trees and grass and cow parsley gone to seed. The grass where she squatted smelt like the country. She could see a cricket on a dandelion leaf.

If Alistair had come on to the Hill it wasn't through that gate. She gave him ten minutes and when he still hadn't appeared began to walk along the path that runs parallel to Albert Road. Her pale cream shoes were streaked with green smears and threads on the hem of her skirt had been pulled by brambles. It didn't seem important.

There must be no chance of meeting Alistair head-on, so Regent's Park Road should be avoided. She began to run again, lightly, not too fast, because running made her feel free. It came to her that she had actually told Alistair she didn't want to see him again. She had told him things were over between them and told him why, and this pleased her; she felt it had been brave of her. Lately she had been

thinking a lot about her own passive gentle temperament, her inability to say no, her politeness and her
acquiescence, and she had wondered if she was one
of those said to be born to be victims. Those people
were attracted to the strong and aggressive and they
to the victims. But perhaps, to coincide with her
meeting Leo, she was changing, asserting herself,
leaving victimhood behind. It was frightening to
think of oneself as doomed to be used and mal-
treated by others, not a free agent and master of
one's fate.

Avoiding Regent's Park Road was impossible, but
she crossed it quickly, into Fitzroy Road. Wherever
Alistair might be, he wouldn't come into these streets
– she was sure he was even more ignorant of the
place than she – and slackening her pace, she slowed
to a walk until she came to Chalcot Road, which
forms the spine of Primrose Hill. She had read
somewhere that there was once an old manor house
of Chalcot here and that Chalk Farm itself was a
corruption of the name. Alistair would be lost here;
he would have turned back by now.

As Mary walked along the pretty, shabby, dusty
street the thought came to her that perhaps it was
unwise to visit Leo out of the blue. She did not know
him well enough yet to drop in on him. The unkind
and prejudiced things Alistair had said had given
rise to these misgivings. Surely she should discard
them, forget them. Those allegations sprang from his
jealousy and unaccountable hatred of 'Oliver' that
had started long before she met him. But even so
might she not be doing a risky thing?

She imagined Leo not alone. Not necessarily with
another girl, not that, but with the brother he was so
close to or even their mother or some friend to whom
he would be reluctant to introduce her, or just – since

he had only yesterday moved in – surrounded by disorder and chaos, in a panic of failure to cope.

The prospect of turning back, going back to Charlotte Cottage and spending a lonely evening with Gushi, kept her walking on. Suddenly she was at Edis Street. There it was, a left-hand turning of mid-Victorian terraced villas, more stucco, plaster scrollwork, untidy flowery front gardens, bicycles chained to fences. Three steps led up to a dark green front door. But first, dividing the small front garden from the pavement, black-painted, spiked, iron railings. She shivered inwardly. Did everybody in North-West One see railings where they had never noticed them before?

There was still time to turn back. In spite of herself, she imagined walking into his room and seeing a woman her own age sitting there, her shoes kicked off, a glass of wine in her hand. A dark woman, she thought, quite unlike herself, with a tangled bush of hair and a bright sparkling face. The idea of it caused a surge of anguish. But she pressed the bell marked with a newly printed card: L. Nash. No voice came out of the grille. He must have seen her from a window. The door trembled and growled, came open as she pushed it. She started to walk up the stairs, more quickly when he called to her from above.

'Come up. How wonderful of you to come!'

He was standing in the open doorway. She was learning that he didn't want to kiss or even touch her when first they met. It was just that they stood close together for an instant, looking into each other's faces. They did this now and she felt her own expression echoing his with a small conspiratorial smile.

It was an ordinary little room that he had, two open doors off it disclosing the whole of his small domain. A very tidy man might have been living there for six months, the kind of man with a place for everything and everything in that place. Roses from a garden, not a florist's, filled a blue vase on the windowsill. He had been hanging curtains. One was up and the other, half its rings inserted, lay draped across the back of his single armchair.

'I was about to phone you and ask you to come,' he said, 'but I didn't need to. You read my mind.'

She looked about her and a warm joy flooded her, filling her body and her head, until it seemed it must break out of her in happy laughter. 'I was afraid – well, a bit apprehensive about coming. I thought you might not be too pleased.'

He put his arms round her and laid his cheek against hers. She was aware as he held her of that peculiar feeling she had when with him of twinship, of being uncannily like him, older certainly, but physically so similar and with the same tentative-ness, caution, shyness, gentleness and fingertip-feeling sensitivity.

'I will always be too pleased,' he said. 'I will be too pleased for words, for anything. I can't tell you how pleased.' He saw her arm and frowned at the angry red marks. 'Who has hurt you?'

'It doesn't matter,' she said. 'It really doesn't matter now, Leo.'

Chapter Seventeen

From force of habit Bean had continued to take delivery of a newspaper after Maurice Clitheroe died and one day he had come upon an article about sixteen homosexual men convicted of assault for practising particularly violent sado-masochism. In spite of the participants' admitted consent all had been sent to prison.

Bean heartily agreed with this verdict. In his view, consent or no consent, people needed protection from others' perversions, and he, he told himself, should know. But he was disgusted to find this sort of thing in a newspaper, reminding him of what he hoped to have put behind him for ever. Anyone might read it and get ideas that otherwise wouldn't have crossed their minds. That was the last time he was going to read that paper, or indeed any paper. What, after all, was the telly for but to provide a pleasanter and easier-on-the-eye alternative to all these *Timeses* and *Daily* thises and thats?

Concentration wasn't required to nearly the same extent. You could get up and make yourself a cup of tea or fetch in a cress and Marmite sandwich and when you got back it was still merrily spilling out the news, same faces, same music, and if the pictures were different you hardly noticed – you couldn't remember what the last ones had been. Thus it was that, although Bean saw all about the murder on Primrose Hill, knew the victim was another vagrant, once again impaled on railing spikes, he had been out in the kitchen making a mug of Earl Grey when the man was identified. He hadn't been much interested. If he thought about it at all it was to reflect that the police hadn't caught Cahill's killer and that the chances were they didn't try all that hard, weren't bothered when the victim was one of those beggars.

He had breakfast television on while he ate his breakfast. It was orange juice, muesli, a Danish pastry and a cup of tea, and in the mornings the news was the BBC's offering, all those teenagers and cartoon bears and dinosaurs being a bit too much to stomach at seven-fifteen am. Nothing on it about the second dead man on the railings, that had been a flash in the pan, and he only kept the set on because he hadn't quite finished his tea. Bean already had his new baseball cap on and his Marks and Spencer's bottle green cardigan, for the early mornings were chilly, and he was thinking about switching off and setting forth to Mrs Morosini's, his first port of call, when the doorbell rang.

Nobody ever called at this hour. Mystified, on his way out with his key in his pocket, he went to answer the door. Two men were there, both young. Bean thought one of them only looked about seventeen. The older one had a hatchet face and pitted cheeks, the way it was quite fashionable to have if you were a pop star or in cowboy films. They didn't look to him like police officers but they said they were, an inspector and a sergeant, and they flashed warrant cards at him while they told him names he didn't catch.

Bean always thought of sado-masochism, even now, after all this time. They had caught up with him, even though he had done nothing more than he was told.

'What d'you want?' he said, his voice squeaky.

'May we come in?'

'I was just going off to my work.'

They seemed to know all about his work and for some reason it amused them. The older one said he could give his work a miss that morning because, on second thoughts, instead of coming in they'd like him to accompany them to the police station. Then the younger one said there would be no harm in his phoning a client – one phone call only, mind – to say he was cancelling this morning's walk.

Bean hardly knew whom to phone, who would be the best bet. He had to make up his mind fast and settled on Valerie Conway, back from holiday the day before, and in his estimation the closest to him of all of them in class and calling. The two policemen stood there watching him in a very laid-back sort of way.

'I'm not well,' he said when she answered. He didn't know what he would have done if Mr or Mrs Cornell had answered. 'I was wondering if you'd give the others a ring and let them know.'

'What, all five of them?'

'It wouldn't take a minute. There's Mrs Morosini and her number is . . .'

'I'll phone her,' said Valerie. 'She can phone the others. What's wrong with you, anyway? Laryngitis? It sounds like you've lost your voice.'

The policemen escorted Bean to their car. He told them he had never had anything to do with those perverts, only opened the door to them and looked after Mr Clitheroe when he was hurt and handed over payment when he was unconscious. They were amused but seemed not to know what he was talking about. He was inside the station and in an interview room before he got an inkling and then it was slow in coming.

'You drew fifty pounds out of your bank account at the end of last week,' said the inspector, now understood by Bean to be called Marnock.

How did they know? How could they know? He nodded and his head went on nodding like one of those toy dogs people used to have in the rear windows of cars.

'What would that have been for then?'

A phrase came to Bean from out of somewhere. 'Day-to-day general running expenses,' he said and he tried to clear his throat.

'Got a cough, have you?' said the young one.

'Must be all that dog-walking in the damp,' said Marnock. 'Funny you've never drawn anything before for these day-to-day running expenses. Not for, let's see –' he looked at a notebook on the table '– seven months. That's right, seven months since you last made a withdrawal from that account.'

Now he was pretty sure none of it had anything to do with Clitheroe and his practices, Bean was gaining courage. He effected a final throat-clearing. 'I don't know what right you've got to go poking about in my private bank account,' he said. 'What's all this about?'

'Now he asks,' said the young one. 'Who's Mussolini, Leslie? I can call you Leslie, can't I? Or do you prefer Les?'

If he hadn't been so shocked at hearing the name of Mussolini uttered like that, Bean would have reacted violently to being called by his given name. He had hated it ever since his schooldays in that Hampshire village and since then no one had used it. He was always Bean. Bean, as far as everyone knew, was what he might have been christened. But hearing himself called Leslie was nothing to hearing the name he personally, he alone, had given to the

206

anonymous hitman encountered once on the Hanover Gate Bridge.

He tried playing the innocent. 'He was Italian, like
the leader of Italy in the war. Like Hitler.'

The change in Marnock was shocking. He seemed
galvanised. He leapt to his feet and stood over Bean,
shouting, 'Don't give me that. Don't you play games
with me. Who's the man you called Mussolini when
you were shooting your mouth off in the Globe?'

'I don't know his name.' Bean's voice was still
strong but he had started to shake. He tried to stop
his knees knocking together. 'I don't know what he's
called. I called him Mussolini because he looks like
him. The spitting image of him, only young like.'

They had this nasty way of changing the subject,
just when you thought you were getting somewhere.
'You don't like homeless people, do you, Les?'

Bean picked what he thought was the politically
correct thing to say. 'It's not right for a great nation
like ours to have beggars on its streets.'

Marnock laughed. It was as if he couldn't help
laughing, though he would have liked to. 'So you'd
solve the problem in Hitler's way, would you?
Couldn't quite call it ethnic cleansing – the Final ·
Solution, is that it?'

Maybe the young one could tell Bean hadn't the
least idea what Marnock meant, for he reverted to an
earlier tack.

'What did you draw the money out for, Les?'

'It was for Mussolini, wasn't it?' said Marnock.
'What was he going to do for it?'

'Nothing. I don't know. I never saw him.'

'You *what*?' Marnock was standing over him again.

'I mean, I saw him once – he never came back. I
never saw him *again*. I went back but he never turned
up. He never did, I swear it.'

'What was he going to do,' said Marnock, 'for this princely sum?'

'I said, I never saw him again.'

'Kill Clancy, that was it, wasn't it?'

'Not kill him,' Bean protested. 'Not that. I never wanted that. Rough him up a bit – and why not? He'd mugged me. He'd taken a good bit more than fifty quid off me, I can tell you. Mussolini, whatever his name is, him, he was going to do the same, that's all, he ...' A gradual, awful, realisation was dawning. The railings, the second vagrant, the vital part of the news he'd missed to make his tea. 'I want a lawyer,' he said. 'I can have a lawyer, can't I?'

'Of course you can, Leslie,' said Marnock. 'I think that's a very good idea.'

Their natures and ways were uncannily the same. And this was wonderful to discover; each shared emotion, reaction, approach, a relief to find. It was not just that he kept his home precisely as she kept hers – clean, neat, airy – that he dressed simply, got up early, was as good-tempered and warm first thing in the morning as when they at last put out the lights, but that they seemed to like and need and want all the same things. She had only to mention a taste or preference for him to confess a similar leaning. He even had the same sort of food in his fridge as she had in hers. In his bathroom, when she went to take her shower, was the brand of soap she used.

It was almost as if he had set out to make himself the same kind of person. When his phone rang he answered it by giving the number, as she did, he said, 'Goodbye', not 'Bye-bye', and when someone downstairs slammed the front door he winced and smiled at his wincing, which would have been just her own reaction.

Their lovemaking, when it finally happened, was

what she had wistfully envisaged but never before quite known. With Alistair, and with a boyfriend or two before Alistair, she had tried to achieve the ideal she had made for herself long before. But, reluctantly, she had faced what seemed a universal truth, that her particular wish and need were not acceptable to men. They might not be violent or aggressive but they were urgent, demanding, determined to make the rules, certain of what was right. If they acceded to her – and from time to time they did – there was always a feeling she had that they were keeping her sweet, being 'patient', giving in so that they might get their own way next time. She had been called frigid by each of them, when they lost their tempers.

Until Leo, she had almost reached a point of seeing herself as wrong and the Alistairs of this world as right. She had almost resolved that next time, whenever that was and with whomever, she would accept the male attitude and try somehow to teach herself to like it. No doubt, that, like anything else, could be learned. But with Leo there had been nothing to learn or unlearn or make decisions about. She needed to ask him nothing, nor direct his hands, nor resist his urgency, nor pull away from the hardness of lips and teeth. He was as gentle as she, as languid, and until the end, when she, for once, was imperative and demanding, as slow and delicate with his caresses. But at that end she had cried out as those others had always expected her to cry and held him in an embrace she was fearful of afterwards, in case her strength was greater than his.

That had been three nights before, the time of her flight from Alistair. The next evening Leo came to her and though she worried that Alistair might arrive, might turn up on the doorstep at any moment, she forgot him after a while. Discovering

Leo, she forgot everything, lying in his arms, talking to him, *caring* for him. For it was inescapable, that feeling she must look after him, that he needed her as much to watch over his health, his fragile body, as for a lover.

Side by side in the warm evening, they were each as white as a marble statue, not a mark, a flaw, a flush of colour on their milky paleness. She could scarcely see in the dusk where the skin of his thigh ended and hers began. Only his face, in repose, the bluish eyelids closed, looked more tired than hers, looked, she fancied, older than hers. But that perhaps was the fantasy of a woman of thirty, wishing to be nearer her young lover's age.

Their hair was nearly the same colour, hers of a slightly finer texture, a clearer gold. The down on her arms was the same thistledown stuff as his. Each had the same kind of freckle sprinkling, pale gold, sparse, on the bridges of their noses. If their features were quite different, it was only as a brother and a sister's may be, each taking genes from a different parent. Their skin was the same matt fine white, skin that perhaps lined early, though hers, in spite of her seniority, had fewer lines than his. She looked at those lines tenderly, touching them with a warm fingertip.

They had talked, earlier, of this similarity and Leo had pointed out what should have occurred to her but for some reason had not, that in people whose blood and tissue types matched so perfectly, resemblance was more likely than not. Wouldn't it have been far stranger if one of them had been dark and the other fair, or one heavy and big-boned and the other slight? She had searched among the Trust's literature and found one of its leaflets, the one with a happy smiling photograph of two young men, donor and recipient, and yes, Leo was right, they were

210

much the same height, with the same colouring, the same smile.

'We may even be distantly related,' she said.

'I'm your lover,' Leo said. 'I don't want to be your cousin.'

He stayed all night with her. She slept better than she had since coming to Charlotte Cottage. Gushi came upstairs in the small hours and snuggled into the space between their feet. Leo didn't mind. He got up first and made her tea. It was gone eight and she was still in bed when the phone rang. He took the receiver off and handed it to her. The voice said it was Edwina Goldsworthy and Bean wouldn't be taking the dogs out. Maybe he wouldn't be taking them out for a couple of days. He was ill. Some sort of inflammation of the throat, Lisl Pring had said.

So she and Leo had taken Gushi into the Park and in a way she had been glad of Bean's bad throat because it meant she could spend the next night with Leo, of course taking the dog with her. For the first time she was feeling the constriction imposed by becoming a house-sitter. She was bound to remain at Charlotte Cottage until September, and once Bean was back, remain there every night because of Gushi. Alistair, in Leo's place, would have told her not to be bound to the Blackburn-Norrises, there had been no formal contract, but Leo did not. In his eyes the agreement was just as binding as if it had been drawn up by a solicitor and witnessed. In short, he felt the same as she did.

'And I don't think I could quite move in with you,' he said. She hadn't suggested it – they had known each other only a few weeks – but it was what she wanted.

'There would be something – not sordid exactly, but not what I want for us, if they were to come back and – well, find us. It will be better for us to be forced to wait until September.' He spoke very seriously. 'I would like everything to be above board.'

She said softly, 'What is it that you want for us, Leo?'

'At the moment,' he said, 'I'm still teaching myself to believe what's happened. That you're who you are, the woman who saved my life, that I've met you, and that you're –' he hesitated and his face flushed the way hers did '– the other half of me.'

'Yes,' she said, 'yes.'

'I'm falling in love with you, of course I am, but it's almost as if I was in love with you before we met; I'd made an ideal image of you and by a kind of miracle you are that image come to life.' He smiled at her, took her in his arms. 'It's not easy getting used to that,' he said. 'I don't want us to have any secrets, Mary. May we tell each other everything about ourselves, tell our whole lives?'

So they had begun doing that. He told her about his childhood with ambitious failures for parents: a father whose career as an athlete had been ruined by a ruptured Achilles tendon while training to run in the Olympic team and a mother who had twice failed to acquire through correspondence courses and evening classes the degree she longed for.

The result had been for them to see him and his brother as fulfilling hopes which in their cases had been dashed. They must be great sportsmen or great scholars, preferably both. His brother Carl had gone to drama school, incurring their father's anger and disgust. Acting wasn't a man's job. The only work Carl could get for a long time was modelling, more cause for outrage. Their father had died. That was when he discovered that all these years his mother had had a lover. Once her husband was dead, she had gone to Scotland to join him, leaving her sons

212

with scarcely a goodbye. It had hurt Leo, for she had seemed never to take his illness seriously and refused outright to be tested for tissue compatibility. Without Carl's devotion, he hardly knew what would have become of him . . .

'And the rest is history. That was where you came in.'

'Yes. That was where I came in.'

'I'm afraid my mother never forgave me for failing to run a three-minute mile and get a double first. Leukaemia's not hereditary, you see. That's known for sure now.'

She looked at him. 'I'm not sure that I understand.'

'If it were, she might be able to blame herself and my father. I mean, it wouldn't be their fault if one of them carried a faulty gene, of course it wouldn't, but people blame themselves for handing on to their children a poor genetic inheritance. Conversely, as I've discovered, they like not having to blame themselves, not having the grounds for it.' He spoke, not bitterly but with amused resignation. 'There's always the suggestion there – it's not explicit but it's there – that somehow I must have caught it or done something I shouldn't have to bring it on. My mother actually said once that nothing like that had ever happened to Carl.' His rueful laughter took the sting away. 'Still, grown-up people shouldn't live at home with their parents, do you think?'

'It's not something I know much about,' she said, 'but, no, you're right.'

She was appalled by what he had told her. The mother he had not much wanted her to meet – though he had not exactly discouraged her, either – she now wanted to keep away from until the time came when she and Leo . . .

'As soon as your time is up at Charlotte Cottage,' he said, 'I'm going to want you to come and live with

213

me. I'm giving you advance notice. Will you, in this tiny place?'

'But, Leo, we won't have to. I'm rich – had you forgotten?'

His face, so ardent and eager, changed. 'I'm afraid I had,' he said. 'I wish I could.'

In the post next morning came two letters. One, she could see by the handwriting on the envelope, was from Alistair. She opened the other first. It was from Mr Edwards, asking her if she was in need of 'funds', as there would be no difficulty in advancing to her from her grandmother's estate any reasonable sum. Bean arrived while she was reading the letter. He looked tired. She could see he had been ill. For the first time – perhaps she had previously not taken much notice – it was apparent to her that he was an old man, vigorous, well-preserved, but old.

He launched into an involved apology. It was all due to circumstances beyond his control; it wouldn't happen again. Mary hardly understood how you could guarantee you wouldn't get a throat infection a second time, but Bean didn't mention his throat. He said, to her astonishment, that he hoped Sir Stewart and Lady Blackburn-Norris would 'never have to know'.

'What, that you were ill?'

'That I missed taking the little chap out, miss. I'd feel easier in my mind if they didn't know.'

Pathetic, the sadness of age. 'I shan't tell them,' Mary said warmly. 'I shall have forgotten it by the time they get back.'

She told Leo and they laughed about it. He had stayed the night but waited until Bean was gone before coming downstairs. Formerly, she would have waited until she was alone before opening Alistair's letter but no longer, not now that she and Leo were so close. She said, 'Here,' and held it up. He put his arm round her and read it over her shoulder.

Alistair wanted to know why she had run away from him the previous week. What was she afraid of? He wondered if she should be undergoing therapy, she was so strange, so unbalanced. Did she realise that in an hysterical outburst she had actually said she didn't want to see him again? He was treating that with the indulgence he was sure she now wanted. In other words, he would forget it.

Could he arrange a therapist for her? He would be happy to do that. Meanwhile, they should meet and talk about money. Where did she want to live and what would she think a reasonable sum to spend on a flat or house, given their changed circumstances?

'I'd like to throw it away and not answer it.'

'But you won't do that,' he said. 'You're too much like me. Too polite and reasonable. You'll answer it and be firm but nice and repeat what you said about not seeing him again.' His voice took a stronger note. 'You won't see him again, will you, Mary?'

'I won't if I can help it.'

He held her. 'Please, Mary. For me.'

The police had given him the phone book to look up solicitors. He knew the names of the man who had acted for Anthony Maddox and the man who had acted for Maurice Clitheroe, but the last thing he wanted was Marnock's attention drawn to his late employers. He found a firm to phone in Melcombe Street and after a little while a young woman turned up. Bean began to feel a whole lot better when she started telling them they couldn't hold her client for more than twenty-four hours without arresting him. Did they intend to arrest him? She told them firmly that they had no evidence against him.

215

But even Bean could see that they had. By the time the solicitor came he had already told them everything they wanted to know – all about the mugging, about Mussolini and his offer, the money and his failed attempt to meet Mussolini again. He had admitted he wanted some injury done to Clancy and, when pressed, that he hadn't been particular as to whether this injury was serious or, indeed, fatal. He hadn't meant to say any of those things but they fetched it all out of him, and once begun there seemed no point in holding anything back.

What saved him, he thought afterwards, was that he still had the money. He actually had it on him. Of course they could hardly know that it was the same money, but possession of it helped his cause. He was with them for a total of fourteen hours and could, in fact, have taken the dogs out next day, was prepared to do his afternoon's duty, only they came back for him. They had found Mussolini.

Another day passed, a day of questions, mockery, teasing, taunting and, from Marnock, outbursts of serious anger. Mussolini had told them all sorts of things about Bean, they said, that Bean was sure was untrue, for Mussolini, real name Harvey Bennett, couldn't possibly have known them, could only have invented them. For instance, he had never said – never in his wildest dreams would have said – that he wanted Clancy killed. He had never boasted to Bennett about having killed a man once but was now a bit past it at his age. When he was told this, the deathbed of Anthony Maddox flashed awfully across his mind, but he had never talked of it, had spoken no word of it to anyone. It was all in Bennett's imagination.

He had never, as they insinuated, offered Bennett fifty pounds to kill Clancy, with another fifty to come when the deed was done. Nor had he sought Bennett out, enquiring indiscreetly in the Globe for someone to do a job for him. His solicitor came back and told Marnock not to forget the Police and Criminal Evidence Act 1984.

After he'd spent hours there in a cell they let him go. He never knew why. He wasn't going to ask, the relief of being free was enough for him, but he felt very shaken. Still, he had his fifty pounds and he knew what he was going to do with that. Buy a new camera.

The shop where the first one had come from, purchased by Maurice Clitheroe some ten years before, was in Spring Street, Paddington. It was still there. He found it in the new phone book, gave them a ring, asked what they'd got and their prices. The shop stayed open till all hours, being bang in the middle of tourist country, so he went over there on the tube after he'd walked his dogs. It was only two stops.

The camera, being second-hand, came to less than he'd thought. The shop manager threw in a film and Bean, doubly departing from custom, bought himself a bottle of whisky and the evening paper. Even if it was only a piece about the release of a man who'd been 'helping police with their enquiries', he wanted to read about himself. Paddington was a lot shabbier, dirtier and more litter strewn than the Marylebone Road and it gratified him that he didn't live there.

He was coming out of the wine shop when he saw the girl again, the one who used to come to the house in Maurice Clitheroe's time that he'd made a face at in Baker Street. She was standing in the doorway of a dingy looking video shop. He nearly missed seeing what happened and would have missed it if for some reason he hadn't turned round from taking a photo of a Highland Collie – a really smashing looking dog – an old woman had out with her on a lead.

217

A red Mercedes had pulled into the kerb and the girl was bending down to talk to the driver. Her clothes were a whole lot more upmarket than the previous time he'd seen her: red sequinned top, tight white mini, white stilettos. Whore's gear, but not cheap. Then Bean saw the driver. It was James Barker-Pryce MP and his red whiskery face, for once without the clamped-in cigar, was framed in the window. Bean took a photograph. He took two shots. The car door was pushed open from the inside and the girl got in.

Bean went home and read the paper. There was nothing in it about him, only a long piece by a psychiatrist the paper called famous, though Bean had never heard of him, about crazy street people and Clancy in particular. The psychiatrist said theories had been put forward as to why the dead man collected keys, some suggesting this was for the purposes of robbery, others that they constituted an armour against possible attack. The truth was that in Clancy's disturbed mind these were the keys to dream homes. Having no home, he had collected keys to the homes of others, keys being the symbol of home-ownership, of possession and of the privacy he could no longer enjoy.

Bean had never read such rubbish. While looking through his collection of dog photographs and selecting negatives for enlargement, he drank rather too much of his whisky and woke with a hangover. Putting on his baseball cap and a T-shirt patterned all over with pictures of endangered species, he was on tenterhooks lest the police come back for him. After all, they had been two days running, why not today? But no one came and he got to Erna Morosini's five minutes ahead of time.

She was rather short with him, not asking if he was better but moaning about how exhausted she was, having to walk Ruby herself. It was easy to see the beagle hadn't been using up enough energy. Like a team of sprightly carriage horses, she pulled Bean up to Park Crescent, puffing and lungeing. He exchanged a glance with the Duke of Kent, who didn't look the kind of man to be intimidated by policemen, before Ruby pulled him on. Valerie Conway appeared at the area door with Boris.

'A Mr Barker-Something phoned me yesterday to ask what I thought you were playing at. He said he hadn't had a word out of you and not to put yourself out to come when you did get back. He's making other arrangements.'

'What's that supposed to mean?'

'He says there's school-leavers round here panting to do the job for a fraction of what you charge. There was one girl said she'd take Charlie out for free, he's so lovely.'

Boris padded up the steps, his claws making a patter like the sound of hailstones on the metal treads. Waiting at the top, tied to the railings, Ruby fell amorously upon him, not much deterred by Boris's low growl and lips peeled back to show yellow teeth. Pity there was no market for dog pornography, Bean thought. He took them into the gardens and through the tunnel under the Marylebone Road. Now Pharaoh was dead, he could do that, and never again feel that trepidation, that tightening of the muscles and tensing of the nerves.

In the Park Marietta was uneasy, missing Charlie, not inclined to run by herself, but wandering aimlessly and stopping for a scratch. Bean got a shot of her standing on the rings of cobblestones round the Parsee's fountain, looking soulful. It would be a good picture and it somewhat calmed him. He had been boiling with anger and the injustice of it ever since Valerie Conway told him of Barker-Pryce's decision. The nerve, after what he'd seen in Paddington!

Two can play at that game, thought Bean.

Chapter Eighteen

The police coming took Hob by surprise. Not their coming – he expected that – but their reason. He must be getting soft in his old age. He'd had a birthday the day before, his thirty-second, or he thought it was his thirty-second, but he couldn't be sure; it might have been his thirty-third. He'd asked his mum and she didn't know either. All she'd said was that he was a few years younger than her but not all that many because she'd been just a kid when he was born.

But he was old enough to be losing his grip because he thought the police came on account of the riot. He thought they'd come to *apologise* for all his windows getting knocked out in the mini-riot of the night before. That came of living on the first floor – he'd have been safe higher up. He still didn't know the cause but there'd been these boys, kids of thirteen or fourteen, running up and down the walkways armed with car jacks and milk bottles, and then it had turned nasty, one of their dads coming out with a crossbow and someone else with what looked like a shotgun.

Hob watched from his window. He'd got some Es, the yellow tabs, from Lew but he knew he'd get so excited if he took one now he'd be down there with the rioters. They were shouting out something about a boy they said the police had beaten up in his cell, some mate of theirs accused of dropping a concrete block off the top floor on to an old man's head. Hob didn't want to get involved.

The first of his windows went while he was out in the kitchen getting himself a vodka as a starter before his main meal of the blow he'd got for the weekend. It was bricks they were throwing now. Hob picked the brick up off the floor and thought about throwing it back but didn't. It must have come off that pile the council builders left behind when they built a wall round that raised flowerbed at the entrance to the car park. Pointless, really, because all the flowers had been torn out overnight and someone had started dismantling the wall. He took a swig of his vodka and wandered towards the settee.

Before he'd even sat down he heard a brick or bottle go through the bedroom window. Someone must have dialled 999, for two police cars screamed in while he was pushing broken glass about with his toe and kicking it into the corner. The police had riot shields. Hob could hardly believe it. Riot shields for a crossbow and a few bricks! He wasn't in a state but the vodka made him a bit rocky. He smiled at his pun, his joke, and went to his jacket pocket for the red velvet bag.

There was a terrible noise going on out there now. All his windows at the front had gone – good thing the weather was getting so warm. He didn't care much. He set to work on his ritual, cutting the straw in half, crumbling up the jumbo, screwing on the Imperial Russian Court cap, drawing in at last the life-giving smoke.

It might have been an hour after that that the police came or a lot longer. He couldn't tell. He'd danced about the room a bit, done some Power Ranger exercises, air punching and karate kicks, and then he'd built a pyramid out of the three bricks that had come through the windows and the broken glass and cut himself in the process but not so's you'd notice. He must have gone to sleep at one point, for the scratching woke him up. Mice. He lay there listening to the mice and thinking it was a nice sound, nice and peaceful, not like rats, he'd never heard of any disease you could catch from mice, when there came a sound that wasn't nice at all, a great pounding on the front door.

He looked out of the broken window and saw their car down there. Unmarked, of course, but still recognisable to him as a police car. They knocked again and he let them in, all smiles, certain this was a routine visit, nothing to worry about, sir, all cleared up now, sorry you've been inconvenienced.

They didn't say any of that, but pushed past him into the flat, looking about them with their noses pinched as if it was a sewer they'd come into. They asked him if he was Harvey Owen Bennett and where had he been on June the something, the night Cahill was killed?

'Here,' said Hob. 'On me tod. Where else?'

They pressed him for more than that and he tried to think. A Thursday it was. It was years since he'd had much of a memory. Maybe that was the day he'd talked to his mum on Leo's phone and asked how old he was and she'd said that about him being younger than her and she'd have to go on account of her and his stepfather going down the boozer for this party they were having for her silver wedding. What silver wedding, he'd said, on account of her only being married for about five minutes, and she'd said, so what, it would have been her silver wedding if she'd not got divorced and the whole family was coming including his dad.

'No, I tell a lie,' he said. 'I was at my mum and dad's silver wedding.'

He hadn't a scrap of faith in it as an alibi but he

had to say something. They weren't going to leave him alone to get to a phone; they took him with them. On the way out he saw that the flowerbed was entirely gone, not a brick left, not a handful of earth. Maybe they'd learn now.

It was like a miracle what happened. People who knocked families ought to think before they spoke. His family was one in a million, solid as a rock, supportive was the word he was looking for. He didn't have to ask them, he didn't have to say a word – well, he couldn't, he was in that police car with the driver glaring at him – they came out with it all without hesitation, his stepfather told him on the phone afterwards. Of course Hob had been at the party, there from nine till they packed in when the extension ended at one-thirty, and he slept the night at their place. Two of his half-brothers and his stepsister's ex and the ex's girlfriend, they all backed him up, and his stepsister's ex who had an imagination said he'd done a beautiful rendering of 'I'll be Your Sweetheart' while they were cutting the cake.

'Any time, Hob, you know that,' his stepfather said. 'You don't have to ask.'

He saw that he didn't.

Effie was up on the Hill, drinking the nuns' tea, and so were Dill and Teddy and the man called Nello. Last time Roman had been up there all the talk had been of Pharaoh and his terrible end, of Pharaoh and of Decker. Who would be next? Would it be one of them? No one talked of it any more. They were as they had been before, or almost. Roman fancied they were more subdued than usual, more wary. They, who had never been afraid of what people with roofs over their heads feared, the streets, the dark, were afraid of them now.

He had taken to leaving his barrow under the arch

at the Grotto. Sooner or later it would be stolen, he knew that, but he didn't much care. It was a relief not to have to lug it around with him. Every time he saw Nello, who had all the marks of the amiable natural, the village idiot, almost the holy fool, the man would remind him of the risks he ran.

'They'll nick it off you, Rome,' he said. 'They'll nick it off you. Don't you know not to leave it about? They'd have it if you chained it up, they would. Don't you know to keep it with you?'

And Effie grinned and nodded and pointed to the empty space, the area four feet in front of him, where she thought the barrow should be.

'You want to go back and fetch your barrow, Rome,' said Nello. 'You'll be lucky if it's still there. There's plenty as'd pay good money for that barrow.'

Someone was killing the street people but he was to worry about the possible loss of a gimcrack box barrow. Psychologists, he thought, called that displacement. They all walked down the hill together, Effie and he, Nello and Dill and the beagle. Dill had told him that when he got a new uncle, when the old one had left and his auntie had found a replacement, the new one had turned him out of the house – well, it was a flat at Woodberry Down, but it came to the same thing. He had given him twenty-four hours to go and told him to take the dog with him. It had been his auntie's dog but she'd seemed glad to see the back of it, so Dill and the beagle had set off together.

'Like Dick Whittington and his cat,' Dill had said unexpectedly, crinkling up his oriental eyes.

But the streets hadn't been paved with gold and the beagle didn't even have a name. They just called it Beagle. Instead of a lead, Dill had a length of rope, but he let the dog off when they were in the Park. Roman saw the fair-haired girl in the distance, walking towards the Broad Walk, and a man with

225

her, as fair and slight as she, not the dark burly one he had sent off in the wrong direction.

The memory made him smile. A couple of weeks ago it had been, and just about this time of day. Then, too, he had been up on the Hill partaking of the nuns' tea and wondering, he remembered, if those charitable sisters were connected in any way with a church he often passed that was dedicated to the Handmaidens of the Sacred Heart. It was a name he loved and that stuck in his memory, and he was thinking of it and of those nuns who were handmaidens to the poor and dispossessed, when the fair girl came running along as if pursued and called out to him a breathless hallo.

That set off another train of thought, this time Russell's contention – or Russell quoting some other philosopher's contention – that at certain times and in certain situations to lie is moral. If, for instance, one should see a man running as if in fear of his life, and within moments his pursuers arrive and ask which way he went, then it is permissible to lie and tell them the left-hand fork when in fact the man fled to the right. This reflection had come into his mind just as he came out at the bottom of Ormonde Terrace and the dark and burly chap appeared, running, red-faced, obviously as mad as hell.

Roman nearly laughed aloud at the opportunity that had been sent him or he, coincidentally, had found. Would the man have asked him? Probably not.

He pointed down the terrace towards Primrose Hill Bridge and the Park. 'She went that way.'

'*What?*'

'The lady you are chasing went down there into the Park.'

The man stopped and stood, indecisive. He had

gone even redder. 'Fuck you,' he said to Roman. 'Mind your own bloody business.'

But he turned and ran down the terrace just the same. Roman watched him, laughing. He hadn't laughed so much for ages, not since before it happened, not since his loss. For a moment or two he had awaited further developments – the man's reappearance perhaps, the fair girl herself to come creeping back – but nothing happened. And since that afternoon he had twice seen her with a new man, this straw-haired pale-eyed one, who looked nice enough, who held her hand and once put an arm tenderly about her shoulders.

This relieved him of a burden, for he had thought, after amusement at the incident gave place to reflectiveness, that she was in distress, and he had come close to constituting himself her guardian or protector. He saw her so often, their paths were always crossing, that he felt he could easily keep an eye on her, see that she was safe. But safe from what? If the railings murderer, the Impaler as the papers called him, sought out young women for his victims, Roman would have made himself at once her watchdog. But she could hardly be further from the type that had so far been his victims. She had a home, probably a nice one, and she was female. Did her femaleness exclude her? He gave Effie a glance, Effie with her bandaged legs and the men's suit trousers she wore and her green bundles, and wondered.

When they came to the Inner Circle he told them that this area, this ring enclosing a few acres, had once been designated by Nash who was the Prince Regent's architect, as the site for the Prince's summer palace. He meant to say no more, for he had no wish to be their didact, but Nello said to go on, to tell them, and Dill said to sit on a seat and tell them a story. Effie only stared, her eyes as empty and as desperate as they always were.

So he told them how the Prince who became George IV had laid out this park, or rather Nash had under his instructions, and how Nash and Decimus Burton had built the villas and the terraces for the Prince's courtiers. He talked about the great road that was to be built all the way from this inner circle down to Trafalgar Square, that it had been begun and Portland Place was the start of it, but the plan had to be abandoned through lack of money. They could appreciate that; they knew about governments' thriftlessness and abandoned schemes. Dill put the beagle back on its lead, or tied the rope to its collar, and they made their way through the Rose Garden that was in full bloom, that was at the glorious zenith of its blooming. The sun was hot and the air perfumed, Roman thought, like those famous gardens of the East, the Shalimar perhaps.

They were a rag, tag and bobtail crew, shuffling along these immaculate paths, and people gave them glances but no stares. The respectable were afraid of the retorts or oaths that stares might evoke. Though dogs were strictly not allowed, no one said a word even when the beagle lifted its leg against a rose called Sexy Rexy. But Effie knelt down by the finest rosebed of all and buried her face in the full brilliant blossoms of Royal William, inhaling and lifting her head and burrowing once more in the rich scented petals.

Roman couldn't think of much more to tell them, though they asked. The summer palace had never been built – what would it have been like? The Pavilion at Brighton? – and the great road had been spoilt by intersections, Regent Street having later been quite destroyed and rebuilt. The Inner Circle had been the province for a while of the Royal

Botanical Society before becoming Queen Mary's Rose Garden. He left them then, Effie and Nello seated side by side on a bench near the bandstand, Dill and the beagle on their way to their pitch outside Tussaud's. It was time to buy his supper, make his way back to the Grotto.

The evening sun awoke in him memories of warm London nights. They were few, it nearly always grew cold, but sometimes, when they had a sitter for the children, he and Sally had gone to a restaurant in Bayswater or Notting Hill and eaten their dinner at a table outside. He was no longer able, when he envisaged these events, to see Sally's face clearly. There were parts of it, a curve, a feature, that whatever constructed such things in his mind failed to build accurately. It was not that she or the children receded from him but rather that a mist or veil had come down between them and himself.

A curious thing was happening: he was able to remember with less pain, with something more like a sweet nostalgia. Something he had believed would never come was coming, a kind of resignation. It was not exactly hope he had, certainly not recovery, but he could, in connection with what he had suffered, repeat to himself Winston Churchill's dictum, that this was not the end nor the beginning of the end, but it was the end of the beginning.

Had he set forth on his pilgrimage then with the aim of being cured? He thought not. It had been escape, not therapy, but perhaps therapy had come just the same. His fate he had begun to see not as something to be fought against with rage and anguish (Why me? Why me?), but as marking him out simply to be a member of that rare band of people – not so rare in many places – whose whole family has been destroyed at a stroke. He could see himself calmly now as one of them, different from the rest of mankind as a dwarf is different or an amputee, destined to live with that difference for ever and to accept.

He went into a shop in Camden High Street, bought a sandwich, an apple and a banana, and because he had wanted it the other day when he only had milk, a bottle of wine. There was a corkscrew in his barrow if no one had come and stolen it and all it contained, as Nello had forecast.

He stopped for his usual contemplation of Durham's figure in bronze. She gazed towards Gloucester Terrace with his old girlfriend's eyes, making him ask himself where she was now, what had become of her. Would he know her if they met? Did she still look like this maiden drawing water from the spring? She was not in the least like the fair girl he had fancied needed protection. He was not ambitious to become one of those men who haunt and harass women, following them, dogging their footsteps, but still he thought as he climbed down into the Grotto, that he would try to watch over her from a distance.

For all that, he was unable to tell himself why he felt she needed a guardian angel. She had the man who looked so uncannily like her. Her brother perhaps? The burly dark one was just a fool who surely constituted no real threat. As he opened his wine, he began to make a little scenario. Her brother had come back from abroad, expected to share her home with her, but found the dark one in residence and they had fallen out ... He couldn't finish the story, couldn't see where it might go next nor account for her being chased to the gates of Primrose Hill. But he thought he would 'look out' for her, and begin in the morning, for he was sure she always entered the Park just here, at the Gloucester Gate, and walked past that sculpted tower of silence.

*

There came back to Bean a conversation he had once had with Clitheroe. His employer was in bed recovering from a particularly serious beating. When he dressed it Clitheroe's back reminded Bean of James Fox's in the film *Performance* that he had seen while working for Anthony Maddox, only Fox was an actor and the weals and cuts on his back were make-up while Clitheroe's were real. He had said something like that, something about Chas in the film, and Clitheroe said, talking of acting, he's a pretty good actor, that chap.

What did he mean, actor, Bean had asked. And Clitheroe said The Beater's name, which Bean couldn't remember, and then he said, he's made himself into what he thinks I want him to be, and he's right, I do want him to be that. I want a savage, Bean. I want someone who enjoys beating someone else more than anything in this world, who gets all his pleasure from it, who wants it better than sex or drugs or money, because to him it *is* sex and drugs and money. Do you understand?

'Sure,' said Bean, 'of course I understand.' Understanding made him feel sick but he didn't say that.

'I love his excitement, Bean. Do you know, I think I love *him*, and why not? It's just what a crazy pervert like me would do. I'd like to do something for him, set him up for life, show him after I'm gone that I had real feelings for him.'

'Turn over,' Bean said, 'and let me have a dekko.' He had stopped calling Clitheroe 'sir' about the time The Beater first began coming. 'Christ,' he said, 'I just hope this lot's not turning septic.'

'It'd better heal up because (the name again) is dropping in for a drink and fifty lashes on Saturday.'

'He'll kill you,' said Bean, not knowing how near the truth he was.

'I can see it in his eyes that he's acting,' said

231

Clitheroe, wriggling – with pain or pleasure, or were they the same? 'There's something dead in his eyes. And I'm glad of it, Bean, because it would be too much for me if it was real. It would be too beautiful to bear.' He shivered and goose pimples came up between the wounds. 'He could act anything. I wonder why he doesn't? Make his living at it, I mean. Maybe he's never had the chance. Or maybe he only wants to act in life, not on the stage. He wants to *be*, you could say, not to act.'

That was all too deep for Bean. He hated that kind of high-flown meaningless speculation. The Beater *had* dropped in for the drink and whatever and again the following Saturday and it was after he had gone that Maurice Clitheroe had his stroke. Sometimes Bean thought himself lucky to have got the apartment under Clitheroe's will, for he might easily have left it to The Beater.

It was satisfying to have remembered, but not much use. Every morning, about this time, Bean still expected the police to come back for him, though it was over a week now since they had hauled him in for a second going-over. While he dressed and had his breakfast he kept running to the front to look out of the window and check.

'Testimonials? I've never heard of such a thing,' said Bean, annoyed, when Valerie Conway told him Mrs Sellers wanted two independent references on top of Valerie's own recommendation before she would surrender her dalmatian to his keeping.

'Suit yourself,' said Valerie. 'But don't expect me to put myself out another time.'

Bean said he'd ask Mrs Goldsworthy and Miss Pring but he wasn't promising anything. This Mrs Sellers should realise she wasn't doing him any favours. A reliable dog-walker was like gold dust, never mind Barker-Pryce and his school-leavers.

'Oh, get a life!' said Valerie, slamming the area door.

Lisl Pring was off on location somewhere so Bean had to use his key to pick up Marietta. He asked Mrs Goldsworthy about the reference and she said, Oh, sure, no trouble, she'd do it later and to remind her again if she forgot. Bean knew she'd never do it. She was the sort who had so much money she never bothered to do anything. He tied the dogs to the gatepost at Charlotte Cottage and pretended to ignore what Ruby was trying to do to McBride. Let them get on with it. He asked Miss Jago for a reference. Something like that would have looked better coming from Sir Stewart Blackburn-Norris but it couldn't be helped. She said, yes, of course, and she'd give it to him next morning, and somehow he thought it likely she'd actually do it.

It was a warm sultry morning, the kind of July day that threatens a storm to come. Swarms of gnats rose and fell above the surface of the lake, and from the bridge over the island the water had a foetid smell. The grass in the open areas was worn and bleached by the sun. Bean walked the dogs over the bridge and almost to the Hanover Gate. This morning the roof of the Mosque was dull as an old copper pot. Watching the gambols of Boris and Marietta, he asked himself if he really wanted another big dog, a dalmatian. Big dogs were unruly and easily got out of hand. Pity they couldn't all be like that little Gushi, who stuck close beside him and only occasionally ran off for some puppyish adventure with McBride.

A man was walking down the Broad Walk from the zoo end. Bean was quite a long way away from him. Flowerbeds and ornamental trees and fountains and urns spilling out more flowers separated them. But he would have known The Beater anywhere, at any distance, by his slouching walk, the lift of his chin, his body movements as elegant as a black man's, the way his arms hung loosely by his sides. Bean had all the dogs on their leash by now and he approached nearer. He had no objection to being seen by The Beater and in the daylight and the warmth had lost the fears of the night.

When their eyes met The Beater's showed not a flicker of recognition. But he was an actor, wasn't he? Bean stared at him before turning abruptly away. How old was he? That had always been a mystery, but he must be all of thirty-five now. He turned round when he was sure The Beater wasn't looking, and took in the jeans, the denim jacket, the longish hair. Was it possible . . . ? He had seemed clean enough but some of them *were* clean. There were hostels now where they could get showers, wash their hair.

So could The Beater have come so low as to be on the street?

Bean had no real reason to think so except that *they* did come in here and loaf about and The Beater seemed to have been wandering aimlessly. Where, after all, could he have come from and be going to? If he really was one of them maybe the Impaler would find him and he'd end up murdered and stuck on railings somewhere. Things would have been very different for The Beater if he hadn't beaten Clitheroe quite so hard and Clitheroe had lived a little longer and changed his will . . .

Marnock and the sergeant were waiting for him when he got back to York Terrace, sitting outside in their car on a double yellow line. They were a lot more polite than on previous occasions which made Bean cocky and say in a testy tone:

'What is it this time?'

They wanted him to tell them all about the man who had mugged him in the Nursemaids' Tunnel. There was no need to go down to the station if he'd be good enough to ask them in. Was he sure the mugger had been Clancy? Was there any room for doubt over the identity of his attacker?

Bean had to rethink the whole thing. Maybe it hadn't been Clancy. He wondered if he dared give them a description of The Beater but he thought better of this as too dangerous and said he couldn't remember. They stayed for nearly two hours, their politeness unflagging, and when they left they said nothing about seeing him again.

He had a Bird's Eye Lean Cuisine for his lunch and watched 'Emmerdale' on television. After that, feeling cheerful, he told himself that nothing venture, nothing have. All his clients' phone numbers were written down in the accounts book he kept. As he dialled Barker-Pryce's number he thought, if she answers or some secretary or whatever I'll just put the phone down. When he heard Barker-Pryce speak his throat dried.

'Yes? Who is it?'

He managed to speak. 'It's Bean, sir. The one who walks the dogs.'

'What d'you want? Speak up.'

'I was wondering,' said Bean, his rising anger strengthening his voice, 'if you'd like to see some really beautiful photographs I've taken of Charlie. They're smashing, sir, I think you'd like them.'

He was well named Barker. The noise he made, a laugh presumably, was much the same sound as that coming from McBride when he put up a mandarin duck.

'That's rich. Coming from you. You walked the

animal, right? When did I give you permission to use it as a model?'

Bean drew a deep breath, expelled it, said, 'Talking of models, sir, I nearly mentioned these pix the other evening when I saw you in Paddington with the young lady.'

Silence. Bean seemed to smell cigar smoke.

'I'd been buying a paper, Mr Barker-Pryce. A newspaper. It was to read that article about the gentleman from the government and the lady in the hotel. I expect you know him, don't you, sir?'

The voice was quieter this time, the tone more polite. 'What exactly do you want?'

'Among other things, a reference, if you please, sir. For a lady with a dalmatian. I wondered if I might drop in after I've taken my *other* dogs for their walk. Say about five-thirty?'

Chapter Nineteen

It took Roman a while to find out where she lived. He felt a natural aversion to spying on her. But one Saturday, he saw her in Primrose Hill and with the utmost discretion followed her home.

He had been in a second-hand bookshop in Regent's Park Road and there found an old work, published in 1840, called *Colburn's Calendar of Amusements*. The bookseller only wanted two pounds for it, for it was in a ragged battered state. Roman stood in the shop doorway, reading a passage from it that touched him, that seemed to parallel in a zany awkward way, his own state.

The lion in the collection of the Zoological gardens was brought, with his lioness, from Tunis, and as the keeper informed us, they lived most lovingly together. Their dens were separated only by an iron railing, sufficiently low to allow of their jumping over. One day, as the lioness was amusing herself leaping from one den to the other, while her lord looked on, apparently highly delighted with her gaiety, she unfortunately struck her foot against the top of the railing, and was precipitated backwards; the fall proved fatal, for, upon examination, it was found she had broken her spine. The grief of her partner was excessive, and, although it did not show itself with the same violence as in a previous instance, it proved equally fatal: a deep melancholy took possession of him, and he pined to death in a few weeks.

Deep melancholy may kill lions, but not human beings. Not even the deepest grief kills them, for men have died from time to time, but not for love ... He was remembering, incongruously, how when he was a boy the zoo's telephone exchange was called Primrose and remembering too a joke about dialling Primrose one, two, three, four, and asking for Mr Lion, when he looked up and saw her pass by on the opposite pavement.

She might not have been walking home but somehow he fancied she was. He put the book in his pocket and began to walk in the direction she was going. If she looked back, he thought, he would abandon his pursuit of her. He would give it up at once, for she must on no account be made afraid of him. How much, how infinitely much, he would have liked to read that account of the poor lion's fate to Sally, for there seemed no one else in the world to whom he could read it or tell it and who would react with the same tender sympathy. But she was not in the world; she was nowhere, ageless, lost, with her dead children.

The fair-haired girl, the Irene Adler girl, crossed the road ahead of him and then Albert Road and made her way into the Park by way of St Mark's Bridge, over the Outer Circle and into the Broad Walk. She hadn't once looked back. But why would she? She wasn't Lot's Wife, leaving the Cities of the Plain, or Orpheus hoping Eurydice followed on behind. The Walk was shady here, much overhung by trees, chestnuts and planes in heavy leaf. The two wolves, penned behind double wire fences, explored and sniffed their territory like dogs. He saw her turn to look at them but not pause. She took the first of the two left-hand paths that led to the Gloucester Gate.

He had been making his nightly home in the

Grotto for nearly three weeks now, the longest time he had spent in any one place. And all the while, it seemed, she had been quite near him, for she had crossed the Outer Circle and was leading him along Albany Street. Park Village West. If she went in there she must live there, for it was a crescent, leading nowhere but back to that northbound artery. It was quiet, a bower of trees and flowers, green, scented, but the leaves a little dusty, for this after all was near the heart of London.

She hadn't once looked back, but she did so at the gate of a pretty Italianate house, and seeing him, not knowing that he had been behind her all the way from Primrose Hill, lifted up her hand and waved.

Only a woman in a million, he thought, would say hallo to me, smile at me, and when there had been some hallos and smiles, wave to me. And he wondered if he should stay a while to see if her brother came home – but it might be hours, or the brother might be in there now. He turned away, opening his book and reading it as he walked along.

Someone had come and boarded up his windows. Hob didn't know who because he had been out most of the day, trying to get what he wanted out of the bunch of stony-hearted people he knew or was related to. He got home late, spaced out and low on the paediatric Valium syrup which was all he'd been able to get out of his half-sister. It didn't do much for him beyond making him sleepy so that at least he was too tired to feel all the intensity of a state.

He'd first gone for help to his half-sister's boy-friend. This man, the father of her youngest child, made crack himself by mixing cocaine and bicarbonate of soda and baking the resultant paste in a microwave. He offered it to Hob at ten per cent less than its street value – or he said it was ten per cent;

Hob couldn't work it out. But Hob had already handed over all his giro money to Lew under the Chinese trees and he was skint. The boyfriend shrugged and said too bad. His half-sister took pity on him, or more likely wanted him out of the house, and said she'd got a bottle of the kids' Valium he could have. They were supposed to have it in their bottles but she and the boyfriend found whisky more effective.

After that he proceeded to his cousin's place in one of the blocks off Lisson Grove. The cousin and two of his mates were sitting in front of a hard-core video smoking weed. They passed the joint to Hob more or less as a matter of course but none of them would give him any money or even lend him any. The cousin said he knew a man he'd met in a pub that might want a job done and he told Hob where he might find this man, giving him a funny look when he saw him swigging out of a kid's medicine bottle.

The paediatric Valium tasted very sweet and of something that brought back Hob's childhood. He couldn't think what it was and he was too sleepy to think much anyway. He hung about the newsagent's the man used for a long while, bought a couple of scratch cards, getting nothing up of course but a couple of Walker's crisps and two diet Cokes. Then he sat on a seat outside on the pavement, but no one came along who remotely fitted his cousin's description. Fruit drops, that was what it was. It came back to him suddenly as he was trudging home – fruit drops that syrup tasted of, what his mother's nan called boiled sugars. His first stepfather used to buy them for him after he'd given him a harder clout than usual.

He was looking up high, to the top of the next block, Blackwater House, to see where the kid had stood when he'd dropped the rock on the old man, which was why he didn't notice the windows till he was almost at the door. Raw planks of wood were nailed up over all his front windows, the two in the living room and the one in the bedroom. It was a warm night and inside the flat it was hot like an oven. He sat on the settee and laid his head on one of the Mickey Mouse scatter cushions.

When the lights in the flats opposite and the lights in the car park went out it would be black as pitch in here. As it was, only thin lines of light, orange-coloured, slipped through the cracks between the boards. It would be as bad in the bedroom. Hob drank more Valium syrup to put himself out and he must have spilt some on the floor, for he was aware in his sleep and his half-sleep of the mice at his feet, licking it up.

'We could live here,' Mary said, 'when the time comes for me to leave Charlotte Cottage.'

She and Leo were in Frederica Jago's house, big, turreted, late-Victorian red brick, set in an over-grown rather dark garden. Mary had not visited it since her grandmother's funeral and the meeting there with Alistair and Mr Edwards. It was stuffy and airless. She felt she should go about opening windows, but as soon as she came through the front door she had been lethargic and reluctant to take any positive steps. The place was filled with her grand-mother. It was not a new feeling, it was how everyone felt in her circumstances, but all the time she expected the dead woman to walk in, to smile, to speak, to hold out her arms.

'I grew up here. It seems forbidding now but it didn't then. I remember being proud of living in such a *distinguished* house and I think I used to boast about it at school. I must have been a horrid child.'

Leo had been silent ever since they came through

241

the front door. Normally, he would have reacted to that last statement of hers, refuted it at once, and she even wondered if she had said it for that reason: to hear him tell her she could never have been horrid. She was growing hungry for praise from him. But he said nothing, only shrugged lightly. She took him upstairs, going from room to room. In one she opened a dressing table drawer but the scent that came from it, vanilla and roses, was so much the essence of her grandmother that she drew back with a little cry.

In the big bay window of the master bedroom she turned to him and laid her head against his shoulder. 'Leo, what is it? What's wrong?'

'Nothing,' he said. 'There's nothing wrong.'

'I'm sure there is. Do you hate the place? We don't have to live here. I don't even know that I want to. There's something retrograde about choosing to live in the house where one was brought up.'

He screwed up his eyes. He said, as if with an effort, 'Your wealth. I suppose it's only now that I'm realising how rich you are. This place has brought it home to me.'

'I told you.'

'I know. Now I'm seeing for myself.'

She had no heart for the rest of the house and led him downstairs and back into Frederica's drawing room. He was looking all the while warily about him. She saw his eyes take in the pictures, the glass, the porcelain, and linger on a tall French clock in a case of brass and glass that began at that moment to strike four.

'If you'd known,' she said fearfully, 'when we first met, would you have still wanted to know me? I mean, would you have pursued it? Or would you just have said thanks and maybe we'll run into each other again one day?'

He paused. It was a long pause. 'I don't know,' he said. 'I can't answer that.'

Her heart seemed to fall through her body, sliding down in a sluice of coldness. 'But you thought at first Charlotte Cottage was mine. When you first heard from me you had my address as Charlotte Cottage.'

'Yes, and I was mightily relieved, I can tell you, when I found out it wasn't yours.'

'But what can I do? I can't give it all away. And, Leo, I don't want to. I want somewhere nice for us to live. I want us to live as we please and you not necessarily to have to go on working for your brother – unless you want to, I mean. I want to buy a car; I haven't even got a car and nor have you.' She found she was talking wildly, 'I can buy us a smaller place, a flat, a little house.'

She put out her hand to touch his but it remained unresponsive. The memory that came back to her was always there but usually suppressed, buried under layers of pleasanter things.

'Why did you leave me that day in Covent Garden?'

He turned uncomprehending eyes. 'What?'

'We were out together. It was the second, no, the third, time we went out together, and you suddenly said you had to go, you had to meet your brother, and you said goodbye and walked away.'

'I suppose I had to meet my brother.'

Some inner cautious voice told her not to pursue it. She stood up. 'Let's go.'

Outside it was very dark. Clouds had been gathering all afternoon and now thunder rumbled from beyond Hampstead and Highgate like distant explosions. Coming here, he had held her hand, but now he walked apart from her, his head down, sullen as she had never seen him. After a moment or two he said lifelessly, almost regretfully:

'I love you.'

Until then he had never quite said it.

The words themselves were gratifying. Perhaps they always were, no matter who said them. Suddenly she was uncertain. She thought she loved him, she loved being with him, she loved their lovemaking, but could she answer him in the way he would want her to? What made her suddenly doubt? A certain sulky childishness because he had difficulty in coping with the difference in their incomes?

They were in a taxi, silent again, and home in Charlotte Cottage before he said another word. By then the storm was full-blown, the lightning splitting a sky of huge black thunderclouds, the rain beating down all the flowers in Park Village gardens. She had put the lights on; it was like a winter evening. Gushi, terrified, hid under the sofa, his cold nose pressed against her ankles. It was the kind of weather when you could take it for granted Bean wasn't coming. Leo said suddenly, in an uncharacteristic outburst:

'I can't bear that man, whatshisname, Alistair, writing to you that you're going to live together, you're going to buy a place together.'

'But we're not. I've told you, all that's over.'

'He wants to marry you, doesn't he?'

'Perhaps. I don't want to marry him.'

A thunder crash seemed to rock the house. Gushi whimpered. She got down on her knees and did her best to stroke his chrysanthemum head, reaching under the sofa.

'Will you marry *me*?'

She turned her head. It was ridiculous to be on all fours.

'Did you really say that?'

'I really did.' He looked almost shamefaced. His

face was her face when she was awkward or embarrassed.

'Leo, I'm older than you. We've known each other for less than two months. And –' she couldn't resist '– I'm rich.' She saw him wince. 'We can live together; we're going to do that. We can get to know each other.'

'We do know each other.' He got down on to the floor beside her and held her shoulders. His eyes were very near hers. 'We are part of each other's bodies, and not just in the way all lovers are, but in a special way. You are my bones, Mary. You are my blood. Who else could we marry? Don't you see that after what we've been to each other, it would be wrong for us ever to marry anyone else?'

She felt a little faint. She shook her head, on and on.

'Marry me, Mary, before he can marry you. Marry me now.'

'Leo, you know we see eye to eye in most things, but this is – isn't it a bit ridiculous? I do want to be with you, I do want to live with you as soon as I can leave here, but why does it have to be marriage? One day, yes. Maybe in two or three years' time. When we know what we both really want.'

He said very quietly, 'There may not be two or three years.'

'What do you mean?'

'I don't think I'm going to live very long.'

It was as if she had put out her hand, expecting to encounter warmth, and had felt, instead, ice. She had been practical, prudent, and she could see he was deadly serious.

'What do you mean?'

There was fear in his voice now. 'Just what I say.'

The ice was touching her spine, sliding down.

'Have they told you that? Have they told you at the hospital?'

'Let's say,' he said, 'they won't answer when I ask. I had a check-up on Wednesday.'

'You didn't tell me.'

'I would have if there'd been a – a favourable outcome. I shall be all right for a while. They talked about a while.'

She said breathlessly, 'Another transplant?'

'You would do that for me a second time?'

'If necessary. Of course I would.'

There was a wild look in his eyes she had never seen before.

'I never thought you'd do that. I never considered it.' He seemed disproportionately distressed. It was as if she had said something that might change his life and his plans – as indeed this might – but not pleasurably, not in a way to be entirely desired. 'I wish I'd known,' he said, half to himself, and then, 'You'd do that?'

'I've just said so. Leo, it's nothing to the donor, nothing but an anaesthetic, and that's quite safe if you're strong and healthy.'

She put her arms round him. She felt a pulse drumming in his neck, his heart beating steadily but fast. Her mind wasn't made up but she knew she was about to act as if it was.

'If you need another transplant, who better to have it from than your wife?'

Chapter Twenty

Before going to St Andrew's Place Bean called in at the chemist and picked up the ten enlargements he had had made. Expensive but worth it. The dog photographs – Charlie sniffing noses with McBride, Charlie in pursuit of a goose, Charlie reclining elegantly on sunlit grass – he had in a cardboard folder and he slipped one of the enlargements in with them. The others he locked up in Maurice Clitheroe's safe.

His new-found power led him to ask James Barker-Pryce not to light another cigar while talking to him. It was bringing on the asthma he thought he had left behind him twenty years ago. They had gone into a small office or study with a view from its long window of the Royal College of Physicians. On the desk was a stack of writing paper with House of Commons printed on it in green and a picture of a gridiron thing that Bean thought meant it was the property of the government. The cigar was· left behind, smouldering in an ashtray in the hall.

He opened the cardboard folder, displayed two photographs of Charlie and then the enlargement. Barker-Pryce snatched it up.

'I have others, sir,' Bean said.

Barker-Pryce didn't even look at the shots of Charlie. Some of these people weren't fit to keep a dog. He picked up his dark green Mont Blanc fountain pen in khaki-stained fingers and wrote a reference on that same crested writing paper. His handwriting was not what Bean would have expected, being small and clear and perfectly legible. Over his shoulder, Bean could read desirable words: 'reliable', 'a true animal-lover', 'unfailingly punctual'.

'I've made other arrangements for Charlie,' Barker-Pryce said in almost the tone he would have used to a neighbour or an honourable friend in the Commons. 'I can't see my way to revoking those, if you understand me. But I'd like these pictures of my retriever.'

The money was there, all ready and prepared. It was placed in his hand, the notes lined up against the edges of the envelope with the reference in it. Bean didn't count them, he could tell it was a hundred pounds. With an awful attempt at a conspiratorial grin, a squeezing shut of the eyes, a lifting of that thick hairy upper lip to expose teeth of the same shade and shape as the mahogany beading on the desk, Barker-Pryce said:

'Buy yourself a few videos instead of the newspaper, eh?'

Bean did speak then. 'I'll call again in a week's time.' He'd dropped the 'sir'. He left the pictures where they were, the one of Charlie and the goose uppermost. The expression on Barker-Pryce's face was frightening, so he stopped looking at it. What those girls went through! No wonder they'd never let a John kiss them.

Charlie burst out of one of the rooms at the back and came boisterously up to him in the hall. Poor innocent creature, thought Bean. He touched the retriever perfunctorily on the head the way Queen Victoria's dad might have patted one of the dogs at Sidmouth. Barker-Pryce didn't say another word but stood in the study doorway, looking at him. Bean pulled the front door closed.

Mrs Sellers and her dalmatian lived in Park Square, which would be convenient, being more or less on the way from the Cornells' to Lisl Pring's. The dalmatian (called Spots, 'not Spot, please,' said Mrs Sellers) was obedient and docile and she took a fancy to Bean from the moment he entered the flat. The interview went well and it looked as if Bean would soon add another dog to his charges. The reference on House of Commons paper made an awesome impression on her but didn't stop her asking for a second one.

Miss Jago at Charlotte Cottage was the sort who when she said she'd do a thing, did it. Except that she hadn't. And he'd already twice reminded her of her promise. He noticed most things about his clients and it didn't escape him that Miss Jago had an engagement ring on her left hand. Not much of a ring – Victorian rubbish of nine carat gold and tourmalines you could pick up for forty quid at Camden Lock. One of the numerous men she entertained was presumably going to make an honest woman of her. He wondered – for he was always on the lookout for a means of money-making – if Sir Stewart and Lady Blackburn-Norris knew, if they would mind, if she had told them. Would she be marrying soon? Would she bring hubby to live *here*? Was there anything in it for him?

More pressing was the matter of his reference. Having hesitated as to whether or not he wanted another dog and a big dog at that, he now desperately wanted Spots. He told himself he needed the increase to his income walking Spots would bring. Besides, it irked him, Mrs Sellers doubtless believing by this time that no one else was willing to vouch for him.

Twenty-three days had elapsed between the first murder and the second and now it was just twenty-three days since the second murder. Bean expected a third at any minute. He believed in psychopaths ruled by the phases of the moon, cycles of madness, bloodlust regulated by multiples of seven, give or take a little. So there should be another one at any time.

He was sure the police believed in it too. That was why they were so jumpy and so polite. He had stopped reading the papers, but the television had a programme about fixated killers, killers with a mission or an obsession, and there was a psychiatrist on it – probably the one who analysed Pharaoh's madness – talking about murderers who killed prostitutes or nuns or almost anyone so long as they could be put into a category.

The twenty-third day went by and the twenty-fourth, and none of the homeless or the jacks men or the beggars got killed. Whoever was doing it had probably gone off somewhere else, Bean thought, gone up north – they always went up north for some reason. He often speculated about The Beater and wondered if he ought to say something to the police next time they paid him a visit. They had been back twice since asking him about the mugger in the tunnel and he had begun seriously thinking of himself as their adviser, as genuinely helping them with their enquiries. But what could he say? That The Beater could act anything, pretend to be anything he wanted? A sadist or, doubtless, a respectable citizen?

Instead of leaving wet weather in its wake, the storm had just made things hot. Summer had come at last. All the rain had made the grass in the Park very green and fed the roses so that they grew lush with dark shiny foliage. The sun shone on velvet lawns and sparkling dewdrops; by noon the temperature had climbed to twenty-five and higher and in the evenings people watched performances at the Open Air Theatre in sleeveless dresses and T-shirts.

Calling for Gushi on the first really hot morning, the sky cloudless, the air clear, he asked Miss Jago for the third time about that reference. She looked genuinely aghast, he had to give her that.

'I *am* sorry. I'm so sorry. I'll have it done for you by this afternoon.'

'I don't see you in the afternoons, miss,' Bean said in his most respectful tone.

'I'll try to be home by the time you bring the dogs back. Or else you can be sure it will be here when you come in the morning.'

The woman who walked ten dogs was out with her troop. It was all right for her; she wasn't a day over thirty-five. She had given up waving at Bean since the day he returned her greeting with one of his looks. But nothing could stop their dogs fraternising. Ruby made the Cavalier King Charles spaniel her prey. It was a lot smaller than she was and those dogs always had poor sight. Bean had to rescue it from gang rape, for McBride and Boris had followed Ruby's lead.

The woman watched his efforts without offering to help. Then McBride found a heap of horse dung – how did a horse get in here? Under a mounted policeman? – and rolled his fat wet body in it, shaking smelly brown liquid all over Bean's trousers. It was no way to make a living, he told himself – he'd be seventy-one in September. But he had to have an income. He couldn't live on the pension, especially in a luxury maisonette designed for a fifty thousand a year man.

Valerie Conway was waiting in the area doorway, well out of the rain of course. Boris would never go down the stairs alone. Bean had to take him, otherwise the borzoi would lie down on the top step and refuse to budge.

'You got the dalmatian on your books yet?' Valerie said as he descended.

'Why do you ask?'

'Just being friendly. As a matter of fact I'd like to think business was good because Mr Cornell has given me a message for you.'

'What message?'

'He's giving you two weeks' notice. Your services won't be required after the twenty-eighth.'

Bean stared at her. He took his hand slowly from Boris's collar and the dog slunk through the doorway, drawing its body to one side so as not to touch Valerie as it passed her.

'What's brought this on?'

Valerie could hardly contain her pleasure and triumph, he could tell that. 'They're going to live permanently at their place in the country. And I'm moving in with my boyfriend.'

'Well, thanks very much. Thanks very much for the courtesy of *two* weeks' notice.'

'I consider I've done very well by you, Leslie Bean or whatever your name is. Why d'you think I found you a new customer? You ought to be down on your bended knees thanking me.'

He looked hard at her. He would have liked to say she could keep her two weeks' notice and she needn't think he'd ever have another thing to do with that foul-tempered dog, that cold-hearted, evil Russian, the animal that hadn't even attempted to defend him when he'd been mugged. But he couldn't; he needed the money.

'Thank you, Valerie,' he said, and was about to add that he'd see her later, but she had slammed the door.

252

The sun grew almost unpleasantly hot by three-thirty. Bean never thought he'd be complaining about the heat but he would gladly have missed out on the afternoon walk. Marietta, always the least controllable of the dogs, the liveliest, the bounciest, went too near a family of cygnets and got a peck on the chest from the swan. She screamed as if she'd been stabbed with a knife, but Bean couldn't see a mark. Little Gushi was too hot under his thick shaggy coat, puffing and whimpering until at last Bean picked him up and carried him. He was heavy for his size and he panted, his tongue hanging out.

All this made Bean late getting back to Charlotte Cottage. He rang the bell, hoping Miss Jago was home as she had said she would be. But there was no answer, so he let himself and Gushi in with his key. She kept it very clean, he always noticed. What he would really have liked was to have taken Marietta in there and left her to run about shaking and splashing the pale walls and silk chair covers with muddy water. But, thinking of his reference, he left the other dogs at the gate, carried Gushi into the kitchen and refilled his water bowl.

Taken all in all, it had not been a pleasant day. Bean had still not been back to the Globe. It was not that he was any longer afraid to go there, or that he believed the police would watch him go there, but he saw himself as punishing the place by ostracising it. All the trouble he had been in was due to the Globe and the Glober's clientele telling tales. Bean had an obscure feeling that a well-run pub wouldn't have those sorts of customers.

So, for the past three Fridays, he had been going to the Queen's Head and Artichoke. He knew no one there but that bothered him very little. He went there to drink and this evening he felt particularly in need.

253

Someone in the pub the previous week had buttonholed him and started giving him a history of the place – how the original house that had stood here had been built by one of Elizabeth I's gardeners, hence its name. Bean wasn't interested and he looked cautiously about him so that he could give the historian a wide berth, but the man wasn't there this evening. He asked for a double whisky, Bell's, and ginger ale, and took it to a table in the corner.

Without the whisky he would probably never have thought of going up to Park Village. A second double emboldened him. After all, he was already in Albany Street, and it was a beautiful evening. At just after nine-thirty, the sky was clear and cloudless, violet-coloured and still stained red in the west. So near the Park, the air smelt of the scents distilled by the sun from grass and leaves and roses.

Twenty to ten, which was the time he would get there, was not too late to pay an evening call. He remembered Anthony Maddox's rules about that – he was talking of the phone but it came to the same thing – 'nothing before nine am or after ten pm.' Besides, she couldn't complain; she had promised him that reference over and over again. On the spot, he could stand over her till it was done. Well, stand there and perhaps be offered a drink while she wrote it.

When she said she was going to be married, Dorothea assumed it was Alistair.

'It's Leo I'm marrying.'

Dorothea had to think who that was. 'How awfully romantic,' she said.

'It is, isn't it? But I'm so glad you think so. I'd thought you'd disapprove. We haven't known each other very long.'

'Knowing the person very long isn't necessarily important. You can have an instinct about someone being right for you.'

'That's exactly it. I have an instinct about it. But I do wish my grandmother was alive to see us, to see *him*.'

'You thought I wouldn't approve but she would?'

'Oh, maybe it's that her generation expected marriage, they thought in the terms of marriage, whereas ours doesn't. I suppose I'm getting married to make, as they say, a public commitment.' And, she thought, but didn't say, because he may not live long. 'I'm older than he is. Why should I wait?'

'Do you know what I'd really like, Mary? I'd love you to wear one of Irene's dresses. Why not *the* wedding dress?'

They looked at it in its glass case. Irene Adler had never existed and nor had Godfrey Norton; she had never been married to him, so never had a wedding dress. This one had been worn by some Edwardian bride, long dead. It was white lace with a high boned collar and long embroidered train. Mary laughed.

'I'm getting married at Camden Register Office. Can you imagine *this*? I shan't even have anything new for it. We don't care about things like that – he doesn't any more than I do. And we shan't have a honeymoon. We can't; I have to stay at Charlotte Cottage for another five weeks. He'll go back to his place and I to mine, I expect – and then, I don't know. But I think we'll be happy, Dorrie.'

'And what about Alistair?' said Dorothea.

Since she had run away from him and hidden herself among the trees on Primrose Hill she had seen and heard nothing of him apart from the letter. She had not yet been able to face replying to it.

'He wants me to let him invest my grandmother's

money. He says I'll never find anyone more competent and more cautious. But I haven't got the money yet and shan't have it for ages.'

'You sound as if you don't much want it.'

'That would be silly, wouldn't it? We all want money. Now I'm going to marry Leo I want somewhere nice to live.'

She said goodbye to Dorothea and took the path straight across the Park but their talk had delayed her and it was only when she reached the gate of Charlotte Cottage that she remembered telling Bean she would be home early, that she would be home before he came back and would give him his reference. He couldn't have long gone. Gushi, with fresh water brimming his bowl, was lying exhausted on the kitchen floor.

Mary sat down to write Bean's reference, the little dog on her lap. It took her a long time because she had never done it before and had no idea what was requisite to say. And to whom did you address it? She had written *To whom it may concern* and 'Mr Bean' – should she try to find out his first name? – when Leo arrived. He looked white and tired, said he had had a hard day; he would have to lie down for a while.

The reference finished, she decided to write to Alistair. She would tell him she was getting married in three weeks' time to Leo, and she had begun, had rejected 'My dear Alistair' for plain 'Dear Alistair', when Leo called her from upstairs. She came into the bedroom and he started to say rather peevishly that she had promised to look after him, to care for him, but although she knew he was exhausted she had virtually ignored him since he got home ... And then, suddenly, he was laughing at himself, apologising, saying how absurd he was; he was only making excuses for wanting her.

So she went into his arms and after a while he began his gentle delicate lovemaking, his fingers with the soft gossamer touch of a moth's wing, his lips as cool as petals, so that it was like being in bed with a phantom. She closed her eyes and thought, when I open them there will be no one there but a shadow. And then his movements strengthened and his body grew real and seemed infused with a sudden great heat. The sound wrenched out of him was like a groan of pain.

They slept and woke to see a red sunset behind the trees of the village and the double spires of St Katharine's. The red dimmed and the sky was blue covered with tiny pink feathers. Mary got up, had a shower, put on loose cotton trousers and a T-shirt, and began to make their supper. But Leo came down while she was tearing lettuce for a salad and gently shepherded her away – he would do it. He was fine now, he wasn't ill.

He laid the table, opened the bottle of wine he had brought. She finished her letter to Alistair. Everything she wanted to say had presented itself clearly, she had had no difficulties with it, and what had seemed an insurmountable problem resolved itself into a simple telling of the plain facts, kindly, precisely, without emotion.

It was nine before they sat down to eat, his pasta dish with black olives having taken detailed preparation. She ate and was glad to see him eating so heartily, a second helping and another slice of *ciabatta*. Remembering Alistair's suggestion, she asked him if they should start house-hunting this weekend. They would be bound to like the same things, they always did, so it should be a delightful exercise. If he agreed, she had quite decided to sell the house in Belsize Park.

The idea seemed to appeal to him and he speculated about houses. Buying a house, buying any
property, had never come in his way before, he
confessed. It was something that the grown-ups did.
And she laughed because she felt just the same. It
was not for them, they were children to whom such
businesslike adult stuff had never occurred, but now
it must, they must be serious; they must realise that,
give or take a little, they could have whatever they
wanted. He had got up and come round the table,
put his arms round her and was holding her close in
a bear hug, when the front doorbell rang.

Mary said, 'It's Alistair.'

'Yes, I expect it is.' Leo hesitated only infinites-
imally. 'I'll go. It's time we met.'

She jumped up. 'I don't want him to hit you!'

Leo laughed. 'He won't hit me.'

She wondered how they would look together, side
by side, the one so slight and fair and with the
unearthly pallor, the other dark and heavy-set and
choleric. Leo came back. The man with him was
Bean.

'Not wanting to put pressure on you, miss, but I
shall be going on my holidays in a couple of weeks'
time . . .'

'Your reference,' Mary said, stammering. 'Your –
yes, I – yes, I have it here. I'll just get an envelope.'

When she came back into the room Bean was
sitting on a chair at one end of it and Leo at the table
facing him. She handed over the reference.

'It's for a dalmatian,' Bean said.

That made Leo laugh. He laughed almost crazily,
throwing back his head, and when Bean had gone, he
shouted the words, still laughing. 'It's for a dalmatian! A dalmatian! A reference for a dalmatian!
What'll it do with it, d'you think? Eat it? Bury it?'

She had never known him so noisy, so wild. She

258

laid her hand on his shoulder but he still shouted, his face convulsed, 'A dalmatian? Can you imagine it reading it? Does it wear glasses? A dalmatian!' And then, suddenly, he was weeping, the tears streaming down his face. He clutched her, pulled her down to him and knelt with her on the floor. His arms held her so tightly she wanted to cry out.

'Mary, Mary, I don't want to die. I want to live, I want to live with you. Why can't I live to be old like others will? I don't want to die!'

At some point in his pilgrimage Roman had made up his mind to settle nowhere for more than a few nights at a time, to be always on the move so as to distance himself as far as he could from an approximation to domestic life. And now he had been at the Grotto for three weeks, had even turned it into a kind of home, storing his barrow under the lee of the archway, sleeping there on his groundsheet, keeping, in a cave of bushes, a store of food. The litter had irritated him and he had gradually tidied the place up, picking drinking straws out of branches, stuffing broken bottles and packaging into the carriers they gave him at the grocery. And the rain had washed the place clean, scouring the coped edges of the little pool, filling it with fresher water.

When the sun came out, a hot sun at seven in the morning, he sat with his back to the ironwork of the bridge, looking at his garden, the rhododendrons, the elder trees. The water in the nearer pool was now so clear that he could see his thin bearded face and gaunt figure reflected in its glassy surface and use it as a washbasin for splashing face and hands. He could wash the mug he used for drinking milk and wine and the knife that was his only utensil. But this domesticity brought home to him an unwelcome

259

thought. Homelessness could not be artificially contrived but must come about through real need and
real deprivation. And again he called himself a
phony and a fake, one who had partaken of others'
misery because it was *there* and available.

He should go now. He should move on. His
reluctance to leave the home he had made – he
would be rigging up curtains next, building parti-
tions from cardboard boxes – brought him a wry
amusement and taught him that he could be amused,
he could even laugh. Hadn't he laughed with pure
glee at the plight of the man, *her* boyfriend, he had
sent off in the wrong direction?

If he left he could less easily keep an eye on her.
But she had her brother now; he had several times
seen them together. Her brother would protect her
from the dark, red-faced pursuer. Perhaps, then, he
would stay just a week longer. He knew where she
lived and where she worked, that she had a little dog
the old man in the baseball cap took out with the
rest, that her brother visited her every day, that she
was harassed by a dark-haired man with, to say the
least, an aggressive manner. His daughter, he sometimes thought, might have grown up to look rather
like her. Elizabeth had that same very slender
fairness, the fairy face, that look of being often
startled by events.

He remembered a camping holiday they had once
had, he and Sally and Elizabeth. Daniel was not yet
born. It had been in the Highlands, a place not in the
least like this Grotto, this spoilt London garden, yet
there had been a cave there and a little pool.
Mountains soared beyond and there was a beach of
silver sand on the loch. Elizabeth, with a child's
passion for place, had wanted to stay there for ever.
It was impossible to make her understand that they
had to go back, that livings had to be earned, the

house maintained, she had to return to school. One night he had let her have her heart's desire and sleep, not in their tent or hired trailer, but in the cave itself. But anxious parent that he had been, he had worried and, unable to sleep, had moved himself into the mouth of this hole in the mountainside and mounted guard there all night.

Now he was doing the same thing in another place, for someone else. He closed his eyes and saw his daughter, his wife, his son, and though their faces were less clear than they had been, their identities remained, his eternal companions. And he thought, in a paraphrase, *for ever wilt thou love and they be fair.* Time could not change them or take them away again and however he became reconciled, however able to find a kind of contentment – for he could feel contentment coming, closing in on him, like fate – they would never be lost or further from him than now or their lives forgotten.

He wept for himself and them, sitting by the pool, his head on his knees, quiet accepting tears. Then he got up and stationed himself below the wall to see her when she came up the street and entered the Park.

Chapter Twenty-One

'Your father was a doctor,' Leo said.

'And yours was a civil servant.'

They were reading each other's birth certificates, sitting in the registrar's drab foyer.

'That's a polite way of saying he worked behind the counter at what was then the Labour Exchange.'

'Mine was a GP, nothing grand.' Mary found herself often reassuring him. She was bent on establishing an equality between them. Leo, she saw, had been born in 1971 and she pointed out to him bravely her own birth date of 1965. 'You were only a baby when my parents died.'

The date of their own marriage was fixed for 17 August, a Thursday. After the formalities were completed Mary asked Leo if his brother would come to their wedding.

'I don't think so. He's not much of a one for weddings.'

'We shall have to have two witnesses and he's an obvious one. I thought I'd ask my cousin Judith and my friend Anne, and Dorothea and Gordon will come. Will you ask your brother?'

'If you want me to.'

'And I should like to meet him first, Leo. Can I meet him?'

They sat down at a table outside a café in Marylebone High Street and ordered coffee. Leo looked as if the long walk had been too much for him and Mary made up her mind to take a taxi home. He had rested his head back against the chair and now he closed his eyes momentarily.

'Can I meet your brother, Leo?'

'Why do you want to?'

'Because he is your brother. I've hardly any relatives of my own.'

He said nothing. She watched him ruefully, his tired face, his spent look.

'Am I nagging you?' she said.

He touched her hand. 'You couldn't nag anyone.'

'It's just that you're so fond of your brother, you're always talking about him. If he's such an important person in your life, won't he be important in mine?'

The coffee came, black for her, a cappuccino for him. 'When I'm married I shall break with my brother,' he said, and he looked away. 'I don't want you to meet him. There, I've said it. I don't want that.'

'But you love him so much. He's done so much for you. I don't understand, Leo.'

Leo said stonily, 'I loved him once. That's all in the past. He won't come to our wedding.'

On one of the hills of Kemptown in Brighton, Bean's sister owned a small two-bedroomed terrace house. From the back garden, if you stood on a chair, you could see between two high-rise buildings a segment of sea. Every August she went to stay with her ex-husband's sister-in-law in the Peak District and while she was away Bean stayed in her house. For years they didn't even meet. Not since their mother died had he spoken to her except, briefly, on the phone.

He made careful arrangements for his holiday. His clients were assured, not once, but again and again, that he would be back one week from his departure.

'I shall be in harness again on Friday the eleventh,' he told them, one after another.

Erna Morosini said she had seen a young woman exercising a bunch of dogs. The woman always wore jodhpurs and had long dark hair. She looked young and strong. Her name was Walker. Didn't Bean think that was funny, her being called Walker and walking dogs? Did Bean know anything about her? Did he think she would take on Ruby while he was away?

'Would you really entrust your much-loved beagle to her, madam?' Bean asked. 'She obviously takes charge of far too many dogs. You can see they're out of control.'

'Well, if you put it like that . . .'

Mrs Goldsworthy caused him even more disquiet by telling him that the school-leaver who had taken on Barker-Pryce's Charlie would be exercising McBride 'as a temporary measure'.

'I can't do it. Not with my knee.'

It was the first Bean had heard of Mrs Goldsworthy's knee.

Giggling and showing off her ribcage, Lisl Pring said she had made the perfect arrangement. She didn't need the exercise but her boyfriend did and he was going to ride his bicycle round the Outer Circle, dragging Marietta behind him.

Bean was shocked. 'That's against the law, miss.'

'The cops are going to bother about that, are they? When they've got this murderer to catch?'

Mrs Sellers said she would simply go back to what she had been doing before Bean was engaged, walking the dalmatian herself. But she looked aggrieved. Perhaps she thought there should have been something in the references about him having holidays.

Lunchtime or late morning were good times to

catch Barker-Pryce, before he went down to the House. Bean encountered the school-leaver on the doorstep, about to exercise Charlie. He had a low opinion of anyone who didn't take a dog out before noon and he gave the tall sixteen-year-old one of his looks, baring his teeth.

This time Barker-Pryce said absolutely nothing. He opened the door, stood aside to let Bean in, closed the front door, opened the door to the study, stood aside to let Bean in, closed the door. Where was his wife? His servant? The cleaner?

Bean had brought more photographs but when offered them, Barker-Pryce shook his head in silence. He had the money ready, five twenty-pound notes in a stack on the desk next to the headed paper. Bean held out his hand and Barker-Pryce put the money into it, saying not a word. He opened the study door, stood back for Bean to go through and left him to let himself out of the house. As he closed the front door Bean heard the rasp of a lighter struck by a thumb and the leap of a flame as a cigar was lit.

Dealing with The Beater would be less straightforward. Or so he believed. He had no knowledge of where The Beater lived, or of his real name, and it was no use seeking him out where they had previously met, for that would defeat the purpose of his enterprise. He could of course wait for him in a likely place and make his demand, but as he walked back to York Terrace he asked himself whether it was necessary at this stage to do anything at all.

They had looked at each other and they had done so speechlessly. The silence, though, had been eloquent and Bean was certain each had read the other's mind. The Beater would know that he had taken in the whole situation and appreciated exactly what the position was. The Beater would need nothing put into words. He would be more silent than Barker-

265

Pryce. Even now, at this moment, he would be thinking of everything Bean knew and just how disastrously Bean could if he chose ruin his life and his prospects.

Bean went home and opened all the windows. In weather like this he wished Maurice Clitheroe had put in air conditioning before he died. He put a pack of frozen Bombay potatoes and another of pilau rice into the microwave. Tucking Barker-Pryce's hundred pounds into the suitcase he'd be taking away with him, he thought that if he went on at this rate he'd soon be able to send out for stuff from Express Tikka and Pizza.

With BBC 1's News at One turned on, sipping at a can of Diet Sprite, he started wondering about The Beater once more. It was becoming clear to him that he need do nothing. The Beater would seek him out. He knew where he lived, for he might well have expected to inherit Maurice Clitheroe's house himself and would have watched closely to see who would occupy it after Clitheroe's death.

The Beater might come at any time.

This thought was vaguely unpleasant. Seated in the very room where so many unsavoury happenings had taken place, Bean seemed to hear again his employer's screams, the swish of the switch and slap of the cane. The Beater was not only an accomplished actor but strong too. Thinness didn't mean much, it was the muscles that counted. Bean fancied he would be quite ruthless. It might be wise not to let him into the house but to suggest, for instance, that they meet in a pub or even talk in the street.

He would do that. When the Beater surfaced – and Bean was sure now that this would happen before his departure for Brighton on Saturday – he would be prepared, leave nothing to chance, above all, never be alone with The Beater where there were no other people, no lights, no life.

He set off as usual at a quarter to four, Ruby didn't want to be walked and dragged her feet all the way up Portland Place, only showing some interest in life when they came to the parking meter with which she conducted a desultory love affair. Passing the Cornells' former home, Bean noticed that the Venetian blinds were pulled down at all the windows and three black plastic bags of rubbish had been left in the area. A stink of something spicy and decaying wafted up to the pavement.

The afternoon was hot and he was wearing his red baseball cap with the perforated crown, his jeans and a short-sleeved T-shirt with a herd of elephants marching across it, but he was sweating. When he was in Brighton he might invest in a pair of shorts. More and more people were wearing them, even men of his age. Into the gardens of Park Crescent where the lawns, green and springy the previous week, were fast drying and turning yellow. Ideally, he ought to find another dog in this area so that he didn't have to walk the solitary one on her own all the way from Devonshire Street to Park Square. That prompted him to ask Mrs Sellers if she knew of anyone but she stared vaguely at him as if she didn't know what he was talking about. Spots started panting as soon as they were out in the street.

A hot wind blew the trees and raised litter on dust clouds. McBride came sleepily out of the house in Albany Street, disinclined to walk, stopping every thirty seconds to scratch himself, but Marietta was quite sprightly, her chocolate skin looking as if it had been shaved, and perhaps it had. He didn't even have to ask Lisl Pring.

She seemed to have forgotten his reproof or never to have taken it in. She said she'd just had a phone call from a friend who'd been ill. The friend had a lively young spaniel and was at her wits' end to know how to get it exercised.

'Where would she be living, miss, this friend of yours?' Bean said. 'Not too far away, I hope.'

'I'll have to think. I mean, I've never been to her place. Gloucester Avenue? Or was it Gloucester Place? Same difference, you know what I mean.'

Bean didn't. He thought there was all the difference in the world, about half a mile's difference.

'I don't mind asking her to give you a ring.'

'Thank you very much indeed, miss,' said Bean, but she didn't notice the sarcasm. She wouldn't.

Miss Jago was out at work. He let himself into Charlotte Cottage and with Gushi running about him, jumping up his legs, had a quick look round. A postcard from Lady Blackburn-Norris, all about the weather in some far-off place and saying nothing of interest, a bunch of junk mail, fliers from a dry cleaner's. Bean tucked Gushi under his arm and went out, back to the other dogs.

Once in the Park, he took a photograph of Spots and McBride, looking sweet side by side. A beggar materialised from nowhere, the way they did, an oldish man with brown teeth and stubble on his face. He held out a hand that was more like one of those toadstools that grow on tree trunks than part of a human being.

'Change for a cup of tea, guv?'

'Bugger off,' said Bean. He'd have liked to kill them all. Whatever they said about that Impaler, his was a mentality he could understand.

It was the hottest day of the year. No one would have chosen to walk across the open centre of the Park, treeless and exposed to the heat of that sun. Walking home, she kept to the shady Outer Circle.

Two men were running on the oval track by the Primrose Hill Bridge but they were dark-skinned and perhaps interpreted the heat as pleasant warmth. She crossed the Circle at the Gloucester Gate and glanced down over the low wall. The man with the beard was lying asleep on a groundsheet spread between the two round shallow pools, a book open and face-down beside him, a bottle of something standing in the water to keep it cool.

Next time they encountered each other, should she give him money? She had always given to beggars but since her accession of wealth, had carried five and ten-pound notes to distribute. Was he the kind of man who would welcome alms? He seemed to be sleeping in total peace, as if he had no cares, or had discovered some secret of life. She walked home and she must have been early, for Gushi was still out.

He trotted in, panting, clearly affected by the heat, five minutes afterwards. Bean's face was glistening and beaded with sweat. He was an old man to be walking so far in temperatures in the upper eighties. She paid him for his week's dog-walking. Gushi in the kitchen noisily lapped water. Mary went with Bean to the gate and was introduced to the dalmatian, a docile dog who licked her hand. 'A member of the company due to your good offices, miss,' said Bean. 'Your reference went down a treat with Mrs Sellers.'

His obsequious manner always embarrassed her. But now it was accompanied by the kind of leer only to be expected from a much younger man. He looked her up and down, as if making some kind of assessment or calculation. She went quickly into the house.

It was too hot to eat, or too hot for human beings. Gushi had recovered enough to wolf down a can of Cesar and she picked at bread and cheese and salad.

When the time came to leave she would miss the little dog. Perhaps she and Leo could have a Shih Tzu of their own. She wrote a letter to Judith in Guildford, inviting her to the wedding, and another to Anne Symonds that she had been at college with, and with Gushi on the lead went out to post her letters.

The pillar box on the corner was out of use, the two slots sealed up. The only other one she knew of was under the main arch of Cumberland Terrace. It was still very warm at nearly nine, the kind of evening that comes only after a day of exceptional heat. A few days before, in a sudden high wind, there had been a premature falling of leaves, plane leaves turning yellow and dropping on to the pavements. Or perhaps it was not premature but a normal happening that occurred always at this time of the year, an early warning of autumn. The leaves, dried and shrivelled, crackled under her feet. She walked through the passage at the Cumberland Terrace.

A haze hung over the Park, soft and mysterious. The trees had become purplish-grey shapes, utterly still. The air smelt of diesel and lavender, a curious combination. Few people were about. They would all be at café tables on pavements, in the gardens of pubs. She posted her letters, watched the locking of the Park gates. The Park police went in, it was said, and rounded up the dossers who tried to spend the night in the shelter of the restaurants and pavilions, but some always escaped their vigilance, sleeping among the bushes or under the lee of the zoo. That reminded her of the man she had seen asleep that afternoon, and carrying Gushi now – 'You are just a baby,' she murmured into his fur – she made her way back into Albany Street at the Gloucester Bridge.

Mosquitos danced in swarms above the water of the pools. The air was crowded with wheeling insects, moths with dusty wings, gnats, blue flies. They seemed not to bother him. He sat among the rocks, resting on a rolled-up sleeping bag, reading his book. It came back to her that once, to herself, she had called him Nikolai, because she had seen him reading Gogol. When he saw her he got up, just as a man might when a woman comes into the room.

'Good evening,' she said.

He smiled. 'Good evening.'

It was an opportunity. He had come a little way up the slope and was looking at her with what she interpreted as concern, though it couldn't be. She could go down there and sit with him and talk. But what about and why? It was an absurd idea. Besides, Leo was coming, would be there in ten minutes. Even more absurd was what she said, in the light of what she had just said.

'Goodnight.'

He nodded, as if confirming something he had suspected. He had very blue eyes, intelligent and kind.

'Goodnight,' he said.

She remembered as she walked away that she had intended to give him money but she had none on her and now, anyway, it seemed an absurd idea, insensitive and wrong.

It was a man's voice on the phone and somehow he had expected a woman. Well, he hadn't really expected ever to hear another word about it. Not from that Lisl Pring, that butterfly brain. The funny thing was that he'd been watching her on television. 'EastEnders' was a favourite programme of his and he never missed an episode. Lisl Pring had been doing her stuff, looking quite different from in the flesh, if that was the term for someone as bony as her, looking fatter for one thing, quite well-covered and shapely, and the credit titles were coming up, when the phone rang. If the programme hadn't been more or less over he wouldn't have answered it.

The voice said what its owner was called, or he supposed it did, and then something about a dog.

'Are you a friend of Miss Pring?' he had said because he hadn't caught the name.

'I just said. It's really urgent. I'd like to see you as soon as possible.'

Bean hadn't cared for the tone. 'I shall want to see *you*,' he had said, 'and the dog. I'm not sure I'm prepared to take on a lively young spaniel. It *is* a spaniel, right, and a puppy?'

'Not a puppy. He's two years old and he's been to dog-training with me.'

'Well, I'll see,' Bean said grudgingly. 'She said Gloucester Avenue.' Or had she said Gloucester Terrace? 'That's seriously out of my way, you know.'

'As a matter of fact, it's Gloucester Place, the top end.'

Maybe the top end wouldn't be so bad. He was starting to say so, not sounding too enthusiastic, when the voice said:

'But I'm moving. I'm moving to Upper Harley Street in a month's time.'

Just exactly where he wanted another dog, half-way between Ruby and Spots.

'I could look in tomorrow,' Bean said. 'About this time tomorrow?'

'Make it half an hour later.'

He'd enjoy himself all the more in Brighton if he knew he'd got six dogs to come back to. Six was a good round number, a number he should make a point of sticking with.

'Say nine o'clock then?'

272

'Nine will do very well.'

Bean switched off the television and went back to his packing. He always packed a little bit every night for a week before he went away and so made sure of not forgetting anything. But he left out the red baseball cap and the elephant T-shirt. He'd travel in those.

Chapter Twenty-Two

Another job for the old dog man. Putting it like that made Hob laugh. It didn't take much to make him laugh these days. And this would be the biggest job ever. The money on offer made him feel dizzy just to contemplate it. He saw it as putting an end for ever to all states; with such a huge sum states could be kept at bay indefinitely. He would always be as he had until now hardly ever been – the happy dancing joker, the Power Ranger, the laid-back man, the laughing man.

He'd come down very low: waited outside the women's toilet at Chester Road and when he'd seen a woman go in and had made sure she was alone in there, gone after her, found her washing her hands and while she screamed taken her handbag. Seventy pounds in cash. Everything else he'd left in the bag, and he'd put the bag on one of the seats so she'd be sure to find it. Coming home, the cash converted into crack, he'd unlocked his front door and stumbled into the hot darkness. Strips of light lay across the floorboards looking as if someone had drawn on them with orange chalk. At first he hadn't seen the note. It was a folded piece of paper, lying on the floor just inside the front door. An envelope was with it.

Hob wasn't much good at reading. Somehow he'd never got the hang of it and he was worse when in a state, as now. The note and the envelope on the floor beside him, he crumbled up one of his rocks and dropped it through the mouth of the watering can rose, then came the cap, the straws, the tin lid, finally the lighter applied to the perforations. He breathed in, a long hauling breath, as if his lungs were engines for dragging and tugging. The smoke in his windpipe felt like the first time he'd tasted ice cream.

Happy as the day is long, he was at his reading best. The envelope had a letter in it from the council, something about putting new windows in at nine am on the fifteenth and to be sure to be in to admit the operatives. Or that's what he thought it said. The note was from Carl, harder to read because it was in handwriting. He was to go up that evening and Carl might have something for him.

It was a long time since Hob had seen either Carl or Leo. He thought Leo had left and he wouldn't have been surprised if Carl had gone too, though where he couldn't begin to guess. No doubt he came back from time to time. Leo was going to die. You didn't have to be a doctor or have Carl's brains to know that. Hob got up and did a little dance, punched the air, sang one of his mum's nan's funny old songs and then he sang 'I'll be Your Sweetheart' and 'Night Train to Memphis' because he wasn't going to die, whatever might happen to Leo.

The mice must sleep in the daytime. He pictured them asleep behind the skirting board, looking like Jerry in the Tom and Jerry cartoon, or Mickey Mouse on his cushions, but furry and soft too. Maybe there were hundreds of them, curled up and cuddling each other. All that boarding up made the place airless but the kitchen smelt fresher than the rest of the flat. He took two Weetabix out of the packet and crumbled them up on the living room floor in front of the telly. The crumbling made him giggle because maybe the Weetabix was for the mice like crack was for him. Then he went upstairs.

It would have been too much to expect the lift to be working still. It wasn't. The stairs were nothing to him when he was well and he pranced lightly up the fourteen flights, making a noise about it presumably, because Carl must have heard him. He was standing there, holding the door open, looking as miserable as sin and his face as pale as Leo's.

'How's Leo doing, then?' Hob said, which he never would have if he hadn't been fit and raring to go.

Carl didn't answer, just shrugged and looked away. 'I'm going out,' he said. 'This won't take long. You can make two K out of it, which is the entire extent of my resources, all I've got till the week after next, rather.'

'Two *K*? You mean, two *grand*?'

'It's no use haggling because, as I said, it's all I've got.'

'I'm not haggling,' said Hob.

'And five hundred grams of E, so long as you'll take the yellows.'

'That's fine by me, Carl.'

Sweat was pouring off him. The medical book he'd been reading told him your sweat didn't smell so much when you got older, but Bean wasn't taking any chances. He'd had a horror of it all his life but his repugnance had increased after those beating sessions, when the house had been filled with the meaty, oniony stench, the result of wildly expended energy.

He had a shower, his second of the day, sprayed himself with deodorant and put on clean clothes: nicely pressed jeans, the elephant T-shirt and his red baseball cap. The T-shirt he'd give a quick rinse to when he got back and it would be dry by the morning, ready for the train.

276

They closed the Park at nine in August. That would just about allow him to walk to the top of Gloucester Place by way of the lake and the Kent Gate. He left home at eight-thirty. It was as warm and as humid as Florida, thought Bean, who had never been there.

The other route would have been shorter but there would have been all those roads to cross and all that traffic. The Park was peaceful and quiet, the lake glassy and the air thickening. When he looked up the darkening blue of the sky was fading under a veil of mist. A moon had risen, a pale oval, blurred and fuzzy, like the corpse of something that had long lain in muddy water.

All the birds had gone to roost. From a distance a black swan, sleeping on one leg with the other and its neck tucked into the plumage of its back, looked like a monstrous mushroom. Green- and chestnut-feathered ducks curled themselves up into silk cushions at the water's edge. But the coming dusk was robbing everything of colour, the grass turning grey, the water like black glass, the trees shapes and shadows rather than living things.

A beggar wandered towards him. He fancied it was the one who had asked him for money the day before, but now there was no one else about, they were alone, passing each other on the lake path, Bean looked the other way, pretending not to see him. You could never tell these days, who would turn out violent. Most vehicles were banned from the Park but a Royal Parks Constabulary police car went slowly past, the kind they called a lettuce sandwich because it was white with a dark green and light green stripe along its side.

To the left of him the Turkish domes of Sussex Place gleamed like an encampment of tents at dawn. The boats were all tied up to the island in the middle of the Hanover pond, bobbing gently on the water. He glanced up that way because he could never pass it without remembering Mussolini, so when he turned back and began to cross the grass towards the gate and saw Mussolini approaching him under the trees he refused to believe his eyes. He actually rubbed his eyes, as if stimulating them to see straight.

It was as if Mussolini had been waiting for him. He wasn't going anywhere; he'd just been standing there, what the police called loitering. Bean could see the street lamps in the Outer Circle. There were people walking up there, traffic heading up to the Macclesfield Bridge. He turned his eyes on Mussolini, making out his pudgy features, skinny body and filthy old clothes in the warm gloom.

'You took your time,' Bean said.

Mussolini was wrapped up for such a hot night, wearing the sort of layers, dark matted rags, favoured by the beggars. He was chewing something and Bean didn't think it was gum. Whatever it was, he eased it into the corner of his mouth, pushing it with his tongue.

'You was late,' he said. 'You dropped me in the shit.'

'That may be but it's you that's too late now. The job I wanted, someone else did it. And a bit more thoroughly than what I bargained for.'

'Could be another job,' said Mussolini. 'There's always jobs folks want doing.'

Bean shrugged. He had lingered for a moment but now he began walking on towards the gate, a wide gate with maybe twenty-five spikes on its railings. Mussolini had got into step beside him and Bean was quickly aware of his smell. Not the cooking smell of fresh sweat but of dirt ingrained, unwashed clothes, the excrement of vermin, the acrid coldness of chemicals. He tried to draw himself aside, but Mussolini was close now, his head bent down to Bean's lesser height, peering at Bean's chest.

'Dig your elephants,' he said, and then he said, 'Jumbo, jumbo,' and started laughing. 'Jumbo, jumbo.'

His laughter made an eerie manic sound in the silence of the Park.

Chapter Twenty-Three

Park Road runs northwards on the western side of the Park from the top of Baker Street to the junction of St John's Wood Road and Prince Albert Road and communicates with the Outer Circle by means of the Hanover Gate and Kent Passage. The London Mosque is in Park Road. So are the Rudolph Steiner House, a defunct pub called the Windsor Castle, Dillon's Business Bookshop and a number of Indian restaurants. There are sandwich bars and a wine bar and a fur shop where no one ever seems to buy anything.

The bookshop is so situated for its proximity to the London School of Business Studies, a graduate school housed in Decimus Burton's most spectacular of all the Park terraces, at Sussex Place. This is on the Outer Circle, an amazing range of Corinthian columns, polygonal bays and cuboid domes, so light and airy that they might be tents of silk rather than towers of stone. Graduate students in need of books need not walk all the way down to Baker Street and up Park Road to reach the shop but may turn left out of the terrace and, once past the College of Obstetrics and Gynaecology, find the opening to an alley called Kent Passage.

The passage is narrow and long and absolutely straight, tree-shaded and confined by high hedges behind chain-link fencing, not railings. On the southern side it is overshadowed by the pale brick walls of the Royal College of Obstetricians and Gynaecologists. The trees and shrubs which grow along its length are planes and sumachs, strawberries and the Rose of Sharon. Near the Park Road end the passage opens out into an oval shape, closes again, and the pavement of the wider thoroughfare is reached. The bookshop is a few paces to the left while on the right lies the Kent Terrace.

This is the only terrace not to face on to the Outer Circle, a plain range of buildings with Ionic columns. Anthony Maddox once told Bean that the terrace had been built in 1827 and named for George IV's brother, the Duke of Kent, but the Duke, as well as being the parent of the Heir Presumptive to the throne, was long dead by then, so there was no need for too much grandeur or originality. Bean thought this was said spitefully, for his resemblance to the Duke's statue had already been pointed out, but he never passed the terrace without thinking of what had been said and wondering if malice was intended.

The Kent Terrace, however, has one peculiarity. As well as the usual black iron railings, a feature of the place is the spikes adorning the tops of the pillars in its grounds.

A pair of these pillars flank the gate that leads into Kent Passage and the steps down into Kent Passage. These are man height, cuboid and very solid, and from the tops of both sprout five iron branches in a cluster, each one terminating in five spikes. They look rather like bunches of thorn twigs, but ugly and menacing too, and it would be hard to say what purpose they were intended for or what was in the designer's mind.

A man's body was impaled on these iron thorns.

It was so arranged as to be invisible from Kent Passage unless you happened to be looking at the sky, and visible from the terrace only if you peered behind the pillar. Besides, a heavy mist had hung over the Park and its environs since dawn, obscuring even those objects that were near at hand in swathes of white vapour.

The body was supported in its position by the splayed spikes penetrating its chest, head lolling forward, arms dangling, legs hanging. Barefoot, dressed in jeans with ragged hems and missing knees, torn grey T-shirt with washed out black logo and a dark red cardigan that was stiff with food stains and blood, it had once been a smallish man. The legs and arms were thin, the white feet pathetic. No doubt its total weight amounted to no more than nine stone. Even so, to lift it up so high must have taken considerable strength.

A great many people passed it during the morning. None of them looked up to the height of the pillar. Even after the mist had gone and the sun come out, the body was not discovered until noon. A police officer on the beat entered the passage from the Outer Circle. First he had walked round the pond where the pleasure boats were moored, crossed the yellowing balding grass and left the Park by the Hanover Gate. His eye had been on a dosser in camouflage pants and grey vest who was fumbling in a litter bin suspiciously close to a parked car whose windows had been left open.

The policeman lingered, watching until the dosser, having found the remains of a takeaway in the bin, shambled off northwards towards the Macclesfield Bridge. Then he stepped into the passage and strolled slowly along it. Someone shook a duster out of one of the high windows in the building on the left. The passage was in deep shade for three-quarters of its length and there the sun came through the leaves, making a dappled pattern, before there were no more leaves but only a sunlit space.

On to this space fell a shadow.

It was like a crab or part of a crab or perhaps it was like a paw, the extended limb of a frog. He looked up. The body hung like a sack in clothes or a guy, limp and slack, and its hanging hand had a trail of blood dried between the fingers.

Chapter Twenty-Four

Dill and the beagle were sitting on one of the seats on the southwest side of the lake, watching an old woman in a tracksuit feeding the geese. There were not so many geese as a year ago and the story was that the street sleepers were catching them to kill and roast over fires on the canal bank. Dill always talked to the beagle as if it were a person. He said that much as he'd like to taste roast goose, for he never had tasted it, he wouldn't know how to go about catching a goose, let alone killing it. And how would you get the feathers out? And the innards? He was talking like this about a goose to stop himself shaking with fear about the dead man.

The beagle's tail started to wag, thumping on the slats of the seat. Roman patted its head, stroked it, sat down next to Dill and Dill told him the goose story just as he had told it to the beagle a moment before. But it no longer had the power to stop Dill shivering.

'What's wrong?' Roman said. 'There's been another, hasn't there? Is that it?'

'The fuzz had me in, mate. They had me look at him.'

'To identify him?'

Dill nodded. He held on to the beagle's collar to steady his hands. 'They said they'd seen me with him but they never had.' He looked up, turning his head in a crooked cautious way. His oriental eyes were puffy as if he had been crying.

'They was OK,' he said. 'They didn't hurt me.'

'What happened?'

'I went in this place.' He wrinkled up his nose. 'There was this geyser lifted up a sheet and showed me what was under. It was just a dead face, mate, you couldn't see no cuts. I didn't know him. I'd never seen him before. They said was I sure and then the geyser put the sheet back. They was OK. There was one geyser give the beagle a bun.'

'Maybe it was one of the jacks men,' said Roman.

'I don't reckon. I don't know what to think, mate. I reckoned I knew every geyser up here. You ever seen a dead person, Rome?'

'My mother.' Sally and his children, but he didn't mention them. Daniel's face had been cut to pieces. 'I saw my mother.'

'Do they always look like they're made of wax? Like they've never been alive?'

'I don't know. You're sleeping at St Anthony's, aren't you, Dill?'

'They won't let me take the beagle. What am I supposed to do about the beagle?'

Roman walked on towards the Clarence Gate. The flowerbeds and the grass here were covered in a soft grey quilt of goose down. Goose feathers floated on to the petals of flowers. He bought a paper at a newsagent's at the top of Baker Street. The front page and four inside pages were devoted to the murder and the two previous murders. On the front page was a four-column spread photograph of a stretch of railings, purporting to be but perhaps not those on which the body had been found; black spiked railings with grass behind and trees shapeless in the thinning mist. Inside were more photographs: Cahill's and Clancy's, more pictures of Park railings and one of a group of jacks men sitting or standing about on the canal bank.

The body was understood to be that of a man in 'late middle age', whatever that meant, of no fixed address. He had not yet been identified. The pockets of his jeans and cardigan were empty. His feet had been bare. The police wanted help from the public in their enquiries . . .

Roman decided not to go away this time. He would stay and sooner or later they would question him. They would question every dosser in the vicinity of the Park, in the whole of London probably. He would stay, do his best to answer their questions, be a good citizen. It was all part of the way his life was changing, turning back on itself, turning him back into something like what he once was.

Blue and white tape printed with the words *Police Do Not Cross* made a flimsy but deterrent boundary around the sturdy column and its crest of spikes. The Kent Terrace looked livelier than usual, most of its windows wide open and from time to time heads poking out. But if there had ever been a crowd waiting and hoping for new sights as when Pharaoh's body was found, there was none here. A uniformed policeman strolled about on the forecourt.

In Park Road the traffic kept up its customary steady roar. Veiled women, men in pairs, snowy-shirted, chatting animatedly to each other, never to the women, made their way up to the Mosque. Roman had come up there because he was interested by descriptions of the column he kept hearing about but which he had never yet seen.

A dark trickle, the colour of burnt umber, ran tear-like down the cream stucco from the roots of the spikes.

'It's not what you're thinking,' the policeman said. 'It's rust.'

'Some strength was needed to hoist a body up there. Was he on the top?'

'It's all been in the papers, mate,' said the policeman, and he turned away, discreet or perhaps only bored.

Next day, by chance, they asked him to come to the police station and talked to him exhaustively about the inhabitants of the Park environs, growing more and more mystified, he thought, by his manner and his accent.

When they asked him if he would accompany them to the mortuary and attempt to identify the latest murder victim, he said, 'Certainly. If you wish it.'

The sergeant – he didn't merit an officer of higher rank – gave him a look and the detective constable with him a look, and if he didn't quite cast up his eyes he sketched the gesture. Roman was taken to the mortuary by car. He could tell the two policemen expected him to smell, were all prepared to go through pantomimes of flinching, shifting their seats and opening windows, and when they found him inoffensive were almost disappointed.

The body was covered by a green plastic sheet. Roman remembered what Dill had said about waxiness. He thought of carvings he had seen out of soapstone or white jade. The face could have belonged to a man of any age over, say, forty. It was somewhat Hanoverian with small mouth and full cheeks and although he could not identify it, he thought he had seen this man somewhere before.

That was all he could tell the sergeant.

'You know him but you don't know who he is?'

'I wouldn't say I knew him but I've seen him before.'

'Where would that be?'

'In the Park, I expect. I spend my life in the Park.'

The sergeant finally asked him what a man like him was doing on the street.

'I prefer it,' Roman said, not wanting to go into the events of his private life. 'It suits me.'

'Some sort of eccentric, are you?'

'Perhaps.'

He resisted asking permission to go but sat in the open-plan office waiting while the sergeant fiddled with papers, giving him from time to time meaningful looks. Once, in such a place, Roman would have been tense and self-conscious, searching his mind for minor motoring offences he might have committed, but now he felt nothing beyond a mild boredom.

The sergeant said, 'That's it then. You can go,' and he added, perhaps unable to resist, 'You want to get yourself together, pull your socks up, put a roof over your head. The street's no place for your sort, as you must know.'

Roman nodded. He walked out and no one tried to stop him. The Grotto, where he returned, had been scoured clean of litter by the police. They had done a better job than he had ever been able to do, taking away every scrap of paper and shred of rag in their search for evidence. His barrow had gone, stolen probably, not taken by them.

It was hot and close, the abode of flying insects. They swarmed above the pool in which the water was no longer clear and fresh but coated in scum. He sat down on the dry ground in the dusty shade. Soon he would have to go out, up into Camden Town, and replace the contents of the barrow. Buy second-hand clothes, another groundsheet, more blankets, a water bottle, and a host of other things. It seemed to him a foolish exercise, absurd, because he *could* buy them – he could within reason buy anything he wanted.

The sergeant's comments only reiterated what he had himself been thinking. What he had done had served its purpose but had now become artificial, a quixotic slumming, and to continue it was self-indulgence.

The real courage would lie in returning to the world.

Leo spent every evening with her but not the nights. He gave as his reason the one they had used before, that Charlotte Cottage was the Blackburn-Norrises' home. So in the mornings she was alone and she took Gushi out alone. He missed his companions and, spoilt baby that he was, often plumped down on the grass like a cushion of chrysanthemums and refused to move. She carried him home, a furry muff in the August heat.

But in the evenings, when Leo came, they walked him together. Leo's mood alternated between a kind of sorrowful brooding and an almost manic brightness. He was going to turn these obligatory walks into adventures, he said, and announced his intention of running to earth Mrs Sellers and Spots.

He even went up to one woman exercising a spotted dog of dubious provenance. 'Did my fiancée give your dalmatian a reference?' he asked her.

She looked panic-stricken and backed away. Another dog-owner, faced with the same enquiry, pointed towards the Inner Circle and asked Leo if he knew there was a police station down there. Mary was amused, then embarrassed. On their way back to Park Village she again asked him what was wrong.

'Are you worried about getting married?'

'That's the last thing I'm worried about. Marrying you is what I want more than anything in the world.'

'Then what is the first thing you're worried about?' she asked him gently.

'Death,' he said and burst into shrill laughter.

Once they were inside the house he began kissing her. He kissed her mouth and her throat and drawing open her shirt, kissed her breasts. She was not used to passion from Leo, rather to something more controlled and gentle, but she responded eagerly. It was as if this was what had always been missing between them.

He whispered, 'Not upstairs, in here,' and pulling her into the living room, kicked the door shut behind him.

Once before, in here, he had held her, both of them kneeling, and asked her to marry him. Now he began to make love to her as if it was the first time. Her whole body seemed to melt into a warm languid liquefaction. He was no longer light and phantom-like but strong and urgent, his mouth holding hers and his arms wound tightly round her. The phone ringing made her cry out in protest at a cruel interruption.

Leo cursed. 'Leave it. Don't answer it.'

She simply shook her head, unable to speak. The ringing went on interminably. They listened to it, stilled and motionless. When it stopped, Leo stroked her hair, her shoulders, turned her on her side and entered her like that, a hand clasping each breast. She gave a clear cry of pleasure, arching her back as he let out a long sigh.

A little before ten he left her to go home to Primrose Hill. They had sat for the rest of the evening with their arms round each other, talking about the future, where they would live. His earlier wildness had been displaced by calm and, she thought, hope. After he had gone she took Gushi on to her lap and fondled him, doing her best not to resent the little dog whose presence stopped her returning with Leo.

Bean would be back from his holiday and in the morning would be at the door as usual at eight-fifteen. The phone rang again as she was watching ITN's ten o'clock news. She turned off the television and picked up the receiver. Alistair's baritone sounded deeper and smoother than usual. The sound of it made her brace herself, her body tensing after the long relaxation of the evening.

'I phoned you earlier,' he said and his tone was accusing, admonitory.

She and Leo had sometimes laughed together about those people who apparently expect you to be sitting close by the phone all day, waiting for their call. She decided not to placate him.

'Yes, I heard it ring. I didn't answer it. I was – occupied.'

'Don't you think it rather irresponsible not to answer the phone? It could be something serious. It could be an accident to someone close to you.'

'Now my grandmother is dead,' she said quietly, 'I have no one close to me except Leo and he was with me.' It was true and her solitariness struck her forcibly as she said it. Dorothea and her cousin she was fond of but really there was only Leo. She breathed in. 'You got my letter, Alistair?'

'That, of course, is why I am phoning. At last, you might say. I've taken my time, haven't I? It was a blow, Mary, it was a heavy blow.'

What could she say? Not that she was sorry, certainly not that. 'Sooner or later there was bound to be someone. There will be for you.'

He didn't like that. 'In your case it was rather sooner than later, wasn't it? As to someone for me, as you put it in your romantic way, don't imagine I've been celibate since you left. I'm hardly that kind of man.'

She didn't believe him. She didn't care. He made it

impossible to resist some kind of apology. 'I'm sorry if I've hurt you.'

It was as if she hadn't spoken. 'I had better get to my reason for phoning. You've rather distracted me from the point. As a civilised man, I wanted to congratulate you. I hope you'll be very happy.'

'Thank you. That's very nice of you, Alistair.'

'And to tell you that I've got something for you. A wedding present.'

She was astonished. 'You're giving me a wedding present?'

'Is that so strange? Didn't you say to me a few weeks ago before you so inexplicably ran away from me that in the time-honoured cliché you hoped we could be friends?'

'Of course I hope that. I didn't think you wanted it.'

'Mary,' he said, 'I have a wedding present for you. Don't tell me to send it, please. I want to put it into your hands.'

She found herself passionately not wanting to see him, have him come there, spoil her weekend with Leo. Just waiting for his arrival, fearing what he might do, would make her apprehensive for hours. She remembered that evening when Bean had arrived unexpectedly and before Leo answered the door she had assumed it was Alistair.

'Monday,' she said reluctantly. 'Would Monday be all right?' Not here, though. 'Would you come to the museum on your way home from work? We could have tea or a drink.'

'You won't run away from me again, will you?'

It was chilling the amount of venom he could put into those innocuous words. Her usual urge to be conciliatory came, departed, driven away by rising anger.

'I've said I'll meet you, Alistair. It will be the last time.'

His barrow gone, the Grotto trampled by police and no longer a desirable home, Roman set off to find another place in which to spend the night. All his possessions were in a rucksack he had bought, blue plastic, very cheap, but still plainly new and costing money. Every step he now took seemed to be leading him inexorably back into the world.

Some people were having a party on one of the houseboats in Cumberland Basin. He paused on the bridge and looked down at them. They were young. One of the men was naked to the waist; a woman was holding up a frothing bottle of champagne; another had a guitar from which she plucked dull reverberating notes. A young girl, holding her glass out to be filled, saw him and waved. Nothing could have made him so certain that his shedding of the street was apparent.

St Mark's Church in Albert Road on the fringe of Primrose Hill was a grim neo-Gothic place, the kind of building that made him wonder why the Victorians wanted to revive in their places of worship the creepy and sinister elements of mediaeval architecture. Its gate and its doors were painted sky blue, an incongruous colour perhaps used to soften the grim effect. A garden rather than a graveyard surrounded it, a place of late-summer blooming shrubs and fluff-headed thistles. He crossed the road over the water, for here the canal turned northwards in its passage up to Camden Lock. The place where he stood was called the Water Meeting Bridge.

A green rectangle on the bridge contained a gold shield bearing the legend, *With Wisdom and Courage*. These were qualities he needed and would have liked to have. And perhaps he had more of them now than ever in the past. On the parapet he looked along the canal to the next bridge. Between the two bridges grass and weeds reached to the edge of the tow-path and the churchyard trees overhung it.

He turned into St Mark's Square, then into Regent's Park Road where the other bridge was. It was with a little thrill of dismay that he noted the row of spiked railings at the chancel end of the church, another set serving as balusters up the steps to what was perhaps a vestry door. Someone had tied a bunch of coloured balloons to one of the spikes. There must have been a children's party. Thinking of Daniel, who had liked balloons but hated the noise they made when burst, he opened the gate into the garden and walked along the path.

White Japanese anemones gleamed in the dusk. The place was alive with mosquitoes and all those cousins of mosquitoes that are smaller but sometimes fiercer, midges, gnats. They danced on the warm air. A bat swooped, then another. He remembered Sally's fear of bats, her curious superstition, the only one she had, that bats had a predilection to get in women's hair and bite their scalps. He didn't mind bats but the mosquitoes in their dense concentration would be unbearable.

There were no gravestones. He wondered why not. Where they might have been were green garden seats, enough to seat a dozen people. Nothing lay below him but the trees and snowberry bushes and long grass descending to meet the path and the dark yellow water. Chain-link fencing made a formidable barrier between the fringes of the garden and the canal bank, but it was climbable. He scrambled over, his sights on the other bridge, a sheltered place. Street sleepers traditionally made their beds under bridges – wasn't there a song about it? A Merle

Haggard song about making a kingdom under the bridges?

He dropped down on to the path. It was starting to get dark, a light up on the bridge reflected in the oily water. A tubular metal rail offered some sort of security to those going too near the edge under the bridge. The light gleamed on its silvery surfaces. He was only a few yards away when he saw that the area under the brown brickwork already had an occupant. Street people, no matter what they wear, or what they started off wearing, always seem to be dressed in darkness. They are blackened, everything muted by time and dirt to the colour of shadows, so that when seen from a distance a group of them look like figures in bronze.

In his early days on the street, Roman had once been no different; this man was no different. He was an incarnation of dirt, a bundling and layering on this warm night of dark greasy rags, string-tied, his skin much the same colour as the shred of cloth round his neck, as his cracked boots. His face peered out from between the knotted neckcloth and his battered hat, a face dark as a black man's but sickle-shaped in profile, with a long hooked nose and rough pitted skin.

He might have spoken when he saw Roman; he might have recognised him as belonging to the same kind, but he didn't. Roman was very aware in that moment of his own cleanness, his washed clothes, some replaced and new, his new backpack. He wanted to laugh when the man under the bridge scowled at him and made a gesture of dismissal, shaking his fist. What did he think he was? Some tourist who had lost his way? But he understood. He looked like that tourist, he had indeed lost his way, and now had only the tourist's recourse.

'OK,' he said. 'I won't disturb you. Goodnight.'

It was the final sign. He climbed up the bank again, over the fence into the churchyard, left by the blue gate, and set off to walk up to Camden Town where, in his new respectable guise, one of the cheap hotels would give him a bed for the night.

Chapter Twenty-Five

When it was eight-thirty and still Bean hadn't come, she took Gushi into the Park herself. It was already very warm. The grass was soaked and beaded with dew. Not a breath of wind stirred the trees, their foliage pendulous and dripping off the branches as if composed of some thick viscous fluid. The sun that was turning lawns and flowerbeds and greensward into a desert seemed burning on her arms and face.

She walked across the Broad Walk, past the restaurant and over the Long Bridge. Gnats had already begun their dance above the scummy brown water. Once, when she first came here, the uneven juxtaposition of the Outer and Inner Circles had confused her and she had been inclined to lose herself in the flower gardens. But now she could have drawn a plan of the Park with her eyes shut. She turned left along the path opposite the back of the theatre, meeting and passing a woman she had never seen before but whose dog Gushi evidently knew well.

The scottie and he encountered each other nose-to-nose, tails wagging, then noses were inserted under tails. The two of them began a play fight, growling, rolling over in the grass. The woman turned back, smiling tentatively. Mary remembered that she had seen this jaunty little black dog among the others tied to the gatepost of Charlotte Cottage.

The woman didn't introduce herself even when

Mary said who she was. 'That bloody Bean has let us all down again.'

'I thought perhaps I'd got the date wrong,' Mary said.

'Oh, no. He was due this morning. Too nice down by the seaside, I expect. He'll be back tomorrow with his tail between his legs.'

The metaphor was so unconsciously appropriate that Mary wanted to giggle but she controlled herself. She called Gushi, eventually had to drag him away, and passed on along the path without learning McBride's owner's name. Back in the Park, on her way to the Irene Adler, it was far hotter. The blue sky was already whitening and the air thick with humidity. The zoo animals she passed seemed to feel the heat no more than the cold but to lumber and munch placidly, bent solely on the getting of food. Up in Albert Road there was a smell of diesel and exhaust, a hot bitter stench. She could see a bevy of street people stretched out on the grass in the church gardens. They could have been taken for sunbathers except for the rags that still covered every inch of them but for stricken faces and coarsened hands.

Dorothea said to take the whole of next week off – why not? Gordon would take over. She should have a whole free week for her wedding. But Mary remembered that Alistair was coming on Monday to bring his mysterious wedding present and she could see that changing this arrangement might lead to terrible difficulties. And she didn't exactly have a lot of preparations to make for the wedding, anyway. So she said she would take from Wednesday morning off if that was all right with Dorothea and Gordon.

'Go home early this afternoon then,' Dorothea said. 'Nobody's going to come looking at corsets and crinolines on a day like this.'

And remarkably few did. Mary was home again

by four, in time for Bean's arrival at a quarter past. But again Bean didn't come. She waited for half an hour and then she dialled his number in York Terrace. No reply. Leo arrived just after five and they sat outside in the shade, drinking tea and then sharing a bottle of wine. The garden was full of brown and orange butterflies and little coppery-winged moths. Gushi lay under a lilac bush, puffing showily, his tongue hanging out.

Leo remembered the name of Spots's owner and they found her in the phone book. But Mrs Sellers hadn't seen Bean for a week or heard from him. Mary and Leo took Gushi out themselves when it was cooler, though it was not very cool. As they walked back, arms round each other's waists, he asked her to come back to Edis Street with him for the night. But if she did that she wouldn't be here for Bean in the morning, and she was sure Bean would be here in the morning. Leo didn't argue. He kissed her and said he would be back in Charlotte Cottage before she woke up. He would come quietly into the house and if she would like that, to bed with her.

'I'd like that,' she said, smiling.

She overslept. She was lying sleepily in Leo's arms, having made leisurely, half-awake love with him, their bodies naked and damp, cooled by sweat, when at last she looked at the clock. It was almost nine.

Bean hadn't come. He had a way of thrusting his fist at the bell and pushing with all his body weight behind it, keeping it there until someone answered. She would have heard. He would have seen to it that she had heard.

She put on a robe and went downstairs. Leo had picked the post up from the doormat when he came in and left it on the hall table for her. The letter postmarked Cape Cod was from the Blackburn-Norrises and announced their return rather earlier than expected. They would arrive back in London on 19 August.

She made Leo tea, took it up and showed him the letter. 'The order of release.'

'I thought it might be,' Leo said. 'You can come and live with your husband a mere two days after we're married.'

For an hour or so it distracted her from the problem of Bean. But at ten-thirty she phoned Mrs Sellers, who hadn't seen him, and then, on the number Mrs Sellers gave her, the actress Lisl Pring. Lisl wasn't just annoyed, she was worried. The chocolate poodle Marietta was all right – Lisl's boyfriend took her out twice a day trotting behind his bicycle. It was doing wonders for his figure and he didn't mind how long it went on. But what had happened to Bean? He would never absent himself like this unless he was at death's door. She gave Mary the names of Bean's other clients.

Mary and Leo took Gushi out. It was too hot to go far. Gushi drank nearly a pint of water when he got back and returned to lie under the lilac bush. After she had called Express Tikka and ordered a *thali* each for their lunch with pickles and *nan* she phoned Erna Morosini.

No, it wasn't her that Mary had encountered in the Park the previous morning. Her dog wasn't a scottie.

'Mine's the sexy beagle,' said Mrs Morosini. 'You must know the one. My partner says I ought to have her doctored but I'm still hoping for pups one day.'

'Bean ...' Mary began but Mrs Morosini cut her short.

'Oh, yes, he's disappeared, hasn't he? He left me his Brighton number, I insisted, and I've called it and talked to his sister. She hasn't seen hair or hide of him. Well, she only came back herself yesterday but there's not a sniff of him in the place.'

300

As if Bean was a terrier that had turned himself into a stray, as if he had run off and would turn up without his collar and with his ear bleeding.

Their lunch came just before one, brought in the red and white van by the man who had removed his chef's hat and was wearing nothing but shorts and a red and white vest. Their *thalis* were eaten outside in the shade of the laburnum and the Japanese cherry and all was peaceful until Leo produced their dessert of raspberries and nectarines. Then wasps drove them indoors. They put Gushi in the coolest place, on a window-seat in the north-facing bedroom. Mary hadn't asked how they should spend the afternoon but Leo anticipated the question. He pulled her down on to the bed.

'Let's not go downstairs again.'

When the gates had only been open for an hour and before the heat mounted, they took the dog into the Park. A marathon was being run. Round the Outer Circle, in at Chester Road, round a segment of the Inner Circle, out at York Bridge and round the Outer Circle again. Then repeat – twice? Three times? The runners were all male, all thin, their faces contorted with effort or agony. Their T-shirts, clinging to bony chests, were as wet as when taken dripping from the wash.

Leo said they made him feel tired. They made him feel ill.

She looked anxiously into his face. 'You're all right, aren't you? All this walking isn't too much for you?'

'It's vicarious,' he laughed. 'I'm feeling it for *them*.'

But as they walked back, arms round each other, hip to hip, she thought back to the transplant and had the strange feeling that it was ongoing, continuous, that when they were together like this or in bed side by side, the flow of strength from her still proceeded into him, like an injection of some serum into a permanently open vein. She leant across and kissed his cheek and felt the arm around her tighten and his hand caress her waist.

'If Bean comes now we shall have to send him away empty-handed,' Leo said when they were back in the house and Gushi was stretched out exhausted on the kitchen floor. 'But I don't think he will come, do you?'

'No, I don't. You know, Leo, he could be in that house of his, collapsed, dead. I don't suppose anyone has gone to see. He's an old man, older than he looks.'

'He's a bit over seventy.'

Mary stared at him. 'How do you know?'

'How do I know? Let's see – he must have told me that night he came here for the reference. Look at me, Mary. Do you like Bean?'

'Like him? I haven't thought about it. No, as a matter of fact I don't. I don't like him a bit.'

'That's all right then. You can stop worrying about him. Forget him.'

Leo went out to buy the Sunday papers. They looked through the property pages for likely houses in St John's Wood and Hampstead and Leo even called one of the numbers given in the small ads but no one answered the phone. Bean hadn't come. Just before lunch Lisl Pring phoned, enthusing about a new dog-walker she had found. A woman called Amelia Walker – Walker the walker, wasn't that hilarious?

Mary thanked her but said she could hardly entrust Gushi to the care of someone unknown to his owners. For the time being she would go on taking him out herself. Leo said it was too hot to do anything but rest and the bed was more comfortable

302

than the Blackburn-Norrises' sofa. The temperature climbed to ninety degrees.

'Why do they always give shade temperatures?' he wanted to know. 'It's so cautious and petty. Why not what it is in the sun? It'll be a hundred and five in the sun.'

'I suppose because the sun isn't always shining.'

'My love, you sound so sad – don't be sad.'

'All right,' she said. 'All right, I won't.'

They made slippery love, their bodies closing together and withdrawing from each other with soft sucking sounds. Sweat became another amorous secretion, thinner and colder, strongly saline. She tasted his salt on her tongue and felt the faint sting of it in her eyes. They fell lightly asleep, wet palms clasped against the wet skin of belly and shoulder. A river flowed between her breasts.

The windows were wide open but no wind moved the heavily hanging drawn curtains. A bumble bee's throbbing buzz, alternately terrified and reassured, awoke her. She lay watching it until at last it found a way to freedom through where the curtains met. Leo slept on. She got up, had a shower, and came back into the bedroom wrapped in a bathtowel. What she saw made her gasp. Tears were running down Leo's sleeping face. They were not perspiration but real tears. He was crying in his sleep.

She knew she must tell him about this, must ask him, but she postponed asking him. He seemed so happy when he got up, suggesting they go out to eat somewhere when it was late, when the warm dusk was giving way to dark. What about that little Italian restaurant they had gone to the first time, the day after they first met?

In the meantime Gushi must be walked. It was too hot to go far. The people in the Park were mostly prone, sprawled on the yellowed grass.

303

'They look dead,' said Leo. 'They look like bodies after the battle is over.'

It was an opportunity. She spoke gently, lovingly. 'Why do you cry in your sleep, Leo? Your face was wet with tears.'

'Wet with sweat,' he said lightly and quickly.

If he had been a frightened child her voice could hardly have been more tender. 'It was tears, my love. You were crying. Really.'

'I had a bad dream. We all do sometimes.'

'It must have been a very unhappy dream.'

He refused to say any more but began instead to talk about people who lay in the sun, about sunbathing being a mid-twentieth century fad that would disappear as fast as it had become fashionable. They put Gushi on the lead and walked back, past the children's playground to the Gloucester Gate. A police car was parked outside Charlotte Cottage. The officers had left the car and sought the shade of the porch. When Mary and Leo came up to the door the elder of them produced a warrant card.

'Detective Inspector Marnock.'

The other man, the sergeant, muttered a name Mary couldn't catch. 'May we come in?'

It was Leo who said, 'What's this about?'

'And you are, sir?'

'Leo Nash.'

'Well, Mr Nash, it's about Leslie Bean. You know a man called Leslie Bean?'

Mary's hand tightened on Leo's arm. 'What's happened to him?'

They were all in the living room. Gushi, a hot bundle of fur, jumped for the sergeant's lap and lay there, gazing into a not very prepossessing face with slavish worship.

'Can you tell us what's happened to him?' Leo said.

'Perhaps. With your help. And yours, Miss Jago. I understand you knew him. He walked your dog. You saw him frequently?'

'Yes. Every day.'

'So you would recognise him?'

'Of course I would.'

She had the feeling that Marnock was struggling with an inhibition on saying too much to the public. It would be ingrained in him to say, 'That I am not at liberty to tell you' or 'We can't answer that', but he was plainly making up his mind how much he could reveal without total indiscretion, and how much he must reveal in order to gain their compliance.

'A Miss Bean has contacted us to report her brother as a missing person. He has not been seen since the evening of Friday the fourth.'

'And?' Leo said sharply.

'On Saturday the fifth the body of an unidentified man was found in the vicinity of the Kent Terrace.'

'But that was one of the street people,' Mary said.

'We thought so at first. We haven't for some days. You don't want to believe everything you read in the papers. Nor do we think this was the work of the man the tabloid press calls the Impaler.'

'But why not?'

'That,' said the sergeant when Marnock hesitated, 'we are not at liberty to tell you.' Evidently a dog lover, he fondled Gushi's ears.

'The clothes on the body weren't his own. They were put on him after he was dead.'

'As some sort of joke, no doubt,' said Marnock. 'Psychopaths can have an unfortunate sense of humour. Now, Miss Jago, Mr Nash, we've been unprecedentedly frank and open with you. For a reason, of course. We want you to do us a favour. Mr Bean's other lady clients feel a natural distaste . . .'

'For what?' said Leo.

305

'For identifying the body, sir.'

Horrified, Mary said, 'Surely his sister could do that!'

'She's eighty years old,' said the sergeant. 'Besides, she hasn't seen him in twenty-five years.' Suddenly more confiding, he gave a little laugh. 'Oh, yes, we know it's peculiar. It's that all right. He stopped in her house while she was away and left before she got back. Every year. Year in and year out. They'd not set eyes on each other for as you might say a quarter of a century.'

They both went.

Inside the mortuary it was cold and there was a strong icy smell. Mary thought it must be the smell of death, of decomposition impossible to mask, but Leo told her it was formaldehyde.

She was there to identify, if she could, the body; Leo to support and comfort her. He had only once seen Bean, and that briefly, in the evening, by artificial light.

The bodies were in drawers, green metal, like filing cabinets. It seemed to her a dreadful depository of a man's life, even though it was not a final resting place. One of the drawers was pulled open and a plastic sheet lifted.

She had expected to feel violent shock and revulsion and had tried to prepare herself all the way here, but when she looked on the face it was calmly and with no particular feeling. The dead man was Bean, there could be no doubt, but it looked more like a waxwork of Bean from Madame Tussaud's. This sculpted head and rigid face seemed as if they had never been alive but had been cast in this shape and turned out of a mould.

'Yes,' she said. 'That is – is Mr Bean.'

'Quite sure, Miss Jago?'

Had she sounded dubious? Impossible to explain to this policeman the awe death induced in this pitiful place, the wonder she felt at what man came to at the last, an effigy in a metal drawer.

'I am quite sure,' she said.

It had shaken them both. She and Leo were subdued, refusing the policeman's offer of a lift home, needing to be away from the police and talk of dead Bean. They would make their own way back. All ideas of revisiting that little Italian restaurant were abandoned, for Mary didn't feel like eating. They walked, hand-in-hand, sometimes giving each other rueful glances, until Leo said:

'Smile. Please. For me. You were wonderful in there. Cool as a cucumber. Why are cucumbers cool, anyway? They are. We all know that. But why are they, when marrows aren't and melons aren't?'

'You'll have to ask a botanist or a vegetable gardener.'

'The tiresome thing about all this for me is that I have to go to a funeral tomorrow.'

She turned to him, distracted by this flat statement where none of his attempts at distraction could succeed. 'You didn't tell me.'

'No. It's an old friend of my family's. A bore – I mean the funeral is, not the friend was.'

He said no more until they were in the house. She noticed that his eyes were puffy as if he had been suppressing tears. His voice had a ragged sound.

'The funeral is in the afternoon. My mother will be there and I'll have to go back with her afterwards. I probably won't see you all day.'

'Leo, if your mother is in London, can't I meet her? And wouldn't she come to our wedding?'

He beckoned her to him, took her face gently in his hands.

'You're so beautiful. I shall never tire of looking at

307

your face. Never a day goes by when I don't want to gaze and gaze at you.'

She smiled. 'I asked you about your mother.'

'I'm leaving my family behind after tomorrow. I'll say goodbye to them then. They won't know it's for the last time but it will be.' She knelt down in front of his chair and he bent forward to put his arms round her. 'So I'm not going home tonight. Wild horses couldn't drag me home.'

'We won't let the wild horses try,' she said.

Chapter Twenty-Six

That night he again cried in his sleep. He made no sound but when he turned his face to meet hers the wetness touched her cheek. It was dawn and she could just see. The tears glistened.

In the morning he was up before her, bringing her tea in bed and the post, the newspaper, more fliers, a tax demand for Sir Stewart Blackburn-Norris, hire car cards. He was so cheerful, pulling rueful faces but making light of the ordeal ahead, that she decided to say nothing. His intention to wear a dark suit for the funeral pleased her, for it was in accordance with her own ideas of what was decorous and civilised.

Still he was unwilling to talk about the funeral, who this family friend was, why his mother would be there. It made her wonder if it was for this dead friend that Leo's nightly tears were shed. She felt she couldn't ask. Perhaps one day he would tell her. He held her hand at the breakfast table. Together they took Gushi into the Park and there, by the Parsee's fountain, Leo left her and went off towards St Mark's Bridge and Primrose Hill.

His parting from her brought back that afternoon in Covent Garden. She watched his receding figure as she had on that previous occasion. He had never satisfactorily explained why he had gone after apparently intending to spend the day with her. Did it any longer matter? This time he had kissed her tenderly, held her in his arms and whispered that he loved her. A party of eleven children came into the museum at four. They were Scots from Lanark on a school trip to London who, having done the Sherlock Holmes house, had come up here in their minibus. Mary showed them round and gave them the guided tour because their harassed teacher preferred that to a Walkman and a tape for each child.

It was the kind of day when she longed for air conditioning, wholly impractical for this little house of small rooms in a climate where the heat would endure for only a short time. The street door stood open, and the window in the shop, but it was still almost insufferably hot. The sun blazed and the air was motionless. In the shop, where the children, like so many visitors, showed more interest in the artefacts for sale than in the museum exhibits, papers and prints on the counters had begun to curl in the heat.

By five it was no cooler and Alistair still hadn't come. Mary supposed she would just have to wait. Running away from him was something she was now ashamed of. There was a childishness about it she wanted to eradicate from her character but knew that Alistair, though censorious, rather liked. Weakness and folly in women made him feel more powerful and in control, more able to justify a superior stance.

Once Stacey had gone home, Mary went outside and sat in the shade on the low wall that bounded the courtyard. On such warm summer evenings London acquired a pavement life. Restaurateurs were putting out tables and chairs and striped umbrellas in preparation for those who preferred to dine outdoors. Shopkeepers, in the half-hour before their shops closed, sat on their doorsteps. Every sunblind was down and at the café opposite in St

John's Wood Terrace someone was casting bucket-fuls of water over the flagstones.

She watched steam rise from the wet pavement. Her thoughts were full of Leo as they had been for most of the day. She sensed that being in the company of his mother and brother might be as troublesome and painful as the funeral itself. The relationship he had with his brother became each day more mysterious. If he loved him so much why break with him? She was resolving never again to ask Leo if she might meet his mother or brother when she looked up and saw Alistair coming down Ordnance Hill from the direction of the tube station. The present must be very small. He wore no jacket and carried only the thin flat briefcase she had once given him but had thought even at the time too small to accommodate more than a few sheets of paper and a diary.

He waved when he saw her but did not quicken his pace. It was too hot to rush. She couldn't fail to remember how once, seeing him approach from a distance, her heart had leapt and a thrill run through her body. She felt nothing for him now, no faint lingering regret. He looked uncomfortably hot, his face red and beaded with sweat, his hair wet with it and sticking to his scalp. His hot hand felt wet through the thin stuff of her blouse as he laid it on her shoulder. She freed herself and began walking back towards the museum. Then she thought, as she had not thought before, This may be the last time we shall ever meet. We shall very likely never see each other again. We were lovers; we once thought we loved each other, perhaps truly did though imper-manently. How sad and awful to terminate it like this . . .

'Alistair, let's go over to the café and have a drink.'

His eyebrows went up. She hadn't noticed till then

311

but now she saw how unpleasant his expression was, how grim. 'Sure,' he said, 'and while I'm inside ordering two Perriers you'll do another of your famous flits.'

'No. I promise I won't.' They had turned back and were crossing the road, he somewhat reluctantly. 'I don't think we ought to part,' she said, 'without some ...'

'Ceremony?'

'I was going to say, without saying goodbye properly, and without saying perhaps that we have no hard feelings for each other.'

He laughed. A waitress came up and he ordered without asking Mary what she wanted. 'You seem to think,' he said carefully, 'that I still feel for you what I used to. I suppose it pleases your vanity. Well, I don't. I'm over you. As for hard feelings, I've plenty of those. You could say, those are all I have. And now I want, frankly, to get shot of you.'

She could find nothing to say. Perrier came, a large bottle of it, with ice and lemon in two glasses. He poured their drinks. She had a sudden dreadful feeling he would fill another glass with water and throw it in her face. She even edged her chair back a little. Her life, she realised, had been shot through for a long time with imaginings of what Alistair might do, fantasies far exceeding what he actually ever did. He drank the last drops in his glass, reached down, opened the briefcase and took out a small flat parcel. It was about the size of a video cassette, rectangular, less than an inch thick. The gift-wrapping, pink and silver paper, narrow silver ribbon falling from its knot in curlicues, looked nevertheless as if he had done it himself. The corners were clumsily folded, the ribbon twisted. On a card he had printed her name 'Mary' in rather large but uneven capital letters.

312

'Thank you,' she said faintly.

'I want to say something, one last thing. It's this. Don't think you can come back to me. When things go wrong, I mean.'

She said, with a spark of spirit she didn't feel but forced to flash out, 'Don't you mean, *if* things go wrong?'

'No, Mary, that's what *you* mean. As long as you know. I won't be available. I won't be carrying any torches. I shall have found someone else.'

Thinking of this meeting, she had planned all kinds of things to say: charitable wishes for his future, even the expression of some impossible hope that they might go on knowing each other. But now she had no words, she simply felt a kind of despair in his presence that she knew would disappear entirely once he had gone. He was the kind of man, she thought, that she would always run away from and she wondered that she had not done so before, long ago.

He paid the bill. He jumped up and struck an attitude. She watched him, appalled, already nervous.

'And whether we shall meet again I know not,' he declaimed. 'Therefore let us our everlasting farewells take. Forever and forever farewell, Mary!'

A group of tourists approaching the next table turned and stared. He said it again.

'Forever and forever farewell, Mary!'

He pushed back his chair and sent it skidding across the pavement where it toppled and fell over. Then he walked rapidly away. Someone laughed. Mary was embarrassed and rather shaken. She picked up the parcel but it was too big to go into the small bag she was carrying. She would have to carry it in her hand. It was too hot to walk far but she would walk. She would keep to the shady side of the street, and hope it was true what they said about endorphins being released by exercise to calm you down, to create a sense of well-being.

More than endorphins she wanted someone to comfort her. Leo, of course. But she knew she really wanted her grandmother. Her grandmother would hold her as she had done when she was a little girl, hug her in warm silence – but her grandmother was dead, was ash, was dust. Leo would be there, eventually he would, though he was spending the evening with his family. When Leo came in at the front door she would go quietly up to him and he would take her in his arms.

The man she called Nikolai came into her mind and she thought, strangely, that he was one of the few people she could think of that she would like to talk to, to have listen to her, to receive from her confidences whose nature she hardly understood. But when she came to the Gloucester Gate and crossing the road by the bronze maiden, looked down into the Grotto, there was no one there and no evidence of his occupancy. A cigarette packet, discarded over the wall, floated on the surface of the pool. Otherwise the place was as neat as a suburban garden.

She put the parcel down on the hall table. Gushi was too hot to run out to meet her. He lay panting on the cold kitchen floor, his tongue hanging out. There was no point in taking him out for hours yet. Perhaps she would wait until Leo came home and they would walk him together. She stroked Gushi's head, gave him fresh water, then went upstairs to shower and put on trousers and a T-shirt.

It was at this point that the telephone rang. It was Leo. Once, several years before, she had spoken on the phone to Dorothea's husband Gordon just after he had come round from an anaesthetic. Leo's voice sounded like Gordon's had then, thick, throaty, half-choked, aged by many years.

'I can't get away this evening,' he said. 'I don't know when I will. Things haven't been too – too good. I'll see you tomorrow.' There was a pause in which she fancied she heard sounds like sobs suppressed. 'Is that all right?'

'Leo, of course it is. But can't I . . . ?'

'No, I don't know what you were going to say but you can't do anything. No one can. I shall be fine. Did you see Alistair?'

'For the last time, I'm sure. He's given us a wedding present.'

'What is it?'

'I don't know. I haven't opened it yet.'

'Perhaps you'd better not open it. Perhaps there's a bomb inside.' There was an hysterical edge to his voice. Had she imagined a sob? 'Mary, I'm sorry I can't come back tonight.'

'It doesn't matter,' she said. 'I understand.'

But she was not at all sure that she did. She was aware of bitter disappointment. Why is it worse to be alone on fine summer evenings than when it is cold or wet? The food in the fridge looked uninviting. She drank some sparkling water, ate a peach, and settled down to put the final touches to the Irene Adler brochure. It was due to go to the printer by the end of the week. By the time it came out she would no longer be Mary Jago but Mary Nash.

Did she want that or would she keep her maiden name? She hadn't thought of that before. Somewhere on the brochure there should be a line saying, 'designed by Mary Jago' or 'designed by Mary Nash'. She wrote the new name to see how it looked, how it felt. Many people would say it was unlucky for a woman to write her new name before it was hers, before she was married. She tried her new signature, disliked it and almost decided to keep the name Jago.

From the hall Gushi gave a sharp yap. She went out to see what had alarmed him and found another flier from Express Tikka and Pizza on the doormat. Alistair's present was on the hall table where she had left it, pink and silver paper, curlicues of ribbon, clumsily bunched corners. She took it back into the living room. Gushi jumped on to her lap and curled up like a cat.

Sticky tape held the parcel together under the ribbon. It was surprisingly hard to get off. She had to disturb the dog to fetch scissors. Leo's words came back to her then, about the present being a bomb. That was absurd, of course, he hadn't been serious, but she held the package up to her ear as if to hear something ticking. She shook it. There was nothing loose inside, nothing to rattle.

She cut the sticky tape, then the corners. Inside the paper was a flat silver box, the kind you can buy from the gift wrapping section in stationery shops. The lid was taped to the base. More cutting and the lid came off. Bubble-wrap, cotton wool, a handful of tissues for padding, and a card in an envelope.

It was a strange choice for Alistair to have made. That was her first thought as she looked at the picture of a bride and groom, doll-like figures, the man in a top hat and morning coat, the woman in white crinoline and bridal veil, the pair of them standing on the carved and scrolled icing of a beribboned cake. Underneath the legend read: *Wishing you Joy on Your Wedding Day*.

Was this his present? Was this all? Inside the card was an enclosure; evidently a letter, the paper folded twice. He had written nothing on the card, not even his name. For a moment she thought of not reading the letter, of throwing it away unread, apprehensive

316

of his insults and reproaches. But it was cowardly not to read it. It could do her no harm. It was only words and from someone who now meant nothing to her. She was holding it between thumb and forefinger, still unfolded, when the phone rang again, and as she picked up the receiver it was still with her, just a sheet of A10 size paper, folded twice.

Leo's voice said, 'I'm sorry. I'm sorry for that – that display just now. I'm at my brother's but he's gone out for a moment and I'm ringing back as soon as I could. Forgive?'

'Nothing to forgive. Are you all right?'

'I'm fine.'

She said wistfully, 'I wish you could come home now.'

'Mary, my mother wants me to stay the night. She's here. I may not see her again for years, if ever. You know what I said about that. That this was the final meeting.'

'That's all right,' she said. 'Of course you must stay. Don't worry about it. I shall be fine.' Afterwards she didn't know why she had told him. 'I've opened the present. It wasn't a bomb. Just a card and a letter and a lot of padding.'

'I love you,' he said. 'I just wanted to ring you and say that. On Thursday you'll be my wife. It's too good to be true.'

'It's true,' she said.

His brother must have come back into the room. He said goodbye, he would see her on the following evening, and put the receiver down. That reminder that he was with his family for the last time was disquieting. It suddenly seemed unnatural, unnecessary. She wished she had asked his reasons, simply asked to know more about it. Anyway, it wasn't too late. Tomorrow she would ask him.

She unfolded the sheet of paper she was still holding in her hand.

The logo of the Harvest Trust, the scarlet mushroom shape, the Battersea address, and opposite this the direction to herself, Ms Mary Jago in Chatsworth Road, NW10. Below it was a line that this was from Deborah Cox, Donor Welfare Officer. The date was six days before.

Her first thought was that the letter shouldn't have gone to her old address. Then she remembered she had never given the Trust a firm change of address, only asked for one letter, the last she thought she would receive from them, to be sent to her care of her grandmother. She read:

Dear Ms Jago,

It is probable I am bringing you news you know already since I believe you have been in correspondence with Mr Nash and have met him. This is confirmed by our receiving no replies from you to our recent letters informing you of his decline and illness.

Therefore I hope it will not be a shock to you, though certainly giving distress, to know that Mr Nash died yesterday. He passed away quite peacefully in the night at the hospice where he had been for the previous two weeks. His mother and brother were with him.

While this must be a cause of great sadness to you, you will know that by your generous donation you succeeded in giving him a longer life, and of higher quality, than he would otherwise ...

Mary laid the letter down in her lap. She was simply confused. How could Leo's death be a shock when she had spoken to him five minutes before? They had made a mistake. They were confusing her with

318

someone else and Leo with someone else, they had their files mixed.

She picked it up and read it again. *This is confirmed by our receiving no replies from you to our recent letters* ... What recent letters? Transplant updates that Alistair had received and opened? She was suddenly very cold and she moved into the sunshine of the open windows, feeling the heat touch her. *Mr Nash died yesterday* ...

Now, at seven, it was too late to phone them and ask for an explanation. Anger and indignation started to replace the initial shock. Alistair was as much to blame as the Trust in perpetuating their mistake, and surely out of malice. He had sent her this letter as a wedding present, the most vindictive act he had ever committed against her.

The phone rang and rang. At last he picked it up and said, 'Alistair Winter.'

'Alistair, Mary. You must know why I'm phoning . . .'

He put the phone down. The dialling tone began. She looked at the receiver in disbelief. Blood rose into her cheek where he had struck her and she put up a cold finger to feel the heat. After a moment or two she poured herself a measure of brandy and drank it down neat. The brandy made her choke but filled her with warmth as if some heating agent had got inside her and sent its rays to travel outwards to her skin. She told herself to take deep breaths. Alistair's malice had shaken her profoundly. She fancied that in his silence at the other end of the phone she had heard satisfaction and glee.

But she reminded herself that it wasn't he who had written that letter. He had only sent it on. It was a real letter, from a real place, not something Alistair had forged. He had only been the instrument that ensured she received it.

319

This was no time for those old hesitations. Avoiding thought, she dialled Leo's brother's number in Redferry Road. It rang and rang; there was going to be no answer. Leo had said he would be there but he wasn't there. That meant very little. He and his brother might have gone out for a drink, or he might have gone back with their mother to wherever she was staying. It just seemed strange – she felt it suddenly as suspicious and odd – that he should have talked to her about breaking with his brother, never seeing his mother again, yet be going out with them, staying the night with them ...

Mary needed someone to be with her, to bring to this letter, to these events, a detached and dispassionate mind. After a while she phoned Dorothea but instead of coming out with all of it, found herself asking if it would be all right not to come in tomorrow. She had arranged to take a week off from Wednesday but could she start her holiday tomorrow instead?

'Sure. Why not?' Dorothea said. 'Gordon will cope. Are you OK? You sound a bit shaky. Pre-wedding nerves?'

'I expect so,' Mary said, and for some reason tried to smile into the receiver as if Dorothea could see her. 'Thanks, Dorrie.'

'It's your wedding, not your funeral.'

'Yes.'

It had been impossible, would have been grotesque, to have read or quoted the letter to Dorothea. To anyone? She picked it up again, read it again and this time saw something that she had not previously noticed. Under the Harvest Trust address was Deborah Cox's own home number. Mary had begun to feel sick. The brandy, perhaps, or not having eaten for so long. She wondered why she had told Dorothea she wouldn't go to the museum tomorrow.

What was she anticipating? What spectre awaited her?

The fear of knowing was starting to overcome the fear of not knowing. Suppose she were to destroy the letter now, tear it into pieces and burn the pieces in an ashtray? Or make a little bonfire outside? Then she could pretend it had never come, that Alistair's parcel had contained only a card, say nothing of it to Leo ... She dialled Deborah Cox's number.

It was answered after the second ring. Scarcely waiting for Mary to say what she wanted, Deborah Cox asked her if she needed counselling. The Trust would be happy to provide counselling. She would advise it, particularly as Mary had written to Leo Nash, had even got to know him.

'You did actually meet?'

Mary hesitated. She had begun to tremble, her knees shaking. How she could tell so blatant a lie she didn't know. 'No,' she said. 'No, we never met.'

'But you had contact? By letter?'

'Yes. We had contact.' Mary had to clear her throat. 'What did he look like?'

'I'm sorry?'

'What did he look like? Leo Nash.' Her voice was hoarse but the lying got easier. 'I asked him for a photograph but he didn't send one.'

'Fair, short, about five feet six, dark eyes. It's probably just as well you didn't meet. A donor can get emotionally involved with a recipient. It's to do with the nature of the transplant, and that makes it all the worse when the recipient dies.'

'You said he had a brother ...'

'That's right. Ten years older. They shared a flat. But I wouldn't advise contact, if that's what you're asking. Now, as to arranging counselling ...'

Mary said no, thank you, and that wouldn't be necessary. She put the phone down very quietly.

Chapter Twenty-Seven

Hob was well.

For more than a week now there had been no states. He was fast forgetting what being in a state was like, or even feeling low was like, for he never let himself decline far enough from being well to find out. He was rich enough to stay well for months, maybe a year, nor did he need to work. The irony was that more work came in than had done for years beforehand, and with it, necessarily, more money to keep him well.

He wondered why this should be and one day he asked Lew. There was no one else he dared ask since Carl had disappeared. Lew was old and weird and had been into all that stuff when he was young in the Seventies and he said it was because of Hob's positive attitude. He was positive and in touch with his inner self. People sensed this and came looking for him when they wanted a job done. He'd done three jobs just since the big one – the biggest of all big ones – and one of them, funnily enough, had been a second roughing up of that git who hadn't the sense he was born with, the one who lived in St Mark's Crescent.

Hob hadn't stayed at home much. Home was a dump, anyway. For all their promises, the council hadn't come to mend the windows. Maybe he hadn't read the letter right, so maybe they'd never said they were coming. Whatever the way of it, he couldn't live in a boarded-up box no different from being inside a microwave, not in this heat he couldn't. So he'd more or less taken to the outdoors and it had been lovely, like a holiday, better than Corfu really. He'd never been much for going in water.

He wandered the Park and Primrose Hill and St John's Church Gardens, sitting on the seats, lying on the grass. By day he'd sit at a table outside one of the refreshment places and he'd drink but he seldom ate more than a Magnum or a packet of kettle chips. When he was well he never much fancied food. Mostly he drank vodka or sometimes tequila for a change. After the first few days he bought a bottle of each and carried them with him, but in a proper rucksack, not plastic carriers like those beggars. The rucksack also held his gear, the watering can rose, the lighter, a batch of drinking straws – he helped himself from the counter when he paid for his drink – and reserve supplies. He never let himself get low, let alone run out. The thought of a state even looming on the horizon made him shudder.

Drinking straws ended up all over the Park. Sometimes he wondered, giggling to himself, if anyone noticed, remarked on it, wondered what the hell was going on: straws caught up on rosebushes, littering flowerbeds, floating on the scummy water under the bridges. Because he was a joker he stuck one in the mouth of the bronze maiden and made a woven crown of six others for Sir Cowasjee Jehangir's drinking fountain. He was happy. One day he bought a postcard of the lake with boats on it and sent it to himself. He had to go home sometimes, for a change of clothes and to catch a bit of the athletics from Trent Bridge on telly, and when he crept into that furnace of a flat he found his postcard on the mat with, 'Great whether, wish you was heer' on it and 'luv from Hob'.

323

That made him laugh a lot. It was the funniest thing he could think of, getting a postcard from himself, wishing he was somewhere else. He fell about laughing and got so excited he needed a shot of vodka to calm him down. He had started to lose weight. Not on his head or face – those bits of him were as big and heavy as ever – but his body was thin and the skin sagged round his middle like an old sock when the leg has been pulled out of it. Leo had once told him about a girl he knew who'd been fat, obese he called it, and for some reason she turned anorexic. Her skin hung on her skeleton like draped material and they'd operated on her, cut bits out and stitched her up, and all on the NHS. He'd started wondering if he could have the same thing, only he couldn't because in hospital he'd never be well but would get into a state the first day.

Now he was rich he'd been buying all the rocks he wanted, and E too, and angel dust when there was any about. Big H was no use to him because he couldn't face needles, which was why the coming of crack had been such a godsend. The only time he'd tried the needle he'd fainted dead away. God knows what had happened when he was a kid and they'd tried giving him those shots for polio and whatever. He'd never asked his mother, but the answer probably was she was too shellacked to take him or too bone idle.

He never cared to think about the time, a year or two back, when he'd been reduced to sniffing ozone unfriendly aerosol stain remover. He thought instead about the other two jobs: breating a geyser's leg in Chalk Farm and a straightforward beating up round the back of Lisson Grove. He got a Hawaii for each of those, though he reckoned he was underpaid for his Chalk Farm effort, as fracturing a leg wasn't the simple task it was cracked up to be. He enjoyed the pun he'd made and had another good laugh.

Most evenings he went through his ritual by the pond in the Grotto. The beggar with the fancy voice had moved out. The people who owned the house that builders were doing up – and months they'd been at it – had put up more barbed wire and more fencing in their inexplicable efforts to keep intruders out. He couldn't understand it. It wouldn't keep him out, or any streetwise person. He sat on the coping of the pool in the insect-infested half-dark, dropped his rock into the watering can rose, screwed on the top, inserted two fresh straws, applied the lighter to the rock and set the apparatus in the tin lid.

The crystalline lump fizzed and crackled. Though he'd been some way off being in a state, his condition took a dizzying upturn when the smooth sweet smoke drew into his lungs. Later on he'd take a tablet of E or maybe smoke some PCP and if he got too excited bring himself down with a couple of cycles – cyclobarbitone calcium to you ignorant buggers, he thought. It takes an alcoholic to be an expert on alcoholism and a junkie to understand the journey to oblivion.

He began giggling uncontrollably. The laughter he allowed full rein, he let it rip, and he lay down there rolling on the flagstones and the dusty earth among the dry crackling leaves. A face looked over the parapet of the bridge. He could just make it out in the dusk, a thin face with pitted skin that watched him for a long moment, fascinated by the sight of this man rolling on his back like a dog in a pile of shit.

When he was ready to stop laughing and rolling he stopped. He was in perfect control. He started putting his gear back into the rucksack, took a swallow of vodka, noticed what he'd been carrying about with him for more than a week now: a red baseball cap and a T-shirt with elephants marching across it. The funniest thing in the world, it seemed to him, would be to take them up to the Oxfam shop in Camden High Street tomorrow, hand them in and make sure they put them on show in the window.

As he clambered out of the Grotto and crossed on the lights at the top of Albany Street he began giggling again at the thought of that. Making sure he was unobserved but still giggling, he climbed over the spiked railings of the Gloucester Gate and disappeared into the soft still darkness of the Park.

Her loneliness left her exposed and vulnerable. She was like someone put ashore on a desert island who watches the boat recede across an empty sea; there is no one left in the world who knows or cares where one is or what has happened.

She held Gushi. Afterwards, long afterwards, she sometimes said that the little dog, snuggling in her arms, licking her fingers, had saved her sanity. Holding him, his warmth necessary in spite of the heat of the day, she understood that some monstrous fraud had been perpetrated against her but not how or why. Even who it was that had done what had been done she didn't know, for she had no means of knowing Leo's identity. Trying to solve this enigma brought on fits of shivering as if it were cold out there, as if snow covered the Park.

She must have sat there for more than an hour, still, scarcely thinking, in a state of shock, for when next she looked at the clock it was nine and dark outside. She switched on a table-lamp and a flock of moths came in, brown and yellow and a black and white one, spotted like a dalmatian. They made for the light, circling the lampshade. She thought of his laughter, of 'A reference for a dalmatian', and gave a little cry of pain. The light off, the room in darkness

326

to let the moths escape, she dialled the Redferry House number again, her throat dry and constricted. There was no reply. She wouldn't phone again. She was resolved on that. For one thing, absurdly, she had no idea what she would say.

The idea of the night was horrible. It would be so long, so lonely, and the small hours unbearable. She went upstairs and in the medicine cabinet in the Blackburn-Norrises' bathroom found a phial of capsules with *Lady Blackburn-Norris* printed on its label, *For the sleeplessness*, and the name of the drug with instructions to take one or two at bedtime.

She put Gushi out into the garden. The night was warm and soft and above her in a velvety violet sky a few stars were visible, a rare thing in London. Gushi started yapping at the bats that swooped overhead, so she brought him in again. When she had locked up and settled him on the foot of her bed, she opened the bedroom windows wide, took her clothes off, fetched a glass of water and swallowed one capsule, then a second. She scarcely had time to lie down. Sleep came at her like a black walking spectre, cloaked and hooded, seizing and absorbing her into itself and its wide wing-like arms.

In the early hours, five or six, she awoke, ponderously limp and weak from the drug, but remembering him beside her and making love to him. Over and over, he whoever he was had made love to her, with sweet gentle touches and strong unstoppable passion and murmured loving words. She got up and just made it to the bathroom. She was sick, the retching painful, tearing at her throat. On and on she vomited until she had collapsed on to the floor, drained dry.

After a while she slept again – until Gushi came asking to be let out, his nose like an ice cube against her naked shoulder. She got up off the floor, put a robe round her. Another splendid day was out there, blue sky, sunshine unhindered but the sun itself an invisible fire.

The phone started ringing just as she had come in from the garden. No one knew this number but for Leo, the man who said he was Leo. Alistair knew it, but she was certain, as if it were a law of nature, that Alistair would never phone her again, that she and Alistair would never speak to each other again. She let it ring and ring, watching the instrument. She picked up the receiver.

It was Deborah Cox.

The question of least importance was the one she asked. 'How did you know this number? I didn't give it to you.'

'I dialled the number that gets you the voice to tell you who made the last phone call.'

'Yes. Oh, yes. Of course. What was it you wanted?' She had never before spoken so rudely to anyone. 'I'm sorry. I mean, what can I do for you?'

'There's something I wanted to tell you. You seemed so interested in Leo Nash, the sort of person he was, what he looked like and all that. I'm not sure I ought to tell you, it's just between you and me, but I know you're discreet.'

The woman knew virtually nothing about her ... 'What is it then?'

'Leo,' Deborah Cox said, 'when he began to get ill again he refused to ask you to make a second donation. You were the only possible donor but he expressly forbade us to ask you.'

Mary said stonily, 'I don't understand.'

'He said he wouldn't put you through the process again – going into hospital, having a general anaesthetic which is always a risk, the convalescence afterwards, all that. He wouldn't. We did everything in our power to persuade him but it was no use. I thought you'd like to know.'

'You mean he was a hero,' said Mary. 'A knight in shining armour, a selfless saint – is that what you're saying? Someone who laid down his life so that I shouldn't have a week's discomfort?'

There was a silence in which, somehow, outrage was apparent.

'Frankly, Mary,' Deborah Cox said at last, 'I didn't realise you were quite so disturbed. You're undoubtedly in need of therapy, so about that counselling . . .'

Asking herself if all this would turn her from a well-mannered courteous woman into a rude one, Mary quietly replaced the receiver in its rest.

The man, whoever he was, the con man, the man who had deceived her, would come to the house as he always came when he had been away for the night. Already the heat was closing in as if a giant lid were held over the steam from a pan. From the comparative cool of Charlotte Cottage, Mary came out into a heat that enveloped her like a blanket. She left Gushi behind. It was too hot for him to walk and he must be content with escape into the garden twice a day. She was leaving the house to avoid the man who had been her lover but whom she dared not think of in those terms in case she was sick again.

It was a matter for regret now that she had asked Dorothea for the day off. The museum would at least have sheltered her, given her a place to be where he wouldn't find her. There seemed nowhere to go but the Park, but even as she entered it, going in by the Chester Gate – further north, nearer the zoo, she might meet him – she told herself this running away couldn't be prolonged. They would meet, they were bound to. He couldn't know Alistair had exposed him and she had found him out. Probably today,

329

sometime today, they must encounter each other. She began to shake again. She felt weak, enfeebled, the sleeping capsules still taking effect, and she sat down on a seat under the trees in the Broad Walk.

The day after tomorrow was to have been her wedding day. He would have married her, of course he would. That had been the purpose of the project, to marry her for her money and that vast barrack of a house up in Belsize Avenue. Tears came into her eyes and ran down her cheeks. He had been so plausible, so *nice*, so gentle, a wonderful actor. But who was he that he could show the registrar Leo Nash's birth certificate and have Carl Nash for a brother and receive her bone marrow and *die*, yet be alive?

The man she had once named Nikolai had come to sit on the other end of the bench. She hadn't heard his arrival; he might have been there for five minutes, ten. Her tears, her thoughts, had cut her off from the external world.

'Don't cry,' he said, and then, 'What is it?'

She lifted her head, turned her eyes. Her sight was blurred by tears but still she was sure he looked different. The change was subtle, not definable, for he still had his beard, he still wore his jeans, his denim jacket, the threadbare T-shirt, the battered trainers. But he was a man now, not a dosser. Whatever it was must be in those blue eyes or in the more confident set of his shoulders.

The classic response, but what else could she say to a stranger? 'It's nothing.'

'You're very unhappy,' he said. 'Shall I go away? I expect you'd like me to go away.'

Her new-found rudeness had its limits. 'No. No, of course not.' She turned her face away. 'I am unhappy. No one can do anything about that.'

He was very hesitant. 'Do you want to tell me? I mean, just to tell someone?' It came to him then how he had told no one about his wife and children. He had talked of them only to that other self inside his head. If the other street people knew, it was only that a tragedy figured in his life just as tragedies figured in all their separate lives. 'The cliché is true,' he said. 'Sometimes it's best to talk to a stranger.'

She shook her head. She got up and when he protested – he would go, the last thing he meant was to drive her away – shook her head again, made a gesture with her right hand indicating he should stay where he was.

'I can't talk,' she said. 'It's not just – well, inhibition. I wouldn't know what to say. I don't *know*, you see, I don't *know*.'

He looked at her neutrally, trying not to encourage or discourage.

'I don't know what's been done to me, only that it's bad and cruel, I think.'

'Sometimes,' he said, 'it helps to get angry. You could try anger.'

She nodded abstractedly. He watched her walk away. He was convinced that something terrible had happened to her and with that thought came a sense of failure. By his presence, near her, he had absurdly thought he could save her from suffering, protect her from life. Who did he think he was? He hadn't been able to save himself, so how could he hope to save another?

But now, while she was out of doors, he would never let her out of his sight.

Chapter Twenty-Eight

Walking down from St Barbara's House in Camden High Street, the women's hostel where she sometimes slept, Effie turned her eyes to the window of the Oxfam shop. She looked at it as another woman might look at the windows of Selfridges or D.H. Evans. Oxfam prices were usually beyond Effie but they were a possibility – they weren't ludicrous; they weren't that other woman's Harrod's. She needed a T-shirt, it was so bloody hot. The only one in the window had elephants on it, a married couple of elephants they were supposed to be, with a couple of babies. Vanity had gone out of Effie's life ages ago – but her with four elephants on her front? Do me a favour. Anyway, it was about sixteen sizes too small.

A baseball cap she could live without. A pimple on an egg that would be on her Humpty-Dumpty face. Maybe she'd try the Sue Ryder place for her T-shirt if she could remember where it was. She wandered on, shifting the heavier bundles she carried from her left to her right hand, heading for the Gloucester Gate.

Dill went up there later to cash his giro but he didn't look in the Oxfam window because he never bought clothes. The nuns who had a soup and bun stall in Eversholt Street five nights a week handed out cast-off clothing for free. He was more interested in food for the beagle, which he'd run out of, so he tied the dog up to a parking meter and went into the Indian mini-market. There he bought five cans of

Cesar, gourmet stuff but light to carry in those little foil cans. The beagle would wolf it down.

Roman passed by on his way from the Hawley Hotel to Lisson Grove, where the Benefit Office and Job Centre is, a long walk but nothing much to one who had walked miles every day for the best part of two years. A slight embarrassment stopped him looking at the Oxfam shop as he passed it. He consciously kept his eyes averted. The previous day he had handed over to them all the clothes – those that survived and were in a reasonably decent condition – he had worn while on the street, having washed them first and worked on them with the hotel's ancient iron. They would very likely be in the window. Naturally, he had not been offered any money for them but it troubled him vaguely that there were people out there prepared to pay for and wear his cast-offs. So he didn't look.

Nor did Nello, also on his way to cash his giro and spend a half of it in the Red Lion. The school-leaver who had inherited Bean's dogs (even managing to poach Marietta from Amelia Walker) dragged his charges past the window, heading for the pharmacy where his mother's repeat prescription for barbs was regularly dispensed. As often as not, the dogs never saw the grass of the Park these days. The school-leaver was too busy shopping or playing the fruit machines.

It had taken him only two days to time the early walk for two hours later. Outside the pharmacy he tied the dogs up so tightly that Ruby couldn't get her leg over or Spots catch a sniff of Charlie's chuff. Another hundred chlorme-something or others, please, and this prescription for his baby brother who never gave any of them a wink of sleep. It was for paediatric Valium in syrup form. The school-leaver was going to divide it up and sell it in forty-millilitre phials. There was a good market among the buffs for coming down from a speed hang-up. Cough mixture would go into the Vallergan bottle and his brother no doubt keep on screaming half the night.

It had to be one of Bean's regulars who spotted the T-shirt and the baseball cap, but few of them ever looked in charity shop windows, let alone went inside. In any case, Camden High Street was too down-market or just Bohemian for the Barker-Pryces, Erna Morosini, Mrs Sellers and Edwina Goldsworthy, and not sufficiently recherché for Lisl Pring. Just as well for the school-leaver, or they might have seen their dogs lashed to lampposts outside the pinball arcade. The one who looked but saw no need to go inside was Valerie Conway.

She was living with her boyfriend just off Camden High Street and was walking down to her new job as receptionist in the Peugeot showrooms. The neighbours in Jamestown Road had been all agog when they found out she'd known Bean quite well, seen him every day and talked to him. It was a wonder it wasn't she the police had hauled in to identify his body.

'I was like Bo-Peep's sheep,' Valerie said. 'They didn't know where to find me.'

But she wasn't without public spirit. And she wasn't too posh for Oxfam shops. Her sister had bought a really nice boob tube from one of them and worn it on her honeymoon in Bodrum. Valerie was on the lookout for a halter top. A red one was in the very centre of the window and the idea apparently was that you wore it with the red baseball cap they'd stuck on the plaster model's head. Valerie went inside, her heart thudding uncomfortably.

'D'you know where you got that from?'

'If you mean who brought it in,' said the sour-faced middle-aged volunteer, 'I do remember the man, but we're not in the habit of asking donors to divulge their names.'

'Suit yourself,' said Valerie. 'I'll have the red halter. I just wanted to know about the baseball cap because the last time I saw it it was on the head of one of those blokes that got themselves impaled on railings.'

The day came and went. The wedding day. He hadn't come, so Mary understood that he must somehow know he was discovered. The scam was over. If he was close to the real Leo Nash, and he must have been, perhaps the Harvest Trust had let him know they had informed her. After all, she would have received that letter much sooner if Alistair hadn't delayed sending it on.

His failure to come was at the same time a relief and a disappointment. A relief because of her shame at the things she had said, her confidings in him, her confessions of love, the relative speed with which she had let him make love to her and, later, her revelling in that lovemaking. The disappointment was because she was angry. Although she had appeared indifferent to it at the time, she had taken to heart Nikolai's advice. *You could try anger.* She had tried, perhaps for the first time in her life.

Anger had come and begun to grow and as it grew brought with it a kind of liberation. Why hadn't she previously let herself be angry? With Alistair, for instance? But the anger she now nourished needed expression and it could only express itself to *him.* And he didn't come, would never come.

The police came instead.

They wanted more identification, this time to tell them if a red baseball cap and T-shirt with elephants on it had belonged to Bean. Had she ever seen Bean wearing them?

'Many times,' she said. 'He wore the hat every day in hot weather. I only saw the T-shirt once but it was his.'

There must have been a new firmness about her, a decisiveness, which she fancied made Marnock give her one or two surprised glances. Had she ever seen Bean with anyone? Had he, for instance, ever been accompanied when he came to fetch or return Gushi? She answered no without hesitation to both questions and the policemen thanked her and left.

Dorothea was coming round in the evening. Mary had phoned her the night before to tell her the wedding was off but giving no further explanation. She had been similarly unforthcoming with her cousin in Guildford. After all, if she didn't understand herself, how could she explain? She found a bottle of wine, the Chardonnay Leo had been so fond of, and dialled Express Tikka and Pizza for Chicken Korma with pilau rice and Bombay potatoes for eight o'clock.

One of the qualities for which she liked Dorothea was her willingness to accept a refusal to explain, her submission without protest to silence on a particular subject. She was discreet, could keep a secret, and understood about other people having private places they wanted to keep inviolate.

'Don't ask,' Mary said. 'I say that because I don't really know why myself. Perhaps I'll have an explanation one day and then I'll tell you. And then maybe you won't want to know, you won't care.'

Dorothea had brought a basket of peaches and a carton of clotted cream. 'Better put this in your fridge till it's time to eat it.' In the same tone she said, 'Are you very unhappy?'

'I don't know. That's a peculiar answer but I really

336

don't know. I'm angry. I've never been so angry with anyone and it feels so strange and new. But I can't be angry *with* him because I don't know where he is.'

They sat on the terrace and drank Campari with ice and orange juice and lime slices. Gushi lay half under the lilac bush and half on the grass, snapping at any moth that came his way. The sky was very pale blue as if long exposure to the fierce sun had faded it. There was a smell of smoke. Not illegal smoke from an illicit bonfire, Mary thought, but a fire somewhere, perhaps on the embankment of the railway line coming out of Euston. Fires kept breaking out from cigarette ends tossed on to tinder-dry grass.

'I brought you a paper,' Dorothea said, 'for distraction. Well, a rag, a tabloid. Have you ever heard of an MP called Barker-Pryce?'

'I don't think so.'

'That man Bean that was murdered used to take his dog out. The dog must have gone out with Gushi. A golden retriever called Charlie.'

'I remember the dog.'

Dorothea passed her the front page. There was not much text. It was mostly photographs and headline: *The MP and his Toy*, with beneath it, *What was the Link with Murdered Man?* One photograph was of a choleric-looking elderly man with bristly whiskers and badly cut hair, sitting at a table in what looked like a drinking club but might have been in a private house, next to a young, heavily made-up girl with waist-length hair. A cigar with a pendulous head of ash pulled down one corner of his mouth. Fingers fat as sausages could be seen gripping the girl's shoulder from behind. Her head rested on his shoulder. The caption read, *A Toy is only a toy but a good cigar is a smoke. James Barker-Pryce, Conservative Member for Somers Town and South Hampstead, parties with a friend.*

The other photograph, snapped on a beach some-where, was of Bean.

It was hard for Mary to take much in. Distraction does not always distract. She seemed to have no concentration. The lines of print danced.

'Here, you read it to me.'

'All right. I like reading aloud. "The missing link. The time has come for the public to be told. What was the connection between James Barker-Pryce MP and Leslie Arthur Bean, the murdered dog-walker?

'"It is several days since the police revealed that Bean was not the Impaler's latest victim but that this was a copy-cat killing. Leslie Bean was well-known to Mr Barker-Pryce's friend Miss Toy Townsende, twenty-three, who has told police. 'I knew Les when he was a butler. That was three or four years ago at my friend Mr Maurice Clitheroe's home. Les was employed by my friend James Barker-Pryce to walk his beautiful retriever dog Charlie but I think there must have been some disagreement between them as the dog-walking ceased, though Les still paid visits to Mr Barker-Pryce's Regent's Park home ...'"

'Can you imagine anyone actually talking like that?'

'It sounds libellous to me. How do they hope to get away with it?'

'Perhaps they don't care. "On the phone today Mr Barker-Pryce, sixty-eight, said he had no memory of any photograph of himself and Miss Townsende. It was possible she was the young lady who made a suggestion to him while he was parking his Bentley in Paddington Street, London W1 two months ago. Mrs Julia Barker-Pryce, sixty-two, Mr Barker-Pryce's wife of thirty-three years, was not available for comment. She and her husband are ... Turn to page two."

'Here's a shot of the girl in a G-string. She can't

really be called Toy, can she? "She and her husband are spending the weekend at their country retreat at Upper Slaughter, Gloucestershire . . ." Upper Slaughter? I don't believe it.'

'There really is a place called that. Dorrie, did you hear the front doorbell?'

'I don't think so. Listen. It goes on, "Mr Barker-Pryce later told our reporter" – I suppose they're all barracking him outside his country house – "'There was no quarrel between me and Mr Bean. That would be impossible. He was a working man and I believe former servant. I dismissed him for incompetence and there is no truth in rumours that he visited my house or that I continued to pay him a remuneration.'" Oh, that must have been the bell!'

The tikka man had come round the side of the house in search of them. He was wearing his red and white T-shirt with red jeans and carrying a tray laden with covered dishes, fastened to his torso with straps like a rucksack.

'I'm so sorry,' Mary said. 'We weren't sure if we heard the bell.'

'Shall I put it in the kitchen for you?'

'Thank you.'

He went indoors, came back, giving Dorothea a doubtful look, then a smile and a, 'I'm not mistaken, am I, madam?'

'No, no. You used to drive the dry cleaner's van, didn't you? Oh, it must be five years back.'

'That's right. Spot on. And you live in Charles Lane up in St John's Wood.'

They began reminiscing. Mary went indoors, turned the oven on low and put the Korma, rice and vegetables inside. Leo's engagement ring that he had bought her in a shop in Camden Passage was still on her finger. She took it off and wondered what would happen to it if she put it down the waste disposal unit and pressed the switch. It might break the unit. Better give it to some poor dosser to sell. She took it off and dropped it inside the cutlery drawer. Then she peeled two peaches, sliced them and looked for a liqueur to pour over them. The Amaretto Leo had brought the previous week . . .

Even in her mind she had better stop calling him that. Leo wasn't his name. He wasn't Oliver either; he couldn't even be called by the pseudonym under which she had so long known the recipient of her donation, for he wasn't that recipient. It wasn't into his bones that her marrow had been induced, but an unknown dead man's.

She took the wine out of the refrigerator, found a corkscrew and put it with two glasses on a tray. Dorothea was lying back in the lounging chair, gazing up at the pale sky, now covered with a network of vapour trails. Gushi had climbed on to her lap. The tikka man had gone.

'That poor man,' Dorothea said, sitting up. 'He went to prison for running someone over when he was driving a laundry van. Of course I didn't mention any of that. But I remembered. I don't think you ought to go to prison if you didn't *mean* to kill someone, do you?'

'Sometimes I think no one ought to go to prison for anything,' said Mary. 'But that's not very practical. Was he on drugs or drunk or what?'

'He'd been drinking,' said Dorothea. 'Talking of which, do you want me to open that for you?'

The traffic in the Marylebone Road speeds up at the weekends. There is less of it, less to slow it down or bring it to frequent stops. On the Sundays of mid-August less traffic uses the road than perhaps on any other days of the year and it seems like some highway in the Fifties or Sixties when driving was pleasurable and the air relatively pure.

But on mid-August Saturdays, with so many people away on holiday and so many tourists and car-less pedestrians, the traffic speeds along, three lanes of it, roaring up to Euston and the underpass or tearing down to Chapel Street, the Marylebone Flyover and the M40. Sometimes brakes shriek when a stop is enforced at Baker Street lights or those at Park Crescent. In the week it is a slow, lumbering battering ram that plods at fifteen miles an hour, but on a late summer Saturday it becomes a swift juggernaut and therefore far more dangerous.

Mary thought all these things as she came back from buying bread in Marylebone High Street on Saturday morning. Gushi was tucked under her arm. She had brought him with her on a supernumerary walk but he was frightened by the traffic noise and buried his face in the palm of her hand. They crossed quickly and she brought him into the friendly green of the Park. He ran down the bank and drank thirstily from the lake. Already a hot vapour hung over the broad expanses of grass, bleached yellow and in places entirely bared by the drought. The water with which the flowerbeds were sprayed first thing each morning had dried by now and some plants hung their heads. She kept to the shady side of the path.

A man on a seat was reading a paperback of *The Catcher in the Rye*, the woman at the other end of the bench a broadsheet newspaper with the front page headline: *MP to Sue over Murder and Sex Allegations*. Mary tried to think about her future, where she would live, what she would do. Leo, Oliver, that man whoever he was, had said, *Two days after we're married my wife will be able to come and live with me* . . .

She remembered then. Today the Blackburn-

Norrises were coming home. He had said that because the Blackburn-Norrises were coming home and she would be free. She looked round for Gushi. He was making friends with a Jack Russell, touching noses, wagging tails. She went back for him, put him on the lead, gently shooed the other dog away.

'They're coming home today,' she said to him. 'Your master and mistress, your people, owners, whatever you call them. Come on, let's get back fast.'

So that's what I've come to, she thought, talking aloud to a dog in public. Gushi licked her fingers. No, he's not sorry for you, he doesn't understand, she said to herself. He's a nice dog but he's just a dog.

They went out into Albany Street by the Cumberland Gate and Cumberland Terrace. As they came into Park Village West the Blackburn-Norrises' taxi was just pulling away from the gates of Charlotte Cottage.

He had slept that Friday night in his own flat for the sake of seeing the horror movie, *How to Make a Monster*. The boards, of raw beech that gave off a strong resinous smell, encased the broken windows and made of the interior a dusty kiln. There was no way of ventilating the place except by leaving the front door open and no one did that; no one dared. He'd gone through his ritual and used two rocks before the film started, then gone on to vodka, neat but with a spot of tabasco and a sprinkling of mustard. He didn't need excuses but if he did he'd have said it was to take his mind off the stink in the flat and the heat. For his health's sake, he nibbled at a Duchy Original, the gingered sort, with his drink.

The telly was still on when he woke up. His watch had stopped and he didn't know what time it was. Dark or light, it was all the same in here, or almost. A strong sun high in the sky penetrated the cracks in the beech boards and laid bright bars across the bit of filthy carpet on the floor. The smell, he realised now, was himself. He smelt like the hamburger stall outside Madame Tussaud's that the people in the mews between the waxworks and the Park complained filled their places with the reek of onions and fatty beef. He wondered if it mattered or if he should do something about it. In the pitch dark something ran over his foot.

Hob yelled. He jumped up, smashed the light on with the flat of his hand and saw the mice flee, scurrying for the honeycombed skirting board. It was only mice, that was all it was. They had been feasting on Duchy Original crumbs. He staggered to the bathroom and urinated copiously. His half-brother had told him blow made you pee a lot and he was right. The bath was full of dirty dishes, the washing-up of weeks. He had long used up every piece of crockery he had, and it lay piled there, dusty by this time, coated with the little waxy white pellets like seeds that were fly eggs. Hob thought he saw things moving between a plate and a glass and he turned away. That was funny, because he'd never hallucinated. He'd never been interested in acid, microdot, mushrooms or any of that stuff.

He decided against a bath. Where would he put the dishes? He went back and turned the telly off. He turned the light off too and lay on the settee. For some reason he started thinking about his brother-in-law that used to be before his sister divorced him. Hob had rather liked him, had felt sorry for him because when he was a teenager he'd done acid, just the once, and he'd been left years later with these visions of rats. They'd come at any time and crawl all over him. Hob's ex-brother-in-law had been dead scared of rats, had a phobia about them, so it was a miserable existence he led. Shame, Hob thought. But he never thought about anything or anyone for long. Like alcoholics with drink, he thought about, talked to himself about, considered, wondered at, the substances he used. He would have talked to others about them, only there was no one to talk to.

The mice were back. He could hear them scuttering. Someone on the floor below had told him she'd woken up in the night and heard this trundling noise and when she shone her torch under the bed she'd seen this mouse rolling a Smartie she'd dropped towards a hole in the wall, pushing it with its nose. You had to laugh. He saw a thread of light appear on the floor, then another. It must be morning.

Sometime today he was due to work over a bloke up in Agar Grove who'd done something that got up Lew's nose – though not what he liked up there. Promised to take a bag of smack along with his dope and then reneged (Lew's word) on the deal. Hob was getting a hundred for putting the shyster out of action for a couple of weeks and four rocks over the odds. His thoughts drifted to those rocks but he'd only got two left in the flat, so when thinking instead of *using* got too much, he wandered off looking for what he'd brought in the evening before. The red velvet bag – the stuff was with the bag. Maybe in the kitchen . . .

He found it and poured the powder into a foil bag that had once held some adjunct, sensitive to light, of a photocopier. Like much of his paraphernalia, Hob had found it in a wastebin in one of the more prosperous parts. He slit open the bottom of the bag and held it over the powder in one of the saucers from the bath, screwed up the open top and put his mouth over the resulting aperture. It wasn't as clever or as satisfying as his watering can rose but it would

344

do for now. Better than one of your ordinary stems, anyway. He lit the powder with a match.

It was angel dust or phencyclidine, out of fashion and therefore relatively cheap. Hob had seen on telly that it was basically the stuff they shot into rhinos and elephants on darts to put them under when they moved them away from ivory hunters or whatever. PCP was a change and, anyway, he liked it because it made him feel unreal, like he was a person in that *How to Make a Monster* movie, living inside the telly and watched by millions, or else invisible and not watched at all. Both sensations were pleasant enough.

Sweat began to break out all over him. That was the effect of the dust as was this floating sensation. He got up and walked about, took a few dancing steps, feeling suddenly like a tall thin man with a small head and ballet dancer's feet. Maybe he'd get out of here and go and do the shyster over before the day had really begun.

He could feel his heart beating. The idea that you couldn't always feel your heart beating amused him and he laughed as he danced about the flat, picking up what he needed. Unthinkable to go out without the red velvet bag, without something to keep him well, without something else to bring him down if the heartbeat got so strong it was painful. All ideas of having a bath or changing his clothes had receded. Who needed that shit?

His heart had stopped. For a moment he was transfixed with terror, for he had forgotten what had just made him laugh, that a beating heart cannot normally be felt. He pranced again, punching the air, and into his ears, squeezing up through his body, came the tick-tick-tick of his heart. Laughing again, he thumped himself on the chest, on the place where, under the skin and ribs, the ticking clock pumped.

The red velvet bag in his jacket pocket, he left the flat and came out on to the concrete walkway. A cannibalised van stood tyreless on what was left of the grass, and broken glass littered the empty aisles of the car park, thick as flints on a beach. Round here they used spray paint for the graffiti and the kind they used was red, like blood. For all that, the morning was beautiful, the sky translucent like a blue pearl, the air as yet cool and almost fresh, as if some breath of it had wafted this way from the Park in the night. Hob noticed only the emptiness, the absence of anyone. This was only so in the very early hours and his watch told him it was not quite half-past six.

He went down the concrete stairs and tried to think about getting to Agar Grove, but for some reason his inner eye could only see the railway line running across the Euston wasteland, the visual part of his mind throwing up bridges and flyovers and cranes with necks like Meccano dinosaurs. He'd have to come down. He needed something to bring him down. Yellow Jackets or Vs – what had he got? He palmed two Nembutal, swallowing them in his own saliva.

The place still had an appearance of emptiness when the police came looking for him half an hour later. It was still only seven. The police car crunched over the broken glass and stopped by the mutilated van. Marnock had a sergeant with him and a man in uniform, the one who was driving. They saw the boarded-up windows, looked at each other and shrugged. There was no doorbell. The sergeant banged on the knocker. He did that twice, then they shouted through the letter box, 'Police, open up!'

No one did, so they broke the door down, no difficult task. It yielded after two shoulder charges

and a thump from the driver's boot. The smell that
came out to meet them was so bad that at first they
thought there must be a dead body inside.

Chapter Twenty-Nine

They had taken a Camcorder with them and had recorded every minute happening, it seemed to Mary, of their long holiday. She agreed to watch the video and they were childishly pleased. They were astonished too, perhaps expecting excuses for avoiding the experience. But Mary was glad of the chance to sit still and speechless in the living room with the curtains drawn. While her eyes focused on Sir Stewart and Lady Blackburn-Norris in bright unsuitable swimwear beside a hotel pool, in ponchos on donkey back, viewing Inca remains and eating lobster in revolving tower-top restaurants, she could give her mind to her future: what she was going to do and where she was going.

Thankful that she had neither said nor written anything to the Blackburn-Norrises about her impending marriage, she had been spared enquiries and possible condolence. They treated her sweetly, charmingly, but at the same time only as the recipient of all their news, a willing ear for their holiday reminiscences and the most wonderful housekeeper and dog-minder they could possibly have hoped to find.

It wasn't until the video was over that they mentioned her grandmother's death and then it was to deplore the loss of a friend rather than sympathise with her, whose only close relative in the world was dead. But she tried to avoid self-pity and quickly changed the subject to tell them about Bean.

They were old and both appeared, in spite of a dark tan that gave their faces a look of distressed leather, more fragile than before they went away. News of a violent death should be broken gently to them and this she tried to do, first by saying that Bean would be unable to continue dog-walking. But when, in response to Sir Stewart's angry bark of, Why the hell not, for God's sake, she said quietly that Bean was dead, adding that he had met his death by violence, fragility was replaced by expressions of avid interest.

'You mean he was murdered?'

'Yes, that's what I mean.'

'By that Impaler fellow?'

The news must have reached them somehow. Possibly in American newspapers. Had they made an exception to their unwritten rule and considered three murders in Regent's Park just important enough for their pages?

'Apparently not,' she said. 'They haven't caught anyone for Bean's murder but they know it wasn't the same one as killed the other two.'

'Bean,' said Lady Blackburn-Norris, who had until then been speechless with the wonder of it. 'Bean,' she said again. 'What had he done to get himself killed, Mary dear? Does anyone know?'

The other implications of the death took a while to reach them but did so at last. Sir Stewart, pouring a pre-lunch sherry for his wife and Mary and a stiff whisky for himself, said, enunciating slowly as if the full horror of his words came clear only as he uttered them:

'Then who's been walking the bloody dog?'

'Well, I have.'

'Oh, Mary darling, how awful for you! And you

had your work and heaven knows what. We would never have asked you if we'd known you'd have to walk the little beast.'

Their lack of enthusiasm at seeing Gushi again had been matched by his apathy at the sight of them. Lady Blackburn-Norris had patted his head and remarked only that at least he hadn't put on weight while Sir Stewart had ignored him altogether.

'I didn't mind walking him. He's a dear little dog. It was only for a couple of weeks. There's a boy, a teenager, who seems to have taken over Bean's job, but I didn't – well, you must see what you think of him.'

'But who can we trust?' Lady Blackburn-Norris threw out her hands. For a moment Mary thought she meant trust with the Shih Tzu. 'To have a key? To come in the house?'

Sir Stewart topped up his glass. 'It's out of the question having some bloody youth no one knows in here.'

'I can't walk him,' said his wife. 'Not at my age. Not with my arthritis.'

'The bloody dog's more trouble than he's worth.'

They asked Mary to stay to lunch. It was that, that invitation to a meal, which, because it specified, brought home to her the fact that she was going to have to leave Charlotte Cottage and leave today. She had had plenty of warning. They had told her well in advance of their return. She could hardly complain of the unfairness of it. Upstairs, in the handbag she hardly ever used, was the key to Lamballe House, Belsize Avenue, a big dark dusty house that no one had visited for weeks. But she had somewhere to go, a far cry from so many out there with nothing and nowhere . . .

The man in Agar Grove made an attempt at fighting

back and in the process cut Hob's lip and blacked one of his eyes. His struggles didn't avail him much. It would have been better for him to have given in and let his assailant get on with it. Hob took his revenge for the eye and the lip, kicking the shyster in the stomach and chest but calling it a day when he heard a rib crack.

He had used the tube to get up there but now he was walking. He had gone quite a long way before he noticed there was blood on the toes of his shoes. Perhaps he was even leaving bloody footprints. Suddenly a host of worries enclosed him and he felt like a marked man. Everyone was looking at him. There was a man close behind him – he kept looking round to see – who must be following him, following the trail of his footprints. It wouldn't matter which way he went. If he doubled back into the hinterland of Kentish Town, the man would be there. Much more of this and he'd have to kill him. He'd have to lead him somewhere quiet, into some narrow tree-sheltered street, and kill him.

But when he next looked round the man had gone. The betting shop on the corner had swallowed him up. Hob remembered it was Saturday, Lottery day. If he won the Lottery he could buy up the world's stock of cocaine and enough PCP to stun a safari park. But he didn't buy a ticket. Buying a ticket meant talking to someone, getting out the money, being *among* people. The idea was vaguely unpleasant.

He went into a shop, a corner supermarket, empty but for its Indian proprietor and a young Indian girl, helped himself to a Coke from the drinks fridge, paid for it, all in silence. They asked him if he wanted a scratch card and he nodded, scratched away and of course it was a dud. The usual two Walker's crisps and two weekend breaks in Tenerife. He opened the

Coke can. It wasn't that he wanted a drink. He wanted something with which to wash down two black beauties and a crystal methedrine. He needed pepping up.

The drink made him need to pee. There was never anywhere and he couldn't wait till he got to the Men's in the Broad Walk. He went into an alley and, like a dog, let forth a flood over someone's dustbin. In the Park he tried to wipe the blood off his shoes on to the grass but by then it was dry. Nothing mattered, though, and anyway you couldn't see the blood in the strong blinding sunlight. By the St Mark's Square Bridge he dropped down on to the tow-path. A boat was coming down from Camden Lock, under Albert Road, and a woman on deck waved to him. Her face was lobster red from the sun. Hob didn't wave back. He was looking for Lew or Carl. Gupta never showed himself in daylight.

There was no one on the canal bank but three or four of the jacks men, and they didn't count. They were scarcely human. One of them was lying on his back with a hand hanging down, trailing in the water, an empty bottle just fallen from his slack lips but kept upright in the crook of his arm. So might a baby lie, its feed sucked dry, sleep overtaking it before its mouth quite relinquished the teat. Hob resisted the temptation to kick him in the groin as he passed. Enough was enough.

He found himself a secluded spot, sat among the trees and went through his ritual with the contents of the velvet bag. Two rocks – why not? But they were all he had. A rare moment of lucidity came and he understood that no matter how many he had, how many little zip-lock packages, he wouldn't be able to save them up and keep them in reserve. He would smoke any given number, any *bought* number. There could be no end to it and no satisfying the craving.

352

But this knowledge passed as the smoke from the two rocks took hold. It passed and was lost as the smoke itself was lost in the diesel air and the canal stink and the serene blue sky.

He felt his heart beat and he heard it. On the move again, no longer bored or uneasy, paranoia past, he danced along the canal bank. The jacks men didn't give him a glance. They saw funnier sights most days than a prancing man with a skinny body and a big head. Gradually he forgot everything but his energy, his happiness and the drug that brought those things. He would go to Lew's place. He wasn't supposed to, but he would.

On his doorstep on the estate Lew didn't let him in – he had a wife and kids and it was Saturday – but he sold him all the rocks he had: fifteen. He'd collect a fresh supply in the afternoon. Hob got a cut rate, especially as he was happy to take some Tueys as part of the deal. He took a taxi back, ignoring the taxi driver's loud sniffs and requests to have the windows opened in the back, but just before the turn-off from Albert Road he asked the driver to drop him there. He didn't want to go home – what was there at home, for God's sake?

'That's a verbal contract, you know, what we had,' said the driver.

'You what?'

'A gentlemen's agreement that I take you to Plangent Road – that's like Euston.'

'I'm getting out at the lights,' said Hob. 'Too bad if you don't like it.' He started laughing. 'I don't have to pay you, it's down to you.'

He got out. The driver muttered something about one pound sixty and Hob handed it over. No tip.

'Wash yourself, why don't you,' the driver called after him. 'I'm going to have to have this cab detoxed.'

353

It was all hugely amusing to Hob. The funniest thing he could think of was him going round to people's houses and sitting in people's cars and them having to spend good money on getting rid of the smell of him. He crossed the road at the lights, spitting on to the bonnet of the waiting Jaguar. The driver couldn't leave his luxury vehicle and come after him, that was the beauty of it.

If the builders were working on the reconstructed house, as it seemed from their materials lying around, they weren't on Saturdays. He was amazed to see it was already two in the afternoon. Where had the day gone? Where did all the days go? He pushed open the garden gate and climbed down in the Grotto, avoiding the barbed wire, ducking and dipping and worming his way, catching his clothes on the sharp barbs.

A condom, half-full of water, floated on the figure of eight pool. He picked it out and threw it into the bushes. Suddenly he was very tired. He knew that feeling. It happened all the time. It was part of withdrawal, the beginnings of a state. But he continued to sit there, taking no action, staring into the water which, though with green bits floating on it, was nevertheless quite clear and through which he could see the brick fragments and broken glass that covered the bottom of the pool.

The sensation he had in his head was not precisely pain. It was more as if someone had put a cap on him and was drawing tight a string threaded through the rim of it. That was how it was for some minutes. During those minutes he sat looking into the pool and beginning to tremble. Then the pain came, a headache which started quite mildly but increased very fast, becoming enormous, as if a metal helmet was clamped over the cap, a helmet that was too small for his huge cranium, but that his head was being forcibly squeezed into, while levers on its sides and doors and bolts were clamped and screwed into place.

With shaking hands he opened the red velvet bag and set to work. Only half a straw was left. He had meant to get replacements but had forgotten. It was impossible to block off one of the holes in the vodka top, so he put his mouth over the whole thing, lit the crumbled rock through the perforation and drew in the white smoke. It seemed more acrid than usual, less delicious. He began to cough but thrust the bottle top back into his mouth just the same.

Something happened then. His hands had stilled, the headache was leaving him, but he felt a sensation in his head like nothing he had previously known. It was like hearing a train come very fast out of a tunnel or even a car hitting the back of another car. It was a clang and a rushing and a long-drawn explosion all at the same time.

He felt his body undergo some change. It frightened him because he had no idea what that change was. It was just that he was not the same as he had been a minute before. A little while before he had been something and now he was something else. He tried to put out his hands but the left hand was dead. It was like those times when you wake up in the morning and your arm is numb, only when you rub it and squeeze it the feeling slowly comes back. The feeling wasn't coming back this time. And he couldn't see shapes. He could only see brightness, and as his legs slid into the water, the rainbow flash of an arc of spray.

> I have no pain, dear Mother, now,
> But oh, I am so dry,
> Attach me to a brewery
> And leave me there to die . . .

*

The time change and their advanced age caught up with the Blackburn-Norrises by mid-afternoon. Sir Stewart's eyelids drooped and he angrily forced them open. His wife said, 'You won't go just yet, will you? You won't leave us?'

Mary said hesitantly, 'Do you mean, stay another night?'

'Oh, darling, I'd like you to stay for ever!' She quickly spoiled the effect. 'What are we going to do about the wretched dog? We only took the dog on because its owner died. I can't walk it.' She pointed at her sleeping husband. 'He *won't*.'

'I'll stay till tomorrow if you're sure. And then perhaps I could find this woman who exercises the dogs, or the boy, and you could interview one of them – what do you think?'

'I wish I didn't have to think,' said Lady Blackburn-Norris. 'I'm so tired I'm sure my time-clock's spring has worn out.'

Mary watched her fall asleep. She drew the curtains against the afternoon sunlight. In the hall Gushi lay panting. She picked him up and carried him into the kitchen, gave him water and laid him on the cool tiles. He licked her fingers. In the short time of their acquaintance she had learnt to read Lady Blackburn-Norris's thoughts and to predict what turn they would take. If the offer were made that she was sure would be made, she would say yes.

One more night in Charlotte Cottage and then she would go. Whatever her fate might be it was not to spend the next months or years of her life as companion to a rich old couple. She went upstairs and put clothes into one of the suitcases. It was nearly six, long past the time for Gushi's walk. The Blackburn-Norrises slept on. Gushi slept. She filled a glass from the cold water tap, drank half of it, listened to the drone of an aircraft passing overhead, the nearer, more vibrant buzz of a wasp at the window pane. There seemed nothing in the world left to do, to read, to see, to care about; no one to talk to or be with. If I stay here, she thought, I will start to weep.

She put the house key into her jeans pocket, glanced once more at the sleeping old people – Sir Stewart had begun a stertorous snoring – went out of Charlotte Cottage and into Albany Street. The day had begun to cool, the shadows to lengthen. She crossed on the lights by the St Pancras fresco, looked back and saw that Nikolai had crossed behind her. A tour bus, crammed with visitors, went past up to Primrose Hill. A Union Jack on a cyclist's handlebars reminded her it was the day of VJ celebrations. National events had passed her by these last few days.

She managed a half-hearted wave to Nikolai. The children's playground at the Gloucester Gate was still crowded. Old men in khaki, covered with medals, wandered ahead of her, looking as if they had strayed from a procession. She asked herself why she had come in here and where she was going. Then someone called her name, a familiar voice, a voice that made a wave break inside her body.

'Mary!'

The man she had known as Leo was sitting on the grey granite steps of the Parsee's fountain.

Chapter Thirty

It was Marnock himself who found Hob.

They had been searching for him since morning in all his known haunts. The latest sighting came from a man in Agar Grove who, from his hospital bed, was able to name his assailant. He had lost four teeth, had two cracked ribs and a broken collarbone, but he was anxious to talk about Harvey Owen Bennett.

It was his opinion that Bennett was the Impaler. Bennett was guilty of both the street people killings. Marnock disagreed but didn't say so. He thought the Agar Grove man entitled to sling mud and make wild accusations. For the time being. He was no angel, had a string of convictions as long as the Broad Walk which Marnock would later make longer. It was his belief the Agar Grove man was responsible for the mugging of Bean in the Nursemaids' Tunnel.

He was always made happy by villains grassing. It gave him hope for the future. Harvey Owen Bennett, for instance. Bennett had killed Bean and stuck him on that five-pointed iron tree but someone had paid him to do it and Marnock now hoped Bennett would tell him. The Agar Grove man had created a happy precedent.

Marnock called that day on every member of Bennett's extended family. They weren't truthful people but this time, with misgivings, he believed them when they said they hadn't seen him. His

358

mother said she hadn't seen him for six months and this amused Marnock in the light of what she had told him back in June: that at the time of Pharaoh's murder Hob had been among guests at an all-night silver wedding party in the Holloway Road.

They scoured the Park for him. Marnock thought of the Grotto as the abode, more or less reserved, of the toffee-nosed dosser with the Oxbridge accent, and he nearly didn't look. It was a drinking straw, spiralled with red like a barber's pole and stuck up in the branches of a tree, that caught his eye from his seat in the back of the car. The ritual that served Harvey Bennett's habit required drinking straws . . .

He was lying half in, half out of the dirty little pond. They heard his breathing long before they reached him and that was how they knew he was alive. Marnock's sergeant was on his mobile calling an ambulance before they had laid a finger on Hob.

'He's young,' Marnock's sergeant said. 'Well, youngish. But I reckon he's had a stroke.'

The ambulance man, getting Hob on to a stretcher, said superfluously that he wasn't a doctor. Then he said that in his opinion Hob had had a stroke.

'Or several,' said Marnock. 'I once knew a bloke, only a year or two older than him, same taste for substances, had twenty strokes in quick succession.'

'Bloody hell,' said the ambulance driver. 'Did it kill him?'

'In a manner of speaking,' said Marnock. 'After a couple of weeks they switched off the machine.'

Be angry, Mary said to herself, you must be angry. You must walk on past him, pretend he's not there. Or stand your ground and tell him what you think of him. She held her fists tightly clenched. He was in front of her now.

359

'I've been here since eight this morning,' he said, 'waiting for you.'

'I didn't come into the Park this morning,' she said.

'It was so hot. I brought a bottle of water but it got warm. I tried to keep awake but I fell asleep and when I woke up I thought I'd missed you.'

She knew he had never heard that note in her voice before.

'What do you want?'

'I suppose that's how you think of me, as always wanting something, as doing everything I do for what I can get out of it.'

'Wouldn't that be a true picture?'

'Not entirely.'

She walked into the shade of the trees, put her hands against the rough cool bark of a tree and bowed her head. 'I thought I'd never see you again. I hoped not. I know what you did. I've thought about it these past days – I haven't had anything else to think about – and there can't be anything you can say to me in extenuation.' She turned to look at him, half look at him, and remembered then what she hadn't thought of for perhaps an hour or two, their lovemaking. It came back and brought hot angry blood into her face. He must see that burning colour and know. 'It won't mean anything to you if I say it was the worst betrayal I've ever known.'

Alistair's small misdemeanours, what were they compared with his offence?

'Would you – could we – is it possible to ask you if we could go back to the house?'

'The Blackburn-Norrises have come home.'

'Then will you sit down here with me or on a seat or somewhere and talk to me?'

Her head bowed again. She found she was shaking it from side to side. The words came out hoarsely.

'What is your name?'

'*What?*'

'I asked you what your name is. I can't call you Leo. You aren't called Leo.'

'My name is Carl,' he said. 'Carl Nash. Leo was my brother.'

She sat down. He dropped on to the grass beside her but moved when she indicated by a pushing movement with her hands that he was too close. She looked at him properly for the first time, a gaze of deepest scorn, and saw that his eyes were full of tears.

'I brought Leo up. He was more than ten years younger than I. Oh, yes, of course I'm not twenty-four, I'm older than you, Mary, not younger. I'm thirty-five.'

'We believe what people tell us,' Mary said. 'Or I do. I believed what you told me. And I saw your birth certificate.'

'You saw his. When the leukaemia was diagnosed and they said he needed a transplant I thought there wouldn't be a problem. There was our mother – not that she'd taken a scrap of notice of Leo since he was ten, she'd left that to me – and there was myself, a couple of half-sisters somewhere about. None of us was compatible. Can you imagine that?'

'You've already told me. Except that you suggested it was you not your brother who needed the transplant. If you're going to explain you should . . .'

'Tell you why I posed as Leo?'

'It was for my money,' she said bitterly.

He lifted his shoulders, not denying. 'I was an actor once. Only there was no work. Then I was a schoolteacher. Funny, isn't it? Then I made a bit of money,' he said. 'Dealing, mostly.'

She knew she was innocent but not what she was

innocent of. The look in his eyes told her he wasn't talking about scrap metal or antiques.

'Drugs,' he said impatiently. 'I'd needed funds to find a donor for Leo. That was before the Harvest Trust. I thought maybe I'd have to go to some Third World country and buy a donor. Then you came along.'

'I wasn't rich then,' she said. 'I'd been living in a one-bedroom flat in Willesden and earning twelve thousand a year. What made you think I was rich?'

He said simply, 'The heading on your writing paper. The address. Charlotte Cottage, Park Village West.'

Briefly she closed her eyes. Unseeing, she sensed he had come closer to her and she drew away. She looked at him.

'And when you found out I didn't live there you dropped me. You meant never to see me again. That was what happened. You weren't ill, you were never ill.'

'True,' he said. 'It was a bitter disappointment.' She looked incredulously at his wry smile. He had aged in the past few minutes. He might be forty, forty-five. The smile creased his pale face into lines and ridges. 'I did need money, you see. I knew Leo would get ill again. I could see the signs; I'd made myself an expert in his illness.' All the ironic amusement died out of his face. 'I loved him so much. Believe me, if you can believe anything I say, believe me, I'm not trying for your sympathy, your compassion, but I'd like you not to think me a total monster. I loved him as if he was my own child..Or I think so – I've never had a child.'

'So that was all right? Using me was all right because you loved your brother?'

'No, Mary, it wasn't all right. But it was all I could think of. Your grandmother died and when I heard

362

that I came back. You told me what she'd left you and it was more than I'd imagined in my wildest dreams.'

She had become curious in spite of herself. The sheer suicidal nerve of it compelled a question.

'I might have found out at any time. The Trust might have told me Leo – your brother – they might have told me he was becoming ill again. What would you have done?'

'What I did when they did,' he said. 'Disappeared. But I used to scrutinise your post. I was – I was usually up first.' He had turned away his eyes.

'So that's why you stayed with me,' she said bitterly, unable to bring herself to use the words. 'That's why you stayed those nights, so that you could get to the post in the morning.' The words were hard for her because she had never used them before. 'That's why you screwed me, *fucked* me.'

He said with a simplicity she had to believe at last was honest, 'It was at first. I came to love you. Couldn't you tell?'

For half an hour she had been unaware of anyone else in the Park but themselves. A child's shriek, a blue and white lightweight ball bouncing across the grass, coming to rest at their feet, reminded her they were not alone. She stood up, brushed dried shreds of grass off her jeans and lobbed the ball back. He watched her, anxiously waiting.

'What do you want me to say?' she asked him wearily.

'Only that you believe me.'

She supposed that she had noticed. It was when the lovemaking changed from a sick man's effete attempts to enthusiasm, when acquiescence became passion, that she had been aware of it without asking why. He had been ill and now he was getting better, that was all.

'I believe you.'

She said it dully, for it was a few moments before relief came and she understood that she need no longer feel humiliation and shame. He had wanted her, he had not had to force himself.

'I wanted to marry you by then,' he said. 'I'd never wanted that before.' He squeezed his eyes shut and sprang to his feet. 'Will you do one last thing for me? Will you walk a little way with me?'

'I don't know.' She nearly called him Leo. 'I don't know, Carl.'

He flushed at the sound of his own name. It seemed to confirm him as its true possessor. 'Do you remember that place we went to for dinner? That first time? The Italian place?'

'When you pretended to be ill?'

He winced at that. 'I'm sorry. I had to. I thought I had to. Mary, I've done worse things than that to get money.'

'I don't want to hear,' she said.

'I thought – I wondered – if you'd let me take you there now, tonight. If we could – it would be the last time, wouldn't it?'

She nodded. She still wanted answers. 'I'll walk with you.'

'And you'll come to the restaurant?'

'Perhaps.'

He got to his feet, held out a hand to help her, but she shook her head. They walked across the grass in silence, across Chester Road and down the Broad Walk.

'Leo knew all about it,' he said. 'He thought it was funny at first. We both thought it was funny at first. He used to want all the details but I – I stopped telling him things after a while.'

'Just as a matter of interest –' Mary knew she was no good at the ironic tone. She found it hard to be scathing, but she tried – 'Just as a matter of interest, why didn't Leo meet me himself, or isn't there anything amusing about being honest?'

'Oh, Mary, he was just a boy, undersized, not educated, never quite well. I loved him and perhaps you'd have come to love him if you'd known him, but not like that, not in that way. You'd never have said you'd marry the real Leo.'

Suddenly, as they came down the path and reached the lake, she stopped thinking about herself and, reluctantly, almost fearfully, began to think about him. The anger had evaporated. It had never been thriving. She put her hand on his arm and looked into his face.

'You must be very unhappy.'

'Thank you for that,' he said.

'Oh, Carl. It was like losing your own child.'

'I suppose so. But it was worse. I killed him, you see.'

'*What?*'

'Oh, I don't mean that. Not actually. Not like that Impaler kills people. I mean I killed him by taking away his only chance of getting well.'

'I don't understand.'

'You would have given another donation, wouldn't you? If it had been asked for you'd have done it?'

'Yes, but . . .'

'You said so. When we'd been to your grand-mother's house, the day I asked you to marry me. You'd have given it to me, to your husband, but it wasn't I that wanted it, it was the real Leo Nash.

'Leo was dying by then. Perhaps you could have saved him but I couldn't ask, could I? I couldn't let the Harvest Trust ask. I thought maybe if once we

were married and I said I had to have money – I had
to have, say, fifty thousand – you'd have given it to
me and I'd have gone to India and bought the right
sort of bone marrow for Leo. But Leo died.'

She thought about it. She had withdrawn her hand
from his arm when he spoke of killing his brother,
but now she replaced it and let it lie there lightly.
They had come out of the Park at the York Gate and
the clock on Marylebone Church ahead of them
began to chime the hour. Perhaps because of the VJ
Day commemorations the traffic was dense and
swift.

'It was a monstrous irony,' he said. 'That I who
loved Leo, who would have done anything for Leo,
who did do anything, spoiled his chances of life by
what I did. By choosing this way to make a fortune
for Leo, I blew it. So I killed him. If by killing
someone we mean that but for us he'd be alive. But
for me, Leo would be alive.'

They had come to the pavement edge and begun
to walk towards the lights at Harley Street. The
traffic noise was so loud that he had to shout.

'The old dog man,' he began.

'Bean,' she said. 'Bean – what about him?'

'He tried to blackmail me. He was going to tell you
– things about me.' He smiled. 'Not the things I've
told you. Other things you'd have liked even less. I
couldn't allow that.'

'I can't hear you,' she said. 'I can't hear you for the
traffic.'

'Just as well,' Carl said, softly now and half to
himself. 'I know you won't forgive me, anyway, but
you'd never have overlooked paying someone to –
deal with Bean.' He turned to look at her, seized her
by the shoulders. 'Mary!' It was very nearly a shout.
'Can you hear me now? I've blown it with you too, I

366

know that. Just for the record, how did you get the Harvest Trust's letter?'

She also had to raise her voice. 'Alistair sent it me. As a wedding present.'

'The bastard.'

She never once looked behind her. Roman saw her put her hand on the man's arm and for a moment he thought things were all right, and then he knew they were far from that. A sense of foreboding filled him. He had been about to turn back but now he wouldn't; he would stick with it.

The charge of emotion between them was so powerful it tensed their bodies. He marvelled at it, walking a dozen yards behind them. She withdrew her hand, recoiled, spoke a name, 'Carl . . .' loud enough for him to hear. So it was Carl. But what was her name? Strange that after so long, so many brief chance encounters, he still didn't know.

'What?' he heard her cry. 'What?'

Carl was explaining something. She shook her head vehemently, but after a moment or two the hand was back, resting on Carl's arm but distantly somehow as if placed there out of pity rather than affection. You are imagining too much, Roman told himself, and you are spying too much. They can take care of themselves. It's no more than a lovers' quarrel being made up.

But he followed them down York Gate. The clock on St Marylebone was chiming seven. The pavements of the Marylebone Road were choked with crowds, the traffic pouring fast down towards the Euston underpass. He was very close behind them now, so close that if she turned round and saw him he would have had to make an excuse for his presence and he had no explanation. But she didn't turn round. She was looking into Carl's face, not

367

with love, not with passion, but still as if no one else in the world existed.

Her voice she kept low, drowned by the traffic's roar, but the man called Carl shouted above it. He shouted as if he didn't care who heard him:

'I don't want to live without him, you see. I can't face life without him.'

For a brief while Roman had been so near her that by putting out his hand he could have touched her, then, as happens in crowds, two people pushed in front of him, squeezing between him and her and forcing him to step back. They were part of the group at the pavement edge, waiting to cross when the lights changed. You could wait ages here for the lights to change, then when they did they were red almost too short a time to allow for crossing. Seven or eight people stood poised to cross and she and Carl were at the head of them, waiting while the traffic pounded down its three lanes.

Things happened very quickly then. Roman, craning his neck, but taller than those in front of him, saw Carl give her a little push back from the kerb. A little saving, protecting push into those waiting behind. He put his head down and plunged into the road, threw out his arms and ran into the traffic, in front of a car, a taxi, into the path of a container, running at bonnets, under wheels.

A woman was screaming from the moment he leapt from the kerb. Roman heard his own rough gasp as he clenched his hands. Brakes screamed and horns brayed. Carl was flung into the air, his body describing an arc in the blue air against the setting sun, splintered by flashes of light from sun-glinting chrome, the sudden full beam of a headlight blazing on him as he fell under wheels and was ground between tangling metal.

There was blood somewhere. Roman thought he

saw a long splash of it fly against white enamel. He was struggling to reach her, catch her as she fell, but the crowd made a wall around her, leaning over her, kneeling beside her. He stepped aside, let it go, and stood holding his bowed head in his hands in the suddenly emptied street.

Sirens were already wailing.

Chapter Thirty-One

For quite a long time Marnock or his sergeant sat by Harvey Owen Bennett's bed, hoping for a name, hoping he would come round sufficiently to tell them who had paid him to kill Bean. One or other member of his large extended family was usually there, a half-brother or sister, a stepsister, his mother, stepfathers and men who said they were his uncles. Some of them touched his lifeless hand.

He never moved. He was fed intravenously and a machine kept his heart beating and his lungs breathing. Sweat occasionally broke out on his large forehead and slab-like cheeks.

Three weeks after he had been brought in the doctor in charge of his case told Marnock that Harvey Bennett would never speak again. His eyes were open and he would never close them. It was unlikely he could think or remember or speculate or even suffer. Large areas of his brain had been destroyed.

James Barker-Pryce sued the tabloid newspaper and was awarded substantial damages. These were not on account of their allegations that he had been consorting with a known prostitute; he had admitted that and there was some question whether his constituency party would readopt him at the next General Election. He had brought the action because the journalist alleged he had been involved in a conspiracy to murder.

The school-leaver went back to school, or rather to a sixth form college to take some A Levels, and all Bean's dogs except for Gushi were walked by Amelia Walker, who seemed to find no difficulty in handling seventeen animals at once.

Mary Jago had always meant to sell her grandmother's house and buy another but having gone there to live after Carl Nash's death, there she remained. She had builders in to convert the upper floors into self-contained flats and her friend Anne Symonds had moved into one of them. The Harvest Trust asked her if she would be willing to remain on their books and in December she gave another bone marrow donation, this time to a girl of sixteen she knew as 'Susan' and who knew her as 'Barbara'.

Roman Ashton rented two rooms in a house in Princess Road, Primrose Hill, where he was not particularly comfortable. All the money derived from the sale of his house he had sunk into a precarious venture with Tom Outram, the Talisman Press having been taken over and absorbed into a massive conglomerate. With some American backing they had started a publishing house that produced only historical novels in paperback originals. So far it had been startlingly successful but how long would such success last?

Their headquarters were in the Marylebone Road and when it wasn't raining Roman walked to work through the Park. He never saw the fair-haired girl. She no longer walked through the Gloucester Gate and south of the zoo to the Charlbert Bridge. She no longer crossed Chester Road or ran through the rose garden.

And then one day he saw her. He was going to work, crossing the Outer Circle, and she and her little

371

dog were getting out of a car she had just parked by the Monkey Gate.

'Hallo,' she said.

'Hallo.'

'Do you know, I've often looked for you in here but I've never seen you. I thought you must have – well, moved away.'

'I've looked for you too,' he said.

They passed through the gateway into the Broad Walk and across on to the grass. She unclipped the lead from the dog's collar, let him go, stood up and held out her hand.

'Mary Jago,' she said.

'Roman Ashton.'

'I was house-sitting for some people when I last saw you. They gave me their dog. They didn't like him much, you see, and I did. I live in Belsize Park now and I've got a car, so I can still bring him into the Park, but I'm rather late today.'

'That's why we've never met,' he said.

'You stopped being a street person?'

'Last August.' He saw her wince at those words and said quickly, 'I did it to get over something. It's something I'll never get over and I don't really want to but I'm glad of the two years I spent sleeping rough. It gave me – something else to think about. I've got a job now and I'm looking for a place to live.'

'When we last met,' she said, 'you advised me to be angry.'

'Did I? I don't remember that. And were you?'

'There was no one to be angry with,' she said, and she looked down at her shoes. 'Except myself. I think I've got a bit stronger. I don't placate people so much. I'm not so trusting. Oh, I don't know why I'm telling you all this. You can't want to know.' She started calling the dog. 'Gushi, Gushi, where are you?'

'I'll tell you something,' he said. 'When you lived in Park Village I appointed myself your guardian. I thought I could watch over you. I told myself you needed protecting. Once when there was a man running after you I sent him the other way.'

She was looking at him, incredulously at first, then with a smile dawning.

'But I didn't do much, did I? I didn't do a thing. I couldn't save you from whatever it was.'

Her face suddenly grave again, 'You couldn't save me from that,' she said. 'I fell into something because I was lonely, something awful. It's over now.'

I know, he thought. I saw. The Shih Tzu came running up, sat at her feet quivering, looking up into her face.

'He always wants to be carried. He's such a baby.' She picked up the dog. 'You said – you said something about looking for a place to live. Only – well, I've got this big house and I've had some conversions done, and I thought if it was a flat you were – but perhaps . . .' she hesitated, as if putting a restraint upon herself, reminding herself of past indiscretion '. . . perhaps we ought to get to know each other a bit better first.'

'That seems a very good idea,' Roman said.

The man on the canal bank had been there for weeks, months, ever since high summer. Not all the time – he had his occupation – but by night, three nights a week at least, watching and waiting. He had been there since before the body of David George Kneller that they called Nello had been found on the railings outside the zoo.

He blamed himself for that. If he had been more vigilant, done what he had started doing in August two months before, Nello would be alive now. No use asking whether the life Nello lived had been

373

worth living – the life he now lived – for that wasn't the point.

The first evening he had come down here the man with the beard they called Rome had also come down, looking for a place to kip. But he had got him to leave with a shake of his fist and a scowl on his ugly face. It *was* ugly – so what? There were things they could do for acne now, drugs and whatever – medication was a *cleaner* word – but there hadn't been when he was fourteen. The scars hadn't stopped him getting a wife and promotion or the right to do what he was doing.

For the fiftieth time, or maybe not quite so many as that, he scrambled down through the churchyard and the brambles and stinging nettles on to the canal bank. The clothes he wore, black, ancient, stained rags, were dead men's clothes from the rotting boots to the greasy cloth cap. Sometimes he wondered what he would do if he found someone else on his pitch, settling down for the night. But he never had and he didn't now. Once he'd sat down he always listened to the traffic passing overhead, fancying but doubtless mistaken that he'd know the sound of the van, the diesel noise that was somehow bigger and more of a gargle than that made by a taxi.

The bridge throbbed when cars went over it, boom-boomed when it was something bigger like a truck. It had been dark for hours, since five in the afternoon, but it wasn't cold. Under the bridge it was always damp, the brickwork oozing moisture, the ground sticky, the canal waters dark, more shiny than he ever expected and with rainbow streaks of oil. There was something uncanny about a river that didn't flow but where the water was stagnant, just water put into a ditch really, and the ditch had been dug by men. He'd never thought of any of that until he came to sit nightly by the canal.

He always tried not to fall asleep but often he couldn't help himself. If what he was waiting for happened that would wake him up all right. When he woke, usually a bit before dawn, his legs ached and his back ached from lying on damp concrete and he felt filthy, as if some sticky substance had been pasted on him in the night, to make a coat between his skin and his clothes.

Tonight he thought it unlikely he'd sleep. It had been his day off and he'd slept away the afternoon. Since that first evening when he'd forgotten, he'd never come down here without food, plenty of it. A pizza – ironical that, really – a couple of mini pork pies or a samosa, cold sausages, a bag of crisps, bananas. His wife called bananas the junk food of fruit and he saw what she meant – not that they weren't good for you but that they were so easy to eat. He ate one. He drank some coffee out of the flask he'd brought.

The barrow he had with him he'd found dumped in the Grotto. God knows who had put it there or had used it. It was his now and he filled it up with groundsheet, sleeping bag, cushions, a torch, the cigarettes he shouldn't smoke but probably would before the night was out, food, the coffee flask, a bottle of water, *Today*, the latest Stephen King – when was Stephen King going to write about canals, the horrible way they just lay there, not moving, just waiting, still or lightly rocking? Maybe he already had.

Up in Camden Town a dog started barking. It barked for a bit, then began howling like a wolf. The wolves in the zoo never seemed to howl. He tore the pizza in half and each half in half and started eating. You couldn't tell from the state of the darkness but it was after eleven, nearly midnight. Overhead the traffic was a lot lighter. For a long while there wasn't any traffic, and then the bridge would thump and rattle.

It was too dark to read his book or his paper and he wasn't keen enough on either to bother with his torch. He contemplated the slightly rocking black water with the skins of light lying on patches of it. He started counting the seconds between one rattle of the bridge and the next, calculating that enumeration at a medium-fast rate was counting seconds. A hundred and ten, next time a hundred and eighty. It was when he was counting for the third time, reaching two hundred and seventeen, that he had this crawling sensation that someone was looking at him from the parapet of the bridge.

He couldn't see the parapet from where he sat, only the underside of the arch, greenish with algae, a single drop of water falling from between two redder bricks. Grubbing with his fingers in the grassy earth, he picked out a flat pebble and first holding it parallel to the ground, sent it skimming across the surface of the water. It made a trail of spray as a toy speedboat might. He thought he heard footfalls on the bridge above his head.

He belonged to a profession whose members are not supposed to feel afraid. It was the same with the armed forces. But these days it is no longer necessary to pretend you don't feel fear, only not to show it. He was afraid and he knew all the ways of not showing it. At least, the hand didn't shake that reached for the cigarette packet, took out a cigarette and brought it to his mouth. He struck a match and watched the blaze of light under the bridge, the glitter on the tubular rail, the black shadows fleeing into the water.

Which way would the man come?

He listened, heard something crushed underfoot, a piece of litter, plastic and hard. It cracked under the pressure of a shoe descending. He looked towards the sound, preparing to act his part, raising a fist to ward off an intruder, the way he had when the Oxbridge dosser came down.

It was over now. For good or ill, for himself or the Impaler, this must be the end. No more waiting and watching. Before he saw anything else he saw the glint of the knife.

He started to get up. Act naturally. The dosser on the canal bank would get to his feet, would start back, drop his cigarette into the dark water. He had his back to the underside of the bridge. It struck cold through the padding of his clothes. The man came down, revealed himself in the dark that is never quite darkness – tall, youngish, a dark combat jacket over that red and white vest, camouflage pants over the red jeans. His lips curled back like a dog's.

The way he hurled himself on to the dosser with his back against the wall was sudden, a violent reflex, but not unexpected. The knife sank into something soft and thick, but not into flesh. There was no blood. It was pulled out to strike again but never reached its target. The poised arm was seized, brought up at an unnatural angle; a leg came out from the bundle of black rags, kicked with practised aim and the man in the combat jacket gave a soft groan. His upraised hand trembled, opened and the knife fell clattering on to the concrete.

It was then that the kick came again, harder, more assured. Arms went up and for a moment the figure was poised on the coping, just a foot away from the guard rail, mouth open to scream. The booted foot slammed in just below the ribcage, a flat ram, and he went in backwards, the scream released, making a huge splash as he struck the water. The spray flew up to the height of the bridge and drenched the man on the bank who cursed and shook himself.

He lay down flat in the wet. He was checking if his

quarry could swim. Not well, but enough, enough to flounder down there in a doggy paddle, treading cold water, spluttering and coughing.

One of the other objects in the barrow was a mobile phone. He fished it out and made his call. As he was speaking, telling them where he was, where to find him, he thought how everyone had speculated as to why the Impaler avoided the Park. What was sacred about the Park, or dangerous about it? What placed an embargo on the Park? But it was simple. The answer was simple. There was no traffic in the Park. It was closed to all but Park Police and Park Administration vehicles – closed to a red and white takeaway van.

The man in the water could hold out for five minutes and that was all it would take. They would be here to help him in five minutes, less than that now. He watched the struggles, the inefficient battling towards the canal rim and feeble grasping of the stone.

His eye on his watch, he waited another two minutes. Then he scrambled up the bank, searching till he found a six-foot long stick, a branch with dead leaves still clinging to it. Down on to the puddled path again, the branch extended for its life-saving purpose. White, water-bleached hands grasped the wood. He pulled, bracing his feet against the place where the brickwork met the concrete path. He spoke the form of the caution and the man's name and said:

'I'm arresting you for the murders of John Dominic Cahill, James Victor Clancy, David George Kneller and the attempted murder of Detective Inspector William Marnock . . .'

ROAD RAGE

To the Chief Constable and Officers of the Suffolk Constabulary.

My thanks are especially due to Chief Inspector Vince Coomber of the Suffolk Constabulary who gave me good advice and corrected my mistakes.

Chapter 1

Wexford was walking in Framhurst Great Wood for the last time. That was how he put it to himself. He had walked there for years, all his life, and walked as well as ever, was as strong, and would continue to be so for a long time yet. Not he but the wood would change, the wood would scarcely be there. Savesbury Hill would scarcely be there or Stringfield Marsh, and the River Brede, into which the Kingsbrook flowed at Watersmeet, that too would be unrecognisable.

Nothing would happen yet. Months must pass first. For six months the trees would remain and the uninterrupted view over the hill, the otters in the Brede and the rare Map butterfly in Framhurst Deeps. But he didn't think he could bear to see it any more.

> And that will be England gone,
> The shadows, the meadows, the lanes,
> The guildhalls, the carved choirs.
> There'll be books, it will linger on
> In galleries; but all that remains
> For us will be concrete and tyres.

He walked among the trees, chestnuts, great grey beeches with sealskin trunks, oaks whose branches had a green coating of lichen. The trees thinned and spread themselves across the grass that rabbits had cropped. He saw that the coltsfoot was in bloom, earliest of wildflowers. When he was young he had seen blue fritillaries here, plants so localised that they were seen only within a ten-mile radius of Kingsmarkham, but that was a long time ago. When I retire, he had told his wife, I want to live in London so that I can't see the countryside destroyed.

A defeatist attitude, she said. You should fight to keep it. I haven't noticed fighting keeping it, he'd said. She was on the committee of the newly formed KABAL, Kingsmarkham Against the Bypass And Landfill. They had already had one meeting and had sung 'We Shall Overcome'. The Deputy Chief Constable had got to hear of it and said he hoped Wexford wasn't thinking of joining as there was going to be trouble, trouble of a peace-disturbing and possibly violent kind, in which the Chief Inspector might well be, at least peripherally, involved.

A little breeze had got up. He came out of Framhurst Great Wood on to the open land and looked up at the ring of trees crowning Savesbury Hill. From here not a roof or tower or silo or pylon could be seen, only birds flying in formation towards Cheriton Forest. The road would pass through the foundations of the Roman villa, the habitat of Araschnia levana, the Map butterfly, found nowhere else in the British Isles, cross the Brede and then the Kingsbrook. Unless the impossible happened and they made a tunnel for it or put it on stilts. Araschnia and the otters would like stilts about as much as they liked concrete, he thought.

Kingsmarkham wasn't the only town in England whose bypass had been swallowed up in building and so become just another street. When that happened a new bypass had to be built, and when that too was engulfed, another perhaps. But he would be dead by then.

With this gloomy thought he returned to his car

2

that he had left parked in Savesbury hamlet. He always came to his walk by car. Would he be prepared to give up his car for the sake of England? What a question!

He drove home through Framhurst and Pomfret Monachorum in pessimistic mood and therefore noticing all the ugly things, the silos like iron sausages up-ended, the sheds full of battery hens, electricity substations sprouting wires and looking like newly landed aliens, bungalows with red-brick garden walls and wrought-iron railings, Leylandii hedges. Nietzsche (or someone) had said that having no taste was worse than having bad taste. Wexford didn't agree. On a happy day he would have observed newly planted well-chosen trees, roofs rethatched, cattle in the meadows, ducks paddling in couples, looking for nesting sites. But it wasn't a happy day, not, that is, till he came into his house.

His wife's habit was to come out of wherever she was to meet him when something good had happened, something she couldn't wait to tell him. He bent down to pick up the card which had been dropped through the letter-box, looked up and saw her. She was smiling.

'You'll never guess,' she said.

'No, I won't, so don't keep me in suspense.'

'You're going to be a grandfather again.'

He hung up his coat. Their daughter Sylvia already had two children and a shaky relationship with her husband. He risked spoiling Dora's pleasure. 'Another scheme for keeping the marriage going?'

'It's not Sylvia, Reg. It's Sheila.'

He went up to her, put his hands on her shoulders. 'I said you'd never guess.'

'No, I never would have. Give me a kiss.' He hugged her. 'It's turned into a happy day.'

3

She didn't know what he meant. 'Of course I wish she were married. It's no good telling me one out of every three children is born out of wedlock.'

'I wasn't going to,' he said. 'Shall I phone her?'

'She said she'd be in all day. The baby's due in September. She took her time telling us, I must say. Give me that card, Reg. Mary Pearson told me her son got a holiday job delivering those cards for this new car-hire firm, Contemporary Cars, and he's taking one to every house in Kingsmarkham. Every house – can you imagine?'

' "Contemporary Cars"? No one'll be able to pronounce it. Do we need a new car-hire firm?'

'We need a good one. *I* do. You've always got the car. Go on. Phone Sheila. I hope it's a girl.'

'I don't care what it is,' said Wexford, and he began dialling his daughter's number.

Chapter 2

The route planned for the Kingsmarkham Bypass was to begin at the arterial road (an A road with motorway status) north of Stowerton, pass east of Sewingbury and Myfleet, cut across Framhurst Heath, enter the valley at the foot of Savesbury Hill, bisect Savesbury hamlet, cross Stringfield Marsh and rejoin the main road north of Pomfret. The minimum of residential area was to be disturbed, Cheriton Forest avoided and the remains of the Roman villa just circumvented.

Probably the first remark on the subject to appear in a newspaper was that made by Norman Simpson-Smith of the British Council for Archaeology. 'The Highways Agency says this road will pass through the periphery of the villa,' he said. 'That is like saying an access road being built in London would only cause minor damage to Westminster Abbey.'

Until then the protest had simply taken the form of representation by various bodies at the inquiry held jointly by the Departments of Transport and the Environment. Friends of the Earth, the Sussex Wildlife Trust and the Royal Society for the Protection of Birds, were the obvious ones. Less expected presences were those of the British Council for Archaeology, Greenpeace, the World Wide Fund for Nature, KABAL and a body that called itself SPECIES.

But after Simpson-Smith's comment the protests came, as Wexford put it, not in single spies but in

5

battalions. The environmental groups, whose members numbered two million, sent representatives to look at the site.

Marigold Lambourne, of the Royal Society of Entomologists, was there on behalf of both the Scarlet Tiger Moth and the Map butterfly. 'Araschnia is found thinly distributed in north-eastern France,' she said, 'and in the British Isles solely on Framhurst Heath. There are probably two hundred specimens extant. If this bypass is built there will soon be none. This is not some minuscule fly or bacterium invisible to the naked eye we are talking about but an exquisite butterfly with a two-inch wingspan.'

Peter Tregear of the Sussex Wildlife Trust said, 'This bypass is a project dreamed up in the seventies and approved in the eighties. But there has been a revolution in global thinking since then. It is all utterly inappropriate for the end of the century.'

A woman wearing a sandwich board with *No, No, No to Rape of Savesbury* painted on it appeared on the hill when the tree-fellers moved in. It was June, and warm, and the sun was shining. She took off the sandwich board and revealed herself entirely naked. The tree-fellers, who would have cheered and whistled if she had been young or had been sent to one of them as a strippergram, turned away and set to even more busily with their chain-saws. The foreman called the police on his mobile. Thus the woman, whose name was Debbie Harper, got her photograph – her large, shapely body wrapped by then in a policeman's jacket – in all the national papers and on to the front page of the *Sun*.

That was when the tree people came.

Perhaps Debbie Harper's picture alerted them to what was going on. Many of them belonged to no known official body. They were New Age Travellers, or some of them were, and if they arrived in cars and

6

caravans, none of these vehicles were parked on or near the site. Debbie Harper had disrupted the tree-felling and only four silver birches had so far been cut down. The tree people drove steel bolts into tree trunks at a height calculated to buckle a chain-saw blade when felling began. Then they began building themselves dwellings in the tops of beeches and oaks, tree-houses of planks and tarpaulin and approached by ladders which could be pulled up once the occupant was installed.

That was June and the site of the first of the tree camps was at Savesbury Deeps.

Debbie Harper, who lived with her boyfriend and three teenage children in Wincanton Road, Stowerton, gave interviews to every newspaper which asked her. She was a member of KABAL and SPECIES, Greenpeace and Friends of the Earth, but her interviewers weren't much interested in that. What they liked about her was that she was a Pagan with a capital P, kept ancient Celtic festivals and worshipped deities called Ceridwen and Nudd, and posed for *Today* wearing just three leaves, not fig-leaves but rhubarb, these being more appropriate for an English summer.

'We're unhappy about the spiking of the trees,' Dora said on her return from a meeting of KABAL. 'Apparently the chain-saws can come apart and maul workmen's arms. Isn't that an awful thought?'

'This is just the beginning,' her husband said.

'What do you mean, Reg?'

'Remember Newbury? They had to get in six hundred security guards to protect the contractors. And someone cut the brake pipe on a coach carrying the guards to the site.'

'Have you talked to anyone who actually wants this bypass?'

7

'I can't say I have,' said Wexford.

'Do you want it?'

'You know I don't. But I'm not prepared to give up driving a car. I'm not happy about sitting in traffic jams and feeling my blood pressure go up. Like most of us, I want to eat my cake and have it.' He sighed. 'I daresay Mike wants it.'

'Oh, Mike,' she said, but affectionately.

Wexford had broken his resolution not to go back to Framhurst Great Wood. The first time he went was to watch wildlife experts building new badger setts (with ramps and swing doors like cat flaps) in the heart of the wood. The tree-houses in the second camp were already being built, which was perhaps enough to drive the badgers to their new homes. The second time was after the tree-fellers refused to endanger their lives by using chain-saws on trees whose trunks were embedded with nails or bound with wire. A few felled trees lay about. The Highways Agency was seeking eviction orders against the tree dwellers but meanwhile another camp took shape at Elder Ditches and then another on the borders of the Great Wood.

Wexford climbed up Savesbury Hill, again, he told himself, for the last time, from where the four camps could clearly be seen. One was almost at the foot of the hill, one half a mile away at Framhurst Copses, a third on the threatened verge of the marsh and the fourth and furthest away half a mile from the northernmost reaches of Stowerton. The countryside still looked much as it always had, except that a field in the neighbourhood of Pomfret Monachorum was packed with earth-moving equipment, diggers and bulldozers. These things were almost always painted yellow, he reflected, a dull, dead yellow, the colour of custard that had been kept in the fridge too long.

Presumably yellow showed up better against green than red or blue.

He walked downhill on the far side, then wished he hadn't, for he found himself up to his thighs in stinging nettles. Their hairy pointed leaves failed to sting through his clothes but he had to keep his arms and hands held high. The nettles filled an area as big as a small meadow and Wexford was thinking that if the road had to go somewhere it would be no bad thing for it to pass through here, when he saw the butterfly.

That it was Araschnia levana, he knew at once. Among all the tens of thousands of words that had been written lately about Savesbury and Framhurst, he remembered reading that Araschnia fed on stinging nettles in Savesbury Deeps. He advanced a little until he was a yard from it. The butterfly was orange-coloured, with a chocolate-brown pattern and flashes of white, and the underwings had a sky-blue river-like border. You could see why it was called the Map.

It was alone. There were only two hundred of them, perhaps now not so many. When he was a child people had caught butterflies in nets, gassed them in killing bottles, attached them to cards on pins. It seemed appalling now. Only a few years ago people who opposed bypasses were looked on as cranks, loony weirdos, hippie dropouts, and their activities on a par with anarchy, communism and mayhem. That too had changed. Conventional figures of the Establishment were as determined in their opposition as that man he could now see peering out between canvas flaps through the fork in a tree branch. Someone had told him that Sir Fleance and Lady McTear had marched in a demonstration organised by supermarket millionaires Wael and Anouk Khoori.

9

Like most Englishmen, he had his reservations about the European Union, but here, he thought, was one instance when he wouldn't mind an absolute veto coming from Strasbourg.

Towards the end of the month, the British Society of Lepidopterists created a new feeding ground for Araschnia, a stinging-nettle plantation on the western side of Pomfret Monachorum. A journalist on the *Kingsmarkham Courier* wrote a satirical but not very funny piece about this being the first time in the history of horticulture anyone had been known to plant nettles instead of pulling them up. The nettles, naturally, flourished from the start.

The badger movers set about a similar reversal of the usual order of things. Instead of preserving habitats, they were obliged to destroy them. In opening and sealing up a sett that, if it remained in occupation would have been in the direct path of the new bypass, they had first to cut away a dense mass of brambles. The growth of brambles had been vigorous, indicating it was new this year, springing from heavily pruned stock, and the prickly trailing runners were heavy with green fruit. They lifted the cut mass with gloved hands and found something lying beneath that made them recoil, one of them shout out and another retreat under the trees to vomit.

What they found was the badly decomposed body of a young girl.

Kingsmarkham police had no real doubts as to who this was. But they made no announcement of their guess as to identity. It was the newspapers and television who named her, with few reservations, as Ulrike Ranke, the missing German hitchhiker.

10

She had been nineteen, a law student at Bonn University, the only daughter of a lawyer and a teacher from Wiesbaden, and she had come to England in the previous April to spend Easter at the home of a girl who had been an au pair in her parents' house. The girl's family lived in Aylesbury and Ulrike had set out to make her journey on the cheap. It had never been quite clear why. Her parents had supplied her with enough money for a return air ticket to Heathrow and her train fare. However, Ulrike had hitched across France and taken the ferry to Dover. That much was known.

'I don't find it at all mysterious,' Wexford had said at the time. 'I would have if she'd done what her parents told her to do. That would have been astonishing, that would have been a mystery.'

'What an old cynic you are,' said Inspector Burden.

'No, I'm not. I'm a realist, I don't like being called a cynic. A cynic is someone who knows the price of everything and the value of nothing. I'm not like that, I just don't like mealy-mouthed hypocrisy. You've had teenage children, you know what they are. My Sheila used to do that stuff all the time. Why spend good money when you can do it for free? That's their attitude. They need the money for music and the means of playing it, black jeans and prohibited substances.'

It seemed he was right, for on the girl's body, in the pocket of her Calvin Klein black jeans were twenty-five amphetamine tablets and a packet containing just under fifty grammes of cannabis. There was nothing on her to show that she was Ulrike Ranke and no money. Her father identified her. The man who had raped and strangled her two months before either had not recognised the contents of her pocket for what they were or had no use for them.

11

The money which she had carried on her in notes, all five hundred pounds of it, was gone.

Framhurst Copses had not previously been searched. None of the countryside round Kingsmarkham had come under scrutiny. There was no reason to suppose Ulrike Ranke had passed this way. Kingsmarkham was miles from the route she might have been expected to take from Dover to London. But someone had put her body in a woodland declivity and hidden her under the fast-growing tendrils of blackberry bushes. In the opinion of the pathologist and forensic examiners the body had not been moved, she had been killed where she lay.

Because there had been no search there had been no inquiries either. But immediately the identity of the dead girl was announced, William Dickson, the licensee of a public house named the Brigadier (he called it an hotel) phoned the police with information. Once he had seen photographs of Ulrike Ranke in the *Kingsmarkham Courier* he recognised her as the girl who had come into his saloon bar in early April.

The Brigadier was on the old Kingsmarkham bypass, one of those roadhouses put up in the late thirties, pseudo-Tudor, thickly half-timbered, apparently huge but in fact only one room deep. A car-park behind was overshadowed by a very large prefabricated building, designed as a dance hall (Dickson called it a ballroom). The car-park was surfaced in macadam but all round the house and the area in front was gravelled. Very unpleasant to walk on, as Vine remarked to Burden, worse than a shingle beach.

'It was just before closing time on Wednesday April the third,' Dickson said when the two policemen came in.

'Why didn't you say so before?' said Burden.

He and Detective Sergeant Vine were sitting up at

12

the bar. Alcohol had been offered and refused by both. Vine was drinking mineral water which he had paid for.

'What do you mean, before?'

'When she went missing. Her picture was all over the papers then. And the TV.'

'I only look at the local,' said Dickson. 'All I ever see on the telly is sport. Folks in the bar trade don't get a lot of leisure, you know. I'm not exactly overburdened with quality time.'

'But you recognised her as soon as you saw her in the *Courier*?'

'Nice-looking chick, she was.' Dickson looked over his shoulder, reassured himself of something and grinned. 'Very tasty.'

'Oh, yes? Tell us about April the third.'

She had come into the bar at about ten-twenty, a young blonde girl 'dressed like they all dressed' in black but with some sort of jacket. An anorak or parka or duffel, he didn't know, but he thought it was brown. She had a shoulder-bag, a big overstuffed shoulder-bag, not a backpack. How could he remember so well after nearly three months?

'I've got a photo, haven't I?'

'You what?' said Vine.

'There was a hen party going on,' said Dickson. 'Girl getting married at Kingsmarkham Register Office on the Thursday. She asked the wife to take their picture, her and her friends round their table, and she handed her this camera, and just as the wife took their picture this German girl came in. So she's in the picture, in the background.'

'And you've a copy of this photograph? I thought you said it wasn't your camera?'

'The girl – the bride, that is – she sent us a copy. Thought we'd like to have it, seeing as it was in the Brigadier. You can see it if you want.'

'Oh, yes, we want,' said Burden.

Ulrike Ranke was well behind the group of laughing women and out of the brightest lights, but it was plainly she. Her coat might have been brown or grey, or even dark blue, but her jeans were unmistakably black. A string of pearls could just be glimpsed lying against the dark stuff of her blouse or sweater. The canvas and leather bag on her right shoulder looked overfull and heavy. She wore an anxious expression.

'When I saw that picture in the *Courier* I said to the wife to find that photo and the minute I set eyes on it I realised.'

'What did she come in here for? A drink?'

'I told her she couldn't have a drink,' Dickson said virtuously. 'I'd called for last orders. It wasn't a drink she wanted, she said, she wanted to know if she could make a phone call. Comical way of talking she had, like an accent, couldn't get her tongue round some words, but we get all sorts in here.'

It never ceased to surprise Burden that the British, the vast majority of whom can speak no language but their own, are not above mocking those foreign visitors whose command of English is less than perfect. He asked if Ulrike had made her phone call.

'I'm coming to that,' said Dickson. 'She asked to use the phone – called it a "telephone", long time since I've heard that expression – and said she wanted a taxi. That's who she'd be phoning, a taxi firm, and did I know of one. Well, naturally, we get a lot of call for taxis out here. I said she'd find a number by the phone, we got a card stuck up on the board by the phone. I said she'd have to use the pay-phone, I wasn't having her using the one in the office.'

'And did she?'

'Sure she did. She came back in here. The clientele

14

was all gone by then and the wife and I was having a clear-up. She started telling us how she'd hitched a lift from Dover in a lorry. The driver'd said he'd take her as far as he was going and dropped her off here, he was parking for the night in a lay-by. I said to the wife I reckon she was lucky he *did* drop her off, good-looking young kid like that.'

'She wasn't lucky,' said Burden.

Dickson looked up, startled. 'No, well, you know what I mean.'

'She called a taxi? D'you know which one?'

'It was Contemporary Cars. It was their card stuck up by the phone. There was other numbers on a bit of paper but that was the only card.'

'And the taxi came?'

For the first time Dickson looked less than proud of himself, the picture of rectitude and earnest integrity slipping slightly. 'I don't rightly know. I mean, she said they'd said fifteen minutes, they'd said it'd be Stan in fifteen minutes, and when I went up to bed like half an hour later I looked out of the window and she was gone, so I reckon he turned up all right.'

'Are you saying,' said Burden, 'that she didn't wait for him in here? You sent her outside to wait for him?'

'Look, this is a hotel, not a hostel . . .'

'This is a public house,' said Vine.

'Look, the wife had gone to bed, she'd had a heavy day, and I was clearing up. We'd had a hell of a day. It wasn't that cold out. It wasn't raining.'

'She was nineteen years old,' said Burden. 'A young girl, a foreign visitor. You sent her out there to wait in the dark at eleven o'clock at night.'

Dickson turned his back. 'I'll think twice,' he muttered, 'before I phone you lot with information next time.'

*

15

Later that day, after hours of questioning, Stanley Trotter, a driver for Contemporary Cars and a partner with Peter Samuels in the company, was arrested for the murder of Ulrike Ranke.

Chapter 3

Sheila Wexford intended to have her baby at home. Home births were fashionable and Sheila, her father said with a kind of fond sourness, had always been a dedicated follower of fashion. He would have liked her to go into the world's best obstetrics hospital, wherever that might be, some four weeks before the birth was due. When labour began he would have preferred the top obstetrician in the country to be present, along with a couple of caring medical assistants and a troop of top-of-their-finals-year midwives. An epidural must be administered after the first contraction and, should labour continue for more than half an hour, a Caesarean be performed – a keyhole one if possible.

That, at any rate, was what Dora said his preference would be.

'Nonsense,' said Wexford. 'I just don't like the idea of her having it at home.'

'She'll do what she likes. She always does.'

'Sheila isn't selfish,' said Sheila's father.

'I didn't say she was. I said she did what she liked.'

Wexford considered this contradiction in terms. 'You'll go up and be with her, won't you?'

'I hadn't thought of it. I'm not a midwife. I'll certainly go after the baby's born.'

'Funny, isn't it?' said Wexford. 'We've come a long way in sexual enlightenment, the equality of women

17

and men, got rid of the old shibboleths. Men are present at the births of their children as a matter of course. Women breast-feed in public. Women talk publicly about all sorts of gynaecological things they'd once have died before mentioning. But you can't imagine that there's anyone who wouldn't balk, to say the least, at the idea of a father being present when his daughter gives birth, can you? You see, I've shocked you. You're blushing.'

'Well, naturally I am, Reg. Surely you don't want to be present at Sheila's . . . ?'

'Lying-in? Of course I don't. I'd probably pass out. I'm only saying it's an anomaly that you can be there and I can't.'

Sheila lived in London with the father of her child, an actor called Paul Curzon, in a mews off Welbeck Street. The baby would be born there. Wexford, whose knowledge of London was shaky, checked it out on his *Geographer's Atlas*, and found that Harley Street was near enough for comfort. Harley Street was full of doctors, as everyone knew, and hospitals too probably.

Contemporary Cars was housed in a prefabricated building of temporary appearance on an otherwise empty lot in Station Road. It had once been the site of the Railway Arms, a pub which was less and less frequented, its one-time customers finding beer prices exorbitant and drink-driving laws draconian. The Railway Arms closed down, then was pulled down. Nothing else was built and there were those in Kingsmarkham who called the windswept, litter-strewn site, fringed with nettles and surrounded by spindly trees, an eyesore. In their eyes, the arrival of the converted mobile home hardly improved matters, but Sir Fleance McTear, Chairman of both KABAL and the Kingsmarkham Historical Society, said that in view of the projected bypass it was the least of their worries.

Peter Samuels, the self-styled chief executive of Contemporary Cars, told everyone his business would soon be moving into permanent premises, but so far there had been no sign of this. The old Railway Arms site offered plenty of parking space for taxis and very convenient exits and entrances into the station approach. It was in these trailer-like offices with their stowaway tables, shower cabinet and pull-down beds from former days on the road that Burden first interviewed Stanley Trotter.

At first Trotter denied all knowledge of Ulrike Ranke. His memory jogged by Vine's quoting from William Dickson and mentioning the German girl's accent, Trotter eventually recalled taking Ulrike's phone call – taking the call, not driving out to the Brigadier. He had intended to do that himself, he said, but was due to pick up someone off the last train from London, so passed the job on to one of the other drivers, Robert Barrett.

The difficulty there was that when questioned, Barrett had no recollection of his movements on the night of 3 April beyond being sure that he had fares throughout the evening, it was a busy evening. The whole week had been busy – something to do with Easter, he thought. But he was sure of one thing: he had never, in the five months he had worked for Contemporary Cars, picked up a fare from the Brigadier.

Burden asked Stanley Trotter to come to Kingsmarkham police station. By then he had discovered that Trotter had form, previous convictions of no inconsiderable kind. His first offence, committed some seven years before, was breaking and entering shop premises in Eastbourne, his second, far more serious, was robbery, a definition which implied

19

assault. He had punched a young woman in the face, knocked her to the ground, kicked her and taken her handbag. She was walking home along Queen Street, quite alone, one midnight. For both these offences Trotter had gone to prison, and would have served a much longer sentence for the second if his victim had suffered more than a bruise on her jaw.

But it was enough, or almost enough, for Burden. He had got Trotter to confess that he did in fact drive out to the Brigadier at ten-forty-five on 3 April. Originally, he said, he had been too scared to admit it. He drove there, reaching the pub just before eleven, but the fare wasn't waiting. If she had been there once she was gone by then.

At this point Trotter demanded a lawyer and Burden had no choice but to agree. A sharp young solicitor from Morgan de Clerck of York Street arrived promptly and when Trotter said he couldn't recall whether or not he had rung the bell at the Brigadier, told Burden his client had said he couldn't remember and that must be sufficient.

Outside the interview room Vine said, 'Dickson said she was out in the street. Trotter wouldn't have had to ring the bell.'

'No, but he didn't know she'd be out in the street, did he? He'd have thought – anyone would have thought – she'd be inside the pub and have rung the bell as a matter of course. Are you telling me he'd have shown up at the pub at eleven at night and finding no one there just turned round and gone back to Station Road?'

'That's what *he's* telling you,' said Vine.

They went on questioning Trotter. The solicitor from Morgan de Clerck took them up on every small point, while providing his client with an unending supply of cigarettes, though not a smoker himself. Trotter, a round-shouldered, thin and unhealthy-

20

looking man of about forty, got through twenty by the end of the afternoon and the atmosphere in the interview room was blue with smoke. The solicitor interrupted everything by incessantly asking how long they intended to keep Trotter and finally asked if he was to be charged.

Recklessly, Burden, hardly able to breathe, gasped out a yes. But he didn't charge him, he just kept him at Kingsmarkham police station. When Wexford got to hear of it he was dubious about the whole thing, but Burden got a warrant and Trotter's home in Peacock Street, Stowerton, was searched for evidence. There, in the two-roomed flat over a grocery market kept by two Bangladeshi brothers, Detective Constables Archbold and Pemberton found a string of imitation pearls and a holdall of brown canvas bound in dark-green plastic.

To Wexford it wasn't much like the shoulder-bag in Dickson's photograph, nor did it conform to the description of his daughter's bag Dieter Ranke had given the police. This one was an altogether cheaper affair and brown and green instead of brown and black. The Rankes were comfortably off, both parents professionals with significant jobs, and Ulrike, an only child, had wanted for nothing. Her pearls were a cultured string, carefully matched, an eighteenth-birthday present for which her mother and father had paid the equivalent of thirteen hundred pounds.

'That poor chap will have to take a look at the bag,' Wexford said, meaning Ranke and thinking of himself and his daughters. 'He's still in this country for the inquest.'

'It won't be so bad as identifying the body,' said Burden.

'No, Mike, I don't suppose it will.' Wexford didn't want to pursue that, he might say something he'd be sorry for afterwards. 'I'm told the Department of

21

Transport are applying to the High Court for leave to evict the tree people.'

Burden looked pleased. The idea of the bypass had always been attractive to him, largely because he thought it would put an end to traffic congestion in the town centre and on the old bypass. 'No one made all this fuss in the old days,' he said. 'If government decreed a road was to be built people accepted it. They took the entirely proper view that if they voted their representatives into parliament they'd done their democratic duty and they must abide by government decisions. They didn't build tree-houses and – and *streak* – is it called streaking? They didn't do criminal damage and cripple tree-fellers who are only doing their job. They understood that a road such as this is being built *for their own good*.'

' "He didn't know what the world was coming to",' said Wexford. 'That's what they'll put on your tombstone.' He gave Burden a sidelong look. 'Big demonstration tomorrow. KABAL, the Sussex Wildlife Trust, Friends of the Earth and Sacred Globe, the whole lot led by Sir Fleance McTear, Peter Tregear and Anouk Khoori.'

'It will just make more work for us. That's all it'll accomplish. They'll still build the bypass.'

'Who knows?' said Wexford.

He didn't question Trotter himself. Burden, harassed by Damian Harmon-Shaw of Morgan de Clerck, succeeded in getting an extension of twelve hours to the time he was allowed to keep Trotter. He knew that when that time was up he would either have to charge him or let him go, as the Magistrates' Court was unlikely to be persuaded by the evidence to issue a warrant of further detention.

The three Vauxhalls and the three VW Golfs used by Contemporary Cars were all examined. Peter Samuels put up no objection. The cars had each been

22

cleaned inside and out at least ten times since 3 April and had each carried hundreds of fares. If there had ever been traces of Ulrike Ranke's brief occupancy of one of them, a hair perhaps, a fingerprint, a thread from her clothes, these had long ago been removed or obliterated.

'You haven't any evidence, Mike,' Wexford said after he had listened to the tape. 'All you have are his previous convictions and the fact that he went to the Brigadier and finding no one there, turned round and went home again.'

'He knows Framhurst Great Wood. He's admitted going to the picnic area when his kids were young.' Trotter's desertion of his wife and small children, and his subsequent divorce, remarriage and very rapid second divorce, were other factors which had prejudiced Burden against him. 'He knows the lane into the wood and he knows all about parking at the picnic place. The body was found two hundred yards from there.'

'Half the population of Kingsmarkham knows that picnic area. I used to take my kids there, you used to take yours. One might say it was pretty open of him to admit knowing it. He wasn't obliged to.'

Burden said coldly, 'I know he's guilty. I know he killed her. He killed her for that string of pearls, the most easily disposable of all jewellery, and for the five hundred pounds she was carrying.'

'Do you know he was short of money?'

'His sort is always short of money.'

Dieter Ranke came to Kingsmarkham two hours before Burden's extension was up. In the meantime he and Detective Sergeant Karen Malahyde had questioned Trotter again but made no progress. Ulrike's father rejected the brown canvas bag after a cursory glance. The cheap pearl necklace found in

23

Trotter's flat provoked an outburst of anger. He shouted at Barry Vine, then apologised, then wept.

'You will now allow my client to go,' said Damian Harmon-Shaw in a very smooth voice and smiling condescendingly.

Burden had no choice. 'He's got off scot-free,' he said to Wexford, 'and I know he killed her. I can't bear that.'

'You'll have to bear it. I'll tell you what really happened, if you like. When that miscreant Dickson had turned her out into the street Ulrike wasn't at all happy being on that road with no other house in sight. If the pub lights were put out there wouldn't have been any light, it would have been very dark indeed out on the bypass. She waited for the taxi, but before it came another car stopped and the driver offered her a lift. A car or a lorry – who knows?'

'And she'd take it, in spite of the dangers?'

'Individual instances are quite different, though, aren't they? People think themselves judges of character. They think they can tell what someone's like from a face and a voice. It's dark, it's late, she's cold, she's no idea where she's going to sleep that night, if she's going to sleep anywhere, she doesn't know when she'll get to Aylesbury. A man comes along in a car, a warm, well-lit car, and he's a nice man, not young, a fatherly man who doesn't make personal remarks, who doesn't ask her what's a lovely girl like her doing out on a dark night, but just says he's on his way to London and would she like a lift. Maybe he says more, that he's on his way to pick up his wife in Stowerton and drive her to London. We don't know, but we can imagine. And Ulrike, who's tired and cold and knows a decent older man when she sees one . . .'

'Great scenario,' said Burden. 'There's only one objection. Trotter did it.'

*

24

But next day Stanley Trotter was back at work, busy along with Peter Samuels, Robert Barrett, Tanya Paine and Leslie Cousins in picking up from the station and driving to the meeting point the hordes of bypass demonstrators who arrived from London.

Some walked. It was only a mile. The young and the poor were obliged to walk. Some of the activists were virtually penniless. A comfortably off élite, most of the Wildlifers, a few Friends of the Earth and a large number of independent but dedicated conservationists, formed a long queue outside the station waiting for taxis from Station Taxis, All the Sixes (named for its phone number), Kingsmarkham Taxis, Harrison Brothers and Contemporary Cars.

The meeting point was the roundabout on the road between Stowerton and Kingsmarkham. Something over five hundred people gathered there, members of a Group called Heartwood carrying tree branches felled the day before, so that, as Wexford put it, they looked like Birnam Wood coming to Dunsinane.

They marched through the town, heading for Pomfret and the site that would be the start of the new bypass. Councillor Anouk Khoori, joint managing director with her husband of the Crescent supermarket chain, had dressed herself from head to toe in appropriate green, even to green eyeshadow and green fingernails.

The dying leaves on Heartwood's green branches dropped off along the route, leaving a trail down the middle of the road. Debbie Harper was there in her sandwich board but this time it was apparent she was adequately clothed underneath it in blue jeans and green T-shirt. Dora Wexford, having met with no opposition from her husband – 'I wish I could join you,' he'd said – marched in the orderly ranks of middle-class KABAL. Its members had all rather ostentatiously eschewed green garments and,

25

indeed, anything in the nature of the gear that might associate them with the New Age.

Wexford, who watched the march from his office window (and waved to his wife who didn't see him) noted some newcomers. Their banner proclaimed them as members of SPECIES. He amused himself for a while trying to think of what this could be an acronym for – Save and Protect Environmental Culture In Ecological Something or Sanctuary for the Preservation of Earth Co-operation and Integration Something Something.

At their head marched a commanding figure. He was tall, at least as tall as Wexford himself and he exceeded six feet by a good three inches. He carried no banner, waved no flag, and his clothes were very different from the uniform that was a mixture of denim and medieval pilgrims' gear. This man, whose head was shaved, wore a great cloak of a pale sand colour that flapped and rippled as he walked. Wexford saw with something of a shock that his feet were bare. His legs appeared to be bare too, as much as could be seen of them. The swinging folds of the cloak hid so much.

If he hadn't been concentrating on this man, staring at his profile of huge forehead, Roman nose and long chin, he might have seen one of the marchers throw a stone through the window of Concreation's offices on the Pomfret Road.

This converted Georgian house, which housed the company building the bypass, was separated from the roadway by a lawn and drive-in. No one seemed to know who had thrown the stone, though there was a lot of speculation, the more conservative partakers in the demonstration suggesting a member of either SPECIES or Heartwood. Wexford asked Dora later, but she hadn't seen the stone thrown, only heard the crash and turned to look at the smashed window.

The rest of the demonstration passed without incident. Three days later eviction notices were issued on people living in the four camps on the bypass route. But before the Under Sheriff of Mid-Sussex could begin carrying out the evictions, building had begun on two new tree camps, one at Pomfret Tye, the other at Stoke Stringfield, 'under the auspices', as the announcement to the press rather grandly had it, of SPECIES.

The crime tape round the area where Ulrike Ranke's body had been found came off and the badger movers returned to their task. The British Lepidopterists announced that eggs of Araschnia levana had been seen on nettles in the new plantation, though no larvae had yet been hatched.

It was August, and the tree-felling had resumed, when the masked raiders came into Kingsmarkham by night and made their onslaught on the premises of Concreation.

Chapter 4

They invaded the building, smashing windows, computers, fax machines, phones and copiers. They pulled open the drawers of filing cabinets and either tore up the contents or slung them in the shredders. The police got there very quickly but while arrests were being made, another group had occupied the headquarters of Kingsmarkham Borough Council. A third rampaged about destroying High Street shops.

Some of those arrested were tree people, but the hooded ones, wearing black stockings over their heads with eye and mouth holes, were newcomers to the town. They had come in during the day and set up a new camp on the bypass route, this one making the seventh. Yet more eviction orders had been applied for.

The day after what became known as the Kingsmarkham Rampage, Mark Arcturus, a spokesman for the campaigns section of Friends of the Earth, appealed for the protest to remain law-abiding. 'Everything we can accomplish,' he said, 'will be lost if the public associates the protest with violence and criminal damage, and we shall lose the public support we have enjoyed, which has been so heartening to us. Until yesterday the action was peaceful and civilised. Let us keep it that way.'

Sir Fleance McTear said that KABAL was dedicated to peaceful protest. 'We do not condone violence even in so good a cause.'

The *Kingsmarkham Courier*, but no other newspapers, carried a statement from a man called Conrad Tarling to the effect that desperate situations called for desperate measures and what choice had the public when government ignored the voice of the people? Tarling described himself as the King of the Wood and the leader of the SPECIES representation on the bypass site. Wexford recognised him from the picture accompanying the story. He was the cloaked man who had marched in the procession.

A team of workers were brought in under guard to remove spikes and wires from tree trunks. The tree people in the camps watched them at work and bided their time until the guards, who for a while kept up a round-the-clock shift system, eventually went home.

Patrick Young, of English Nature, announced in *New Scientist* the discovery in the River Brede of a rare caddis, Psychoglypha citreola, its larva a tiny worm in a mosaic-like cast, the adult form a yellow-winged fly, about an inch long. As a result the government's conservation advisers considered whether parts of the river should be designated as an area of special scientific interest.

'Under the European Habitats and Species directive,' Young said, 'super-reserve status gives the highest level of protection. Psychoglypha could still save this unparalleled area of beauty and rare species. Its discovery highlights the Department of Transport's failure to carry out an adequate environmental assessment of the Brede and Stringfield Marsh.'

One of the tree-houses in the camp at Elder Ditches caught fire on a hot afternoon towards the end of the month. Its occupants, a man and a woman, were leading lights in SPECIES. The tree-house and its tree were both destroyed but after some initial alarm it was decided that the fire was an accident, caused by a spirit stove used for tea-making falling over.

'These people,' said Burden to Wexford, 'destroy more of the environment than they save.'

'One tree. You're ridiculous.'

'Being right often seems ridiculous at first,' said Burden sententiously. 'How's Sheila?'

'She's fine. The baby's due in three weeks. I'd feel a lot better if she'd have it in hospital.' Wexford went on, principally to rile the inspector, 'One of her friends has joined the protest. He's called Jeffrey Godwin, he's an actor, owns the Weir Theatre.'

'That converted mill at Stringfield? He ought to know better.'

'He's got the Weir to stage a protest play, opening next week. It's called *Extinction*.'

'Sounds a bundle of laughs,' said Burden. 'I for one shan't be buying any tickets.'

On the last Monday in the month Concreation shifted its earth-moving equipment from the meadow at Pomfret Monachorum and the first digger plunged its great spiked shovel into the green hillside.

Wexford had been mildly worried for six months, waking up in the night sometimes and imagining the icy emptiness, the great yawning abyss opening at his feet, if Sheila should die in childbirth. He had never known of childbirth death, since the sole occurrence of this in his own life had happened to an aunt of his when he was only four, but he was still worried. The coming child he thought of too, not especially about it, but about the effect on Sheila if it should be less than perfect, about her grief which would in the natural course of things be his grief too.

But he knew during those months that the anxiety

30

he suffered would be nothing to what he would suffer when Sheila's due date arrived, in the days that followed that due date, for first babies, they say, are never on time, and – unbearable to contemplate – once he knew labour had begun. This worry, though, was yet to come, not to start until 4 September. He told himself not to be a fool, to banish it from his mind, at least until that due date, for there is no point in worrying twice, once for real and once about the prospect of future worry. 'Most of the things you have worried about,' he said to Dora on the evening of 1 September, 'have never happened.'

'I know,' she said, 'I taught you that axiom,' and as she spoke the phone rang.

He picked up the receiver.

'Hi, Pop,' said Sheila. 'I just had the baby.'

He had to sit down. Fortunately, the chair was there.

'Can you hear me, Pop? I had the baby and she's fabulous. She's called Amulet. She's got black hair and blue eyes. And do you know, it wasn't half as bad as I expected.'

'Oh, Sheila . . .' he said, and to Dora, 'Sheila had the baby.'

'Well, aren't you going to congratulate me?'

'Congratulations, darling.'

'She weighs three point four four kilos. I don't know what that is in pounds, you'll have to find conversion tables. I could have phoned you when labour started but I knew it would only worry you and then things happened so fast . . .'

'Here's your mother,' he said. 'Tell your mother all about it.'

Dora talked for fifteen minutes. When she finally put down the phone she said to Wexford that she'd be going to London in two days' time. 'She asked me to come tomorrow.'

'Why not go tomorrow?'

'Too many things to see to here. I can't just up sticks and go off like that. Besides, I think I should give her a day or two. Let her get used to the baby. It's not as if there'll be anything for me to do there except be with them. She's got a private nurse.'

'Amulet,' said Wexford. 'I expect I shall get used to it.'

'Don't worry. She'll be called Amy.'

SPECIES and the tree people swarmed over the earth-moving equipment during the night, removing metal parts, cutting cables, immobilising engines and mixing iron filings with diesel. A number of arrests were made, a guard was put on the diggers and James Freeborn, the Assistant Chief Constable of Mid-Sussex, appealed for a government grant of £2.5 million for policing the bypass.

Wexford asked for a meeting with him to discuss the outbreak of shop-breaking and petty thieving in Sewingbury and Myfleet. Four hundred security guards, hired by the Highways Agency, were housed in decaying huts on the former Army base at Sewingbury. Local residents put the blame on them, complained that they were responsible for pub brawls and that the buses which transported them to the bypass site caused traffic congestion, noise and pollution.

'An irony, isn't it?' Wexford said to Dora. 'Who shall have custody of the custodian? But thanks to this meeting I shan't be able to drive you to the station.'

'I shall get a taxi. If I weren't carrying all this stuff, all these presents you insist on, I'd walk it.'

'Phone me this evening. I want to hear all about this child. I want to hear her *voice*.'

'The only voice they have at that age,' said Dora,

'is crying, and we'll have as little of that as possible, I hope.'

He left the house at nine for his meeting. Before he went he meant to tell her not to phone Contemporary Cars. It wasn't particularly important but he didn't care for the idea of Stanley Trotter driving his wife. Of course it might not be Stanley Trotter, it might be Peter Samuels or Leslie Cousins, and even if it was Trotter the chances were he wouldn't mention Wexford, or his arrest, or Burden's unfounded suspicions. That really depended on whether Trotter was paranoid or aggrieved, or just relieved to have been released when he was. Anyway, he hadn't warned her, but at the time he hadn't said a word to her about Trotter so if the worst came to the worst she could justly plead ignorance.

His meeting ended without any firm policy being agreed on, but his presence there seemed to put ideas into Freeborn's head. If he hadn't anything better to do that afternoon perhaps he would like to accompany the Deputy Chief Constable on a tour of the conservation sites. It was being undertaken prior to the environmental assessment of the Brede and Stringfield Marsh and the bodies represented would include English Nature, Friends of the Earth, the Sussex Wildlife Trust, KABAL and the British Society of Entomologists.

Wexford could think of a lot of better things to do. He couldn't imagine why Freeborn's presence was required, still less his own, and he remembered rather sadly his resolve not to go near Framhurst Great Wood again, a decision that had already once been broken.

Of course he said he would come, he hadn't much choice. It was no good being an ostrich about these things, he must confront the prospect like everyone else. Perhaps he could even tell the Entomologists of

33

his sighting of the Map butterfly. He was thinking about this and about how animals and insects and even some plants dislike the moving of their habitats, even when this is no more than a mile or two, when the call came in to Kingsmarkham police station from Contemporary Cars.

Not Trotter but Peter Samuels. It was a little after noon. He had come back to the offices in Station Road to find his receptionist bound and gagged and tied to a chair, the place turned over and the petty cash stolen.

Barry Vine went down there with Detective Constable Lynn Fancourt. The door to the mobile home was open and Samuels was standing on the steps.

Inside, it was a squeeze for the four of them. Tanya Paine, whose job it was to answer the phones, the one for the cars and the one for potential fares, sat on the pull-down bed rubbing her wrists. The cord that tied her had been tightly bound round wrists and ankles. A pair of tights had been used as a gag and another to blindfold her. She wasn't hurt but she was frightened and shaken, a young woman in her early twenties, white-faced under the heavy make-up, her elaborately done long hair coming down from its chignon where the gag and blindfold had been tied.

'I'd been driving a client to Gatwick,' Samuels said. 'I was on my way back. Couldn't make out why I hadn't had a call from Tanya here. I mean, it was unheard-of, an hour going by without a call. I thought maybe the phone was down. So I come back here. I mean, I never come back here, not till my dinner-time, but being as I hadn't had a call not in all of an hour and a half . . .'

'All right, sir, thank you very much,' said Vine. 'Let's hear from Miss Paine. Just one man, was it, Miss Paine? Did you get a look at him?'

'There was two,' said Tanya Paine. 'They had

34

black masks on with holes for their eyes and mouth. Well, not masks, hoods. It was like the pictures in the paper of that lot that broke into the bypass builders' place. And one of them had a gun.'

'Are you sure of that?'

'Of course I'm sure. I was scared. I was dead terrified, actually. They opened that door and came up the steps and shut the door and the one with the gun pointed it at me and said to get in here. So I did – well, I wasn't going to argue, was I? They made me sit in that chair and one of them tied me up. At gunpoint. I hadn't got no choice, it was at gunpoint.'

'What time would that have been?'

'Ten-fifteen, ten-twenty, something like that.'

'And you were gagged and blindfolded?' said Lynn Fancourt.

'I don't know why. I couldn't see their faces anyway, not with them masks. They blindfolded me and I couldn't see a thing. I heard them moving about. Then they shut the door on me, that door, and I couldn't hear either. Oh, well, I heard the phone ring a few times, I could hear that. They was here a good while after they tied me up, a long time, I don't know how long it was before I heard the door bang.'

The room where they were had originally been the bedroom of the mobile home. To the built-in furniture, pull-down bed, hanging cupboard and two foldaway tables, had been added a fireside chair and two Windsor wheelback chairs, to one of which Tanya Paine had been tied. Beyond the door was the kitchen, equipped with microwave, fridge and cupboards with counters, and beyond that the living area, currently used as the office. With both interior doors shut not much of what was going on in the office could have been heard by a gagged and blindfolded woman shut in the bedroom.

35

Vine and Lynn Fancourt looked it over. 'Contemporary' as a title for this company was something of a misnomer. The two telephones were the only evidence of modern technology. There was no computer and no safe.

'We don't need no safe,' said Samuels. 'Twice a day I bank the takings, once at dinner-time and once at three.'

'So what was in the petty cash box?' asked Vine, holding up an empty tin that long ago had contained cream crackers. He held it in a clean handkerchief between thumb and forefinger, though whatever fingerprints might have been there had by then been irrevocably smudged by Samuels' and Tanya Paine's handling of it.

'Maybe five quid,' said Samuels, 'and that'd be pushing it. I'd got my takings on me and the same would go for Stan and Les. They'd bring them in round about midday and I'd bank the lot.'

Vine shook his head. It was a long while since he had heard of anything so slapdash.

Tanya Paine came out, her hairdo reassembled, her lipstick renewed. 'I thought you'd want to see me the way they left me,' she explained, 'before I repaired the damage. There was three pounds forty-two in that cash box, Pete. I checked it out on account of thinking I'd pop out for a capuccino and a Mars bar when Stan came back and I'd not got no change myself. Three pounds forty-two exactly.'

They had taken it. But had they been looking for something else? A drawer had been pulled out from under the counter where the phones were. A book of receipt stubs was on the floor. The VAT book had been opened and left face-downwards. But policemen get to know when a place has been ransacked or conversely, made to look as if it has been ransacked. This effort to deceive had not even been wholehearted. The two masked men had come for something Contemporary Cars had but, as Vine said to Lynn on the way back to the police station, it wasn't three pounds forty-two and it wasn't some vital document among the VAT inputs.

'What were they doing then for what she calls a long time after they'd left her tied up in there?'

'I don't know,' said Vine. 'The chances are though that it wasn't the long time she says. She was scared, understandably so, and it seemed like a long time. It was probably a couple of minutes.'

'So they tied her up, shut the two doors on her, took the petty cash and dropped a few things on the floor to make it look like a search? And they had a *gun*?'

'That'll have been a toy or a replica. No one was hurt, it's a small sum that's missing, there was no damage – and we're never going to find those two, you know that.'

'That's a bit of a defeatist attitude, Sergeant Vine,' said Lynn, who was twenty-four, new from her training and ardent.

'You watch it, young Lynn. I don't mean we're not going to check the place over and see if the prints are those of any villain known to us. We shall observe the usual routine but there's been rather a lot of this sort of thing lately, though I'll admit the masks and the gun are novelties.'

When Burden heard of it he immediately seized on the fact that one of Contemporary Cars' drivers was Stanley Trotter. One of the two intruders could even have been Stanley Trotter.

'Tanya Paine would have recognised him,' said Vine. 'Anyway, why would he need that? He was on the spot or could be. He could look for whatever it was without tying the girl up.'

'Where is he now?'

37

'Down there, I reckon. They all come in at midday with their takings. They're all there. Well, not Barrett, he's away on his holidays.'

Burden went down to Station Road, accompanied by an enthusiastic Lynn Fancourt. Tanya Paine was back on her phones, apparently none the worse for wear. She sent them through to the kitchen area, where Trotter was sitting in front of the black-and-white television set, eating a hamburger and with a plate of chips on his knees.

'Maybe you'd like to tell me where you were between ten and midday,' Burden said.

Trotter took a bite out of his hamburger. 'The station trade,' he said with his mouth full. 'And when that come to an end after the ten-nineteen'd come and gone, I got a call from here to fetch a fare from Pomfret. Masters Street, Pomfret, number fifteen, to be precise, which I took to the station, picked up a fare as was waiting and drove them to Stowerton, and by then it'd have been half-eleven, so I had my tea break. I was back in the cab by ten off twelve and I hung about down by the station, but when I never got no more calls from here, I thought, funny, that's very funny, that's never happened before.'

'What then?'

'I come back here, didn't I?'

'I'd like the name of the fare you picked up in Pomfret.'

'I don't know his name. Why would I? Tanya said to go to fifteen Masters Street, Pomfret, and that's what I done.'

Burden asked Tanya Paine for the fare's name. Presumably she kept a record. She looked at him blankly.

'I'd have to write them down.' She spoke as if writing by hand was comparable to mastering some difficult language, Russian, for instance. 'Pete's thinking of getting a computer,' she said, 'if he can pick one up second-hand.'

'So you've no idea how many calls come in or who from?'

'I never said that. I know how many. I sort of jot it down.'

She showed him a sheet of paper on which perhaps thirty or forty dashes had been made in pencil.

'What about the fare you picked up at the station after that?' Burden asked.

'I took him to Oval Road, Stowerton. Number five or it might have been seven. He'll remember me and so will the Pomfret chap.'

Trotter fixed Burden with a stony glare. He didn't look guilty, though. He looked as if he had nothing to hide. Burden was unable to imagine how the incidents of the morning at Contemporary Cars could have any connection with the murder of Ulrike Ranke, but that was what police work was about, discovering connections where none seemed to exist. He went back to the office where Tanya Paine had retreated. Squinting into a small hand mirror, she was applying violet-coloured mascara, her lips pursed and her nostrils narrowed.

'Is it possible,' he said, 'that one of the two men who tied you up could have been one of the drivers here?'

'Pardon?' She turned round and passed her tongue wetly across her lips.

'The two men' – he rephrased it – 'could one or both of them have been known to you? Did you have any sort of feeling of familiarity?'

She shook her head, stunned by this new turn the inquiry was taking.

'Did they speak?'

'One of them did. He said to keep quiet and I'd be OK. That's all.'

'So you didn't hear the other one's voice?'

Again that amazed shake of the head.

'The other one, then, he was masked and you didn't hear his voice. You can't really say he couldn't have been known to you, can you? If you couldn't see his face and didn't hear his voice, it could have been someone you knew very well.'

'I don't know what you mean,' said Tanya Paine. 'I'm confused now. They tied me up and gagged me and it was *horrible* and I want counselling. I'm a victim.'

'We can arrange that, Ms Paine,' said Lynn sympathetically.

Burden took Lynn Fancourt down to Stowerton with him where they established that no one from number five Oval Road had been brought by taxi from the station that morning. Nobody was at home at number seven, so they had either gone out again or Trotter was lying, an alternative Burden preferred to believe. A woman at number nine told them her neighbour was called Wingate, but she had no idea whether he had been fetched from Kingsmarkham station that morning or where he was now.

The Pomfret fare, if he existed, might still be in London or Eastbourne or wherever the train had taken him, but more than three hours had elapsed, so it was equally likely he was back again. Lynn rang the bell at fifteen Masters Road, a between-the-wars bungalow with a view over the bypass site.

The woman who answered the door had been doing some interior decorating. She had magnolia gloss paint on her hands, her jeans and shirt, and streaks of it in her hair. She looked cross and hot. No, she hadn't got a husband. If Burden meant her partner, he was called John Clifton, and yes, he had gone to London that morning on the ten-fifty-one. A taxi had taken him to Kingsmarkham station but she hadn't heard him phone for it, she hadn't seen it come and she had no idea which firm it was or who was driving the car. John had called out goodbye and said he was off and ... 'What's happened to him?' she said, suddenly alarmed.

'Nothing, Miss ...'

'Kennedy. Martha Kennedy. You're sure nothing's happened to him?'

'It's the taxi driver we're interested in,' said Lynn.

'In that case, perhaps you'll excuse me. I want to finish these bloody doors before John gets back.'

Burden said they would call again later. The door was shut rather sharply in his face. On the way back to Kingsmarkham they passed Wexford who was driving himself to Pomfret Tye for his meeting and tour with the Deputy Chief Constable and the conservationists.

The day, which had started dull and misty, was such a one as all lovers of the countryside should be given for their viewing of natural wonders. Or perhaps should not be given, should be denied, lest the soft air, the sunshine, the blue sky and the rich green of vegetation give too painful and nostalgic an edge to a pastoral loveliness that must soon pass away. Better for all, Wexford was thinking, if the day were dull and cold, and the sky the colour of the concrete soon to spread itself across these hills, these deeps and marshes, and bridge on stark grey pillars the rippling waters of the Brede.

Today the butterflies would be out, the tortoise-shells and fritillaries as well as Araschnia, and wild bees on the eyebright and the heather. There were goldcrests in the fir trees of Framhurst Great Wood. He had seen a pair of them once when on a picnic

41

with Dora and the girls, and he and Sheila had looked, though looked in vain, for the nest that is like a little hanging basket. Dora – he had meant to phone her at lunch-time, in spite of what he'd said about her phoning him in the evening. But he hadn't, he'd decided to wait. By now she would have seen the new child, his granddaughter Amulet. Alone in the car, he laughed out loud over the name.

Freeborn hadn't yet got there, much to his relief. If the Deputy Chief Constable had arrived first he would have had something snide to say about it, even if Wexford himself had been on time, even if he had been early. Somewhat to his dismay, Anouk Khoori, chairperson of the Council's Highways Committee, a woman with whom he had crossed swords in the recent past, was representing the local authority. She was fetchingly dressed in a yellow T-shirt with green jodhpurs and green wellies, her bright blonde hair tied up in a black-and-yellow bandanna, and she was exercising her wiles on Mark Arcturus of English Nature, smiling into his eyes, one scarlet-tipped hand resting on his sleeve. All smiles ceased when she became aware of Wexford's presence and she gave him a very brief, frosty glance.

Wexford said in his best stolid-policeman voice, 'Good-afternoon, Mrs Khoori. A fine day.'

The Entomologists introduced themselves and Wexford told them about Araschnia. Anecdotes on the theme of rare butterflies spotted in unlikely places were interrupted by the arrival of Freeborn accompanied by Peter Tregear.

The Deputy Chief Constable took it upon himself, like a primary school head teacher, to count heads. 'If we're all here we may as well begin.'

'We're surely not going to walk, are we?' said Anouk Khoori.

Wexford couldn't resist. 'They haven't built the road yet.'

'And let us hope they never will,' said Arcturus, as if the earth-moving equipment wasn't busy a couple of miles on the other side of Savesbury Hill even while they spoke. 'Let us be positive. Let us remember hope is one of the cardinal virtues.'

It wasn't a very long walk that the party undertook. They took the footpath across the meadows from Pomfret Tye and at Watersmeet, where the Kingsbrook flowed into the Brede, Arcturus was able to point out, under the clear, golden water, clinging to a round, gleaming pebble, the mosaic cylinder of the yellow caddis. Mrs Khoori was disappointed. It wasn't big enough for her taste.

Half a mile along the river, perhaps not so much, Wexford could see the old mill building that Jeffrey Godwin had converted into the Weir Theatre. Dora wanted to see that play, *Extinction*, and no doubt Sheila would come down for it ... He switched his mind from that train of thought. Janet Braiswick, of the English Entomologists, was walking with him and he told her about the goldcrests, and about seeing scarlet tiger moths when he was a boy. She told him how as a child in Norfolk she had once, but only once, seen a swallowtail in the fens.

They came to the nettle plantation at Framhurst Deeps, treading softly now, even Anouk Khoori silent and anxious. The sun was hot, it was butterfly weather, and they waited and watched almost reverently, but no Map butterfly appeared. No butterfly at all rose from the long grass and the ox-eye daisies that whitened the meadows like summer snow.

The dismantled badger setts were studied, for here at this point the bypass would run, through Araschnia's nettles, through the outskirts of the wood and into Stringfield Marsh. In the distance Wexford could see the latest camp, the cluster of houses put up by tree dwellers. Eviction notices had been applied for but not yet issued. Meanwhile the tree dwellers had spiked every oak, ash and lime in a half-mile stretch. Perhaps Sir Fleance McTear wanted to avoid the controversy these spikes might evoke or the indignation of Mrs Khoori, who was known to disapprove of all protest that was not a matter solely of the written or spoken word, for he suggested they turn back and make a small detour to take in the area designated for the new badger setts.

They were too far away to hear, still less see, the diggers working at the start of the site. Much too far to see the guards brought in by bus to protect the construction workers, the watching tree people, the witnesses. This was no more than a nature walk, Wexford thought, reminiscent of distant schooldays when Kingsmarkham infants were brought to these meadows to see the dragonflies and the water beetles. He asked Janet Braiswick when she had last seen tadpoles in an English pond but she couldn't remember, only that it was at least thirty years, when she had been a small child.

At five they were all back in Pomfret. Sir Fleance suggested tea in a local teashop, at least a cup of tea if no one wanted to eat, but this proposal met with no enthusiasm. They were all depressed by what they had seen, they were saddened. Even Freeborn, Wexford noticed, was subdued. He and Anouk Khoori were country dwellers who never went out into the country, who had been obliged to do so today, and had in some strange way been frightened by what they saw, by its existence and its ephemerality.

> And that will be England gone,
> The shadows, the meadows, the lanes . . .

44

They would rather not have seen it and then they could have pretended it wasn't there, just as he had thought he wouldn't go back so that he also could pretend. Avoid that place, don't pass that way, avert the eye, until there were no more ways to pass or places to be in . . .

And now he might as well go home. He remembered then that he would be alone at home. Well, he had plenty to read. He could start on those George Steiner essays everyone said were wonderful. And at some point there was always television, accompanied by a small single malt. Dora would probably phone about seven. She wouldn't expect him to be home much before seven, but she would phone then because whoever cooked for Sheila, and there was certain to be someone, would put dinner on the table at half-past.

The house was hot and stuffy. Today it had felt more like July than early September. He opened the french windows, drew a chair up to the garden table, went back into the house for beer from the fridge and the book of essays: *No Passion Spent*. Was it necessary to begin at the beginning or could he dip? He thought it would be fine to dip.

The french windows blew shut. He wouldn't hear the phone but Dora wouldn't phone before – well – ten to seven. At a quarter to seven he considered eating. What should he eat? When Jenny Burden went away she left her husband home-made frozen dinners in the freezer, one for every day of her absence. Wexford wouldn't submit his wife to such slavery, but he didn't like cooking, the fact was he couldn't cook. Bread and cheese and pickles for him, and maybe a banana and ice-cream. Soup first, Heinz tomato. Burden said that this was every man's favourite soup . . .

When it got to ten-past seven and Dora hadn't

45

phoned he began to wonder. Not to worry; to wonder. She was a punctual, meticulous woman. Perhaps they had people round for drinks and she couldn't just slip away. He would postpone eating until he'd spoken to her and he turned off the gas under the soup.

The phone rang at seven-fifteen.

'Dora?' he said.

'It's not Dora, it's Sheila. Where have you been? I've been phoning and phoning. I phoned your office and you weren't there, I phoned home over and over.'

'I'm sorry. I didn't expect a call till seven. How are you? How's the baby?'

'I am fantastic, Pop, and the baby is perfectly fine, but where is Mother?'

'What do you mean?'

'Mother. We expected her by one at the latest. Where is she?'

Chapter 5

He had done all the things one does in these circumstances: phoned hospitals, checked at the police station what road accidents there had been that day – only a car going into the back of another on the old bypass – phoned next door and talked to his neighbour.

Mary Pearson hadn't seen Dora since the afternoon of the day before but she had seen a car parked outside that morning. At about ten-forty-five, she thought it was. Maybe a few minutes earlier.

'That would be for the eleven-o-three,' said Wexford.

'She was allowing herself a lot of time.'

'She always does. Was it a black taxi?'

'It was a red car, I don't know the make, I'm afraid I don't know about cars, Reg. I didn't see her get in it.'

'Did you see the driver?'

Mary Pearson hadn't. She sensed at last that something was wrong. 'You mean you don't know where she's got to, Reg?'

If he admitted it the whole street would be talking within the hour. 'She must have told me but it's slipped my mind,' he said, and added, 'Don't worry,' as if she would worry and he wouldn't.

Kingsmarkham Cabs used black taxis, so Dora hadn't gone with them. And she couldn't have used Contemporary Cars because they were out of action

47

from about ten-fifteen until just after midday. So much for the caution he'd forgotten to give her, yet for which there had been no need ...

He phoned All the Sixes, Station Taxis, and every local company he could find in the phone book. None of them had picked up Dora that morning. He was beginning to have that feeling of unreality which comes over us when something utterly unexpected and potentially terrible happens.

Where was she?

Now he wished he had been discreet, had told Sheila some lie as to her mother's whereabouts, for he had to phone her again and say he had no idea what had happened, he had no clue. Holding old-fashioned ideas about post-parturitive women, he thought shocks would be dangerous, a shock would dry up her milk, fear would delay her recovery. It was too late now.

Sheila wailed down the phone at him, 'What do you mean, you don't know what's happened, Pop? Where is she? She must have had some ghastly accident!'

'That she has not had. She'd be in hospital and she's not.'

He could hear Paul saying soothing things. Then the baby began to cry, strong, urgent staccato screams.

It can't be true, was what he wanted to say, this can't be happening. We are dreaming the same dream, nightmaring the same nightmare, and we shall wake up soon. But he had to be strong, the paterfamilias, the rock. 'Sheila, I am doing everything I can. Your mother is not injured, your mother is not dead. These things I would know. I'll phone you as soon as I find out more.'

He went into the kitchen and poured the soup down the sink. It was nearly half-past eight and dusk, darkness coming. An oval orange moon was climbing up behind the roofs. He asked himself what he would think if this were someone else's wife. The answer was easy: that she'd left him, gone off with another man. Women did it all the time, women of all ages, after many years of marriage or a few. As a policeman, he'd ask that husband if such a thing was possible. First he'd apologise, say he was sorry but he had to ask, and then he'd inquire about her friends, any particular man friend.

The husband would be affronted, indignant. Not my wife, my wife would never ... And then he would think, remember, a chance word, a strange phone call, a coldness, an unusual warmth.

But this was Dora. *His* wife. It wasn't possible. He realised he was reacting just like the husband of his experience, his small fantasy. My wife would never ... Well, Dora *would* never and that was all there was to it. It was insane to think like that and he was ashamed of himself. He had no strange phone calls to remember, devious behaviour, unguarded coldness, feigned warmth. It wasn't just that she was Caesar's wife, she wouldn't want to.

He poured himself an inch of whisky, then returned it to the bottle. He might have to drive somewhere. Instead he picked up the phone and dialled Burden's number.

It took Burden seven minutes to get to him. Wexford was grateful. He had a funny thought: that if they'd been Italians or Spaniards or something, Burden would have put his arms round him, embraced him. Of course he didn't do that, just looked as if the thought had crossed his mind also.

Wexford made them tea. No alcohol tonight, just in case. He told Burden the whole story and described what he had done, the hospitals, the taxi companies, checking the road accidents.

'It's hopeless going to the train station,' Burden said. 'There's never anyone there. The days are gone when there was someone to check your ticket and watch you go through. I suppose she'd even get her ticket out of the machine?'

'She always does. They've got a new one that takes credit cards.'

'What does Sylvia say?'

Wexford hadn't even thought about his elder daughter. It would be true to say that for the past two or three hours he had forgotten her existence. A flood of guilt swamped him. Always he tried desperately to pay her the same attention he did to Sheila, to need her as much, to love her as well. Sometimes this had the effect of making him pay her *more* attention and give her more consideration, but now in a crisis, all that had fled, had disappeared as if he had made no such resolve, and he had behaved like the father of an only child. He said abruptly, 'I'll phone her.'

It rang and rang. The answering machine came on, Neil's voice with the usual formula.

Exasperated, Wexford wasn't going to give his name and the date and time of day – what nonsense! – but just said, 'Please phone me, Sylvia. It's urgent.'

Dora must be with *them*. Everything was coming clear. Some dreadful thing had happened, an accident, or one of the children had been taken ill. He hadn't asked hospitals about Sylvia's children. Dora had been told before she could phone for a taxi and had gone to them – yes, been fetched by one of them. Sylvia had a red car, a scarlet VW Golf . . .

'Would she have gone like that?' Burden asked. 'Without telling you? If she couldn't get you, wouldn't she have left a message?'

'Perhaps not if it was' – Wexford looked up at him – 'bad enough.'

'You mean, she'd have wanted to spare you? What are you thinking, Reg? Someone terribly injured? *Dead*? One of Sylvia's boys?'

'I don't know . . .'

The phone rang. He snatched it up.

'What's so urgent, Dad?' Sylvia was cool, pleasant, sounding more contented than usual.

'Tell me first if you're all all right?'

'We're fine.'

He couldn't tell whether his heart sank or leapt. 'Have you seen your mother?'

'Not today, no. Why?'

After that he had to tell her.

'There must be some perfectly simple explanation.'

He had heard those words a thousand times, had even uttered them. He said he would call her back as soon as he had news.

'Thanks for not asking if she could have left me,' he said to Burden.

'It never crossed my mind.'

'I'm wondering if she decided to walk to the station after all.'

'In that case, what about the red car?'

'Mary just saw a red car. She didn't know it was a taxi. She didn't see Dora get into it. It might have been any car parked outside.'

'What are you saying? That she set out to walk to the station and something happened to her on the way? She collapsed or . . .'

'Or she was attacked, Mike. Attacked, robbed, left there. There have been a lot of strange goings-on in this place lately: that masked lot on the rampage, the breaking into Concreation, that business at Contemporary Cars this morning.'

'D'you want to go out and follow the route she'd have taken?'

'I think I do,' Wexford said.

His daughters would phone in his absence, but he couldn't help that. Burden drove. The only route Dora could reasonably have taken was along roads that were built up all the way. There was no stretch of open country, no area of waste ground, no alley to pass through and only one footpath to take as a short cut. It had been a misty morning but the sun had come through bright and strong by ten-thirty. People would have been about, in the street, in their front gardens.

Before they came to Queen Street Burden parked and they explored the footpath. It led between the backs of shop yards and of gardens, was overhung with trees on both sides. A couple of teenagers were standing up against a garden gate kissing. There was no one else, nothing else. Burden drove across the High Street, entered Station Road, the station approach.

'It's not possible, is it?' Burden said, turning round outside the station.

'I ought to be relieved.'

'Let's say she walked it, and I reckon she must have done if none of the taxi firms took her, could she have met anyone on the way who gave her some sort of news so grave or so important as to distract her from going to London?'

'That's the idea I had about Sylvia all over again really, isn't it?'

'Well, could she?'

Wexford thought about it. He looked at the houses they passed, some of whose occupants he and Dora knew, well or slightly, but none were friends. The United Reformed Church, the Warren Primary School, a row of shops, then roads that were purely

52

residential. Some acquaintance comes running out of one of these houses, calls out to Dora, rushes her indoors, pours her heart out, appeals for help ... Denies her the use of a phone? Frustrates her visit to a new grandchild, the longed-for granddaughter? Compels her attention for *eleven hours*? 'No, Mike, she couldn't,' he said.

All the stories he had ever read of people going missing, all the cases of missing people he had ever come across ... He thought of them now. The woman who had gone into a supermarket with her boyfriend, left him waiting at the fish counter, to go herself to the cheese counter, and was never seen again. The man who went out to buy cigarettes but never returned. The girl who checked into a Brighton hotel in the evening but who wasn't in her room in the morning, was nowhere. All those others who just weren't where they should have been at some given time, who had disappeared without clue, without trace.

Still, it was only eleven hours. A day, he thought, a whole lost day. In his house the phone was ringing. Sheila. No, he had no news. He told her – absurdly – what he had told Mary Pearson, not to worry.

'Don't say there must be some perfectly simple explanation, Pop.'

'That's what your sister said. Maybe she's right.'

Burden offered to stay the night with him.

'No, you go home. I shan't sleep anyway, I don't suppose I'll go to bed. Thanks for coming.'

He didn't say aloud what he was thinking. He let Burden go, watched him depart and went back into the dark house, switching lights on. She must be dead, he said to himself, then said it to the empty room.

'She must be dead.'

He amended it to: she must be dead or badly hurt.

53

And not found. Somewhere she lay. There was no other explanation for her not phoning him or one of the girls, or somehow getting a message to him. Then he thought of the note that might have been left for him, the note that blew off the mantelpiece or fell down behind the furniture. He crawled about the floors, looking for the scrap of paper that would explain everything, tell all. Of course there was no note. When had Dora left him notes?

The small whisky he had poured back into the bottle he poured out again. Someone else could drive him if need be. The need wouldn't be tonight, he knew that by some kind of intuition.

Everyone knew. Because of his phone calls of the previous night and because Burden got in first, they all knew. They didn't expect him but he went in because he didn't know what else to do.

He had slept in the armchair for about an hour. Then he got up, had a shower, made himself a mug of instant coffee. You can phone hospitals at any hour, so he phoned a few, all ones he had phoned the evening before. No Dora Wexford had been brought in. He phoned both daughters and found that they had been talking to each other half the night. Sylvia was going to London to give Sheila support once she had found someone with whom to leave her sons, school being still out for the summer holidays. Would Dad like Neil to come and stay with him?

Dad would not, but he said it politely: 'No, thank you, my dear. You're very kind.'

He had been at the police station for an hour, not doing anything, sitting at his desk, when Barry Vine came in to say there had been a phone call from someone wanting to report a missing boy, a teenager. Vine, who wouldn't normally have been anxious to regard a boy of fourteen, six feet tall, gone from his grandmother's house for twenty-four hours as missing, thought the circumstances justified special attention.

'What circumstances?' said Wexford.

'This boy was going to London. He was going to the station in a cab.'

'My God,' said Wexford softly.

'Do I get the grandmother down here, sir?'

'We'll go to her.'

Rhombus Road was two streets from Oval Street where Burden had come with Lynn Fancourt on the previous day to check on the fare Trotter said he had fetched from Kingsmarkham station. Since then Wingate had confirmed Trotter's statement: he had been picked up from the station at about eleven, having come off the ten-fifty-eight train, and deposited in Oval Street at eleven-twenty. Wexford and Vine passed his door, turned left and left again and parked outside seventy-two Rhombus Road.

It was a street of small terraced houses, put up at the end of the nineteenth century, as so many in Stowerton had been, to accommodate workers in the chalk quarries and their families. All were now owner-occupied, affordable by young couples and first-time buyers. Most front doors were painted various bright colours, flowery window-boxes attached to sills and front gardens concreted over to give room for one parked car.

No car stood in front of seventy-two, which though not shabby, retained its original glass-panelled front door and sash windows, had flower beds full of chrysanthemums and Michaelmas daisies and a gravel path. The door was opened by a woman who looked far too young to be the grandmother of a fourteen-year-old. She had frizzy dark hair, pulled back with two slides from a pale, freckled face that

55

appeared as if make-up had never touched it. Denim dungarees were loose around her waist and over the check shirt. Her eyes were frightened, too wide open.

'Come in, please. I'm Audrey Barker. Ryan is my son.'

They went into a small, exquisitely tidy living-room that smelt of lavender polish. The woman who had got up from her armchair was in her seventies, plump, white-haired, in a heather-and-green tweed skirt and a twinset the colour of the scent.

Wexford said, 'Mrs Peabody?'

She nodded. 'My daughter came this morning. She came as soon as she knew about the muddle we'd got in. She's not well, she's just got out of hospital, that's why Ryan was staying with me, because she was in hospital, but as soon as we didn't know – I mean, as soon as we knew . . .'

'Why don't you sit down, Mrs Peabody, and tell us about it from the beginning?'

It was Audrey Barker who answered him. 'Basically, my mother thought Ryan was going home yesterday and I wasn't expecting him till today. We should have phoned and checked but we didn't. Ryan himself thought yesterday was the day.'

'Where do you live, Mrs Barker?'

'In south London, Croydon. You get the train from Kingsmarkham and change at Crawley or Reigate. You don't have to go into Victoria. Ryan had done it a good few times. He's nearly fifteen and he's tall for his age, taller than most grown men.' She evidently thought they were condemning her, though their faces were quite blank. 'He could have walked to Kingsmarkham station,' she said.

'It's over three miles, Audrey. He had his bag to carry.'

Vine steered her back to the previous morning. 'So Ryan was going home, Mrs Peabody, and you

56

thought he ought to have a taxi to the station. Is that right?'

She nodded. Slowly she clenched her fists and held them in her lap. It was a controlling gesture, a way of containing panic. 'The stopping train is the eleven-nineteen,' she said. 'The bus would have got him there an hour ahead of time and the next one would have been too late. I said why not have a taxi. I'd give him the money, it would be my treat. He'd only once been in a taxi before and that was with his mum.' Her voice slipped a bit. She cleared her throat. 'He didn't know what to say so I phoned up. It was a bit before half-past ten, five-and-twenty-past ten. I asked the man for a taxi for a quarter to eleven. That was to give Ryan time to buy his ticket. A nice bit of time, I don't like rushing. Oh, I wish I'd gone with him – why didn't I, Audrey? I was just too stingy to pay the fare back again.'

'That's not being stingy, Mum. That's common sense.'

'Who did you phone, Mrs Peabody?'

She thought. One hand went up and briefly covered her mouth. 'I said to Ryan to do it. Phone up, I mean. But he wouldn't, he said he didn't know what to say, so I didn't push it. I said, find me the number in the book, the local Yellow Pages book, and I'll do it. He gave me the number and I did it.'

'Wrote the number down, do you mean? Or brought you the phone book and pointed at it, or what?'

'He just said it. I put the phone on my lap and he said the number and I dialled it.'

'Can you remember it?' Wexford asked, knowing how hopeless this was, registering her bemused shake of the head. 'It wasn't double six, double six, double six, was it?'

'It was not,' she said. 'I'd remember that.'

'Did you see the car? The driver?'

'Of course I did. We were waiting in the hall, Ryan and me.'

They would be, Wexford thought, they would be there on the spot waiting, these two inexperienced taxi takers, the old woman and the boy, he could picture them. Mustn't keep the driver waiting, have you got the money ready, Ryan, and a fifty-pee piece for his tip? Here he is now. You want to go to the station, that's all you have to say to him, now give Nan a nice kiss . . .

'He came on the dot,' said Mrs Peabody, and Ryan picked up his bag and that bag they all wear on their shoulders, a back-something, and I said lots of love to Mum and to give me a kiss and he did. He had to bend right over to kiss me and he gave me a big hug and off he went.'

She began to cry. Her daughter put an arm tightly round her shoulders. 'You're not to blame, Mum. Nobody's blaming you. It's just all so mad, there's no explanation.'

'There must be an explanation, Mrs Barker,' said Vine. 'You didn't expect Ryan till today, you said?'

'They start back at school tomorrow. I thought he was coming the day before they started but him and my mother, they thought it was two days before. We should have phoned, I don't know why we didn't. I did phone when I got home from hospital. That was Saturday and I was sure Ryan said it was Wednesday he was coming home, but now I reckon what he said was I'll be home all day Wednesday or something like that.'

'So you weren't worried when he didn't turn up?' said Wexford.

'I wasn't worried till first thing this morning. I phoned Mum to check up on his train. It was a shock, I can tell you.'

'It was a shock for both of us,' said Mrs Peabody.

'So I got the next train down here. I don't know why, it was just instinctive, to be here with Mum. Look, where is he? What's happened to him? He's not what you'd call big but he's very tall, he's not stupid, he knows what he's doing, he wouldn't go with some man who offered him something. I mean, money, sweets, he's *fourteen* for God's sake.'

Dora's a grown woman, Wexford thought, a middle-aged woman who knows what she's doing, who wouldn't go with any man who offered her anything . . .

'Have you got a photograph of Ryan?'

On the verges of Framhurst Great Wood men worked all day, under the supervision of a tree expert, at extracting metal spikes from the trunks of oaks, limes and ashes, at chain-saw-felling height. One of them injured his left hand so badly that he had to be taken as a matter of urgency to Stowerton Royal Infirmary where it was feared at first he would lose two fingers. The tree people in the high branches were peaceful and silent, but those in the tree-top camp at Savesbury Deeps bombarded the workmen with bottles, empty Coke cans and sticks. From the top of a noble sycamore someone poured a bucket of urine on to the head of the tree expert.

Clouds had been gathering since lunch-time and the rain began at three. It descended delicately at first, pattering on a million tired summer-weary leaves, increasing in volume until it became a deluge. The Elves, as some called them, retreated into their tree-houses, drew up their tarpaulins, while some of them descended into the tunnel they had dug to link Framhurst Bottom with Savesbury Dell. Lightning lit up every Elves' nest in the high branches and a great gust of wind shook the trees so that their trunks swayed like the stems of flowers.

Over the whole panorama of woods, hills and green valleys (as seen from the air) the wind, weighted with heavy rain, flew in great silvery grey sweeps that glittered when the lightning came. The thunder rolled, then clattered with a sound like trees falling or heavy objects flung down on top of each other from a great height.

The workmen and the tree expert went home. Down in Kingsmarkham, Wexford also went home: a brief visit to check on his forlorn hope that there might be something significant or even vital on his answering machine.

He found both his daughters there.

The three-day-old Amulet lay in Sylvia's lap. Sheila leapt up and threw herself into his arms.

'Oh, Pop darling, we thought we ought to be here with you. We both thought that simultaneously, didn't we, Syl? We didn't hesitate, we didn't *think*. Paul drove us down. I didn't even bring the nurse – well, I couldn't, could I? Where would we put her? And I don't really know anything about babies, but Syl does, so that's OK. And poor, poor you, out of your mind about Mother, you must be!'

He bent over the child. She was a pretty little girl with a round rose-petal face, tiny prim features and hair as dark as Sylvia's was and Dora's once had been. 'Lovely blue eyes,' he said.

'They all have blue eyes at that age,' said Sylvia.

He kissed her, said, 'Thank you for coming, dear,' and to Sheila, 'You too, Sheila, thank you,' though he didn't want them, they were an added complication and his heart had sunk when he saw them, ungrateful devil that he was. Many people would give all they had for the devotion of not just one daughter but two. 'I have to go back for a couple of hours,' he said. 'I only came home to see if there was a message.'

'There's nothing,' said Sheila. 'I checked. It was the first thing I did.'

When one has children one has no privacy. They take it for granted that what is yours is theirs, personal things and the secrets of your heart, as well as possessions. He ought to be used to it by now. But how kind they were, his daughters, how good to him.

'Surely you're not indispensable at a time like this?'

It was a remark characteristic of his elder daughter. He ignored it, though looking at her kindly. How different they were, the two of them. Most of the time he didn't see it but now, inescapably, he saw her mother in Sylvia, the same features, the same almond-shaped dark eyes, hardened in Sylvia's case just as Sylvia was taller and altogether a bigger woman. But the likeness ... It made him gasp and turn his gasp to a cough.

Sheila took his arm, looked into his face. 'What can we do for you, darling? Have you had lunch?'

He lied, said he had. She was so absolutely the successful young actress who has just had a baby, she was it and playing it in her muslin tunic and white trousers, strings of beads, fair hair loose and flowing, soft, fruit-coloured make-up. Yet Sylvia in jeans and loose T-shirt, looking down with unusual tenderness at the baby on her knees, seemed more the child's mother.

'I'll see you both later,' Wexford said and plunged back through the torrents to his car.

They had mounted a hunt for his wife and Ryan Barker, mainly concentrated on inquiries in and around Kingsmarkham station. Every taxi company had been investigated. The drivers had no more knowledge of Ryan than they had of Dora and the station staff, such as they were – three ticket clerks and four platform staff – remembered nothing of either.

By five, Vine and Karen Malahyde with Pemberton, Lynn Fancourt and Archbold had come up with only one certain thing: neither Dora Wexford nor Ryan Barker had reached Kingsmarkham station on the previous morning. Somewhere between their points of departure and the station they had been spirited away.

It was Burden to whom the Roxane Masood phone call was relayed at five in the afternoon.

'I want to report my daughter missing.'

Something cold touched the back of his neck and flickered down his spine. He nearly said that he supposed she'd taken a taxi to the station the morning before. But it was his caller who said that.

'Pomfret, you said? We'll come.'

It was a cottage at the end of the short High Street where the shops came to an end, an ancient lath-and-plaster dwelling with eyelid gables and tiny latticed windows. Rain streamed off the eaves of the thatched roof. Pools of water lay on the path and inundated the tiny lawn. Wexford and Burden had to stand inside .on the doormat and shed dripping raincoats, so heavy had the downpour been between car and front door.

She was in her early forties, thin, intense-looking, with big dark eyes and chestnut hair hanging in a shaggy mane to her shoulders. She wore a garment that in any other time in history would have been called a night-gown, white, diaphanous, floor-length, with flounces and bits of lace. The ethnic painted beads round her neck removed any such illusion.

'Mrs Masood?'

'Come in. It's my daughter that's called Masood,

62

Roxane Masood. She uses her father's name. I'm Clare Cox.'

The interior looked as if it had been decorated and furnished in the early seventies and then frozen. Indian and African artefacts littered the place, the walls were hung with strips of Indian printed cotton and brass bells on strings, and there was a heavy odour of sandalwood. The only picture was framed in dark polished wood inlaid with mother-of-pearl.

It was a photograph of a young girl, the biggest photograph Wexford thought he had ever seen, and she was almost too beautiful to be real. When you looked at it you could understand those fairy-tales in which the prince or the swineherd is shown the likeness of some girl unknown to him and falls instantly in love. 'This portrait is of magical beauty, such as no eyes have seen before,' as Tamino sang. Her face was a perfect oval, her forehead high, her nose small and straight, her eyes huge and black with arched eyebrows, her hair a gleaming black veil, long, centre-parted, water-straight and fine as silk.

Wexford reflected upon these things afterwards. At the time he quickly turned away from the portrait and having ascertained that this was Roxane herself, asked Clare Cox to tell him what had happened on the previous day.

'She was going to London. She had an appointment at a model agency. She's got a fine arts degree but she wasn't interested in that, she wanted to be a model and she'd tried everything, all the agencies. Mostly, they didn't want to know; she was too beautiful, they said, and not thin enough, but she's *extremely* thin, believe me . . .'

'Yesterday morning, Ms Cox,' Vine prompted her.

'Yes, yesterday morning. She was going to London to this agency and then to see her father. He's got a business in Ealing, he's done very well for himself and he takes her out to some very grand places, I can tell you.' She caught Vine's eye and collected herself. 'She didn't turn up. Anyone else would have phoned to find out why not but not him, of course not. He thought she'd changed her mind, if you please.'

'How do you know then . . . ?

'He did phone. An hour ago. Some pal of his thought he could get her modelling work. I hope it's bona fide, I said, you hear such terrible things, porno rings and whatever, and I said why don't you ask her yourself and he said, put her on, and that's when it came out. He hadn't seen her.'

'Did you check with the modelling agency?'

She put out her hands, raised her shoulders. Her voice was a thin scream. 'I don't even know where the bloody place is!'

'So yesterday morning,' said Wexford, 'she went to Kingsmarkham station by taxi? Which taxi?' He was sure she wouldn't remember. 'Did you hear her make the call?'

'No, but I know when it was and who it was. She always had taxis, her father makes her an allowance and it's liberal, I can tell you. She'd always used the same company since they started. She phoned just before eleven. She knew the girl who worked for them, answered the phone, I mean. Tanya Paine. They were at school together.'

'Roxane can't have gone to Contemporary Cars yesterday, Ms Cox,' said Burden. He thought of how to put it. 'Their phones were down. They were out of order. She must have called another company.'

'Well, she didn't,' said Clare Cox. 'I was up in my studio, painting. That's what I do, I'm a painter. She came in and said the cab was coming in fifteen minutes and she'd catch the eleven-thirty-six. I don't know why I said it, but I did, I said, right, and then I said, how's Tanya, and she said, I don't know, I didn't talk to Tanya, it was some guy answered.'

'You mean she phoned Contemporary Cars at – what? Ten-thirty? And they answered?'

'Of course they did. And the cab came for her at ten to eleven. I saw her get in it and that was the last I saw of her.'

Chapter 6

Wexford finally got home to his daughters and his granddaughter at ten at night. But he was glad to have been busy, up to a point to have been distracted. Sylvia's insistence that he must be exhausted irritated him, though he gave no sign of annoyance. Her emphasis on the unfairness of it, on the way he had to do everything himself if he wanted it done, sent him to the dining-room in quest of a small whisky. Upstairs Amulet was screaming the place down.

'My posterity is driving me to drink,' he said to himself.

Then he thought how wonderful it would be to have Dora here to say it to. It was years since he had actually thought, in positive words, that to see his wife would be wonderful. How quickly, he reflected, disaster or potential disaster disturbs that which we accept as normal, shifts the aspect, makes us see the truth. You could so easily understand those who said, I will never be rough with her again, never offhand, never take her for granted, if only . . .

Earlier, once they had left Clare Cox, he and Burden, with Vine and Fancourt, had moved in on Contemporary Cars. They had gone over the place once again and then fetched Peter Samuels, Stanley Trotter, Leslie Cousins and Tanya Paine down to the police station.

Burden was looking at Trotter rather in the way a

Nazi-hunter might have looked at Mengele if he had found him lying low in a suburb of Asunción: with satisfaction and vengefulness and something like glee.

Who had driven Roxane Masood to the station? Who had driven Ryan Barker?

'I've told you enough times,' Peter Samuels said. 'We never got no calls between half-ten and twelve midday. We couldn't have on account of Tanya here being out of action.'

Tanya Paine was becoming aggressive. 'I didn't make it up, you know. I didn't tie myself up. I'm a victim and you're treating me like a criminal.'

'I'll need the name or at any rate the address of the fare you drove to Gatwick,' Burden said to Samuels. 'I don't understand how you all just accepted not getting any calls for an hour and a half. Didn't it occur to you to go back and find out why not?'

'We was busy,' said Trotter. 'You know where I was, going from Pomfret to the station and then to Stowerton, you know all that. It was a *relief* to me there weren't no calls, I can tell you.'

'Anyway, it wasn't all that abnormal,' Leslie Cousins said. 'I can think of dozens of times when it's been slack.'

Burden rounded on him. 'I'll have the addresses of the fares you took, please.' He said to all of them, 'I want you to think. Have you any idea, even a suspicion, who it could have been that came into the place and tied Tanya up? Anyone you've talked to? Anyone who knew no one ever went back there before twelve noon?'

Peter Samuels asked if they minded if he smoked. He was a stout, heavy man with three chins and split veins on his cheeks, probably no more than forty but looking older. He had the cigarette packet out before anyone replied.

Burden said rather unpleasantly, 'Not if it helps your concentration.'

Trotter didn't ask if anyone minded his smoking. The moment their cigarettes were lit Tanya Paine began an artificial coughing. Cousins, the youngest of them and Tanya's contemporary, grinned and cast up his eyes. He said that any of their fares might know they never went back there before midday.

'A regular fare might notice. I mean, one of us could have said. Why not? No harm in that, is there? I mean, one of us only has to say we're busy, none of us never goes back to the office before twelve.'

At last Samuels said he sometimes had occasion to tell a fare he hadn't a radio link with the office but worked a car-phone system. That was if the fare asked. Sometimes a fare wanted to be picked up when he came back on the train, for instance. Could he call directly from the train on his mobile? 'That's when I'd tell him. I'd say to call the office and Tanya'd get through to one of us, depending on who was likely to be available.'

'So you're saying that anyone you've ever driven might know?'

'Not *anyone*,' said Samuels. 'Only them as asked.'

It was after this that they were allowed to go home and Vine, with Lynn Fancourt and Pemberton, started house-to-house inquiries in the vicinity of Kingsmarkham station. Only there weren't many houses. Contemporary Cars' office stood on half an acre of waste ground overlooked by nothing much, bounded on one side by the blank brick wall of the bus station and on the other by a tall, thin building that housed a shoe repairer on its lowest level and an aromatherapist, photo-copying agency and a hair-dresser on the upper floors. Outside, and for a few feet inside, the chain-link fencing which bounded the land, thin, straggling trees, poplars and elders, grew out of six-foot-high nettles.

Opposite, beyond a row of cottages, was a pub called the Engine Driver, then a cash-and-carry hardware store, then the station car-parks.

Two hours later they knew very little more than when they started. Housewives, shoppers, drivers bent on catching trains, pub patrons, don't notice two men parking a car and mounting the steps of a mobile home unless they have reason to do so. The men could easily have put on masks once they had entered Contemporary Cars' office, for they would not have been seen by Tanya Paine until they had opened a second door.

Wexford pondered on how much more *noticeable* women were than men. If the intruders had been women someone might well have noticed them. Would this change as the equality gap between the sexes narrowed even more? Would women dressed like men, women in jeans, dark jackets, short-haired, without make-up, be as easily ignored?

He went to bed, then got up again when all was quiet. Sleep was impossible, unthinkable. Sheila's bedroom door was ajar and he stood in the doorway for a moment, watching her sleeping, the baby also sleeping beside her, in the crook of her arm. Such a sight would once have given him intense pleasure. For the first time in his life he understood what it was to want to roar aloud one's misery and terror. The thought of his children's reaction if he actually did that, their panic and fear, almost made him smile. He sat downstairs in an armchair in the dark.

Reading was as impossible as sleep. He thought of the Contemporary Cars business, knowing now for certain what had happened. The two men, with several accomplices, were arranging the taking of hostages. They had immobilised Tanya Paine in order to have uninterrupted access to the phones for an hour and a half – or as long as it took. Very likely they weren't particular as to who their hostages were. They only had to be three people who phoned Contemporary Cars for a taxi between ten-thirty and eleven-thirty. The three they got were enough.

Ryan Barker, or his grandmother representing him, had phoned from Stowerton at ten-twenty-five for the eleven-nineteen, Dora from Kingsmarkham at ten-thirty for the eleven-o-three, Roxane Masood at ten-fifty-five for the eleven-thirty-six. Why was there a gap of twenty-five minutes before they responded to another call? Because no calls came in? Because none came in from one person alone and they felt unable to handle two passengers? (He winced at that, at that word 'handle'.) Because they had only two drivers working with them? It was possible too that one of them was one of the drivers, leaving the other to deal with the phone . . .

And then what? Ryan Barker might not have been too sure of the way to the station. His driver might have taken him almost anywhere within, say, a five-mile radius, before he realised. But Roxane Masood would have known within five minutes, Dora much sooner. Wexford didn't think his wife would simply have accepted, have wept, have pleaded. She would have tried to do something. Not to the extent of jumping out of the car, not that.

He clenched his fists, squeezed his eyes shut. Verbal protest, no doubt. A threat to leave the car. They must have taken steps to guard against such an eventuality. There must have been an accomplice waiting at, say, the first stop, red traffic light, halt sign, road junction. Then the rear door is opened, the accomplice enters, another one of those toy or replica guns is brandished . . .

Yes, that was how it was done in each case. But why?

Look at the alternative. Kidnap three people picked out of the street in broad daylight? It would have to be in daylight because there was never anyone about after dark. These days there never was. People stayed at home in front of the television or if they went out, went in cars. They even drank at home and pub after pub was closed. Like the Railway Arms. Beer was expensive and you couldn't go to a pub by car anyway, not with the current laws as to driving over the permitted limit. This way, the way the kidnappers had done it, there was no suspicion, no resistance, no struggle, until the route became unfamiliar, and then, with the accomplice at hand, it would have been too late.

Another reason for that twenty-five minute gap might be that they wanted women because women were physically less strong. And, even in Ryan Barker's case, it was a woman who had made the call. If she told them the fare would be a fourteen-year-old boy that wouldn't be enough to deter them. So they had a girl, a teenage boy and a middle-aged woman as their hostages, and the last-named happened to be his wife.

They must *be* hostages, surely? There couldn't be any other reason.

Another why remained. None of the three had any money, not real money. He and Dora were more or less comfortably off, Roxane Masood's father was prosperous, but Wexford doubted if he was in the millionaire league, and Ryan Barker's family seemed in straitened circumstances, if not positively poor. What ransom therefore could they be looking for?

Sometime during the night he made himself a cup of tea and fell asleep in the chair for an hour. A bit later he brewed coffee, went to the front of the house

71

and watched the dawn come. The dark sky began to grow pale at the horizon, a rim of lightening that was not quite light. Upstairs Amulet gave one cry before Sheila silenced and comforted her with the breast. Dark clouds shifted and positive light, pale-green and gleaming, showed clear and cold.

With the coming of dawn over the bypass site, the Under Sherriff for Mid-Sussex, Timothy Jordan, moved in on the Savesbury Deeps camp with his bailiffs. It was the largest of the camps and its occupants had been served with eviction notices some time before.

The protesters were either in the seven tree-houses on the site or sleeping in hammocks strung between the oak, ash and lime trees which predominated in this area. Before the sun came up Jordan had them corralled inside a circle of yellow-coated policemen. He woke them by announcing with the aid of an amplifier that he had a court order granting him possession of the land and that they should vacate it. The amplifier was essential because the forest birds' dawn chorus was so loud: jug-jug, tweet-tweet, tu-witta-woo.

Meanwhile, in Sewingbury, the fleet of buses were picking up security guards from the old Army camp and ferrying them to the site north of Stowerton where the earth-moving would begin in half an hour. In Framhurst Great Wood, inside the secret tunnel, whose existence they supposed unknown to all but the members of SPECIES, six people who regularly slept there were rousing themselves from sleep. The other end of the tunnel came out near the foot of Savesbury Hill.

The last of the six to emerge were a self-styled professional protester called Gary and the woman who had been his companion since they were both

72

fifteen and whom he called his wife. No one knew her name but everyone called her Quilla. Gary had never trimmed his blond beard and it hung nearly to his waist. His clothes would have been more appropriate, and have attracted less comment, if the date had been 1396. He wore breeches, cross-gartered, and a brown canvas tunic, and Quilla a long cotton gown. They turned back for blankets because the morning was chilly and came face to face with a German Shepherd dog. At the Savesbury end the bailiffs and police had penetrated the tunnel mouth.

Once Gary and Quilla were out, Timothy Jordan sent a tunnelling expert known as the Human Mole into the tunnel to check it was empty and then put a guard on each end. Another bailiff, called the Human Spider, shinned up the tallest tree towards the house in its top branches. A rain of chopped wood, tin cans and bottles descended on him, for a while impeding his progress. On the ground Jordan's men began pulling people out of the bender tents and emptying them of their contents, before ripping the structures apart.

Somehow the quieter and more organised bands of protesters had got to know about it and a growing number of them assembled outside the security line: KABAL, SPECIES and Heartwood. When they saw one of the big rough-coated dogs come out from the tunnel mouth they began a low angry chanting. Up in the tree the Human Spider encountered a woman on the threshold of her tree-house and as the two of them struggled with each other fifty feet up, the crowd chanted, 'Shame, shame, shame!'

Patiently and in silence, Gary and Quilla assembled their property which had been flung out of the tunnel. They looked as if about to go on a pilgrimage to Canterbury with a Pardoner and a Wife of Bath. Neither of them would have touched, still less owned, anything made of plastic, so they stuffed their clothes, their blankets, their pots and pans, into old-fashioned jute sacks. Quilla began to sing the madrigal 'April is in my mistress' face' and the other dispossessed protesters joined in, with the tune if not always the words.

Up in the tree the woman whom the Human Spider had laid hands on had either fainted or, more probably, staged a faint, and hung limp between the two men who supported her. They began to lower her down the ladder, a perilous exercise, as her passive resistance gave them no help.

'Shame, shame, shame!' chanted the crowd.

Gary and Quilla sang:

> 'April is in my mistress' face,
> And July in her eyes hath place.
> Within her bosom lies September,
> But in her heart a cold December.'

By now the sun had risen, a fiery ball between black rails of cloud. The birds' calling was more subdued. Jug-jug, tu-witta-woo . . . A sharp gust of wind blew through the tree-tops.

On reaching the ground the woman who had appeared to faint sprang from the arms of the men who had brought her down. She was dressed in rags, some of which flowed and others which wrapped her like a mummy's bandages, and now, as she stood there and raised her arms to the crowd in a gesture of triumph or encouragement, her tattered garments streamed and fluttered in the wind. She ran to Quilla, embracing her and crying.

'We'll go to the Elder Ditches camp,' said Gary. 'I've had it with tunnels. You can show us how to build a tree-house, Freya. We'll build a big tree-house for the three of us.'

74

'I am a tree,' cried Freya, once more spreading out her arms.

'We're all trees here,' said Gary.

While Wexford's daughters made the kind of breakfast for him that he never ate, fussed over him and begged him to rest, Burden went in to work half an hour earlier than he need have done. His mind was full of Stanley Trotter. No amount of argument was going to convince him Stanley Trotter wasn't involved in this up to his neck and deeper. The man had murdered Ulrike Ranke and now he was engaged in a conspiracy to kidnap. It was probably a perverts' ring. The German girl had been raped before she was strangled and Burden believed this was developing into some sort of elaborate sex crime.

He had been at his desk ten minutes when a call was put through to him from the front desk. 'The editor of the *Kingsmarkham Courier* to speak to someone in authority. The governor's not in yet.'

'I suppose I'll do,' said Burden.

'He said you failing the governor.'

The editor, who had been there for some years now, was a man called Brian St George. Burden had met him once or twice, often enough, apparently, for St George to feel justified in calling him by his Christian name in full.

'I've received a funny sort of letter, Michael. Came in the post just now. It was the first one my personal assistant opened.'

If St George had a PA, Burden thought, he was Sherlock Holmes. 'What do you mean, a funny letter?'

'Maybe it's a hoax, but somehow I don't reckon it is.'

Trying to keep sarcasm out of his voice, Burden suggested St George tell him the letter's contents.

'Or do you think you'd better come down here, Michael?'

'Tell me what's in it first.' Suddenly Burden had a warning feeling, what Wexford called *fingerspitzen-* something. 'Don't handle it too much. Read it to me without handling it if you can.'

'OK, Michael. Will do. Funny, isn't it? A letter in these days. I mean, a phone call, a fax, e-mail, whatever, but a letter! Wonder it wasn't brought round by a guy on horseback.'

'Could you read it?'

'Right. Here goes. "Dear Sir, We are Sacred Globe, saving the earth from destruction by all means in our power. We are holding five people: Ryan Barker, Roxane Masood, Kitty Struther, Owen Struther and Dora Wexford ..." They have to be wrong there, don't they? I mean, that's your boss's wife, isn't it? Since when's she been missing?'

'Go on.'

'OK. "... Owen Struther and Dora Wexford. They are safe for the moment. You will not find them. We will be in touch today to tell you our price for them. Inform all national newspapers and Kingsmarkham police for maximum publicity. We are Sacred Globe, saving the world." '

Burden said quietly as Wexford came into the room, 'We'll come to you now and take possession of that. In the meantime tell no one. Is that understood? No one.'

Chapter 7

The sheet of paper was A4 size, Wexford guessed, 80 grammes weight, plain white, the kind you can buy by the ream from any office supplier. Once the letter would have had to be handwritten, later typed – and typing was almost as great a giveaway as handwriting. Now, with computers, detection was nearly impossible. The expert would probably be able to say which software had been used, which word-processing program, and that was all. No spelling mistakes any more, no capitals in error for lower case, no slipped letters, no chipped digits.

There might be fingerprints but he doubted it. The writer had folded the sheet once and then, in the same direction, once more. The envelope it had come in lay beside it. Laser printers are unable to print envelopes but a program is available for printing envelope labels and this facility had been used. It was, he thought, dreadfully anonymous.

They sat round Brian St George's desk, the letter lying in the middle of the leather inlay. St George was immensely pleased with himself, a complacency he had stopped trying to deny. He kept smiling wonderingly, amazed at the plum of a story which had come his way.

He was a cadaverous grey man with a hatchet face and a big belly that hung like a half-filled sack from his bones. His pale-grey chalk-striped suit was in serious need of dry-cleaning. A woman may wear a crew neck or an open-collared shirt under a suit but on a man this gives the appearance of his being half dressed and it was a long time since St George's sweatshirt had been the white it was when it started life. He could hardly keep his hands off the letter. They strayed towards it and he pulled them back, like a boy teasing an insect. 'I suppose I can photocopy it?' he said.

'You can have that PA of yours in here to copy it by hand,' said Burden. 'But it's not to be touched.'

'They're not used to copying by hand.'

'Do it yourself then.' Wexford had never previously encountered the editor of the *Kingsmarkham Courier* that he could remember and he didn't much like what he saw. 'Which national newspapers did you have in mind to release this to?'

'The lot,' said St George, suddenly nervous, fearing the worst.

'You can do that but with the strict embargo that nothing is to appear until we give the go ahead. That goes for the *Courier* too, naturally.'

'Yes, but hold hard a minute, publicity's the best thing out in a case like this. You want publicity. You've a lot more chance of finding these people if everyone knows what's going on.'

'Nothing at all till we give the go-ahead. I hope that's understood. This is a very serious matter, the most serious you're ever likely to be involved in. Mr Vine will stay here with you to see my instructions are carried out.'

'It is your wife, isn't it?'

Wexford didn't reply. He had read the letter on the desk: '... Ryan Barker, Roxane Masood, Kitty Struther, Owen Struther ...' and then, when he reached his wife's name, the four syllables had come at him and struck him like a blow; black, hard letters

78

leaping off the sheet. His eyes had closed involuntarily. He hoped now he hadn't recoiled, actually stepped back, but he feared he had. Feeling the blood recede from his face, as if it retreated like a withdrawing tide into the centre of his body, he had had to sit down suddenly.

His voice had deserted him but it was back now, deep and strong. 'Who beside yourself has seen this letter, Mr St George?'

'Call me Brian. Everyone does. No one but my PA, Veronica, has actually seen it.'

'Keep it that way. Mr Vine will speak to Veronica. At present silence is absolutely imperative. You will speak to these national newspapers and we will have a meeting with their editors later today.'

'OK, if that's the way you want it. It seems a crying shame but I bow to the inevitable.'

'We shall ask British Telecom to put a trace on your phones,' Burden said, lifting the letter in gloved fingers and slipping it between plastic. 'How many lines are there?'

'Only two.' St George said it in the tone of a man who would like to have said 'twenty-five'.

'These Sacred Globe people have expressed their intention of making contact again today. Everything that comes over the phone into these offices must be recorded. I shall send you an officer to take Mr Vine's place in due course.'

'By God, you're taking things very seriously,' said St George, still smiling.

Wexford got up. He said, 'I expect you know it's an offence to attempt to pervert the course of justice.'

'No need to look at me. I'm a law-abiding sort of chap, always have been, but I suppose I'm allowed to express an opinion, and in my opinion you're making a grave mistake.'

'I'll be the judge of that.'

Wexford could think of half a dozen nastier things to say but he hadn't the heart for any of them. Going down the stairs they passed a young woman coming up. She had black curly hair hanging to her waist and a scarlet skirt that measured about nine inches from waist to hem. The personal assistant, probably.

'I'm not going to hang about,' Wexford said. 'I'm going straight to the Chief Constable. Meanwhile we'll need a trace on all our phones.'

'Yes. I wonder how many BT can do. It won't be an unlimited number. Who are these Struthers, Reg? Kitty and Owen? Why weren't they reported missing?'

Donaldson opened the car door and they got in the back. Wexford punched out one of the numbers of the Mid-Sussex Constabulary headquarters in Myringham, then asked for the Chief Constable's extension. He seldom saw the Chief Constable, most of his dealings being with Freeborn, the Deputy. Montague Ryder was a distant, lofty figure who suddenly seemed approachable when, in response to Wexford's insistence on urgency, he came to the phone and agreed instantly to a meeting as early as possible.

'I'll go over there now, or once we've dropped you. I don't think it's odd the Struthers haven't been reported missing, Mike. They're probably a married couple living alone. I expect they intended going away on holiday. I've been wondering about the interval between Dora calling for a car at ten-thirty and Roxane at ten-fifty-five, but this accounts for it. There wasn't an interval, these Struthers called for a car around ten-forty-five. The probability is they phoned Contemporary Cars to catch one of those trains between the eleven-nineteen and the twelve-o-three . . .'

'Or to go to Gatwick. If it was a holiday they might have been going by air.'

'True. But whatever it was, if they left an empty house behind them, who would know they were missing? If a family member was there, he or she wouldn't expect to hear from them. It would be odder if they *had* been reported missing. What is peculiar is that there were two of them and one could be a man maybe in the prime of life.'

'You mean, it's harder to abduct such people than ...' Burden tried to be tactful, failed abysmally '... well, one on his – her – his own.'

'Yes.'

'Maybe he's an elderly man. They could both be in their seventies for all we know. I'll have them checked out. The phone book may be enough. Struther's not a common name in this neck of the woods. Are we going to say anything about this to the boy's mother and grandmother and the girl's mother?'

'Not yet.'

'What do they want, Reg? What's this price of theirs?'

'I think I know.'

Wexford turned his face away and Burden said no more. He got out of the car and went into the police station. There, though there were others to do it for him, he looked up Struther in the phone directory himself. There were two Struths, fifteen Strutts but only one Struther: O. L. Struther, Savesbury House, Markinch Lane, Framhurst.

He punched out the number. Four double rings and then, of course, one of those damned answering machines. Burden hated them. At least the greeting message on this one wasn't facetious, not the kind that said, 'Call me back if there's money in it,' or 'If you want to take me out to dinner I'm on.' A man's

81

voice, which could have been middle-aged or old, but certainly wasn't young. The English it used was very correct, even pedantic. Courteously, it named the woman first.

'Neither Kitty nor Owen Struther is available at present to answer your call. If you would like to leave a message, please do so after the tone, giving your name, the date and the time. Thank you.'

Burden thought it worth a try. He left a message, asking whoever might be there – a slim chance but a possibility – to contact Kingsmarkham police as a matter of urgency. Then he got on to British Telecom.

The Regional Crime Squad's Major Crime Unit, consisting of a detective chief inspector, one inspector, six detective sergeants and six detective constables, all specially trained, was housed in an unpretentious building in Myringham. Once it had been a set of auction rooms. It was built of brown bricks with vaguely Gothic windows and a door round the side. Through these windows computer screens could usually be seen, with people staring into them.

Wexford had passed it on his way to the Constabulary headquarters, an altogether more impressive place put up in the eighties when architecture was beginning to take a turn for the better after the lamentable previous ten years. The headquarters, out on the Sewingbury Road, had an ambitious roof, a kind of terraced mansarding, with a large square tower in the middle, curved wings and a pillared portico. On the lawn in front stood a statue of Sir Robert Peel, who, as well as being the founder of the police force, was said to have occupied a house at Myfleet for ten months between the autumn of 1833 and the summer of 1834.

The Chief Constable had a suite in the tower. An ante-room was full of the usual computer operators.

One of them left her machine and took him through, knocking on a brass-fitted mahogany door. Wexford had that feeling of the heart rising into the throat, though he wasn't in the least nervous of Montague Ryder. It was rather that, at present, every happening seemed fraught with foreboding, every moment in passing time pregnant with dread.

The room was huge, like a lounge in a good country hotel, with armchairs, sofas, low tables, a big bowl of dahlias and Michaelmas daisies standing on an antique cabinet. Windows, designed less for opening and letting in light than for viewing panoramas, afforded the sight of green hills, deep valleys and the distant rolling downs.

Montague Ryder got up from where he had been sitting at a desk and came to Wexford with outstretched hand. 'I've been talking on the phone with Mike Burden,' he said. 'I think he's pretty well filled me in. You did right to hesitate but we must tell those parents at once. Anything else isn't feasible.'

He was a small man, slight but strong-looking, many inches shorter than Wexford. Abundant uniformly pale-grey hair covered his head like a neat cap and his eyes were the same clear dove-grey. 'This is a bad business about your wife.'

Wexford nodded. 'Yes, sir.'

'Won't you sit down?'

A green leather sofa accommodated them both, one at each end, facing one another. On the desk, a few feet away, stood a framed photograph of a pretty fair-haired woman with a child of maybe ten and another of eight. Wexford found he couldn't look at it. He said, 'These people, this Sacred Globe, will make contact again today. How or where we don't know.'

'Burden told me. You were quite right to embargo newspaper coverage. I shall set up a meeting with

83

newspaper representatives for later today myself. I shan't need you at that.'

Wexford hesitated, then said, 'I hardly suppose you're going to need me at all, are you, sir? I mean, once I've given you the facts. You won't want me on the case.'

Ryder got up. He was recognisably the kind of person who never sits still for long, a pacer, a fidget, a man with too much energy for the ordinary uses of daily life and one whom exhaustion probably hit at the end of each day. He said, 'Would you like coffee? I'll have it sent in.'

'Not for me, sir, thank you.'

'Right. I drink too much of the stuff anyway.' He perched on a chair arm. 'You mean, of course, that I'd take you off the case because of your wife's involvement. In other circumstances that would be so, but I can't here.' Perhaps for the first time ever, he essayed Wexford's first name. 'I can't, Reg. We'll call in the Regional Crime Squad, but even so I don't have enough senior officers to dispense with you. I need you to lead this investigation. I'm putting you in charge of it.'

The first call from a national newspaper came in at ten-thirty. They wasted no time, Burden thought, referring the speaker, and the two others who called within minutes, to the Chief Constable's office at Myringham. As far as he was concerned, the sooner they got on with that restraining press conference the better.

Where would it come to, the phone call from Sacred Globe? He presumed it would be a phone call. The post, after all, had come and there was no second delivery. A message by fax or e-mail would be too dangerous to send, its very existence a clue to the transmitter. So a phone call it would be. To the police station? To the *Courier*? Somehow he didn't think so. One of those insistent national newspapers perhaps, or the local authority, the mayor's office, even the Constabulary headquarters. No, not that last. It would be somewhere they would least suspect, yet to someone certain to pass it on ...

To one of Wexford's daughters?

He'd see about a trace on Wexford's home phone. And then he was going to take Karen Malahyde and the two of them would go up to Savesbury House, home of the Struthers. If his message had been received it hadn't been answered. Probably there was no one there. He couldn't place the house, couldn't see it in his mind's eye, but big country houses were two a penny round here, he'd probably know it when he saw it. If the Struthers had neighbours there was a good chance of one of them having seen something.

Facially, Karen looked like a dedicated police officer. She had been promoted to detective sergeant the previous year. Her expression was serious, her dark eyes steady, but her face was too scrubbed-looking, her hair too grimly cropped, for her to be considered good-looking. That was above the neck. Below, she had all the attributes of a catwalk model, perfect figure, and legs, as Burden's son John had once said, to die for. Burden himself didn't think of women in those terms and had been congratulated on this negativity by Wexford who, perhaps ironically, praised his political correctness. Karen herself was almost too PC for Kingsmarkham, particularly in her dealings with men. He didn't care whether she liked him or not, yet he rather fancied she did.

She was an excellent driver and it was she who drove the two of them. In Savesbury Lane they were stopped by the police cordon, for the bailiffs were

85

still busy breaking up treehouses and clearing occupants. When the sergeant in his yellow coat realised who it was he would have made an exception and let them through, but Karen good-humouredly turned round and took an alternative route via the Framhurst byroad.

The village of Framhurst would be the most badly affected of all conurbations in the Kingsmarkham neighbourhood. 'Conurbations' was a Highways Agency word which had made Wexford laugh grimly, for Framhurst was no more than a village street, a crossroads, three shops and a church. The school, built in 1834, had long since been converted into a house that its occupants whimsically called Lescuela.

Of the shops, one was an old-fashioned family butcher's to which customers came from all over the neighbourhood, another a general store, newsagent and video library, and the third a teashop with a striped awning and tables on the pavement outside. Framhurst had traffic lights at the point where the Kingsmarkham road crossed the one that passed between Pomfret and Myfleet. No one was sure how much of the new bypass would be visible from the houses which lined the village street, but there was no doubt about the coming destruction of the view from the hill to which that street led. The whole valley lay spread out below, woods, marsh, round, tree-capped Savesbury Hill, and the River Brede threading through the light-green and the dark-green like a long, crinkly strand of white silk.

Burden looked down on it. Of course you couldn't see any of those people from here. You couldn't see the pilgrims transformed into refugees, moving on with their bundles to pastures new. One day, not far off now, a twin-track road, three lanes each side, would change the entire face of that panorama, like a white bandage covering a long never-to-be-healed wound.

They found the house with some difficulty. It was concealed in shrubbery and tall trees, and was invisible from the road. Its nearest neighbour was a cottage on the outskirts of Framhurst village. They went past the house, realised they had gone too far and turned round. A sign on the gatepost was overgrown with tendrils of wild clematis. Karen had to get out and pull away the leaves to disclose a name: Markinch Hall in almost obliterated letters with Savesbury House printed boldly over the top of it.

'Interesting,' said Burden. 'I wonder if what-are-they-called, Sacred Globe, had problems finding the place.'

'Mr and Mrs Struther probably gave directions over the phone.'

The gates were open so they drove in and up a gravelled drive bordered by cypresses with tall alders and sycamores making a backdrop behind them. Brick and timbered walls gradually appeared as the trees thinned, and the varied colours, red, yellow and purple, of a well-tended garden replaced much of the green. The house looked like two houses joined together, the one ancient and picturesque, gabled and lattice-windowed, the other a tall Georgian building with portico. The whole must be very big, Burden thought, big enough for several families and with outbuildings or even wings behind.

There are gardens and gardens, his wife said. Most of them are full of stuff from the local garden centre, but the other kind, the rare kind, contain plants you hardly ever see, plants her father called 'choice', the ones that only have Latin names. The gardens of Savesbury House came into this latter category.

Burden would have been hard put to it to name a single one of these flowers, these bedding plants and climbers, but he could tell the effect was very pleasing. The sun which succeeded the rain of the day before brought out a subtle sweet scent from whatever it was that spread its blossoms over the Georgian façade.

A Gothic front door on the older part of the building, black and worn, arched and studded, looked as if it hadn't been opened since Queen Victoria's Golden Jubilee. Burden was approaching it, his eye on a curly iron bell-pull, when a man came round from the side of the house. He glanced at Burden, curled his lip at Karen, eyed Burden again and said, 'What d'you want? Who are you?'

It was the kind of accent that the majority of the British people laugh at and Americans can't understand, a plummy drawl that is never acquired by public school alone but requires parental back-up and preparatory education from the age of seven.

Burden had no incentive to be nice. He said, 'Police' and produced his warrant card.

The man, who was young, no more than in his mid-twenties, looked at Burden's photograph and back at the original as if he seriously expected a hoax. He said to Karen, 'Have you got one too or are you just along for the ride?'

Karen exhibited warning signs, familiar to Burden, though not perhaps to her questioner. Her eyes snapped, then stared unblinking. 'Detective Sergeant Malahyde,' she said and put her card in his face.

He stepped back a little. He was tall, well-built, in riding breeches and hacking jacket over a white T-shirt, his features copyable by an artist or photographer as the archetype of the English upper class: straight nose, high cheek-bones, tall forehead, firm chin and the kind of mouth that was once called clean-cut. His hair, of course, was straw-blond and his eyes steel-blue. 'All right,' he said. 'What have I done? What misdemeanour have I committed? Have I driven without lights or subjected some young lady to sexual harassment?'

'May we go inside?' Burden said.

'Oh, I don't really think so, do you?'

'Yes, I do think so, Mr Struther. It is Mr Struther, isn't it? The son of Owen and Kitty Struther?'

He was temporarily disconcerted and returned Burden's look in silence. He walked up to the front door and pushed at it. The door came open with a long, drawn-out groan. Over his shoulder he said, affectedly casual, 'Has something happened to my parents?'

Burden and Karen followed him into the house. The hall was low-ceilinged, half-timbered, a huge, sprawling place with a stone-flagged floor on which black carved furniture stood about, the kind that looks as if Elizabeth I might have sat on it or eaten off it. They all had to duck under the lintel to get through the doorway into a living-room. Here were floral chintz, Indian rugs, arts-and-crafts tables, and all was exquisitely clean and sweet-smelling.

'Do you live here, Mr Struther?' They hadn't been asked to sit down but Burden did so.

'I look the sort of guy who would live at home with Mummy, do I?'

'May I know where you do live?'

'London. Where else? Fitzhardinge Mews, West One.'

He *would* have a West One address, Burden thought. 'Then I suppose you are here to take care of the house while your parents are away on holiday?'

That did surprise him. He looked at Karen's legs, pursed his lips. 'Something like that,' he said. 'It's scarcely a hardship to come here on my own holiday.

My mother fears burglars, my father has some phobia about an inefficient drain, ergo . . . ! Now can we come to the point?'

'You were here yesterday morning,' Karen said, 'when a driver from Contemporary Cars came to collect your parents and drive them to Kingsmarkham station?'

'Gatwick airport, actually. Yes, why?'

'Where were they going?'

'You mean, where are they now. Florence. A city more familiar to you as Firenze, no doubt.'

'If you make a phone call to their hotel, Mr Struther, you will find that they are not there. They never went there.' Burden had been about to say that Kitty and Owen Struther had been abducted but he waited. The man's hostility was almost tangible. 'If you make that phone call you will find that your parents are missing.'

'I am not hearing this. I do not believe this.'

'It is true, Mr Struther. May I know your first name, please?'

'Not to call me by it, I beg. I'm old-fashioned about things like that. My *Christian* name is Andrew. I am Andrew Owen Kinglake Struther.'

'You do know where your parents are staying, Mr Struther?'

'Certainly I do and I consider that question impertinent. You've had your say, I've registered your absurd news and now I'd like your space.'

Burden decided to give up. He was under no obligation to make this man believe in his parents' abduction. He had done his best. Later in the day, no doubt, Andrew Struther would be on the phone to Kingsmarkham police station, having had what he had been told confirmed at Gatwick and in Florence, but instead of showing contrition and asking for more facts, demanding to know why the whole story hadn't been imparted to him earlier.

But as they entered the hall once more and crossed the stone flags there was a sound of running footsteps from above and a girl came down the staircase, followed by a German Shepherd dog. She was about Andrew Struther's age, a white-faced, red-lipped girl with a mass of untidy mahogany-coloured hair, wearing jeans and what looked the top half of baby-doll pyjamas. The dog was young, black and tan, not unlike the bailiff's dogs, with a dense, glossy coat. At the bottom the girl stopped, holding on to the carved banister post.

'Cops,' said Andrew Struther.

'You're kidding.'

'No, but don't ask. You know how low my boredom threshold is.'

The dog sat at the foot of the stairs and stared at them. Burden and Karen let themselves out but the front door slammed behind them before they could close it. Burden made no comment to Karen and she drove in silence. The sun had gone in and a light rain splashed the windscreen, too scanty for wipers to be needed. He thought of the various places Sacred Globe might phone, the places they would know about, a group practice surgery, a hospital, a high-street shop. Once they had done that the story would be out and there would be no way to stop it, never mind high-level newspaper conferences. Somehow he knew they would phone somewhere he hadn't thought of and couldn't cover. British Telecom were obliging, but they couldn't put a trace on every possible phone and no one else but BT was permitted to do it.

Karen found a parking space almost outside Clare Cox's cottage, just where the double yellow line ended, and tucked the car behind a black Jaguar of last year's registration. Its owner – Burden guessed it before he was told – opened the door to them. He was a small, neat man, improbably dressed in a denim suit. His skin was waxen-cream, his hair and moustache inky black and Burden thought he looked like a not very old artist's rendering of Hercule Poirot.

'I am Roxane's father. Hassy Masood. Please come in. Her mother isn't feeling too good.'

Though obviously Asian, or of Asian parentage, Masood spoke with the accent of west London. The background, created by Clare Cox, of Indian artefacts and vaguely central-Asian rugs and hangings, suited his appearance but not his voice, manner or, apparently, his taste. In the living-room he shook his head disparagingly, cast up his eyes and, gesturing with his hands, exclaimed, 'This junk! Can you believe it?'

'We'd like to see Ms Cox if that's possible,' said Karen.

'I'll fetch her. You've no news of my daughter, I suppose? I came down here last night. Her mother was in a rare old state.' He smiled tightly, wrinkling up his eyes. 'So was I, in point of fact. Families should be together at a time like this, don't you think?'

Burden said nothing.

'I'm not staying here, of course. One gets used to big places, large rooms, don't you find? I should feel stifled here. I'm staying at the Kingsmarkham Post-house. My wife and our two children and my stepdaughter will be joining me later today.'

'Ms Cox, please, Mr Masood.'

'Of course.' Please sit down. Make yourselves at home.'

They found themselves both staring at the portrait. Roxane was the offspring of two not specially good-looking people whose genes cunningly combined to produce a rare beauty distant from either of them. Yet it was her father's black, liquid eyes that looked down from the wall and his thick, smooth skin like whipped cream that covered those fine cheek-bones, that rounded chin, those perfect arms.

'That photograph,' Clare Cox said, entering the room and seeing them looking. 'It's not good of her, not really. I tried painting her but I couldn't do her justice.'

'No one could,' said Masood. 'Not even . . .' he sought for a suitable name, came up with one highly inappropriate '. . . Picasso could.'

Clare Cox was a pitiful sight. Perpetual crying had soaked and swollen her face and made her voice hoarse. The tears still lay on her red, puffy cheeks. She collapsed into a chair that was swathed in a red-and-purple shawl and lay back in an attitude of absolute despair. Burden, who had begun to have doubts after the Andrew Struther experience, now felt that telling the parents must be right. Hope, even vain hope, was better than this.

Karen told them what had happened, the bare facts, that at any rate at the moment, Roxane was safe. Roxane wasn't dead or injured, or the victim of a rapist. All Masood and Roxane's mother could do for a moment was stare in stupefaction.

Then Masood said, 'Abducted?'

'It seems so. Along with four others. As soon as we know anything we'll keep you informed. I promise you that.'

'But at the moment,' Karen said, 'we don't know any more. We'd like to have a trace put on your phone.'

'You mean you . . . someone will come and . . . an engineer?'

'No. BT can do it without coming here.'

'But they – these *abductors* – could phone *here*?'

'We don't know where or when the phone call will come, but yes, we think it will be by phone.'

Quietly, Burden explained how important it was to have their silence. No one must be told. 'Not your wife and children, Mr Masood. No one. As far as they are concerned, Roxane is simply missing.'

He gave the same injunction to Audrey Barker and her mother in Rhombus Road, Stowerton. They too were asked for their permission to have Mrs Peabody's phone monitored. Audrey Barker's reaction to the knowledge that her child was missing had been quite different from Clare Cox's. There were no signs of tears but her face was whiter than ever, her eyes seemed larger and she looked as if she had lost even more weight off her thin, stringy frame. Burden remembered that she had been ill, had recently left hospital. She looked as if she needed to be back there.

Mrs Peabody was simply confused. It was all too much for her. She took her daughter's hand and held it in both of her own. Over and over she kept saying, 'But he's a big boy, he's big for his age. He wouldn't get into a stranger's car.'

'He didn't think it was a stranger, Mother.'

'He wouldn't have got into it, he's too big for that, he knows better, he's big for his age, Aud, you know that.'

'Can I see the other mother?' Audrey Barker said. 'Can we meet? You said there was a young girl taken too. We could form a support group, the other mother and me, and maybe the other women – have they got family?'

'That wouldn't be wise just at present, Mrs Barker.'

'I don't want to do anything out of turn but I just thought ... well, it helps to talk about it, to share your experience.'

You haven't had an experience yet, Burden

94

thought grimly, and let's hope to God you won't have. Aloud, he repeated what he had already said, that it was better not at present.

'They won't want you interfering, Aud,' said Mrs Peabody.

'These people who've got my son, what do they want?'

'We hope to know that today,' said Karen.

'And if they don't get it what will they do to him?'

At the police station they waited for Sacred Globe to call. They waited at the *Kingsmarkham Courier*, Barry Vine's vigil having been taken over by DCs Lambert and Pemberton. It was still only noon.

It was an ill-assorted group who had been taken away and imprisoned somewhere, Wexford thought. He thought in this way to distract himself from terrible ideas, from actually picturing Dora and imagining how she must feel. A twenty-two-year-old potential model who looked like an Arabian Nights princess, an over-tall schoolboy of fourteen, a married couple who, if Burden wasn't exaggerating, belonged to that county set of an anachronistic but still surprisingly powerful élite – and his wife.

She would get on better with the boy and the girl, he thought, than the two whose horizons were perhaps bounded by the hunt, paternalistic good works and pre-Sunday-lunch sherry parties. Then he reminded himself that, after all, the Struthers had been going to *Florence*. There must be something redeemable about a couple who would spend a holiday there instead of on a Scottish grouse moor.

Dora would be all right. 'Your mother will be all right,' he had said hollowly to his daughters. And they believed him, as they always did when he spoke, as it were, *ex cathedra*. The doubts were all inside himself. He knew the wickedness of this world as they didn't. But he knew Dora too. She would be sensible, practical, she had a great sense of humour and she would make it her business to comfort those young people. If they were all together, the five of them. He hoped they were together, not each in solitary confinement.

Would they know who she was? She wasn't the sort of woman to say, 'Do you know who I am?' Or even, 'Do you know whose wife I am?' Would they recognise the name? Not unless she told them, he was sure of that. Only those he had had dealings with knew his name. But if she had told them, then it might well be to his house that the call would be made. They would expect him to be there, not here. They would ask Dora and she would tell them he would be at home, waiting to hear about her.

At one o'clock he and Burden sent out for sandwiches. He tried to eat but he couldn't. Having one's wife abducted was a fine way of losing weight, except that he'd prefer obesity. Once the rejected sandwiches had been removed he went down to check the progress being made in setting up an incident room.

Some five years before, an annexe to the police station had been fitted up as a gym. This was at the height of the great fitness craze when it was thought advisable, at least for the younger members of the force, to work out as often as possible on exercise bikes, treadmills, skiers and stair-steppers. Wexford had read somewhere that most people who start exercising keep it up for a maximum of six weeks and this proved to be the case. Recently the gym had been used entirely as a badminton court but, as Burden had said, not really intending a pun, that would have to be shuttled out of the way.

The inevitable computers were going in, the modems, the phones. He walked about, looking at things, not seeing, aware that eyes were on him in a new and curious way.

He had become a victim.

Now her son was at school, Jenny Burden had gone back to teaching history at Kingsmarkham Comprehensive. It was a pity, as far as she was concerned, that the continental system didn't operate here and schools start at eight and finish at two. Perhaps that would eventually come about through the European Union, a body her husband had no time for but which Jenny tended to think of as a good thing. As it was, she had to find someone to look after Mark between the time he stopped at three-thirty and the time she finished at four.

But things were different on Thursdays, not just this Thursday, the first day of term, when her last class ended at twelve-thirty and she could go home. The nicest thing about it was being there when her friend who did the afternoon school run brought Mark home at three-forty, when he ran in and jumped into her arms. In the meantime, having eaten the one lunch she got all week that didn't have chips or pizza in it, she was curled up in an armchair reading Roy Jenkins' *Gladstone*.

The phone ringing slightly annoyed her. People shouldn't phone during these lovely quiet two and a half hours, her only alone time. But she answered it, she had never managed to get into the way of letting a phone ring. 'Hallo?'

A male voice. Absolutely ordinary, she said afterwards, as accent-free as a voice could be, somewhat monotonous, impossible to say if young or middle-aged. Not old, she could say that. A dull voice, perhaps purposely geared to be without a regional note or a peculiarity of pronunciation.

'This is Sacred Globe. Listen carefully. We have

97

five hostages: Ryan Barker, Roxane Masood, Kitty Struther, Owen Struther and Dora Wexford. I will tell you our price for them in one moment. Naturally, if the price is not paid, they will die one by one. But you know that.

'Our price is that you stop the bypass. All work on the Kingsmarkham Bypass must be discontinued and not resumed. That is our price for these five people.

'We will be in contact again. Another message will be sent before nightfall. We are Sacred Globe, saving the world.'

Chapter 8

'Did you guess right?' Burden said.

'I'm afraid so.'

Wexford was reading the transcription Jenny had made, as accurately as she could, of Sacred Globe's phone message. There was nothing in it to surprise him, it was in fact routine stuff, but the threat to kill the hostages if the 'price' was not paid still reared up off the page at him.

His new team had come into the room and it would shortly be time to address them. As well as Burden from Kingsmarkham there were Detective Sergeants Barry Vine and Karen Malahyde with the four DCs, Lynn Fancourt, James Pemberton, Kenneth Archbold and Stephen Lambert. The Regional Crime had sent him five officers from their complement of fourteen: DI Nicola Weaver, DS Damon Slesar paired with DC Edward Hennessy, and DS Martin Cook paired with DC Burton Lowry.

Nicola Weaver, Wexford had met for the first time ten minutes before. A woman had still to be very good to have risen to where she was at her age. She couldn't have been more than thirty. Hers was a sturdy figure, not very tall. She had strong features, black hair severely cut, the fringe at right angles to the sides, and she wore a wedding ring. Her eyes were a clear turquoise-blue and though she seldom smiled, when she did she showed perfect white teeth. She had shaken hands with him, a firm handshake, and said as if she meant it, 'I'm very glad to be here.'

Slesar was dark, handsome in a strained, bony way, one of those tall, skinny people who can eat anything without putting on weight. His very short hair was a dull lamp-black, his skin the olive of the Welshman or Cornishman. Wexford had a feeling he had seen him somewhere before, met him, but for the moment he had no recollection of where. DC Hennessy was his opposite, thickset, of medium height, with a pudgy face, reddish hair and light-hazel eyes like a ginger cat's. The other sergeant was thickset and heavyish, with bright, sharp eyes. DC Lowry was black, skinny and elegant, like a cop in a television serial.

Karen Malahyde greeted DS Slesar like an old friend – or something more? At any rate she didn't favour him with the short, cool look and tight nod she gave most male newcomers, but smiled, whispered something and sat down next to him. Could he have encountered Slesar in her company? Was that the solution? Somehow he didn't think so. It was something of a mild joke among them all that Karen never seemed to have a boyfriend.

He began by telling them what some but not all of them knew already, that his wife was among the hostages. Nicola Weaver, who evidently didn't know, said something to her neighbour, Barry Vine, and raised her eyebrows at his answer.

Wexford told them about the two messages, beginning with the one to the *Courier* which had resulted in the Chief Constable's press conference and an undertaking secured from all national newspapers that they would print nothing until he lifted the embargo. The second message, he said, had been received by Inspector Burden's wife at their home

100

and he had a copy of Jenny's transcript shown on the screen.

'I think and hope this may be an instance of someone being too clever – and in his opinion amusing – for his own good. We might have expected the message to come to my house, since my wife may well have told her captors who she is and who I am. To choose Inspector Burden's home took us by surprise as was the aim. We must try to avoid being taken by surprise again.

'But in being clever he may also have been unwise. How did he know about Mike Burden? How did he know of his existence? Perhaps because Mike had had dealings with him and it's unlikely these were of a – how shall I put it? – a social nature.' A ripple of laughter made him pause. 'That is something we have to go into,' he went on. 'No doubt Sacred Globe found his phone number in the book, but we have to investigate how he knew whom to look up.

'The hostages were taken at random. We know that. Therefore there's little point in much investigation of their backgrounds. That isn't going to help us find where they are or who has them. We have to begin from the other end, with Sacred Globe itself. That's our starting point and getting on with it is imperative. This means contact with all the pressure groups protesting currently at the building of the bypass.

'Most of them – a couple of days ago I'd have said all of them – are legitimate groups of sincere people protesting against what they see as an outrage in a peaceable way. But in these instances there are always the others, those in it for the pleasure of causing disruption, for example, the rioters who invaded Kingsmarkham one Saturday night a month ago and many of whom, perhaps like our hostage takers, were masked and seemingly unidentifiable.

101

'Someone in these groups, in SPECIES or KABAL, is going to be able to help us. Even someone with Sussex Wildlife or Friends of the Earth, both legitimate, concerned societies, may well have come in contact with very different elements while on other protests. These people have to be talked to and any clues they may give us quickly followed up. The tree people and those in the camps have to be talked to. They may be our most valuable sources of information.

'I've said that the hostages' backgrounds aren't apparently of much significance but, on the other hand, I would draw your attention to a connection between Tanya Paine, Contemporary Cars' receptionist, and the hostage Roxane Masood. Miss Masood and Miss Paine appear to have been acquaintances if not close friends. They knew each other, which is the principal reason for Miss Masood's calling that particular taxi firm. This may mean nothing, it's probably no more than coincidence, but it is a tiny lead that shouldn't be neglected.

'The Chief Constable is at present with the Highways Agency. What will come of that meeting I don't know. I do know, as sure as I have any certainties about this business, that the government isn't going to say, "OK, forget about the bypass, let the hostages go and we'll build it somewhere else." Nothing like that is going to happen. That isn't to say there won't be some sort of interim compromise. We must wait and see what he has to say when he returns from his meeting.

'Meanwhile, because time is very important, we all have to get going on the lines I've just laid down. Principally, to find out who Sacred Globe are, their members, their leaders. We have to wait too for the message we are told will be sent before nightfall.

102

'Are there any questions?'

Nicola Weaver got to her feet. 'Is this to be classified as a terrorist incident?'

'Doubtful,' Wexford said. 'Not at any rate at this stage. As far as we can tell, Sacred Globe isn't attempting to overthrow the government by force.'

'Wasn't there a group or an individual who planted bombs on new housing estates?' This was Inspector Weaver again. 'I mean, bombed them to discourage new building? They're a possibility, I should think.'

'What about the guy who made concrete hedgehogs and put them on motorways?' This was DC Hennessy's contribution. He added, 'The idea being simultaneously to avenge squashed hedgehogs and wreck cars.'

'Anyone like that can be a lead,' Wexford said.

Turning with a slight frown from Karen Malahyde, who had apparently been whispering information to him, Damon Slesar asked, 'I understand Inspector Burden's wife is a schoolteacher at a local school. Could one of these Sacred Globe folks have been in her class at school or be a parent of such a child?'

'It's a good point,' said Wexford. 'Good thinking. That way he might know whose wife she was.' At once, as he uttered those words, his own wife came powerfully into his mind, seemed to stand before his eyes. He blinked, resumed, 'This is another lead to look into as soon as you leave this room. Talk to. Inspector Burden and find out where his wife taught up till five years ago and where she has begun teaching now. Right. That's all. I hope you're all happy to work late tonight.'

It was still only four o'clock. Before nightfall, Wexford repeated to himself, before nightfall the third message would come. Now, in early September, night didn't fall until eight o'clock, if by the term

103

one meant after sunset and when dusk has begun. In the next four hours that message might come to almost anyone. The same options as earlier applied and earlier they had been wrong.

Jenny had, with commendable presence of mind, immediately punched out the number 1471 that summons a recorded voice telling the subscriber the caller's number. But the caller had, prior to the call, put in the number that negates this procedure, so there was no result. These days any call could be traced if the caller's number was known, except that a call box was almost certainly being used and this time it would be a different one. Were they in the vicinity, he wondered, or a hundred miles away? Were the hostages together or held separately.

He asked himself, knowing he shouldn't ask, shouldn't touch it, shy away from this, whom they would kill first? If things didn't go the way they wanted – and how could they? – who would be first?

The only call to come in during the next hour in connection with the hostages was from Andrew Struther, son of Owen and Kitty Struther, of Savesbury House, Framhurst.

Burden was rather surprised to hear the voice of a reasonable man using reasonable words, even apologising. 'I'm sorry, I'm afraid I was a mite discourteous. The fact was this tale of my parents being missing seemed to me so totally incredible. However – I've phoned the Excelsior in Florence and they're not there. They've never been there. I'm not exactly worried . . .'

'Perhaps you should be, Mr Struther.'

'I'm sorry, I don't entirely follow . . . Hasn't there simply been a mistake?'

'I think not. The best thing would be for you to come down here and we'll give you the facts as we

104

know them. I'd have done so this morning, but you were' – Burden endeavoured to be polite – 'not particularly receptive.'

Struther said he would come. He didn't know the whereabouts of Kingsmarkham police station and Burden had someone give him directions. Pass through Framhurst, over the crossroads, keep straight on, follow the signs for Kingsmarkham ...

DCs Hennessy and Fancourt had gone to the bypass site to interview tree people at the Elder Ditches and Savesbury camps, where Burden was to join them. Detective Inspector Weaver was with the KABAL hierarchy and Karen Malahyde, with Archbold, was researching SPECIES, where their headquarters was, how many members they had nation-wide, what they did and if it ever involved breaking the law.

A phone call came to Wexford from Sheila to say Sylvia was going home. Neil had been in touch with the news that their younger son, Robin, had chicken-pox. She was going home, but would be back next day, as soon as she was certain she couldn't carry the chicken-pox virus or bacterium back to Amulet. Wexford had given up arguing, protesting, telling them both to go home. He just uttered, 'yes, darling, that's fine, anything you like,' adding that he didn't know when he'd be back. The message wouldn't come to his home anyway. Sacred Globe would know very well he wouldn't see much of the inside of his house at the moment.

A promise had been extracted from Peter Tregear of Sussex Wildlife to be with him by five-thirty, when Andrew Struther arrived, accompanied by his girlfriend whom he introduced as Bibi. Both wore sun-glasses, though it wasn't a bright day. The girl's were the mirror kind that you can see your own face in. She wore a red-and-white-striped Breton top, so skimpy that every time she moved an inch of tanned midriff showed. She seemed highly conscious of her good looks and allure, fidgeting her body into provocative poses. Wexford left them to Burden. He felt Burden was owed an apology, though he doubted if it would come.

Perhaps because Burden had told him he should be worried, Struther had brought with him a photograph of his missing parents. They were standing in snow in bright sunshine on some ski slope. Both were smiling and screwing up their eyes. It would have been hard to identify the originals from this, but Burden didn't think he was going to have to. He saw a tall man in a dark-blue ski suit, a rather shorter woman in red. From what could be seen of it under woolly hats, both had fair hair fading to grey, light eyes and were strong, straight and lean. Owen Struther might have been fifty-five, his wife a few years younger.

'I must ask for your silence,' Burden said. 'We are taking a very serious view of this. I don't think I'm overstepping the mark if I say that a leak to the press will result in prosecution for obstructing the police in their inquiries.'

'What is this?' said Struther.

Burden told him. He didn't name the other hostages. A reluctance to name Wexford's wife had seized him.

'Unbelievable,' Struther said.

The girl gave a shriek. She sat up awkwardly, forgot to be provocative, took off her glasses. Hazel eyes, verging on the golden, had the look of an animal's, empty of emotion, though greedy and purposeful.

'Why them?' Struther asked.

'Chance. A random selection. There have been threats. Threats to kill unless conditions are met.'

'Conditions?'

Burden saw no reason why not to tell him. All the next-of-kin of the hostages would have to be told. Much as he would have preferred to shy away from it, he said, 'That the building of the bypass be stopped.'

Struther said, 'What bypass?'

He lived in London, he might not read the papers, watch television. There were such people. 'I rather think the proposed route can be seen from the windows of your parents' house.'

'Oh, that new road? The one people keep demonstrating about?'

'That one.' Wexford watched Struther digest this information, nod, put up his eyebrows. 'Thank you, Mr Struther,' he said. 'We'll keep you informed. Remember what I said about not speaking to anyone about this, won't you? It's of the greatest importance.'

Dazed now, as if in a dream, Struther said, 'We won't say anything,' and then, 'Christ, it's just beginning to hit me. Christ.'

Peter Tregear must have passed him going out as he came in. The secretary of the Mid-Sussex Wildlife Trust was not to be told of the abductions, only of a subversive group called Sacred Globe. What did he know of them? Had he even heard of them?

'I don't think so,' Tregear said. 'There are so many of these groups and splinter groups. It's never simple. Have you ever read a book about the French Revolution?'

Wexford looked at him in astonishment.

'Or the Spanish Civil War, for that matter. I mention those world-shaking events because in both of them, and the Russian Revolution too, it was so far from simple and straightforward. Not just two sides, I mean, but dozens of splinter groups and factions, almost impossible to follow. Human nature's like that, isn't it? Can't keep things simple, people always have to have a lot of internecine squabbles; one little thing they don't agree with and they're off forming a collective of their own. Give me animals every time.'

'So you think the members of Sacred Globe were part of one of the other groups but they disagreed with the rules or the aims or whatever, maybe wanted more action, less talk, more violence even, so they broke away and formed their own.'

'Or didn't break away,' said Tregear. 'Stayed *and* formed their own group.'

'Before Mark was born,' Jenny said, 'I'd been teaching first at Sewingbury High School as it then was, and later at Kingsmarkham Comprehensive. Oh, and I did a bit of part-time at that private school, St Olwen's, when Mark was three and going to that nursery in the mornings.'

Wexford had found her in her husband's office where she had been since receiving the call. Her little boy was with his school friend, siblings and parents.

'I've told half a dozen people everything I can remember about that phone call,' she had said when Wexford came in. 'And soon I'll be telling them what I *can't* remember.'

'Don't do that,' he had said. 'We've picked your brains enough on that. Now we want to know how he came to phone you.' He listened in silence to the enumeration of her teaching experience. 'Did your pupils – sorry, you call them students now, don't you? – did they know who Mike was, what Mike did?'

'I suppose so. Some of them did. Kids aren't like they used to be when we were young, Reg.' She was flattering him there, he thought, considering she was getting on for twenty years his junior. She smiled at him. 'We'd never have asked teachers personal questions. We'd have got short shrift if we had. It's different now. For one thing they genuinely want to know. They're interested in people the way we weren't. Or I wasn't. At the Comprehensive they call me by my Christian name.'

'And they'd ask you about your husband? What he did?'

'Oh, all the time. The ones I taught five years ago, ten years ago, and the ones now. Except that now *every one* of them knows he's a policeman.'

'And back then? Say seven years ago? I'm thinking of seventeen-and eighteen-year-olds at that time. Is there anyone you can think of who specifically asked?'

'I think pretty well everyone knew then, Reg. They were all interested in my wedding – you remember what a big, showy wedding we had, all my mother's doing – and it was in the local paper then what Mike did.' She looked at him doubtfully. 'Where's Mike now?'

'Somewhere at the bypass site. Why do you ask?'

'I hoped he'd be coming home. But he won't, will he, not for hours? Can I go, Reg? I need to fetch Mark.'

Not for hours ... It would have been the end of a normal day, but Burden knew that for him it was only half over. Eyes peering at you from forest depths and forest trees was an image constantly recurring in children's literature. He was always reading such descriptions to his son, but the eyes in the child's book belonged to animals and these were human. He was aware of them from the branches above him and the scrubby coverts beneath. A sacking curtain was pulled aside at the entrance to

109

one of the tree-houses and a man stepped out, saying nothing, staring down, his face impassive.

They had left the car in a lay-by on the lane and walked first along the green ride, then taken the path that wound its way through groves of man-high birch saplings. Lynn Fancourt knew the way better than he did, a good deal better than Ted Hennessy who trod warily, rather as if he was being taken on a tour of an unexplored rain forest. Twittering birds gathered in the tree-tops, preparing to roost. Burden thought he could hear the sound of a guitar ahead of them, but soon the music and the keening voice stopped and all that could be heard was the birds' tuneless murmuring.

Then, as the birches were left behind and the great trees began, he saw the eyes. Their approach had been heard, their footfalls on the twigs and leaf-mould and dry grass, and that was why the guitar had been put away. Everyone in the trees prepared to watch for them. Burden had been used to believing that it was only animal eyes that shone in dark places, but these gleamed in exactly the same way. He had just taken in the fact that their arrival had interrupted the activities of three people who seemed to be involved in the building of a new tree-house, when the man on the platform spoke.

'Can I help you?'

He said it like someone serving in a shop, with the same degree of friendly politeness, but he wasn't much like a shop assistant, more a leader of men, tall with a commanding air, a cloak wrapping him. He might have been a general surveying the battlefield before the fighting starts.

Archbold said very correctly, 'Kingsmarkham Crime Management. We'd like a word.'

'What are we supposed to have done now?'

'We're making inquiries,' Burden said. 'That's all.

We'd just like to talk to you.' He moved his hand, a half-wave. 'Nothing to do with this camp. It won't take long.'

'Wait.'

The cloaked man disappeared into his tree-house. There wasn't much he could do about it, Burden thought, if he didn't come out again. And there were fewer eyes staring now. He looked up at the tree-house which was in process of being built. A wooden framework had been constructed on the firm foundation made by the two huge limbs and lopped-off trunk of a long-ago pollarded beech. A woman in an awkward-looking long dress clambered down the trunk and began searching for tools in a canvas bag on the ground. She passed a hammer up to the man with the long fair beard who had come half-way down for it. At that moment their leader – Burden somehow knew he was that – came out from behind the curtain, his cloak left behind, and shinned down his ladder, suddenly transformed into a normal person in jeans, sweatshirt and trainers.

Not quite a normal person perhaps. For one thing, this man was exceptionally tall, exceptionally long-legged, with long-fingered, attenuated hands. His head was shaved, his features like those Burden had seen in pictures of Native American chiefs, harsh, razor-sharp, fleshless bones and skin. 'Conrad Tarling.' He nodded as he spoke, a kind of substitute for a handshake. 'They call me the King of the Wood.'

Burden could think of no rejoinder.

'Would you prove your identities, please?'

A glance at the warrant cards and the nod came again.

'We've been through a lot, had a good deal of trouble,' said Conrad Tarling in the tone of someone who has spent six months in a refugee camp. 'What is it you want to ask about?'

111

Lynn Fancourt told him. While she was explaining, the hammering started. The man building the tree-house had begun attaching lengths of timber to the beam construction. Lynn raised her voice. She had to shout above the noise and Burden went over to where the woman in the long dress was standing.

'Would you mind stopping that for the time being?'

'Why?' the man in the tree said.

Burden had never seen such a long beard except in illustrations to children's books: the wizard, the woodcutter. He didn't know why he kept on thinking of children's books. 'Police,' he said. 'We have some inquiries to make. Just hold off for ten minutes, will you?'

For answer, the hammer was flung out of the tree. Not, however, in Burden's direction or anywhere near him. The woman in the long dress picked it up and scowled at him. He heard Lynn Fancourt ask Tarling in her normal voice if he had ever heard of Sacred Globe or knew anyone in the camp who might have, when a girl in mummy-like wrappings and draperies appeared, running from nowhere, from a tree-top or out from among the trees perhaps, but who erupted into the midst of them, shouting and throwing out her arms.

'You turn us off our land, you drag us out of our homes, and now you come here and ask us to betray each other. It's not enough that you wreck this country, this world, you've got to wreck the people too. Not just their bodies, not just the way you carried me unconscious down a ladder at dawn this morning, not just that, though I might have fallen and been disabled for life, not only that, but you'd wreck our souls too. You'd make us betray our friends and when you do that you smash the spirit!'

112

There was a silence which Burden broke. 'Your friends?' he said.

'She's upset,' Tarling said. 'And no wonder. I don't suppose it was you, was it? It was the bailiffs. But you all get tarred with the same brush and who's to blame for that?'

'As you do, Mr Tarling, and who's to blame for *that*?'

Tarling began a lecture on environmental issues, the destruction of ecological balance and the danger of what he called 'emissions'. Burden nodded once or twice, then left him and went home, from where he phoned in to the old gym and announced where he would be that evening. They had agreed to keep each other constantly informed of whereabouts.

'They weren't exactly co-operative,' he said to Jenny while eating a fast supper at the table with his son. 'I got started on the wrong foot, I suppose. This Quilla – how does a woman get to be called Quilla? What's it short for or long for? – she gave me a name. And the other one, the Freya one, softened up a bit and gave me a place. I strongly suspect neither exists.'

'I suppose you're going out again?' Jenny said it neutrally, not at all in a tone of exasperation.

'Well, what do you think? That we're going to have a nice evening watching a detective series on telly?'

'Mike,' said Jenny, 'I've remembered something – well, someone. At the Comprehensive before Mark was born.'

He stopped eating.

'I don't want to remember it in a way because it's so – well, isn't it awful in our society, the way people with morals and high ideals and courage get labelled as subversives and terrorists? The way that happens and other people who never did a thing in their lives

113

for peace or the environment or against cruelty, they're the ones that are respected?'

'No one's talking about terrorists,' said Burden.

'You know what I mean. Or I bloody well hope you do. I've made you see things a bit more my way, haven't I?'

'Yes, love. I'm sorry. I'm a bit tired.'

'I know. Mike, there was a boy at school – it would be six years ago, he was seventeen then, so he'd be twenty-three now, he was an animal rights person when animal rights were mostly about being against the fur trade and saving endangered species. He was an idealist and I don't think he'd have hurt anyone, though when I come to think of it he never seemed to care much for *people's* rights. He left school and went up north somewhere and later on, it was after Mark was born, someone, one of the teachers, I happened to meet her, told me he'd been convicted of stealing a lot of animals or maybe birds from a pet shop and releasing them somewhere. And the thing was, he asked for ten other offences of that kind to be taken into consideration. So I thought . . .'

'Why did you never tell me?'

'You wouldn't have been interested.'

Burden said quietly, 'No, you thought I'd say, serves him right, or, these people are a menace to society, and perhaps I would have. What was his name?'

'Royall, Brendan Royall.'

His little boy was beginning to read. Burden had never before come across a child who, instead of being read to, now wanted to read to the parent who had done so for him night after night for four years. But he hadn't known a parent like that before or many children, come to that. He kissed his wife and for a moment laid a loving hand on her shoulder.

' "I really couldn't eat mouse pie," ' read Mark. 'Mummy, you're not listening.'

Mouse pie, said Burden to himself, mouse pie. The things these writers thought of. Upsetting to an animal rights activist, that would be, a source of distress no doubt to this Brendan Royall ... He drove himself to Clare Cox's. The Jaguar was still outside. Hassy Masood had returned with his second family, for the front door was opened by a young girl in a sari.

The tiny living-room was full of people. Masood, who had changed his denim suit for one of dark-grey broadcloth, proceeded to introduce them. 'My wife, Mrs Naseem Masood, my sons, John and Henry Masood. My stepdaughter, Ayesha Kareem, who is Mrs Masood's daughter by her first marriage to Mr Hussein Kareem, now alas dead. Roxane's mother, Miss Clare Cox, you of course already know.'

Burden said good-evening. Something about Hassy Masood made him feel tired before he got started. Unlike her daughter, Naseem Masood wore western dress, a very tight red suit with a short skirt, a great deal of expensive costume jewellery, gold with red stones, high-heeled white shoes. Her black hair, teased into tendrils, was nearly as long as Gary the tree man's beard. Her daughter was tall and willowy, had coppery skin, strangely light-brown eyes, long nose and curved lips, the look of a girl from Omar Khayyám. She made Burden think of the only bit of poetry he knew and the lines about bread and wine and thou beside me in the wilderness, came back to him. The little boys, pale, neat, black-haired, stared at him in a way he wouldn't have cared for his own son to stare at anyone.

On the sofa Clare Cox lay with her feet up, her eyes closed. She made a gesture to him with her hand, a movement of greeting possibly, or more likely, despair. She wore the same night-gown-like garment he had always seen her in, reminding him of Quilla, for it was soiled now, stained down the front, perhaps with her tears.

'I am sorry to disturb you, Miss Cox,' he began, 'but I know you understand that in the circumstances . . .'

Masood interrupted him. 'Now what can we get you in the way of refreshment, Mr Burden? A drink? A sandwich? I doubt if you have had time today for much in the way of sustenance. I don't of course touch alcohol myself but having seen fit to provide Miss Cox with supplies in the way of wine and brandy, I can with no trouble at all . . .'

'No, thank you,' said Burden. 'Now, Miss Cox, this won't take a moment.'

She opened her eyes. 'Do you want to speak to me alone?'

'That won't be necessary.'

After he'd said it he realised he might have relieved her of the rest of them, but he wasn't thinking fast enough. He thought only that if Hassy Masood had been obedient his wife would not know about Sacred Globe, but the questions he needed to ask could have been asked of the parent of any missing person.

She sighed. The girl called Ayesha turned on the television, lowered the sound to a murmur and sat on the floor staring at it, six inches away. Mrs Masood took her sons by the hand, then put an arm round each of them and pulled them to her. Masood, who had left the room, came back into it with glasses of what looked like orange squash on a tray.

Sticking to his refusal to drink, Burden said, 'What can you tell me about your daughter's friendship with Tanya Paine?'

'Nothing. She just knew her.'

Clare Cox had turned her face away, pushing it into a cushion. The girl on the floor drank her orange squash noisily, with slurps.

Burden said, 'Were they at school together?'

For a moment he thought she wasn't going to answer. Then she turned over and half sat up. 'They were at Kingsmarkham Comprehensive, but they weren't close friends, they just knew each other. Roxane's cleverer than her. She was in the top group for art and English.'

'I don't suppose he wants to know that,' said Naseem Masood to no one in particular.

Clare Cox spoke rapidly. It was a way of getting it over quickly, of getting rid of him. 'Roxane had a job – well, it started as a holiday job – working in the instant print place in York Street and she ran into Tanya who had a job next door and they'd got into the way of having a coffee together. Then Tanya went to work for Contemporary Cars and Roxane left to be a model, but when she wanted a car she'd always go to Tanya.'

As she was speaking the eyes of everyone in the room apart from the girl on the floor had turned to the portrait on the wall. The beautiful face looked back at them.

Mrs Masood was the first to remove her gaze. Having derived the maximum from this interview, she had apparently decided she had had enough. She got up, smoothing and pulling down her skirt. 'We should be getting back to the hotel now, Hassy,' she said. 'The boys want their dinner and Ayesha's a growing girl.' She addressed Burden. 'That Posthouse is a very good hotel for a place like this.'

He asked Clare Cox if she had Tanya Paine's address and was given the name of a block of flats in Glebe Road. Tanya, Clare Cox seemed to think, shared with three others. He waited until the

117

Masood family had left, Ayesha, in spite of her height and her grown-up clothes, tearful and stamping her foot at being taken away from the silent screen.

'Have you no one to be with you overnight?' he asked.

'God,' she said, 'give me the chance to be alone.' She wiped her eyes with her fingertips, though there had been no tears in them. 'Mr Burden? It is . . . er, Burden, isn't it?'

'That's right.'

'I wanted to tell you something about Roxane. Oh, it isn't helpful, it isn't anything, but it's worrying me so . . .'

'What is it?'

'It's . . . do you think they're keeping her somewhere like a – oh, God – a small room, a cupboard even, I mean. She's claustrophobic, you see. I mean, she's really claustrophobic, seriously, not the way people just say they are when they don't like going in lifts. She can't be shut in anywhere, she can't stand it . . .'

'I see.'

'This is quite a small house but she's all right here when the doors are open. She always leaves her bedroom door open. I shut it once by mistake, I forgot, and she got in an awful state . . .'

What could he say? A couple of soothing sentences that offered very little comfort. But her question remained with him as he got into the car and drove back to Kingsmarkham. Sacred Globe weren't likely to be keeping the girl in some spacious apartment with french windows open on to lawns and terraces. The probability was somewhere small and confined, and he thought about cases he had known or read of, people kept in sheds or tanks or chests or car boots. How was Dora Wexford about claustrophobia? Did any of the rest of them have phobias or, come to that, allergies, special dietary requirements? It seemed to serve no useful purpose to find out . . .

He found Tanya Paine by herself, her flatmates all out. Solitary evenings she evidently devoted to beauty treatments, for her head was wrapped up in a towel, her nails were newly painted and there was a powerful foul smell in the room of some kind of depilatory.

At first she took his visit as that of a concerned social worker checking up on whether she had been given the counselling she had asked for. He recognised her as a total solipsist, with no interest in anyone but herself or in anything but her immediate concerns. In a way, this was an advantage, because telling her about the abductions would be out of the question.

Almost anyone else would have asked. She remained unsurprised by his questions, confirmed what Clare Cox had said, but volunteered no further information. To her, it appeared, Roxane Masood was just a girl she knew, not a girl who had affected her much; a mate to have a laugh with (as she put it), someone to meet for a coffee and a Danish. As soon as she could she steered the conversation back to her counsellor, a woman whom she had seen once, but who was not giving her the satisfaction she hoped for. 'She never asked me what sort of childhood I had. Don't you reckon that's funny? I was all geared up to tell her a few bits about my mum and dad and she never even asked.'

The phone ringing saved Burden from making any answer. Afterwards he had no idea how he knew, how the sense of what it was, of who was making this call, came to him in an inspiring flash, almost from the moment she picked up the receiver.

Perhaps it was the tone in which she said, 'What?'

119

or the expression on her face, her lower lip dropping, her eyes widening. He got up, was across the room in two strides, met her eyes and took the phone from her. She seemed relieved to be rid of it, dropping it into his hands like a snake or a hot coal.

A couple of sentences had already been uttered. Burden concentrated on listening as he had never listened before.

... Globe. You know the hostages we have. You know our price.'

It was as Jenny had said, a dull, accentless, monotonous voice.

'By morning we need a public assurance of cessation of work on the Kingsmarkham Bypass. We are not exigent, we are not draconian. A moratorium will suffice. Stop the work for the time being while we negotiate.

'But a public assurance via the media we must have and by nine tomorrow morning. If not, the first of the hostages will die and the body be returned to you before nightfall.

'Pass this message on to the police and the media.'

Burden didn't speak. He knew it would be useless and, in any case, he didn't want the possessor of this voice to know it wasn't Tanya Paine listening to him.

'I repeat, pass this message to the police and the media. The embargo on publicity is not of our doing. Remember that. Publicity is what we desire.

'We are Sacred Globe, saving the world. Thank you.'

The phone was put down, the burr began and Burden turned round to see Tanya Paine staring at him, open-mouthed and with clenched fists.

Chapter 9

The second meeting was at nine that night and it was in the old gym. The Chief Constable and the Deputy were both there, but Wexford presided. His team had brought in a mass of information but the most useful, it appeared, came from Burden who had discovered a positive lead in Brendan Royall and, by the purest coincidence, been present when Sacred Globe's phone call came to Tanya Paine.

'Why her?' Nicola Weaver wanted to know.

'That's been puzzling me,' Burden said, 'and those words he used, "draconian" and "exigent" and "moratorium". I'm not sure I know what "draconian" means myself. She's not what you'd call bright.'

The message, rendered as accurately as he could by Burden and put on the word processor, was up on the screen in front of them in a hugely magnified version.

'But it doesn't matter, does it?' Damon Slesar said. 'The sense is what matters, the crux of it, that unless there's a public announcement by nine one of the hostages . . .' He had been going to say, 'get the chop' and, apparently remembering Wexford's wife, quickly changed it to '. . . one of the hostages' life is endangered. She'd pass that on all right.'

'Still, it was a piece of luck for us you were there, Mike,' said the Chief Constable. 'Or could they have known you were there?'

'I don't think so, sir. I told no one.'

'How about the voice, Mike?' Wexford asked.

'Possibly the same voice as the one that delivered the earlier message to my wife. On the other hand, she thinks the voice she heard was accent-free and not disguised, while I'm pretty sure the one I heard was. All those long words but a hint of a cockney accent. You know how you sometimes hear an actor talking cockney on TV and it sounds good – they learn it from tapes and they've learnt well – but at the same time it's not genuine, it's not the real thing, it's telly cockney that we've got used to and accept. Well, that's what this voice was like, someone who'd learnt his cockney from a tape, and dropped his voice and took the inflections out of it. Altogether too much of a good thing, if you get my meaning.'

Lynn Fancourt and Archbold then had something to say about the name they had picked up at the Elder Ditches camp. A woman called Frances, known as Frenchie, Collins arrested in Brixton for being involved in an affray, was put forward by Freya, the dispossessed tree woman, though she spoke of her with such vindictiveness that Lynn suspected she was attempting revenge or settling a score. But it would have to be followed up.

Karen Malahyde, making inquiries at Framhurst Copses camp, was on to two leads which directed her to a house at Flagford that had long been a commune of activists of various sorts. Slesar and Hennessy were working on the Brendan Royall angle and Barry Vine was set for a renewed interrogation of Stanley Trotter.

The Chief Constable told them what he had achieved that day. Against everyone's will – but they had no choice – Sacred Globe's condition would be complied with and publicly announced.

'It goes against the grain,' Montague Ryder said. 'You know that. You all feel that. But "moratorium" is the word, a good word, and that's all it will be. That bypass is going to be built.'

The atmosphere in the gym was very different from what it would have been if the hostages had not included Dora Wexford. If the rest of them only sensed or intuited that, her husband knew it. However serious the matter, in other circumstances there would have been a degree of light-heartedness, a grim humour, a derisive profanity. As it was, they were wary, even embarrassed, and each one of them, in his or her own way, was afraid.

Not a single face was lit by a grin, no witticism or crack was exchanged, as they parted. The Chief Constable and his Deputy left together. Damon Slesar, departing with Karen, the two of them side by side, made a point of saying good-night to Wexford, and saying it very respectfully. 'Good-night then, sir.'

They made for one car between them, but not looking into each other's faces or speaking. Burden made the expected offer of accompanying Wexford home, staying the night if he wanted it, and Wexford again refused, though giving him heartfelt thanks.

Nicola Weaver caught up with him as he came into the car park. He thought how tired she looked. Someone had told him she had two children under seven and a not very co-operative husband. Her eyes were a curious shade of dark, bluish green, the same colour as the malachite in the ring she wore. 'There's something I thought you should know,' she said to him. 'You probably know already, but in case not – in this country the vast proportion of kidnap victims, more than a majority, turn up unharmed. With kids it's different but adults, getting on for a hundred per cent.'

'I did know, but thanks, Nicola.' He wasn't going

to tell her she was the fifth person to impart these facts to him that day.

'Nicky,' she said. 'What good would it do them, anyway, to kill someone? It's an empty threat.'

'I'm sure you're right,' he said. 'Good-night.'

She got into her car and he got into his. The night was dark and moonless. He could see some tiny stars, infinitely distant pinpricks in black velvet. Lines came into his head and he repeated them as he drove home.

'Setebos, Setebos and Setebos,
Thinketh he dwelleth in the cold of the moon,
Thinketh he made it, with the sun to match,
But not the stars,
The stars came otherwise.'

A white sports car was parked on his drive. He recognised it as belonging to Paul Curzon, Amulet's father, and when he went upstairs he saw that Sheila's bedroom door was shut. The two of them were in there and their baby with them. Instead of causing him pain, it pleased him, gave him a tiny idea of peace, if not comfort.

If he was going to get any sleep it was better to get it not immediately but later in the night. Sleep that came at once would vanish after an hour and leave him wakeful and a prey to every kind of dreadful anxiety for the long hours to come. But sleep came, he lost himself in it after a short struggle, and slipped into a dream of Dora, of Dora and himself when young.

Why is it always our younger self in dreams, and even more so, the younger selves of those close to us? No book had ever offered him the answer to that, no dream expert analyst, for dreams are not expressive of our wishful thinking or surely they would all be happy and optimistic. In his dreams his daughters were children, his wife a young woman, and he, though unseen by himself, the dreamer, *felt* young. This time he had come up to a tower, like a castle rising out of a great empty plain, and she was leaning out of an upper window, extending her arms to him.

Her hair was very long, as it had been in the early years of their marriage. It hung over the window-sill and down the stonework of the tower like Rapunzel's in the fairy story, only Dora's hair was dark, black as a raven's wing. He came close to the tower and took hold of the hair in his two hands, not intending to climb it, of course – even in the dream he knew real people didn't do that and in any case he was far too heavy to attempt it. She still smiled down but suddenly a terrible thing happened. The weight of her hair was too much for her, or his hold on it was too much, and with a cry she toppled forward and plunged from the window. He awoke, uttering a continuation of that cry, shouting as if they were calling out a protest together.

No one came. His room was far enough away from Sheila's for her to hear nothing. Besides, like most dream shouts, it had come out strangled and muffled. He lay for a while in the dark, then got up and walked about. We are all mad at night, someone had said. Mark Twain, maybe. It was true – or, in his case, was it? Didn't he have something to go mad about?

In the morning that announcement would come. Presumably via radio and television, later in the newspapers. But what if it didn't come? What if the assurance given Montague Ryder came to nothing because some higher decision affected it, because someone – the Home Office? The Department of the Environment? – thought it would smack of giving in to the demands of terrorists?

Nicky Weaver had told him what he already knew, that it was highly unlikely the hostages would come to harm. On the other hand, her assumptions were based on statistics of the kind of kidnapping carried out solely for monetary gain. These Sacred Globe people were fanatics, money didn't come into it with them. If they killed, whom would they kill first?

Stop it, he said to himself, stop it. They'll kill no one. It wouldn't be Dora, anyway, if it was the youngest or the oldest they chose. He looked at the time, then wished he hadn't. It wasn't yet two. If he must think he ought to be thinking of possible connections between this suspect and that, this suspect and that place – only there were no suspects. As for the place, maybe that was an angle they had neglected up till now and should neglect no longer.

He was at a loss. Where did you start? With the people always. Find a suspect and you were a good way to finding a place. If that announcement didn't come ... The Chief Constable had given a guarantee it would come. He put the light on and tried to read. It was a history of the American Civil War, lent him by Jenny Burden, well-written, exhaustively researched, containing many descriptions of the carnage in that terrible conflict, of wounds, of slow death.

He kept seeing Dora afraid. She was strong, but she would be afraid. Anyone would be. His mind was partially distracted by a thought for that girl, Roxane Masood, whose mother had said she was claustrophobic. Confinement in a tiny room wouldn't bother Dora any more than confinement in a banqueting hall, but the claustrophobe ...

At about four he fell into a jerky, fitful sleep. Waking just before six, reflecting on the events of the evening before, he remembered where he had previously encountered Damon Slesar. It was that 'Goodnight then, sir' that brought it back to him. That spurious word 'then', inserted like an apology.

It had been at a conference he had attended more out of curiosity than anything, for its subject was the differences between British and continental European police practice. There had been speakers from France and Germany and Sweden. Nothing strange about Slesar's being there, of course, except that most of the others had outranked him. In many ways it was admirable to see a man of his age and rank so wisely putting himself in the picture. On the Saturday night Wexford saw him again, this time in the local pub, where he was dining with a *commissaire* he knew from an investigation that had once taken him to the South of France. Slesar and some cronies sat at the next table, drinking whisky.

Afterwards, having stuck meticulously to fizzy water Wexford, with Commissaire Laroche, was making for his car when he saw Slesar heading for his. It hadn't occurred to him that after drinking as he had been Slesar would attempt to drive. But, accompanied by the two friends he had sat with, he was unlocking the driver's door.

Wexford had spoken almost involuntarily. 'Better not.'

Slesar looked at him, his eyes glazed. There was a loose, uncoordinated look to his face, the muscles out of control. He said, 'I'll be fine.'

By now there must have been half a dozen people around them. Wexford kept his voice light, almost jovial. 'Come with me. I'll drive you back. Someone can fetch your car in the morning.'

Slesar seemed to realise how many witnesses to all this there were. His dark face reddened. You could see it clearly in the lamplight. 'You're right, sir,' he said, and then, 'Jim'll drive me.' He touched the man behind him on the shoulder with more perhaps of a stagger than a touch, holding on to the car for support. He looked at Wexford and said, 'Goodnight then, sir.'

A sensible man. A man who could take reproof and remain cheerful. Wexford was glad he had remembered, as far as he could be glad about anything, and pleased to have Slesar on his team. He got up and went downstairs in his dressing-gown, a dark-red affair more like velvet than towelling, which Sheila had given him for his birthday. Paul was in the kitchen, making a cup of tea, the baby, awake but not crying, in the crook of his left arm.

Wexford asked himself if it was good for an actor to be quite so good-looking these days. Paul Curzon had perhaps been born half a century too late. Amulet's black hair was his, or perhaps it was Dora's ... Wexford put out his arms for the child, for he wasn't best pleased to see someone holding a baby and boiling a kettle at the same time.

'How are things?'

How much did Paul know? Only that Dora was missing? 'Just the same,' Wexford said.

The first local news, Newsroom South-East, would be just before seven. There might be something on the radio before that. He didn't want to hear it – or not hear it – in anyone else's company, he wanted to be alone.

'You didn't mind me staying the night, did you? I miss them – well, I miss Sheila and I rather want to get to know that baby so that I can miss her too.'

Wexford managed a sort of laugh. 'I'm glad you did.' An idea came to him. 'You know, Paul, I wish you'd take her home, take *them* home.'

'But you need her here. She says you need her. She

says she doesn't know what would happen to you if she wasn't here.'

Wexford shook his head. Misunderstandings always depressed him. It was even worse when they happened between people who were close, who thought themselves knowledgeable of the other's mind. He would have to be tough. 'Frankly, it only adds to my worries having her here. Don't look like that. She's very important to me, I love her dearly and that's an understatement, but while she's here on her own with the baby I keep wondering about her, if she's all right, what she's doing, and I can do without that, Paul. I never see her, you know. I'm never here except at night. Take her home. Please.'

Paul passed him a cup of tea. 'Sugar?'

'No, thanks. Take her up a cup and tell her you're taking her home.'

'OK. I'd love to. There's nothing I'd like more. If you're sure . . .'

'I'm sure.'

He had forgotten how simply comforting it was to carry a baby about. A stupid feeling came over him that if only he could walk about the house like this for hours with this warm, cuddly child held close against his chest, things would be better, he would worry less, he would be less prone to terrible fancies. The large blue eyes looked calmly up into his own. Did such young babies normally have eyelashes of that length and thickness? Her skin was like cream and like mother-of-pearl too.

He carried her into the living-room and looked out of the window at the sun coming up and into the dining-room out of the french windows at the garden full of long shadows. She pursed her mouth and blinked when he told her he was waiting for Newsroom South-East, that an hour had never passed so slowly before.

Paul came back and took her from him. 'Breakfast,' he said, and to Wexford, 'She only woke once in the night.'

'What did Sheila say?'

'She'll come home with me, but she won't promise to stay.'

Radio Four had nothing to tell him. He left it on because it was better to have voices and music and a weather forecast than silence. It occurred to him that a way of using up the time would be to shower and shave and get dressed, so he did all those things. By the time he was done – and he had tried to dawdle – it was still only a quarter to seven.

He put on the television as well as the radio. They only talked about money and business at this hour, and the inevitable sport. He heard the letter-box as the daily papers came through. Nothing on the front pages of either of them, nothing inside either. He reminded himself that to the vast majority of the population of the British Isles this wasn't really news. You only cared if you lived nearby – or if you were a fanatic. It would be news all right if they *knew*. If they had been told of the hostages and the demands and the conditions. That would drive the Lebanon and European Monetary Union off the front pages and prime time.

Newsroom South-East, here it was now: the pretty, dark young woman talking first about a visit Princess Diana would be paying to a Myringham hospital, and then . . .

'The Highways Agency announced last night that all work on the Kingsmarkham Bypass is to be suspended. This is due to an environmental assessment of the River Brede and Stringfield Marsh which must be carried out under a European Habitats and Species directive before work can continue.

'Though certain to be no more than a temporary

suspension, it may last for some weeks. We talked to Mark Arcturus, of English Nature. Is this good news for the protest groups, Mr Arcturus, or is it only . . . ?'

Wexford switched it off. A great wave of something more than relief, something like happiness, had flooded him. He put his hand up to cover his mouth, the way children do not only when they have said something injudicious but when they have thought it. That he could be *relieved* at these people's victory! That he could be filled with joy!

It was all nonsense anyway. What was he thinking of? Dora was still in their hands. All the hostages were still in their hands, and he was nowhere nearer finding who Sacred Globe were and where their headquarters was than he had been twenty-four hours ago.

The news travelled fast. When Burden, with Lynn Fancourt, began his inquiries at the camp at Pomfret Tye, the tree dwellers were already celebrating. Someone – Sir Fleance McTear's name was suggested – had supplied them with a good imitation of champagne. A fire had been made on the edge of the heath and they were sitting round it, singing 'We shall overcome' and drinking sparkling wine.

'It's strictly in contravention of a by-law,' Burden said sourly to Lynn, 'lighting bonfires. These so-called nature lovers, ecologists or whatever, they're always the worst.'

He recognised the couple whose tree-house had burnt down back in the summer, admonished them for the fire and started on his questions. They asked him if he didn't think it was great news, man, and didn't he reckon that word 'suspension' was a nonsense? What they really meant, man, was that they were giving up on the bypass altogether and

131

'suspension' was just a way of saving face, didn't he agree?

Neither Lynn nor he got very far with rooting out clues to Sacred Globe and they moved on to Framhurst Great Wood. There, to Burden's surprise and considerable dismay, they found Andrew Struther and the red-haired Bibi sitting on a log in conversation with half a dozen tree people.

Struther jumped up, looking guilty. 'I say, I know what you must be thinking, I'm frightfully sorry but it really isn't that way. I haven't actually disclosed a thing.'

'Come over here, will you, Mr Struther?'

Bibi seemed to take his departure as an excuse for getting to know the tree people better. She got up off the log and followed a young man in nothing but a pair of shorts and a big straw hat to where a ladder was placed up against the trunk of a massive chestnut. He indicated to her to go ahead of him and went up close behind her as she took her first upward steps, giggling wildly.

Burden said, 'May I ask what you're doing here, Mr Struther? You have friends among these people? Yesterday you indicated to us that you didn't even know a bypass was planned.'

'That was yesterday.' Struther had gone rather red. 'You can actually learn quite a lot in twenty-four hours, Inspector, if you put your mind to it. I thought I'd better learn something, considering what's happening to my parents.'

'I hope you've said nothing to any of these people about that.'

Now it was an aggrieved look that Burden got. 'No, I haven't. I was bloody careful about that. I made a point of it. I was told not to and I haven't.'

'Then what exactly are you doing here? I don't

suppose *you're* making an environmental assessment.'

'I thought if I talked to them one of them might give me a clue about who would do a thing like that, who's likely to be . . . well, a sort of terrorist.'

Precisely, in fact, what he and the rest of the team were doing. It sounded strangely feeble on Struther's lips.

'I'd leave that to us, if I were you, sir,' Burden said. 'It's our job, you see. Leave it to us and get off home. Someone will be along to see you later.'

'Really? What will that be about then?'

'I'd prefer to leave that till later, Mr Struther, as I've said.'

The girl had disappeared inside a tree-house. Struther looked wildly about for her, began shouting, 'Bibi, Bibi, where are you? We're going home, darling.'

The tree people watched him impassively.

Karen Malahyde had run the woman called Frenchie Collins to earth at her mother's home in Guildford. Nicky Weaver, Damon Slesar and Edward Hennessy were working on flimsy material given them by the SPECIES cadre and Archbold and Pemberton were tracing, by phone and computer, environmental activists nation-wide. Wexford had a meeting scheduled for two-thirty. He had already spoken to the Chief Constable and his Deputy and talked on the phone to Brian St George.

The editor of the *Kingsmarkham Courier* sounded indifferent and Wexford thought he knew why. If he had been allowed to use the story when the letter first came from Sacred Globe on the previous morning, he would just have got it into this week's edition of his newspaper. Now, on Friday, it was too late. As far as he was concerned he would have been

133

happiest if nothing more had been heard from Sacred Globe, the hostages or the police until the following Wednesday evening. 'I still think you're making a mistake,' he said. 'When something like this happens the public have a right to know.'

'Why do they?' said Wexford rudely. 'What right? Who says so?'

'It's a first principle of journalism,' said St George sententiously. 'The right of the public to know. Muzzling the press never did anyone a mite of good. Not that it's any skin off my nose, I couldn't care less, only I don't mind it going on record that I think you're making a grave mistake.'

But the Chief Constable said, 'We're going to keep it dark, Reg, as long as we can. Frankly, I'm surprised we can. But since we can, let's keep at it.'

'It's Friday now, sir. I've a hunch the press isn't going to be all that interested. They'd think of it as a waste, using a piece of news like that at the weekend.'

'Really? I hadn't thought of it like that.'

'What they'd like,' said Wexford, 'is to have the embargo lifted on Sunday evening. Great stuff for Monday morning's papers.' He suppressed a sigh. 'If you approve, sir, I'd like to tell the hostage families of the ... well, the conditions and the threat. I think we ought to. I'll do it myself.'

Audrey Barker and Mrs Peabody first. He would go to Stowerton on his own, then to Clare Cox in Pomfret, finally to Andrew Struther, as soon as the meeting was over. The Chief Constable seemed to think it a good idea. You could keep it from the press but not from those families, not in fairness and humanity.

His own family were just as much involved as the Masoods, Barkers and Struthers, and saying goodbye to Sheila that morning he had promised to phone her whether there was news or not. He would keep in touch daily, twice daily. Before he left he phoned Sylvia, told her that her sister had gone back to London, that he was all right, he was fine, but there was no news.

They were all assembled in the old gym ten minutes before time, all, that is, except Karen Mala-hyde who was still off somewhere in pursuit of Frenchie Collins, and Barry Vine who was beginning to share Burden's view of Stanley Trotter. Wexford walked in and everyone stopped talking. It wasn't just respect and courtesy, he knew that. They had been talking about him among themselves, and about Dora. For the first time he found himself wishing that what he had thought would happen had happened, that the Chief Constable had put someone else in charge of this business.

Nicky Weaver, looking a lot less tired and ener-vated than on the previous evening, looking brisk and energetic, had a good many leads to talk about from SPECIES and KABAL. A SPECIES officer, now apparently a reformed character, had once, quite a long time ago, been sent to prison for attempting to sabotage a nuclear power station. This man had given her a comprehensive list of names of people he said were anarchists.

'Why did he tell you?' Wexford wanted to know.

'I don't know. Probably because he's currently only in favour of peaceful resistance. Someone took him on a tour of the power station at Sizewell and he was so impressed he completely changed his tune.'

'It looks as if we've done all we can at the camps,' Wexford said. 'The computer can deal with all the names we've come up with and make cross-referen-ces, if any. With this suspension of work on the bypass we've bought ourselves time and that's

135

important. There should be, some time today, another message from Sacred Globe.

'They haven't promised it. There was no undertaking in last night's message that another would follow, but something will come. We have traces on as many Kingsmarkham, Pomfret and Stowerton phones as BT can provide us with. BT have done us proud and there are no complaints in that area. But Sacred Globe are vain people, they're arrogant. Such people always are. They'll want to congratulate us on having the good sense to fall in with their demands. They'll phone or get in touch by some means or another. It won't have escaped their notice that the suspension is temporary. It's a suspension, a postponement if you like, not a full stop.

'Unless I'm much mistaken they are going to want a full guarantee that the Kingsmarkham Bypass is cancelled. And that, of course, we can't give them. That we can never give them, come what may.'

Nicky Weaver raised her hand.

'Nicky?'

'This guarantee – it's struck me that this is something no one, no authority, would, could, ever give. For instance, such a guarantee could be given, the hostages would be released and an immediate reneging on the undertaking could follow. Or even if their intention was sincere, even if they promised not to build this bypass, once there was a change of government, even a change of the Secretary for Transport, it could be built. So how are Sacred Globe ever to get round that?'

'I suspect they live for the moment,' said Wexford. 'Get a guarantee and if it lasts five years they've done well. If a bypass is proposed later – well, maybe they start again. Nothing is certain in this world, is it?'

He thought he saw a shiver run through her, but perhaps it was his imagination.

Chapter 10

From Stowerton Dale to Pomfret Monachorum silence prevailed over the bypass route. It was rather cold for early September, windy with a touch of Siberia in the breeze, and from time to time a sharp shower of rain rattled down. Birds which had sung tweet-tweet, pu-wee, jug-jug at dawn were silent now and would make no sound until roosting time. In the camps the early euphoria had subsided, it was anticlimax time and the tree people were discussing, thinking, planning and, above all, wondering.

The heavy earth-moving equipment had been returned to the meadow where it had first been assembled. The buses that carried the security guards to the site had not run that day and the guards in their dilapidated air-base huts talked among themselves about the chances of being laid off.

Stowerton children, hitherto kept away by the guards, clambered over the heaps of earth, playing at guerrilla warfare in a mountainous region. KABAL called an emergency meeting at which a decision was reached. Lady McTear and Mrs Khoori were to draw up a petition to the Department of Transport for all members (and any other supporters that could be found) to sign that, in the light of a need for environmental assessment under an EU directive, and the unique ecological phenomena present at the site, work should never be resumed on the bypass.

*

When Mrs Peabody was young you tidied up the bedroom and put the child into a clean night-dress before the doctor came. If anyone in authority was coming you cleaned the whole house. Going shopping 'into town', you dressed up in your best. These habits die hard and it was plain that a kidnapped grandson wasn't enough to deflect Mrs Peabody from her conditioning. She was the kind of woman who would put clean sheets on her own deathbed.

He felt deeply, painfully, sorry for her in her pink twinset and pearls, her pleated skirt and shiny shoes. She even had on lipstick. All the cushions in the living-room were plumped up and magazines were set out in a fan shape on the little table. She could powder her face but not summon up a smile for him, just managing a subdued, 'Good-afternoon.'

Her daughter, from a generation who saw things quite differently, from Clare Cox's generation, looked as if she hadn't washed herself or combed her hair since she heard. He knew all about pacing, he had done plenty of it himself these past days and nights, and he thought she paced this house for long hours. It was apparent she couldn't keep still, though she looked ill, in need of a long convalescence.

'I have to be here, on the spot,' she said to him. 'I ought to go home, I've just left everything, but it would be even worse at home.' She sprang up, walked across the floor to the window, stood there clenching and unclenching her hands. 'You said on the phone you had something to tell us.'

'It isn't bad news?' Mrs Peabody was a marvel of self-control, he thought, and wondered what her nights were like, when the bedroom door was shut. 'You did say it wasn't bad.'

He told them of the condition, that work on the

139

bypass must stop. Audrey Barker walked across the room again, nodding, silent and nodding, as if she had thought of this or as if she wasn't surprised. But Mrs Peabody looked as bewildered as if he had told her the hostages would be released only if the entire population of Kingsmarkham agreed to learn Swahili or pilot helicopters.

'What's our Ryan got to do with that? That's the government.'

'I quite agree with you, Mrs Peabody,' Wexford said, 'but that's the condition.'

'They *have* stopped,' Audrey Barker said, coming up close to him; her hands working once more. 'It was on the TV. Is that why they've stopped?'

'There's been a suspension of work, yes.'

Mrs Peabody seemed overawed. He could see her digesting what had been said, interpreting it into a form she could understand. 'And all on account of our Ryan?' she said. 'Well, and the rest of them. Our Ryan and the rest of them.'

She shook her head in wonderment. This was fame, this was to be lifted out of obscurity, get into the newspapers, have one's name on television. 'Our Ryan,' she said again.

Her daughter glanced angrily at her. She said to Wexford, 'If the work's stopped, why hasn't he come back?'

Why hadn't he? Why hadn't any of them? It was now four in the afternoon, nine hours after that announcement of suspension had been made. Not another word had been heard from Sacred Globe. The message Burden had happened to receive was the last one and had been made twenty hours before.

'I don't know. I can't tell you because I don't know.'

She had forgotten that his wife was among the hostages. 'But what are you doing to find them? Why

140

aren't you out there now looking for them? There must be ways.' She was tearing at her hands now, as if to pull them off the wrists. They were marked already with self-inflicted bruises. 'I'd go and look myself only I don't know how. You know how, you must do, it's your job. What are you doing for them? They could kill Ryan, they could torture him – Oh God, Oh Christ, what are you doing?'

Aghast, Mrs Peabody laid a small wrinkled hand on her daughter's arm. 'You mustn't speak like that, Aud. No good can come out of being rude.'

'There's no question of torture, Mrs Barker.' At least, that was something he could be sure of, especially if he didn't let himself think too much about it. 'And I don't think any of the hostages will be killed. If Sacred Globe kill them they lose their bargaining power.' Every word he uttered was a jab of the knife. He almost gasped. 'I'm sure you can understand that.'

She turned away, then rounded on him once more. 'Then why haven't they come back to you now the bypass has stopped?'

It was the same question. Clare Cox had asked it half an hour before when he had been with her in Pomfret. Alone, the Masood family having – incredibly – 'gone out for the day' to do the tour of Leeds Castle, she had been trying to paint to distract herself. At any rate, there were smears of paint on the smock she wore over one of her flowing dresses.

'Why haven't they done what they said they would?' she had asked him.

It wasn't then but now that he repeated to himself the words delivered to Tanya Paine that Burden had remembered: *Stop the work for the time being while we negotiate. But a public assurance via the media we must have by nine tomorrow morning. If not, the first of the hostages will die and the body be returned to you before nightfall ...*

While we negotiate ... But no overture of negotiation had come, no request for any kind of talk. And the message said nothing about returning the hostages, only about killing them if work on the bypass wasn't suspended. There had been nothing at all about what must be done before the hostages could come back.

'We'll keep you informed as soon as anything happens,' he said to Audrey Barker.

The phone rang as he was speaking. She picked up the receiver and was instantly calmed by the voice at the other end. A little colour came into her face. She spoke in monosyllables but gently, almost sweetly. It occurred to him as he left and set out for Framhurst that he knew less about her and her son than about any of the hostages. There was something about her and her mother that inhibited asking, and this was increased by their plight.

Who and where, for instance, was Ryan's father? Was there anyone else at home in Croydon? Probably Mrs Peabody was a widow but he didn't know that. Audrey Barker had been in hospital for an operation but he didn't know what for or how serious it was or even if she was fully recovered now. Who was the caller that she had talked to on the phone? Perhaps it didn't matter, any of it, perhaps these things were simply their private business that in the circumstances no one should inquire into.

Hadn't he told his team himself that the backgrounds of the hostages should be of no particular interest to them or their operation?

Rain had begun to fall more heavily as he entered that part of the country now inevitably associated with the bypass. Here, the apocryphal visitor from Mars would have suspected nothing, have received

142

no hint of destruction, pollution, environmental damage. The deep lanes wound between overgrown banks and high hedges, the wind sighed in the high branches of beech trees, the woods slept quietly under the soft patter of rain and a few still-green leaves fluttered down.

In Framhurst a dozen or so tree people sat on the pavement under the teashop's striped awning, drinking Coke and one of them a cup of tea. Robin Hood's Merry Men probably looked rather like that, Wexford thought, not in the orange knee breeches and fringed green tunics of cartoon film but a medieval version of denim with brown cagool-like garments on top, bearded, dirty, but strangely the representatives now of those who cared about preserving England. But why did they always look like this? Why weren't they ever men in grey suits? He slowed as he passed them, then quickly drove on to Markinch Lane.

Savesbury House was impressive. Burden had described it as half barrack, half architectural hotchpotch, but Wexford saw the mixture of styles as charming, as essentially English. The drive ran deep between groves of tall trees, their branches reaching for the sky. Then the lawns opened out and the flower beds were displayed with their rare unnameable herbaceous plants. If you stood on the edges of those lawns and parted the foliage with your hands you could doubtless see the whole great panorama of Savesbury and Stringfield, and the river winding below you.

A dog padded from the side of the house as he left his car. The animal approached him with stealthy, silent menace, a shaggy black German Shepherd, behaving in the intimidating way such dogs sometimes do, curling its upper and lower lips back about an inch to show a trim double row of bright white teeth.

Wexford's father had been one of those people of whom it is said that they can 'do anything with dogs'. He hadn't quite acquired that art himself but some of his father's talent had come to him, by association or by genes – perhaps he just wasn't afraid – and he put out his hand to this creature and said a casual hallo. He didn't like dogs, he had never liked the various dogs Sheila had foisted on him and Dora to 'mind' while she was away, but they liked him. They fawned on him, as this one did, stuffing its nose into his coat pocket when he bent down to it.

The white-faced girl called Bibi, a cigarette hanging from her mouth, opened the door. He had seen her before but in the distance, just as he had seen Andrew Struther, when the two of them came to see Burden at the police station. Her face, that Burden and Karen Malahyde had simply found good-looking, reminded him of a cartoon character the artist wants to look beautiful and evil, the Snow Queen perhaps or Cruella De Vil. That red hair was a most peculiar colour, nearer crimson than mahogany, and he didn't think it was dyed.

She grabbed the dog by its collar, cooing at it, 'Come here, Manfred, come to mother, sweetheart,' as if he had been sticking pins into it.

Burden had said the interior of Savesbury House was beautifully furnished and 'squeaky' clean. Two days in the care of Andrew Struther and Bibi had changed all that. A plate of Chum or some such stood almost in the middle of the hall floor with a bowl of water alongside it. Manfred had been chewing bones between meals and Wexford nearly tripped over half a femur that lay on the drawing-room threshold. In there, cups and glasses stood about on shelves and table tops, a plate with a half-eaten sandwich sat on the seat of an armchair. Several large ashtrays had been filled to overflowing. The place was stuffy and there was an unpleasant smell compounded of cigarette smoke and old marrowbones.

Andrew Struther, entering the room, also nearly fell over the femur. Before uttering a word to Wexford he said crossly to the girl, 'Can't you put that bloody Manfred in kennels? You said you would. You absolutely promised when I agreed to have him here *for no more than two days*. Right? Remember?'

The face he turned to Wexford was sullen and aggrieved, a very handsome marble-hewn face though, lightly tanned, a shade darker than the butter-coloured hair. He and the girl were today both dressed like tree people in elegant green and brown – Elves who shop at Ralph Lauren. His parents, Wexford thought, were by far the richest of the hostages. They made Dora look poor and the others on the breadline.

'Chief Inspector Wexford, I think you said?'

'That's right. I believe you already know the condition these people have imposed.' He remembered the elucidation that had come to him while he was at Mrs Peabody's. 'Sacred Globe, as they call themselves, have not undertaken to release the hostages on suspension of work on the bypass, only to negotiate. However, there has so far been no move made by them towards negotiation.'

'Why do you say that?' the girl asked in a petulant voice. ' "As they call themselves" – why do you say that?'

Wexford said stoutly, 'People who commit acts of this kind aren't deserving of respect or dignity, do you think?'

Bibi didn't answer but Struther rounded on her. 'I

145

just hope to Christ you aren't starting to feel *sympathy* with a bunch of shits who have kidnapped my mother and father.'

His pale-brown face had become bright red. Wexford had seldom seen calmness so swiftly transformed into violent rage. Struther took a step towards the girl and for a moment he thought he would have to intervene, but Bibi stood her ground, put her hands on her hips and stared insolently up into his face.

'Oh, what's the use!' Andrew Struther shouted. 'But I want that dog out of the house first thing tomorrow. Is that understood? And this place cleared up. My mother will be coming back – do you realise that? My mother will soon be back. Isn't that right, Chief Inspector?'

'I very much hope so.' Wexford remembered his caution about the private lives of the hostage families being of no interest, but he disobeyed it again. 'What is your father's occupation, Mr Struther?'

'Stock market.' Andrew Struther spoke shortly. 'Same as me,' he added.

Manfred, in the hall, was chewing a chair leg. Whether it had mistaken the leg for a bone or just liked reproduction Chippendale Wexford didn't know and wasn't staying to find out. He drove slowly down the drive between the trees. The rain had stopped while he was inside Savesbury House and a pale, misty sun appeared in the blue triangle among the clouds. His car thermometer told him the outside temperature in Celsius and Fahrenheit: 13 and 56, not brilliant for the time of year.

Five minutes later he was in Framhurst village street. Most of the tree people had gone from outside the teashop but two remained. The teashop owner had rolled up the awning, perhaps when the rain had stopped, and optimistically placed more tables and chairs out on the pavement. On two of these, with a single teacup between them on the table, sat a man with the longest beard Wexford had ever seen, a golden beard like a skein of embroidery silk, and beside him a bedraggled young woman in the kind of clothes Clare Cox favoured, a dirty cotton gown with a spotted scarf tied around the waist.

He saw them so clearly and observed so much because the teashop was on a corner of a crossroads, one turning leading to Sewingbury, the other to Myfleet, and boasted Framhurst's single set of traffic lights. The light had turned red as he approached. He had already identified the man (from Burden's description) as Gary and the woman as Quilla, when she suddenly sprang to her feet, jumped off the pavement and placed herself in front of him in the middle of the road. Wexford shrugged, wound down the window.

'What do you want?'

She seemed taken aback that he wasn't angry and hesitated, both hands up to her face. He waited. There was no traffic behind him, none ahead. She brought her face up to the car window.

'You're a policeman, aren't you?'

He nodded.

'Not one of the ones who came talking to us at the camp?'

'Chief Inspector Wexford,' he said.

She seemed taken aback or shocked, shaken anyway. Perhaps it was only his rank, a higher one than she had expected.

'Can I talk to you?'

He nodded. 'I'll park the car.'

There was a space round the corner on the Myfleet road. He walked to where she was now sitting at the table with the bearded man. 'Your name is Quilla,' he said, 'and you're Gary. Shall we have a cup of tea?'

They seemed astonished that he knew their names, almost superstitiously affected, as if a name taboo were in existence and he had broken it. He explained, it was simple. Gary smiled diffidently. You could have sat there till Doomsday, Wexford said, before anyone would come out to serve you. He went into the shop and presently a girl of about fifteen came out to take their order.

'I could do with something hot inside me,' Quilla said. 'You're always cold in our business. You get used to it but a hot drink's a welcome thing.'

'Would you like something to eat?'

'No, thanks. We all had some crisps when the others were here. That was when we saw you go through and the King said you were a policeman.'

'The King?'

'Conrad Tarling. He knows everybody – well, he knows them by sight. The others went back to the camp, but I said I'd wait and see if you came back and Gary waited with me.'

'You want to tell me something?'

The tea came, three cups and saucers, a large pot, synthetic sweetener in packets and the kind of liquid in plastic cups that looks like milk but never originated in a cow. Wexford thought it was disgraceful in the midst of the countryside and said so.

'Take or leave it,' said the girl. 'That's all there is.'

'We campaign to stop that sort of thing too,' said Gary. 'We're against everything that's unnatural, everything that's synthetic, pollutant, adulterated. We've dedicated our lives to that.'

Instead of saying that it was extremely difficult in modern life to sort out the natural from the unnatural, if indeed anything natural remained, Wexford

148

asked them how long they had been professional protesters.

'Since I was sixteen and Quilla was fifteen,' Gary said. 'That's twelve years ago now. I'm in the building line but we've never had jobs – well, paid jobs. The work we do is pretty hard.'

'How do you live then?'

'Not on the benefit. It wouldn't be right to be kept by a government and taxpayers when we're opposed to everything they think and everything they live by.'

'I don't suppose it would,' said Wexford, 'but it's a novel viewpoint.'

'We don't need much. We don't need transport often and we make the roof over our own heads. We do itinerant farmwork when we can get it. I do the odd building job. I cut grass. She makes straw dollies and sells them and she makes jewellery.'

'A hard life.'

'The only possible one for us,' said Quilla. 'I heard – well, I don't know how to say this.'

'What did you hear? That we were looking for names?'

'Freya said. Freya's the woman the bailiffs nearly dropped out of a tree yesterday. She said you were looking for a terrorist.'

Wexford drank the last of his tea. The undertaste of non-lactic soymilk creamer ruined it. 'That's a way of putting it.'

'What's he supposed to have done?'

'I can't tell you that.'

'OK. But if you're looking for someone who doesn't care that for human life, who'd do anything, abominable things, to save a beetle or a mouse, I can tell you who you want. Brendan Royall, he's called. Brendan Royall.'

Chapter 11

It was the only name to have come to them twice, from two completely separate sources. Brendan Royall was Jenny Burden's ex-pupil, the boy who had 'never seemed to care much for people's rights' but had committed eleven offences in connection with the theft and subsequent liberation of animals.

To Quilla – her surname was Rice, Wexford discovered – Brendan Royall was the enemy, the activist who not only got protest a bad name but did things in the course of his campaigning that were opposed to all she stood for. It was her indignation over the very case Jenny had mentioned, he thought, which had led her to speak to him.

'They died, all those creatures he *liberated*. The birds didn't know how to fly and he didn't know what to feed them on. He was carrying the animals in the back of a van down the motorway and the back doors came open. It was carnage, it was abominable. I don't believe he cared, it was done for the principle, he said.'

'I'm surprised he's not here,' Gary said. 'I've been expecting him to turn up ever since we came and the first camp started. It's his sort of thing, you see.'

Quilla nodded eagerly. 'Not the spoiling the countryside so much as those insects and whatever. The Map butterfly and the yellow caddis. He'd kill a hundred people to save a stick insect. I once heard him say people weren't necessary, they were just parasites.'

Wexford offered them a lift back to the tree camp. They refused at first, they could walk, they wouldn't be beholden, but the rain started again and Wexford said it seemed a shame when he was going that way anyway. Quilla said she didn't know where Brendan Royall was at present. He ought to have been *here*, putting up some sort of demo along the Brede and she couldn't understand why he wasn't. When Gary had last heard of him he had been in Nottingham, but Quilla said she had come across him later than that, in some connection with making a tunnel for weasels under the A134 in Suffolk. The difficulty was that, like them, he never really lived anywhere.

'His parents are round here somewhere,' said Quilla. 'I've got an idea he may have gone to school here.'

'That's right,' said Gary. 'He did. I don't know about living round here but he told me his grandad used to have a big house near a place called Forby and it should have been his, only his dad cheated him out of it.'

'He *would* say that.'

'He wanted to turn it into a sanctuary for animals that had been illegally imported. It was a great big place with a lot of grounds. Only his dad came in for it and sold it. His dad gave Brendan some of the money but that wasn't good enough for him. He wanted the house or all the money for the cause.'

It was almost six when Wexford got back to the station. Nothing more had been heard from Sacred Globe. They would have reached him on his mobile if it had, but still he'd hoped . . .

'This Brendan Royall is the most positive lead we've got so far,' he said to Burden. 'He's just the sort we're looking for, obsessed with what they all

151

call Nature with a capital N, and with a total disregard for human life.' He winced when he said that part, but Burden pretended not to notice. 'Gary Wilson says he can't understand why he's not here, protesting with them, but I can. I hope I can.'

'You mean because he's one of those Sacred Globe people? He's not in a tree camp because he's somewhere else holding the hostages?'

'Why not? I want everyone to stop whatever they're doing and go out after Brendan Royall. Someone – you, if you like – should talk to Jenny and see if she can remember where the Royall parents lived. Or live. It's only six years ago, the fellow's only twenty-three now. Then there's the house that was the grandfather's. Someone in Forby is bound to know. It shouldn't be hard. Let's get the team in here, Mike, and brief them.'

The third meeting of the day was at six-thirty. Everyone was back from what had proved largely fruitless searches. Karen Malahyde had been to the council flat in Guildford, had been redirected by a tired old woman who said she never wanted to see her daughter again and finally found Frenchie Collins ill in bed in a dirty room in Brixton. She had been in Africa, had picked up some infection and was still far from recovery. Karen saw no reason to doubt this, nor to disbelieve her when she said she had lost four stone in weight.

Barry Vine had been talking to KABAL and DS Cook with his DC to the Heartwood collective, whose leader, a bold young woman, had asked Burton Lowry if he was doing anything that evening. Lowry replied coolly that he was hunting hostage takers, so she said some other time and gave him a long, heavily charged look. None of that was passed on to Wexford. He told them about Brendan Royall,

152

the parents, the grandfather's house, the eleven offences.

'You can sort it out among yourselves how you do it. I'm going to talk to Mrs Burden again but you can proceed as you like. I don't need to tell you that there's been no more word from Sacred Globe.

'One last thing. Make a start tonight. But don't keep at it too long. The great thing is to prepare the ground for tomorrow. We're all under a good deal of pressure and must have our sleep. Needless to say again, all leave is cancelled and we're all coming in tomorrow bright and early. So let's try and get some sleep tonight. That's all.'

He caught a flash from Nicky Weaver's blue-green eyes. It seemed to him, perhaps erroneously, full of empathy and compassion. She attracted him. She wasn't the sort of woman he had ever admired, she was a frightening departure from those sweet, young, pretty girls, and it was all the worse for that. Why did he have to feel this now, to bring him guilt and remorse, when all he really wanted in the world was to have Dora back? Inescapable, though, this appalling feeling of how wonderful it would be to have Nicky come home with him, drink with him, listen while he talked, take his hand – and then?

Someone had told him she adored her husband, a man who had nagged her to give up work when the children were very young and since then punished her for not agreeing by doing nothing himself. She had to employ a nanny for the evenings because Weaver, though not in general averse to staying at home, refused to do so if it might involve minding his own children. But Nicky would never hear a word against the man . . .

'Wake up,' said Burden. 'You're coming back to have a bit of supper with me and pick Jenny's brains – remember?'

153

'I know. I'm coming.'

'Brendan Royall or no, I'm convinced that Trotter's involved in this somehow. I talked to him again this morning, Vine's talked to him, in that pigsty he lives in. I know he murdered that girl, Ulrike Ranke, and I've a theory he's set himself up as a hit man. You can understand that, a man kills once, he gets used to it, he'll kill again, but for money this time . . .'

'Trotter didn't murder the girl, Mike.'

'I wish I could be as sure as you.'

'No, you don't. You don't wish that at all. What you wish is that I'd listen seriously to all this rubbish about Trotter and the girl, only you know damn well I won't. As for his other calling, where does a hit man come into all this? No one's been killed yet.' Wexford was aware of Burden watching him carefully, almost with tenderness. 'Don't bloody look at me like that! I'll say it again, no one's been killed yet, and if they are it won't be Trotter that's responsible. Trotter was just like all the rest of that Contemporary Cars lot, a fool who knows about as much about running a business as I do about Psychoglypha citreola and as little about the environment as my granddaughter Amulet. So forget him, will you? Stop wasting your time on him. We've other things to do.'

Jenny put her arms round him and kissed him sweetly. It took your wife being abducted to make women really nice to you, he thought wryly. He sat down in the Burden living-room and let Mark read to him. At any rate he'd never been read to by a five-year-old before. Life was full of new experiences.

It was *The Wind in the Willows*, old-fashioned stuff but none the worse for that, and when he had finished Mark said very politely, 'I hope you don't mind, Mr Wexford, but Badger reminds me of you.'

He didn't mind. Mike brought him a stiff whisky

154

and he accepted it because it had been preceded by an offer to drive him home.

They ate salmon mousse, chicken casserole and blackberry-and-apple crumble. No doubt it had been put on in kindness to him because he thought it unlikely Burden ate like that every night. Jenny told him all she could remember about Brendan Royall, every word he had ever uttered to her, every principle and theory of life he had aired. More to the point, she now recalled mention of Royall's grandfather's house, a paranoid rambling on about Royall's being cheated out of his inheritance and vague threats – which she, as his teacher, had tried to discourage – of getting even.

'The Royalls lived outside Stowerton somewhere, north Stowerton, I do remember that. A smallholding or a . . . I do believe it was some kind of wildlife sanctuary. In a small way, that is.'

'Now it'll have a fine view of the bypass approach road.'

'I expect they moved after the grandfather's house was sold. Brendan used to say that he would get even with his father and then he boasted that he was going to get half the proceeds – as soon as he got it he was going to leave school.'

'Did he show any particular concern for animals when he was at school?'

'Not that I know of, Reg. But then they didn't practise vivisection in the biology class.'

'All right. I asked for that. You said his parents had an animal sanctuary, so I wondered.'

'I honestly can't remember. But I think it was more like a . . . do they call them petting zoos? Rabbits and a pony and a couple of goats.'

Wexford smiled. 'Did he get money from the sale of his grandfather's house?'

'I don't know. But he did leave when he was seventeen.'

Wexford got on the phone to Nicky Weaver with this new information, but Nicky already knew most of it. The grandfather had lived in some style at a house near Forby called Marrowgrave Hall and the sanctuary or petting zoo had become something more in the nature of a theme park.

'Don't keep it up too long, Nicky,' Wexford said. 'Remember what I said about sleep.'

'I know. I'll get off home now. My kids are alone or they will be in ten minutes.'

'You'd better remember about sleep too, Reg,' Burden said, catching his last words. 'It's nearly ten. I'm going to drive you home in your car and Jenny will follow us to drive me back.'

'Have I really had that much?'

'Who's counting? But, if you must know, it was two double whiskies and three glasses of burgundy.'

'You drive me, Mike. And thanks.'

He ought to have felt swimmy but he was stone-cold sober. He let himself into his house, closed the door behind him and stood in the dark for a moment, making himself aware of the silence, the emptiness. Sylvia was gone, Sheila was gone. He was alone now. He walked into the living-room and sat down in an armchair, still in the dark.

The members, or whatever you called them, of Sacred Globe would go to prison for years for abduction, for threats, for holding people against their will, depriving them of liberty, he couldn't remember the words of the charge. They wouldn't be inside for much longer if they killed the hostages. On the other hand, if they killed them there would be no one alive to describe their captors.

He thought of Roxane Masood, the claustrophobe, of the questions Audrey Barker had asked and of the

156

couple who had been going on holiday to Florence. But he couldn't think about Dora, not now, he would have cried aloud if he had allowed himself to do that.

Why do we always go to bed at night? Most of us do. When the time comes, even if we aren't tired. Why don't we sleep in chairs, vary bedtimes, think, now is the time, fall into bed, slip into sleep? Because there must be a routine to life, a framework to hang life on. Routines were what kept you sane, gave you something to do at this moment and at that, definite places to go, positive things to do. Abandon it and that way madness lies.

He went upstairs. He got into his pyjamas and the crimson velvet dressing-gown and lay down on top of the bedclothes. The Civil War book was on the bedside cabinet and he thought how much he would like to pick it up and throw it through the closed window. The sound of the glass shattering would be satisfying in a curious, brief sort of way. Only it was Jenny's book.

Jenny ... Her story of Brendan Royall matched Gary Wilson's. That didn't mean Royall need be involved with Sacred Globe. Gary and Quilla could be involved with Sacred Globe and have told him about Royall as a diversionary tactic. Suppose no outsiders were involved with Sacred Globe, suppose they stood alone. It had been taken for granted that activists in other peripheral or ancillary fields would know about or even be attached to Sacred Globe, but there was no rule about that. They could be a group of people who were individually opposed to environmental damage and had linked up as the result of a word spoken, a passion shared, a spontaneous decision.

But no. Because normally law-abiding people don't behave like that. And amateurs would need one person, or more than one, to organise them into this form of active violent protest. But the truth might well be that they were a mix of ardent amateurs and ruthless professionals, which brought him back to where he started: that someone up in those trees, or someone in KABAL or SPECIES, or in any organisation represented in Kingsmarkham to fight that bypass, must know or have a clue or a tenuous connection.

Why hadn't Sacred Globe sent another message? Why the silence, a silence that was now more than twenty-four hours long?

They had sent a letter. They had been in contact twice by phone. Short of the methods obviously closed to them because of ease of identification, what means of communication was left?

The personal one, the face-to-face contact. They had talked last time about negotiation and now, he thought, they meant to send a representative. Next time the message would be brought to them by word of mouth. What, by someone who just walked in wearing a Sacred Globe T-shirt? Carrying a white flag of truce? Anyone who was sent must face immediate arrest and yet . . .

He must stop thinking about it. He must sleep. Revolving these things in his mind was the worst way of aiming for that. Better try one of the recognised methods that were variations on counting sheep. He took off the dressing-gown, turned over and started repeating to himself all the names of houses in Jane Austen: Pemberley, Norland, Netherfield Hall, Donwell Abbey, Mansfield Park . . .

Trying to think what Lady Catherine de Burgh's house was called, he fell asleep. It was the drink and sheer weariness. Even as he slipped into it he knew it wouldn't last long.

The moon that had been covered on the previous

night rose into spaces between the thin cloud, into a clear sea of darkness. It was a white full moon with a greenish iridescence, the light from it very bright and cold. Wexford thought it was the moonlight, a shining path of it in the gap between his half-closed curtains, that awakened him. A strip of moonlight lay across his face and neck, like a white arm.

He got up and pulled the curtains till they met. If he had only done that before he went to bed perhaps he wouldn't have wakened. The hour of sleep he had had might be all he was going to get for the night. He looked round the bedroom in the greyish pearly light. Dora's things were everywhere. Hairbrushes and a bottle of perfume on the dressing-table, a scarf hanging over the back of a chair, on her bedside cabinet a box of tissues and her other watch, the one she wasn't wearing. In closing the cupboard door he had inadvertently caught up the stuff of one of her skirts in it. The pale, silky material, a handful of it, gleamed in the half-dark. He opened the door, pushed the material in, moved a hanger along the rail, smelt her scent and closed the door again.

He was back in bed when he heard the sound and immediately knew he had heard it before, one minute before, and it was that which had awakened him, not the moonlight.

Sitting up, he listened. It came again. A crunch, made and repeated, footsteps on the gravel of the path. He got out of bed and reached for the clothes he had taken off, just the trousers and socks. Over the back of a chair was a round-necked sweater. He pulled it over his head, stepped softly to the bedroom door and opened it silently. From down below came another sound, a different sound, a click, a screwing, a release. Someone was trying the back door.

It was bolted on the inside. What did they think he

159

was, a policeman who'd leave his back door unlocked all night? This was Sacred Globe, he had no doubt about it. As he had thought, they had sent a representative and to him, to his home, in the night. The digital clock on Dora's side told him it was twelve-fifty-two.

The moonlight hadn't penetrated the thick curtains at the landing window and it was darkish. His eyes grew accustomed to it as he waited. He could see the outlines of windows now and the moon's pale ambience, over the banisters to the hall, the window there, the open door into the living-room. Below the landing window, at the side of the house, there came another footfall, then another. They had tried the back door and were returning to the front. Tap, tap, quite light footfalls, but loud too. They weren't making silence a priority, that was for sure. Whoever they were, whatever they wanted, they weren't afraid of him.

How would they make him let them in? By ringing the doorbell, presumably. Yet why had they tried the back door first? It came to him suddenly. *They would have Dora's keys.*

They would have a key to the back door and one to the front door, and for some reason they had tried the back first, but it had been bolted on the inside.

Now for the front door.

He didn't want to be seen straight away. He went to the front of the house, into the front bedroom, and looked out of the window, but the porch overhang blocked his view. Padding back, he heard a key turn in the front-door lock. The door opened and someone entered the house. The door was softly, almost stealthily, closed.

The last thing he expected was light. He heard a switch click without realising what it was, then light streamed up on to the landing. He marched out of the bedroom to the head of the stairs, prepared to confront them.

Dora was standing in the hall, looking upwards.

Chapter 12

He held her in his arms. He was afraid to slacken his hold in case she vanished again. It couldn't be a dream because she was the age she really was and he was his real age too. She laughed weakly when he told her that in his dreams he and she were always young, but her laughter broke raggedly and she began to cry. He held her and pressed her wet face against his cheek.

'What can I do for you? What would you like? Shall I carry you upstairs? I used to be able to do that. Shall I try?'

'Like Rhett Butler,' she said through her tears. 'Oh, Reg, don't be so silly.'

'I'm a fool. I know. Oh God, I'm so happy.'

She said drily, but with a break in her voice, 'I'm not exactly down in the dumps myself.'

'A drink,' he said, 'a stiff one. Have you had proper food? I won't ask you anything about what's happened, not tonight. The entire Mid-Sussex Constabulary will want to ask you tomorrow, but not tonight.'

She stepped back a little from him, looked into his face. 'Why weren't you in bed, Reg? What's happened?'

'I thought you were a representative of Sacred Globe and I wasn't going to meet them in that cardinal's robe.'

'Is that what they call themselves? I suppose I am

in a way,' she said, 'though not what you'd call an official one. I don't know why I was released. No one said. They just put that foul hood over my head again and drove me here.'

'You don't have to talk about it now. My God, no one was ever so happy to see someone else since the world began . . . What would you like? Tell me.'

'Well, most of all I'd like a bath. Washing facilities weren't all they might have been. I'd like a bath and you to bring me a very stiff gin and tonic in the bath, and then I'd like to go to sleep.'

When he came back with her drink he found all her clothes in a heap on the bedroom floor. The first time she had ever done such a thing, he thought. And grinning to himself, then actually laughing aloud with happiness, he picked up every garment and dropped them all into a large, sterile plastic bag.

Six-thirty in the morning was too early to call the Chief Constable but Wexford called him.

Montague Ryder sounded as if he had been up for hours and had already run twice round Myringham Common. 'I am sure you know, I don't have to tell you, that we are going to have to talk exhaustively to your wife and she is going to have to tell us all she knows. It must be taped and probably gone through twice, with a time interval in between, to make sure nothing gets missed out.'

'I know that, sir, and she knows it.'

'Right. Good. Time is of the essence and the sooner we get started the better. But don't wake her, Reg. Let her sleep till nine if she can.'

She had been fast asleep when he crept out of the bedroom to make his phone call. He hadn't slept much himself, getting only fitful bursts of sleep, because he kept waking to see if it was real, if she was really back and there in bed beside him. Down in the kitchen he made tea, squeezed orange juice, then brewed coffee as well for good measure. The time passed like a flash. He thought of the previous morning when he had been walking Amulet about, waiting for the news, and time had dragged, had seemed to stand still. Time travels in diverse paces with diverse persons. I'll tell you who Time ambles withal, who Time trots withal, and who he stands still withal . . .

Sylvia was the first daughter he phoned because he wanted to phone Sheila first.

'You should have called me last night,' Sylvia complained.

'No, I shouldn't. It was one o'clock. She's asleep now but you can come over and see her tonight.'

Sheila answered the phone in a tearful tone. He told her.

'Oh, Pop,' said Sheila, 'how absolutely amazingly wonderful, darling. Shall I bring Amulet and come over now?'

When he went upstairs at half-past seven Dora was awake and sitting up. She put out her arms and hugged him. 'I got plenty of sleep in that place, so I wasn't tired. There was nothing to do but encourage the others and sleep.'

'Do you know where you were?'

'I haven't a clue,' she said. 'Of course I knew that would be the first thing you'd all want to know – and so did they. They were scrupulously careful about that from the very first.'

He brought up her breakfast and she chose coffee. He had a shower, singing bits of Gilbert and Sullivan at the top of his voice. She was laughing at him and he loved that.

'But, Reg, tell me something,' she said when he came back into the room in the crimson dressing-gown, 'who's in charge of this? It can't be you, they

164

wouldn't have had that, not with me being one of the hostages.'

'It was. It is.'

He explained why and she said, 'poor you' and then she said, 'Last night you said you expected their representative and I said I was one in a sort of way. They gave me a message, you see. That was the only time any of them spoke. They handcuffed me, they brought me out and put the hood on.' She shivered a little. 'One of them spoke. It was quite a shock. Up till then it had been as if they were dumb or deaf mutes. He called it "the next message". Does that make sense?'

He nodded.

'Well, he said they'd noted the suspension but suspension won't be enough. They want cancellation. Negotiations start on Sunday, he said.'

'How do negotiations start?' Wexford asked.

'I don't know.'

'They didn't say any more?'

'That was all.'

Wexford, Burden and Karen Malahyde. Not an interview room. Everyone but Dora jibbed at that, she said she wouldn't have minded, she rather liked being the centre of attention and she'd never seen the inside of an interview room except on television. But they had the recording equipment taken to the old gym and four armchairs too, to make it more like a party and less like an interrogation. The Chief Constable came over specially, shook hands with Dora and told her she was a brave woman.

'Where do you want me to start?' she said when she was sitting down with her third cup of coffee of the day beside her. 'At the beginning, I suppose?'

'I don't think so,' said her husband. 'As you said yourself, the most important thing at the moment is

165

where. Tell us what you can about the place you were held in.'

'But you know I don't know where it was.'

'We must hope to find where it was from what you tell us.'

'That almost means beginning at the beginning because it was the journey that took me there. But I don't know which way he went or how long it took, you don't when you've got a hood over your head. But I'd guess we were driving for an hour, not more, and for some of the time we were on a big road, possibly a motorway.'

'Could it have been in London?' Karen asked. 'London or just outside London?'

'I suppose it could have been the southern suburbs, Sydenham, Orpington, somewhere like that, but I don't know, I haven't a clue really. I wasn't in the car long enough for it to have been north London. It could have been almost anywhere in Kent or Hampshire, it could have been the coast.'

Dora was very pale, her husband thought. And in spite of having slept heavily, she had had less than six hours and she looked tired. He had wanted to drive her straight to Dr Akande at the medical centre but she had refused, she had almost laughed at him. They shouldn't delay, she had said, she was all right. But when she was dressing he had seen her stagger and have to catch hold of a chair.

Disapproval was no uncommon feeling for Burden to have and he disapproved of the whole thing. Dora should have seen the doctor, been given a thorough examination and probably a tranquilliser if not a sedative. He had no time for counselling himself – though giving lip service to the whole counselling theory because it was police policy – but he firmly believed in the principle of shock hitting victims a

166

good deal later than one would expect. Shock would hit Dora and then she'd have a breakdown.

She had dressed in a grey skirt and grey-and-yellow-checked blouse, oldish clothes, comfortable and familiar. When she left to go to Sheila she had been wearing a new suit, caramel-coloured linen. She had worn it for four days, it had got crumpled and creased as linen does and now she never wanted to see it again. The other clothes in her suitcase she hadn't seen since that hood was first put over her head, for they had taken the case away and, for all she knew, still had it in their possession. She had been allowed to bring her handbag back with her but not the suitcase, nor the presents she had been taking with her to Sheila.

She had paused to drink her coffee and when she began again seemed to realise for the first time that she was being recorded. Her voice grew more stilted and became slower.

'The hoods we wore – we all had them on sometimes – were like small sacks with eyeholes and the sacking had been sprayed, I think, with black spray paint. Or soaked in paint. My hood was quite thick and heavy. They didn't take it off till I was inside.'

'Talk naturally,' Wexford said. 'Forget the machine.'

'I'm sorry. I'll try.'

'No, it's OK, you're doing fine.'

'Well, then, you're going to want to know inside what and that I can't tell you.' She gave the recorder a glance, cleared her throat. 'But it was on the ground floor and I think partially below ground. I went down two steps to get into it. Like a basement but not like a cellar. Am I explaining that properly?'

'I think that's perfectly clear,' said Burden.

'I want you to know that I took pains to notice

everything from the start, to note the size and shape of everything and all the time to try and pick up clues to where I was. I thought it might be necessary and it has been.'

'Good for you, Mrs Wexford,' said Karen. 'You're a marvel.'

Dora smiled. 'Wait till you hear. The results didn't match up to the intention. The boy was already there when I arrived. Ryan Barker he's called but I suppose you know that. He was in the room, sitting on one of the beds. He was just sitting there, staring. The room was quite big, about a third the size of this gym, and oblong, but there was only one window and that was on one of the shorter walls and quite high up. Not all that high up, though, because the ceiling was rather low. I'd say not seven feet. Reg wouldn't have bumped his head on it but he'd have been scared of doing that. I can't do the room measurements in metres but I'd say it was about thirty feet by eighteen to twenty.

'There was the door I came in by and another door that led into a very tiny washplace with a lavatory and basin. There were four beds in the room, narrow, single, foldaway beds. Later on they brought in another one and I think it was because they only intended to take four hostages but in fact took five . . .'

'What makes you think that?' Karen asked.

'You don't want me having opinions, do you? Well, if you think it could be useful. I had a feeling they thought there'd be only one of the Struthers when in fact it was both. And later on Owen Struther said his wife had phoned for a car, so they thought they'd be picking up a woman on her own. Anyway, they brought in a fifth bed. The beds were the only furniture apart from two kitchen chairs.'

'What sort of a room was it?' Wexford asked.

168

'You mean, how old, in what state of decoration, was it a sort of kitchen room or a sort of living-room, don't you? Well, it definitely wasn't a living-room. The walls were uneven, with peeling whitewash, and the electrics were rather primitive, all the cables showing. Under the window there was an old sink, a large butler's sink, but there were no taps. There were rough wooden shelves all along one of the longer walls but there was nothing on them. It was rather like a garage except that there was no garage door for a car to come in by. It could have been a workshop. I thought about that aspect of things a lot and came to the conclusion it could once have been a small factory.'

'Did you look out of the window?' This was Karen.

'The first chance I got. A sort of box had been built round the outside of it. I can only describe it by saying it was like a kind of rabbit hutch in which the rabbit wouldn't have got much light. You could open the window – or you could have if it hadn't been locked – I mean it was openable, and outside, fixed over it, there was this structure, this contraption of wood and wire netting that was more like a chain-link fence. I climbed up on the sink that first day and tried to have a look out and I could see green. Green and brickwork and a lump of concrete like a broken step, and that's all. It might have been the country or a suburban garden. All I can say is that it wasn't an outlook on to some inner city place.'

'Could you tell which way the window faced. Its orientation?'

'The sun came in in the afternoons. It faced west. I'd say due west. I've said there was a little room to wash in with a loo. Well, that was quite interesting because it was new. I mean, it had never been used before. The walls were painted white and the basin and lavatory pan were absolutely new, only there was no lavatory seat or lid. There was no window either. It looked as if it had been a cupboard which had just been converted and done as cheaply as possible, as if it had been done for *us*, I mean, on purpose to accommodate the hostages.

'We stayed in the main room for three nights and four days. Or I did. And Ryan did. The others were moved after a while. Shall I go back to the beginning now?'

'We'll take a break,' said Wexford.

'Are you sure?'

'I'm quite sure. I'm going to pass on what you've told us to the rest of the team and see if it sparks off any ideas. We'll start again in an hour.'

Three children from Stowerton arrived at the police station at eleven with a bagful of bones. They had discovered them, they told the duty sergeant, in one of the heaps of earth, now temporarily abandoned, at Stowerton Dale. One of them put forward the opinion that the bones were Roman, the others that they were of recent origin, the detritus of a serial killer's massacre.

'Sounds like Manfred's been busy,' said Wexford when he heard about it, and explained about Bibi's German Shepherd.

'They'll have to go for analysis,' said Burden despondently.

'I suppose so. Anyone can see most of them are spare ribs and the rest are what's left over from an oxtail stew.'

'What did they mean about negotiations starting on Sunday?'

'I wish you hadn't asked me that question.'

Karen Malahyde sat with Dora drinking coffee. She thought Mrs Wexford shouldn't have another cup, she had already had three, and told her so very

170

kindly and politely. Dora said all right and please to call her Dora, she couldn't be doing with that Mrs Wexford stuff, and did Karen think there might be any orange juice available? If she wasn't expecting the freshly squeezed kind, Karen said, something could be rustled up, the sort they called 'made from concentrate'.

Dora fell asleep in the quite comfortable armchair but woke up when Karen came back. Why did Karen think they hadn't sent her suitcase back with her? And those presents she had been taking to Sheila, babyclothes and a kimono and books? What possible use could they be to them?

'I think we ought to wait and talk about that when Mr Wexford and Mr Burden come back, Mrs ... er, Dora.'

'I'm sure you're right. You only know orange juice is the real thing when it's got bits in it, don't you?'

Wexford and Burden came back together and Burden started the recorder.

'I was asking about my suitcase,' Dora said. 'It doesn't matter all that much. In a way nothing matters but that I'm back and so far the other hostages aren't, but why would they want it? It's just an ordinary medium-sized fibre case, dark-brown, with my initials on it. And there were the other things I was carrying, presents for Sheila and the baby.'

'It's possible,' said Burden, 'that in their haste to get rid of you they simply forgot.'

'Can we go back to the beginning now?' Wexford shifted his chair out of a shaft of sunlight coming through one of the gym's long windows. 'Can we start at last Tuesday morning?'

'Right.' Dora sat back, curled her legs up under her. 'I had to phone for a car. There is a taxi firm called All the Sixes and I phoned them because their number's easy to remember. It was getting on for half-past ten. I wanted to catch the eleven-o-three, which was allowing plenty of time. Anyway, what I got from All the Sixes was one of those recordings that are so maddening. You know, "Please hold the line" and the voice goes up on the "please" and up again on the "line". And then it goes, "Your call will be answered as soon as possible" and then a burst of *Eine Kleine Nachtmusik*. So I found that flyer they'd sent us and called Contemporary Cars.'

'The voice that answered,' Karen said. 'What was it like?'

'A man's. Ordinary, rather flat and dull. No accent. Quite young. It was exactly ten-thirty, by the way. I happened to look at the digital clock on the video while I was talking. He came very promptly – about seven minutes later, I should think.'

'Can you describe him?'

'Not very precisely. I've thought a lot about it. I can only say he wasn't very tall, maybe five feet eight, he was thickset and he had a beard. He walked a bit stiffly, he was bandy-legged. Oh, and he smelt. There was a peculiar smell about him.'

'D'you mean BO? Sweat? A sweetish fried-onion smell?'

'No, not that. More like nail varnish remover. Acetone, is it called?' She looked from one to the other of them, suddenly much livelier, her tiredness driven away by the excitement of talking about it all. 'Like nail varnish or remover, not exactly unpleasant, just odd.

'The doorbell rang and I fetched my case and the parcels – well, carrier bags, from the living-room before I answered the door. The idea, you see, was that he'd carry them to the car for me. But when I opened the door he was standing at the front gate with his back to me. I suppose I should have called to him to take the case but I didn't, I just said good-morning or hallo or something and he nodded. I put the case and the parcels outside the door on the mat, pulled the door shut after me and locked the deadlock.

'He was in the car by then, in the driver's seat. I didn't think it was odd, I just thought he was rather rude. He hadn't even opened the car door for me. I did just glance at his profile before I got into the car, but most of his face was covered by this black curly beard. The car was full of his smell. He had longish, thick, dark curly hair and a pullover or sweatshirt on that was a sort of greyish-blue.'

'What sort of car was it?' Burden asked.

'Small, red, a VW Golf, I think. Anyway, it was like my daughter Sylvia's.' Dora added drily, 'If I were a detective with reason to be suspicious I'd have taken the number, but I'm not and I didn't.'

Burden laughed. 'Were you wearing a seat-belt?'

'What a question! Of course I was wearing a seat-belt. Remember whose wife I am.' Dora shook her head, exasperated. 'I had the suitcase in the car with me, on the seat beside me, and the parcels on the floor. He drove the usual route to the station but he did a sort of detour in Queen Street. There was a bit of a hold-up, there mostly is, and I didn't think anything of it. Taxi drivers go all sorts of odd ways these days to avoid traffic.

'We stopped at a red light on the junction of York Street and Old London Road. The light there is a pedestrian crossing that's operated on a button. Now, of course, I know it was deliberate that he drove to that particular crossing. The lights are pedestrian-controlled. Someone waiting there pressed the button as the car approached, the light turned red and we stopped. The nearside rear door was opened and this man got into the car.

173

'It all happened so quickly, I couldn't have struggled or cried out. For one thing I was trapped in the seat-belt and, you know, it takes a moment or two to extract oneself from a strange seat-belt, it's not like the one in one's own car. And I didn't get a look at him either, no more than a fleeting glimpse of someone young and tall with a stocking over his face.'

'You mean he was standing at the lights with a stocking over his face?'

'There was no one else about,' Dora said, 'but I think, I have the impression, he pulled a stocking over his face with one hand while he opened the car door with the other. It meant I couldn't see his face at all, only that it looked rubbery. But that would be the effect of a stocking on anyone's face, wouldn't it?

'He pulled a hood over his own head and one over mine. I couldn't see anything for a moment, I was struggling and trying to shout, and I was aware of handcuffs going on. It wasn't pleasant. No, much worse than that, it was . . . it was terrifying.'

'Would you like to take another break, Dora?' Wexford asked.

'No, I'm fine. I expect you can understand that I was very frightened. I suppose I was more frightened than I've ever been in my life. After all, I haven't been in that many frightening situations; I suppose I've been sheltered. And there was nothing I could do. It was a bit better when I could see. He had adjusted the hood, pulled it down.

'I could see outside for a moment and that we were on the old bypass. He pointed to the floor, indicating I was to get down there. So that I couldn't be seen from outside, I suppose, or see out. I obeyed him, of course I did, and sat on the floor.

'I think I was in the car for about an hour. It might have been longer but I don't think it was less than an hour. I didn't struggle any more because it wasn't any use. I was terribly afraid. It's not much point saying that now, so I won't go into it. I was afraid I'd lose control of myself in various ways and I wanted to avoid that more than anything. I tried to stay calm, to breathe deeply, but that wasn't easy sitting on the floor with the hood on.

'The car turned in somewhere, through a gate or just into a narrow street or even round the back of a factory or warehouse, I just don't know. But it went much more slowly and it kept taking bends to the right and left. Then we stopped. The hood was still turned so that the eyeholes were at the back. I think he'd only adjusted it at the beginning to show me it did have eyeholes. Anyway, I couldn't see a thing, just a stuffy blackness, and my hands were hand-cuffed in front of me.

'My arms were taken by one of them on each side of me. I think it was the driver on the right-hand side because he didn't seem all that much taller than me and his arm felt quite thick and pudgy. And the smell of him . . . The one on the other side held my arm very hard, you could call it an iron grip. I had the impression of long, thin, strong fingers. He didn't smell of anything. I can't say if it was country air or town air and it was the same sort of temperature as at home.

'I sensed, I heard, a heavy door being unlocked, then opened, and I was taken inside. I wasn't pushed in or flung in or anything, just walked down the steps and in, brought to one of the beds and helped to sit on it. They took the hood off me first, then the handcuffs, but they kept their own hoods on. He had stubby brown hands and the other one had long fingers. That was when I saw Ryan. They went away, closed the door and locked it behind them.'

175

'We'll break for lunch,' Wexford said, 'and then I'll want you to have a rest.'

The best thing would have been to take his wife out to lunch. Wexford kept reverting in his mind to ways of doing this, even if it meant having Burden and Karen Malahyde along as well. But he really knew he couldn't do it. Not today, not in these circumstances, not the Olive and Dove's new La Méditerranée restaurant, a nice bottle of wine, salades de crevettes, sole meunière and crème brulée. Another time. Next week but not today. He sent out for assorted sandwiches, smoked salmon, cheddar and pickle, ham and tongue.

She was looking a bit better. The talking must be doing her good. Of course, tiredness and shock notwithstanding, it *would* do her good. That was what psychotherapy was about, talking to people who not only listened but wanted more than anything else to listen. It was much better for her than keeping it all inside, lying in bed stuffed full of Akande's sedatives.

He let her have another cup of coffee. A lot of nonsense was talked about coffee, about its speeding effects and its caffeine, but you never heard of anyone who actually came to harm through drinking it. She put cream in hers and sugar, which she never would have done at home. The rest he had tentatively said she should have she had rejected.

Burden started the recorder. It was he who asked the first question. 'You were alone in the room with Ryan Barker, is that right?'

'For a while, yes. He was very frightened, he's only fourteen. I talked to him. I told him not to worry too much. If they were going to hurt us they would already have done so. I think I realised by then that we were hostages, though I'd no idea what the

176

ransom could be. Ryan said he knew he ought to be brave – being a male, I suppose was what he meant – and later he said his father had been a soldier who'd died in battle, in the Falklands – but I said, no, he didn't have to be, he could bawl the place down if he liked and that would fetch them back and we could ask them why we were there. Mind you, I was scared stiff myself, but having him there was good for me, because I couldn't show it in front of him.

'Anyway, we weren't alone for long. Roxane was brought in. I'm taking it you do know Roxane Masood is one of the hostages?'

'Roxane Masood and Kitty and Owen Struther are the others,' Karen said.

'That's right. Roxane was a good deal less passive than I was, I can tell you. She was struggling as they brought her in and when they took the hood and the handcuffs off her she tried to fly at them.'

'Who brought her in?'

'The driver and another man. Another tall one, taller than the driver, but not as tall as the one who was in the car with me. As far as I could tell, in his late twenties, maybe thirty. It was he took the handcuffs off Roxane and the driver took the hood off her.

'Roxane made for their eyes with her fingernails even though they had hoods on. The thin man fetched her a great blow across the head and she fell over. She fell on the bed and I think she passed out for a while. I went to her and held her and she came round and started to cry. But that was only because he'd really hurt her. It wasn't crying like Kitty Struther.

'They brought the Struthers in about half an hour later. He was the stiff-upper-lip sort. He reminded me of Alec Guinness in *The Bridge on the River Kwai*. You know, very stiff and straight and *English*, refusing to have any dealings with his captors, that sort of thing. The other man that brought me, the one with the rubbery face, he brought Kitty in. She spat at him when the hood came off her. He didn't do anything, just wiped it off.

'I once read in a book how amazed someone was to hear a really refined ladylike woman use foul language in a situation that was ... well, like this one. They wouldn't have believed she'd known it. Well, that was how I felt about Kitty Struther. The spitting and then the words she used. I suppose it was hysterics, but she screamed and yelled and pounded on the mattress with her fists. After a bit Owen tried to calm her down, so she started punching him. I don't think she knew what she was doing, but she screamed for a very long time. The rest of us just sat there, appalled. And then she began this soft, awful weeping. She curled up like a foetus and buried her face, and at last she fell asleep.'

Dora stopped, sighed, slightly lifted her shoulders. 'I expect you'd like me to tell you what I can about the rest of the people who were holding us.'

'Would you have a look at this, please, Dora.' Burden had produced a photograph which he held out to her. 'Could the dark one, the driver, be this man? Forget the beard, beards can come off and go on at the drop of a hat. Could this be your driver?'

Dora shook her head. 'No. I'm sure not. He's thin, this man, and older. Somehow I know the driver wasn't very old, and he was heavier.'

When Karen had taken her away to get a cup of tea, 'Who is it?' Wexford asked.

Burden put the photograph away. 'Stanley Trotter,' he said. 'He also smells. We had a bit of news in today. I haven't bothered you with it, you had enough on your plate. It's from the police in Bonn, Bonn in Germany.'

178

Wexford thought. 'Where Ulrike Ranke was at university?'

'That's it. You remember the pearls? The eighteenth-birthday present of matched cultured pearls for which her parents paid thirteen hundred pounds?'

'Of course I do.'

'Well, she sold them. Needed the money rather than jewellery, I reckon. The Bonn police have found it and the jeweller who gave her seventeen hundred Deutschmarks for it.'

'Not generous,' said Wexford, having done his mental arithmetic.

'No. Did she buy herself another string for twenty, something to show the parents if need be? Certainly she bought one because we know she was wearing a string of pearls in the Brigadier photograph. And was that the one . . . ?'

'It's not Trotter, Mike,' said Wexford. 'He's not her killer and he's not Dora's driver.'

Chapter 13

The signboard, planted in the grass verge, read: Euro-Fun, The Only International Theme Park in Sussex. The lettering was white on a blue ground and underneath it someone had painted, not very expertly, a small deer or chamois, a windmill and what might have been the Leaning Tower of Pisa. Damon Slesar swung the car in through the open gates, or rather, the one open gate, the other being off its hinges and leaning against the fence, and up a track that would be two ruts of mud in winter.

The theme park had been arranged as a series of paddocks, through which the track wound in a haphazard way. Its distant appearance was slightly redeemed by an abundance of trees which hid some of Euro-Fun's worst excesses, though most of these were revealed as prospect became foreground. Each section bore the name of the country represented there, lettered on a swinging sign suspended from tall pillars rather like barbers' poles. The whole had grown shabby with the years and there were few visitors. Five people, three adults and two children, were walking about in bemused fashion in the area labelled Denmark, dubiously eyeing a wooden dolls' house with a green roof and a plastic facsimile of the Little Mermaid seated on the edge of a stagnant pond lined with blue polythene.

What precisely visitors to the place were supposed to do wasn't clear. Perhaps only walk, look and wonder. A man and a woman were doing that, especially from their expressions the wondering part, among rain-damaged wax tulips in the shadow of a monstrous red-and-white plastic windmill, while a couple of pre-teens sat on the steps of a chalet staring at a cuckoo clock. The cuckoo had come out in front of the clock face and, the mechanism breaking down at this point, stayed out, silent, its beak permanently frozen open in the cuckooing position.

'You ever brought your kids here?' Damon Slesar asked.

'Please,' said Nicky Weaver, 'do me a favour. Oh, look at the Parthenon! Can you believe it?'

It looked as if made of asbestos but was probably plasterboard, the pillars whitewashed drainpipes. A figure, that properly belonged in a shop window but was now dressed in white pleated skirt and black jacket, stood in front of the Acropolis strumming at a stringed instrument. Next door was Spain with a papier-mâché bull and matador, and then came the ticket office and car park. Adjacent to the car park stood a sprawling bungalow in need of a paint.

The man who came out was middle-aged, in cable-knit pullover and grey cord trousers. He was one of those men who have practically no hair on their heads and a great deal on upper lip and cheeks. In his case it was grey and shaggy, a thick, drooping moustache and slightly curly side whiskers.

'Will that be two, then, madam? Car park straight on.'

'Police,' said Nicky, showing him her warrant card instead of the expected cash. 'I'm looking for Mr or Mrs Royall.'

He was no stranger to police inquiries. Nicky could tell. The police can. He thumped his chest with his fist, said, 'James Royall at your service, ma'am. What can I do for you?'

Nicky knew that 'ma'am' wasn't politeness or deference, but intended as a joke, a parody of the style policemen use when addressing a senior female officer. James Royall was being funny.

'I'd like to talk to you about your son. Brendan – is that right?'

'Now I can't leave my post, can I, ma'am?'

Damon Slesar turned his head, craning from side to side. 'I don't see any rush, do you? They're not exactly queuing up.'

'We'd like to talk to you *now*, Mr Royall,' Nicky said. 'Whether you leave your post or find someone else to man it is immaterial to me.'

The little office or hut had an inner room. Nicky opened the door to it, walked in and beckoned to James Royall. There were two kitchen chairs and a table doing duty as a desk. The walls were lined with shelving on which stood dozens, perhaps hundreds, of artefacts from the theme park: figurines, plastic animals, sections of tree, dolls' house, boat, all broken, all apparently awaiting repair.

Royall picked up the phone, said into it, 'Mag, can you get down here. Something's come up.' He looked towards Damon, 'What about his nibs, then?'

'We're anxious to get in touch with your son, Mr Royall. Do you know where he is?'

'Ask me another.' Royall shrugged his shoulders. 'You've come to the wrong shop, you know. Him and me and his mum, we're what you might call *estranged*. In other words, not exactly on speaking terms.'

'And what accounts for that, Mr Royall?'

He transferred his glance to Nicky whose appearance and tone, and perhaps also her rank and profession, he seemed to find amusing. A small smile lifted the corners of his mouth under the drooping moustache. 'Well, ma'am, I don't know that that's any business of yours, but speaking as an easygoing man, I'll tell you. In the first place my son Brendan thought for some mysterious reason, unfathomable to me, that when I came into my old man's property I should pass it over lock, stock and barrel to him. Nice expression that, don't you think? Lock, stock and barrel. Refers to guns, of course. But you'd know all about that, ma'am. The twenty K I did give him from the sale of said property wasn't enough, oh dear, no. So he kept coming back for more. But he didn't care for our Euro theme. The bull and the matador, they were among what he took exception to . . .'

'And the moles, dear,' said a woman's voice from the doorway.

'Oh, and the moles, Mag. You're right. Not wanting this place to resemble the Alps, being as we already had our Swiss area, we had the cheek to call in the mole exterminator without consulting his nibs first and that, you might say, cooked our goose.'

Mrs Royall, called to the receipt of custom and now perhaps unwilling to relinquish it, hovered in the doorway, continually glancing over her shoulder lest a car or party should slip past her unawares. She said to Nicky in a rather helpless way, 'I'm Brendan's mother.'

'Can you tell us your son's whereabouts, Mrs Royall?'

'I only wish I could. It's been a cause of great sadness to me being cut off from my only child and all over this passion he's got for animals. We love animals too, I said to him, only you have to be practical in this world.'

Royall made the sound usually written as 'pshaw!'. 'It's not animals, it's money. And you know damn well where he is. Keeping an eye on his future prospects. Sucking up to them as are in his grandad's shoes.'

'And where might that be, sir?'

'Marrowgrave Hall, *ma'am*. As I sold to my cousin, Mrs Panick, some seven years ago and passed on a fair whack of the proceeds to that greedy, grasping monkey-lover . . .'

'Oh, Jim!' wailed Mrs Royall.

They left as another car arrived, this time with Austrian registration plates. Nicky wondered what its occupants would think of the section devoted to their motherland with its gilt-caparisoned plastic horse, bust of Mozart and musical box which played Viennese waltzes on the insertion of a ten-pee coin.

'It wasn't the same people who brought Roxane or Kitty and Owen in,' said Dora. 'Or, rather, I'm not sure about the tall one, it might have been him, but the driver, it wasn't him this time. This man was taller, though not so tall as the tall one, and he was thinner, and I think he was younger.

'The tall one, his was the only face I ever saw, and I saw it through a tan-coloured stocking. A fairly thick stocking, twenty denier, if you know what that means. He was white, Caucasian, as they say, his features might have been sharp or they might actually have been rubbery. I couldn't identify him. If you showed me photographs I could say he looks a bit like that or that or that, but I couldn't positively say. I've no idea what colour his eyes were. There was only one of them whose eye colour I actually saw.

'The driver I've told you about. I don't think I can add to that. I never saw his eyes. I never heard any of them speak, they never spoke to us. The third one, the one who helped bring Roxane in – there was a

184

fourth but he didn't appear till the next day – the third had a tattoo on his arm.'

'A *tattoo*?'

Wexford and Burden had the same thought. This is the detective story clue, even the old-fashioned detective story clue, the ineradicable mark that is the perfect giveaway. But now, today, in reality?

'He had a tattoo on his arm?' Wexford said. 'Are you sure?'

'I'm sure. I didn't see it till next day. Not till the Wednesday. It was a butterfly tattoo, red and black, but I suppose all tattoos are. I'll tell you more about it when I come to that, shall I?'

'Right.'

'I said there was a fourth man,' she went on. 'He was one of those who brought our breakfast next day. He was another tall one, the same height as the first tall one, and I honestly don't know what to say about him. He even wore gloves, so I don't know what his hands were like. He was just a tall, masked figure, thin, straight, with an athletic stride, frightening really, though I'd stopped being frightened by then. I got angry, you see, and that kills fear. I couldn't identify any of them and I don't think the other hostages could.'

'But you didn't see this fourth one, the gloved one, till the next day, the Wednesday?'

'That's right. I shouldn't have got on to him now. I shouldn't have got on to the tattoo. You're telling me off in the nicest possible way, aren't you?'

'I wouldn't dream of it!' Karen Malahyde laughed. She hesitated, then said, 'Why did they let you go?'

'I don't know.'

'You said one of them spoke to you?'

'It was yesterday evening. About ten. I was alone by then with Ryan, just the two of us. The others had been taken away. The tall one who wore gloves came in with the tattooed one. I was sitting on my bed – I mostly was. They motioned me to get up and hold out my hands and I did. And then they put handcuffs on me.'

Wexford made a sound, turned it into a cough. He clenched his fists and unclenched them. She looked at him, made a rueful face.

'They took me outside. I didn't struggle or protest. I'd seen what they did to those who did that – well, to one who did that. I didn't even say goodbye to Ryan. Well, I thought I'd be coming back. Then they put the hood on me. That was when the tattooed one spoke to me. It was only about a minute after I'd been led out but – well, that was a bad minute. I thought they were going to kill me. Still, let's pass on. It was a shock hearing his voice.'

'What was it like?'

'His voice? Cockney, but not natural. I mean, it was like cockney that's been learned.'

Burden caught Wexford's eye and nodded. The man who had phoned Tanya Paine had a cockney accent he thought sounded as if learned from tapes. He said to Dora, 'What exactly did he say?'

'I'll try and remember accurately. Now then – "Tell them the suspension has been noted. Suspension isn't enough. Work has to stop permanently. Tell them negotiations start on Sunday." Then he told me to repeat it and I did. I'd lost my voice from nerves but it came back because if they were giving me a message I knew they must be sending me home.'

'They put you in a car? Did you see the car?'

'Not then. They turned the hood round so that I couldn't see anything. I couldn't see any more of the place where we were than when I arrived. They put me in the back seat of a car and fastened the seat-belt on me. The drive took about an hour and a half. I'd have moved the hood round so that I could see out but what with the seat-belt and the handcuffs I couldn't. When the car stopped the driver opened the door, came round and took off the hood. It was dark but I could see it was the same man who had brought me, the short, dark, bearded man. The one who smelt. He still smelt. He'd put on dark glasses. Shades, do they call them?

'He took off the handcuffs, undid the seat-belt and helped me out. He gave me my handbag – it was the first I'd seen of it since Wednesday. He didn't speak, I never heard his voice. The car was parked alongside the cricket field, which is about a quarter of a mile from our house. I think he parked there because it's just field on one side and the Methodist church and graveyard on the other. No one to see, I suppose.

'It was past midnight and all the street lamps were out. He got back into the car, leaving me there. I tried to see the registration but it was too dark. As for the make and colour, it was lightish, it could have been any of those creamy-grey colours or greyish or light-blue. He didn't put his lights on until he was a good fifty yards away. The number started with an L and ended with a five and a seven.

'After that I walked home. My house keys were in my bag. I tried to let myself in the back way but the door was bolted on the inside, so I went round to the front. But you asked me why they let me go. I'm sorry, I never really answered that. Just to deliver the message? It couldn't be just that. I honestly don't know why.'

'All right,' said Wexford, 'that's enough for today. You can talk some more to me at home, if you like, but that's an end of the formal stuff for now. You've given us plenty to go on.'

It was as ugly a house, as only the Victorians in their

later architectural phases could build. The remarkable thing, as Hennessy said to Nicky Weaver, was that it had evidently been intended as a dwelling house and not an institution. The principal building material was brick of a yellowish khaki, the sickly colour occasionally broken by lines of red tile. Eight sash windows were close up underneath the shallow slate roof. There were eight more below, these slightly deeper, but on the ground the three on either side of a front door that stood plumb in the centre were set in pointed Gothic arches. It had a mean, squat front door without benefit of panelling, with no porch, not even set in a recess. Still, Marrowgrave Hall was an enormous place, as Damon Slesar saw when he walked round the side, for the whole front edifice was repeated on the back, the roof merely taking a kind of dip in the middle.

The only outbuilding was a garage, a prefabricated affair that stood separate from the house. Hennessy looked through the single window at the back but there was nothing inside except a pile of empty sacks. Nicky rang the doorbell. It was answered by a woman of enormous girth, one of those people who are so hugely fat that it is a wonder they can bear the daily heaving of this mass of flesh from place to place. She was probably still in her forties, with a pale moon-face and loose mouth, a little thin, reddish hair. A floral tent enveloped her, reaching to her heavily bandaged knees and shins.

'Mrs Panick?' said Nicky.

'You're the police, dear. We've been expecting you. We had a call.'

'May we come in?'

The smell was of food. It was quite a nice smell, especially if you happened to be hungry, a compound of vanilla and burnt sugar and something fruity. An occasional whiff of cheese joined in as they

188

were led down a dour corridor, then frying bacon, finally as they entered a cavernous kitchen a heady amalgam of the lot, rich, hot, almost succulent. Their progress was necessarily slow as Patsy Panick lumbered ahead of them with difficulty. In the kitchen she stood, hanging on to a chair, getting her breath.

An elderly man was sitting at a long pine table, eating a meal, presumably his lunch, though it was not much past eleven-thirty. He was nearly but not quite as fat as his wife. Women and men put on weight differently and while his wife's was distributed more or less evenly all over her, Robert Panick's had rested, accumulated, swelled and become mountainous, only on his stomach. Slesar remarked afterwards, when they were on their way back through Forby, that he had read somewhere about Thomas Aquinas having to have a great ellipse cut out of the table at which he worked, to accommodate the Angelic Doctor's huge belly. Robert Panick could have done with an ellipse cut out of this one, but no one had thought of it and he was obliged to sit some two feet back from the table and bend as far forward as his girth allowed to eat his food.

It had apparently been a plateful of fried meat, liver and bacon perhaps, with chips, peas and fried bread. More of the same sizzled in two pans on the stove. A plate of Mrs Panick's half-eaten meal was also on the table and, approaching it, she absentmindedly lifted a forkful to her mouth.

'Give them something to eat, Patsy,' said Panick, who hadn't otherwise seemed to notice their presence. 'Some of those chocolate biscuits with the jelly in or we've got some frozen Mars in the freezer.'

'No, thanks,' said Slesar for all of them. 'Very good of you, but no thanks all the same. We wanted to ask you about the house. You bought it off a Mr James Royall about seven years ago, I believe?'

189

'That's right, dear. Only it was six years. Jimmy's my cousin. His daddy that lived here was my uncle. We'd always loved this house, hadn't we, Bob? It's a lovely old house, a real lovely antique, and when we got the chance to have it – well, Bob had done ever so well in business and just sold up, and why not blow some money on the house of our dreams? That's what we said.'

Her husband nodded and, having finished up the last scrap of fried bread, passed his plate to her for a refill. Most of the contents of the two pans went on to it. Mrs Panick sat down in front of her own plate and the chair emitted a long, painful creak.

'You don't mind if I go on with my meal, do you? I wish you'd have something yourselves. A nice piece of Victoria sponge? I made it myself this morning. Well, all right, if you're sure. Our needs are very modest, dear, as you see, and we don't run a car, there's a very nice delicatessen in Pomfret that delivers twice a week, so we felt we could afford the place and the upkeep, and we manage quite OK, don't we, Bob? Mind you, I think my cousin Jimmy made a special price for us, us being family.'

'The son, Brendan,' Nicky said. 'I suppose you know him too?'

'Know him? He's more like a son to us. I mean, first cousin once removed, that's a laugh. He's like our own. And he won't have anything to do with Jimmy and Moira, dear. Says his dad's cruel to animals as well as cheating him out of his inheritance and it is true my uncle John often said Brendan could have the place when he went. His dad did give him a bit of the money we paid over but he spent most of it on his Euro theme. Still, I said to Brendan, don't you worry, dear, it'll be yours one day.'

'Meaning?'

'That we'd leave it to him in our wills.'

'So you see him?'

'See him? He always pops in when he's down this way. I say to Bob, Brendan's made us his parents since his own was so unsatisfactory. We're – what's the term I want? – yes, surrogate. We're surrogate parents for Brendan. And I think he knows he'll always get a good meal here. Now you've eaten all the rest of that fry-up, Bob, I'm going to have to find myself something else.'

'There's a pudding, isn't there?' said Panick in the tone of someone asking a bank manager if it can possibly be true his account is in the red.

'Of course there's a pudding. When have I served you a meal without a pudding? Not in all our married life. But I've got an empty corner wants filling now and I reckon I'll have to attack the Camembert the way the French do, before the dessert, right?'

'Do you know where Brendan is now, Mrs Panick?'

'Well, he won't be with his mum and dad, dear. That's for sure. Nottingham maybe? He was down here a couple of weeks back, no, I tell a lie, more like a month, something to do with butterflies or frogs. He loves animals, does Brendan. That's his work, you know, saving animals, a bit like the RSPCA. And he came in to see us and we happened to be having pheasant that night, frozen of course, the season not starting till next month, but none the worse for that, and I did bread sauce and orange sauce though that's not strictly the thing with pheasant, and oven chips and a suet roll to fill up and a chocolate roulade with clotted cream.

'He came rolling down our drive as happy as a lark at just on five and parked the caravan right outside the kitchen window, so that he could get the cooking smells, he said.'

'He lives in a caravan?' said Hennessy, trying not to sound too aghast.

'Well, a Winnebago is the correct term, dear. He's always on the move, you never know where he is from one moment to the next.'

'He hasn't a fixed address?'

'Not what you'd call fixed. Not unless you count this one.'

'We'd appreciate it if you'd let us know if he turns up here.'

'You can be sure of that,' said Patsy Panick, which wasn't at all what Nicky expected.

'Where are you hiding that pudding, Patsy?' said Bob.

Driving back through Forby, once designated (or damned) as the fifth prettiest village in England, Nicky Weaver said, 'Didn't you think they were too good to be true?'

'No one's too good to be true,' said Hennessy, after the manner of Wexford, whom he admired. 'What are you suggesting, ma'am, that they were acting?'

'I suppose not. The way they were going at that food, Brendan Royall won't have too long to wait for his inheritance.'

'Isn't it too bad, him living in a Winnebago?' said Damon. 'Just our bloody luck.'

'What, you mean you're envious because you want a Winnebago or sick because it means he's always on the move?'

'Both,' said Damon.

Four men, one of them tattooed, one smelling of acetone, one wearing gloves. A red Golf, a basement room, a newly converted washroom, masks of spray-painted sacking, handcuffs, a light-coloured car, registration L something something five seven. A man with a learned cockney voice. These were what

192

Wexford presented to those of his team who were not in Nottingham or Guildford at a meeting in the old gym at four. They told him about a paranoid man who had quarrelled with his parents and a Winnebago Nicky Weaver had begun tracing.

'I'd very much like to know if Brendan Royall has a tattoo,' he said. 'Presumably, his parents could tell us.'

'Or Mrs Panick might know,' Nicky Weaver said.

Rather shyly, Lynn Fancourt said she didn't want to appear ignorant, but what was a Winnebago? Burden explained that it was a luxury mobile home, not far removed from a bungalow on wheels. Royall could range the country in it, parking in lay-bys overnight if he chose.

Then Wexford played the tapes to them. The Chief Constable arrived unexpectedly after the first one had been running for five minutes. He sat and listened. When it was over he accompanied Wexford up to his office.

'Your wife must have a lot more to tell us, Reg.'

'I know she has, sir, but I'm a bit afraid ...'

'Yes, I know what you mean. And so am I. Would it help her to have counselling, do you think?'

'Frankly, sir, talking to me *is* her counselling. Just talking and having me listen. We shall talk more this evening.'

The Chief Constable looked at his watch, the way people do when they are going to talk about time. He said, 'Do you remember saying to me the newspapers wouldn't be all that interested if the embargo on this story was lifted on a Friday or a Saturday? That what they'd like best would be to have it late on Sunday?'

Wexford nodded.

'Then we'll lift it tomorrow.'

'All right. If you say so.'

193

'I do. We'll have the whole pack of them down here, we'll have phone calls pouring in all day with sightings of the Struthers in Majorca and Singapore, we'll have people who know the basement room is in the house next door, but nevertheless, we may also get help. And we need more help now, Reg.'

'Yes, sir. I know we do.'

'Sometimes I think it would be better if we adhered more to the continental system, like they have in France, for instance. Kept investigations secret, made them more in the nature of undercover operations, low-profile stuff, not all this sharing everything with the public. Keep the press, the public and the victims' families at arm's length while the investigation goes on. Once you recruit the public, the pressure on us increases.'

Shades of that conference on continental methods ... 'They expect instant results,' said Wexford.

'That's right. And then mistakes are made.'

After that, Wexford went home. As he drove down the High Street he passed a straggling line of tree people, laden with packs, heading for the best places to hitch lifts to somewhere, anywhere. They were leaving, or some of them were. While the environmental assessment went on they were off to protest elsewhere.

The red Golf parked outside his house made his heart lurch. But, of course, it was Sylvia's. He was so involved in all this he couldn't recognise his own daughter's car. He let himself into the house and found not one but both daughters there. Dora was holding Amulet in her arms. He had to remind himself that this was the first time she had seen the baby.

'I'll be staying the night with Syl, Pop,' Sheila said. 'Just in case you're feeling aghast.'

'I could never feel anything but delight at seeing

you,' he said untruthfully and, with a smile at Sylvia, 'both of you.'

'Don't strain yourself.' Sylvia got up. 'We're going. We just had to see Mother. Don't you think we've been good, not saying a word about this to anyone? I mean, Sheila knows masses of journalists, she could easily have let something out, but we've been *clams*.'

'You've been magnificent,' said Wexford. 'You can talk all you like on Monday.' He gave Sheila a severe look. 'I never heard of a woman junketing about the countryside with a week-old baby the way you do. Now give me a kiss, both of you, and get out of here.'

After they had gone he hugged Dora and felt her heart beating fast. He was aware that the hand which reached up to rest on his shoulder was shaking.

'Do you want a drink? Something to eat? I'll take you out to dinner if you like. It's late but not too late for La Méditerranée.'

She shook her head. 'I started to shake when I got home. Karen drove me home and came in with me and made me a cup of tea, but once she'd gone the shaking began. Then the girls came. Sheila had a hired car all the way from London. I don't want to start shaking again, Reg. It's very disconcerting.'

'Would it help to go on talking? I mean, about that place and those people?'

'I think perhaps it would.'

'I'll have to record it.'

'That's all right,' she joked, her laugh a little ragged. 'I'm spoilt now. I'll never want to have an ordinary conversation unless I know it's gone on tape.'

Chapter 14

'If they didn't speak,' he asked her, 'how did they find out who you all were?'

There were dark smudges under her eyes and lines round her mouth he didn't think had been there before. But the shaking had stopped. Her thin hands lay calm in her lap. And her voice was steady.

'After the Struthers were brought in Tattoo came back and gave us each a bit of paper. They were torn-off scraps of a lined writing pad. He didn't say anything, but as I've said, none of them ever did. Kitty Struther was lying on the bed crying and moaning that she wanted to go away on her holiday. It was bizarre. There we were in that awful situation and she kept whining about her holiday that had been ruined. Tattoo just put her bit of paper beside her, but her husband picked it up and filled it in for her.

'It just said, "name", which we took to mean they wanted our names. Owen Struther said they were criminals and terrorists, and he wasn't doing anything to gratify criminals, but when Roxane told him how they'd hit her – she had a great bruise on the side of her face by that time – he did it all the same. He said he'd compromise for his wife's sake. We all wrote our names down and after a while Tattoo came back and collected them.'

'You didn't tell him who you were?'

She looked at him inquiringly. 'I wrote down Dora

196

Wexford, if that's what you mean. Oh, I see. I didn't say I was married to you. I suppose I thought they'd know that – but no, maybe not.'

How many people would recognise his name? Not all that many. True, in the past he had several times appeared on television in connection with previous cases, to appeal for witnesses, for help from the public, but no one remembers the names of policemen in these broadcasts, or of those who get their pictures in the papers.

'Remember they never spoke to us, Reg,' she said. 'And on the whole we didn't speak to them much. Well, Roxane spoke to them. And the first time they brought us food Kitty said thank you and that made Roxane laugh, only Tattoo got hold of her by the shoulders and shook her till she stopped. But the rest of us hardly said a word to them. I don't think they ever knew the investigating officer was my husband.'

They did by Friday afternoon, he thought, they found out, and that's why they let her go. It was too much for them, the idea of having his wife among the hostages, a hassle they could do without. It must have come as a shock to them. Besides, releasing her was a sure way of getting their message to him. But how had they found out?

'You've said how Tattoo struck Roxane Masood when she tried to attack him and Rubber Face, right? Why didn't he or they strike Kitty Struther?'

Dora considered. 'Kitty didn't attack him, she only screamed and yelled.'

'She spat at him. Most people would find that pretty inflammatory. Later on Tattoo got hold of Roxane and shook her, and that was only for laughing when Kitty thanked him for the food.'

'Well, I don't know, Reg, I can't answer that. I know they didn't like Roxane. You see, she was

197

trouble from the start. Owen Struther talked a lot about not doing anything conciliatory, "not giving any quarter to the enemy" was his phrase, he wasn't old enough to have been in the Second World War, though he talked as if we were all prisoners of war, but it was Roxane who put up more resistance than any of us. Not that first time but the second evening we had food brought, it was The Driver and Rubber Face, she took one look at it and said, "What's this filth?" and threw it on the floor. It was cold baked beans and bread, quite edible, really, if you're hungry and we were, but she threw it on the floor. Rubber Face hit her again and she was going to fight back. It was horrible, but this time Owen Struther intervened and they stopped. He didn't do much, just told them to stop and put his hand on Roxane's shoulder. Anyway, I suppose he had an authoritative manner or something and it was effective. Kitty started crying again and he sat with her, stroking her head and holding her hand. Then Tattoo came in and cleared up the mess on the floor.'

'You all slept in the basement room that night?'

'At about ten Rubber Face and Tattoo came in, switched off the light and took the bulb out of the socket. Oh, and they did the same in the washroom. They always came in pairs, by the way. After all, we were five, although I don't suppose Kitty or I could have done much. It was very dark in there, though after a while a little light filtered in through the rabbit hutch on the window.'

'Artificial light, you mean?'

'Light that might have been from a street lamp or the outside light on a house or a porch light. Not the moon, though we did get moonlight on the Thursday night. There was a blanket on each bed but no pillows. It wasn't cold. We none of us took our clothes off – how could we? Well, I took off my skirt and jacket. One thing that will make you laugh . . .'

'Really?' he said. 'I doubt it.'

'It will, Reg. I'd got a toothbrush in my handbag. They took my bag away next day but I had it then. I'd bought three new tubes of toothpaste the day before and it was one of those offers you get everywhere now, buy three and you get a free toothbrush with a small tube of toothpaste, all in a plastic case for travelling. Well, I don't know why, but I'd put this in my handbag and there it was. We all shared it. If anyone had ever told me I'd share my toothbrush with four strangers I'd never have believed them.

'We all lay there in the dark and Owen Struther started talking about its being the first duty of a prisoner to escape. There was no way out of the washroom, so the main door remained and the window with its bars and its rabbit hutch, but he said the window was a possibility. In the morning he'd examine the window.

'Ryan Barker had hardly said a word while the light was on, but he seemed to gain a bit of courage in the dark. Anyway, he said he'd like to try and escape and he'd help. Owen said, "Good man," or something equally daft and Ryan said his dad had been a soldier. It was as if he was talking to himself in the dark. He said his dad had been a soldier in some war, he didn't say which war then, and had died for his country. It was quite strange hearing him say that in the dark. "My dad died for his country."

'Anyway, Kitty was crying again. She wanted Owen to "hold her", she said, which was a touch embarrassing for the rest of us, and anyway he couldn't. Those beds were only two feet wide. She lay there moaning that he had to care for her, he had to look after her, she was so alone, she was so frightened.

'I didn't think I'd sleep but I did. After a while. I was trying to work out how they'd done it, managed the Contemporary Cars driving, I mean. With four of them it could quite easily be done. Anyway, there were more than four and I'll come to that. Working that out must have sent me to sleep, but the bed next to me shaking woke me up. It's funny – or perhaps it's not – but talking to you like this has stopped *me* shaking. I feel quite reasonably OK.

'I didn't shake in there but Roxane did. It was Roxane's trembling making the bed shake. I put out my hand to her and she clutched it and said she was sorry but she couldn't stop, it wasn't fear, I mean fear like Kitty's, it was claustrophobia.'

'Ah,' said Wexford. 'Yes.'

'You mean you knew?'

'Her mother told me she was claustrophobic and that it was a severe form she had.'

'It was. It is. She whispered to me that it was all right in the light but in the dark it affected her badly. It would have been all right if the door had been open, but of course it never was.

'She was really a very sensible girl, Reg, in many ways, only she was too brave for her own good. We pushed our beds a bit closer together. Holding her hand seemed to help, so I went on doing that and after a time we both went to sleep.

'In the morning our breakfast was brought in by Gloves and Rubber Face. That was the first time we'd seen Gloves. He had a gun.'

'He had a gun?' Wexford said. 'A handgun?'

'If that's the name for a pistol or a revolver, yes. It might have been a toy or a replica, I wouldn't know, and Owen, who surely would know, said afterwards

200

that it wasn't real. So probably the gun Rubber Face had in the car wasn't real either.

'The gun got used later. Oh, don't look like that, no one was hurt.' Dora reached out and took hold of his hand. 'They didn't put the bulbs back, they never did. It wasn't very light in there, though the sun was shining outside. Light never really penetrated through the bars and the rabbit hutch. Gloves unlocked the window and opened it. That wasn't as generous a move as I've made it sound because the bars made it impossible to squeeze anything thicker than an arm between them. At any rate, we got some air into the room.

'Our breakfast was slices of white bread – you know, Mother's Pride or something, pre-sliced – an orange each and a cake each, a sort of dry muffin thing, jam in small containers, the kind you get in hotels, five mugs of instant coffee and three plastic pots of non-lactic soymilk stuff. I suppose we got such a big meal because we weren't to have anything else till the evening. Owen talked a lot of nonsense about sharpening the one spoon that came with it and turning it into a screwdriver – he was thinking of unscrewing the door hinge – but Rubber Face came back and checked on everything before taking the trays. Shall I tell you about the rest of the day now?'

'No, my dear, I'm going to send you to bed. I'll bring you up a hot drink. More talk tomorrow.'

He sat there alone for a while, trying to think what it was that she had said which rang such a jangling of bells in his mind. It came to him at last. The non-lactic soymilk, that's what it was, the milk substitute the hostages had been brought for their breakfast. He had had it in the tea he had with Gary and Quilla on the previous afternoon and it had left an unpleasant taste in his mouth. It all seemed a hundred years ago now, so much had happened since.

But those two had known he was a policeman though not his name. He had told them he was called Wexford and, now he looked back, he remembered how Quilla had seemed to start at the name. At his rank, he had thought then, but suppose it had been at the name?

At around five-thirty on Friday afternoon outside the Framhurst teashop he had told Quilla and Gary his rank and his name. Four hours later preparations were under way for releasing Dora.

It was strange ground for him, all unfamiliar, new, untried. Some of the time he felt as if he was finding his way through a dark wood where all the trees were exotics, the obstacles unidentifiable and the wild animals threatening in an indefinable way. The taking of hostages, the demanding of a ransom that was of a political nature, all that was something he never expected to have to handle and if asked would have suggested its handling by some different, even remote, authority.

So on this Sunday morning he seemed to have reached an impenetrable part of the wood, but one which he must penetrate. He hardly knew what his next move should be. The computers now held a mass of information, details of every lead that had been followed, background – curricula vitae, if you like – of every person named in the investigation, coincidental and cross-matched activities, possible sites and 'safe houses', transcribed interviews. Then there were the tapes. There was the letter to the *Kingsmarkham Courier* and the versions of the later messages. In it all he could see nothing concrete, nothing to make him feel the time was approaching when he could order a certain place to be pinpointed and one or more persons to be targeted.

He had sent DS Cook and DC Lowry to find Quilla

and Gary and bring them to Kingsmarkham police station. If they were still at the Elder Ditches camp, he thought, if they hadn't departed the day before with so many others. Dora had still been asleep when he was preparing to leave and he was wondering what to do when Sheila phoned. Sheila, who had spent the night at Sylvia's, would come in on her way home, now or as soon as the hire car arrived, and stay with her mother until he returned. He had left, feeling one anxiety lifted.

Blind in the dark wood, he had nevertheless come to a decision. All the hostages' families should be fetched in, assembled in the old gym with those of his team who were available and told the present state of things, told, too, that the story would break on Monday morning. Whatever the Chief Constable might say about continental practice, they had involved the hostages' families and must continue to do so. Now, as he looked at them all sitting there, he wondered if he had done the right thing – but how did you know the right thing when there was no precedent?

He remembered how Audrey Barker had asked him if she could be put in touch with the other mother and form a support group. He had refused, largely to reduce to a minimum the chances of a breach of secrecy. They could do it now if they wanted to, perhaps discussion would be a comfort to them, but he had noticed that now the opportunity had come each sat isolated, silent, giving no more than an occasional suspicious glance at the others.

Mrs Peabody hadn't come, so her daughter was the only member of the group without support. Hers was a lonely figure, her head bowed, her hands folded in her lap, her face paper-white. Despair seemed to enclose her, a misery that the news of her son's safety had done nothing to dispel. By contrast,

Clare Cox had a hopeful air. She looked practical, resolute, above all she looked *different*. A jacket and skirt, a pair of black pumps, transformed her appearance. Her hair was tied back with a black silk ribbon. Masood, in a smart dark suit with a purple sheen, had accompanied her but without his second family. Wexford noted with as much amusement as he was capable at present of summoning up for anything that they were holding hands.

Whispering from time to time in Bibi's ear, Andrew Struther looked tired and strained. The girl wore white shorts and a red tank top which left her midriff bare. But he was formally dressed in a white shirt and tie, linen jacket and dark trousers. They too were holding hands but in a far more demonstrative way than Roxane's parents, an almost libidinous way. Bibi's hand enclosed his caressingly and moved it to rest on her pale-golden thigh. Distress hadn't touched her, but then why should it? It wasn't her parents who had been kidnapped.

Wexford got up on the impromptu platform and began talking to them. He told them how the facts of the case which had been presented to the press on the previous Wednesday would no longer be embargoed after this evening. The media would be free to use them with the other more recent information which Kingsmarkham CID would pass on to them today.

He believed they already knew that Sacred Globe had released his wife. It was she who had been able to give them so much information about the present condition of the hostages and to tell them that on Friday when she left all were alive and well. She had also carried with her the message that Sacred Globe would begin negotiations today, Sunday, but no word had yet been received as to what they might have in mind. Nor, he said, could he say that these putative discussions were of a kind into which the police – or, come to that, the hostages' families – would be prepared to enter.

They listened. He asked them if they had any questions. He knew he hadn't been entirely open with them or perhaps he hadn't been entirely open with himself. That 'alive and well' business – how true was that? Now he thought he had forborne to question Dora any more, had postponed further questioning, because there were things about Roxane Masood particularly, and the Struthers to a lesser extent, he hadn't wanted to hear before he spoke to these people. Their fears were somewhat allayed. Was there any point in giving rise to more fear at this juncture?

Audrey Barker put up her hand like a child in a classroom – or a child in a classroom in his day.

'Mrs Barker?'

Her eyes, her strained, stretched face, had the look of someone who has just witnessed something terrifying. Seen a ghost, perhaps, or a bloody motor-way pile-up. 'Can you tell me a bit more about Ryan?' she asked. It was the voice of a woman on the edge of tears. 'How he was, I mean, how he's taking it?'

'He was fine on Friday evening. His spirits were good.' Wexford didn't add that from then on the boy would have been alone. 'The hostages appear to be adequately fed, there is no problem there. They have washing facilities, beds and blankets.'

Don't ask me if they are all together, he prayed silently. Don't ask where the girl is. No one did. Clare Cox seemed to take it for granted that Roxane was also in that room when Dora left it.

Masood, having disengaged his hand from hers, had been writing something in a small leather-bound

205

notebook. He looked up and asked, 'Can you please tell us who's looking after them?'

'There appear to be five men or four men and a woman.'

'And perhaps by now you have a clue as to where they are?'

'We have clues, yes, many clues. Leads are being followed all the time. As yet we have no firm knowledge of where the hostages are being held, only that it's somewhere within a radius of about sixty miles. Tomorrow's publicity may be of considerable help to us there.'

The question was bound to come. It always did. Andrew Struther asked it.

'Yes, all right, that's all very well, but why haven't you done more to find them? It's how many days now? Five? Six? What exactly have you been doing?'

'Mr Struther,' Wexford said patiently, 'every officer in this area is working all out to find your parents and the other hostages. All leave has been cancelled. Five officers from the Regional Crime Squad have joined them.'

'Miracles we do at once,' said Masood, as if the aphorism was witty or new. 'The impossible will take a little longer.'

'We must hope it won't prove impossible, sir,' Wexford said. 'If there are no more questions perhaps you'd like to confer among yourselves for a while. There has been talk of forming a support group that might be helpful at the present stage.'

But they hadn't quite done with him. The other question he had almost believed wasn't inevitable was suddenly put by, of all people, Bibi.

'Bit funny, wasn't it, I mean, a bit peculiar, that your wife was the one to be released? I mean, how do you account for that?'

The kind of rage he must never show welled up

inside him, the kind that made hypertension an actual physical sensation, blood pressure pounding. He drew breath, said calmly and at that moment with perfect truth, 'I can't account for it. I can only hope that the truth about that and everything else will soon emerge.' Another long, deep breath and he added, 'You will of course all be prepared for a good deal of media attention. As far as the police are concerned, no restriction will be placed on anything you may choose to say to the press or any interviews you give.' He raised his head and looked at them all. 'Keep your spirits up. Be optimistic.' They stared back as if he had insulted them. 'Thank you for your attention,' he said.

He stepped down from the platform, feeling a strong desire, which must not be indulged, to get away from these people. They stood about, rather, he thought, as if they expected refreshments. Then a strange thing happened. The two mothers gravitated towards one another. Until then he could have sworn there had been no rapport between them, scarcely recognition of a shared plight, but now, as if the things he had said had brought home to them their common anxiety, they approached each other, eye meeting eye. And as if following stage directions on the same script, each reached out and they closed together in an embrace; they fell into each other's arms.

Men would never do that, he thought. So much of awkwardness, of embarrassment, had been left out of women. He was aware of a certain degree of embarrassment even in himself, something that surprised and very nearly amused him, while Masood looked the other way and Struther said something to the girl that made her giggle.

Wexford coughed tactfully. They would keep in

touch, he told them, and to remember that all this would break in the media by the morning.

Dora, fetched by Karen, sat in his office, a pleasanter place than the old gym. A good night's rest had improved her appearance, taken away that tired, drawn look. Some of her natural vivacity was back and she had dressed herself carefully in a skirt and top he hadn't seen before, blue and beige, flattering colours for her.

Burden was also in the room and the recorder had just been switched on. At first a little stiff and inhibited by the device, Dora now spoke as freely as if it hadn't been there.

'Chief Inspector Wexford has entered the room,' said Burden, 'at ten-forty-three.'

That seemed to amuse Dora who smiled. 'Where was I? Had I got to the first morning?'

'The morning of Wednesday, September the fourth,' Burden said.

'Right. I'll go on calling them The Driver, Gloves, Rubber Face and Tattoo, if that's all right.' Their smiling nods encouraged her. 'Oh, and the fifth one, the – what's the word? – not transvestite. Oh, yes, hermaphrodite.'

'What?' said Burden. 'You're not serious?'

'I don't know if it was a man or a woman. No faces, you see, and no voices. It was wise of them not to speak, wasn't it?'

'Clever villains don't speak,' Burden said. 'We know all about that round here. Go on, Dora.'

'The others wore black trainers but The Hermaphrodite wore those big clumping shoes with heavy tops and thick soles – are they Doc Marten's? – and I did wonder if that was to make the feet look bigger – if it was a woman, that is. He/she moved like a woman, a bit more graceful than the others, less deliberate, lighter – oh, I don't know, does one know?

'As soon as we were left alone that morning Owen Struther got hold of Ryan – well, sat beside him and started talking to him. It was this doctrine of escape of his and I think he picked on Ryan because although he wasn't yet fifteen, he was the only other male there. And Ryan is six feet tall. I didn't like it because, after all, he may be the size of a man but he's only a child still in many ways.

'Owen kept telling Ryan to be a man. It was up to them to defend us women because they were men, that was part of their role in life, and the most important thing was for Ryan never to show fear, and a lot of other rubbish like that. I left them to it, went into the washroom and did my best to wash myself all over. I spent a good deal of time in there trying to keep clean, and apart from anything else it was a way of passing the time.

'Roxane washed herself too and we both used my toothbrush. I told Kitty the washroom was free but she barely took any notice of me. She'd paced about earlier, pounded her fists on the walls and all that, but then she'd collapsed on to her bed, she'd had some coffee but no breakfast, and she seemed simply to have succumbed to despair.

'It was strange, her husband so active and determined and full of energy, so much the audacious officer in an old war film, and she as feeble as if she were actually going through a nervous breakdown. Well, there was the spitting and the bad language, but that was momentary and all in the past by then. You couldn't understand how two people who were married to each other and presumably had been for years and years, could have such different attitudes to life.'

'What were these escape plans?' Wexford asked.

'I'll come to that. I spent the morning talking to Roxane. She told me about her parents, her father is this quite rich entrepreneur. He was born in Karachi but came here as a child and worked his way up from nothing. She's very proud of him, but more sorry for her mother than proud. Her mother would never marry Mr Masood, though he wanted her to. Roxane could remember him still pressing her mother to marry him when she was ten years old. But Clare – she calls her Clare – put her career first and said marriage was obsolete, though apparently her career never amounted to much. Then Mr Masood married someone else and had more children. Roxane minds a lot about that, she's jealous, she doesn't like her stepmother, I'm afraid she gets a tremendous kick out of her stepmother being over-weight while she, of course, is slim as a reed.

'She told me about wanting to be a model and her father helping her, and then we got on to her claustrophobia. She said it came from her grand-mother – that is, Clare's mother – shutting her in a cupboard as a punishment when she was a toddler. I mean, if that's true it's quite terrible – one can hardly understand such a thing – but I did wonder myself if it could really be the cause. These psychological things are always more complex than that, aren't they?

'Anyway, I mustn't go on about her. She was claustrophobic, but she could just about manage in that room, only it did make me wonder how she'd get on if this modelling got off the ground and she had to stay in small hotel rooms. But maybe she'll be another Naomi Campbell and only stay in suites.

'They didn't bring us any lunch. They didn't come near us for hours. Owen Struther examined the whole room, taking Ryan round with him, paying particular attention to the window and the door. The

210

window was open but it was still impossible to see much, only the greenness and that grey something that was a sort of concrete step, and it was virtually impossible to reach out of it either. Owen's arm was too thick to get between the bars, but Ryan could squeeze his out. Not that there was any point in it. He put his arm through the bars as far as he could and managed to touch the wood of the rabbit hutch. He said he felt rain on his hand but we could already see it was raining ...'

'Could you hear the rain?' asked Slesar.

'You mean, drumming on the roof? No, nothing like that. I had the impression there was at least one and probably two storeys above the basement room. It wasn't a barn or a free-standing garage.

'I'll come back to Owen Struther. His idea was that the only possible method of escape would be while they were inside feeding us or fetching our tray and the door was unlocked. Closed but unlocked. He and Ryan would do it with Roxane to help them. I don't think he thought much of any potential strength I might have and, of course, his poor wife was hopeless.

'Roxane was to distract the attention of one of them. I don't know what he had in mind at that point, maybe make another attack and we all knew what that resulted in. But I don't think he'd have cared. He was obsessed. They would pick a time when The Hermaphrodite was one of the pair because he/she would be easier to handle. Incidentally, that would have been all very well if they'd been in and out every few minutes, but as I've said we hadn't seen them for hours. Still, the whole escape plan wasn't very practical. While Roxane was busy with one of them – being beaten up, I suppose – he would handle the other and Ryan would make his escape by way of the door.

211

'I intervened then and asked him if he realised Ryan was only fourteen. For one thing, he couldn't drive a car. What did he think he was going to do out there in the middle of God knows where? So the plan was changed and he was to go out through the door while Ryan and I handled the other one.

'In the event it didn't work. It was disastrous. But I'll come to that later, shall I?'

There are about twenty-five different varieties of wild blackberry growing in the British Isles. Most people think only one kind is to be found, but you have only to look at the difference in leaf formation, not to mention the size, shape and colour of the berries, to understand how they vary. The frail-looking young woman in a faded tracksuit who was picking blackberries, filling a wicker basket and eating as many as she picked, informed Martin Cook of these facts unasked.

'Interesting,' said Cook. 'What are you going to do with those?'

'Cook them with elderberries and crab-apples. Make an autumn compote.' She gave Burton Lowry an appraising look. Cook was used to that. His DC attracted black and white women alike. 'I don't suppose you've come here for a lesson in Elves' cuisine, have you?'

'I'm looking for Gary Wilson and Quilla Rice.'

'You won't find them here, they've gone. Had a bit of harassment in mind, did you? I'm afraid you'll have to make do with me.'

Cook ignored that. He wouldn't go on ignoring such provocation but he would for a while. 'And what might your name be?'

The young woman shrugged. 'It *might* be any number of things. My mother wanted to call me Tracy and my father liked Rosamund, but in fact

212

what they actually called me is Christine. Christine Colville. What's yours?' When she got no answer she said to Lowry, 'Would you like a blackberry?'

'No, thanks.'

Cook turned away and looked into the depths of the wood. The first tree-houses at Elder Ditches were just visible in the distance. He could see someone sitting in a clearing, apparently holding a musical instrument, but all was silent. 'Is there someone' – he hardly knew how to put it – 'well, in charge here?'

'You want me to take you to our leader?'

'If you've got one, yes.'

'Oh, we have one,' she said. 'The King of the Wood. Haven't you heard of him?'

The name came back to Cook. He remembered the statement to the *Kingsmarkham Courier*. 'He's called Conrad Tarling?'

She nodded. She picked up her basket, turned to them and beckoned. 'Follow me.' As she walked along she plucked bunches of elderberries from the bushes which filled about an acre before the tall trees were reached. Cook and Lowry walked along behind her.

'I'll come back for the crab-apples,' she said. 'I don't suppose you've ever heard of the King *in* the Wood, have you?'

'You just said it was Tarling.'

'Not that one,' she said scornfully. 'In Italy, by the lake of Nemi, in ancient times. This man was called the King in the Wood. He walked round and round this tree, nervous and afraid, armed with a sword, ever-watchful, because he knew men would come and fight him, would try to kill him, so that the killer could be the next King.'

'Oh, yes?' said Cook.

But Lowry said, 'He was a priest and a murderer, and sooner or later he would be murdered and the man who killed him would be priest in his stead. Such was the rule of the sacred grove.'

Christine Colville smiled but Cook said, 'The what?'

It sounded a lot like Sacred Globe to him. She eyed his puzzled face and began to laugh. Cook hadn't the faintest idea what she and Lowry had been talking about, but he was pretty sure she at least was sending him up. When they reached the trees, once they were among them, Christine Colville set down her basket, lifted her head and whistled. It was a whistle like a bird calling – pu-wee, pu-wee.

Faces appeared among the branches.

'Someone needs to talk to the King,' she said.

It was then that Conrad Tarling showed himself, as if called forth by the magic word 'King', the Open Sesame word. He emerged from a tree-house on to the platform on all fours. He was naked to the waist, his shaven head bluish and gleaming.

'Police,' said Cook. 'I'd like to talk to you.'

Tarling retreated behind the flap of tarpaulin which served his crow's nest as a front door. Cook was wondering what to do now when he reappeared, wrapped up this time in his all-enveloping sand-coloured cloak. For a moment Cook thought he would swing down from this considerable height, hand over hand on this branch and that, foot over foot on protuberances on the gnarled trunk. But instead he flicked his fingers at someone unseen and within minutes Christine and a man in shorts and anorak had propped a ladder up against the tree.

Face to face with Cook in the clearing, he was a good six inches taller. His head was rather small, his neck long. The face was an arresting one, hard, clean-cut, as if carved from wood.

Cook asked him about Gary Wilson and Quilla Rice but the King of the Wood wanted identification

214

before saying a word. Having gravely studied Cook's warrant card, he asked in a grand manner what the police wanted them for.

'To ask them a few questions.'

Tarling laughed. He had an audience now, half a dozen Elves squatting on the platforms of their tree-houses, listening, while Christine Colville and her companion in the anorak, sat close by, cross-legged on the grass. Tarling's voice was very deep and soft, yet ringing. They could probably hear what he said in Pomfret, Cook thought bitterly.

'That's what you always say. The words of totalitarianism. A few questions. A spot of interrogation. A smidgen of inquisition. And then the fun and games in the police cell – is that it?'

'Where do you people keep your vehicles?'

Another laugh, this time directed at the gallery. 'Ugly sort of word that, isn't it? "Vehicle". It's what I'd call a police word, like "proceeding" and "inquiry". Those of us who have *vehicles* keep them in a field kindly – very, very kindly, and I mean that – lent to us by Mr Canning, a farmer who is an angel of light compared with others of his kind and, like us, opposed to this damnable bypass.'

'I see. And where might this angel's field be?'

'Between Framhurst and Myfleet. Goland Farm. But Quilla and Gary didn't use it. They haven't a *vehicle*. They must have hitched, they usually do.' Picking up his basket and turning his attention to an elder tree, Tarling said less aggressively, 'They'll return in a week or so. For your information, as you'd doubtless put it your *good* self, they've gone to the SPECIES rally in Wales and they'll soon be back. No one believes this environmental assessment is the end, you know. Things don't happen so easily as that.'

'And you?'

'I beg your pardon?'

'Do you have a' – Cook rejected the offending word – 'a car?'

If Cook was unacquainted with the works of Lewis Carroll, Lowry was not. Wexford too would have recognised the quotation but to Cook it was gibberish. He turned away in disgust. Tarling's words and the tree people's consequent laughter pursued him.

> ' "I have answered three questions and that is
>   enough,"
> Said his father, "Don't give yourself airs.
> Do you think I can listen all day to such stuff?
> Be off or I'll kick you downstairs." '

Walking back to the car, he said to Lowry, 'I'm getting a bit pissed off with you pulling your university rank on me.'

'What did I do?' said Lowry indignantly.

Barry Vine was in the car with Pemberton. They had been at the Savesbury Deeps camp but appeared to have learnt less than Cook had. Half the tree people had gone, many of them on other pilgrimages to seek out other violations and injustices.

'Your words?' said Cook belligerently.

'Theirs,' said Vine with a shrug. 'I'm off to Framhurst, have a cup of tea in the village.'

A surprised glance was the response to that. Vine explained.

'I'd like to know where they get that muck from they call non-lactic soymilk. I mean, can you buy it in a supermarket or is it only supplied to restaurants as against retail outlets? And when we've refreshed ourselves Jim and I will go and have a word with Farmer Canning.'

Nicky Weaver knew a lot about Brendan Royall's Winnebago by this time. She knew its registration number, that its colour was white, that it was three years old and that he was usually but not invariably alone in it.

The best piece of information she had about it was that it had been seen that morning on the M25, heading for the M2, by a police car on speed control. That rather reduced the impact of the piece of news she had just had phoned in from the Elder Ditches camp by DS Cook, that Royall might be found at a SPECIES rally in Wales. Of course, she had checked out the rally and discovered it was to be in Neath, near Glencastle Forest, and due to start on Tuesday. Please God, they would have found those hostages by Tuesday . . .

If Royall was planning to go there he had been heading in the wrong direction. It wasn't likely he would go near his parents but she couldn't take that for granted. On the other hand, it was practically certain he would pay a visit to the Panicks.

She walked among the desks in the old gym, looking at computer screens, watching for anything new that might have come in. Everyone knew about the SPECIES rally by now. It was an important event in the protestors' calendar. Should the force be there, a presence, among all those activists?

She glanced out of one of the long windows on the car park side. A car was coming in that she didn't recognise, a small white Mercedes, probably come to fetch Dora Wexford. Back in Myringham, at the Regional Crime Squad, she would have known every car that came in and out, and would have questioned any unfamiliar ones. They were nearly all unfamiliar here . . . No harm in noting down the registration number though. Better safe than sorry. She did so as the car turned the corner round the back of the building and disappeared from sight.

'Let's just get this straight,' said Burden. 'Gloves, the one in gloves, you saw less of him than of any of the others. You saw him on the Wednesday morning at breakfast, but not again till you were due to leave. Is that right?'

'Not quite. I saw him on the Wednesday but not again till the Friday, only it was at midday on the Friday.'

'Right. Now food. What did they give you to eat? No, I'm perfectly serious. Food could be a clue as to where you were.'

'Do you mean, what did they give us that Wednesday evening?'

'For a start, yes.'

'I don't think it will be of much help. There were three large pizzas, cooked but cold, some more of the white bread, five slices of processed cheese and five apples. The apples were badly bruised. Oh, and more instant coffee and that non-lactic stuff. If we wanted anything else to drink we just got it ourselves from the water tap. And since we didn't have a cup or a glass or anything we had to put our mouths under the tap.'

Dora drank some of the tea Archbold had brought in to them and took a chocolate biscuit with the appreciation of someone who has recently subsisted on a diet of cold pizza and sliced bread.

'It was Tattoo and The Hermaphrodite that evening. Tattoo and Rubber Face were probably the strongest and the most . . . well, the most ruthless of them, or that's the impression I had, but The Hermaphrodite was certainly the weakest, and I could see the moment they came in what Owen had in mind.

'What Roxane did, it wasn't deliberate, I mean it wasn't part of a plot, it was just spontaneous. She jumped up and said to Tattoo that she wanted to talk

218

to him. "I want to talk to you," she said. And then she said, "And I want you to talk to us." He just stood there, looking at her. Or I suppose he was looking at her – you can't tell when a person's wearing one of those hoods.

' "You've left us all day without food," she said, or something like that. "You've left us all day without anything to eat. It's outrageous what you're doing," she said. "What have we done? We are innocent people. We have done no one any harm. You give us hardly anything to drink," she said, "and this is the first food we've had for ten hours. What is it you're doing?" she said. "What do you want?" He didn't say a word, just stood there, very close to her.

'The Hermaphrodite was holding the tray, a large, heavy tray with all that food on it. I could see Owen keying himself up and Ryan too, poor kid, playing at adventures. The door was shut but it wasn't locked. Roxane – oh, she's a courageous girl – she looked into Tattoo's face, his mask, it was about six inches from her face, and she said, "Answer me. Answer me, you bastard!"

'He hit her. He hit her as hard as he could across the head. That was when his sleeve fell back, he was wearing a shirt with quite loose sleeves, and I saw the tattoo, a butterfly on his left forearm. As Roxane fell over on the bed Ryan made a rush for The Hermaphrodite. Well, The Hermaphrodite dropped that tray and food went everywhere, pizzas upside down on the nearest bed, apples rolling across the floor and the tray making a terrific crash. Ryan had hold of him/her by the shoulders, Tattoo sprang round and pulled out a gun. Owen had got the door open but he never actually got out.

'Everything happened at once, it's quite hard to sort it all out, but the gun went off. I still can't tell you if it was real or not. It made a loud bang and

219

whatever was fired out of it went into the woodwork round the window. Would a replica gun make a noise like that?'

'It might,' said Burden. 'Any sort of gun makes a noise.'

'I don't actually think it was aimed at anyone. Kitty was screaming her head off. She was lying on her bed, drumming her fists into the mattress and screaming. Maybe it was that or maybe it was the gun, but Owen hesitated and you know what they say about the person who hesitates. The Hermaphrodite aimed a kick at Ryan, a really high, hard kick, and it caught him in the stomach and sent him flying, clutching at his body. Roxane was groaning, holding her face. I didn't do anything, I'm afraid, I just sat there. That gun going off had rather mesmerised me.

'Tattoo must have had handcuffs with him because he got them on to Owen. It was quite remarkable the way while this was all going on neither of those two spoke a word. Owen was shouting and cursing, threatening them with all sorts of punishment to come, "They'll shut you up in high security for ever," that kind of thing. Ryan was rolling on the floor whimpering, Roxane was groaning and Kitty was screaming, but those two were utterly silent. I can tell you, it was sinister, it was a lot more effective than anything they could have said.

'It dehumanised them, you see. People are people because they speak and these two had become machines. They were science fiction creatures. Anyway, you don't want the philosophy. I'll tell you what happened next. I suppose they always carried handcuffs because they put a pair on Ryan and another pair on Kitty who sobbed while they did it. Tattoo manhandled Roxane into the washroom and locked the door.

'That frightened me because I knew how she felt

about enclosed spaces. But I thought that if I told them that, it would make things worse, not better. So I said nothing. Tattoo stayed with us while The Hermaphrodite went away and came back with hoods for the Struthers. The hoods were put on and the Struthers were taken away and that was the last I ever saw of them. It was at about half-past seven on the Wednesday evening.'

Burden interrupted the narrative once more. 'You never saw them again?'

Dora shook her head, realised this movement would be recorded and said. 'No, I never did.' She went on, 'But I've no reason to think any harm came to them. I think they were just taken to somewhere Tattoo thought would be safer. Kitty was sobbing all the time they were being taken out of there.

'Ryan was more or less all right, just very shaken. Later on a terrific bruise came up on his stomach. He got himself up and said something about knowing better than to have tried that on. But I was extremely worried about Roxane. There was an awful silence from behind that door and I thought perhaps she'd fainted. I considered trying to break it down. Have you ever tried to break a door down?'

They all had. All had succeeded but it hadn't been easy. It hadn't been like on television where a shove and a kick will do it.

Wexford said, 'Did you try?'

'Yes, because the silence didn't go on. She started screaming and pounding on the door. It wasn't like Kitty's screaming, this was real phobic terror. I put my shoulder to the door and I kicked it. Maybe I'd have succeeded but after a moment or two Rubber Face and Tattoo came in. They moved me out of the way, Rubber Face just lifted me and dumped me on my bed. Don't look like that, Reg. I wasn't hurt.

'They let Roxane out but not at once. It was nasty

221

what happened. They looked at each other, those two – well, the heads in the masks turned – and I just had this feeling they knew and they, or one of them, was enjoying it. They'd discovered her fear of enclosed spaces and they were *pleased*. They stood there listening to her pounding on the door and her pleading.

'Eventually, they unlocked the door. She staggered out and fell on her bed, sobbing bitterly. It was awful, it really was dreadful. But life in there had to go on. I hugged her and tried to comfort her.

'Then Rubber Face and Tattoo found my handbag and Kitty's – Roxane didn't have one, they don't at that age – and took them with them and went away, I don't know why, having left Ryan handcuffed. The handcuffs didn't come off him till next morning and he was very uncomfortable and in pain.

'We just settled down, the three of us, to make the best of things. I picked up the food that wasn't filthy or otherwise ruined; the pizzas were all right and I washed the apples. I got them to sit down with me and eat as best they could and then we talked. We played a sort of game, each of us to tell a true story about a member of our families. It was dark, you see, they never brought the light bulbs back.

'Well, I started the ball rolling by telling a story and then Roxane told one about her aunt meeting Gershwin when she was a child. It was in New York. And Ryan told one about his father winning some county athletics championship. Still, you won't want to know any of this. We all went to sleep. Even Roxane did, though she was in pain with her face. It was very swollen and black with bruises, and a cut on her temple was bleeding. They were to take her away next day but I didn't know that then.

'I was the only one who hadn't been hurt in some

222

way and that made me feel guilty. Ridiculous really, but I suppose people do feel guilt in my situation . . .'

DC Edward Hennessy went out to the car park just before four. His car happened to be parked alongside Chief Inspector Wexford's. Between the two cars, on the tarmac, stood a dark-brown fibre suitcase, with the initials on its side: D.M.W., and beside it two large, full plastic carriers, one green, one yellow.

Hennessy didn't touch any of it. He went back inside, knocked on the door of Wexford's office and told him. Dora Wexford was still there, taking a break from recording. She jumped up. 'That has to be my case,' she said. 'And it sounds like my parcels.'

She was right. The carriers contained her presents to Sheila: babyclothes, a shawl, a kimono for a nursing mother, two new novels, a flagon of perfume and one of body lotion. She identified the case as hers and watched while it was opened to reveal her undisturbed, carefully folded clothes. On top of them was a sheet of paper, on which were printed the words of Sacred Globe's next message.

No more delays, please. The media must be told at once. This is the first step in our negotiations. We are Sacred Globe, saving the world.

Chapter 15

The contents of the suitcase were, as far as she could tell, as Dora had packed them. 'This is like what they ask you at airports,' she joked. 'Did you pack your case yourself? Has it been left unattended at any time? It's yes to the first one and heaven only knows to the second.'

'I think I saw the car it came in,' Nicky Weaver told Wexford. 'A white Mercedes. For some reason – God knows what guardian angel inspired me – I took down the number. It's L570 LOO.'

'That'll be the car they brought Dora home in. The L-something-five-seven car.'

'Cheeky bunch, aren't they?' Burden sounded half admiring. 'Not your usual villains.'

'Let's hope they're too clever for their own good.'

'I don't like it,' said Wexford, and when they looked at him inquiringly, 'I don't like their jokes and I don't like it that our decision to lift the embargo coincides with their demand to lift it. It can't be changed now, but it looks as if we're complying with what they ask.'

Dora had been having a cup of tea with Karen Malahyde. She had at first seemed awestricken by the reappearance of her suitcase and parcels, almost as if it evinced supernatural powers on the part of Sacred Globe, and her husband recalled what she had said about science fiction characters who were not quite human. He sat down opposite her and the recorder was started.

'Can we come to Thursday morning, Dora?'

'Well, I'm still on Wednesday night really. Something happened on Wednesday night. Two of them came in while we were asleep, or they thought we were asleep. Roxane and Ryan were, and I pretended I was; I thought it was safer.

'I saw and heard the door open and two of them came in. I think it was Gloves and Tattoo but I can't be sure. They were in their usual hoods. That was when I shut my eyes, so I don't know what they were there for, what they did, but they were wandering about in there for some minutes. Before they left they came and stood over us, checking we were asleep, I suppose. You know how you can always tell something like that, you can sense it.

'On Thursday morning,' Dora began. 'Roxane's face was dreadfully bruised and her left eye was quite closed up. I know it shouldn't, but it somehow made it worse, doing that to such a beautiful girl.

'Rubber Face and The Driver brought our breakfast. It was more white bread, dry bread, and a slice of some sort of tinned meat, the cheapest sort like spam, and three packets of crisps. That must have been to sustain us through the day because again we got nothing else till the evening. Nothing to drink either but water from the tap.

'But they did come back for the tray. Roxane didn't shout at them this time. She just started asking when they were going to let us go, what they wanted, how long this was going to go on. You have to understand that we didn't know they called themselves Sacred Globe. We didn't know they wanted the bypass stopped or their threats or anything. And Roxane desperately wanted to know. Of course neither of them answered. As I've said, they never spoke. They never even seemed to hear, though it's hard to tell a thing like that when someone's face and head are covered up.

'In the middle of the afternoon Roxane began hammering on the door. Ryan had been very subdued after being thrown on the ground the evening before, and his stomach hurt, but once she'd started he helped her. They banged on that door and kicked it and this went on for a good half-hour.

'At last the door was opened and Rubber Face came in with Tattoo. I was very frightened, I don't mind admitting it, because I thought they were going to beat Roxane up and maybe Ryan too. But nothing like that happened. Tattoo simply got hold of Roxane and pinned her arms behind her. She screamed and yelled but he took no notice. He handcuffed her like that with her hands behind her. Rubber Face manhandled Ryan out of the way and when he tried to put up a bit of resistance, grabbed him and locked him in the washroom.

'They had a hood with them and they put it over Roxane's head and took her away. They just took her away, I've no idea where or what happened to her. She spoke to me, she said, "Goodbye, Dora," through the hood, it was sort of muffled but that's what she said. I never saw her again.' Dora paused. She shrugged a little, shaking her head. 'I never saw her again,' she repeated. 'They may have put her with the Struthers, wherever they were, I just don't know. All I can say is that about ten minutes afterwards for the first time I heard footsteps overhead, but that may have had no connection with where they put Roxane.'

'One set of footsteps or more than one?'

'I don't know. More than one set, I think. Ryan was let out of the washroom after an hour. Tattoo and The Driver came in and let him out and after

226

that he and I were alone. We just sat there and played word games. I don't think I've ever in my life so longed for something as I longed for a pad of paper and a pencil – or, come to that, Scrabble or Monopoly. After a time we just talked. He told me things I don't think he'd ever told anyone before.

'His father had been killed in the Falklands war. They'd been married just three months, his father and mother. She was pregnant when the news came and he was born seven months later. The reason she was in hospital was to have a cone biopsy – that's the operation where they take off a bit of the cervix because of pre-cancerous signs. It was the second she'd had. She was going to get married again and she wanted more children – she's only thirty-six now – but it's not likely she'll have any after all that. I'm sorry, I don't suppose you want to hear all this, it's not relevant. It just seemed to me a heavy burden to lay on a boy of fourteen, confiding it all to him.

'Anyway, he confided in *me*, and that's how we passed the evening. They were very late bringing our breakfast on Friday morning. I suppose they'd seen to the others first, I mean to Owen and Kitty and Roxane, wherever they were. It was Tattoo and Rubber Face. They brought us bread rolls, very stale, jam in those individual containers and an apple each.

'Ryan and I had decided we'd ask them what had happened to Roxane, though we didn't think we'd get an answer. We did ask and we didn't get an answer. I think that was the longest day of my life. There was nothing to do. Ryan went completely silent, maybe he thought he'd said too much the evening before, maybe he was embarrassed. Whatever it was, he didn't answer me when I spoke to him. He lay on his back on his bed, staring at the ceiling. For the first time I seriously began thinking

227

we'd never be released, we'd go on like this for weeks and then we'd be killed.

'Gloves appeared at lunch-time. It was the first time we'd seen him since the Wednesday morning. I thought it was Rubber Face at first, but his build was much slighter than Rubber Face's. Tattoo was with him. That was when I saw Gloves's eyes. I said I only saw the eyes of one of them, didn't I? Well, it was Gloves's eyes.

'The holes in his hood must have been bigger than in those worn by the others. Anyway, I could see his eyes quite clearly. They were brown, a clear, deep brown. He came close to me for a moment, peered at me as if he was trying to ... well, verify something about me, and that's when I saw his eyes. But it's not much help, is it? I suppose half the population have brown eyes.

'It was that evening they let me go. I've told you all about that. Oh, they fed us first if that's of any interest. Tinned spaghetti in tomato sauce, cold of course, bread, more jam. Tattoo and The Hermaphrodite brought it. I was preparing for another night in there when they came in and took me out. Ryan was left there alone. As I've said, I've no idea what happened to the others.'

Wexford got up as Barry Vine put his head round the door and asked if he could have a word. 'It's about food, sir,' he said when they were outside. 'And it's all pretty negative. You remember the non-lactic soymilk at the Framhurst teashop?'

'Of course I do.'

'I don't know why, but I got it into my head that if that place was the only outlet for the stuff in the south of England ... Anyway, forget it, because you can buy it everywhere. You can buy it in supermarkets. Thanks to Sunday opening, I've done a pretty thorough check on that. You can buy it at the

Crescent in Kingsmarkham and every one of their other branches too. Nation-wide.'

'Another lead bites the dust,' said Wexford.

In the Chief Constable's living-room in his house outside Myfleet, Wexford sat eating pistachio nuts and drinking a single malt. Donaldson had driven him there, would drive him back and was at this moment sitting in the car eating a ham sandwich and drinking a can of Lilt. No one had time for proper meals any more.

Wexford was there to talk about the release of the hostage story to the media. In the morning. Tomorrow morning. But they had agreed on how it should be done, how limited it should be and how free, the hour of release and the defensive measures they would take. And now Montague Ryder wanted to talk about Dora. He had listened to the tapes, all of them, and had heard the last one twice.

'She's done very well, Reg, superlatively well. She's an observant woman. But yet . . .'

I do not like 'but yet', reflected Wexford, quoting someone or other. Cleopatra, he thought. He said quickly, 'I know. There's a lot there and at the same time there isn't much.' But could you have done as well? Could I? In a misogynistic way, normally quite foreign to him, he thought how most women he knew would have collapsed under Dora's ordeal, caved in, been stricken dumb. 'They were clever, sir,' he said. 'Clever and cocky. They must have been, to take the risk of letting her go.'

'Yes. Odd that, wasn't it? We still think it was because they found out who she was?'

Wexford nodded, but dubiously. The Macallan bottle was raised along with the Chief Constable's eyebrows and he was tempted, but he said no. He could have gone on drinking all evening, but what was the point? He had to stay sensible tonight and be alert tomorrow.

'You know what I'm thinking, Reg?'

'I think so, sir.'

'Hypnosis. Would she consent?'

It was a method, newly fashionable, of extracting information and observations which lay buried, which would probably remain buried, unless unearthed by means other than the subject's own volition and intent. Wexford hadn't much experience of it. He knew, or had heard, that it often worked. He felt a sudden violent revulsion against putting Dora through it. Why should she have to suffer this ... this *assault*? This taking away of her free will, this indignity.

'I don't know if she'll consent,' he said. Surprisingly, he had no idea what her reaction would be. Horror or interest, recoil or even attraction? 'I must tell you' – this was very hard to say, to express, to a man of so much higher rank and power, but he wouldn't sleep if he didn't say it – 'I must tell you, sir, that I'm not prepared to persuade her.'

Montague Ryder laughed, but pleasantly. 'Suppose I ask her?' he said. 'Suppose I ask her tonight and then, if she agrees, we'll get hold of the psychologist to hypnotise her tomorrow? Would you mind that?'

'No, I wouldn't mind,' said Wexford.

Chapter 16

Television stole the press's thunder and the Kingsmarkham kidnap story appeared on ITN's news at eight-forty-five and BBC1's at nine-fifteen, prefaced in each case by the words, 'News is just coming in . . .'

By the later time Dora was in bed with a gin and tonic and a hint from her husband that Monday could be the day of her encounter with a hypnotherapist. Wexford regretted now that the hostages' names had been released, or rather that the name of a former hostage had. But even he was unprepared for his doorbell ringing at seven in the morning and for the arrival of three reporters and four cameramen on his doorstep.

The two daily newspapers he took had already come. Both used the story as their front-page lead. Somehow, one of them had got hold of a photograph of Roxane Masood, and this, with pictures of the bypass site, a facsimile of the first Sacred Globe letter and a picture of himself – the hated portrait of him all smiles, holding up a beer tankard, that they kept in their archives – dominated the broadsheet. He was glancing through the text when the doorbell struck his eardrums with a reverberating peal.

Luckily he was dressed. He could imagine another photograph featuring the crimson velvet dressing-gown. Before he opened the door he knew who it was. The chain was on, he had put it on for some reason ever since Dora had come back, and the door opened only six inches. His grandmother, a Pomfret native, used to open her front door a couple of inches to unwelcome callers and snap, 'Not today, thank you.' He had been very small when she died but he remembered, though he restrained himself from repeating her words now. 'Press conference at the police station at 10 a.m.,' he said.

Flash bulbs went off and cameras clicked. 'I'd like an exclusive interview with Dora first,' one of them said impertinently.

And I'd like your head on a plate. 'Good-morning,' he said and shut the door. The phone rang. He snapped into the receiver in his grandmother's words, 'Not today, thank you,' and pulled out the plug.

A photographer had got round the back and was looking through his kitchen window. For the first time he was glad of the 'Roman' blinds Dora had had put up the previous summer. He pulled them down, drew curtains, made the tea, poured a cup for Dora and a mug for himself, and took them upstairs. She was sitting up in bed with the radio on. News of the Kingsmarkham Kidnap – the title had been coined and would be kept – had displaced everything else: Palestine, Bosnia, party political wrangling and the Princess of Wales.

'Is there a ladder in the garage?' he asked her.

'I believe so. Why on earth do you ask?'

'Show no surprise if a head appears at the window any time now. The media are here.'

'Oh, Reg!'

On the previous evening the Chief Constable had been to see her. She was very tired, had been lying on the sofa in her dressing-gown, but even though she had been warned of his coming, hadn't dressed. Wexford was glad she hadn't. He welcomed her independence of spirit and expected a further show of it when the request was made. She would say no. She would say it politely, even apologetically, but she wouldn't agree to some shrink putting her in a trance.

She said yes.

And now she was saying it again, even apparently looking forward to it. 'I must get up. I'm being hypnotised this morning.'

As far as he could remember, there had never been so many press men and women in Kingsmarkham. Not for a serial killer. Not even for the murder of Davina Flory and her family. They had parked their cars everywhere and traffic wardens were out in force, taking numbers, leaving tickets. Wheel-clamping would soon start.

He could picture the invasions of the cottage in Pomfret, Mrs Peabody's little house in Stowerton and the onslaught on Andrew Struther at Savesbury House. He could picture it without going to see. They must defend themselves as best they could, and perhaps it was all to the good, maybe this tremendous publicity would help.

Already, at nine, the phone lines into Kingsmarkham police station were jammed by callers with information. He looked over the shoulder of one of the busy phone operators at the computer screen on which everything that came in was recorded. Roxane Masood hadn't been abducted, she had been seen in Ilfracombe; Ryan Barker was dead and his body would be released for £20,000. The Struthers had been seen in Florence, in Athens, in Manchester, looking out of an upper window of a factory in Leeds, on a boat in Poole harbour. Dora Wexford had never been abducted but had been planted as a spy, a decoy, a detective. Roxane Masood was going to be married in Barbados to the son of a woman who would tell them the whole story for a sum to be negotiated . . .

Wexford sighed. All these people's calls would have to be followed up and all of them would either be mistaken or malicious. Unless, of course, one was authentic, just one provided a lead . . .

He had got Dora out of the house, a big hat and tent-shaped coat concealing most of her, into a car driven by Karen Malahyde. After what she had been through she didn't want anything covering her face and he hadn't argued. The press had run after the car for a bit, taking photographs. When he came back from the old gym, where he left her listening to her own tapes and checking what she had said, he found Brian St George waiting for him.

The editor of the *Kingsmarkham Courier* was deeply aggrieved. In the same grey pinstripe and dirty white sweatshirt, he came up to Wexford, pushing his face close to him. His breath smelt of periodontal gum disease. 'You don't like me, do you?'

'What makes you say that, Mr St George?' Wexford retreated a couple of feet.

'You lifted the embargo on this story on the worst possible bloody day of the week for me. Lift it on a Sunday and I've got five days before the *Courier* comes out. *Five days*. The story'll be dead by then.'

'I'm sure I hope so,' Wexford said.

'You did it out of spite. It might just as well have been last Thursday or have waited till this Wednesday, but no, you have to do it on a Sunday.'

Wexford appeared to reflect. 'Saturday would have been worse.' As the red mounted fiercely up in St George's face, he said imperturbably, 'You'll have to excuse me, I have work to do. You'll no doubt be getting a lot of calls from the public, even though you haven't the advantages of the nationals, and we'd like everything passed directly here, please.'

234

Craig Tarling, older brother of Conrad Tarling, was currently serving a ten-year prison sentence for his animal rights activities.

'It's not a common name,' Nicky Weaver said. 'I spotted it on the computer and checked him out.'

Damon Slesar raised his eyebrows. They were on their way to Marrowgrave Hall and he was driving. 'A man's not responsible for what his relations do,' he said. 'My father grows fruit and veg on the old bypass and my mum spins yarn out of animal hairs. People send her their pets' fur in bags.'

'There's nothing wrong with that. It's perfectly respectable.' Nicky spoke rather sharply. Her mother worked in a greengrocer's part-time – in the rest of her time she helped look after the Weaver children – and Nicky didn't like his tone. 'And so is fruit-growing. You shouldn't talk like that about your family.'

'OK, OK, sorry I spoke. You know me, my wit runs away with me. What did this brother do?'

'Conspired – master-minded might be the better word – to set off fifty firebombs. His targets were rabbit and chicken farms, butchers' shops, an agricultural college and an agency selling tickets for circuses, among others. I expect he'd have targeted ostrich farms, only this was five years ago and there weren't any then.'

'What went wrong? I mean wrong for him and right for law and order?'

'A shop assistant thought it strange for one man to buy sixty timing devices and told the police.'

On the horizon, standing out against a yellow and black sunset, stood ruined Saltram House where, long ago, Burden had found the body of a missing child in one of the fountain cisterns. Nicky asked Damon if he had ever heard that story, it had been about the time Burden's first wife had died, but he shook his head, his brown eyes contrite.

The car turned into the drive. In the pale sunshine of morning Marrowgrave Hall looked no less forbidding and seemed more than ever closed up, secured against the outside world. Nicky got out of the car and stood for a moment staring at the façade, at the windows and the brickwork in its shades of dried blood and baked clay.

'What is it?' Damon asked.

'Nothing. It just seems such an unlikely place for those Panicks to live in. I'd expect a nice big seaside bungalow at Rustington.'

Dressed up for Sunday, Bob in a dark and shiny suit, Patsy in a flowered silk tent, the Panicks had been at table. Perhaps they always were and when they got up it was only for the clearing away of one meal and to begin the preparation of the next. Patsy carried a large white linen napkin to the door with her and was still wiping her mouth when she opened it. Once more she lumbered ahead of them down the passage towards the kitchen. The smell today was of a breakfast, the kind seaside cafés call a 'full English breakfast', served almost late enough to be brunch, but Panicks no doubt made their own gastronomic rules. At the table, opposite Bob Panick, sat the woman called Freya, Elf, tree-house-building expert and recent resident of the Elder Ditches camp.

She made a strange contrast with her hosts, for she was as thin as they were fat and dressed as unconventionally as they were formal. Face and hands were an unhealthy waxen white but what the rest of her was like it was impossible to tell. She was swathed from head to foot in something like a very old faded sari, frayed and tattered, which, bundled round her though it was, still provided no illusion of adding bulk to her emaciated shape. But she was eating as heartily as the Panicks. In front of her was a plateful of bacon, scrambled eggs, fried bread, fried sausages, fried mushrooms, tomatoes and potato crisps, identical to those set before Bob and Patsy.

She showed no sign of alarm at their entry, unless giving Damon Slesar a long assessing glance was the result of fear. More likely she fancied him, as Nicky said to him afterwards. Patsy said she was sure they wouldn't mind if she went back to her meal and wasn't it funny the police always seemed to call while they were eating?

'Hungry, I dare say,' said Bob with his mouth full. 'Give them something to keep the pangs away. There's a nice bit of ham from last night and if they don't mind carving it themselves, so as not to interfere with your meal *again*, Patsy, that would go down a treat with some of that granary loaf and Branston pickle.'

'Nothing for us, thank you,' said Nicky.

Damon said, in a way she thought uncalled-for, that it was very kind of them, and then he redeemed himself by asking Freya if she was a friend of the Panicks.

Patsy, helping herself to more bacon from the pan, answered for her. 'She is *now*. I hope anyone who comes here and enjoys our hospitality can be termed a friend, don't you, Bob?'

'You're right there, Patsy. Is there another sausage going?'

'Of course there is. And give Freya one. As a matter of fact, Freya is Brendan's friend. A special friend, is that right, Freya?' The woman's tiny eyes twinkled deep in the piled flesh, like lights at the ends of tunnels. 'Brendan brought her here last evening, just had a quick bite and then had to be on his way.'

Nicky remembered Mrs Panick's undertaking to

237

let her know if and when Brendan Royall turned up. She had been surprised by that promise and wasn't surprised it hadn't been honoured. 'On his way where?' she said.

The woman called Freya reacted as if her patience, sorely tried for the past ten minutes, had come to breaking point. She threw down knife and fork, sending a splatter of fat to strike the centre of the napkin that was tucked inside Bob Panick's shirt collar. 'Why can't you leave him alone? What's he done? Nothing. Do you know what a visitor from Outer Space would think if she came to this planet? She'd think you were all psychotic. Not only do you fuck up the whole planet, but you punish people who try to stop it being fucked.'

Bob Panick shook his head almost sorrowfully and helped himself to bread.

His wife said conversationally to no one in particular, 'That's what they mean on the TV when they say the next programme contains strong language. Have you noticed that?' She smiled, eyes twinkling, at Damon Slesar. 'I always take it as a sign to come out here and get us a cup of tea and a packet of bikkies. Brendan,' she said to Nicky, 'has just popped over to the bypass site, dear.'

'Why do you have to tell them that?' shouted Freya. 'What's your motive, that's what I'd like to know? You don't have to talk to them, you know. You've done nothing. Brendan's done nothing. Brendan never talks to them, he doesn't speak, he just stays silent, you want to take a leaf out of his book. Why d'you let them fuck you over? Brendan wouldn't say a word to them, he wouldn't utter.'

'So where is Brendan now?' This was Nicky, being patient.

'Something about going to have a look at a – what was it, Bob?'

Bob Panick considered, rubbed his forehead. 'Folks from Europe, that Common Market, some environment they're making. He's gone in the Winnebago.'

The environmental assessment. Yes, Brendan Royall would want to take a first-hand view of that, would probably photograph the proceedings, having parked at Goland Farm.

The meadows here were steep hillsides on which sheep grazed, the hedges tight and dark-green and the woods clustering, and the sudden sight of a field packed with cars, vans and trailers, few of them in pristine condition and most downright shabby, jarred the imagination. The farmhouse that they expected to be a picturesque half-timbered building looked instead like a converted chapel.

Such conversions had become quite common in the south of England as congregations grew smaller. They provided large, comfortable dwelling houses, if you didn't mind church windows and what Wexford called an 'odour of sanctity'. This one, called Goland Farm, was of red brick with a grey slate roof and a lot of unsuitable window-boxes. Any of its shabby outbuildings might have been the original farmhouse, wedged now between tall, uncompromising silos.

Damon parked by the gate, they walked in among the tree people's cars and there they found Barry Vine contemplating an empty Winnebago.

A fax had arrived from the Neath police, a Chief Inspector Gwenlian Dean. Crowds were gathering for the SPECIES conference, but so far everything was proceeding in orderly fashion. The rally was to be conducted in the open, a good many delegates had arrived in caravans or with tents, but the hierarchy were staying in an hotel where the AGM would take place on the following morning. Gary and Quilla had not yet arrived or had not been located. Gwenlian Dean would be in touch again as soon as she had anything to report.

Wexford went into the old gym to assist the Chief Constable at the press conference. They photographed him as he walked in and he wasn't sorry. Anything to replace that beer tankard picture that constantly reared up to haunt him.

Montague Ryder gave a reasonable, measured and civilised explanation of what had happened and what was being done.

'You must have some idea where they are.' This was a stiletto-eyed young woman with long blonde hair. 'After all this time you must have some clue.'

'We have a good many ideas.' Wexford tried to speak calmly, to follow the Chief Constable's example. 'It must be obvious that we can't disclose any of these ideas at present.'

'Are they in the London area or somewhere in the south of England?'

'I can't answer that.'

And the inevitable question that maddened him, asked this time by a fat reporter, male, in a grey suit and with shoulder-length shaggy grey hair. 'How come it was your wife they let go?'

Ryder answered for him, simply, 'We don't know.'

'Yeah, well, they must have had a reason. Was it they found out she was your wife? D'you reckon they were scared to hold on to her? She wasn't ill, was she? I mean, not a diabetic, not someone takes regular medication?'

'Oh, no,' said Wexford, calm again. 'Nothing like that. Nothing at all.'

Burden had Christine Colville in his office, believing correctly that if she saw the inside of an interview

240

room she would send at once for a lawyer. She was less aggressive and superior with him than she had been with DS Cook and seemed more than willing to give him Conrad Tarling's history.

'You an anthropologist, are you, Miss Colville?'

She gave him a long look, the kind usually called withering. 'I'm an actress. That doesn't mean I have to be ignorant about everything but dramatic art.'

He nodded. 'Resting, I presume?'

'You do presume. I'm not resting, as a matter of fact. Apart from taking part in this protest *with my friends* I'm acting in Jeffrey Godwin's play at the Weir Theatre.'

It came back to him. Wexford had mentioned it. A play about the bypass, the environment, the activists. What was it called? He wasn't going to ask her. Ah, yes, *Extinction.*

'Have a big part, do you?'

'The female lead.'

The only love affair of his life – it had happened between the death of his first wife and his second marriage – had been with an actress. But she had been beautiful, a white-bodied, red-headed woman with a strawberry mouth and grape-green eyes. Not at all like this small, compact creature, short and sturdy with a round brown face and dark, wiry hair, cut to within an inch of her scalp.

'You were telling me about the King of the Wood.'

'From which you distracted me,' she said, quick as a flash. 'Conrad's family live in Wiltshire. Sometimes when he goes to see them he walks. It's eighty miles from here but he walks. People used to do that a hundred years ago, they used to walk huge distances but no one does now. Only Conrad.'

'He's got a car,' said Burden sceptically.

'He hardly ever uses it. Mostly he lends it to others. Conrad's a sort of saint, you know.'

King, god, leader, and now saint. 'Right. Go on.'

'His brother Colum's in a wheelchair. He'll never walk again. He gave his strength and his *mobility* for the cause of animals. And the other brother Craig's in prison for his own part in the struggle.'

'Sure,' said Burden. 'He was going to blow up a couple of hundred innocent people.'

'People are never innocent.' In her words and her look he recognised the authentic voice of fanaticism. 'Only animals are innocent. Guilt is exclusively the attribute of mankind.' She tapped her fist on his desk. 'Conrad has never had a job,' she said, as if speaking of some spectacular achievement and, slightly amending what she had said, 'He has never been gainfully employed. But he survives by his own efforts.'

'Like Gary Wilson and Quilla Rice.'

'No, not like them. He isn't in the least like *them*.' Christine Colville used an expression he had thought long dead and gone. 'They are very small fry. Conrad is above the sort of odd jobs they do. His family are very poor, they are aristocratic but poor. His followers keep him.'

'What, the other tree people? What money do they have?'

'Not much,' she said. 'It mounts up if everyone contributes.'

'I'll bet.' Burden repressed what he had been going to say, that Tarling had a nice little earner going. 'Does he have contacts round here?'

She misunderstood him or affected to do so. 'Everyone in the woods knows the King.'

'Maybe I'll come and see your play,' he said and escorted her out.

A throng of reporters and photographers rushed her. Burden went back into the old gym where Wexford had sent out for lunch from the new Thai

242

takeaway. He drank from the can that had come with the green curry and coconut, and made a face. Pushing it away he said, 'What is this stuff?'

'It would seem to be alcoholic lemonade.'

'God.' Burden read the label. 'Whose idea was that? There's probably some law or rule about not bringing alcohol on to these premises.

'It tastes disgusting anyway. If I drink alcohol I want it to taste like alcohol, I want to feel the kick, not lemonade with a mystery sting in its tail. It'll be alcoholic milk next.'

Wexford glanced out of the window. He wouldn't have put it past some wily cameraman to be lurking out there, hoping for a pot shot of him holding a drinks can, *any* sort of drinks can. But there was no one in the car park. 'Mike,' he said, looking at his watch, 'it's gone two. We haven't heard a word from Sacred Globe since five yesterday. I don't understand it, it doesn't add up. It must appear to them, much as I regret it, as if we're simply yielding to their demands. Firstly by calling a halt to work on the bypass, secondly by releasing the story to the press when they asked us to. The fact that we were going to release it at that particular time anyway is neither here nor there. They don't know that. So, why, if it seems as if everything is going the way they want it, don't they take advantage of their apparently strong position and come right back with their final demand?'

'I don't know. I don't understand it either.'

'I'm going to see how Dora got on under hypnosis.'

Chapter 17

As soon as he saw him Burden recognised Brendan Royall. He didn't know he knew him but when he was brought into the police station, into Interview Room One, Burden remembered him from six or seven years back. It had been one afternoon when he had gone to meet Jenny from Kingsmarkham Comprehensive. Royall was standing on the school steps, on the top just outside the entrance, holding forth to a group of his contemporaries who surrounded him.

He had been only sixteen then, a tallish, weedy boy with a light aureole of Harpo Marx hair. It was the eyes that Burden remembered. They were astonishingly dark, as if the hair must be dyed, and burning bright, the eyes of the fanatic, under thick, sprouting eyebrows like animal fur. And the voice was memorable too, harsh, haranguing, with an ugly flat accent, the vowels hollow, the ends of words gabbled.

The years between had brought about little change in his appearance. The hair was rather darker and longer than Burden recalled but the eyes were still fierce and with that crazy brightness, the eyebrows still like a strip of rabbit skin. How he had been dressed in those days Burden had forgotten but on this Monday afternoon Royall was dressed from head to foot in green-and-brown camouflage. In woodland he might have melted into the background, which perhaps was the idea. As to the voice,

Burden couldn't tell if it had changed or not, for Royall declined to open his mouth.

He had brought his lawyer with him. Or this solicitor, not a local man, summoned on the Winnebago's phone, had appeared on the police station steps coincidentally with Royall's own arrival. He had very little to do and could have given his client no better code of conduct than that adopted by Royall without his advice.

The man, who looked as if about to take part in some jungle assault course, sat silent and grave on one side of the table, his solicitor next to him. Even while he was starting the recorder, announcing that the interviewee and his lawyer were present, along with DI Burden and DC Fancourt, Burden knew it was a farce. The solicitor could barely conceal his smiles.

Next door, in Interview Room Two, Nicky Weaver with Ted Hennessy confronted Conrad Tarling, the King of the Wood. His solicitor had taken longer in arriving and Tarling had waited there for nearly an hour before the young woman called India Walton turned up.

Tarling sat in his chair in his robes, the long, full sleeves of his outer garment ostentatiously turned back to show his bare smooth arms, heavily laden with silver and copper bracelets chased in Celtic patterns. He too at first was silent, still as stone, his eyes fixed on the small, high window as if a fascinating scene could be discerned through it instead of the brick wall of the Magistrates' Court.

Wexford was tempted to put his head round the door, but the Codes of Practice for the Police and Criminal Evidence Act prohibit the interruption of interviews in all but exceptional circumstances. A senior officer's curiosity would hardly fall into this category so he had to content himself with a glance through the tiny interior window. The sight he saw reminded him of a story he had heard in his schooldays in the Latin lesson of those old Roman statesmen who went to into the Senate when they heard the Goths were coming and sat marble-like and unmoving on their thrones. Taking them for statues, the Goths prodded and poked them until one rose up and struck back, whereupon all were slain. Wexford, tired and frustrated, would have liked to prod Tarling into life, into some reaction, but knew how untenable such a course must be.

DC Lowry had just told him that the white Mercedes whose number Nicky Weaver had taken had been found abandoned on the Stowerton industrial estate. A stolen car, of course, dumped outside a disused factory building where there were no witnesses, its windscreen smashed and its tyres deflated.

Now Lowry came up to him again and said, 'Can I have a word, sir?'

The man looked like a black Marlon Brando, Wexford thought, but Brando in his *Streetcar Named Desire* days. 'Yes, what is it?'

'Your wife mentions a man who always wore gloves. It occurred to me he might have done that because his hands were like mine.' Lowry held up his long-fingered narrow hands, the colour of a plum on which the bloom still lingers. 'I mean because he was black.'

'Good thinking,' Wexford said and he went back to Dora, who was in the old gym listening to her own voice speaking as if she had never heard it before.

Tarling became as vociferous as Royall was silent. In spite of India Walton's discreet suggestions that he had no need to answer this or that, that he was not obliged to respond to that question and that this one

246

was in the circumstances outrageous, Tarling talked. He held forth. Not that he answered any questions or even appeared to have heard them. He simply talked as if he was making an inflammatory political speech, even as if there was no interrogator present but only a silent, receptive audience.

He talked about his brother Craig, his high principles, his love of animals and his equating of all animals from the humblest to the greatest with mankind. Therefore, if animals could be used in vivisection, human beings could, with equal justification, be blown up. In his eyes, the only difference was that the human beings died a quicker death. He talked of the injustice of Craig Tarling's fate, his courage and undaunted demeanour in prison. When he had finished with his older brother's biography he talked about his younger brother who had been seriously injured under the wheels of a lorry transporting live sheep to Brightlingsea. He paused quite courteously for Nicky to question him and responded by talking about himself, his history, his devotion to the English countryside and what he called the 'restoration of Nature'.

'It's particularly interesting,' he said, 'that all three of us children of bourgeois conservative parents, all the products of distinguished public schools and the two great universities, have each committed his life to a different branch of the protection of created things: my brother Craig to ill-used small mammals, my brother Colum to the beasts of the field and myself to the whole of the natural world. You may well ask yourselves why this has happened . . .'

'I might ask *you* if the name Sacred Globe was your personal invention, Mr Tarling,' Nicky said. 'It's very much in accord with the sort of thing you've been telling us. After all, you call yourself the King of the Sacred Grove.'

247

. . . and what was the nature of the inspiration that came to us individually to reject what is known in our society as a "normal" life and take up the despised cause of the vulnerable, the tender, the fragile, without whom, however, life as we know it on this planet must face hideous destruction . . .'

Her face was different. No doubt it would later revert to normal but at the moment her expression was not only bemused, it was if he were seeing her face slightly out of focus, a little blurred, as if she had lost control of it and the features had become untidy. She was like someone asleep whose eyes were nevertheless open, a sleepwalker who isn't walking.

Karen must have left her for a moment, perhaps to get tea. She hadn't seen him. The voice which spoke, her own voice, dwindled and faded away and there was silence. He saw her reach up to switch off the device but she didn't know how to do this. She shrugged, turned, saw him.

'Dora,' he said.

At once she was herself again. She smiled at him radiantly and said, 'It's amazing, Reg. I not only didn't know I knew all that, I didn't know I'd said it. Not till it was played back. And yet my voice sounds just like it always does.'

'I'm glad you weren't upset.'

'Not at all, not a bit. Dr Rowland was very nice. He just asked me to make myself comfortable and relax as much as I could. Then he said all that stuff you read about hypnotists saying, only it was very reassuring and not a bit mumbo-jumbo-ish. I thought it would be like the dentist when they give you that drug that doesn't send you to sleep but puts you into a sort of half-doze and when the tooth's out or the root canal's done or whatever, it seems as if only a moment has passed. But it wasn't. It was like a

248

dream. Yes, like a dream, the kind you don't know you're dreaming. And then the tape was played back to me and I found I'd said all that about the blue thing . . .'

'The what?'

'I remember now, of course I do. But I don't think I would have if I hadn't been hypnotised. I could tell you all of it now or you could listen to the tape. What would you like?'

'Both,' he said, 'but I can't now. I've got to go on television.'

The camera crews were already coming in. A trestle table was set up for them at one end of the room. The Chief Constable sat in the middle with Wexford on his left, Audrey Barker on his right, Andrew Struther next to her and Clare Cox with Hassy Masood on Wexford's left.

The hostage families had been instructed to say nothing in the nature of a plea to Sacred Globe, to say nothing at all if possible, just to be there.

As it turned out, Andrew Struther answered for all of them, and as he was probably the most articulate, this was just as well. In answer to the inevitable question he said, 'We're leaving this to the police to handle, the best and only possible thing to do in the circumstances. This isn't the time or the place for airing the grief and anxiety we all feel. All we can do is wait and leave it to the experts.'

Audrey Barker began to cry. It was good television, but it didn't help the determined and business-like atmosphere Wexford had hoped to create. Someone asked if it was true Chief Inspector Wexford's wife had originally been among the hostages and if so, why was she released? The scene was cut before anyone answered.

The phones that had quietened during the past

few hours began ringing immediately the next news item came on. A man in Liverpool had seen Roxane Masood going into a cinema with a dark man, probably an Indian. A Mr and Mrs Struther had just left a Little Chef restaurant on the A12 near Chelmsford. Were the police aware that a huge conservationists' rally, master-minded by Sacred Globe, was about to take place near Glencastle Forest?

By coincidence, another fax had arrived from Gwenlian Dean in Wales. Gary Wilson and Quilla Rice had arrived at the SPECIES rally and their camping place noted by her officers. Did Wexford wish her to have them questioned? He sent back a message to the effect that he was anxious to know their movements after his encounter with them at Framhurst, when they had left for Glencastle and what connection they had with Conrad Tarling.

Awaiting him was a report on the white Mercedes L570 LOO. It was the property of a William Pugh, of Swansea, and had been stolen three weeks before from outside a house in Ventnor, Isle of Wight, where the Pughs were spending their summer holiday. Forensic work was proceeding on the car's interior.

'I'm going to listen to my wife's hypnosis tape now,' said Wexford, 'and then I'm going home to hear it all over again from her own lips.'

Barry Vine, pale and tired, said, 'I don't think you are, sir. I don't think you will when you hear.'

'Hear what?'

'A body's been found. On that bit of waste ground where Contemporary Cars park. It's in a sleeping bag dumped up against the fence . . .'

Chapter 18

The barren piece of waste ground where the Railway Arms had once stood was bounded by chain-link fencing, up against which grew the kind of trees and bushes always found on sites of this sort, elders and brambles and the suckers from felled sycamores. Nettles abounded, at this time of the year waist-high. On the wall of the bus station on the right-hand side graffiti faced faded lettering on the opposite building. Long before the aromatherapist and the photocopiers and hairdresser came, but not before the shoe repairer, the words Cobbler and Bootmaker had been printed on the pale brickwork. The graffiti consisted of the single rubric, Gazza, and the paint used had run from the brush in long red drips.

Around Contemporary Cars' trailer the turf had become a dusty hayfield, sprawled with litter. Visitors to the pub and the discount store discarded their cigarette packets and crisp bags over the fence. The sleeping bag, camouflage-patterned, was in the farthest corner among the nettles, half under the brambles. The zip which fastened it along the whole length of the right-side had been opened about eighteen inches to disclose what appeared at first to be only a mass of black silky hair.

'I didn't undo the zip,' Peter Samuels said, anticipating censure that never came. 'I knew better than that. I could see what it was, I could see that hair, without touching it.'

'I undid it,' Burden said. 'Her knees have been bent to get the whole of her inside that bag. When did you find her?'

'Half an hour ago. It was a bit after six. I'd been in there watching you on the telly and I came out to my car, looked over here and I saw. I don't know what made me look, I just glanced up and saw it: a brown-and-green sleeping bag. I reckoned someone had just dumped it. You'd be surprised the rubbish people unload here. I saw the hair, I thought it was an animal at first . . .'

'All right, Mr Samuels. Thank you. If you'd like to wait in the trailer we'll come and have a word with you in a moment.'

'As soon as he had arrived at the site Wexford had felt a sinking of the heart, a dread and apprehension he didn't want justified, that he would have liked to run away from. There was, of course, no running away and no help. A glance at Burden's face had been enough anyway, his pale, cold face and the set mouth. Vine said nothing and Karen said nothing. They turned and watched Peter Samuels walking back across the scrubby grass and then they looked at Wexford. He trod heavily across the nettles to the other side of the sleeping bag, closed his eyes, looked.

The face, of which only the left profile was visible, was badly bruised and with death the bruise colours had become livid, yellowish, green and brown. But the features were unmistakable and he thought of a portrait, a tranquil, gentle, beautiful face and clear, dark eyes. 'It's Roxane Masood,' he said.

Dr Mavrikiev, the pathologist, took no more than fifteen minutes to get there. The photographer arrived at the same time with Archbold, the Scene-of-Crimes officer. Mavrikiev undid the zip to its fullest extent and knelt down in front of the body. It was now possible to see that what Burden had guessed was true and the girl's legs had been bent to an angle of ninety degrees. The body was dressed in black hipster trousers, a red T-shirt and red velvet jacket. A hand, waxen yet delicate as ivory, slid off her thigh as the pathologist gently turned her over.

Wexford had come if not to like, to have a certain respect for Mavrikiev. He was a young man, of Baltic or Ukrainian descent, very fair with pale eyes like crystal quartz, an unpredictable creature, rude or charming according to his mood. Unlike his seniors, particularly Sir Hilary Tremlett, he never indulged his wit at the expense of the corpse, never talked about the 'dead meat' or speculated unkindly as to how the body might have looked in life. But it was impossible to tell what he was thinking, or to read anything in the cold face that might have been carved out of birch wood it was so immobile.

'She's been dead for at least two days,' he said. 'Maybe longer. I will, of course, be able to be more accurate about that later on. But a time-honoured method of assessing the time of death will show you that, for rigor mortis has come on, established itself and worn off again. Note the limpness of that hand. If it's of any help to you at this stage' – he looked up at Wexford – 'I'd very approximately put the time of death as late Saturday afternoon.

'Now when she was brought here I can't tell you but she must have been put in that bag fairly soon after her death because once rigor was established it would have been impossible to bend the legs into that position without breaking the knees. Incidentally, the legs *are* broken but not in aid of getting them into the bag. So you can calculate that the body was placed into the bag on Saturday evening, at any rate before midnight on Saturday.'

253

'And the cause of death?' said Wexford.

'You're never satisfied, are you? You want everything and you want it at once. I've told you before, I'm not a magician. She's obviously been the victim of a violent attack or attacks. Look at her head and face. As to the *cause* of death, you can see for yourself she hasn't been shot or stabbed and there's been no ligature round her neck.' Sir Hilary would have made jokes about poisoning at this stage but Mavrikiev simply got to his feet without even a shake of the head or rueful smile. 'You can do whatever you have to do and take her away. I'll do the postmortem tomorrow, 9 a.m. sharp.'

Photographs were taken. Archbold went about measuring things and got badly stung by nettles. Wexford, free to touch the inside of the bag now, began to search it, felt the padded cover, slid his hand under the body.

'What are you looking for?' Burden asked.

'A note. A message.' Wexford stood up. 'There's nothing. I don't understand this, Mike. Why? Why do this, any of it, why this girl, why *now*?'

'I don't know.'

Peter Samuels was repeating his story of his discovery of the body when Wexford went into the trailer. 'How d'you know it hadn't been there all day?' he asked.

'What, all day since the morning? No, it couldn't have been, no way.'

'Why not? Did you go over to that corner? Did you look? Did any of you? You were busy, no doubt, with your fares, in and out. Did you even look?'

'If you put it like that, well, no. I don't reckon we did. Well; *I* didn't. I can't speak for the rest of them.'

'So it could have been put there on the previous night? It could have been put there on Sunday night?'

'No. No way. Well, come to think of it, I suppose it could, I mean, I doubt it, I doubt it very much, but it *could*.'

A mounting anger was making Wexford's head swim. Not with Samuels. Samuels was no one, of no account. The rage that filled his head and drummed in his brain was with Sacred Globe. He found himself feeling above all a bitter resentment. This, when everything must seem to them to be going their way, when, however politic and previously planned, events must seem to them to be in compliance with their demands . . .

And now no more demands, no promised 'negotiation', not even an impudent thanks for an apparent meeting of ultimata. A murder instead. But he thought sickeningly how often in the history of abductions that happened, just that. All was going well, all seemed to be progressing both from the point of view of the hostages and the hostage takers – and then a hostage murdered, her body sent home, presented to those who searched for her.

At least they hadn't returned the poor child to her mother. It was a measure of the kind of life he led and the sort of people he encountered, he thought, that his imagination could conceive of such a thing. But it reminded him of what he had to do now. He would do it and he would do it himself.

No message from Sacred Globe had come in on the police phones, though there had been plenty of the other sort, from those deluded or fake witnesses claiming to have seen the hostages in far-flung cities or to live next door to where they were held. The screens he glanced at as he passed carried list upon list of names, addresses, descriptions, offences committed, of everyone closely or remotely connected with nature, wildlife and animal protest. Cross-references, possible connections, records of . interviews.

He forgot, briefly, his sympathy with so many of these people, their aims, their laudable desires, their ideal, fading world, and lost everything in a red tide of anger. Breathing deeply, calming his racing heart, he found a voice with which to make a phone call. The Posthouse Hotel. Mr Hassan Masood, please.

'Mr Masood is in the dining-room. Would you like me to page him?'

As so often happens when contact is made with a reasonable, polite person from what seems another world, anger was quenched. Wexford thought of the horror of fetching the man from his dinner, from his wife and sons perhaps . . .

'No, thank you.' He would go himself. He phoned his home, got his daughter Sylvia.

'Dad, what on earth happened to you? Mother's been waiting for you for hours.'

He said he had been delayed, knowing it wasn't Dora but she making the fuss, put the phone down softly on her expostulations. The media, yes. They could wait till tomorrow, even till late tomorrow. He drove out to the Posthouse, walked into the pine-and-glass and tweed-carpeted interior and there the first person he saw was Clare Cox. It hadn't occurred to him she might be there too. It never crossed his mind. She was back in her floor-length dress, a shawl round her shoulders, her greying, tawny hair flopping from its combs. Masood and she had their backs to him. They were side by side at the reception desk, ordering, as he later discovered, a taxi to take her home.

'I had to bring her here,' Masood said when he saw who it was. 'Reporters, photographers, they were all over her house and garden. One of them followed us but I shut her up in my room and the hotel kept them out. This is an excellent hotel, I recommend it.' He beamed at the receptionist and the receptionist simpered back. 'I think maybe it's safe to go home now – what do you think?'

It seemed not to have occurred to him to see Wexford in his angel-of-death role. But Clare Cox, herself rather resembling a Fury or a Fate with her dishevelled hair and trailing clothes, went white in the face and came up to him with outstretched hands. 'What is it? Why are you here?'

Not the mother if he could help it. He made that a rule. 'I'd like you to come back into Kingsmarkham with me, Mr Masood, if you would.' The euphemisms, the circumlocutions! But what else at this moment? 'There's been a ... development.'

'What kind of a development?' She clutched at his sleeve. 'What's happened?'

'Miss Cox, I think this is probably your taxi that has just arrived outside. If you would like to go home in it I promise you Mr Masood and I will come straight to you if need be.' It sounded as if he was promising hope, relief, yet his voice had been grave. 'I can tell you no more at present, Miss Cox. If you will just do as I ask.'

The taxi wasn't from Contemporary Cars but All the Sixes. He felt an obscure relief. Immediately it was out of sight Masood began asking about this 'development'. They got into Wexford's car and Wexford stalled for a while, but when they were nearly there he told him. A sanitised version. The sleeping bag, the waste ground, the bent legs weren't mentioned. He would see the bruising for himself and nothing could help that.

There had never been any real doubt. Masood looked at the beautiful, discoloured face, made a small sound, nodded, turned away.

Wexford thought that if it had been one of his daughters, so foully dead, beaten in the face before

257

her death, he would have rounded on this policeman, in his grief and misery yelled at him, perhaps
seized him by the shoulders, shouted into his face,
Why? Why have you allowed this?

Masood stood meek, with head bent. Barry Vine,
who was with them, offered him tea. Would he like
to sit down?

'No. No, thank you.' He looked up, turning his
head in a curious sideways manner as if his neck
hurt him. 'I don't understand this.'

'I don't understand it either,' said Wexford.

He remembered then that he had told Burden he
thought Sacred Globe were getting cold feet, Sacred
Globe were at a loss with no notion how to proceed
. . . Well, they had proceeded.

'I have sent my wife and sons home to London,'
Masood said in a calm, almost conversational tone. 'I
am glad now. It was just as well.' He cleared his
throat. 'My duty now will be to Roxane's mother.
You will come with me?'

'Of course. If you wish it.'

In the car, on the way to Pomfret, Masood said, 'If
anyone had told me my daughter would die young I
can think of many things I might have said but not
what I *feel* now. It is the waste I feel. So much beauty,
so talented. Such a waste.'

Remembering what Dora had told him, Wexford
wanted to say what is sometimes said to the parents
of dead soldiers, that Roxane had surely died
bravely. But he lacked the heart for it, he doubted if
he would be able to speak the words.

Clare Cox had been drinking since she got home.
A reek of whisky came from her. If it had been drunk
to save her, to anaesthetise her against what she
feared was coming, it was ineffective. Standing close
to her, holding her hand, Masood told her, and there
was no waiting for the news to sink in, for shock to

pass, for a stunning to yield to grief. Her screams began at once, like a chemical reaction, as sharp and insistent as a starved baby crying for the pain of hunger to go away.

'Go home, Reg,' the Chief Constable said on the phone. He was in bed himself. He too had had a long day. 'Go home. There's nothing more you can do. It's ten-past eleven.'

'The press have got it, sir.'

'Have they now. How did that happen?'

'I wish I knew,' Wexford said.

Dora was asleep. He was glad, because it meant he didn't have to explain. The thought of telling her Roxane was dead horrified him almost as much as being with Clare Cox had done. The woman's screams still rang in his ears. Yet Hassy Masood had passed on the news of his daughter's death to the media. In spite of what he had said to the Chief Constable, Wexford was sure of it. Masood had told the news to Roxane's mother – had done his best, no doubt, to calm her – and then told the media his daughter was dead. Well, Masood had other children, a second family, a new life, and to him Roxane had been the grateful recipient of his largess and someone to take occasionally to expensive restaurants. Her death was no more than the waste of her beauty, looks that in her case meant capital. Because Dora was there beside him, he slept like the dead. It took the alarm to wake him and it woke her first.

'I'll go down,' he said quickly, seeing her already up and in her dressing-gown.

He had to get to the papers first. There it was, all over the front pages: HOSTAGE MODEL FOUND DEAD, ROXANE THE FIRST TO DIE, ROXANE MURDERED, A FATHER'S GRIEF ... So he had been right. He went back upstairs and told Dora.

At first she refused to believe him. It was too much. There was no *reason*. With tears running down her face, she said, 'What did they do to her?'

'Don't know yet. I have to go in a minute. I'm sorry but I must. I have to be at the post-mortem.'

'She was too brave,' Dora said.

'Very likely.'

'She said goodbye to me, she said, "Goodbye, Dora".'

Dora turned her face into the pillow and sobbed bitterly. He kissed her. He didn't want to leave her but he had to.

Tuesday. One week since the hostages were taken. The press reminded him of that as they crowded him on his way into the mortuary.

'Two down, three to go,' one of them said.

'How did you get your wife out, Chief Inspector?' asked a girl from a television news programme.

Mavrikiev was already there. 'Good-morning, good-morning. How are you today? Mr Vine is about somewhere. Shall we get started?'

They all got into green rubber gowns and put on gauze masks. This was Barry Vine's first time and though not particularly squeamish when faced with a dead body, this, Wexford thought, might be different. The sound of the saw got to people, that and the smell, more often than the sight of organs being removed.

Now that the body was exposed, Wexford saw what he hadn't seen the night before. The right side of the head was shallowly stove in, the hair matted with dark clotted blood. It seemed to him, though, that the facial bruising was less marked, less violently coloured, appearing as yellowish-green streaks and blotches on the waxen skin.

Mavrikiev worked swiftly and always in silence.

While other pathologists might extract an organ, hold it up and comment on some peculiarity in its structure or progress of its deterioration, he proceeded coolly, speechlessly and deadpan. If Barry Vine had turned pale it wasn't obvious to Wexford. The mask and green cap hid so much, but after a few moments and a muffled 'Excuse me' he left the room with one gloved hand over his mouth.

Breaking his rule, Mavrikiev gave a small, tight laugh and said, 'A case of the eye being stronger than the stomach.'

He worked on, picking something out of the head wound with tweezers. Plastic containers now held the stomach, lungs, part of the brain and whatever it was he had picked from the wound. He finished, stripped off his gloves and came across the room to where Wexford had retreated. 'I'll stick to what I said about the time of death. Saturday afternoon.'

'I suppose I can ask my other question now?'

'What did she die of? That blow to the head. You don't need any medical degrees to see that. Skull's fractured, brain severely damaged. I won't go into a lot of technical stuff, it'll be in the report.'

'You mean someone struck her a violent blow to the head? With what? Can you say?'

Mavrikiev slowly shook his head. He handed Wexford one of the containers. It held a dozen or so small stones, some black with blood. 'If someone struck her he must have hit her with a gravel path. I picked these out of the wound. I don't think she was hit, I think she *fell*. I think she fell from a height on to a gravel path.'

Barry Vine came back into the room, looking sheepish. He kept his eyes averted from the slab on which the body, now neatly covered in plastic sheeting, lay. Wexford ignored him.

'Fell? Or was pushed or thrown?'

'For God's sake, you're at it again. I'm not a magician, how many times do I have to tell you? I don't know. If you expect a great handprint in the middle of her back, that kind of thing doesn't happen.'

'You could tell if she'd struggled,' said Wexford coldly.

'Fingernails full of flesh and blood, eh? There was none of that. If someone did it he'd likely have been left-handed but there was no someone. Her right arm is broken, two of her ribs are broken, her left leg is broken in two places and her right in one. The body's bruised down the right side. I think she fell from a height, perhaps as much as thirty feet, and she fell on to her right side.

'And that's it for the time being, gentlemen. I'll thank you for your attention' – here a supercilious glance at Barry Vine – 'and be off home to my brunch.'

Vine nodded to him.

'Feeling better?' asked Wexford breezily. 'It's just occurred to me that Brendan Royall, when we saw him, was dressed from head to foot in camouflage. Can it be coincidence?'

Chapter 19

Stanley Trotter was still in bed in Stowerton, in the two-roomed flat in Peacock Street, when Burden called on him early on Tuesday morning. One of the Sayem brothers who kept the grocery market downstairs let him in, took him up and pounded on Trotter's door. Perhaps he bore a grudge against the upstairs tenant for something or other, for when Trotter came to the door in pyjama bottoms and dirty vest, Ghulam Sayem smiled smugly to himself. His face had worn much the same expression when Burden announced himself as a police officer.

It was quite a warm day, sultry and windless, but Trotter's windows were tight shut. The room smelt unpleasant. It was exactly what Burden had expected and he analysed the smell as compounded of sweat, urine, Malaysian takeaway and mould, the kind that forms on damp towels that are left about unwashed. Somewhat vain of his appearance and careful of his clothes, he didn't like sitting on the greasy chair with the cigarette burns on its arms, but he hadn't much choice. He dusted it with a tissue he had in his pocket.

Trotter watched him. 'I don't know what you think you've come for,' he said.

'Seen a paper this morning, have you? Seen the telly? Listened to the radio?'

'No, I haven't. Why would I? I was asleep.'

'You're not interested then? You don't want to know what I'm on about?'

Trotter didn't say anything. He rooted about in the pockets of a garment lying across the bed, found cigarettes and lit one. It brought on a liquid, spluttering spasm of coughing.

'You should put yourself down for a heart-lung transplant, Trotter,' said Burden. 'They tell me the waiting list's as long as your arm.' He coughed himself. It was infectious. 'How long were you going to leave the body there?' he snapped.

'What body?'

'How long were you going to leave the sleeping bag there, Trotter? Or were you going to find it yourself? Was that the idea?'

'I'm not saying anything to you without my lawyer,' said Trotter. He put the cigarette down on a saucer, but without stubbing it out, got into bed and pulled the clothes over his head.

The sleeping bag had gone off to the forensic science lab at Myringham. It was made by a company called Outdoors and according to its label manufactured from a fabric that was part polyester, part cotton and part lycra, lined with nylon and thinly filled with polyester fibre.

Meanwhile, an examination of the stolen car had yielded a mass of cat hairs, pebbles from a south-coast beach and sand, which in the opinion of the earth and soil expert, was from the Isle of Wight. There wasn't a fingerprint on it anywhere, inside or out.

The car had been stolen from Ventnor, Isle of Wight. But the hostages couldn't be there, Wexford thought. Dora would have known if she had crossed water. Her captors would never have taken the risk of using the ferry and that was the only way to reach the island.

William Pugh, of Gwent Road, Swansea was the owner. Wexford put through a phone call to him and asked if he had a cat. Two cats, in fact, for the hairs were from a Siamese and a black. Pugh said he hadn't but he had a Labrador, which had been in kennels while he and his wife were away, as if Wexford were conducting a survey into pet statistics.

'I suppose you went on the beach, Mr Pugh?'

'We did not. I am seventy-six and my wife is seventy-four.'

'So you couldn't have transferred sand from your shoes to the inside of the car?'

'The car was stolen within three hours of our getting there,' said Pugh.

Another fax had come from Gwenlian Dean in Neath. Gary and Quilla had been interviewed by one of her officers. At first they claimed to know nothing of any meeting with Wexford in Framhurst but when their memories were jogged Quilla realised who was meant and they both talked with apparent frankness about that encounter. Chief Inspector Dean wrote that her officer had no reason to doubt the truth of what they said, that if they had even heard Wexford's name when he gave it to them it had scarcely registered and they had soon forgotten it.

They didn't intend to return to Kingsmarkham for the time being but were going on to north Yorkshire where a protest was being mounted over the proposal to build a housing estate. Only one factor in all this had surprised Inspector Dean and this, contrary to what she had been led to suspect, was Gary's and Quilla's ownership of a car. They had arrived by car and were going to Yorkshire by car, a respectable-looking four-year-old Ford Escort. Had Wexford any further interest in them?

The inquest on Roxane Masood was fixed for the following day and still there had been no message from Sacred Globe. It was as if Sacred Globe had died or disappeared, taking its hostages with it. Wexford found himself constantly looking at his watch, counting up the hours since they had last been in touch, forty, forty-one ... He phoned Gwenlian Dean, thanked her for her trouble and said he would see Gary and Quilla on their return. By then he hoped, he said stoutly, that he wouldn't *need* to see them.

Meanwhile he had Karen Malahyde keep Brendan Royall under surveillance and Damon Slesar tail the King of the Wood.

Tanya Paine told Vine she had never looked in the direction where the sleeping bag was found. She never did, she never had cause to. They were in the trailer and her phones kept ringing. In the lulls between calls she craned and twisted her neck, leant forward, shifted her chair, in an effort to prove to him that no matter what contortions she had put her body through she couldn't have seen that corner where the sleeping bag was, an area now cordoned off with blue-and-white crime tape.

Vine had never before seen fingernails like hers. He couldn't imagine how they were done. Each one had a design on it like a piece of blue, green and violet paisley-patterned satin. Was it printed or had some artist done it with a very fine brush? Or did you buy transfers, stick them on and lacquer over the top? It was as much as he could do to keep his eyes off those fingernails while Tanya stretched and craned. 'I'm not talking about when you were in here, Ms Paine,' he said. 'But when you arrived and when you left,' and remembering her tastes, 'and when you went out for your chocolate bar and your capuccino.'

'I could have seen it then, I suppose, but I didn't.' She gave him a sideways glance, resentful, cagey. 'And I don't eat things like that any more. I'm trying to lose weight. It was an apple and a Diet Coke.'

No distress over the other girl's violent and shocking death was apparent in her manner. She had seen about it on breakfast television and bought a newspaper on her way to work, the kind of newspaper – it lay between her phones – that carries the maximum of black seventy-two-point headline and the minimum of text. This one's front page said only, MY LOVELY GIRL framing a model agency's photograph of Roxane in a bikini.

'You were a friend of Roxane's, you were at school with her.'

'I was at school with a lot of girls.'

'Yes,' said Vine, 'but this is the one who was abducted and is now dead. It's a bit strange, isn't it? Let me put it like this. First of all the people who abducted her, this Sacred Globe, first of all they choose a car-hire firm where *you* work, and when one of the hostages is dead they return the body to where *you* work. The body of your friend. Bit of a coincidence, wouldn't you say?'

One of her phones rang. She answered it, wrote down a time and a place on her pad. It seemed an inefficient and old-fashioned way of doing things. The design on the ballpoint pen matched her fingernails.

'Bit of a coincidence?' Vine said again.

'I don't know what you mean. You keep saying "my friend". She wasn't my friend. I just knew her.'

'She made a point of booking taxis from here because you were here. She liked a chat on the phone to you.'

'Look,' said Tanya, 'I can tell you why she liked talking to me, it was so as I knew she'd got a rich dad and how she was going to be a model – fat chance, I thought – and that she could afford taxis when others have to get the bus. I thought, for two pins I'd say to you, at least my mum and dad was married and are still together.'

So that was a point of advantage in today's youth meritocracy? Wexford would be interested. No one got married any more, but if your parents were married and *still* married, status was conferred on you.

'You didn't like her?'

Tanya seemed slowly to have realised that it might be unwise to tell a policeman that a victim of violence was personally antipathetic to you. 'I'm not saying that. You're putting words into my mouth.'

'Why do you think her body was put here?'

'How should I know?' Now evidently seemed to her the time to tell an essential truth. 'I'm not a murderer.'

'Have you a boyfriend, Miss Paine?'

He had astonished her. 'What do you want to know that for?'

'If you'd rather not answer . . .'

She watched him write something down, said, 'No, I haven't, since you ask. Not right now.' It was an admission she would infinitely have preferred not to make and she fidgeted uncomfortably, twisting her body and showing him that she did indeed need to lose weight. 'Temporarily, right now, I don't, no.'

Her phone rang.

Neither Leslie Cousins nor Robert Barrett could give Lynn Fancourt any idea of when the sleeping bag containing Roxane Masood's body was brought to the parking area. But while Barrett would only repeat monotonously that he hadn't seen any strange cars about, Cousins was able to state firmly that it hadn't been there at midnight on Saturday when he returned from taking a fare from Kingsmarkham station to Forby.

'How can you be so sure?'

'I went down there. To the back fence.'

'Why? Because you saw something?'

Lynn could tell he didn't want to say. His face had reddened. She remembered the occasional behaviour of her father and her brothers, and marvelled at the curious ways of men who often, even when they have bathrooms or public conveniences not far away ... 'You went down there for a natural purpose, did you, Mr Cousins? To relieve yourself against the hedge?'

'Yeah, well, you know ...'

'It was easier in the days when police officers were always male, wasn't it? Less embarrassing.' Lynn gave the rather hard, bright smile she had seen on Karen Malahyde's face. 'You went down to the back fence to relieve yourself and at that time, midnight, there was nothing lying among the nettles under those trees – right?'

'Right,' said Cousins with a sigh of relief.

The bus station might have been a mile away instead of next door, for all anyone working there could have seen. The high, blank brick wall blocked off everything. On the other side the shoe repairer had closed up and gone home at five on Saturday afternoon, the hairdresser at five-thirty and the photo-copiers at the same time. Only the aromatherapist lived on the premises.

The windows of her first-floor flat looked towards the Engine Driver at the front – she had had those double-glazed – and at the back over the comparative peace of the waste ground. She invited Lynn into a strongly scented living-room that obviously also did duty for client consultations. The walls were covered with photographs and highly stylised drawings of flowers and grasses. A much larger photograph was of the aromatherapist herself, apparently thrown into a state of ecstasy by the scent emanating from a flagon she held to her nose.

She told Lynn her name was Lucinda Lee, which sounded unlikely, but the truth was that people did have unlikely names.

'Half the time I get no sleep here at all,' she complained. 'What with the pub at the front and those cars going in and out at the back. They're threatening to put my rent up and when they do I'm going.'

Had she seen anything untoward between Saturday midnight and Sunday evening? To Lynn's astonishment she had.

'They don't usually work that late,' said Lucinda Lee. 'Or maybe I should say that early. I'd just got off to sleep, it was all of one in the morning, and this car came in making an unbelievable noise.'

'What sort of noise?'

'I don't really approve of cars. I mean, they're the biggest agent of pollution of all, aren't they? I haven't got one, I wouldn't, and I don't know much about them. I can't actually drive. But this one sounded as if he'd got in here in it but he couldn't get it to start again.'

'You mean the engine stalled?'

'Do I? If you say so. Anyway, I got up and looked out of the window. I was going to shout at him. I mean, midnight's bad enough. They use the end there as a toilet, those fellows, it's disgusting – are they allowed to do that?'

Lynn said gently, 'You were telling me you looked out of the window.'

270

'Well, I didn't shout. The car was standing there and he was doing something up the end, bending over something – well, it's embarrassing, isn't it? Worse than dogs, at least a dog is natural.'

It was necessary to deflect her from her pet subjects of pollution, Contemporary Cars and lavatorial lapses. Lynn interrupted her again. 'Could you describe him and the car?'

Soon it became plain that the car used was small and red. At first Lucinda Lee had thought the man was Leslie Cousins, but he was too tall to be Cousins and too thin. She described him as wearing jeans and a zipper jacket.

Later on Sunday morning, mid-morning it had been, when she looked out again she had seen the camouflage sleeping bag but she was so used to seeing rubbish dumped there that she took no further notice.

Brendan Royall had spent the night at Marrowgrave Hall. Karen left her car at its gates and made her way into the grounds, wishing there were more cover than these second-growth trees, scarcely more than saplings, and these ubiquitous nettles. Wexford had once said to her that we were lucky in that the English countryside wasn't dangerous as some places were, the worst to fear being adders and nettles, and whoever saw adders these days? Luckily, she didn't react much to nettle stings.

Rabbits were everywhere, hundreds, in her estimation. They had cropped the turf so that it looked as if someone had shaved it, but still they went on eating what was left. She had been there about fifteen minutes when Royall came out of the front door with a camera. He stood there photographing the rabbits, which must have been too far away to appear as more than dark dots on the film. This done, he began

271

walking forward, and Karen could hear the strange high-pitched whistle he was making. If it was intended to pacify the rabbits, or even attract them to him, it failed and had the opposite effect. Each animal seemed to freeze, before running helter-skelter for the safety of the bushes.

Then Freya came out, draped like a statue on a Roman frieze. She said something to him and handed him something. Royall hung the camera round his neck and got into the Winnebago. This was enough to send Karen racing back to her car. By the time the Winnebago emerged she had moved back on to the edge of the ditch and under the shelter of overhanging branches. Royall turned left towards Forby. It was a cumbersome vehicle to be driving along these narrow lanes. He took them slowly and Karen stayed a long way behind.

There was no way of bypassing Kingsmarkham from this direction and Royall took the Winnebago right through the town, causing a severe hold-up in York Street which was already double-parked. He was heading for the bypass site, Karen thought, or at any rate for its environs. She wondered how Damon Slesar was getting on – Damon who, by coincidence really, had the other surveillance task, that of keeping Conrad Tarling under observation. If anyone got the evening off, if there was any let-up in the hunt for Sacred Globe, she was meeting Damon for a meal in Kingsmarkham at eight. It wouldn't be the first time they had been out together, but it was the first time a meeting between them had happened by design and not by chance or from simple convenience.

Brendan Royall was heading for Myfleet, she supposed, by way of Framhurst. If he was going to one of the camps he would have turned off sooner, certainly by the time they reached Framhurst Cross.

The lights were against him, she could see from a long way away, and she slowed almost to a stop. He had moved off up the Myfleet road before she got to the junction and by then the lights had turned red again. Karen thought maybe she wasn't very good at this and she wondered if Damon was making a better job of it.

A lot of tree people were sitting at tables outside the Framhurst teashop. She could even see, from the car, those little pots of non-lactic soymilk. The lights changed and she accelerated after the Winnebago, but it had disappeared from her view round one, or several, of these bends between the twelve-foot-high banks. Of course she had to meet another car, it was just her luck. She had to reverse about fifty yards before she found, not exactly a lay-by but a slight widening of the lane. She pulled into it and saw the Winnebago, the unmistakable large white mobile caravan, far away on the horizon, pursuing its course over the hillside and now disappearing into the valley.

She hadn't much choice but to continue in the same direction, down into the dip, up the hill, bends and windings everywhere, down into the valley, and there ahead of her was a field full of cars. Goland Farm. The car park for the tree people's vans and bangers. The Winnebago in the middle of it was like a swan in a pond of ugly ducklings. She sat in her car waiting and watching it. It couldn't have been there for more than five minutes before she arrived.

There were people outside the house that had once been a chapel. She looked at them through her binoculars. A woman and two men, neither of whom was Brendan Royall. He must be sitting in the cab or in the back, the living area. After all, that's what it was, a place to live in as well as drive, to sleep in, eat in, read in and probably watch television in for all she knew. She moved the car to where she had the Winnebago well in her sights. The binoculars showed her an empty cab.

The Winnebago had curtains, but these were all fastened back. Her excellent glasses had no difficulty in revealing the entire interior to her. Unless Royall was hiding under the bed he wasn't in there; no one was, it was empty. Suddenly she knew exactly what had happened. The something Freya had handed him outside Marrowgrave Hall was a set of car keys. He had come here in the Winnebago and left again in Freya's car.

The message might come by letter, as the first one had. Wexford could think of about a hundred addresses, authorities, companies, firms, public bodies, to whom such a letter might be sent. He could only trust to it that if any of them received a letter they would pass it on. It wouldn't be fax or e-mail, he had been through all that before. A letter or a phone call or nothing.

Nothing until the next body ...

After all, though they had talked of negotiations, they had no need of them. Their demands were known, their *demand* really. The building of the bypass was not to be postponed or suspended, but cancelled altogether, presumably in perpetuity. It was a ridiculous condition because even if any government were prepared to promise such a thing, the guarantee couldn't be binding on its successors – or could it? Suppose the land was set aside and preserved in its present state, as he had heard certain royal forests were, or Hampstead Heath was? Suppose it was purchased, for instance, by the National Trust?

He found himself ignorant of the law in these

274

respects. But Sacred Globe would have made themselves conversant with it. It was well within the bounds of probability that they would ask for a promise from the National Trust as to the future of the bypass site.

He asked the Chief Constable for permission to address Sacred Globe through the medium of television, appeal to them, ask for the return of the remaining three hostages and require them to state their demands. Permission was refused.

'These people may not fulfil the definition of terrorists as we know it, Reg, but terrorists they are. We can't be seen to negotiate with them. They can address us, but we can't address them.'

'Only they don't address us,' said Wexford.

'How long is it now, Reg?'

'Forty-eight hours, sir.'

'And in that time they've done what you might call their worst.'

'Their worst so far,' said Wexford.

Damon Slesar caught up with him as he was making his way into the old gym. Wexford, turning round, thought he looked tired. Those dark, almost emaciated people showed their tiredness in bruise marks round the eyes and Damon's eyes were sunk in grey hollows. He wondered how his showed – in a general ageing, no doubt.

'Tarling hasn't been anywhere apart from the Elder Ditches Camp,' he said. 'He's been back home since mid-afternoon. He went to take a look at the environmental survey, met Royall there and they went back to the camp together. And that's about it.'

'Perhaps you'd like to tell Karen,' Wexford said not very pleasantly. 'She'll be interested to know where Royall was, seeing that she lost him.'

You could tell so much from a person's eyes, he thought, the subtle changes to the whole face.

Criticism of Lynn Fancourt or Barry Vine would scarcely have affected Slesar, but when Karen was its object he became as vulnerable as if it had been directed against himself. Still, all he said was, 'I'll tell her, sir.'

Something in the tone of his voice told Wexford Slesar would make occasion to speak to her, but if Brendan Royall came into the conversation it would be purely incidental.

'OK. After the meeting you can call it a day.'

They assembled in front of him with their news, their successes – not many of these – their ideas – even fewer. He saw the exchanged glance between Karen and Damon and told himself now was no time to take an interest in the involvement of human beings. In passing only would he notice and be pleased that the exacting Karen, feminist, sharp critic, perfectionist, had perhaps at last found someone to suit her.

The day was over. An hour of peace had come and he was going to use it to listen to Dora's hypnosis tape. At last.

Chapter 20

The voice he expected would be a sleepwalker's, bemused, proceeding as from a medium in a trance. He prepared himself to be unnerved by it. Instead, what he heard were Dora's measured tones, steady, sane, almost conversational. She sounded perfectly at ease, occasionally excited by what had been dredged up out of her unconscious and what she immediately seemed to recognise as truth.

'It was the boy,' she said now. 'Ryan. He had such a thing about his father, he was always talking about him. His father died months before he was born. In the Falklands war. Did I tell you that?'

Silence. Dr Rowland didn't speak.

'It's rather strange, isn't it, having so much love and admiration for someone you never knew and couldn't have known?'

This time the hypnotherapist said, 'People idealise a lost or far-distant parent. That, after all, is the parent who doesn't punish, who never says no, who doesn't get exasperated or tired or cross.'

'Yes.' Dora seemed to be considering this. 'His father left him a book of drawings of ... wildlife, I suppose you'd call it, that he'd made. Well, he didn't exactly leave it to him, he left it behind, and Ryan's mother gave it to him when he was twelve. They were drawings of pond life, frogs and newts and caddises, and all the things he'd seen when he was Ryan's age and which now weren't there any more, had disappeared or were greatly endangered. He treasures that book. It's his most precious possession.'

The hypnotist said, 'Talk about the room.'

'Big, thirty by twenty. Feet, I mean, not metres. I can't do metres. Whitewashed walls. Five beds. Three up one end, those were mine and Ryan's and Roxane's, and two up the window end for the Struthers. Owen Struther moved their beds up there himself. To be away from the rest of us, I suppose. And when Owen and Kitty were gone they didn't take the beds away.

'The floor was concrete, cold underfoot. It was always cold to touch. The door was very heavy, made of oak, I think. When they opened it I could see green and grey outside, and some red brick. The green was grass. The grey was stone.'

The other voice said very gently, 'What could you see out of the window?'

'Green and grey, a stone step, I think. Oh, and there was blue too. Patches of blue.'

'Blue sky?'

There was a silence. Then Dora said, 'It wasn't the sky. It was something else blue. Opposite the window. Sometimes it was high up and sometimes lower down. I don't mean it moved while I watched it. I mean that one day, the Wednesday, I think, it was a small blue patch high up, about eight feet up, and on the Thursday it was a smaller blue patch about three feet up.'

Silence again, a silence so protracted that Wexford knew it was the end. Disappointment had succeeded earlier euphoria. Was that all? Dora had been put through an involuntary – she couldn't have refused and remained a responsible member of society – changing of her consciousness and therefore a loss of her dignity, for that?

He felt like kicking the recorder but he switched it off instead and went home. She was asleep and that didn't surprise him. A message was on the answering machine from Sheila to the effect that she would come back to Kingsmarkham whenever they liked but wouldn't Mother like to come and stay with them?

'Look what happened last time she tried,' Wexford said aloud.

He went to bed and dreamed. It was the first dream he had had since she had come back. He was in a place of vast buildings, warehouses, factories, mills, old railway stations, some of which were recognisable. The Molino Stucky in Venice, the Musée d'Orsay in Paris. He wandered among them, awestricken by their size, by John Martin's *Pandemonium* and Piranesi's *Imaginary Prisons*. It was as if he had strayed miraculously into a book of old illustrations and at the same time, more prosaically, into the Stowerton Industrial Estate. That it was a dream he knew from the first, there was never a moment of illusion. He passed along a street of Blake's dark satanic mills and, turning a corner, came upon Westminster Abbey. Then he knew. He was looking for the place where the hostages were.

Without finding them or their prison he woke up and it was morning, inquest day. His newspaper, on an inside page, carried an article by a well-known feature writer suggesting that any more concessions made to Sacred Globe would constitute a 'Terrormentalists' Charter'.

Dora, making coffee, getting breakfast, said, 'I didn't sleep very well. I kept thinking about them all. That poor Roxane, when she was locked in the washroom. I don't think I'll ever get her cries and her panic out of my head. And the Struthers, they were both so pathetic really. She simply collapsed, she

279

hadn't any inner resources at all. Well, I wasn't very enterprising but at least I didn't cry all the time.'

'Or at all.'

'I was pretty near it sometimes, Reg.'

'I heard your tape,' he said. 'You must be unique.'

'What do you mean?'

'You must be the only person on earth without an unconscious. It's all in your consciousness. You told us everything, didn't you? Kept nothing back. Well, except that blue thing.'

She looked sideways at him, smiling warily.

'What kind of blue was it?'

'Sky-blue,' she said. 'A perfect, true sky-blue. The blue of the sky at noon on a fine summer day.'

'Then it was the sky you saw.'

'No.' She was adamant. She hooked two pieces of toast out of the toaster on the tines of a fork, flipped them on to a plate, reached into the cupboard for the marmalade jar. 'No. It wasn't the sky. You want some coffee? Oh, sit down, Reg. You can take half an hour off for your breakfast.'

'Ten minutes.'

'It wasn't the sky, it was just sky colour. Anyway, was there any cloudless blue sky while I was in there?'

'I don't believe there was.'

'No. This was more like something hung out of a window or painted on, but the difficulty with that is that it moved. It was high up on the Wednesday and low down on the Thursday. And on Friday at lunchtime Gloves boarded up the window a bit more. Did he do that so that I wouldn't be able to see the blue thing?'

'You didn't come up with any reason for why they let you go?'

'If they knew I'd seen things they'd have been more likely to keep me, wouldn't they? Or killed me.

Oh, don't look like that. I was telling you about the Struthers. Owen Struther was too young to have been in any war yet he behaved like an old soldier, all that courage-in-the-face-of-the-enemy stuff, the obligation to escape. It was ridiculous.'

'Perhaps he was an old soldier. You can be a soldier without a war to fight.'

'He wasn't. I asked him. He didn't like being asked, he seemed quite affronted. Ryan admired him. I think he'd have followed wherever Owen led. I suppose the poor boy is always looking for a father figure – or is that too psychological?'

'The trouble with psychology,' said Wexford epigrammatically, 'is that it doesn't take human nature into account.'

Mavrikiev gave his evidence as an expert witness to the Coroner's Court, most of it technical and obscure, an analysis of the nature of certain wounds and fractures. When he was asked if in his opinion Roxane Masood had been pushed from or thrown off a height, he replied that he had no opinion, he was unable to say. The inquest was adjourned, as Wexford had known it would be.

Sacred Globe's silence hung over Kingsmarkham like a fog. Or so it seemed to him. Not to the rest of the world, the country, perhaps. The kidnapping, someone had told him, had even got into the American papers. There was a tiny paragraph on the foreign pages of the *New York Times*. To Wexford it was as if the hostages had been removed as far away as that, thousands of miles. The sun was shining, it was a bright day, but all the time he was conscious of this enveloping mist.

'Sixty-eight hours,' he said to Burden. 'That's how long it's been.'

Burden had the morning papers. POLICE IN THE

'I'm not in the dark about how she died,' Wexford
said. 'I think I know exactly how that happened. Last
Thursday, when they took her out of the basement
room, they put her somewhere else and it wasn't
with Kitty and Owen Struther. The Struthers may not
even have been together at that stage. They put
Roxane on her own somewhere and it was somewhere high up.'

'On one of the floors above the basement room?'

'Maybe. The trouble is – one of the troubles is –
that we don't know what kind of a building we have
to deal with here. Or even if it's only one building. It
could be a factory complex or a barn or a big house
with a basement or a farm with cats. On the coast,
somewhere with a beach. Whichever it is, Roxane
was taken to an upper floor, perhaps three or four
storeys high, and shut up in a room. I think it was a
small room, Mike.'

'You can't possibly know that.'

'Yes, I can. She was claustrophobic and they knew
that. Sacred Globe knew it. Dora saw them look at
each other, the pair who were outside the washroom
door while Roxane was inside screaming and beating
on it. They knew and they acted on that knowledge.
To subdue her. To punish her.

'I was thinking the other day that whatever Sacred
Globe might be, they aren't cruel or stupid, but I've
had to revise that view. So many people are cruel
when they have the opportunity, don't you find?'

Burden shrugged. 'I dare say. I wouldn't be
surprised.'

'Give them power and someone or something
weaker than themselves. That seems to be enough to
make them torment that someone or something.
Have psychiatrists ever investigated this? Have they

tried to find out why something weak and vulnerable inspires compassion in some people and cruelty in others? I don't know and I don't suppose you do.' Wexford shook his head, in sorrow, in anger. 'They put her in a small room high up. That would have been some time on Thursday. She endured it for nearly two days, at what cost we'll never know.' He was silent for a moment. Then he said suddenly, 'Have you got a phobia?'

'Me?' said Burden. 'I'm not very partial to snakes. I get a bit jumpy in a reptile house.'

'It's not the same thing. If it was a phobia you couldn't go *near* a reptile house. I've a phobia.'

Burden looked interested. 'You have? What is it?'

'That's the last thing I'd tell you. Oh, not you, anyone. My wife knows. The point about being phobic is that you don't tell anyone, you daren't. *Phobos* means fear. Suppose some joker sent you the thing you're phobic about through the post in a parcel? That was why Roxane should never have let Sacred Globe know about her phobia, but she couldn't help herself, poor girl. They couldn't send her the thing she was phobic about, but they could shut her up in a small room.

'On the Saturday afternoon, when she was nearly mad with terror, she tried to escape. Perhaps there was a drainpipe, or some climbing plant to give a foothold, perhaps there was a roof that could be reached, or a ledge. Or she thought could be reached. But it couldn't and she fell. She fell thirty feet to her death, Mike.

'In falling she broke her arm, her ribs, both her legs, and she struck her head a great blow. Perhaps she wouldn't have fallen if she had been – how shall I put it? – in her right mind? But phobics aren't, not when they've been exposed to the thing they're phobic about for two days and a night.'

283

Reflecting on this for a moment or two, Burden said, 'Sacred Globe couldn't have expected that. It's possible they were appalled by what happened.'

'If they were amateurs who'd bitten off more than they could chew, they'd be appalled all right. The likelihood is that they hoped to get what they want and release all the hostages unharmed. That's no longer possible. There they were with a body on their hands, a body they hadn't killed.'

'You could say they murdered her when they put her in that room,' said Burden.

'You and I could, Mike. It wouldn't stand up in court.'

'Why did they bring her back here?'

Wexford considered. 'Perhaps because they didn't want the body. The body was a further liability to them. What were they to do with it? Burial is the only real possibility if you've a body on your hands. We can forget about weighting it down and dumping it in water unless they're on the coast. And we've no reason to think they are. They'd have to have access to a boat, total privacy, darkness.

'But *they didn't kill her*, Mike, they only put her into a position for her to kill herself by accident. If they compounded it by burying the body and it was found later, as it surely would have been, who would then have been made to believe they weren't directly responsible for her death? This way a pathologist would soon discover her death almost certainly to have been accidental. So they got rid of the body. They took it away on Saturday night, in the small hours of Sunday morning probably, first putting it into a sleeping bag they happened to have.

'I think they took it to Contemporary Cars because they had a grievance against them. Thus they kill two birds with one stone. Maybe they've got it in for Samuels and Trotter and co. because they so quickly contacted us after the hold-up. I'm beginning to think they're a vindictive lot.'

They were interrupted by the arrival of Pemberton, who believed he had found the source of the sleeping bag.

'London?' said Wexford. 'Where in London?'

'Outdoors don't supply many retail outlets,' Pemberton said, 'and they only deal with sports shops, not department stores. Most of their stuff goes to the north of England, but they do supply a shop in north London in NW1, and one in Brixton.'

Brixton . . . why did that ring a bell? It would be on the computers somewhere, whatever it was there would be a record. 'Go on.'

'The north London one's in Marylebone High Street. That's when I had a bit of luck, sir. They'd taken six of those sleeping bags, the camouflage kind, and six in green and purple, but while the coloured ones had all sold, they hadn't been able to shift any of the camouflage.'

'Negative sort of luck, wasn't it?' said Burden.

'I went to Brixton. The shop's called Palm Springs in High Street, Brixton. They told me they only had four of those sleeping bags and two of them were still in stock. The manager himself took one of them, they came in just before he went on a camping trip, that was August twelve months. He remembered it without any trouble, but then I reckon you would. Better than that, though, he remembered selling the other one because it was on the same day.'

'I don't suppose he knows who he sold it to?' said Burden.

'Yeah, well, that's too much to expect, isn't it? It was a woman, he knew that. And he remembered she was going to Zaïre. Well, he said Zimbabwe at first but then he corrected himself.'

'Right,' said Wexford. 'Well done. And now you

285

can get yourself in front of Mary's computer and go through a million kilobytes to find the connection.'

'There's a connection?'

'Oh, yes, I'm sure of it.'

Seventy hours and not a word from Sacred Globe.

Having swapped cars with Damon Slesar, Karen sat outside the gates of Marrowgrave Hall, awaiting developments, awaiting anything at all. It had seemed wise to be in a grey car today and let Damon have the blue one, though she didn't think it had registered with Brendan Royall on the previous day that she was following him.

She had started off at Goland Farm, parked among the tree people's cars. The Winnebago was there, but whether or not Brendan Royall was she couldn't tell. His curtains were drawn and all her binoculars could do for her was show her that the cab was empty. Today there was no one about and all the windows in the house were shut as if its occupants had gone out for the day.

She was tired. She and Damon had met for a meal the evening before at a much more up-market place than she had had in mind. La Méditerranée, the Olive and Dove's newly opened restaurant. They had eaten and talked and found they had a tremendous amount to talk about, that they were interested in all the same things, the state of the world, the millennium, what was happening to their own environment, the equality of the sexes, as well as crime and punishment. It had made the conversation at their previous meetings seem like small talk, and after the restaurant indicated that it wanted to close up, they had gone on to a drinking place in the High Street that stayed open till all hours.

By that time they were only drinking Cokes but really she should have been at home in bed. He wanted to come up to her flat with her but she'd said no regretfully and they'd kissed good-night, passionately but like stars in an old Hollywood movie, the kiss leading nowhere except to the mutual promise to see each other again soon. So now she was tired when she shouldn't be and sitting here in a warm car, the sun shining outside in a mild sort of way, she was afraid she might fall asleep.

Fear of that sent her out to walk around a bit. She didn't really look like a tree person but she could just have passed for one in her jeans, black T-shirt and cotton jacket. No one, in any case, would take much notice of her in her flat shoes, neutral clothes and with her long hair scraped back tight and her face as nature made and coloured it.

Somewhere a dog was barking, or several dogs were barking, yapping and howling. The noise was coming from the Winnebago. Well, Royall was said to be an animal lover. No doubt he had dogs of his own, but that they were there meant he would be back, and soon.

Near the house were a lot of concealing trees and high hedges. She had a look at the back of it, with its churchy windows. Would a church or chapel, which was what this had once been, have a crypt? There was no sign of anything like that and the windows weren't hidden or any arches plastered over. She had just returned to her car and was winding down a window to let in some fresh air, when a yellow 2CV came tearing into the field and swept round between the rows like something taking part in the Monaco Grand Prix.

Royall got out of the car, followed by Freya. She opened one of the rear doors and four small beagles bounded out. It took her and Royall some minutes to catch them and thrust them into the Winnebago. Freya was in her usual mummy wrappings and she tripped on the hem of her skirt and fell sprawling. Brendan made an attempt to brush mud off her and then she got back into her car and he got into the cab of the Winnebago.

Karen expected them to return to Marrowgrave Hall and they did. Patsy Panick appeared outside the front door as they drove up and laughed and clapped her hands when all the dogs were released. Karen had heard of someone shaking like a jelly but never before witnessed this phenomenon. Patsy's fat shook as if balloons were inside her clothes.

The beagles ran around in circles, wagging their tails. Karen counted eleven of them. Brendan and Freya managed to catch the dogs, carrying them or otherwise propelling them into the house and Patsy, no doubt exhorting everyone, dogs and all, to have something to eat, shut the door behind them.

The sleep problem reappeared. It was hotter now and Karen did in fact doze off but only for a split second. Barking awakened her. The two people she was keeping under surveillance had re-emerged from the house in the midst of their gambolling pack. While they got them into the Winnebago and Brendan also stowed a suitcase, backpack and large draw-string bag, Karen called in to Kingsmarkham police station.

'They're leaving,' she said. 'I'm going to stay with them, see where they're going, but I think they're going a distance.'

'Chief Inspector wants to talk to you. I'll put him on.'

Wexford said, 'When you're done with that I want you back here. Remember a woman in London who was ill, who'd been in Africa?'

'Yes, of course, sir.'

'She's your pigeon. When you've done with Royall and his girlfriend.'

The Winnebago was packed now with dogs and luggage. Freya, it seemed, wasn't going with him. For a moment Karen thought she was leaving separately but she was only putting her car away in the big empty garage. Patsy and Bob had both come out now, Bob with a slice of something in his hand, a piece of pizza or pie or even a sandwich. All Freya got from Brendan by way of farewell was prolonged eye contact while he held both her hands, but Patsy was hugged and perhaps kissed too, only Karen was too far away to tell. Brendan gave Bob a slap on the back, waved goodbye, apparently to the house, and jumped into the cab. Karen retreated under the trees.

He drove out a lot more cautiously than he had when at the wheel of the 2CV. The beagles were all barking and yelping. Karen followed the Winnebago through Forby and along the Stowerton Road. She had been right, he wasn't going anywhere near Kingsmarkham or the bypass site, but heading for the M23 and then perhaps for its link to the M25. She kept behind him until he came to the approach road to the motorway, watched him enter it and then she turned back for the old bypass and Kingsmarkham.

At the police station the first thing she did was ask if there had been anything from Sacred Globe. Damon, who told her how he had followed Conrad Tarling about all day on foot – it was true the man never used a car – said there had been nothing. It was more than seventy-two hours, or three days which sounded even more, since the message in Dora Wexford's suitcase. Damon had left Conrad Tarling up a chestnut tree, where he had retreated into his tree-house, pulled down the tarpaulin curtain and no doubt curled up inside like a squirrel.

'I'm hoping we can meet this evening.'

Karen, who had turned back to her computer

screen, said they could in a way, of course they could.

'What do you mean, in a way?'

'You and I can both go up to London and talk to a woman called Frenchie Collins who may just possibly have bought a camouflage sleeping bag. Will you drive?'

'Sure,' he said. 'I'd love to.'

'The bones those kids found in the heap of earth at Stowerton Dale,' Wexford said, leafing through the forensic reports that had come in, then sitting down and reading. 'Shin of beef and pork knuckle, much as we thought. Now the clothes Dora was wearing, brown linen suit, amber-and-white spotted voile blouse – what the devil is voile, Mike, or should it be "vwahl"? – tan calf pumps – that's shoes – tights in a shade called 'nearly brown', bra and pants in white silk and lycra, white silk slip with coffee lace. Sounds right.

'A small food stain on the blouse has been identified as made by instant coffee and a liquid soya compound. That'll be the non-lactic soymilk. Dora kept herself very clean, I must say, I should have been coated in spaghetti and jam. Now here's something rather more encouraging. A great many interesting substances were taken from her skirt: her own hairs and someone else's, a young person's, long and dark, therefore most likely Roxane Masood's; a cocktail of grains of chalk, breadcrumbs, cobwebs, powdered limestone, sand and cats' hairs. Rather a large quantity of hairs from a Siamese cat and a black cat.'

'There are seven million cats in Great Britain,' said Burden in a neutral tone.

'Are there really? There aren't, however, seven million cases of a black cat and a Siamese found in

290

conjunction.' Wexford referred back to the report. 'Iron filings, which rather points to some kind of factory or workshop. But listen to this. They also found the kind of dust they suggest could be the substance that adheres to the wings of butterflies and moths.'

'*What*?'

'Apparently – there's an explanation here – butter-flies' and moths' wings aren't solid colours, painted on, so to speak. They're not like the colours of a bird's feathers or an animal's fur, but the patterns are made up by an arrangement of coloured dust. If this is worn away or rubbed off, the insect can't fly. The suggestion is that what may have happened is that Dora's rather long full skirt brushed against a cobweb in which a butterfly or moth had been caught and had died . . .'

'What is it? What's the matter?'

Wexford had fallen silent. His eyes moved up the page again. He laid the sheets of paper down, looked up. 'Mike, the dust was rose-pink and brown.'

'So? A lot of butterflies are pink and brown.'

'Are they? I can't think of any. Black and red, white, yellow and orange, but pink? The only insect I can think of that is predominantly pale-brown with pink wings, *rose-pink underwings*, is the rare Rosy Underwing. They're found in Europe and in Japan, but in this country only in parts of Hampshire and east Wiltshire.'

'How on earth do you know?'

'I've been interesting myself in this sort of thing lately. Must be this bloody bypass. Anyway, I read up about this rare Map butterfly and in the course of that I came across a lot of other stuff.'

Burden looked at him, half smiling. The Chief Inspector never ceased to give him cause for wonder.

'I don't know why I remember about the Rosy

291

Underwing but I do. Of course we'll check all this out. Maybe on the Internet? But I do remember that part about the few specimens being native to Wiltshire. Who do we know lives in Wiltshire?'

It took Burden only a few seconds to remember. 'Conrad Tarling's family.'

'Exactly. Do we have an address?'

'On the computer.'

Twenty minutes and they had it all in front of them: British and European butterflies and the Conrad Tarling printout with biography and family history. The Tarling parents' address was Queringham House, Queringham, Wilts. Wexford had already been studying the *Great Britain Road Atlas*, calculating distances. He felt a small anticipatory shiver that came with a sense that this could be it, this could be the breakthrough.

'Queringham's right on the Hampshire border, Mike, half-way between Winchester and Salisbury.'

'Not the seaside, though, is it? And it's too far away. We've fixed on a radius of sixty miles, remember.'

'This *is* sixty miles. Sixty-three or four, I'd reckon. Your actress friend was wrong when she said Tarling walked eighty miles, a spot of sycophant's hyperbole, that was. This is a big country house by the sound of it, Mike, no doubt with a lot of outbuildings, right in the middle of Rosy Underwing country – and Rosy Underwing dust came off Dora's skirt.'

'The home of known activists, of one terrorist,' said Burden. 'Of a man who half killed himself in an animal transport protest.'

'We'll put through a polite phone call to the Wiltshire Constabulary and, with their consent, we'll make our way to Queringham Hall. Now. No time like the present.'

Chapter 21

Did they need back-up?

The Wiltshire Constabulary had armed-response vehicles patrolling their roads, as Mid-Sussex had. If Wexford was in need of that sort of assistance . . . ? The whole country was on the alert for the Kingsmarkham Kidnappers.

Wexford said he wasn't in need, thanks. All he was doing was taking a look. He hadn't even a search in mind, unless the Tarling family would agree, for he wasn't going for a warrant at this stage. But there would be four of them, himself and Burden, Vine and Lynn Fancourt. There was even a certain amount of relief in getting away from the police station and from the incident room in the old gym. They would let him know at once if a message came from Sacred Globe, but at least he wouldn't be there waiting.

Seventy-two hours exactly since the last one.

It wasn't a bad run, not as much traffic as he had feared. They crossed into Wiltshire at six-thirty and the River Avon a few minutes later. Queringham was between Mownton and Blick, a gentle pastoral countryside of downs and quiet meadows, surrounded by areas of beauty designated NT for National Trust.

These old landowners, as Wexford remarked, knew how to conceal their properties from the curious eyes of the populace. You could never see them from the road. They built the house – whenever it was, a couple of hundred years ago – and then they planted the trees. So that now, as you approached, what you saw was apparently a forest. Entering the drive, you had the impression that you might not succeed in penetrating, that the track might come to an end up against a wall of foliage.

Suddenly, all trees ceased and open land was displayed with the house behind it. But here were no gardens of rare plants, here was no view. This was literally a clearing, from which everything seemed to have been scraped or seared away but for a few small stunted bushes and two large stone urns in which grew withered cypresses. Wexford had been right about the outbuildings. There appeared to be a stables wing with a small central clocktower, while to the left, behind the house, was a large barn and an even larger, very ugly, cylindrical silo.

The first thing that struck him was that their visit, the surprise visit of four police officers, two of whom were of considerable rank, was hardly a cause of astonishment to Charles and Pamela Tarling. Like the Royalls, they were used to this sort of thing. Whatever they might be, however self-effacing and law-abiding, their children constantly attracted the attention of the police. No doubt officers from other forces, possibly from all over England, had come up this path, rung this doorbell, asked these questions, and many times before.

Not quite these questions, though.

They were invited in, led into a large English country house drawing-room. It was shabby and weary and worn as only such places can be, the great blue-and-yellow carpet threadbare and faded to grey and straw, the upholstery frayed, the long yellow curtains, hundreds of yards of them, transparent with age. A huge chipped bowl of dead flowers stood in the centre of a table, dead flowers, not dried ones, dropping grey pollen on the white-ringed mahogany surface.

The place suited its owners. They too looked as if they had started life in colours, in strength and trimness and with a certain polish, but time and the expense of this house and the trials of those children of theirs and of living with those children, had stained and bleached and worn all that away. They even looked rather alike, thin, tall, round-shouldered people with small heads, wrinkled faces and untidy grey hair.

'We're interested primarily in your son, Mr Conrad Tarling,' Wexford said.

The father nodded wearily. It was as if he had heard it all before. He had perhaps answered all the questions before as well, the ones about where Conrad was now, when he had last seen him, if he frequently returned to Queringham Hall. Then Burden mentioned Craig, one of the other sons, the bomber.

Pamela Tarling reddened. A dark and painful blush suffused that faded, lined face. She put her fingers to her cheeks as if to cool them. Somehow you knew those fingers would be icy cold.

'They *are* our children,' she said gently. It was something she had probably said many times before. 'We have always tried to be loyal to our children. And ... and they are brave, dedicated people with the right aims and principles, it's just ... just that they ...'

'All right, Pam,' said her husband. 'Actually, I endorse that. May I ask you what you want to do now?'

'Have a look outside here, Mr Tarling, if we may. It's up to you to refuse if you wish. I'd like to have a look in some of these outbuildings of yours.'

'Oh, I never refuse,' Charles Tarling said. 'I never

say no to the police. There seems no point. They always come back with a warrant.'

He might, of course, have been a very good actor. Wexford simply couldn't tell. He went outside with the others but the Tarlings stayed where they were, sitting opposite each other on a pair of decayed sofas, eyes meeting despairing eyes across a battered late-Victorian table.

To what use had that silo been put? Had the place done duty as a farm? The stable roofs were missing half their tiles and the doors of the loose boxes hung off their hinges. The clock was going but no one had altered the hands when clocks went an hour forward in March and now it would soon be time to put them back again. Wexford looked inside, Burden looked inside. Vine pushed open the door of a place that might have been a dairy or a woodshed or even a grain store. A big blind moth flew blundering out and Wexford got a good look at it. But it wasn't a Rosy Underwing, more like one of the giant hawk-moths.

No one had used the place for fifty years and more. That was apparent. It had a stone floor, shelves covering one wall, a window high up and under it a large stone sink. But no washroom built on, no upper floors overhead. Wexford looked out of the window and instead of giving on to greenness and greyness – and an occasionally occurring blue patch – the outlook was to a brick wall criss-crossed with half-timbering.

'It's a dairy,' he said. 'Where they're kept, the basement room, is a dairy.'

'But not this one,' said Vine.

'No, not this one.'

The sound of wheels, rapidly trundling, made Wexford turn round. The man had come across the cluttered courtyard, propelling his wheelchair as fast as a bicycle. It might have been Conrad Tarling himself, the resemblance was so great. Were they twins? If you could imagine him brought down from his graceful eminence, reduced to what sat in the chair before them, his golden cloak discarded, his strength laid waste, this might have been the King of the Wood.

Like Conrad's, his head was shaved. He could have been as tall as Conrad but his body was reduced and bent, his knees drawn up under the rug that covered them. Large but stubby-fingered hands lay on those knees. The face was Conrad's but even more the Last of the Mohicans, sharp, dark, as if made of bronze, and it was full of pain.

'What are you looking for?' The voice was beautiful, low-pitched, scornful.

Burden's answer made Colum Tarling laugh. 'Just a routine check, Mr Tarling.'

Colum laughed bitterly, without amusement, it wasn't even a genuine laugh, but staged, contrived. To force laughter is much easier than to achieve real tears. 'We get a lot of those,' he said. 'Don't let me stop you. Well, I can't stop you, can I? I can't do anything. Not any more. You can't do much when your spinal cord has been destroyed.'

If such people as he have any compensation, Wexford thought, it must be that of a unique power of embarrassing others. If that was what you liked and wanted.

Colum Tarling evidently liked it, for he said, 'You love all the good things and you work for those good things, to keep them and make them endure, civilisation and living creatures and decent behaviour and mankind, and they punish you for that by cutting up your spine under the wheels of a truck. Have you got an opinion on that?'

Wexford had. He could have talked about it for

half an hour without pausing or hesitation. 'You kindly said we should continue, Mr Tarling, so if you'll excuse us, we will.'

Such courtesy he hadn't expected. 'Christ,' he said, 'a gentleman, a real gentleman. In the wrong job, aren't you?'

His father had come out and was standing behind him. Wexford had noticed a spasm of pain pass across Charles Tarling's face when his son spoke so brutally of his destroyed spine. He laid a hand on his son's shoulder and whispered something. More loudly he said, 'Come inside, Colum, come inside now.'

'They're only doing their job,' Colum said. 'Is that what you whispered to me? I didn't quite catch.'

But he turned the wheelchair and moved back to the house, more slowly than he had come out. That father no doubt endured more of the same daily, Wexford reflected, and yet more of the same when the King of the Wood came visiting, walking his sixty miles across country, sleeping under hedges, and even more when he went to see his son in prison. And the mother would hear morning and evening the details of the horror under that lorry's wheels, its precise physiological results, the clinical details, the pain. That would be the conversation in this house, with genteel poverty its backdrop. It didn't bear thinking of. And yet . . .

Tarling, the father, was still there. He said to Wexford, low-voiced, 'His mind is rather badly disturbed. You mustn't think . . .'

'I am not thinking anything in particular, Mr Tarling.'

'I mean, his spine, "destroyed" isn't the word. Not at all. His back was broken but they can mend backs these days, and of course he's lost a lot of height. But it's all, so much of it, in his poor mind . . .'

Wexford nodded. 'I'd like to take a look in those sheds,' he said, 'and then we'll go upstairs if you'll allow us.'

Rebuffed, Tarling said an indifferent, 'Oh, certainly.'

His son Colum seemed to think, or affected to think, they were searching for explosives. He sat in his wheelchair at the foot of the stairs, haranguing everyone, his parents and the four police officers, on vivisection, endangered species, game hunting and, more obscurely, the destruction of the dodo.

Since neither Charles nor Pamela Tarling objected, they investigated the two top floors. Here again, in some curious, almost supernatural way, features of Queringham Hall resembled aspects of the place Wexford had constructed for where the hostages might be held. No, 'resembled' wasn't the word. Mirrored, provided a kind of mirror image? Rather, it was as if Queringham Hall was in one dimension and the hostage house in a parallel universe where things were similar but subtly different because in some past time events and structures had developed in different ways and along different paths.

Just as the basement room presented itself here as a disused dairy, so among the attics they found what might have been Roxane Masood's prison, small, square, low-ceilinged. But the window was too small for even a very thin woman to squeeze out of and six feet below the flat roof of a bathroom protruded far enough to break a fall.

It was only that English country houses often resembled each other, Wexford thought. It told him one thing, though. A country house was what he was looking for, not a factory or workshop or barn.

If she had shown disapproval of this room and perhaps its occupant on her previous visit, Karen

Malahyde was unaware of it. She always tried to maintain a neutral expression and demeanour, no matter how dirty or poor, or come to that, ostentatious and luxurious, a place might be. But she must have given some hint of her true feelings all unawares, must have put something of disapprobation into her tone, or distaste into her cool eye, for Frenchie Collins refused point blank to talk to her.

'I'm not saying a word to a right little tight-arse like you.' She appealed to Damon. 'Look at her face, real sour apple, like she's walking around with a bad smell under her crinkled-up nose.'

'I'm sorry, Ms Collins,' Karen said rather stiffly, 'but I truly don't have any feelings of that sort.'

It was, of course, an outright lie, for she was even more horrified than last time by the squalor of this tiny back room, its view of a grey brick wall and, indeed, by the smell which reminded her of something she hadn't smelt since the chemistry lab at school: the rotten cabbage stink of calcium carbide.

'We simply wanted to ask you a few questions.'

'You simply wanted that before,' said Frenchie Collins. 'And you simply acted like I was something the dog brought in – no, correction, like something the dog did on the floor.'

You could tell she was young, though it was hard to say how, yet she had all the lineaments of age: dry, greying hair, coarse, lined skin, two missing front teeth, wrinkled hands which shook. Her skeletal body was wrapped in a once-white towelling dressing-gown and her feet buried and lost in grey woolly socks.

'Ms Collins . . .'

'I said I wouldn't talk to you. I don't mind talking to him. He seems a nice enough young guy.'

Karen and Damon exchanged a glance.

'All right,' Karen said, 'if that's what you'd like. I won't say a word.'

'I don't want you *here*,' said Frenchie Collins. 'Right? Understood? I'll talk to him on his own, though Christ knows what I can tell him, I don't know anything about those Sacred Globe people. You,' she said to Karen, 'can sit in the car. No doubt there *is* a car?'

Karen went down and did just that. She had a feeling Frenchie Collins knew something that she could get out of her but that Damon couldn't. Of course it was absurd to think like that about a person who refused to talk to her. Because she was a sensible woman and ambitious, with an eye to rising in the police force, she spent the time waiting for Damon in some honest analysis of her own behaviour, examining recent attitudes towards some of the people Wexford called 'our customers'. If you had very high standards of hygiene and method and order it was hard not to apply them to others, but she would try. The great thing was to be aware of your shortcomings, for that was the first step in setting things to rights.

Am I smug, she was asking herself, am I complacent? An honest answer – yes, I am, yes, I am, and intolerant and near to bigotry – was being forced out of her when Damon came back.

It had all been in vain. Frenchie Collins had bought the sleeping bag, as they thought, had taken it to Zaïre but had abandoned it there along with much of her other property. She had been too ill and weak by that time to carry more than the bare essentials.

'So she says,' said Karen.

' "Africa has killed me", she said. Those were her words. And you have to admit she looks in a bad way. I suppose it could be AIDS.'

'No, it couldn't. Hasn't been time. I don't think

she'd have thrown that sleeping bag away, abandoned it or whatever she says. People like her never have any money and they don't abandon things like that. She'd have been more likely to have got inside it at the airport and had herself carried on to the plane.'

'The sleeping bag could have been bought in the north of England where Outdoors' other outlets are.'

Karen remembered that she was supposed to be nice and tolerant, not prejudiced and not smug. Especially with this man she wanted to be nice. It was a long time since she'd known any man she wanted to seem as nice to as she did to this one. 'The rest of the evening is ours,' she said and she smiled. 'We could spend it up here, but it would be nicer to go home, wouldn't it?'

It was after nine when Wexford got back. No message from Sacred Globe. He knew there wouldn't be, or they would have called him, but he was still disappointed. More than disappointed. A feeling he seldom had these days, one he hadn't experienced much since he was young, flooded over him. It was panic and he clenched his hands, suppressing it, breathing deeply.

He had been in his office ten minutes. He didn't know why he had come up here. There was nothing to do tonight. Go home, tell Dora all those things he was beginning to have doubts about. Oh, no, they won't kill them, of course not. We'll find them. We'll find Sacred Globe. We'll find the man with the tattoo on his left forearm and the one who smells of acetone. What kind of illness could you have that made you smell of nail varnish remover? Something wrong with the kidneys? The pancreas? The body manufacturing too many ketones?

But we'll find them. The man who has to wear

gloves because something disfigures his hands. Eczema perhaps or scars. Or because he is black. The woman who wears heavy boots to help her look like a man. The house with a black cat and a Siamese which has a dairy from whose window you can see a shifting patch of blue that's as blue as the sky but isn't the sky.

He went down in the lift, walked across the foyer as Audrey Barker burst through the swing doors.

The duty sergeant called out, 'Excuse me!'

She looked, he realised, as he had never seen her before. She looked happy. More than that – elated, almost manic with happiness. Hair is supposed to stand on end through shock or horror but hers flew out in that wild way from joy. She was smiling, laughing, as if she couldn't stop. 'He phoned me,' she shouted. 'My son phoned me!'

Wexford said, 'Mrs Barker, just a moment . . . What exactly are you saying?'

'I didn't want to phone you, you don't know who you're talking to on the phone, but my son, Ryan, he phoned me half an hour ago. I thought you'd be here, you'd still be here. At a time like this . . . I couldn't keep still, I had to move, run, I came straight here, to tell you myself.'

Wexford nodded. He said very steadily in an effort to calm her, 'Yes, you tell me. Tell me all about it. Let's go upstairs to my office.'

'His voice, I couldn't believe it, I thought I was dreaming, but I knew it was real, and he's all right, he's fine . . .'

'We'll go upstairs, Mrs Barker. The lift's on its way.'

They got in. She jumped into it. She clutched his arm with a shaking hand.

'He's all right. He's quite all right. He likes them

and they like him. He's *joined* them, and now they won't hurt him!'

Chapter 22

Audrey Barker sat opposite him on the other side of his desk with a cup of tea in front of her. She was calmer now and some of the wild joy had gone out of her face. The anxious look was returning, the mouth-pursing that prematurely pleated her upper lip. He let her sip the strong, sweet tea, noticing the shaking of the hand that held the cup, the chatter of teeth against the china. Let her take her time. It was, in any case, now far too late to attempt a tracing of the call.

Sweat broke on her upper lip. 'I should have phoned you, shouldn't I?'

'I'm not sure if it would have made any difference, Mrs Barker. Will you tell me what Ryan said?'

'I nearly fainted when I heard his voice. I couldn't believe it. I was stunned. I thought I was dreaming or going mad. He said, "Mum, it's me" and of course I knew it was him, but I still said, "Who is that? Who is it?" and he said, "Mum, it's Ryan, calm down, it's Ryan" and then, "Listen," he said, "this is a message from us," so I said, "Who's us? What do you mean?" And he said, "Sacred Globe. I'm one of them now." I mean, it was something like that he said, I may not have got his exact words.'

'But you're sure he said that. He said, "I'm one of them now"?'

'Yes, I'm sure. "I'm one of them now." I didn't know what he meant and I asked him.' She had been looking down, her hands clasped in her lap, as she made an effort to remember accurately, but now she raised her head and met Wexford's eyes. 'He said he simply meant what he said. He'd joined them. They'd asked him to join them. He was flattered, of course, he was *proud*. He's only a *child*. He can't make those sort of choices. I was feeling happy and I'm not any more. It was stupid of me, wasn't it? I was happy because he's all right, he's alive, but now I realise he's one of *them* I . . .'

'What else did he say?'

'He said – and it didn't sound a bit like him talking – he said, "Our cause is just. I didn't know, but I do now. We want the best for the world. It's 'we', Mum, do you understand?" '

'Did you ask him where he was?'

She put one hand up to her head. 'Oh God, I didn't think of it. He wouldn't have told me, would he? He said something like, I can't remember exactly, "We want the bypass rerouted" or he may have said re- something else, I don't know. But that's what he meant. "I'll come back to you tomorrow," he said, and I didn't know, I *don't* know, what that meant. I mean, could it be he meant he's coming *home*?'

'It sounds more as if another message will come. Mrs Barker, I'd like you to repeat what you've told me and we'll record it on tape. Will you do that?'

At first Wexford had been astonished by Ryan Barker's allying himself with Sacred Globe. But, of course, it wasn't new, it certainly wasn't unknown, this defection of a hostage to his captors and the espousal of their cause. And this cause in particular held a special appeal for young people. It was the young who were fired with outrage at the destruction of the environment – their future environment – and with a burning fervour to reverse 'progress' and restore some unspecified natural paradise.

He said to Audrey Barker when she had finished recording her conversation with Ryan, 'He idealises his father, doesn't he? I wonder if he sees Sacred Globe as something his father would have approved of, or that he thinks he'd have approved of. I understand his father was particularly keen on natural history.'

She looked at him as if he had suddenly, inexplicably, begun speaking to her in a foreign language. A huge weariness had settled on her, causing a sagging of her face and a slumping of her shoulders. He repeated what he had said, embellishing and rephrasing it.

'I know your husband was killed in the Falklands. I know about the album of drawings. My impression is that Ryan has done what some children who have lost a parent do, make paragons of them, idolise them, and model themselves on them. Erroneously, of course, Ryan sees Sacred Globe as an organisation his father would have admired and wanted to support. So he supports it in his stead.'

She shrugged her shoulders, lifting them to an exaggerated extent, as if to make a total denial. Her voice was bitter. 'He wasn't my husband. I've never been married. I told Ryan his father was killed in the Falklands – well, he was killed at the time of the Falklands, that was true.'

Wexford looked at her inquiringly.

'Dennis Barker was killed in a knife fight. In Deptford. They never got anyone for it. Didn't bother, I dare say, they knew the sort he was. I had to tell Ryan something, so I made up all that and my mother stuck by me and told the same tale.'

'And the natural history?' said Wexford. 'The drawings? The album?'

'They were my father's. John Peabody's. Look, I

never told him otherwise but kids ... well, they deceive themselves to sort of make things better.'

And adults too, thought Wexford. 'The point here,' he said, 'is not what is fact but what he has taught himself to think of as fact. In doing this he's putting himself in his father's shoes, he's being his father.'

'His father, my God! A backstreet thug. Well, he's going the right way about it, isn't he, joining up with a bunch of terrorists?'

'I'll have someone drive you home, Mrs Barker. I shall have a trace put on your mother's phone. I shall have all your phone conversations recorded and take the precaution, with your permission, of having one of my officers in the house with you tomorrow for when Ryan calls again.'

If he called. If they didn't send a letter or another body ... He had to tell Dora.

She surprised him by not being surprised. 'He was waiting for something like that,' she said. 'I had that impression when we talked. I thought he'd found it in a person, in Owen Struther, a father-hero. But Owen let him down, or he must have seen it as letting him down, when he and Kitty were handcuffed and taken away. I see now that Ryan was waiting for something to aim at, a cause, a reason for living. Of course he's only a child ...'

'That's what his mother said.'

'The poor woman.'

He told her about the real father and the fantasy father, expecting her to be at least a little affronted. None of us likes to be deceived, even if the deceiver is barely aware that he is lying and his listener a dupe. But she only shook her head and held out her hands in that gesture of submitting to the inevitable.

'What will become of him?'

'When we catch them, d'you mean? Nothing, I should think. As everyone keeps saying, he's a child.'

308

'I wonder what happened,' she said.

'What do you mean, what happened?'

'I told you they never talked to us. There was no communication. How did they come to change that and talk to him after I was gone and he was alone? Did they approach him or he approach them? I'd think the latter, wouldn't you? I mean, he must have been lonely and desperate for a human voice, so he started talking to them, perhaps asking them why they were doing this, what they wanted. And they saw their chance. It was to their advantage, wasn't it, to have a willing guest rather than a hostage? All hostage takers with a real cause must want that.'

'Only up to a point,' said Wexford. 'If all your hostages convert you lose your bargaining power.'

'The Struthers would never convert. Never. That just leaves them now, doesn't it? Owen and Kitty, just the two of them.'

'It's almost as valuable to Sacred Globe to have two hostages as to have five,' said Wexford.

They were both awake early next morning and she began talking to him about the two people of whom, up till now, she had said least. It was as if she had either been thinking about them during the long watches of the night or else her thoughts and analyses had crystallised while she slept. She brought him tea and sat on the bed. It wasn't yet seven.

'Kitty was only in her early fifties but still I'd say she belonged to a dying breed. All their lives they're protected by men, they do nothing for themselves, make no decisions, have no enterprise. Oh, I know I'm just a housewife myself, but not in that helpless way, doing nothing but a little cooking, a little gardening, a little telling the cleaning woman what to do. They always have just one child, these women, it's funny but it usually seems to be a boy, and they send him away to boarding-school as soon as they can.

'That was Kitty Struther. She hardly talked, but somehow I knew all that. Confronted by something different, something threatening, she just went to pieces, she collapsed like a jelly. All she ever said really was, "Owen, you have to do something" and "Owen, *do* something". And his response was to behave like a prisoner of war bent on escaping from Colditz. You could tell what their marriage was, she utterly dependent on him for everything and he sustaining the illusion of being brave and admirable, finding it necessary to impress her all the time.'

'The little woman? That's what empire builders used to say.'

'The big man and the little woman ... It makes you shudder. Do you remember when Sheila was married to Andrew and his mother used to refer to her as his "little wife"?'

'I'd better get up,' said Wexford, 'or I won't be impressing anyone.'

'They won't kill them, will they, Reg?'

It was the only question he'd anticipated that she had actually asked. 'I hope not,' he said, and then, 'not if I can help it.'

Savesbury House and a trace on Andrew Struther's phone, a trace too on Clare Cox's, though Wexford thought it unlikely Ryan Barker would call her. Her daughter was dead and her involvement, as far as Sacred Globe was concerned, was over. Most probably the call would come to Audrey Barker once more. At least the messages were coming. Anything was preferable to that silence.

Burden, taking Karen Malahyde with him, had gone to Rhombus Road. There, in Mrs Peabody's front room, they would sit it out till the call came. If it came. The computers in the old gym continued to store information, hundreds of thousands of bytes of it, adding now Dora Wexford's comments on the Struthers, Audrey Barker's tape, Karen Malahyde and Damon Slesar's negative results from the interview with Frenchie Collins. Wexford sat in front of Mary Jefferies' screen, reading the document he hoped would at last lead him to Sacred Globe.

A basement room, rectangular, twenty feet by thirty, one heavy door in, one lighter door out to a washroom. One window high up with a sink under it. The window barred with a cross-hatched wooden structure outside it. Something green and a grey stone step visible. The floor of stone flags, the walls whitewashed. A dairy, he knew that now – did that knowledge do him any good?

The non-lactic soymilk, which at first had seemed so promising, was obtainable all over the country. That damned Rosy Underwing had only led them on a wild-goose chase – a wild-moth chase – half across the south of England.

There remained the blue thing that came and went outside the window. Washing hanging out to dry? Did people still hang out washing? A car? It could be a blue car. That would be moved from one place to another and blue was always a popular colour for cars. Yes, but eight feet up in the air? A window which when opened revealed a blue lampshade inside or a blue curtain? He didn't much like any of those ideas. It was the way the blue thing moved that was confusing.

A report had just come in of the theft of twenty beagles from a research laboratory near Tunbridge Wells. The dogs had been taken and the premises set on fire. Kent that was, not his responsibility, not Montague Ryder's responsibility.

Someone, he saw, had already made the connection with Mid-Sussex. Karen Malahyde had all the evidence against Brendan Royall. Did that mean Royall was, after all, unconnected with Sacred Globe? Probably. And Damon Slesar had had no success with Conrad Tarling, who, though occasionally going off for long walks to inspect different areas of the site, was mostly holed up in his tree-house.

Driving to Savesbury, Wexford passed near the camp. A stillness hung over the whole bypass area. At this point, roughly the centre of the proposed construction, no work had yet been done. No trees had yet been cut down. It was still the unspoilt countryside of deep lanes, rich meadows, hilly terrain and, distantly, high downs. The farmer who had removed his sheep from the fields here had brought them back again. Savesbury Hill was still unravaged, a single-standing tor with its crowning ring of trees, its roots in the feeding ground of the Map butterfly. Still. He had no time to waste but for all that he made enough of a detour to see if he could spot evidence of the environmental assessment, but there was no sign of it, unless he was looking in the wrong place.

Last time he had passed this way a fitful sun had been shining. The wind was high enough to blow clouds constantly across the sun's face so that the bright light came and went, and cloud shadows were swept across the green hillsides like flocks of great dark birds. But today it was dull, the thick grey sky threatening rain. The woods must be full of tree people, biding their time, waiting to know what the next move would be, but he could see none of them. Someone had told him that up at the Stowerton end of the bypass site, where the children had found the bones, grass and weeds were already growing on the mounds of upturned earth.

Outside the Framhurst teashop tree people sat at tables, or they might only have been walkers back-packing. No Conrad Tarling, no Gary nor Quilla, no Freya. Perhaps they were all somewhere guarding the Struthers, but he didn't think so. Somehow he knew it wasn't that way at all, it was quite different, he had been looking at this whole thing from the wrong angle. But what was the use of that if you didn't know how and where it was wrong?

Bibi opened the door to him. She had been alerted to his coming, said Andrew was about somewhere and Wexford might find him 'round the back'. He walked through a brick archway on to an area with a floor like a checkerboard of stone squares and turf squares. Tubs of striped petunias and Jamaican daisies stood about, evidence of Kitty Struther's horticultural skills. The dog Manfred was in the act of lifting its leg against a leafy climbing plant which rambled across one of the walls. Wexford turned as Andrew Struther appeared round the side of the Georgian building and followed him back to the house.

The house seemed tidier, better tended, more the way poor Kitty Struther would want to find it when she came home. Sitting in her gracious living-room with its chintz and its rugs in their muted colours, its silver and its Chinese porcelain, Wexford looked once more at the framed photograph of the two remaining hostages, a copy of which Andrew had brought him. You wouldn't guess from this, he thought, that Kitty Struther would bend and break so quickly under pressure and her husband transform himself into a strutting Blimp. In the picture she looked rather more adventurous than he, a well-kept almost athletic skier who had long ago graduated from the nursery slopes. Owen Struther reminded him of photographs from his youth of Sir Edmund

Hillary, and Owen appeared as capable of climbing the world's highest mountain.

'You have some news?' Andrew Struther asked.

'Nothing to comfort you much, I'm afraid. I'm here to tell you that your parents are now the only hostages that Sacred Globe hold.'

'What about the boy?'

Wexford told him. Struther clenched his hands and after a moment or two bowed his head and brought his fists up to his forehead. He seemed to make a massive effort at self-control, breathing deeply and tensing the muscles of his shoulders. He was very different now from the arrogant and supercilious man who, a week ago, had shown Burden and Karen the door. Stress had broken him.

'A call may come here. We have a trace on your phone, but I would like you to co-operate just the same.'

'If by that you mean telling the little bastard what I think of him I'll co-operate all right.'

'I mean exactly the reverse of that, Mr Struther. I would like you to keep him talking for as long as you can. Don't antagonise him. Talk about your parents if you like. It would be natural for you to ask after their welfare, and the more you ask and talk the more likely he is to give you some indication of where they are.'

'You think he'll phone *here*?'

'No, I don't think so. I just want to be prepared.'

If royalty had been visiting Mrs Peabody could hardly have cleaned and garnished her house more thoroughly. She had had notice of the coming of the two officers since eight o'clock on the previous evening and that had been enough. The spring-cleaning must have taken place between then and nine in the morning when Burden and Karen arrived.

314

Mrs Peabody had probably got up at five. One of the antimacassars on the back of an armchair was still slightly damp from the wash, though carefully starched and ironed. Karen touched it with her fingertip and smiled. Then she told herself that she could become like that if she didn't watch it. In about thirty-five years' time she could be a Mrs Peabody, plumping up cushions before guests came, even making someone, whoever it was – Damon Slesar? – take off his shoes when he came in the front door.

'Penny for your thoughts, Sergeant Malahyde,' said Burden because she had gone rather pink.

'I was just thinking I could turn into a finicky old *hausfrau* like Mrs P. if I wasn't careful.'

'And so could I,' confessed Burden, 'or the male equivalent.'

Audrey Barker was to answer the phone herself. If it rang, when it rang. She hovered, coming and going, helping her mother with whatever was left for Mrs Peabody to do, returning with creased-up face and anxious eyes. Alone for a moment with Karen in the kitchen she volunteered, unasked, the information that her operation had been for gallstones. So much for Ryan's more sensational version of that surgery, repeated by Dora Wexford on tape. Karen marvelled at the mind, not to say the imagination, of a fourteen-year-old boy who could give his mother a cone biopsy.

The first time the phone rang was at twenty-past ten. Mrs Peabody had just brought in cups of milky frothy coffee, the Rhombus Road version of capuccino. A lace-trimmed cloth was on the tray and a paper doily on the biscuit plate, the sugar was the loaf kind and there was an apostle spoon in each saucer. Audrey Barker looked at it with the loathing of a woman who cares very little for the appearance of domestic appurtenances but has all her life suffered under the reproofs of a houseproud mother. The phone ringing made her jump and bring her hands up to her head. Burden nodded to her and she picked up the receiver.

It was immediately clear this wasn't Ryan. Burden – and Wexford – had wondered about the man Ryan had told Dora his mother was engaged to. Was this another figment of his hungry imagination? Apparently not, though, as Audrey Barker explained, putting the phone down after a minute or two. 'My friend' she called him. 'He phones me every day. Well, two or three times a day.'

The time went by. To Burden it passed very slowly. Mrs Peabody took away their coffee cups, picked up two invisible biscuit crumbs from the area of carpet between his feet. For something to do, he asked Audrey Barker about her son, his tastes, his interests, his progress at school, and she told him, manifestly becoming less tense. Ryan shone, apparently, at biology and geography, a prowess which surprised no one. He possessed a considerable library of books on natural history. She had given him a field guide to British birds for Christmas and had already bought a set of wildlife videos for his coming birthday . . .

The phone rang again at midday and because it was precisely twelve noon, which somehow seemed a likely time for Sacred Globe to phone, when Audrey lifted the receiver Karen got up and stood close enough to her to hear her caller's voice. It might have been a likely time but it wasn't the right time. The caller was Hassy Masood.

'He phones every day too,' Audrey said when the short conversation was over. 'It's what he calls being my support group. Very kind, I suppose, though frankly I could do without it. She's not up to talking and I don't wonder. He always explains she's not up to it.'

Next time the phone rang it was a wrong number. Watching Audrey, Karen thought she had never before quite seen the significance of the phrase 'jumping out of one's skin'.

The forensic science laboratory naturally gave Wexford no clue as to the provenance of the sleeping bag. Nicky Weaver had made tracing it her task, now that it was clear they had been wrong in supposing it to be identified with the one bought in Brixton and sold to Frenchie Collins. She had also eliminated the north-London source, and she and Hennessy had widened their search to the Midlands while Damon Slesar kept up his surveillance of Conrad Tarling.

But if there was nothing in the lab report on the sleeping bag's origin, a great deal of evidence had been gathered as to where it had been after it came into the possession of Sacred Globe.

It was made of washable material and had been washed at least once in its lifetime. After the Collins woman brought it back from Africa, thought Wexford, only she hadn't brought it back, it wasn't hers. She had told Slesar it wasn't hers and why should she lie?

Few of the substances on Dora's clothes had been found on the inside or outside of the sleeping bag, except for the cat hair. There was plenty of that. Small stains on the outside of the bag had been made in one case by coffee, black coffee without milk, and in the other by red wine. Three small irregular stones inside the bag were the constituents of gravel, all of them tiny flint fragments, but perhaps the most interesting find was a withered leaf. It had been in the bottom of the bag and in the opinion of the forensic scientist had very likely adhered to one of

Roxane's shoes. The leaf was not from a wild plant but from the cultivated climber Ipomoea rubro-caer-ulea, the Morning Glory.

Wexford read that part of the report again. He had once tried growing Morning Glory in his own garden but the summer had been so bad that the first flowers on the sickly attenuated plant failed to come out till October, only to be immediately nipped by frost. Parts of it – seeds? Root? Leaves? – were alleged to produce hallucinations, Sheila had told him, she knew people who chewed it, but when he looked up Ipomoea in a herbal he had found only that it was a source of the purgative, jalap.

On Roxane's clothes had been found stains made by her own blood, by body lotion – presumably deposited before her abduction – by non-lactic soymilk and by tomato sauce. He turned the pages back to the beginning and looked, unseeing, out of his window.

Ryan Barker phoned his mother at the very moment when Burden was giving up hope, was thinking they were in for another of those long waits. Days of waiting once more perhaps, God forbid.

Mrs Peabody made them the kind of sandwiches that are called 'dainty', little crustless triangles of white bread with wafer-thin ham or cress between the slices. She sat and watched them eat. An hour later she made tea. She brought in a cake, the kind of confection Patsy Panick might have admired, chocolate with chocolate icing and ornamented by choco-late flake bars. To Burden's astonishment the sight and smell of it brought a breath of nausea up into his throat, but thin, tense Karen took a small slice.

Her eye drawn to a speck of something on the mantelpiece that shouldn't have been there, Mrs Peabody came back with a duster and got to work.

She rubbed feverishly, polishing ornaments. It reminded Karen of a cat who suddenly senses some trace of scent or dirt on its apparently spotless paw and begins a manic licking.

The phone gave a preparatory click. It hadn't done that before or if it had they hadn't noticed. The bell seemed disproportionately loud, a shrill shattering sound. Audrey gave the number as they had instructed her, in monotonous dalek-speak.

The fiancé once more. Burden wished he had asked Audrey to tell him not to call again that day. He did it now. She nodded but she didn't ask. She put the phone down and it rang at once.

Karen was immediately at Audrey Barker's side as she grabbed the receiver. Again the number was given in that mechanical monotone.

A boy's voice, long-broken but unsteady and perhaps pitched high through nervousness.

'Mum? It's me.'

Chapter 23

'Did you pass on the message, Mum?'

'Of course I did, Ryan. I did what you said.'

Audrey Barker was no actress. Her voice sounded stilted, as if the words had been learned by heart for the dramatic society's play.

'They have to reroute the bypass, you got that?'

'I got it, Ryan, and I passed it on. Like you said, Ryan.'

That stilted voice made him suspicious. 'Is there anyone there with you?'

She almost screamed. 'Of course not, of course not!'

'It has to be announced. Officially. By the government. And if it's not Mrs Struther dies. Have you got that? Before nightfall tomorrow or Mrs Struther's dead.'

'Oh, Ryan . . .'

'I think you've got someone there. I'm going to ring off. I won't call again. Remember our cause is just. It's the only way, Mum, it's the way to save the planet. And when it's a matter of saving the planet one woman's life is of no account. I'm going now. Goodbye.'

That was the conversation Karen Malahyde heard directly. Later on, Wexford was to listen to a tape of it, but before he could do so the call had been traced.

To the Brigadier public house on the old Kingsmarkham bypass.

*

It had started to rain. The rain, which had been gloomily forecast, which had been expected for days, fell rapidly out of swiftly gathered black clouds, then in torrents, fountaining, crashing rain. It held them up. They might have been there in fifteen minutes, that was the minimum it took, but the rain was the kind that doesn't merely slow traffic, it drives it for safety's sake off the road.

Pemberton, driving Burden and Karen, was forced to pull into a lay-by. It was like being under some great waterfall, he said, maybe Niagara Falls. Barry Vine and Lynn Fancourt, in the next car, caught them up and pulled in behind them. By the time the rain had lessened, had been reduced to a normal heavy storm, twenty minutes had gone by. Half an hour had passed by the time they got to the Brigadier, roaring in over that crunchy gravel approach like cops in an LA car chase.

Twenty-five minutes to six, and William Dickson had opened for the evening trade thirty-five minutes before. He was serving the couple in the saloon bar with a pint of Guinness and a gin and blackcurrant when the five policemen came in – crashed in as hard as the rain – and Vine, with Pemberton behind him, strode across to the door into the public bar.

Burden snapped, 'Who else is in the house?'

'The wife. Me,' said Dickson. 'What is this? What's going on?'

Vine came back. 'There's nobody in the public.'

'Of course there isn't. I said. There's this lady and gentleman and me, and the wife's upstairs. What is all this?'

'We'll take a look,' said Burden.

'Suit yourselves. You might ask. Politeness never did no harm. You're lucky I'm not asking to see your warrant.'

The couple in the bar, the woman at a table, her

companion at the counter preparing to pay for his drinks, stared with cautious pleasure. The man kept his eyes on Burden while pushing a five-pound note towards Dickson.

Vine went into the back hallway where the pay-phone was. This was the phone Ulrike Ranke had used back in April when she had made the last call of her life. He looked inside various rooms, an office with another phone, a small sitting-room or snug. There was no one about. Karen followed him. Pemberton and Lynn Fancourt went upstairs.

The rain was coming down heavily again. Sheets of it, falling on the empty car park, almost obscured the outline of the dismal building Dickson called a ballroom. Burden told the man and the woman he was a police officer, showed them his warrant card and asked them how long they had been in the pub.

'Now you wait a minute,' said Dickson.

Burden rounded on him. 'Your wife is being fetched to take over the trade in here. I'd like you to go into that snug place of yours and wait for me. I want to talk to you.'

'What about, for Christ's sake?'

'I regret having to speak to you like this in front of your patrons, Mr Dickson, but you'll go into that room *now*, or else I'll arrest you for obstructing me in the execution of my duty.'

Dickson went. He kicked the doorstop in a petulant way, like a cross child, but he went. Pemberton came back with Dickson's wife, a top-heavy blonde woman of about forty wearing black leggings and high-heeled sandals. Burden nodded to her and asked the couple with the drinks if they would mind his joining them at their table. Rather bemused, the man shook his head. He said his name was Roger Gardiner and his friend's was Sandra Cole.

Barry Vine said, 'I'd like to ask you a few

questions' and repeated the one Burden had already asked.

'We came in when it opened,' Gardiner said. 'We were early and we waited outside a bit. In the car.'

'Other people were here then. A boy of about fifteen? And others with him?'

'He was older than that,' Sandra Cole said. 'He was taller than Rodge.'

'We were in here by then,' Gardiner said. 'Been in here a couple of minutes. A man and a woman – well, a girl – they came in, ran into the bar with the boy, and the girl asked the manager, the owner, whatever, if they could use the phone.'

'She said the boy was in something-shock, ana-something shock, and they had to get an ambulance.'

'Anaphylactic shock?'

'That's it. It was urgent, she said, and the owner, he told them where the phone was ...'

'I told them where the phone was,' Dickson said to Burden. 'Not that pay one, the one in my office. It was urgent, see, she said the kid might die if he didn't get to a hospital. So I reckoned they didn't want to be messing about with a pay-phone ...'

'Developed a conscience since the Ulrike Ranke business, have you?'

'I don't know what that's supposed to mean. They went off into the office and I never saw them again.'

'Come on, Dickson, you can do better than that. You let them use your phone, you were worried the boy might die, but once you'd seen the back of them the whole thing went out of your head?'

'I did go in there,' said Dickson, 'but they was gone. I asked the wife if she'd heard the ambulance because I hadn't, but she didn't know what I was on about.'

'Show me the phone.'

It was on the desk among the welter of papers and

magazines, a brown telephone constructed of a substance that has a glossy surface.

'Has it been touched since?'

Dickson shook his head. A tic had started at the corner of his mouth.

'Don't touch it. And close the place. Most likely you can open again tomorrow.'

'What's all this about? I can't close just like that!'

'You don't have a choice,' said Burden.

He had heard a car arrive. You could hear anything on that gravel. A sparrow walking across it would have been clearly audible. He had heard a car and thought it was customers for the Brigadier but it was Wexford, driven up here by Donaldson. He was in the saloon bar, talking to Linda Dickson, who was now holding a diminutive Yorkshire terrier in her arms, its face pressed up against her brightly painted cheek. Gardiner and his girlfriend were doing their best to describe to Karen Malahyde the appearance of the man and the woman who had accompanied Ryan Barker.

'I never saw them,' Linda Dickson said. She looked around for her husband, but he was locking and bolting the front doors. 'I thought I heard a car, but it must have been that lady and gentleman.'

'Why "must have been"?'

'You can hear everything on that gravel. If this was a free house I'd have that concreted but the brewery won't spend the money.'

'There's no need to go over the gravel if you drive straight into the car park at the back, is there?'

'That's what they must have done.'

'I'm not much of a hand at describing what people look like,' said her husband. 'See too many of them, I reckon. The boy was tall, he was a very tall lad, tall as me . . .'

'We know what the boy looks like, Mr Dickson,'

said Wexford, his eye on the tattoo on the man's left forearm. Butterfly? Bird? Abstract design? 'The boy is Ryan Barker, one of the hostages. You keep asking what this is about – well, it's about Sacred Globe. Do you think that will jog your memory when it comes to describing these people?'

Dickson's mouth fell open. 'You have to be kidding.'

'No, I don't have to be. If I was in the mood for it I could think up a better joke that that.'

'Sacred Globe. Bloody hell. You do mean those lunatics that kidnapped those people and killed the girl?'

'Try describing those lunatics, will you?'

His description, when it finally came, tallied with those of Roger Gardiner and Sandra Cole. None of the three was particularly observant, none apparently much interested in his or her fellow human beings. The plausible tale of anaphylactic shock which, it now appeared, had been told solely by the woman, and which might have been expected to attract their interest, had registered only as an account of something alien and unpronounceable. They considered. Roger Gardiner had actually scratched his head. After a massive shrug of his heavy shoulders, William Dickson came up with the best he could do.

The woman was small but wiry and fit-looking. She wore no make-up and her hair was hidden under a baseball cap. She was young but no one could suggest her age more precisely than to describe her as between twenty and thirty. Her companion was a tall, thin man, also wearing a baseball cap and a pair of dark glasses. Their clothes were so unremarkable that no one could specify what they wore. Jeans, perhaps, jackets of dark or neutral colours. No one had noticed eye colour or a single peculiarity. The man had spoken. The woman's voice was ... just an ordinary voice.

'Like *EastEnders*,' said Roger Gardiner.

Wexford knew what he meant, or thought he did. London working class, only it wasn't politically correct to use expressions like that these days. Cockney – did anyone use the word anymore? Or did he mean like an actor in a television soap? Asked, Gardiner didn't know, couldn't answer, could only repeat what he had said. Like *EastEnders*.

'I'd like to have a look outside,' Wexford said to Dickson.

'Be my guest, guv'nor. I hope I'm a reasonable man, I hope I know how to co-operate. Only there are some not a million miles from where I'm standing who don't know the meaning of the word manners.'

The car park was awash. Puddles were more like shallow lakes and rain dripped off the eaves of the barrack-like building which loomed over the sheets of water. By now the rain had stopped but the dark-grey sky was heavy with more to come. A wind had got up, tearing at the branches of the chestnuts in the meadow beyond the fence.

Wexford hadn't much hope. The truth was that now he had no hope, but he was going to look inside that building just the same. A dance hall – well, if you stuck a few bits of neon on the outside, flung open those double asbestos doors, had some cheerful people selling tickets ... No, it would always be a dreary dump, a cavernous barn of a place, and the best thing for it would be to pull it down.

Cavernous was right. The whole area must have been sixty feet by forty and the ceiling – or roof of girders and plasterboard – a good thirty feet high. There were metal-framed windows all along both sides, a stage of sorts at one end. Vine opened the door that seemed to lead behind the stage and they trooped through. But nothing was to be seen apart from two lavatories, one with a picture of a peacock with fanned tail on the door, the other of a drab peahen – the most sexist thing she'd seen in years, Karen said angrily – a passage and a large unfurnished room that might once have been used for making tea and even preparing food. The place was dusty and untended, and when Dickson said it hadn't been used for years no one had any difficulty believing him.

Yet why had those two brought Ryan here? What was the point of it? Returning to the main premises of the Brigadier, Wexford wondered if it might be from fear of returning to the phone or call box they had used three times before, while they obviously couldn't use any phone that might be installed where the hostages were. Did they know the pub would be largely unfrequented at that time of day? That Dickson and his wife were scarcely perceptive people?

'You've closed up, Mr Dickson,' he said. 'You'll be at a bit of a loose end this evening, so with your permission I think we'll use it to have a talk about your patrons. Who comes here, who's a regular, that sort of thing.'

Still clutching the Yorkshire terrier, Linda Dickson said shrilly, 'You're taking him to the police station?'

Wexford regarded her calmly. 'Would that present a problem, Mrs Dickson? But no, I'm not. I thought we might talk here. In your office.'

Hennessy was unplugging the phone with gloved hands, dropping the instrument into a plastic bag.

'He can't have my phone!'

'The property of Telecom, as a matter of fact, Mr Dickson. We'll clear it with them. You'll soon have it back.' Wexford sat down without waiting to be asked. He was pretty sure he wouldn't be asked. 'Now, you'd never seen these people before, I take it?'

'Never. Not one of them.'

'Do many of the locals use the Brigadier or do you depend on a passing-through trade, people on their way to the coast?'

Once it was plain to Dickson that Wexford's questions were not to involve him directly, not aimed at jeopardising his livelihood or discourage his clientele, he began to enjoy himself. People usually did, Wexford had found. Everybody likes imparting information, and the ignorant and unobservant correspondingly enjoy it more.

'Well, it's all the lot, isn't it?' said Dickson. 'We get a lot of the young. There's not many senior citizens, on account of you need transport to get out here and that they don't have a lot of. Mr Canning from Framhurst, he's in here a lot.'

'He means Ron Canning from Goland Farm,' said Linda Dickson, putting the Yorkshire terrier on the floor where it stood shivering. 'You know, him as lets those tree people use his field for their cars. If ,' she added, 'you can call them cars.'

The dog sniffed Wexford's shoes, gave his left toecap an exploratory lick. He shifted his feet, not easy in so confined a space. 'What's that tattoo on your arm, Mr Dickson? Some sort of insect, is it, or a bird or what?'

'A swallow, it's supposed to be.' To Wexford's surprise, Dickson flushed. 'I'm going to have it removed, the wife's not keen on it. Haven't got round to it yet, that's all.' He picked up the dog, pressed its face against his red cheek and reverted quickly to the original subject. 'Those Weir Theatre people come in. From Pomfret. They call themselves the Friends of the Weir Theatre and the leading light

328

in that's a chap called Jeffrey Godwin. He's like an actor.'

'Been in *Bramwell*,' said Linda. 'No, I tell a lie, it was *Casualty*.'

'I don't mind that, I can tell you,' said Dickson, holding the dog against his shoulder and rubbing its spine as if in an effort to bring up wind. 'I mean, folks like him coming in. Attracts trade, that's what it does. Lot of punters come in just to get a look at him and I always point him out, the least I can do. I always say, that's Jeffrey Godwin, the actor. He's very gracious, I must say.'

Dickson spoke as if he were the proprietor of a restaurant in mid-town Manhattan where Paul Newman was frequently to be seen at a particular table. He smiled reminiscently and settled the dog on his lap, where it immediately fell asleep.

'Look at him,' said Linda fondly. 'You can see he loves his daddy. Can I get you a drink, Mr Wexford? I'm sure I don't know what's happened to my manners. Must be all this upheaval.'

Wexford refused.

'Little something for you, Bill?'

While Dickson was considering this offer, Wexford asked him if he'd noticed any newcomers recently who had become regulars. Did any of the protesters, for instance, use the Brigadier?

Dickson made no secret of his contempt for those involved in any kind of protest against, or even dissent from, totally orthodox convention. Wexford knew at once, from the expression on his face, from the curl of his lip, without his having to say a word, exactly what his attitude would be to those who attempt to save whales, ban fox-hunting, prohibit chemical fertiliser, favour organic foods, are thrifty with water, use lead-free petrol or recycle anything at all.

329

'Needless to say,' said Dickson, 'I haven't got a lot of time for those gentry. And don't get me wrong, that's not on account of they don't *drink*, not to say *drink*, because they're the sort that imbibe a good deal in the way of your mineral waters and Britvics, and that's where your licensee makes his profit, so no, it's not that. It's not that they've got no money for their Perriers and Cokes and whatever. I'll tell you what it is, it's like the way they're interfering in life, our life, yours and mine, guv'nor. Life what has to go on, if you take my meaning. *What has to go on*. Right?'

He drew breath, reached for the tankard his wife had brought him. 'Thank you, my sweetheart, that's very kind of you. Now who else can I tell you about? Well now, there's this lady Stan drives up here now and again. Don't know her name – d'you know her name, Lin?'

'I don't, Bill. Quite an elderly lady she is, from Kingsmarkham, and she comes up here regular Tuesdays and Thursdays to meet a gentleman. I said to Bill, that's very sweet, I said, that's touching, them being not a day under seventy. But I don't know her name and I don't know his. Stan would know.'

Wexford wondered what possible connection the Dicksons thought a pair of superannuated lovers who chose to meet in the Brigadier of all places – was one of them married? Were both of them? – could have with Sacred Globe. 'Stan?' he said.

'Stan Trotter,' said Linda. 'Well, Stanley, to give him his full name. He drives her up here on account of her not driving herself, not having a licence, I dare say. I say "drives her" but it's not been going on for more than – what would you say, Bill? A month?'

'The first time, a Tuesday it was, Stan came into the lounge bar with her and that was the first time I'd seen him since April, as a matter of fact, since the night that German girl got herself killed.'

Wexford looked at her and watched the colour flood her face.

Chapter 24

For the second time in six months Stanley Trotter had been arrested, but this time he would appear on the following morning at Kingsmarkham Magistrates' Court, charged with the murder of Ulrike Ranke.

'I owe you an apology, Mike,' Wexford said. 'You were right all along. I dare say I was rude to you – can't remember what I said but I expect it was nasty.'

'I didn't *know*, you know. I was doing your intuitive thing. It was just a very powerful feeling. I didn't know Trotter's second wife was Linda Dickson's sister. I didn't go into his family tree, though maybe I should have.'

'He was only married to her for five minutes,' said Wexford.

'The mystery is the woman feels she owes him some sort of loyalty. She came out with it quite involuntarily. "Well, he's my brother-in-law, isn't he?" was what she said. She seems to subscribe to the curious notion that once a brother-in-law always a brother-in-law, irrespective of intervening divorces and remarriages. These days that must give some people very large extended families.'

'Dickson didn't mention it, though?'

'Dickson didn't know his wife saw Trotter. Or maybe he just didn't want to know. When she was questioned she said she'd gone to bed and to sleep. Only in fact she was looking out of the window. They're not exactly a compassionate couple, are they? Not what you'd call well endowed with empathy? Can she actually have been *concerned* about Ulrike?'

Burden shook his head, but in the way someone does when he doubts rather than denies. 'She's a woman and Ulrike was a young girl. There's always so much we don't know in a case like this, so much we'll never know.'

'Are you saying this was simple anxiety as to Ulrike's ultimate welfare?'

'I don't know. Do you?'

'Maybe I do. Suffice it to say for now that she did look out of the window, she sat in the window waiting and saw Trotter arrive at about eleven. Trotter didn't ring the bell or knock on the door because he didn't need to. Ulrike was waiting out there and he didn't even have to drive across that gravel and thus announce his coming to Dickson who was clearing up in the bar.'

'And when Dickson finally went upstairs Linda didn't say a word about seeing Trotter come for the girl? Didn't say anything then or when the girl went missing, or when her body was found?'

'Look at it this way, Mike. Linda was relieved when Trotter came, a load had been taken from her mind, so she got into bed and fell asleep. Remember she'd had a heavy day. Next morning she'd no reason to feel anxious about Ulrike. Trotter had picked her up and driven her wherever she wanted to go. But when Ulrike was missing, when the papers were full of it, what did she think then?

'We've never gone any more deeply into why Dickson performed the callous act of sending Ulrike outside to wait for the taxi. He hasn't given a reason, just said they were closed and it wasn't a cold night. But suppose it was Linda who made him send her outside? Linda who even took her to the door, closed it and locked and bolted it? Poor Ulrike isn't alive to tell us.

'My idea is that Linda is a jealous woman, who's been given reason in the past to be jealous. She wasn't leaving Dickson alone with a young woman in the middle of the night, but for herself, she was exhausted, she was dying for her bed . . .'

'Yes, but Reg, Ulrike was a personable young woman of nineteen and Dickson – well, he's not exactly love's young dream, is he?'

'Not to you or me or Ulrike maybe, but perhaps he is to Linda.' Wexford smiled. 'When someone asked James Thurber why the women in his cartoons weren't attractive he said, "They are attractive to my men." Dickson is attractive to Linda and therefore she thinks he must be to everyone else. So she sent Ulrike outside and watched from upstairs to see the taxi come. Because if it hadn't come Ulrike might have come back inside, been *allowed back inside* by Dickson.'

Burden nodded. 'And later?'

'After the body was found, d'you mean? By then she knew Dickson had nothing to do with it. But she had her loyalty to her ex-brother-in-law. To be fair to her, she was probably quite unable to confront the fact that a member of her family, however briefly and tenuously a member, could be a murderer. Few people can do that. He picked Ulrike up, he was driving the taxi, but someone else killed her.'

'I'll never understand human beings.'

'You and me both,' said Wexford. 'Trotter drove Ulrike to Framhurst Copses, raped and strangled her. Perhaps she'd offered him a large sum of money to drive her all the way to Aylesbury and he'd seen what money she'd got. He took it and the pearls. She may have offered him the money and the pearls as the price for her life, so he must have been disappointed when he only got tuppence halfpenny for a necklace he thought worth over a thousand.' He shook his head. 'As for Sacred Globe, they fetched us there for fun. To amuse themselves.'

Ryan Barker's last message, his demand, had not reached the media. A blanket of not so much silence as negativity had fallen over Sacred Globe and the inquiry, drawn down by Wexford, as if he had pulled a cord and released some heavy drapery. The newspapers carried stories of failure, of police ineptitude, of hostages' lives at increased risk, but they held no *news*, no single new development. No word of Ryan Barker's defection had been released to them.

It was as if Sacred Globe and its three captives – its two captives? – were passing into the realm of hostage-taking terrorists associated with a Middle Eastern political scene. The hostages were taken, there was international outcry, demands were made, all negotiation was repudiated, more demands were made with more threats, and then gradually the whole situation grew stale, to be replaced by new excitements. And meanwhile the hostages remained, languished, half forgotten as the days passed, the weeks, the months, the years.

The new excitement in Kingsmarkham was Stanley Trotter's court appearance. A brief one it would be, followed by an immediate remand to a higher court, but the press were on the scene in good time, the same faces, the same cameras, as on the morning the news of Sacred Globe broke.

It had been a big story, Ulrike Ranke's disappearance and the discovery of her body. She was female, young, blonde, good-looking. If that wasn't enough, she had been wandering by night in what was to her

335

a foreign country, carrying drugs, money, jewels, the stuff of sensation.

The aim would be to establish some link between her death and Sacred Globe, or her death and Roxane Masood's. Unfortunately for this pack of people, speculation as to Trotter's links with Sacred Globe would now be *sub judice* and strictly to be kept out of print until a guilty verdict could be returned some months afterwards. Unfortunately, too, the cell in Kingsmarkham police station where Trotter had been held overnight was no more than fifty yards from the entrance to the Magistrates' Court.

A coat was thrown over his head and he was bundled across the paving, while the television cameramen got their shots for early evening news programmes and Newsroom South-East. A small crowd of the public, none of whom had known Ulrike or Trotter or had any personal interest whatever in her murder, waited about in time to boo and yell imprecations, while the hooded figure made his short journey. They too would be on television, which was perhaps what they most wanted.

Nicky Weaver said she couldn't understand it. She never wanted to hear the words 'sleeping' and 'bag' coupled together again as long as she lived. But she knew as surely as it was possible to know anything of this nature that every Outdoors camouflage sleeping bag sold in the British Isles had now been traced. There had been thirty-six, the green-and-purple version being more popular.

'It's a blessing we weren't trying to track down the coloured ones,' she said to Wexford. 'There were ninety-six of them. The thing is, of the camouflage type, Ted or I have seen every one of them. I mean, actually cast our eyes over them. Most hadn't been sold, as I say they aren't popular, people think they look like old army surplus. But we also tracked down a couple to people's homes, one in Leicester and one in a village in Shropshire.'

'So what are you saying?'

'I'm saying it has to be the bag Frenchie Collins bought in Brixton and says she abandoned at the airport in Zaïre.'

'Why would she lie, Nicky?'

'Because she gave or sold that bag to a friend who's involved with Sacred Globe and she knows it. She's probably a sympathiser herself, or maybe more than that.'

Burden would appear in court but not Wexford. He had brought Dora in again and she sat in the old gym. She joked that she never went anywhere but the police station. Did he realise she hadn't been out at all since her release except here and on a single visit to Sylvia?

'Permission to go out tomorrow night, please,' she said.

Like the kind of husband he had never been, would never be, he asked, 'Where do you want to go?'

'Oh, Reg. They're not going to grab me again. Be sensible. I want to go to the Weir Theatre to see Jeffrey Godwin's play. Jenny says she'll go with me.'

'Because I'll say you need a keeper?'

He knew he couldn't shut her up at home, like a woman in purdah, like one of Bluebeard's wives. She had become more precious to him than she had ever been since the first year of their marriage. Now he knew he had undervalued her and wanted years ahead of them in which to show constantly his appreciation.

'I will never stop you doing anything,' he said.

Nicky Weaver came in and he started the recorder.

'It's the distance we're interested in, Dora,' he

began. 'It's a matter of how long you were actually in the car. Now, according to what you've already told us, you were in it for only about an hour when you were taken to wherever it was.'

'That's right.'

'But when they brought you home you say you were taken out of the basement room at about ten, yet you didn't get back to Kingsmarkham, to within a quarter of a mile of our house, until half-past midnight. Rather later than that, in fact. Because you came in through our front door just before one.'

'Yes. On the return journey I think I was in the car for nearly three hours. I assume he was just driving round and round. I've got a theory about that.' She looked from one to the other of them almost shyly. 'Sorry, I shouldn't have, should I? But do you want to hear it?'

'Of course we do,' said Nicky.

'Well,' Dora took a deep breath. 'Well, on the way out it didn't matter so much to them, the distance, I mean. They didn't know then that I'd ever come back. Maybe they thought they'd kill me, I don't know. But on the return journey to Kingsmarkham they knew the first thing I'd do was talk to Reg, then to you all. I'd be bound to and it would be fresh in my mind. So they really had to deceive me and they made the journey as long as they reasonably could.'

'Sounds feasible,' Wexford said. 'But were they deceiving you on the outward journey as well? You see, you've said you could have been taken anywhere within a radius of about sixty miles, but could it have been far less than that?'

'I suppose it could.'

'Could it have been within thirty miles? Or twenty? Or ten?'

She put one hand up to her mouth. It was as if the possibility of this frightened her. 'You mean, were

338

they driving round in circles? Sort of on to the old bypass and round the roundabout and back again and out to Myringham and turn back and up the old bypass again?'

He smiled at her. 'Sort of, yes.'

'It never occurred to me,' she said. 'But I don't see why not. I really don't see why not. I wouldn't have known. I couldn't see a thing. We did go round corners and I think we went round roundabouts. Now you mention it, I think we went all the way round one roundabout. It didn't seem important when I was talking to you the first time but now – I think we did go all the way round.'

A satisfied expression on his face, Burden came back from the court after less than an hour. The proceedings had been swift, Stanley Trotter having been committed for trial and remanded in custody. He found Wexford in the old gym, talking to Nicky Weaver.

'What do we do then, bring her in? It's the Met's ground, Brixton, but I doubt if they'll have any objection. I wonder if she'd ever lived round here, if she has any connection with this neighbourhood.'

Burden said, 'Who are you talking about?'

'This woman called Frenchie Collins. I'm wondering if she knows any of these tree people. If, for instance, she's acquainted with the King of the Wood.'

'Why do you ask?'

Wexford said slowly, 'Because we've been talking about the hostages being within a radius of sixty miles, but that was much too wide, that was too generous. They're not in London or Kent or down on the South Coast. They're here, very near here, and the radius is going to be more like five miles.'

'That's just guesswork.'

'Is it, Mike? The non-lactic soymilk isn't proof of anything but it's evidence. It may not have come from the Framhurst teashop but it very likely did. Ryan Barker made his second phone call from the Brigadier, and though that again proves nothing, it does give a strong indication.'

Wexford sat down. He hesitated, then said, 'Who would be most likely to want this bypass stopped? Environmental activists, yes, professional protesters, maybe. Any green group opposed to destroying England, that's for sure. But more than that would be someone, or more than one, who would be personally affected by the building of the bypass.'

'You mean, people whose livelihood might be endangered by it?' Nicky asked.

'That of course. By what I mean is simpler. People whose outlook, view, of the countryside would be spoilt. Those who'd see the bypass when they looked out of their windows or hear it when they walked in their garden. Wouldn't they have a deeper, more emotional interest than a professional protester who doesn't care where whatever is happening is happening, whether it's a power station in Cumbria or a flyover in Dorset?

'Imagine a group of people – *amateurs*, mostly – getting together in . . . well, in despair, deciding that desperate situations call for desperate measures, all or some of them householders whose views, whose domestic peace and quiet really, will be wrecked by this bypass. Maybe one of them meets someone in the know, someone who's used to this sort of thing, who's not an amateur, and then they start getting things organised.'

'Meets them how?'

'Well, through KABAL, or going to that actor-manager's theatre, the Weir Theatre – where, incidentally, our wives are going together tomorrow

340

night – or maybe on a demonstration. Even on the big march of July.

'One of the group is already in possession of a large suitable house, probably a beautiful country house. After all, that's the point, isn't it? Once the bypass is built it won't be beautiful any more, or its surroundings won't be. In the outbuildings is an old dairy, not exactly underground but half subterranean, for coolness's sake when it *was* a dairy. They have a washroom built on and a guard to half cover the window. Say there are half a dozen of them, an ample supply of guards. They haven't much else to organise, have they, except to do it?'

Builders are hard to find. The regular, steady, orthodox firms are a different matter. They advertise, they are in the phone book. As for the others, the money-in-the-back-pocket brigade and the moon-lighters, the cowboys here today and gone tomorrow, recommendation of their skills, or more likely their low prices, are passed on by word of mouth or begin with an unsolicited knock at the door.

One of these had built the washroom on to the basement room for the specific purpose of answering the needs of a group of hostages; more likely the cowboys, the Bodger and Sons, than a limited company with premises in the High Street. At some point a phone call had been made to them and an estimate asked for. Or not an estimate. Simply a request to do it. Do it as soon as you can and never mind the cost.

In a way, Wexford thought, it was interesting that the washroom had been built on at all. So much was implied by it, so much could be inferred from it.

'They're terrorists, Mike,' he said to Burden. 'However we may shy away from that word, that's what they are. My dictionary defines terrorism as an

341

organised system of violence and intimidation for political ends. But look at what we know of these particular examples of the breed. In most parts of the world terrorists wouldn't worry about their hostages' hygiene arrangements. A bucket in the corner would do for them. But these people went to the trouble of having a washroom with basin and running water and flush lavatory built on to their prison. Not so much civilised as essentially middle-class, wouldn't you say?'

Burden wasn't very interested. He disliked listening to Wexford's disquisitions on social vagary and psychological symptom. What was the point of it except to distract? He had already got Fancourt, Hennessy and Lowry on to Kingsmarkham, Stowerton and Pomfret builders. The ones in the phone book were easy, the others, those who did this work after their legitimate jobs, were the hardest to find. Kids leaving school who have painted their mothers' front rooms think of taking up building work, Wexford had once said, in the same way as anyone who can type thinks he has a book inside him.

'I'll tell you what I'd say. It's that they did it themselves. Sacred Globe. One of them's an amateur plumber, there's a lot of it about. A frequent visitor to the DIY on the old bypass.'

Wexford brightened. 'We should get someone out there as well then. See if they have a regular customer or did have a regular customer, who bought a lavatory pan from them and a basin and the pipework and whatever back in, say, June.'

'Reg,' said Burden.

Wexford looked at him, looked hard and silently.

'That washroom could have been built ten years ago. It could have been built on to that basement . . .'

'Dora said it was new,' Wexford interrupted. 'And it's not a basement, it's a dairy.'

342

'If you say so. I was going to say as a part of a flat conversion that was never finished. It doesn't have to have been built on in the past few weeks, just as the non-lactic soymilk doesn't have to have come from Framhurst or that damned moth from Wiltshire. Sherlock Holmes worked like that, making huge leap assumptions, but we can't do the same.'

'They're in a house near here,' said Wexford stubbornly. 'A house that overlooks the bypass or is seriously threatened by the bypass.'

'I'll take you to the theatre,' he said. 'I know I'm being absurd but I don't want you going out alone. Not yet. Jenny can make her own way but I'll take you.'

Instead of saying she wouldn't go, Dora said, 'You haven't got time, Reg.'

'Yes, I have.'

By the middle of Saturday afternoon, when most builders in Kingsmarkham and Stowerton had been eliminated from the inquiry, Nicky Weaver came up with a positive lead. A. and J. Murray Sisters, an all-woman firm based in Pomfret and specialising in small building jobs, volunteered the information that they had built a shower room on to a flat conversion at a farm in Pomfret Monachorum. The job had been carried out in the previous June.

Ann Murray, an electrician and the elder of the sisters, told Nicky that they had been glad of the work, had jumped at the chance, in fact. Even though the recession was over, they hadn't found it easy to convince the locals that women made as effective building contractors as men, that they all had City and Guilds qualifications and kept their estimates low. The Holgates, of Paddocks, a one-time farmhouse on the Cambery Ashes Road near Tancred, had approached them, she thought, because Gillian

343

Holgate also had a trade usually confined to men. She was a motor mechanic.

The work required was to convert an old larder in a cottage next door to the main house into a shower room. The cottage, then consisting of one room up and one down with a kitchen, was to be a home for the Holgates' daughter. A. and J. Murray Sisters had started the job on 10 June and completed it on 15 June, the plumbing being carried out by Maureen Sheridan and the electrics and decoration by Ann Murray herself. It was the right time and the right place. Or it seemed to be.

Wexford went up there, taking Nicky and Damon Slesar with him. Outside the gate to Paddocks he got out of the car and looked down across the valley. It was hard to say from this point if the bypass site would be visible or not. The woods of Tancred lay between here and the distant river and they would certainly muffle any traffic sound. Perhaps when the bypass was built it might be possible to see a segment of it, a triangle of double white highway between the dark trees and the green hillside.

Slesar opened the gate and they drove in, up a long, straight driveway, macadam, not gravel. The farmhouse had a red shingled façade and a low roof of red tiles. On the hard, dark-grey surface, in a broad patch of sunlight, lay two cats, one asleep, the other on its back, green eyes wide open, white paws gracefully waving. One of the cats was a Siamese, the other a tabby.

Next door, the building that was evidently the cottage was in the process of external painting. A woman up on a pair of steps was applying cream-coloured emulsion to its plasterwork with a roller.

Wexford and Nicky got out of the car, and the woman, who looked about forty, was tall and thin and wearing paint-stained dungarees, came towards them rather diffidently.

'Mrs Holgate?'

She nodded.

Slesar said, 'We're police officers.'

Very taken aback, she said, 'What is it? What's happened?'

'Nothing at all, Mrs Holgate. Nothing for you to be worried about.'

By now Wexford was almost certain this was true, in spite of the cats. The cottage was too small to contain the basement room. Even from here you could tell that the ground area measured nothing like twenty feet by fourteen. But he had to look. Might they look?

Rallying a little from her initial shock, Gillian Holgate said she would like to know what it was about. Nicky said they had information that a room in the cottage had been converted into a bathroom three months before.

'I had planning permission,' Mrs Holgate said. 'Everything was above board.'

Wexford was rather amused to be taken for an official of the county planning department. But Mrs Holgate seemed satisfied without further explanation and ushered them in through the front door of the building she had been painting. The place was obviously occupied, though its occupant wasn't at present at home. The downstairs room was furnished, was rather comfortably untidy and a generous estimate would set its measurements at ten feet by twelve.

Wexford had been uneasy about this annexe or conversion ever since he had heard it described as a shower room, since Dora had been emphatic the room she had used had contained only a lavatory and basin. Of course it was possible the shower had been removed or walled in before the hostages were brought there – possible but unlikely.

And they saw now that this was another dead end. The room the Murray sisters had converted was large, its walls tiled, its shower cabinet of generous size. Its window was of frosted glass and curtained. From the main room quite a big picture window had a view of Tancred woods.

'It must have something to do with those hostages,' Mrs Holgate said wonderingly. 'The Kingsmarkham Kidnap.'

They neither confirmed nor denied. Wexford nodded enigmatically. He stepped out once more into the afternoon sunshine and a young woman who had come running out of the main house almost cannoned into him.

She said breathlessly, 'Are you Chief Inspector Wexford?'

'I am.'

'There's a phone call for you.'

'For me? Are you sure?'

But he had his own phone. Who would know he was here? No one knew.

He followed her into the main house. The phone receiver lay off the hook on a small hall table. He lifted it, said, 'Wexford.'

'This is Sacred Globe.'

'Ryan Barker,' said Wexford.

'We haven't heard from you. You haven't complied with our request. If there is no announcement on the evening news bulletins of a complete revision on the plan for the Kingsmarkham bypass Mrs Struther dies.'

Someone had written it for him. He was plainly reading it and reading it nervously, his voice growing squeaky.

Under his breath Wexford cursed this group of

people who could so exploit a child. He said, 'What do you mean by evening bulletins, Ryan?'

'Wait a minute, please.'

Wexford could hear him conferring with a companion. Then, 'By seven. If it's not, Mrs Struther dies and we will deliver her body to Kingsmarkham tonight.'

'Ryan, wait. Stay where you are. Are you at the Brigadier on the old bypass?'

No reply, only an indrawn breath.

'What you ask,' Wexford said, 'isn't possible. You know that.'

'You have to make it possible,' Ryan Barker's voice said, growing cold now, growing remote. 'You have to tell the press and tell the government. Tell them she's going to die. We're ready to kill her.'

He added stiffly, obviously prompted. 'We are Sacred Globe, saving the world.'

Chapter 25

When he had phoned the Chief Constable and told him of Sacred Globe's latest message, he walked out of the Holgates' house, drove out of their drive and stood on the road, looking through binoculars across the valley.

Somewhere, in a house, a big house, one of those out there among the hills and woods . . . There were hundreds such. And if he couldn't find which one in the next four hours a woman would die. The second woman. Only this one would be deliberate murder. But it would happen because government would never, not in any circumstances, these or similar, not under any threat, announce the cancellation of the bypass. Therefore it would happen unless, in the next four hours, he found which house among so many held the two hostages.

'Nothing to the media,' Montague Ryder said when Wexford walked into the suite at the Constabulary headquarters. 'We must keep it dark from them as long as we can.'

'As long as we can' had a sinister ring. It meant, until Kitty Struther's body is found.

'I know they aren't far from here, sir,' Wexford said.

He glanced at the map on the wall. It was a blown-up sheet from the Ordnance Survey, the central part of the Mid-Sussex area. Ryder nodded to him and he drew with his right forefinger an oval shape that encompassed Kingsmarkham, Stowerton, Pomfret and Sewingbury, the villages of Framhurst, Savesbury, Stringfield, Cambery Ashes and Pomfret Monachorum. Places south of the town were excluded. None of them would be menaced by the new bypass. No house in their vicinity would have a view of it.

'And that's your criterion?'

'One of them,' Wexford said. 'Maybe the most important one.'

Did she know they intended to kill her? He didn't ask Montague Ryder that because Ryder could only guess as he could. She had been, and no doubt still was, the most fearful of the hostages, the most vulnerable, the least self-contained and with the fewest inner resources. Was she with her husband or had they too been separated?

And now he found himself in the dreadful position at this juncture of having nothing to do. For ten days they had all worked so hard, had worked to the utmost of their capacity, and the result had been only to narrow down the place they were looking for into something like fifty square miles. Nothing remained but to pick out the needle in the haystack or wait for the discovery of another sleeping bag containing another woman's body.

'We'll keep Contemporary Cars' ground under surveillance,' he said to Burden. 'I doubt if they'd come to the same place twice, but I daren't take the risk.'

'The police station's another possibility. So is Ms Cox's and Mrs Peabody's. The Concreation building. The Brigadier.'

'Your house. My house.'

They were there now, sitting in Burden's living-room. Or, rather, Burden was sitting. Wexford was pacing.

349

'The *Courier* offices,' he said. 'The Stowerton end of the bypass site. The Pomfret end.'

'You said that kid said Kingsmarkham.'

'That's true. He did. We can't police all these places, anyway. We haven't got the back-up.'

'Has anyone thought of using a helicopter? To find where they are, I mean. We know they're in our fifty square miles.'

'What could you see from a helicopter, Mike? A house with outbuildings? There are hundreds. The hostages aren't going to be up on the roof, waving distress flags.'

Burden shrugged. 'Sacred Globe will watch the BBC's early-evening news, which is at five or five-fifteen on a Saturday, and ITN's half an hour later. If there is no announcement, and of course there can't be, they proceed to kill Kitty Struther. Is that what will happen?'

'I don't know about "will", Mike,' Wexford said bitterly. 'It's twenty to six now. It may be happening now and we can't do a thing to stop it.'

Upriver from Watersmeet, where the stream that ran under Kingsmarkham High Street met the larger waterway, the Brede flows among wide meadows and winds between groves of alders and stands of willows. At one point the stones of the river bed are large enough and regular enough to form a dam, over which the determined water gushes and spouts into the deep pool below. This is Stringfield Weir and it is overlooked by Stringfield Mill, built long ago when some of the farming was arable and the means were needed for grinding corn.

The waterwheel was long gone. Sails there had never been. The building of white weatherboard and red brick, a huge, graceful structure, had been converted some ten years before into a theatre and

350

became the regular venue of repertory companies. The lane that led down to it from Pomfret Monachorum was of reasonable width and serviceable surface. Once there, the theatre-goer had everything the civilised in pursuit of culture could wish for: a large car park concealed by tall trees, a restaurant with river frontage, a splendid view across Stringfield Bridge to the woods, meadows and downs beyond and, of course, the auditorium that was big enough to hold four hundred people.

One of its disadvantages was that actors on stage were bedevilled by flying insects, drawn in by the light, moths and lacewings and daddy-long-legs. Legend had it that a bat had tangled itself in an actress's hair while she was playing Juliet. Wexford, who had never been there before, thought there might be mosquitos and he counselled Dora and Jenny to avoid the river terrace and stay inside for their pre-performance glass of wine.

'I'll come back for you,' he said. 'Will ten-forty-five suit?'

'Reg, we can call for a taxi,' Jenny said. 'I should have brought my own car, I don't know why I didn't. It's not as if we intend to go boozing.'

'Well, now you can. A bit. I'll come back for you so you needn't worry.'

Extinction, with Christine Colville and Richard Paton, ran for three hours, not including the two intervals. He read that on the programme up on the foyer wall. This play, by Jeffrey Godwin himself, alternated its performances with a modern-dress version of *Twelfth Night* and with Strindberg's *The Ghost Sonata*. An ambitious company, who set their sights high.

A voice behind him said, 'How's Sheila?'

He turned and saw standing at his shoulder a tall genial-looking man with brown curly hair and beard.

351

'You must be Jeffrey Godwin,' he said. 'Wexford –
but you know that. Sheila's fine, got a baby daughter.'

'I saw it in the paper,' said Godwin. 'Lovely. I
hope to see mother and child in the not too far
distant future. Are you coming to tonight's performance?'

Wexford said he wouldn't be and explained that
he was particularly busy at the moment. But his wife
was here and her friend. He said goodbye to Godwin
and made his way back to the car park, skirting the
mill's still sunlit gardens, from which came a heavy
scent of late-flowering roses.

Back in Kingsmarkham he went to the police
station and into the old gym. Damon Slesar was
there with Karen Malahyde and three staff working
at computers. Wexford said to the two detective
sergeants that the witching hour was past, it was
gone seven-thirty now. Give Sacred Globe a couple
of hours and the time would come for the returning
of Kitty Struther's body.

'It may be an empty threat,' Damon said.

Karen looked at him, shaking her head. 'I don't
think so. Why would they start being merciful and
civilised at this stage? They're more likely to be made
cruel by desperation.'

'Merciful' was an interesting word for her to have
used, Wexford thought. He asked her what duties
had been arranged for her and Slesar that evening.

'I'm doing Contemporary Cars, sir, and Damon'll
be at Mrs Peabody's.'

A pity they couldn't be together, he thought. It
was obviously what they would have liked. But he
hadn't got the personnel, the back-up. They needed
everyone, even himself, for surveillance duties. On
the watch, there was a good chance of catching
Sacred Globe, he thought optimistically. But what a

352

price to pay for catching them! Kitty Struther's death. He imagined Monday morning's papers. Tomorrow's television, come to that. He switched off, because thinking like that was negative and pointless, and saw Slesar's hand just close quickly over Karen's before leaving the old gym.

After Karen too had gone he sat at the window, eyeing the precincts of the police station and its car parks, front and back, the entrances to both of which could be seen from this point. If they caught someone tonight and followed him – or her – back to where they had come from, what would he need in the way of assistance?

He thought of the gun which Rubber Face had had with him in the car when Dora was taken. Rubber Face had again had a gun when bringing food to the hostages in the basement room, and on that occasion he had fired it, probably only to frighten, but could they be sure of that?

Very likely, since Rubber Face had it both times, there was only one gun. Perhaps Rubber Face was the only shot. Possibly the gun was a replica, very possibly, or a child's toy from a toyshop. If Kitty Struther was shot they would know, he thought grimly, that would be a way of knowing for certain.

And when they knew, when they had followed the driver of the car that brought Kitty Struther's body, would he need arms himself?

Armed response vehicles patrolled the roads for sixteen hours each day. In Mid-Sussex there were two such on patrol and carrying arms. Authority to utilise and deploy firearms officers could only be given by an officer of the rank of Superintendent or above except in special circumstances. These would certainly be such circumstances but armed officers could never be interspersed with unarmed in any operation. If the severity of risk was great, all officers involved in the attack would be fully armed and work as a team of four as a minumum, or more likely eight.

Wexford and his own would be a hundred yards away, watching through binoculars. And the price of all this was Kitty Struther's life.

At eight-thirty he left his watch for Lynn Fancourt to take over and drove to Pomfret and Clare Cox's house. Ted Hennessy was outside in his car on the opposite side of the road, but Wexford ignored him, went up to the front door and knocked.

She came to the door after he had knocked again and rung as well. Hassy Masood had gone back to London with his second family – what interest had he in any of this, now his daughter was dead? She was alone. Her bereavement had aged her twenty years and now she had a madwoman-in-the-attic look, her face gaunt and grey, her hair a shaggy fleece with the colour and texture of dried grasses. Deep down in dark sockets her eyes stared wildly at him. Impossible for him to say now that he wanted to talk to her about the remaining two hostages, that he held the strong belief – he hardly knew why – that a woman's body would be delivered here within the next few hours.

'I came to see how you are.'

She stepped aside to let him enter. 'As you see,' and then she said, 'Not good.'

There are some situations in which there is nothing to say. He sat down and so did she.

'I do nothing all day,' she said. 'I'm alone and I do nothing. The neighbours get my shopping.'

'Your painting?' he hazarded, thinking of what they all said, that work was the remedy for sorrow.

'I can't paint.' She smiled, a ghastly, shadowy smile. 'I shall never paint again.' Tears in her eyes

354

began to flow down her face. 'When I think at all I think of her in that room being afraid. So afraid that she lost her life trying to escape from it.' She put up her hand and wiped the back of it across her eyes. It induced a little shiver the way she read his thoughts. 'That other woman they've got, they'll kill her, won't they? Do you think they'd take me instead? If I offered? If I got it in the papers somehow, that they could have me? I'd like them to kill me.'

Despair he had seen before in all its forms. This was just another example. To suggest counselling to this woman, some kind of bereavement support, would be insulting. All he could do was look at her and say, feeling how wretchedly inadequate it was, 'I am very, very sorry. You have my deepest sympathy.'

As he left, his phone began to bleep. He sat in his car and listened to Burden's account of the car with two men in it who had driven into the car park of the Concreation building. They had got out, opened the boot and lifted out a black plastic bag, sealed at both ends and the length of an average human body.

'I really thought this was it, Reg. The only thing was that one of them could easily lift it on his own. But he held it the way one *would* carry a body – carry a living person, for that matter.'

'What was it?'

'They'd been clearing out a loft,' said Burden. 'It was the usual sort of rubbish from a loft, old newspapers, old clothes, most of it recyclable.'

'Then why didn't they take it to the dump to be recycled?'

'They explained all that. They were scared stiff. Originally they'd been going to stick all the stuff in dustbins – they're brothers-in-law, by the way – but they've got environmentally conscious neighbours

355

that they didn't want seeing paper and cloth disposed of like that. But the dump, with the recycling bins, is three miles away, while Concreation's yard, with a council skip that was brought in empty yesterday, was two minutes from home.'

Wexford sat in his car for a few moments, but it was too near Hennessy's, it would attract attention. He drove back to Kingsmarkham and along the deserted, coldly lit High Street. All those shops, he thought, with bright lights in their windows and not a soul about to look into them. Cars in plenty, though, parked cars whose owners were in the Olive and Dove, the Green Dragon, the York Wine Bar, and who would move on to Kingsmarkham's only nightclub, the Scarlet Angel, when it opened at ten.

The sky was dark now, and bright with scattered stars. There was no moon, or none had yet risen. He tried to remember whether there had been a moon on the previous night and if there had been, whether it had been full or a mere curve of light. His phone rang again while he was parked in Queen Street.

Barry Vine. He was at the station. One of the taxis in the Contemporary Cars fleet had just dropped a fare on the station approach. The fare had one large suitcase and a long bundle, so heavy that the driver couldn't lift it out of the boot. A porter was sought but, of course, there had been no porters at Kingsmarkham station for twenty years.

'The chap just disappeared,' Vine said. 'I mean, I thought he had. There was this bundle lying there on the pavement, the cab had gone and this fellow had vanished into the station. I was looking at it when he came back.'

'What was it?' said Wexford for the second time that evening.

'Golf clubs.'

356

'I trust it's not still there.'

'Someone found him a trolley in what used to be the left luggage department.'

He looked at his watch. It was nine. He would go to Rhombus Road, Stowerton, and then to Savesbury House on his way to the Weir Theatre. Maybe not to go into either place, just to run his eye over them, to check for he hardly knew what. Sacred Globe, after all, had said Kingsmarkham, not Stowerton or Framhurst.

Nicky Weaver must have had the same idea, for she was in her car parked in front of a house a few doors down from Mrs Peabody's. This time Wexford interrupted the surveillance. He went over to her car, tapped on the window and got in beside her. She turned to him her pretty face, the intent eyes, the look of sharp intelligence. He saw all this in the momentary light brought by the door opening. Her geometrically cut black hair, turned under at the tips, reminded him that when he was young such a style was called a pageboy. And he saw her tiredness too, the permanent strained pallor of the woman who has a high-powered job and is a wife and mother too.

'Has anything happened?' he asked her.

'A man called at the house. At about seven. I think he must be Audrey Barker's fiancé. Anyway, he hugged her on the doorstep and he's been inside ever since. Mrs Peabody went out. I thought she was being tactful, leaving them alone together, but she'd only gone to the corner shop for a pint of milk.'

'That Indian place Trotter used to live above?'

'Small world, isn't it?' said Nicky.

'They won't bring Kitty Struther's body here. They'll do something entirely unexpected.'

Driving in the Framhurst direction, he passed the start of the bypass site. If it was never built and those now grass-grown earth hillocks never removed, scholars in future ages would describe them as tumuli or the burial mounds of Saxon heroes. But it would be built. It was a matter not of protest, nor of environmental assessment, but only of time.

Framhurst was as empty as the town but for three boys standing by their motor bikes and smoking outside the bus shelter. Bright strip lighting in the window of the butcher's illuminated nothing but empty white trays and sprigs of plastic parsley. The teashop was locked up and its canopy furled. Night obscured the view of the valley from the ascending lane. It was merely a dark spread, punctured by many lights, a mirroring of the starlit sky. The winding river had vanished but the Weir Theatre shone brightly, a torch on the invisible waterside.

DC Pemberton was in his car outside the gates of Savesbury House.

'It's the only way in, sir. I checked. But the grounds are big and there's only fences or hedges round them. Anyone could get in almost anywhere across the fields.'

'Stay where you are. But they won't come here. It's too far out. It's not Kingsmarkham.'

Ten-fifteen. The play wouldn't yet be over, but he would drive down to Stringfield Mill, take it slowly. How pleasant and comfortable it must be not to be endowed with imagination! He didn't want his, he'd had enough of it, anyone could have it. But imagination wasn't something you could get rid of, any more than you could determine not to love. Or not to be afraid.

That was the worst thing, thinking of her fear. All her life she had had someone else to take the strain, to – what were the words of the marriage service? – love her, comfort her, honour and keep her. Literally, it appeared, those things had been done for Kitty Struther. By parents once, by a husband of course, by

358

a son too. She had never lived alone, earned her own living, known want or even straitened circumstances, never probably even travelled alone. But now she was alone. For ten days she had lived on a diet the like of which she had never previously known, had slept – if she had slept – in the kind of bed she had never even seen before, had been cold and hungry, deprived of all the small comforts of life, without a bath or a change of clothes. And now they had taken her husband from her and were going to kill her.

Imagination, the curse of the thinking policeman. He laughed wryly to himself. The lights of the Weir Theatre blazed ahead of him, dazzling out the stars. He put the car into the car park, walked slowly up the lane towards the river. Ten minutes yet before the curtain would fall. Consolations were always to be found in this life and one thing he could be glad about was that he hadn't just sat through three hours of *Extinction*.

A gate in the stone wall led into the mill's gardens. It would provide a short cut and a pleasant one. He unlatched the gate and pushed it open. The lights were all directed away from here and the gardens lay in a cloud of pale shadow, but as he looked southwards he saw the moon rising, a perfect orange-coloured crescent. A waning moon, and now he remembered. It had been full the night Dora came home, eight days before.

Most flowers close up at night. He found himself surrounded by flowers whose blossoms had become buds again, shut at dusk, but still giving off their various perfumes. But the roses, whose scent had come to him when he was here before, remained open, rosy-gold clusters on long stems and flat yellow faces pressed against the mossy grey wall.

Was this a private garden? Godwin's own garden? There was no sign that visitors to the theatre ever came out here. He turned a bend in the path and saw Godwin himself sitting on the topmost of the crescent-shaped steps that splayed out from closed french windows. The wall behind him was hung with roses, white and red, and with other climbers whose flowers had folded themselves away for the night.

'I'm sorry,' he said. 'I'm using your private gardens as a short cut. I didn't realise there were parts of the mill grounds shut off from the public.'

Godwin smiled and made a deprecating gesture with his hand. 'The public won't want it when the bypass comes.'

'It will pass very near here?'

'At the nearest point about a hundred yards from the end of this garden. I was born here – not *here*, I mean, but in Framhurst – and I lived here till I was eighteen. It's twelve years since I came back. There have been more changes in those twelve years than in all the rest – I won't tell you how many. Too many.'

'All changes for the worse?'

'I think so. Destruction and spoliation but additions as well. More petrol stations, more white and yellow paint on the roads, more road signs, more hoardings, more stupid useless information in print everywhere. That Framhurst's been twinned with a town in Germany and another one in France, for instance. That Sewingbury is the floral capital of Sussex. That Savesbury Deeps has been designated a picnic area. And all the new houses. The Dragon pub in Kingsmarkham renamed Tipples and Grove's wine bar turned into a night-club and called the Scarlet Angel . . .'

Wexford nodded. He was going to say something that he didn't believe about progress and inevitability, but he said nothing at all for a moment because

360

he was looking at the climber which ascended the wall to a height of perhaps ten feet between the red rose and the white.

It was a delicate-leaved plant with fine, pointed leaves and curling tendrils. Flowers it had had and by day they must make a considerable show, but now all were closed up, some furled like rolled umbrellas, others withered.

He spoke now. He said to Godwin, 'What is it? This plant, what is it?'

'Now, look.' Godwin got to his feet. His voice, formerly so gentle and meditative, changed in a flash and became immediately surly. 'Now, look, if you're going to search for hallucinatory drugs or whatever in garden plants, you've got your work cut out. There are hundreds of them. Ordinary poppies, for instance. But this isn't cannabis, you know. This is Morning Glory, it's quite hard to grow, it doesn't bear much, you wouldn't get enough seeds to fill an egg-cup, you . . .'

'Mr Godwin. Please. I am not in the drugs squad. I am looking for two hostages at present in the hands of those who abducted them ten days ago. This plant' – Wexford thought he could postpone too detailed an explanation – 'this plant, or one like it, may be visible from the place where they are kept.'

'Well, for God's sake, they're not kept here.'

Wexford looked about him, at the gardens, the rising moon, the flower-hung rear wall of the mill. No outbuildings, no sheds or garages in sight. The moonlight, strangely white for a radiance that proceeded from that golden crescent, now lit everything, showed every detail of the garden. 'I know that,' he said. 'Please don't be so defensive, Mr Godwin. I am not accusing you of anything. I only want your help.'

The look he got was warmer. There couldn't be much doubt in the mind of anyone who knew about

361

these things that Godwin was guilty and suspicious because he had himself sampled a good many of these garden drugs, probably grew cannabis somewhere, smoked catalpa beans, chewed magic mushrooms. The list, as he had implied himself, was endless. But now was no time for taking an interest in that.

'Tell me about this plant, will you? It's blue?'

'Look.' Godwin picked a closed flower off a stem. He unwound the spiralled petals and disclosed an interior the brightest and richest of sky-blues. 'Nice colour, wouldn't you say? The wild one that grows here as a weed is white, of course, and its little cousin is the pink convolvulus.'

'Does it come up every year?' Wexford sought for the unfamiliar word. 'Is it a perennial?'

'I grew it from seed.' Godwin's geniality had returned. 'Come into the theatre. I'll buy you a drink while you're waiting for your ladies. Mind you,' he added in a challenging tone, 'I'd kidnap a few people myself if I thought it'd stop that goddamned bypass.'

Wexford followed him up the steps, round the side of the mill, out of the moonlit shadows and into bright artificial light. He held in his hand the flower bud and the leaf Godwin had given him. Where had he seen buds and leaves like that before? Seen them very recently?

'Would it move?'

They were in the empty bar now, Wexford confining himself to sparkling water, Godwin with a pint of lager. He said, 'How do you mean, move?'

'Would the flowers be out in one place one day and another the next?'

'Each one only lasts a day, so broadly speaking, yes. You're quite likely to get all the flowers out in one patch and then another lot out on a higher patch.

362

If I make myself clear. Mind you, they wouldn't come out at all on a really dull day.'

On a dull day, such as they had had recently ... Where had he seen that plant before?

Chapter 26

His mobile was silent. There were no messages on the phone at home. When he had driven Dora to their home and Jenny to hers, when Dora had gone to bed and at once to sleep, he put through calls to all those people who were on the watch. There was nothing. The town was quiet, less busy at night than usual, less traffic, it seemed. Only two incidents had been reported: an attempted break-in at a shop in Queen Street, a case of driving over the permitted limit.

It was eleven-fifty. Nearly five hours had passed since Sacred Globe's deadline. He realised how he had been measuring this case out in minutes. Time, time, it was all a matter of time. Had they killed her? Would they kill her? Her body could even now be no more than half a mile from where he was, sitting silently in the dark in his own house.

He remembered another midnight, the night Dora had come home. Moonlight falling on his face had awakened him or else it was the sound of her footfalls on the gravel. Gravel had been in the sleeping bag with Roxane Masood's body. Hold on to that. And the dust from the wings of a moth only found in Wiltshire had been on Dora's clothes. Cat hairs and a smell of acetone. A butterfly tattoo. He opened the french windows and went out into the garden. A dreadful idea had come to him.

Last time, when Dora had come home, he had

thought it was a messenger from Sacred Globe. He had thought they would target him personally. Suppose, now, they brought Kitty Struther's body here? They could have done so while he and Dora were out.

The sickle moon was overhead now, sailing silver-white in a wrack of cloud, not full enough or bright enough to shed much light. He fetched a torch, searched the garden. His heart knocking, he opened the garage doors, flashed the torch inside. Nothing. Thank God. The garden shed remained. For fifteen seconds he knew what he would find when he unlatched that door, but he held his breath and unlatched it and found what was always in there, a lawn-mower, tools, old plastic bags and other junk.

It proved nothing. Of course it didn't, yet that wasn't the way his mind saw it. He began to see all sorts of unreasonable things and he sat down in his chair in the dark and started to think.

The blue thing. He knew what that was now and and, suddenly, he knew where it was. It came to him clearly, a revelation, a picture in green and grey. Only that wasn't possible, that couldn't be. After a while he fetched the London phone book, the S–Z section. He punched out the number he found but there was no reply. Then he phoned Burden.

It was gone midnight but Burden wasn't asleep. He wasn't even in bed. When he heard Wexford's voice he said, 'Have they found her?'

'No.' Wexford could state it categorically and with perfect confidence. 'And they won't.'

'What do you mean?'

Instead of replying, he said, 'When would you like to go to London? Now or at six in the morning?'

There was a short silence and then Burden said, 'Do I have a choice?'

'Sure you do.'

'I shan't sleep. I'm too strung up. So let's go now.'

Once, driving must always have been like this. Deserted lanes, empty roads, a scent in the air of fields overgrown with camomile, not petrol and diesel. For the first ten minutes even the motorway was empty until a Jaguar passed them, roaring up the fast lane at twenty over the limit. The bright, cold lights drowned the moon in their white haze. In the outskirts of London they saw an owl sitting on a telephone cable and in Norbury a fox crossed the road in front of them.

'It's Sunday now,' Wexford said, 'but I've got on to Vine and told him to dig up someone in the morning and swear out a warrant.'

Burden, who was driving, said, 'Should I take the turn for Balham and go over Battersea Bridge?'

'Turn left or go straight on, doesn't matter so long as we cross the river more or less in the centre.'

Neither of them knew London well. But it was easier at this time of night, at two o'clock as it now was, though the traffic had thickened and begun to hold them up. The journey from the river up through Kensington and Notting Hill seemed interminable. Burden, who had been hoping to go through the park, found it closed and took Kensington Church Street instead. Then came the confusions of the Bayswater Road and Edgware Road.

'Easy to see you never did the knowledge,' Wexford muttered.

'The what?'

'What taxi drivers do before they get to be taxi drivers. Going about on bicycles with maps in their hand, learning one-way streets.'

'I'm a policeman,' said Burden austerely, 'thank you very much.'

366

But five minutes later he had to ask if it was all right to park on a single yellow line.

'Quite OK after six-thirty,' Wexford said, sounding more confident than he was.

They were in Fitzhardinge Street, off Manchester Square. No one was about and the place was as silent as anywhere ever is in central London. A thin stream of traffic continued to pass down not-far-distant Baker Street, making a ceaseless throb of background noise. They got out of the car, crossed the street and stood in the entrance to the mews.

This was approached by means of an archway in the terrace on the south side of Fitzhardinge Street. The street was well lit so that it was almost as bright as day, but inside the mews, on the other side of the brown sandstone arch, a single lamp burned, casting its yellow radiance over the cobbles. Of the buildings in there, some consisted of one storey above a garage, others were narrow Victorian houses, flat-roofed or with a single gable, designed for the coachmen employed by the dwellers in Manchester Square or Seymour Street. Poor little artisans' houses, all of them, but prettified with roof gardens and window-boxes, porches and new front doors, grown punishingly expensive to buy.

'If you lived up here,' Wexford said softly, 'in London, I mean, you wouldn't have to worry about wetlands and yellow caddises and butterflies' habitats. There aren't any to lose.'

Burden looked at him in amazement. 'I don't worry about those things and I like living in the country.'

'Yes,' Wexford said. 'I know.' And then, not to be patronising and mean-spirited, 'You did well remembering this address. I'm not sure I would have.'

'My mother's maiden name was Fitzharding,' Burden said simply, 'only without the e, of course.'

They walked into the mews through the arch. Outside the house they had come to, number four, stood two green tubs in which grew standard bay trees, their crowns spheres of dark leaves. The front door was at the side, with two sash windows to the right of it and two more above. No lights showed. In the entire mews, apart from the single street lamp, only one window had a light behind it and that was at the farthest end up against the wall of Seymour Street.

Wexford rang the bell of number four. Although the house wasn't divided into flats, there was an entryphone with a brass grille. He didn't expect an answer to his ring and he didn't get one, neither then nor when he rang again. He knocked on the door, pushing at the letter-box lid so that it rattled loudly.

All was in darkness, all was silent and no window was open. But he knew the house wasn't empty. He could feel the presence of occupants, he hardly knew how, perhaps by some strange sense long discounted as feasible to human beings, but which animals understood. An emanation of tension, of strain growing intolerable, communicated itself to him through the pale walls of the house, through the sealed windows. It almost throbbed as if, instead of people, a crouching monster waited inside, breathing rhythmically, flexing its stubby claws.

And the sense of this reached even Burden who said, 'There's someone there all right. They're in there.'

'Upstairs,' said Wexford. 'In the dark, behind those curtains.'

He rang the bell again, putting his ear to the grille. And this time a strange thing happened. A receiver was lifted at the other end, making a sound like a sigh or the opening of a door that lets in a gust of wind. The sighing sound, the wind blowing, should have been followed by a voice but there was no voice. Up there someone crouched with the phone to his ear, not speaking.

Wexford said, 'Detective Chief Inspector Wexford and Detective Inspector Burden, Kingsmarkham CID.' Too late he remembered he should have said Crime Management. 'Open the door and let us in, please.'

The receiver went back before he had spoken that last sentence.

'Do you remember what Dora said?' he asked Burden. 'When she talked of breaking down that washroom door and asked us if we'd ever done something like that? And we all had.'

Grinning, Burden pressed the bell again. Once more the receiver was lifted. He said harshly, 'Open up or we'll break your door down.'

He had already taken the necessary steps backwards and was running up to give the door a mighty kick, when it opened. A man stood there in a dressing-gown of dark-blue foulard over cream-coloured pyjama trousers. He was tall and lean, and the vee of the dressing-gown showed a mat of whitish-blond hair covering his chest. The hair of his head was pepper-and-salt and, if he wasn't quite recognisable from his photograph, his resemblance to his son both in facial features and colouring was unmistakable.

He said nothing. He stood there. On the narrow staircase behind him a woman was slowly descending. Her feet in red slippers came first into view, then her bare legs with the stiff skirts of a red quilted housecoat reaching to the calves, then the rest of her and her white face, set and grim and ready for what must come.

'Owen Kinglake Struther?' said Wexford.

The man nodded.

'You do not have to say anything. But it may harm your defence if you do not mention when questioned something which you may later rely on in court. Anything you do say ...'

Chapter 27

The morning had started off hazy and cool, an autumn morning of mist penetrated by shafts of pale sunshine. But the mist had lifted now and the sun was no longer pale but bright and strong. Wexford looked up at the brilliance in the blue where the sun was and blessed it for shining when he wanted it to shine. It would show him and all of them what he wanted to see.

Vine had the warrant. They would go in two cars and Wexford would ask for back-up if he needed it. Maybe even if he didn't need it. He should have been tired. In the event, he and Burden had had perhaps two hours' sleep. But he felt elated, adrenalin running, every nerve in his body alert and waiting.

It had worked last night. After entry to the house in Fitzhardinge Mews everything had gone straight-forwardly. The Struthers had capitulated in an entirely middle-class, stand up, speak up and play the game way. The curious thing was that neither of them seemed to see that they had done anything particularly wrong.

'My husband planned it all,' Kitty Struther said proudly. 'It was his idea, absolutely his brainchild. The rest of them – well, we had to bring them in. For sheer force of numbers, you understand.'

'Kitty,' Owen Struther said.

'Well, it's all over, isn't it? It doesn't matter what we say now.' She had looked up at Wexford. 'That

was your wife, wasn't it? There was the boy and the
... well, the coloured girl. She jumped out of a
window, she wasn't pushed. I wonder what your
wife said about us. We put on a jolly good act, you
know. Good as professionals. Owen was Colonel
Blimp and I was the terrified little woman.'

'Kitty.'

She started laughing. The laughter caught in her
throat on a sob and she began to cry, rocking herself
back and forth. Wexford thought how Dora had said
she cried so much. What had been acting and what
real?

'You haven't asked why,' Owen Struther said.
'Personally, I think we were justified. I longed for
that house all my life and managed to buy it ten
years ago. It was all going to be taken from us, it was
going to be ruined by a ghastly road more suited to
Los Angeles or Birmingham.' He touched his wife's
arm. 'Kitty.'

'I can't help it,' she sobbed. 'It's all so sad.'

'You should be more discreet.'

'What does it matter now? If they build the road
what does anything matter? They can execute me if
they like.'

'Get dressed now,' said Wexford, 'and we'll be
off.'

They were back in Kingsmarkham at twenty-past
four. He had snatched his bit of sleep, woken
promptly and checked on the warrant with Barry
Vine. Now, in the first car, he directed Pemberton
where to go.

Pemberton didn't question it. He knew the area
and he had his map, and if he was surprised he
didn't say so. It would all be over in an hour,
Wexford had said, and this afternoon he, James
Pemberton, was playing golf with his brother-in-law.
The Chief Inspector was in the back with Inspector

Burden and DS Malahyde next to him, riding shotgun.

He had used that phrase and Wexford heard it and said, 'I don't believe in Sacred Globe's gun. Not a handgun.'

'Dora said a handgun,' said Burden.

'I know she did and that's why I don't think it was real. Let me put that another way. If she'd said they had a shotgun or even a rifle I'd believe in the possibility of its being real because dozens of people round here have shotgun licences.'

They went the Pomfret way. Marginally quicker, Pemberton said. It would be a lot slower, though, when the bypass was built. Unless they built underpasses or bridges. Burden said his wife had told him of a new proposal she had heard rumoured, that they were going to put a tunnel under the Brede at Watersmeet to save the yellow caddis.

Framhurst was even quieter this morning than it had been last evening, but as they passed over the crossroads church bells started ringing for some early-morning service. For the first time Wexford took note of the car behind him, the car Hennessy was driving. He looked back, craning his neck. Vine was next to him and his heart took a little lurch because of who was in the back with Nicky Weaver.

But he had to be wrong about that. He really knew he was. It was just that he had a horribly suspicious mind, the kind of antennae that locate ugly things, awful things that wouldn't cross other people's minds. But if Brendan Royall hadn't furnished Sacred Globe with Burden's name and telephone number, who had? He had to be wrong. He *was* wrong and since he would never tell anyone, not a soul would know of the doubt in his heart, his nose for the scent of treachery.

Frenchie Collins wouldn't talk to Karen Malahyde,

only to her companion. And before he went to the Holgates he had told only those standing close to him that he was going up there in quest of recent building work. Yet Ryan Barker had phoned him while he was there. And as for Tarling's movements . . .

'I think it may all go quietly,' was all he said aloud.

They were climbing Markinch Hill. The bright sun lit up the whole valley, the green and the black-green, the dark massy woods, the sparkling silver river, white houses and red houses, flint and brown, chalk scree on downland slopes. The shadow of a thin strip of cloud floated lightly across it all.

'House up here, is it, sir?' Pemberton asked.

'On our left now,' said Wexford.

Pemberton got out to open the gates.

'Leave them open,' Wexford said. 'Leave the car here. We'll walk up. We'll go quietly.'

The other car had been close behind them. He walked over to it, repeated to Vine what he had just said and said to Nicky and Damon Slesar, 'I'd like you to stay in the car. Wait here till you're called for. I've got more back-up coming.'

The six who weren't staying anywhere began to make their way towards the house. Not on the drive, not to crunch the gravel, but through the shrubberies, between the trees where, through the branches, here on the ridge, the panorama of the valley opened out and spread itself like a great green tapestry unfurled. The sun made dapple patterns on the fine pale soil, the brown leaves of last autumn. On an island in a sea of trees the house stood with its outbuildings, the double house, Jacobean at one end, Georgian at the other. The trees thinned and the house emerged, the lower floors of the Georgian part hidden by a two-storey building of cut flints with a slate roof.

'Sacred Globe are probably asleep still,' Wexford said. 'Why not? They've nothing to worry about. Or they don't think they have.'

Burden was behind him and Karen now. They came up alongside a wall with a gate in it, opened the gate and passed through, entering an almost enclosed courtyard with a checkerboard floor of stone squares and mown grass squares. Tubs stood about filled with pink-and-white-striped petunias and yellow Jamaican daisies. Ahead of them was an arched opening between the Jacobean part of the house and the encircling wall, an arch he had passed under and seen a dog and a man, greenness and greyness ...

He pointed in silence at the flint-walled building. Its single window faced the rear of the Georgian part of the house, a wall hung with a creeping plant that covered it to a width of about four feet and a height of eight. As he had expected, the sun which was already high in the sky had brought out its flowers, and on the left-hand side at the top and the right-hand side half-way up, had opened perhaps twenty blue trumpets.

Half close his eyes and he could see a patch of blue and another smaller patch. The isolated blossoms disappeared, returned when he opened his eyes. Blue as the sky at noon on a summer's day.

'I wonder if the door's locked,' he said softly.

A stout, heavy door, oak probably, with locks top and bottom. He tried the handle and the door opened. It was a strange feeling, seeing the place at last. The basement room. The prison. It was very much as Dora had described it, about twenty feet by thirty, with the stone sink under the window, the shelves, the door into the washroom. The five camp beds were still there and the blankets folded quite neatly on top of them.

Two stone steps down to the stone-flagged floor. A chilly place, cool enough once to have kept dairy products sound, with shelves on the wall and a lot of cobwebs hanging. He went to the window, saw a sky-blue patch about six feet up, and saw it, because the rabbit hut structure had been taken down, much more clearly than Dora would have. The wood in the window frame was splintered and there was a hole where that bullet had gone in.

Outside again, he half expected a Siamese cat to come sauntering out from one of the outbuildings or, when he looked up, to see a black cat sunning itself on top of a wall. But, no. He knew almost for certain now that he wouldn't see them, just as he wouldn't find any sand from the Isle of Wight.

He had calculated that there were very likely four people in that house, six if he was lucky. Who would answer the front door?'

Andrew Struther. It was usually Andrew Struther, and so it was this time. Probably they had fixed it that it was always he who came to the door. To be on the safe side. But not quite safe enough. Andrew hadn't long been up, you could see that, had perhaps only this minute got up. He was wearing khaki shorts and a dirty white T-shirt, trainers on his feet, no socks.

'I expect you thought policemen took Sundays off, didn't you, Mr Struther?' said Wexford.

'Should I know what you're talking about?'

'We'll have the explanations inside.'

They pushed past him into the hall. Bibi was there in jeans and the heavy boots Dora had described, holding the dog Manfred by its collar.

Wexford said to her, 'Lock that dog up somewhere. Anywhere. Do it now.'

'What?'

'If it touches one of us it gets destroyed, so for its protection, lock it up.'

'The Hermaphrodite,' said Karen softly.

'Exactly. Where are the rest of you, Andrew?'

Burden remembered the man's insistence on his surname and style, and Struther remembered too. It showed in his face but he made no reference to it, only said again, this time more querulously, 'Should I know what this is about?'

'We have your parents in custody. They were arrested in the early hours of the morning,' Burden said. 'Now, where is Ryan Barker?'

'You're making a mistake.'

The girl came back without the dog, went up close to Andrew Struther, looked into his face. 'Andy?'

'Not now.' Struther said to Wexford, 'He's not here. He's been kidnapped, remember?'

'Search the house.'

'You can't do that!'

'Show him the warrant, Mike,' said Wexford, and to Vine, 'If you go down the back here and turn to the left it should bring you into the tall part of this house. On the top floor you'll find the room where Roxane Masood was kept. The window is in the wall where that blue climber is in flower.' He said to Andrew Struther, 'Where's Tarling?'

Andrew said nothing. He took hold of Bibi and put his hand over her mouth. She quailed a bit, shrinking into herself.

'Let her go!' Wexford said, and to Burden, 'Have they been cautioned?'

'They have. I've phoned for back-up.'

The door opened and Vine came in with a tall gangling boy in jeans and a sweatshirt. His face looked bewildered, his mouth slack. When he saw Andrew and Bibi he made a little sound.

'Sit down,' Wexford said. 'Over there. You too.' He

377

nodded in the direction of Andrew and Bibi, who now stood trembling, rubbing her arm where Andrew had clutched her. 'You sit down over there and wait. Where's Tarling?' he asked again.

'Locked himself in his room next to where the kid was,' said Vine.

Andrew laughed. 'He's got a gun, you know.'

'No, I don't know.' Wexford shook his head at him. 'I find it hard to believe a word you say.'

'Pemberton's gone to fetch Nicky and Slesar,' Burden murmured to Wexford. 'The three of us can get him out and by then the back-up'll be here.'

Andrew half rose out of his chair. He clenched his fists, said, 'What did you say?'

No one answered him. Bibi came up to him, took his arm, said, 'I want my dog. Make them let him out.'

He ignored her, repeated, 'You said Slesar. What else did you say?'

Wexford heard the police vehicles' sirens. They were coming up Markinch Hill. He left the room, crossed the hall, walked out through the front door. Emerging from the shadowy avenue were Pemberton and Slesar, coming on to the wide gravel sweep, Slesar a little way ahead. Tarling he didn't see until it was too late but he heard the cry behind him, up at a window, a howl of rage and despair, 'You betrayed us!'

The bullet must have passed quite close to his own head. It was at the sound that he ducked, involuntarily, the deafening report. Even then he thought, a rifle, not a shotgun. Damon Slesar stood utterly still, his hands slowly rising up, even from this distance the hole the bullet made clearly visible on his white shirt, by his heart.

He said something. Perhaps it was 'no', but Wexford couldn't hear, no one could have heard.

378

Slesar's knees buckled and he fell forward and sideways, blood pouring out of his mouth.

The two cars, the van, came up the drive, and the first one, its siren still wailing, had to swerve to avoid the dead man on the gravel and the two who bent over him. Car doors burst open and the men came out. Wexford turned back to the house as Karen Malahyde came from the front door, calm, cold, staring, but uttering the same small sound of protest as Ryan Barker had made not long before.

She stood and looked at Slesar's body but, unlike the others, she resisted kneeling beside him.

Chapter 28

'Kitty Struther described it as her husband's "clever idea",' Wexford began, 'but it looks as if the original plan came from Tarling. He had been at school with Andrew Struther and though they might appear to have little in common, in fact they both shared with Andrew's father Owen a hatred of authority interfering in their lives, or rather, imposing its will on their lives and thus changing them for the worse.'

He was filling in the details for Montague Ryder, and Burden was there too, in the Chief Constable's suite at Myringham. It was Monday and that morning five people had appeared at Kingsmarkham Magistrates' Court charged with abduction and unlawful imprisonment, and one of them with the murder of Detective Sergeant Damon John Slesar. They had all, in spite of Wexford's guesses and belief, been charged with the murder of Roxane Masood.

'Tarling,' Wexford said, 'was also, of course, very much concerned with protest over green issues and with animal rights. He and Andrew Struther encountered each other by chance in Kingsmarkham, back in the spring when the bypass looked as if it would become reality and the activists first began coming here. I don't know how yet and perhaps it doesn't matter. Suffice it to say that they did – Struther was down here visiting his parents – recognise each other and began discussing the bypass.

'Now the occupants of Savesbury House would be a good deal less affected by the bypass than would almost anyone living in a semi on the outskirts of Stowerton or a cottage in the neighbourhood of Pomfret, but the threat seemed appalling to them. Devastating. That's a word that everyone bandies about these days and I don't like it, but here it's appropriate. The valley which their windows overlooked, which they could see from their garden, would indeed be devastated – that is, laid waste. And they would hear the traffic. Their peace would be broken, their silence that hitherto was only disturbed by birdsong, would be lost to the muted but pretty well incessant roar of the bypass users.'

Burden interrupted him. 'But why should Andrew Struther care enough to involve himself in this? He doesn't live at Savesbury House. He's young and young men aren't usually much concerned about birdsong and peace and quiet. Yet he was prepared to risk his liberty . . .'

'Money, Mike. Money and inheritance. Savesbury House would be his one day. Perhaps he wouldn't want to live in it, he lives in his London mews, but he'd want to sell it. Estate agents in Kingsmarkham are saying the bypass will reduce the value of all property in its vicinity, some of it by as much as fifty per cent. In this case that means cutting the value of Savesbury House from three quarters of a million to not much more than three hundred thousand, not to mention making it unsaleable.'

The Chief Constable glanced at Burden. 'It's a different league, Mike, but it's there.'

'I suppose it is, sir.'

'There was money available,' Wexford went on. 'For instance, the building and plumbing of the washroom. I'm pretty sure Gary Wilson did that. He's a builder by trade. He told me so, only it didn't register at the time. Oh, he didn't know what he was doing it *for*. But he was glad of the work and the money, and even more happy, if mystified, when he and Quilla were presented with a car to get them to Wales and thence to north Yorkshire, on the understanding he was to stay out of the way for a couple of months.

'It was money accomplished that. Owen and Kitty Struther had money and they were just as keen on the plan as Tarling and their son. And it was Owen Struther's idea to set it up by using Contemporary Cars. He had used them a few times to get himself to Kingsmarkham station and he knew that the last thing they were was contemporary, he knew their slapdash arrangements. But before the plan could be put into operation they had to have a place to put the hostages and, so to speak, a staff to guard them.

'Three of them would, of course, be Tarling, Andrew and Andrew's girlfriend Bettina Martin, known as Bibi. It wasn't enough – well, it was enough for the guard duty, bearing in mind that Owen and Kitty would only need to *appear* to be guarded – but the car abduction plan necessarily must involve more manpower. So Tarling brought in a man we've called The Driver just as we know Tarling as Rubber Face – it was the stocking over his face that turned his features from sharp into rubber – Andrew Struther as Tattoo and Bibi Martin as The Hermaphrodite. And there was one more.'

Wexford hesitated. He got up and walked over to the window where he stood for a moment, looking across another garden, another view. On some mental retina he saw it happening again and heard the shot, he saw the shocked, whitening face and the blood on the shirt where the heart beat beneath. And then beat no longer.

He turned round, said, 'I didn't suspect him until

382

the night before we left for Savesbury House. And then I didn't exactly . . . Frankly, I thought it was me, seeing villains everywhere, believing nothing and no one. I should have stopped him from coming with us. I only knew he *was* coming when I looked round and spotted him in the car behind. And then, believing nothing and no one as I've said, I didn't believe Tarling had a gun. Or if he did that he'd use it in those circumstances.'

'You have no need to blame yourself, Reg,' said Montague Ryder.

Wexford shook his head, a gesture of self-anger, not denial. He glanced at Burden, knowing what he was thinking, some monstrous version of its being all for the best anyway. What kind of a future, a life, would there have been for Damon Slesar?

'He wasn't at school with them, was he?' the Chief Constable asked.

'Not so far as I know, sir. Myringham Comprehensive, I believe. But he was a member of KABAL, which is perfectly respectable, and of SPECIES, which is perhaps not quite that. Strictly speaking, he shouldn't have joined that latter organisation, but then his life for the past six months has been a catalogue of things he shouldn't have done.

'We have to believe that all these people thought their plan would work. They thought that taking hostages would stop the bypass because they thought the government would give in. This wasn't the Middle East, this wasn't Thailand. This was England and English people holding English people, a monstrous act that would have the desired result. They really thought that. Slesar thought that.'

'He had some special reason for being opposed to the bypass?'

'I suppose you could say that,' Wexford said

thoughtfully. 'Like Andrew Struther, he was concerned for his parents, though in his case it was their livelihood, not a question of his future inheritance. All he could inherit would be a smallholding out on the old bypass, not far from the Brigadier pub.'

'That place where they sell veg and pick-your-own strawberries?' asked Burden. 'I didn't know that.'

'Most businesses on the old bypass will be threatened by the new one,' said Wexford. 'The old one won't be used much, or that's the theory, there won't be many people stopping off for PYO strawberries. Slesar was against the bypass because it would bankrupt his parents. His father grew fruit. His mother had a subsidiary business spinning thread and weaving garments from animal hair.'

'But how did he get into all this?'

'Through SPECIES, I think. Probably at one of their rallies. Prior to the one that's just ended in Wales they had one in Kent in the spring. Very likely he met Tarling there and the rest followed. They would have worked pretty hard on him, the Struthers particularly, because they really needed someone like him, an insider.'

'Why do you say the Struthers "particularly", Reg?'

Wexford said bitterly, 'Struther's a rich man. Not far off a millionaire.' He shrugged. 'Happily for all of us in this country – there are still some things to be thankful for – there is no one a rich man can bribe to stop something like this bypass. It can't be done. But the Damon Slesars of this world are corruptible. I don't know this yet, but my theory is that Struther bribed Slesar considerably, probably went on raising the price until Slesar yielded. No doubt he got enough to set his parents up elsewhere even if they did lose their livelihood.

'Being their mole inside the force,' Wexford went

on, 'Slesar knew Mike Burden's address and phone number for Tarling to phone there with the second message – it was usually the voices of Tarling and Andrew Struther that were heard – and knew I would be at the Holgates' on Saturday afternoon to receive another message there. Of course the sleeping bag which Frenchie Collins bought in Brixton was the one in which Roxane Masood's body was found, as she told Slesar once she was alone with him.'

'She knew?' Burden asked.

'I don't know. Maybe not. Maybe she just took against Karen Malahyde. Anyway, whatever she told Slesar wasn't going to find its way back to me.'

'Poor Karen,' said Burden.

'Yes. But I don't think it had gone very deep with her. And knowing what she now knows will have its effect. While she was tailing Brendan Royall he should have been tailing Conrad Tarling. Needless to say, he wasn't. Tarling went back and forth between the camp and Savesbury House as much as he pleased. Doubtless he went down to Wiltshire, also whenever he pleased. At some point, on his clothes, he brought back moth-wing dust from Queringham Hall and by chance transferred it to the room where the hostages were kept.'

Wexford was silent for a moment. They were all thinking, he supposed, the same sort of thing, the horror of a police officer succumbing in this way, and with bribery added to treachery. And then he wondered what thought had passed through Slesar's mind as he saw Tarling at that window with the gun, his fanatical face, the shotgun aimed. He had stared, the blood drawn from his face, his hands rising as if in an ineffectual warding off of death.

'You said something about the place where the hostages were kept,' said the Chief Constable in a welcome changing of the subject.

Wexford nodded. 'A lot of these old houses that have been farms as well as country houses have a dairy. Mostly they're just used to store stuff in, repositories for junk. This one probably was. My wife called it a basement room but it wasn't really, just rather dark and with one small window slightly high up. I expect they renewed the door, had new locks fitted and so on. Of course they didn't dare get a building firm in to convert a cupboard into a washroom, but Tarling knew someone who would do it and say nothing, someone who lived nowhere and would very likely disappear after a few weeks.

'So they took their hostages, and I think we know already exactly how they did that. Of course, in the case of the Struthers, Owen and Kitty just walked across from the main house and put their hoods on outside the dairy door. Then they had their fun, playing the hysteric and the brave soldier. I suppose it helped pass the time for them until Owen staged his mock escape and they were taken away, first back to the comforts of Savesbury House and then off to London to hide themselves in Andrew's house. Incidentally, I wonder what Tarling thought when she carried her act as far as spitting at him. Still, you don't give the boss a smack in the face.

'It must have been a shock for them when they realised they'd got my wife and they would have done much earlier than I thought at first. They didn't have to know the name or be told who I was. Slesar knew on the day he came along with the other two from the Regional Crime Squad. No doubt he was on the blower to Sacred Globe immediately.'

'You've done well, Reg,' the Chief Constable said.

'Not well,' Wexford said. 'I could have saved a man's life and I didn't.'

Dora said she ought to have known. She ought to

have guessed about the Struthers. After all, they weren't actors, were they?

'Everyone's an actor these days,' said Wexford. 'They learn it off the TV. Look at all those people who get interviewed after disasters. They've no shyness, they all behave as if they've learnt scripts by heart or got monitors in front of them.'

'Why did they let me go, Reg?'

'At first I thought it was because they'd found out who you were, through Gary and Quilla. But that wasn't so. They knew who you were. They knew because Slesar knew. Incidentally, he wore gloves not because he had something wrong with his hands, but to make you think there was something wrong with them. And not because they thought you might have seen the Morning Glory . . .'

Dora interrupted him. 'I don't understand why they didn't just cut that thing down.'

'Probably because Kitty Struther wouldn't let them. She grew it from seed, remember. No doubt she loved it. On no account are you to cut down my Ipomoea, she'd have said, and you don't argue with the boss. No, they let you go because they'd planted false clues on you.'

'They did what?'

'You were my wife, so when you got home they knew the first thing that would happen would be questioning you in depth and subjecting your clothes to forensic tests. If Roxane, say, or Ryan had been released, who knows what would have happened to their clothes before they reached us? Maybe gone into a washing machine or at any rate been carefully brushed by Mother.' Wexford paused for a moment, thinking of Clare Cox, who would never again tend her child's clothes. He sighed.

'They knew that would never happen here. They knew what would happen and did happen, that I'd drop your clothes into a sterile bag as soon as you took them off. They planted clues on that skirt of yours. Iron filings. Cats' hairs, easy for Slesar to obtain from his mother who spins and weaves with pet animal hair. Just as they made sure you'd carry away a picture in your mind of a tattoo on a man's arm and a smell of a man with some kind of kidney disease, a tattoo easily achieved with a transfer and a smell produced by pocketing a tissue soaked in nail varnish remover.

'A lot of this was Slesar's brainwave. And some of it, I think – I hope I'm not being paranoid – was Slesar getting back at me. He bore a grudge against me, you see, for what he saw as my humiliating him in public.'

'Did you do that?'

'Let's say he saw it that way.'

She shook her head wonderingly, 'Reg, you've accounted for them all but The Driver. You still don't know who The Driver was.'

'I do. He'll be arrested tomorrow. And then those unfortunate Tarlings may be the only parents in Britain with three sons serving life sentences. The Driver was Conrad's brother Colum.'

'Isn't he in a wheelchair?'

'Anyone can sit in a wheelchair, Dora. So much of it, as his father told me, was in "his poor mind". You did say he walked oddly, stiffly, but none of us thought much of that.'

'So it's all over?'

'All over. It was all for nothing. A young woman with all her life before her is dead, a misguided young man is dead, a boy who can't tell truth from fantasy is going to present the shrinks and social workers with a problem for years to come, and six people are going to prison. And the bypass will still be built.'

'Not if we can help it,' said Dora stoutly. 'There's a meeting of KABAL tonight to prepare for next Saturday's demo. If all this has taught us anything it's that the Brede Valley and Savesbury Hill are worth fighting for. There'll be twenty thousand people pouring into Kingsmarkham at the weekend.'

He sighed and nodded. Probably this wasn't the first case of an investigating officer being entirely in agreement with the aims of hostage takers, while hating the way they tried to secure their ransom. Probably not – if it mattered. He smiled at his wife.

'And, Reg, after that I'd like to go up and see Sheila and the baby for a few days.' She looked at him with a half-smile. 'If you'll drive me to the station.'